W9-BUO-108

WITHDRAWN

# Sanctuary

# Sanctuary

## An Epic Novel of Thieves' World

Lynn Abbey

HIGHLAND PARK PUBLIC LIBRARY
494 LAUREL AVE.
HIGHLAND PARK, IL 60035-2690
847-432-0216

A Tom Doherty Associates Book
*New York*

SF-F

This is a work of fiction. All the characters and events portrayed in this novel are either fictitious or are used fictitiously.

SANCTUARY: AN EPIC NOVEL OF THIEVES' WORLD

Copyright © 2002 by Lynn Abbey

Thieves' World™ and Sanctuary™ are registered trademarks belonging to Lynn Abbey and are used with permission.

All rights reserved, including the right to reproduce this book, or portions thereof, in any form.

This book is printed on acid-free paper.

A Tor Book
Published by Tom Doherty Associates, LLC
175 Fifth Avenue
New York, NY 10010

www.tor.com

Tor® is a registered trademark of Tom Doherty Associates, LLC.

Library of Congress Cataloging-in-Publication Data

Abbey, Lynn.
Sanctuary : an epic novel of Thieves' world / Lynn Abbey.—1st ed.
p. cm.
"A Tom Doherty Associates book."
ISBN 0-312-87491-X (acid-free paper)
I. Title.

PS3551.B23 S26 2002
813'.54—dc21

2001059660

First Edition: June 2002

Printed in the United States of America

0 9 8 7 6 5 4 3 2 1

For the readers and fans

of

Thieves' World

Acknowledgments

Thieves' World would not have been reborn and *Sanctuary* would not have been written without a lot of support and encouragement.

My thanks go first to Brian Thomsen, who *believed* even when I didn't, and to everyone at Tor Books, especially Jim Minz, who was very patient, and Tom Doherty, who thought it was a good time to bring Thieves' World home.

My thanks, too, to my agent, Jonathan Matson, who did all the things I could never do, and to my close friend, Elaine, who deduced that I wasn't getting enough pizza and, despite the thousand miles separating us, arranged to have it delivered regularly.

And, last but not least, to the super-cell tornadoes that ripped through Oklahoma on May 3, 1999. For ten years I'd insisted that I'd return to Sanctuary "when pigs fly"; that night, the swine, along with everything else, were airborne.

# Chapter One

A full moon shone over Sanctuary, revealing boats in its harbor, dwellings within and without its coiled walls. The city appeared prosperous, but Sanctuary always shone brightest at night. In sunlight, a man standing on the eastern ridge overlooking the city would see that the largest boats tied up along the piers were rotting hulks, that roofs were missing all over town, and the great walls had been breached by neglect in several places.

Sanctuary could have looked worse and had many times during the half century that Molin Torchholder had—however reluctantly—called it home. *Gods* had fought—and lost—their private wars on Sanctuary's streets, but the city went on, resilient, incorrigible, just possibly eternal. Its citizens repelled catastrophe as readily as they squandered prosperity. Time and time again, Molin had watched fire, storm, plague, invasion, and sheer madness sweep through the city, carrying it to the brink of annihilation, only to ebb away, like the tide shrinking from the hard, black rocks wrapped around its harbor.

And should Molin Torchholder call himself a citizen of Sanctuary?

In the morning years of his ninth decade, no one would deny Molin the right to call himself whatever he wished. He preferred to think of himself as Rankan. Born in the Imperial capital, raised by priests of the war-god, Vashanka, and risen to the heights of their hierarchy before his twenty-fifth birthday, Molin Torchholder had been marked as a man with a glorious future. Then he'd come to Sanctuary, a city on the edge of nowhere, a city so far removed from the Imperial Court of Ranke that an insecure emperor had thought it a safe place in which to exile an inconvenient half brother when a sudden attack of conscience stopped the fratricide the Imperial advisors—including the high priests of Vashanka—had suggested.

*I'll be here a year,* Molin had thought the first time he'd ridden down this road. One insufferable year, then he'd be back in Ranke, accumulating power, wealth, and a legacy for the ages. His god had had other ideas. Molin's god had a taste for blood and chaos and once He'd gotten a taste of Sanctuary's particular squalor, Vashanka couldn't push the plate away.

Vashanka had amused Himself with children, thieves, and the pangs of lust. The war-god of the mightiest empire in the world had made an immortal fool of Himself for years. Spurred by immortal embarrassment, divine powers both great and small had allied to erase Vashanka's name from the white-marble lintel of His own temple—from the temple Molin himself had raised in His honor. Reduced to little more than an itch on the world's behind, the great Vashanka had slunk out of Sanctuary on a night very much like this one more than forty years ago.

Molin hadn't felt his god's departure until the next morning when he'd encountered an indescribable absence during his daily prayers. *Vashanka's come to His senses and returned to Ranke*; Molin had thought, little realizing that Vashanka had gone not home, but into exile. Worse—the divine powers that had run Vashanka out of Sanctuary had condemned him—*him!*—to remain within its walls.

From the beginning Molin had loathed everything about Sanctuary: its wretched, soggy climate; the brackish taste of its water; and, especially, its citizens. He swore he could never be reconciled to an unjust fate; then the moon would rise and he'd be drawn to the roof above his palace apartment—or find himself delayed on the East Ridge Road. His thoughts would wander, and Sanctuary would take his soul by surprise, flexing its claws, reminding him of what he tried so hard to forget: This place, and none other, was *home*.

Footfalls drew Torchholder's attention away from the rooftops of Sanctuary. He turned in time to see his escort, a man scarcely a quarter his age, climb out of the roadside ditch. Atredan Larris Serripines' face was paler than the moon and shiny with sweat but, on the whole, he looked a good deal better than he had when he'd staggered into the grass.

"Better now?" Molin asked pleasantly.

Atredan favored him with a scowl. "So much for Father's Foundation Day Feast."

In another time and place, Lord Serripines' second son might have amounted to something. He had the golden hair and hazel eyes of a true Rankan aristocrat, an amiable personality, and the sense not to get caught when he succumbed to temptation. Lesser men had ruled well in Ranke. But in Sanctuary, a generation after an eastern horde had brought fire, rape, pillage, and death to the Empire's heart, Atredan was doomed to ambition without prospects.

No commemoration of the Imperial Founding, however precisely observed, could change that.

Molin dug into his scrip and found a sprig of mint twisted with other herbs, which he offered to the younger man. "I think you'll find it settles what's left and takes the taste away." When one indulged as the Imperial court in its prime had indulged, one never forgot its remedies and kept them forever close to hand.

Atredan had refused the digestive when Molin had first offered it, but took it gratefully now and chewed hard. Within moments his face had relaxed.

"Gods all be damned, Lord Torchholder, I can't believe any emperor has ever sat through a meal like that! The food. The wine—especially *that* wine. Anen's mercy, *what* did my lord father put in it this year?"

Never mind that Anen was the Ilsigi god of vineyards and anathema to the Rankan pantheon, Atredan had a valid argument.

"Honey," Molin replied with an honest sigh. "A comb of Imperial honey, straight from the Imperial hives, the Imperial garden, and the Imperial pantry. The genuine article—or so he told me. Very rare these days."

"Very expensive," Atredan corrected. "Very old, very spoilt, and fit only for swine or my lord father's Foundation Day table."

"That is not for me to say," Molin said diplomatically and—because he was, among many other things, an accomplished diplomat—he made it clear that he would have agreed with the young man, had it been necessary to do so.

Diplomatic nuance was wasted on the Serripines' cadet heir. "Did you actually *drink* that swill?"

"I'm an old man, Lord Larris, and my palate is as old as the rest of me. Swill or ambrosia, it all tastes the same now— Yet, I am sure the wine we drank in Ranke was not so sweet . . . or gluey. And neither did we ferment it ourselves. Truth to tell—we seldom drank Imperial wine, with or without Imperial honey. All the best vintages came by ship from Caronne. They still do, I suppose, but not to Sanctuary. Have a care for your lord father. He was a babe-in-arms when Ranke fell. He dreams of Rankan glory, but he doesn't remember it."

Atredan muttered words too soft and slurred for Molin to catch. The indignities of age! His reputation had been built on his eyes and his ears. Time was when no word or gesture had escaped his senses; that time was gone. It was true that younger men still complimented him and relied on his advice, but they had no idea how much of his edge he'd lost.

Or how tired he had become.

"Come," he urged his escort, "it's time to get me home to my bed."

"You could have stayed at Land's End. My lord father loves nothing better than to have *the* Lord Torchholder sleeping beneath his roof. A veritable hero and not merely of Sanctuary—as if Sanctuary could nurture a true hero—but of the *Empire*."

"For all the good my heroics have done me." Molin chuckled. "After two nights beneath your lord father's roof, I've told all the stories of Imperial glory that I can remember. I've drunk his wine and lit his bonfire. The Imperial ancestors have been properly honored, a new Imperial year is safely begun, and I'm ready to go home."

Atredan cocked his head in the moonlight. "You think we are all fools, don't you, Lord Torchholder? My father, the Rankans he shelters at Land's End . . . me."

"All men are fools, Lord Larris—you, me, your lord father, and all the men and women beneath his roof. The nature of men is foolishness. Never forget it."

"But the Serripines more than others, because Father believes Ranke will be mighty again, and that will never happen."

"Only a fool says 'never' when speaking of the future."

"There's no future for the dead. There is no future, not for us, not for Ranke. We're like fish in a weir. We sing praises each time it rains, but the fact is, we're trapped, and if the rains don't come, we die. Only sooner, rather than later."

Molin gave Atredan a second look—he'd never before suspected that the young man had a bent for philosophy, and although he generally agreed with Atredan's dreary assessment of Rankan prospects, he offered up a scrap of encouragement: "Sanctuary's a coastal town, my boy. The tide comes in twice a day, no matter the rain. A man may drown, but he'll surely never shrivel."

"My lord father has shriveled. He hasn't set foot in Sanctuary since the Bleeding Hand killed my mother. He lives in his own world at Land's End with his back to the sea, waiting for an army that will never come to take back a city that was never his."

Molin didn't like to talk about the years when the Dyareelan fanatics had ruled Sanctuary. Neither did anyone who'd managed, somehow, to survive. The Serripines had gotten off lightly, retreating behind the walls of their fortresslike estate. But Molin would never say that to a son who'd seen his mother disemboweled, nor to her shattered husband. He temporized instead. "Your lord father feels obligated to comfort those whom the emperor has abandoned."

And, in truth, it wasn't Lord Serripines who made each Land's End visit feel like an early trip to the boneyard. If the sack of Ranke had been the most unexpected event in Molin's lifetime, the transformation of the Sanctuary hillsides from scrubland to fields and meadows should be counted a close second. The Serripines paterfamilias might have his head in the clouds where the Imperial past and future were concerned, but in the present he was a shrewd man who knew what to plant and when and—most important—who would pay the most once the fields were harvested.

Lord Serripines would have preferred to sell his harvest to Ranke—for a profit, of course—but there was no one along the eastern coast who could match the bids made in the resurgent Ilsig Kingdom to the north and west. Lord Serripines practically, but reluctantly, listened to his head, not his heart, and sold his harvest to Ilsigi sea captains, who sold it again to men who no longer paid tribute to the emperors in Ranke. Then, to assuage his guilt, Lord Serripines opened his estate to an ever-growing community of Imperial exiles and freeloaders.

The irony was not lost on Molin. With few exceptions, the elder Vion Larris Serripines was the most successful Rankan to dwell in—or *near*—Sanctuary in decades. He was also the unhappiest man Molin had ever met—which was a dubious accomplishment all by itself—but worse, to Molin's jaundiced eye, was Lord Serripines' willingness to shelter any noble-blooded Rankan who washed up in Sanctuary's harbor.

Indeed, two nights at Land's End were more than enough. Molin almost pitied young Atredan and his elder brother, Vion, coming of age in their father's bleak shadow.

"You should thank me, Lord Larris." Molin changed his tone and thirty years dropped from his bearing.

"For what?"

"For giving you an excuse to leave before the bonfire was burnt down to ashes. Lord Serripines would never have agreed, and a son must obey his father."

Atredan grimaced. "My lord father doesn't understand—our future, what there is of it, is bound up with Prince Naimun, and tonight the prince will be in need of a friend's ear. Better it were my brother escorting you back to the palace and Naimun's table, but there's no escape for Vion."

Molin couldn't resist a jab at the youth's defenses. "Naimun's table or his upper room at the Inn of Secret Pleasures?"

The young man contrived to keep his pale cheeks from darkening, but his darting eyes gave his secrets away quicker than his tongue. "You are mistaken, Lord Torchholder."

"I think not, and I care not. The Inn's whores are clean enough, but not tonight, Lord Larris. If you have Naimun's ear, tell him to stay at home. There's apt to be trouble, and the Inn's guards won't withstand a visit from the Dragon."

"Pox on Arizak per-Arizak," Atredan said boldly, giving the Dragon his proper name. "Sweet Sabellia's tits—what brings the Dragon and all the rest of the Irrune to Sanctuary today of all days?"

"The Irrune are a gathering people," Molin answered mildly. "They're entirely unlettered. How else are they to communicate amongst themselves if they do not gather?"

"But not in Sanctuary and not in such numbers. I woke up

yesterday morning, looked over the wall, and saw the whole damned Irrune nation riding down the road."

"The Irrune come together around their chief. Arizak's their chief, and this year Arizak's in Sanctuary because this year Arizak's leg is rotting and he can't sit his horse. As long as Arizak was out in the hills, the Dragon was confident of his inheritance, but since Arizak's butt has settled on a silk cushion instead of a saddle, the Dragon began to worry. His mother, his uncle, and the rest of the riders are worried, too, so they've followed their favored son here in number to make certain that Chief Arizak doesn't forget who he is, or more importantly, which son he's named to succeed him."

"Prince Naimun doesn't give a fig for the damned Irrune. He wants Sanctuary."

"So does the Dragon, just not in the same way. The Dragon wants the city's wealth, its wine, and its women—" Molin paused for effect. "Well, perhaps the half brothers *do* each want Sanctuary for the same reason, but Naimun is so much easier to distract."

"It is not a crime, Lord Torchholder, to drink with a prince," Atredan asserted, showing more spine than Molin had expected.

"No, indeed it is not. Nor is it a crime to call Naimun a prince when he is no more than the eldest son of his father's second wife—unless the eldest son of Arizak's *first* wife is about and your man gets himself killed in a whore's bed."

Atredan had the sense to look embarrassed. "His friends look out for him."

"And that, of course, is why you want to be in Sanctuary to-night—to look out for your friend. So be it. Naimun's weak and biddable and you think that makes him an ideal ruler. You're wrong in more ways than I can count, so be that, too. But think, if you dare, about loyalty—"

"I am loyal, Lord Torchholder." Atredan lowered his voice then raised it as his indignation swelled. "I am loyal to my father, to *my* brother, to my family, to my emperor—should he come to claim my service—and I'm loyal to Naimun."

"Of course you are, Lord Larris—but to whom is Naimun loyal? And why?"

"Don't play with questions, Lord Torchholder," Atredan bristled. "If you suspect Naimun can't be trusted, say so."

Molin waved the young man's anger aside. "Did I say that? Did I say that Naimun can't be trusted? Did I say he wasn't loyal? What I *am* saying, Lord Larris, is that while you may, indeed, be Naimun's friend and, no doubt, loyal to him, do not think for one moment that you are the only man—or woman, for that matter—in Sanctuary who's figured out that our Naimun follows flattery. Trust Naimun, if it pleases you, cultivate his love and his loyalty, but be damned wary of your companions within his charmed circle."

Atredan could not have looked more displeased if he'd had a plate of worms set before him and his father's undrinkable wine to wash it down. "Is that what this is about—the great Lord Torchholder dispensing advice on the road to Sanctuary? You're wasting your time, old man. I know everything I need to know about Naimun and the Dragon, their father, and every other Irrune who matters, and I learned it without your help or my lord father's, either."

He'd hoped for a better response, but Molin was too much the diplomat to reveal his disappointments. "Then, forgive an old man who's seen too many men fail because they forgot to watch their backs."

"When Arizak's gone, Naimun will bring Rankan rule to Sanctuary—without the emperor, of course, and without the Dragon. It's all been settled. I'd think you'd be pleased, Lord Torchholder. Isn't that what you had in mind all along?"

"Of course," Molin agreed, and the words weren't utter falsehood.

The laws of Ranke, when wielded by a strong, yet subtle, ruler were worthy of admiration. Molin would like to see Rankan law return to Sanctuary, but Naimun was neither strong enough nor subtle enough to do so. There was a man in the palace whom Molin liked better for the task—a boy, actually: Raith, Naimun's brother and the youngest of Arizak's sons. Raith had it all—the strength and comeliness, the quickness of mind, the flair for leadership and decision. What Raith lacked was experience. He was all of sixteen and needed another four years, three at least, before he could lay claim to the palace.

*Damn Arizak for getting drunk and falling off his horse!*

"Come," Molin said with unfeigned weariness. "An old man

needs to get moving if he's going to see his own bed before midnight."

Molin set the pace, which was slower than he would have liked—another concession to age. He relied on a staff for all but the shortest walks. The wood was gnarled and blackened and older than Molin. He'd found it in a palace storeroom and had no idea to whom it had once belonged. Probably a prince or priest of the Ilsigi; they rarely went anywhere without some symbol of authority clutched in their hands. Molin had made a few improvements. He'd burnt down the shaft and hidden Sanctuary's Savankh—the scepter with which an Imperial prince-governor ruled an Imperial city—in the tunnel. As an instrument of justice, a Savankh drew the truth out of a man, will he or nil he. The Savankh had transferred its power to the staff, but Molin, like the princes and governors before him, was immune to its sorcerous power.

In competent hands, the blackwood staff was a serviceable weapon, and, despite their years, Molin's hands were competent. He'd gotten his war-name, Torchholder, in part because of a willingness to use whatever object lay closest to hand when he fought. His strength had ebbed a couple decades earlier and his balance was going, too, but his instincts remained sharp, and the Savankh wasn't the only trick hidden beneath the staff's amber finial.

But it was a staff, a plain ordinary staff, that Molin needed as the road widened, and the iron-reinforced Prince's Gate loomed ahead. He'd been thinking with his heart, not his head, when he'd decided to return to Sanctuary. Night travel was harder on the eyes and every other part of a man's body. At the very least, he should have insisted on a pony cart; he'd given up riding not long after his seventy-fifth birthday.

"They're drunk again," Atredan grumbled, and pointed up at the guard-porch atop the gate, where no men could be seen keeping watch.

"Pull the cord anyway."

Atredan reached into shadow and hauled on a thick rope. A bell clanged within the tower. Molin, who remained in moonlight, watched for movement on the roof or any of the tower's barred windows. He saw none.

There were other ways into the city, ways that didn't involve visiting the west gate on the opposite side of the town. A three-foot-wide breach lurked behind rubble a mere thousand paces to the north. Molin would have preferred the gate, for obvious reasons, but he knew the path to the breach and had used it only a few months back to trap a smuggler who'd overreached herself.

Ever the master and merchant of knowledge, Molin would give Atredan the opportunity to lead him to the breach, to see if the younger man knew the path. The youth gave no indication he knew the path—though surely he knew that Sanctuary's walls were not a solid, impenetrable ring. He tugged continuously on the rope, setting up a din within the tower.

At length, a small, firelit opening appeared in the wall.

"'S'locked," the guard said in the coarse Ilsigi dialect that passed for Sanctuary's common language, a dialect almost everyone referred to as Wrigglie.

Molin's native language was the pure, elegant, and nuanced Rankene of the Imperial court at its height. He spoke a handful of other languages as well, but he dreamt, sometimes, in Wrigglie, and suffered a headache every time. Wrigglie was a rapid-flowing speech, punctuated with silences—as though invisible hands had suddenly squeezed the speaker's throat. At its root, it was the language of the Ilsig Kingdom some two hundred years earlier, but it had matured—or rotted—far from that root.

"We know it's locked, pork-sucker," Atredan countered, demonstrating a grasp of Wrigglie street insults, if not diplomacy. "Open it and let us in."

"'S'locked until sunrise. Come back at sunrise."

"We're here *now,* and we have affairs at the palace. The *palace,* do you hear that, pork-sucker? Open the damned gate."

The nameless guard and the cadet heir exchanged insults until Molin hissed, in Rankene, "Flatter him, for mercy's sake, or we'll be standing out here until the sun has indeed risen."

"Flatter him?" Atredan exploded, also in Rankene. "The man is stinking drunk! Flatter him yourself, Lord Torchholder. I don't stoop that low."

"Lord Torch?" the guard inquired. More of Sanctuary's swarthy natives understood Rankene than could—or would—speak it, and, anyway, names remained the same, regardless of language.

Molin stepped into the torchlight beside Atredan. "It is I," he confessed.

"Come with another army, eh?" The guard laughed heartily at his own joke. His breath was sour enough to light a fire at four paces.

Molin Torchholder had never intended to become heroically famous in Sanctuary. He had never intended to save the city from itself, either. But he'd done both when he'd led a hundred mounted Irrune warriors through a conveniently unlocked gate and put an end to the Dyareelan reign of religious terror. In gratitude, every unwashed survivor counted Molin Torchholder among his closest friends.

On occasion, gratitude could be useful. "No army, this time," Molin said with better Ilsigi pronunciation and grammar than the guard had used. "I've been out lighting bonfires at Land's End, and now I just want to sleep in my own bed."

"Bonfires, eh? You could've done your lighting right here, Lord Torch, never mind them folk at Land's End. Them Irrunes, they been lighting fires since they got here yesterday." The guard whistled through absent teeth. "Burggit's done pulled everyone in close, leavin' me here by my lonesome with orders not to budge the gate 'til sunup. 'Git's not taking chances the Dragon'll light something wrong. Only thing worse'n a loose fire is a dead Dragon, eh?" Once again, the guard rewarded his humor with aromatic laughter.

Crude as the analysis was, it was also correct. "Good man, you say you know who I am. If the Dragon's setting Sanctuary ablaze, I *need* to get to the palace. Unbar the gate for me and my companion."

" 'Taint just the Dragon, Lord Torch. All them Irrune been setting fires, same as if they been riding Lord Serripines' tail. 'Git had the name for it, but it's passed clean from my ears."

Silently Molin berated himself for growing old and forgetful. The year he'd spent among the Irrune—the year before he'd led them to Sanctuary's gate—they'd heaped up huge mounds of straw and set them afire, saying their divine ancestor had entered the world through similar flames. Irrunaga's birthday was a movable feast. The bonfires Molin had watched had been lit beneath the first full moon after the autumn equinox, a full month before the Rankan Foundation festival—*that* year.

This year? Molin did the calculations. (Any priest worth his prayers knew the sky calendars as well as he knew the civil ones.) This year, the moon overhead this very night was the first full moon since autumn equinox had passed.

He begrudged the coincidence and the inconvenience, then, with a second thought, reconsidered the coincidence. The Irrune were as raw and rowdy a nation as ever galloped out of the eastern heartland. Their superstitions put Sanctuary's Wrigglie-speaking mongrels to shame, and their language was so primitive that they'd borrowed words left and right to describe their new homeland, yet they *looked* Rankan; and the Rankan myth said that before there'd been a Rankan Empire or even a Rankan kingdom, there had been a band of horse-riding warriors from the east.

If he'd been a full-blooded Rankan, Molin might have been appalled to think that the likes of Arizak and his kin were distant cousins, but he wasn't full-blooded anything except tired.

"Open the gate, good man," he pled with the guard. "Which are your barracks? I'll see that Burggit knows I'm the one who countered his orders."

The guard resisted. "Them Irrune— The streets ain't safe, Lord Torch, and you—pardon me—ain't no youngster to skip from trouble. No, no—trouble finds you, Lord Torch, and 's'my head will roll twice over for forgettin' my orders and for lettin' trouble find the Lord Torch."

"I have an escort." Molin indicated Atredan, who needed no encouragement to scowl and draw his sword.

The guard made one more protest, then relented. Moments later, to the clank of metal and the scrape of wood, the smaller of the two heavy doors cracked open. Atredan slipped through first. Molin followed.

"Don't forget," the guard called after them. "Tell Burggit 'twas on your orders, Lord Torch, that Leaner Vurben opened the gate. 'Tweren't no thought of Leaner Vurben's, 'twas your orders, Lord Torch." The clatter of the closing gate drowned out anything else Vurben might have said.

"Did you hear that? The brazen cur," Atredan complained.

"You're not thinking of running this Burggit to ground, are you? Let the man suffer."

"For what? I did countermand his orders. Common men expect protection from their officers."

"That man presumed to give *you* an order! He gave orders to an Imperial *lord*. He spoke to you as though you were another Wrigglie pud. He should be made an example of. Forget this Buggit; go to Captain Eraldus—he knows who puts food on his damn plate. He'll take care of that Vurben fellow."

Molin sighed quietly. He was a lord, and he enjoyed his privileges, but he wasn't an aristocrat. "I've found it useful, over the many long years of my life, to keep my word when I can. Oddly enough, if you honor the small things, the big ones are less significant. It took me years to learn that lesson."

"But a common Wrigglie pud! Who cares if you keep your word to him?"

Molin didn't bother to answer. When he'd given the orders to expand Sanctuary's walls, he'd imagined a plaza here between the old wall and the new—a place where visitors could be scrutinized from front and back, and cut down with impunity, when necessary. As with so many of his plans for Sanctuary, the final result bore little resemblance to his original vision. Instead of an empty plaza, there was the Tween, a relatively peaceful quarter populated largely by smugglers and hostlers.

The Tween's main street—such as it was—connected the new gate to the old gate, once called the Gate of Gold, but an empty arch these last fifteen years. Past the arch, the Wideway opened up between Sanctuary's wharves and its warehouses. Midway down the Wideway, the Processional branched north to the unbreached walls of the palace, which had hosted as many rulers as the great god Savankala had had mortal mistresses.

Both the Wideway and the Processional were lit by public lanterns—an Irrune innovation that spoke well of Nadalya, Arizak's second wife, who'd initiated it. There were torches, too, stowed in old barrels here in the Tween and at other intersections. It was said, though not in their hearing, that the Irrune feared the shadows and sounds of Sanctuary at night. Neither the torches nor the lanterns were necessary on a full-moon night, but, as Molin had learned, people took note of the small ways in which their rulers kept faith with them.

Molin took a stride in the Wideway direction. An unexpected shiver shook his spine, and he stopped. As a boy he'd been taught to equate such moments with his god's presence. The prayer of welcome and acceptance came reflexively to his tongue and waited for his mouth to open, but Molin swallowed instead. There was still a god bearing Vashanka's name and attributes somewhere, maybe within the Rankan Empire, maybe sulking somewhere in Sanctuary—immortals faded, but they never quite died. Molin Torchholder dutifully dedicated his rituals and daily prayers to his hidden god; but when a cold finger touched him, the erstwhile priest looked in a different direction.

The gods alone—all the Rankan gods, not just Vashanka—knew how Molin's life might have gone if his priestly teachers had guessed the nature of the talent he'd inherited from his temple-slave mother. Most likely, he'd have had no life at all. Indeed, Molin, in his role as a Rankan priest, would never have allowed himself to be born if he'd had the opportunity to take his mother's measure.

Of all the sorceries known to the world, witchcraft was the darkest, the most mysterious, and the one favored by the Empire's northern enemies. Officially, witchcraft did not exist in the Empire. There was prayer, which directly invoked divine power, and there was magic, which—according to priests, if not magicians—used spells for indirect invocations to the same gods. Witches, in the Rankan scheme, were witless mages who'd surrendered their souls to gods so foul and evil that mortal tongues could not pronounce their names.

Rankan priests, especially the warrior-priests of Vashanka's hierarchy, were adept at piercing a witch's deception. The fate of a witch in the bowels of a Rankan temple was necessarily bleak: interrogation by torture and punitive mutilation, followed, inevitably, by a gruesome execution. In light of that fate, it was not surprising that a northern witch usually chose suicide over capture. But Molin's mentors in Vashanka's hierarchy had failed to detect the taint of witchcraft in a nubile, northern slave and, having failed to detect her heresy, taught her to dance. At a decennial Commemoration of the Ten-Slaying wherein Vashanka had freed his divine father, Savankala, from his siblings' treachery, they'd given her to Vashanka's lucky, wealthy avatar for a night of feasting, music, and ritual rape.

Molin had never met the woman who birthed him. She'd died, he'd been told, moments before his birth, taken up in his divine father's arms. He'd known that for the lie that it was before he'd turned six, but he'd never worried about his bony face, his black hair, or his pale skin—so unlike the golden features of the Rankan aristocracy, so similar to Ranke's enemies. Molin had never wondered at all until he found himself in Sanctuary and face-to-face with powers that Vashanka would not—or could not—vanquish.

Molin won the battle against those powers one dark Sanctuary night. He lost both his god and his faith after the victory, but the talent for witchcraft lingered. He denied it publicly, of course, and there was no north-witch mentor to whom he could turn for training. But he practiced diligently, exploring his limits and gradually expanding them, so that when the great nerves in his body shivered he understood that witchcraft had given him a message.

Gripping his blackwood staff, Molin spun right, toward the Tween's tangled streets.

"This way."

"The Wideway's safer," Atredan insisted.

"The wharves are never safer after sundown, and neither is the Processional, if the Dragon's men are celebrating." Molin was confident, but not entirely honest. Witchcraft—*his* witchcraft—did not deal in precise premonitions. He'd felt danger when he'd looked down the Wideway, no more, no less. The rest was his own logic, his own decision. "We'll take the Stairs."

"The Stairs will take us up into the Hill. I'd sooner swim the sewers of Sanctuary than get lost in the Hill!"

"Nonsense. Once we've climbed the Stairs, we'll be at the end of Old Pyrtanis Street, nowhere near the Hill. From there it's an easy walk along the Promise to the Gods' Gate behind the palace. You're not afraid of a few whores or empty temples, are you Lord Larris? See me to the Gods' Gate, Lord Larris, and I'll show you a way through the kitchens to your prince's door *and* the fastest way between the palace and the Street of Red Lanterns . . . We never could have the whores traipsing up the Processional you know—Or has your brother already shown you the postern trap?"

Molin asked his last question with the sweetness of a cat about to pounce. It was unlikely that elder-brother Vion Serripines knew about the trap, ten times unlikely that Vion had told Atredan, and ten times again unlikely that Atredan could resist a gift his brother had never received.

"I've heard about that passage," Atredan lied unconvincingly. "Not from Vion. Vion doesn't know. Vion wouldn't go anywhere where the hem of his robe might get dirty. Vion's no better than our lord father."

Molin led the way without commenting on the young man's assessment of his kinfolk. Every time he took the Stairs, it seemed they were both steeper and less even. He was breathing hard when they cleared the wall and entered into the old city.

Pyrtanis Street was paved with tidy cobblestones, recalling the day when its part of the city had been home to its most prestigious artisans—jewelers, goldsmiths, and their ilk—and not a few of its aristocrats. The shape-shifting mage, Enas Yorl, had dwelt on Pyrtanis Street as well. The jewelers and aristocrats had fled Sanctuary at the first sign of trouble; their fine houses were among the first to burn when plague had threatened the town. Some said the shape-shifter never left, that he still haunted the town, but any man could claim to be Enas Yorl; the man never showed the same face twice to the world.

What was plain for any eye to see on Pyrtanis Street was that the corner where Yorl's basilisk-guarded mansion had once stood was empty, even of weeds—as if the stones were simply elsewhere, like their owner, and might reappear at any moment.

Nothing in Sanctuary went to waste. One season's rubble was next year's construction, and if the new hard-laboring residents were less exalted than their predecessors, they were also less likely to abandon their homes at the first hint of trouble. Whatever havoc the Dragon and his cronies might be raising in other parts of Sanctuary, they had sense enough to stay off Pyrtanis Street.

"We could do with a torch or lantern," Atredan said when they'd come far enough to see the emptiness of the Promise of Heaven and the dark wall of the palace beyond it.

"Nonsense, the way is clear, and moon's brighter than any torch."

Atredan balked. "This place is haunted. We should go the other way, Lord Torchholder."

"The Hand's been gone for ten long years," Molin countered. "Nothing passes here now except a few whores on their way home to the Hill. You're not afraid of a few whores?"

"The gods remember. The gods marked this place."

Atredan was young—not yet twenty—and born outside the city walls at Land's End. He could have few personal memories of the Bloody Hand of Dyareela doing its awful work on the Promise, nor of Arizak leading his warriors against them in a battle that left the last of the old temples in ruins. When the last of the bodies had been collected it had been Arizak, the Irrune chieftain, who'd decreed that while *he* ruled Sanctuary, no god or goddess would be worshiped within its walls.

Those who'd dwelt within the walls and survived the madness had accepted Arizak's decree. They'd been silently grateful to turn their backs on the place where so many had died for so little reason. But the exiles of Land's End—who'd been conspicuous that day by their absence—*they* mourned the loss of the Rankan temples they had not visited in years. They nurtured that mourning—that sense that fate had conspired against their beloved Empire—in their children.

"The gods— All the gods, Ilsigi and Rankan alike and every other god ever worshiped here, do not care about an empty piece of earth, Lord Larris."

"But, Vashanka—!" the young man protested. "Surely—"

"Surely if Vashanka had cared, Vashanka would have done something, but He left this mess for men to clean. Come, Lord Larris. If we'd walked rather than talked, we'd be halfway across by now."

Molin slipped his free arm beneath Atredan's elbow to nudge him forward. A rooster in one of the yards nearby chose that moment to mistake the moon for the rising sun. The sudden sound surprised them both, and another man—to judge by the moonlit silhouette—out on the empty Promise who darted into the ruins that had once enshrined Thousand-Eyed Ils of the Ilsigi, another god who'd done nothing for Sanctuary when it could have used divine help.

"Let's take the other way, Lord Torchholder," Atredan pled, no longer hiding his fear.

When he'd been a young man—or even a middle-aged one—Molin would have pursued the straggler into Ils's temple. He had no quarrel with some Ils-worshiper who preferred chiseled stone to the pile of bricks outside the wall, but once the Hand had driven Ils's priests out of His temple, they'd chosen His marble hall as the site for an altar to their bloodthirsty goddess.

Molin had worked beside a score of priests representing almost as many gods to destroy that altar, that abomination. He'd take no chance that some misbegotten soul could undo his work—

*Tomorrow,* Molin chastened himself. *Tomorrow,* and with a handful of men walking ahead of him. Tonight he would sate himself with the view from the weedy steps.

"The other way, Lord Torchholder. My lord father charged me with your safety—"

Molin led the way, one hand gripping his staff, one eye stuck on the Temple of Ils.

*Were those flame-shadows flickering on the walls?*

So intense was Molin's interest in the distant temple that he heard nothing, saw nothing move in the nearer shadows until a man with daggers in his hands blocked the street some five paces ahead of him and Atredan.

"Prepare to die, Torchholder," the stranger snarled with a man's voice, and flung the metal in his hands.

Molin pressed his staff against the ground and called upon his mother's accursed power. He swayed left, then right as his witchblood quickened. One knife missed completely; the other tangled in his cloak and rang down against the cobblestones. Molin swung the staff into a two-handed grip across his chest and sought his attacker's face in the moonlight. What he found disturbed him to the core of his old bones—the man concealed his features beneath tightly wrapped, dark cloth which was almost certainly silk, almost certainly dyed bloodred, almost certainly worn by a worshiper of the Bloody Mother, Dyareela.

Nonetheless, Molin replied with confidence: "It will take a better man than you to lay me in my grave."

Witchcraft demanded tribute in exchange for its gifts, and Torchholder could not guess what price he would pay for drawing down to the depth of his talent, but for now and the next little while, he was the man he'd been—quick, strong, and cunning. The would-be assassin had not expected a fight from an old man; even less had he expected one from a man in his prime, but he stood his ground and drew another, longer, dagger from his belt. That was more than could be said for Atredan Larris Serripines, who shrieked like a maiden and ran for the Stairs.

The long dagger flew toward the youth; Molin let it pass and closed with the Dyareelan. Old man or young, witch or priest, he'd never been one to waste time defending a coward's back.

That much the stranger expected and, with yet another knife in his hand, tried to get inside the Molin's defense. Molin struck fast with the staff's amber finial, clouting his attacker on the left thigh. It wasn't the blow he'd hoped it would be—no bones cracked or broke. Molin struck again, as close to the same place as he could—witchcraft had restored his vigor, but it couldn't replace the practice he'd missed over the last many years. The stranger cried out in pain. He curved over his leg like a reed in the wind, but backed away from a killing blow.

"Prayer will not save you, Torchholder. You tore her children from her breast. You fed them poison and let them die. You wasted their blood! Wasted blood! She has thirsted all this time for yours—" The Dyareelan had proved that he knew whom he was attacking.

Molin's heart skipped a beat. He clamped his lips together, which the stranger mistook for a prayer.

"Your puny god cannot hear you. Dyareela has chosen my hands to take your blood."

They were mad—that was the first thing a man had to realize about the priests who served the goddess of discord, destruction, and chaos. Only madmen could believe that the world needed to be reborn in blood. Madmen or children. Children, in their innocent ignorance, could be taught to believe anything, and the teaching, if it got hold of their souls, could not be undone.

Molin feinted at the stranger's battered thigh, leading him in a sun-wise dance until moonlight fell on his silk-shrouded face. Morbid curiosity drew Molin's attention to the man's hands. They were as dark as his face from wrist to fingertips. In sunlight they would have been bright crimson.

*How?* Molin demanded of himself. *How had a Bloody Hand priest kept himself hidden for ten years?* And, *How had a Bloody Hand learned about the poison?*

Arizak knew, and his brother, Zarzakhan, the Irrune's high shaman. The three of them had agreed that there was only one sure way to solve the problem they'd found living inside the liberated palace: sevenscore children, stolen from the streets and fed on blood and terror until their very souls had withered. That fateful day of Sanctuary's liberation—before word of the Hand's collapse spread through the streets—Molin, Arizak, and the shaman had examined each child in the light of prayer, witchcraft, and human cunning. No more than one in five had shown a spark of conscience; those they sent aside to be reunited with whatever remained of their families. For the rest, for the young, dead-eyed killers who preferred their meat raw, Molin and Zarzakhan had—with Arizak's express permission—prepared a deadly feast: horse carcasses larded with poison and left where hungry hands could reach them.

By midnight, all the children were retching. By dawn the problem had been solved. Molin and the shaman buried the bare-bone carcasses, replacing them with the corpses of red-handed priests. Then they'd set the carnage alight and sent an ignorant Irrune warrior to awaken Arizak. With his armor hastily buckled around him, Arizak proclaimed to the newly liberated Sanctuary that for its final atrocity the Bloody Hand had sacrificed their captive children.

No one who'd seen what the Hand could do doubted the Irrune chief's declaration.

Back on the Promise of Heaven, the Dyareelan lunged. Molin dodged and pivoted his staff. The amber finial made glancing contact with the attacker's chin. He reeled backward, grunting each time his right leg took his weight, but caught his balance before he fell.

"She is with me," the Dyareelan decided with a crazed laugh. "Strangle spoke the truth! *She* gives me strength. My hands—*My* hands!—will take your blood!"

Molin put a stop to the wild laughter, landing several blows in quick succession on the Dyareelan's neck and along his weapon arm. The last blow cracked the attacker's knuckles, loosening his grip on the knife. It clattered to the cobblestones. When the Dyareelan tried to retrieve the knife with his off-weapon hand, Molin pivoted his staff a second time. This time the amber knob struck true, shattering the stranger's jaw. He dropped to his knees, too stunned to scream or defend himself. Molin stepped in for the kill—a vicious thrust with the knob that drove the Dyareelan's nose into his brain and left him lying still on the stones.

Molin had no time to savor his victory; he barely had time to get the staff planted between two stones before his witchcraft-fueled vigor ebbed. His joints ached, his muscles burnt, and it took all his will to keep himself upright. When the worst had passed and he'd reopened his eyes, Molin saw not only the man he'd killed, but the awkward heap where Atredan Serripines had fallen.

Slowly, painfully, and knowing what he would find, Molin made his way to the young man's side. Kneeling, he felt for a pulse; there was none. After closing Atredan's eyes, Molin withdrew the fatal dagger and studied it in the moonlight. To his mild surprise it was an Imperial dagger bearing—unless he was very much mistaken—the crest of Theron the Usurper carved into its hilt. Thirty years had passed since such knives had been common in Sanctuary and, notwithstanding Theron's failings as emperor—he'd established the dubious and ongoing custom of usurpation rather than political compromise as the means of Imperial governance—a man who owned one of the Usurper's steel knives wasn't apt to part with it willingly.

Which said what—if anything—about the red-handed assassin?

Still hobbling, Molin returned to the corpse he'd created. He loosened the knotted silk. The lifeless face confirmed his worst suspicions: beardless, browless, and bald, with lips as dark as the silk; equally dark patterns swirled like serpents across his cheeks. Though it was hard to be certain between the tattoos and the moonlight, Molin judged the Dyareelan to be a man in his midthirties, too young to have received the knife direct from Theron.

He'd gotten it from someone else. An accomplice?

Molin shivered at the thought. No one in Sanctuary had offered a word of protest when Arizak banned Dyareela's cult and sentenced Her red-handed minions to one of the many traditional Irrune executions: tied hand and foot to the tails of four horses. Molin accepted that there were those in the town who secretly worshiped the outlaw goddess—She spoke to a need, as old and dark as night itself—but no man dared walk the city's streets with bloodstained hands, and another generation might pass before gloves were fashionable.

Perhaps he'd mistaken paint for tattoos?

Molin took the Dyareelan's lifeless hand, spat on its wrist, and rubbed the border where light flesh met dark. The line remained sharp, his own fingers unstained. The stains were permanent and, recalling the assassin's words and accent, he'd been no stranger to Sanctuary. Muttering curses as if they were prayers, Molin let the hand drop and searched for other clues.

*Arizak won't like the sound of this; and Lord Serripines*—Molin shook his head, imagining the Rankan patriarch's reaction to losing his second son and losing him, after all these years, to the Bloody Hand. He tore into the stranger's clothing, even pulled off his worn but serviceable boots. Aside from his tattoos and the silk, there was nothing—nothing at all—to distinguish the assassin from other men—no additional weapons, no jewelry, no luck charms, not even a sprinkling of the blackened metal bits that passed for money in the poorer quarters of Sanctuary.

The absence of identity was uncanny and, for a moment, Molin regretted that final blow. But, with or without witchcraft, he was an old man, and he couldn't afford generosity; besides, the Hand didn't respond well to interrogation. They broke quickly enough . . . and succumbed to the madness inherent in their creed.

Wearily, Molin wrapped his fingers around the staff. He felt the weight of all his years climbing to his feet. In part, that was the aftermath of witchcraft, but not all. If the Bloody Hand of Dyareela were back in Sanctuary, then he'd failed when it had mattered most, and every sacrifice he'd ever made for this gods-forsaken city had come to naught.

*Something. There must be something, some loose end I can trace to its source. If it's not in his clothes, then where? The other stranger, the silhouette running into Ils's ruined temple? The rooster's crowing—a bird or a signal? Had he been betrayed—by the Serripines? Atredan hadn't wanted to come this way. Could that have been pretense? Was the youth that good an actor?*

Molin was returning to Atredan's corpse when a bolt of memory scattered his thoughts—"*Strangle spoke the truth*."

Strangle. A red-handed priest calling himself Strangle. Or herself.

Dyareela was a goddess with unusual attributes and appetites and, though every image Molin had seen portrayed Dyareela as a woman with crimson lips and breasts, it was said that She was hermaphrodite beneath Her skirts. The Irrune had found mural-painted rooms in the liberated palace that Molin could not recall without breaking into a cold sweat. It had taken more than sermons or knives to turn boys and girls into remorseless killers.

By the time the Irrune finished cleansing both the palace and the defiled temples, they'd killed or captured more than three hundred red-handed veterans of Dyareela's cult. The people of Sanctuary had cornered forty or fifty more. No one could say for certain; the tattooed bodies had been in pieces when the Irrune collected them. A few more Dyareelans had turned up in alleys and sewers—suicides, mostly—but the last four years had gone by without so much as a red-handed rumor, and Molin had begun to relax.

Never again.

Never as long as he lived—which didn't allow much time.

Molin knelt uncomfortably beside the red-handed corpse. He pressed his staff across its chest. He'd pay—surely he would pay a high price for indulging in witchcraft twice before the setting of the moon, but it would be worth it, if he could lure Strangle into the light.

The theory was simple—slip into another mind, ransack its memories for a particular face, a particular name; then call that person and wait for him—or her—to appear. In the north, among his mother's people, witchblooded children learned the trick early, but Molin Torchholder had come into his talent late and without a mentor. The theory was all he knew, and a dead man's mind was a bleak midnight sinking toward oblivion.

Once, Molin thought he'd captured the prize—a gaunt face, scared and malefic; stained hands with mutilated fingers. It was accounted an honor among the Bloody Hands to lop off a knuckle or two in the goddess's honor. He whispered the name—*Strangle*—and felt a tug, as if from the far end of a long, slack, rope.

Satisfaction proved Molin's undoing. One heartbeat he was the fisherman hauling in his catch; the next he was the fish. The fish got lucky. It threw the hook and swam free.

Molin awoke with his forehead resting against the dead man's chest. He was chilled to the bone and stiff to the point of paralysis. Tears trickled from his eyes as he straightened his neck—

The moon had set. The street was dark, but in the east, the stars had begun to fade. He'd been kneeling on the stones for the better part of the night. It was a miracle—a sign, perhaps, that Vashanka had not completely forgotten His old priest—that he had survived the night.

Then Molin tried to stand. Something was wrong with his hands. He could feel the staff against his palms but his fingers would not grip it strongly enough to lever him up. He attempted to straighten his spine and the pain of a lifetime lanced through his right hip. Moaning softly, Molin collapsed. When he'd found the strength to try again, the sky was bright enough for shadows.

Molin reached for his staff and stopped short. His hands . . . his hands were not his hands. Yes, he was an old man with blotched, crinkled skin, but the hands that moved, grudgingly, according to his will were bone and gristle wrapped in parchment.

*The price,* Molin thought in horror. Witchcraft always extracted a price, and foolish, clumsy witchcraft exacted the highest price of all. His heart raced, or it tried. He had been old, now he was decrepit, too, and the least effort left him panting and dizzy. With exquisite slowness, Molin wrapped first one hand, then the other around the staff. He had visions of his bones crumbling when he tried to stand, but he foresaw worse if he couldn't drag himself off the streets.

The hip pain was not as severe as it had been before dawn. Molin could stand but knew, even as he balanced on the cobblestones, that he could not walk. The long, black wool robe he'd worn to the Foundation feast was stiff and sticky with blood. *His* blood, Molin thought incredulously and at the same time remembered the stranger throwing a knife that had tangled in his cloak. It had nicked him; and he hadn't noticed. No doubt it had been slick with poison—the Hand was especially fond of paralytic poisons; and he hadn't noticed. He'd plunged into witchcraft, not noticing that he bore an open wound.

Molin had killed himself. It was as simple as that. A man who'd prided himself on his cleverness had slain himself with carelessness. The only thing Molin felt more keenly than the pain in his hip was shame. He hid his face behind a frail hand while with his mind's eye he beheld all his unfinished intrigues.

*Not now,* Molin complained to fate, which was never known to answer prayers. *Not with Arizak crippled and his family divided. Not with the Hand loose in Sanctuary again. I've got work to do; I can't die now, not without an heir . . .*

Vashanka was not a chaste god, nor did He expect His priests to live a celibate life. Molin had been married once, long ago. He'd sired children then and later, but none had lived more than a handful of years. Something to do with the witchblood, he suspected. He'd had other opportunities to choose an heir; and he'd rejected them all. Intrigue was Molin's life. Without intrigue he'd have no life, so he'd never surrendered, nor even shared his web of secrets.

Shame weighed on Molin's shoulders. His chin sank to his breastbone. His hand fell to his side. He stared, seeing nothing but failure and his feet until he blinked and saw himself.

If there were rules to witchcraft—predictable consequences to repeated actions—Molin Torchholder had never learned them. He certainly couldn't account for what lay on the cobblestone—a corpse wearing his face, the face he'd worn yesterday at Land's End—save for the shattered jaw and devastated nose. Its hands were his, too, gnarled and mottled with age, but unmarked by blood-colored tattoos.

When the street awakened, as it surely would now that the eastern sky was gold and crimson, they'd find two corpses on the street—a youth with Rankan features, wealthy clothes, and a single wound; and Arizak's longtime advisor, brutally beaten and stripped to his loincloth. Arizak would be outraged, Lord Serripines of Land's End, too. Lord Serripines would insist that Arizak search the city inside out for the murderer; and Arizak would comply . . . and proclaim a hero's funeral. The Irrune chief had promised as much many, many times, and he was a man of his word.

*What would Strangle make of that? Would he come to see the pyre, hiding his telltale hands? Could a decrepit and crippled old man sniff out the villain and expose him before his ruined body failed completely?*

The man who had been Molin Torchholder had to try. It was better to be dead on the streets of Sanctuary than hobble before Arizak to admit his carelessness and his failures.

# Chapter Two

More asleep than awake, Cauvin lay on his back thinking about gray.

Grabar's stoneyard, where Cauvin lived and worked, had begun to fill with daytime noise. The cow wanted milking. The chickens and goats squabbled over whatever slops Mina had thrown out the kitchen door at the start of breakfast. The dog barked itself silly at the yard's Pyrtanis Street gate. But when Cauvin set himself to thinking about fog and twilight a few household animals didn't stand a chance.

As a boy, Cauvin had mastered gray because his life had depended on it. *Don't think,* the Hand would say as they'd taught him the lessons they wanted him to learn. *Stop thinking. Nobody wants to know what you think about anything. And don't ask questions, either. You're just another lazy pud. Almighty lazy and sheep-shite stupid. Dyareela didn't make you for thinking; She made you for listening and doing what you're told—exactly what you're told, and when you're told to do it. Maybe someday—if you don't die of dumb first—the Mother of Chaos will visit you and you'll hear Her voice. Until then, you belong to the Hands of Chaos so you froggin' sure stop thinking, stop asking questions, and DO WHAT YOU'RE TOLD.*

Cauvin did what he was told, and he didn't ask questions. He'd seen what the Hand did to disobedient orphans. But he couldn't stop thinking, so he'd made himself think about fog and twilight. The Hand didn't seem to notice; neither did Grabar—not that Grabar was anything like the Hand. Grabar was a good-enough man whose worst crime had been seizing an opportunity to turn a sheep-shite orphan into a fake son. If Grabar had Cauvin working stone each day until his shoulders ached, it was honest work with hot food afterward and a place to call his own in the loft above the work shed.

Froggin' sure he argued with his foster parents, but everybody argued. In ten years Grabar had never raised a fist to Cauvin, nor he to Grabar, not even in the early months when Cauvin hadn't known one kind of stone from another. Cauvin hadn't needed the gray since he'd come to the stoneyard—except late at night when he got to remembering life *before*. Then, when his froggin' memories were sore and throbbing, Cauvin dove so deeply into fog and twilight that it was almost like being dead—except that last night he'd had a dream.

Cauvin could count all the dreams he remembered. That's how few there'd been in the twenty-five, maybe twenty-six, years he'd been going to sleep at night and waking up the next morning. He wasn't complaining. What would a sheep-shite idiot like him dream about, anyway? The past? It was bad enough he froggin' remembered his froggin' past. If he'd dreamt about it, too, the way memories got twisted up in dreams, then froggin' sure he'd have drowned himself the way Jess did.

Or Pendy.

Pendy had slit her own throat. Just picked up a knife one morning after she'd been dreaming and damn near sliced her own head off.

Froggin' sure Cauvin didn't want to wind up like Pendy.

Froggin' sure Cauvin didn't want to have any more dreams like the one he'd just awoken from.

In Cauvin's dream, the Hand was back on the streets of Sanctuary. They were looking at everybody through *Her* eyes—through Dyareela's eyes, the Mother of Chaos. They were looking for someone to kill, someone to make *Her* happy.

Looking for loose children.

The Mother of Chaos *loved* children.

In his dream, Cauvin had hidden himself in gray fog and twilight. He'd been the self he was now, full-grown and not the child he'd been when the Hand had caught him. He'd remembered what the Hand had taught him about fighting and about hiding when fighting wouldn't be enough. In his dream, Cauvin would have been safe from the Hand, except that his father had been looking for him, too.

Cauvin had a father. Everybody had a father. You couldn't crawl out of your froggin' mother's belly without your father had put you there first, but Cauvin had never met the man who'd fathered him. Froggin' sure, he could scarcely remember his mother; still, he could have understood if she'd appeared in his dream. But—no—it was his gods-all-be-damned father wandering through the froggin' fog and twilight, shouting "Where's my son? I need a son! Give me a son!"

Worse, Cauvin's sheep-shite sire was leading the Hand through the fog like it wasn't there. Leading them straight to Cauvin, who'd outgrown the need for even Grabar's fathering years ago.

Thank the gods-damned gods, he'd woken up before push came to shove. That froggin' dream had been different. Not that Cauvin had had a lot of experience with dreams, but last night's had felt like a warning: *Hey, pud, we're back, and we're looking for you.*

The dream had been more exhausting than a sleepless night. Cauvin lay on his back with his arms and legs feeling heavier than all the stone in Grabar's yard. He'd feel better if he could drag himself down to the well and stick his head in a bucket of autumn-chilled water but, so far, he couldn't let go of the froggin' dream. The Hand was all that had ever frightened him. The thought that they could return to Sanctuary turned Cauvin's blood into the thick, green sludge that clogged the stoneyard well in summer. He hated sliding down the rope and sending bucket upon froggin' putrid bucket up to the surface until what was left merely stank rather than froggin' crawled. The work always left him gut-sick for a week afterward, and that was froggin' sure how he felt with a rotten, Bloody Hand dream throbbing in his head.

The Hand would find him easy enough, if they were truly back in Sanctuary and looking. They'd taken too many orphans. When Arizak and his Irrune warriors stormed the palace, the Bloody Hand wound up making martyrs of themselves in battle and of the orphans afterward, making sure that the Mother of Chaos got every froggin' drop of blood they'd ever promised her. Better death at the edge of a knife than an angry Mother of Chaos.

It was pure frog-swallowing luck that Cauvin hadn't gotten himself sacrificed with the rest of the orphans the night after the palace fell. Before the fighting had stopped, he'd been prodded into a bare room to face the men who'd beaten the Hand. When a gray-haired man with an Imperial accent had asked him what it had been like to live in the pits for a decade, he'd told them the gods-all-be-damned truth about the killing and the cruelty and hiding in the gray to keep himself from becoming the enemy he both hated and feared.

Honesty had gotten him bolted up alone in a windowless room. He'd been sheep-shite terrified that *She'd* find him that very night, but the Hand had kept Her busy drinking blood in the pits so She'd missed him, like She'd missed Jess, Pendy, and everyone else whose answers had convinced the gray-haired man—Lord Torchholder, according to Grabar; he hadn't given his name to a sheep-shite orphan—to lock them up alone, like Cauvin.

Of course, the Mother of Chaos had froggin' sure gotten Jess and Pendy in Her own good time, and She'd gotten them through their dreams. Cauvin had felt safer because he didn't dream. He'd have prayed that he never dreamt again, if he'd believed that any god in Sanctuary gave a froggin' damn about him. The gods of Sanctuary froggin' sure didn't give a damn to anyone who didn't lay down a padpol or two when he prayed. Better yet, a silver shaboozh.

Froggin' gods, froggin' priests, and froggin' town.

Maybe it was time to leave. There wasn't anything binding Cauvin to the stoneyard. Whatever Grabar had paid to get him out of that room in the palace, he'd more than sweated off the debt, and now that Grabar and Mina had a son of their own—a real son, not a bought son like him—it was froggin' sure that he wasn't going to inherit the yard, no matter how many times Grabar said otherwise. Grabar would be moldering at the bottom of a grave when the time came for inheriting, and Mina wasn't going to give Cauvin anything she could keep for her flesh-and-blood son.

Leorin never missed an opportunity to remind Cauvin of Mina's hostility.

Leorin.

He and Leorin had been paired up for-froggin'-ever. A few years older than Cauvin, Leorin had taught him the tricks of life on the streets after his mother died. When their luck had run out and the Hand had claimed them both, they stuck together in the pits. They weren't separated until a year or so before the Irrune came to Sanctuary. Cauvin had thought Leorin had died after a night with the Hand the orphans called the Whip.

Froggin' sure, death was the best that could happen to anyone after a night with the Whip.

Froggin' sure Cauvin hadn't seen Leorin after the Whip had her, and froggin' sure the Irrune hadn't dragged her before Lord Torchholder. Probably just as well. There was no guessing what Leorin would have told the Torch if he'd asked her the same froggin' questions he'd asked Cauvin. Leorin hated the Hand, but it was a different sort of hate, colder, and just shy of jealous.

Cauvin had damn near forgotten Leorin when their paths had crossed while he was delivering stone in the Maze two years before. Froggin' sure, she'd made the moves on him; then again, Leorin was a dreamer, like Jess and Pendy. She needed someone to hold her when the screaming started.

Leorin had a room for herself above the Maze tavern where she worked. Cauvin would stay with her a few nights each week, eyes wide-open and wedged into a corner, waiting for her dream-self to rise through her body. There wasn't anything the dream-self could say or do that shocked Cauvin; he'd been wide-awake in the pits. He'd just keep her from hurting herself while she dreamt, then hold her while she cried afterward.

Leorin had wanted to jump the broom after the first night they spent together. Cauvin was the one who didn't want to take chances. No sheep-shite way he was chancing a son until he had a better idea what he was going to make of his life, or it of him. Leorin had laughed. She'd said she'd been taking chances for years—with the Whip and countless others—and never caught a bastard.

The others—the countless others—hurt Cauvin's pride, but that was Leorin: sharp as a knife and hard as stone unless you knew—as Cauvin knew—what the pits had been like. If Cauvin said he was ready to light out of Sanctuary on the East Ridge Road, Leorin would follow.

Her face floated through the gray: a Rankan beauty with dark hazel eyes and sleek, gold hair as long as her arms and coiled like summer vines. A man was no froggin' man if he didn't want her, but Cauvin was the man *she* wanted. It was getting harder and harder not to take chances.

Cauvin was imagining the feel of Leorin's breasts beneath his fingertips when his bed shook from below and a voice that was not at all Leorin's bellowed—

"You up there! Cauvin! Get your bones down here before I have to come up there and move them for you. The sun's been up an hour and you're no Irrune prince to lie in your bed all morning!"

Grabar's threat—empty though it was—was enough to get Cauvin moving. He shivered into breeches, boots, and a heavy, homespun shirt, washed in the yard, and hurried through the back door of the kitchen, where Mina cooked their meals.

"Watch your feet!" Mina snapped, as Cauvin opened the door to warmth and breakfast. "Don't you come trailing dirt and straw in here—"

Cauvin leaned against the doorjamb and scuffed his boots with a broom.

"And close that door! This is a respectable house, not some damned barn!"

"Froggin' sure good morning to you," Cauvin replied in the same tone. He shoved the door and let it slam shut. He and Mina were alone together—a circumstance they both preferred to avoid.

Mina looked up from the porridge pot she had simmering on the hearth. "Mind your damned language." She gave Cauvin a good glower, which he returned, then reached for a wooden bowl. "Here, take your breakfast."

There were peas in the porridge and enough bacon to start Cauvin's mouth watering. He took the steaming bowl from Mina's hands with genuine thanks.

"There's more if you want it, and drippings in the melter. Help yourself, but leave plenty for Grabar and the boy."

That was the essence of their relationship: So long as Cauvin left plenty for Mina's husband and her nine-year-old son, Bec, maternal resentment wouldn't boil over. Fortunately, the stoneyard was thriving, and there was enough oil in the melter to spread a golden puddle atop everyone's porridge.

"You slept through the day's excitement," Mina announced,

while Cauvin stirred his breakfast. "Sunup found not one, but *two* bodies up at the crossing! That's what comes of letting the damned Dragon carouse throughout the town!"

"Couldn't have been the damned Dragon," Cauvin countered between spoonfuls.

Grabar swore that Cauvin and Mina were so contrary toward each other, they'd argue about the sun and tides. Grabar had a point of the truth.

"I'd have heard him and his gang carousing, if they'd been anywhere near this quarter of Sanctuary. There's nothing but one lousy wall between my bed and the crossing and those Irrunes froggin' sure sound like jackasses when they jabber to each other."

"You sleep dead, Cauvin; nothing short of a kick to the head wakes you. You were like that the day you walked through the door, and you'll be the same when you walk out. Batty Dol says no one heard the two men die, but she saw the palace guard come to claim the bodies."

"Batty Dol?" Cauvin rolled his eyes. "You're listening to froggin' Batty Dol and believing her?"

Mina banged her iron ladle against the iron pot. "Mind your language! Batty gets mixed up sometimes, but she doesn't lie—not like some I could name. She came running here soon as she saw the guard in the street picking up bodies with drawn swords. Gave her a damned fright, it did. She had a hard time during the Troubles."

Nobody on the topside of the Stairs knew what hard times were, not compared to what had gone on in the pits, but the Troubles were the one subject that Cauvin and Mina held taboo. Not many people talked about the Troubles—except to say that times had been hard and that lots of people still couldn't sleep.

"So, did old Batty say who'd gotten himself killed?"

"No names, but one was a Land's End sparker—all fancy clothes and a fancy sword that was still in its scabbard. She said there wasn't a mark on him save for the hole from the knife that killed him. The other was an old man, stripped near naked—now, that'd be a sight to give any woman a damned fright. No knife in him; he'd been beat to death, she said. But he must've been somebody important, though, 'cause the guards took him away with the Ender."

Cauvin scraped the last of the porridge from the side of his bowl.

He thought about seconds and decided not to, at least until Grabar showed up and told him what they'd be doing all day.

"Someone better knock on all the doors and make sure no old man's turned up missing overnight. A Land's End sparker's got no good reason to be topside of the Stairs after dark."

"The Enders still own half the properties on this street. Pyrtanis Street was their street when my grandmother lived here. The grandest street in Sanctuary. When the Enders come back into Sanctuary—this is where they'll live. They'll rebuild their houses and serve dinners that last all night. Imagine it, Cauvin! My grandfather's house—the house that stood right here—was four stories high. It was built from dressed stone and had twenty rooms! The whole top floor was divided into two rooms: one for the menservants, the other for the ladies'. Grabar, he pulled it down right after we married. Sold the stone to a sea captain. He built a warehouse down by the wharf . . ."

Cauvin looked up and caught Mina with tears in her eyes. Some people had problems because of the Troubles; Cauvin understood that. Mina's problems were older than the Troubles. Grabar had told Cauvin that by the time he married Mina, her Imperial grandfather's house had burnt and rotted. Froggin' sure, Mina and her father were still living on the property, but in a root cellar under the chicken coop. That was the real reason why Mina wouldn't gather the eggs: She didn't dream about the Hand, she dreamt about froggin' chickens.

When Mina hit the wine harder than she ought, she'd put on airs and talk about how she'd be living with the Enders if they knew who her grandfather had been, and if she'd been willing to set aside her marriage vows to Grabar. She bleached her hair because the best Imperials had golden blond hair—only hers looked more like last year's straw. If the Enders came back to Pyrtanis Street—a froggin' big if: It was ten years since the Irrune wiped out the Hand and not one of them had returned. But if the Enders did return, they wouldn't pay attention to a stonemason's blowzy wife.

If he'd wanted to make Mina miserable, Cauvin could have started cursing in the gutter Imperial he remembered from the pits, but making people miserable wasn't something Cauvin ever *wanted* to do. He had to be froggin' mad before he let his temper go because shite for sure, he always regretted losing it afterward. A dream about the Bloody Hand made Cauvin jumpy, not angry. He sought peace with his foster mother:

"Grabar's a good man. The quarter respects him . . . and you. When something happens, people come to the stoneyard to talk about it. Just like Batty Dol did this morning."

Mina swiped her eyes with her sleeve, but not because Cauvin had calmed her. Grabar himself had come through the door, and not two steps behind Grabar came Bec with the egg basket. She wouldn't let her boy see her crying.

Grabar got the biggest bowl and rashers of crisp bacon laid one by one atop the porridge until the man of the house said stop. Bec would get bacon, too. If there were any rashers left when those two were through, then Cauvin would get another taste. Cauvin's eyes were on the bacon; he almost missed Bec grabbing for his empty bowl.

There were bowls enough on the sideboard, but the boy would rather have Cauvin's. Every chance she got, Mina made froggin' sure Bec knew that Cauvin wasn't kin, wasn't even an apprentice or a journeyman with a claim on the stoneyard. The sheep-shite boy was too young still to care about kinship or inheritance. He wanted Cauvin's bowl for the same reason he wanted Cauvin's cast-off shirts: anything was better if Cauvin had used it first. When Cauvin looked at Bec, he saw the trust and love he'd never had for himself.

He teased the boy a moment, then surrendered the bowl with a grin.

Bec darted past his father, who sighed heavily but kept hold of his porridge and mug of small beer.

"'S'gonna be a dead-slow day," Grabar groused while straddling a table bench. "The Dragon's loose on the Processional. Even if a man wanted to do an honest day's work, we can't get him the stone. And you know that if Mioklas hears about our little problem with bodies piling up at the crossing, there's no way he's coming up to settle his account. He'll ask us to risk our damned necks getting bluestone to him, but that's different than him paying for it."

"I could knock on his high door," Cauvin offered.

He'd been persuading the stoneyard's laggard customers to pay their debts since Grabar brought him home from the palace. The good people of Sanctuary didn't know half of what had gone on in the palace while the Hand held it, but they knew better than to argue with anyone who'd survived it.

Grabar waved him off between bites of bacon. "Not today. Mioklas can keep his coin box locked for another day, and we'll keep our stone. You harness up the mule, instead, and take the wagon out to the old red-walled place. I've got a hunch Tobus the tailor's going to be marrying off his son this winter. His wife won't take another woman into her kitchen, so Tobus'll be needing a new house next door to the one he's got. Sure he'll want the fronts to match, so you break out ten or twelve paces of those red walls and bring 'em here."

Cauvin nodded and tried to hide his disappointment. He'd rather knock on Mioklas's high door.

"You know the place?" Grabar misinterpreted Cauvin's hesitation. "I showed it to you once. The roof's been down for years, and there's trees older'n you growing in the master's bedroom."

"Where we got the bricks for Mistress Glary's garden?"

"The very same. No sense letting those bricks go to waste in the sun and rain. You knock out enough of those bricks to front Tobus's new house."

Cauvin calculated the work and suppressed a groan. As bad as breaking out old stone was, breaking bricks was worse. Stone was harder than mortar, but bricks weren't. For every hour he spent swinging the mallet, he'd spend three or four chipping mortar away with a chisel.

"There's bacon for you," Mina called, as if any number of rashers would make any difference to Cauvin's shoulders by the end of the day.

Yet, Cauvin would have to be dead before he'd turn down bacon. He left the table to retrieve his treat from the hearth.

"How about me?" Bec asked, and not about the bacon. "I want to help Cauvin smash bricks. Please, Poppa? Please—I'm big enough now." The boy preened with his skinny arms and mimed a swing with the mallet.

"No," Mina decreed from the hearth. "Cauvin can work alone. I don't want my Becvar pretending he's more bull than man like the two of you—especially not outside the walls. He's fine-boned, like my father, and not made for heavy work. What if something happened out there beyond the walls?" She shivered dramatically.

"He could chisel mortar off the bricks," Cauvin suggested.

Bec wouldn't waste much time working, no matter what, but Cauvin would be glad of his company. The boy had named all the household chickens, and the stories he made up about them were better than the ones Bilibot and Hazard Eprazian told for drinks and padpols in the Lucky Well at the other end of Pyrtanis Street.

"Grabar!" Mina trilled. "I won't have it! Bad enough when you're with him in the yard, but Cauvin's sheep-shite stupid. Becvar could chisel off a finger, and Cauvin wouldn't notice 'til he'd bled to death!"

"Calm yourself, wife. The boy's fingers are safe for another day. Not that they'd be at risk. Like as not, our Bec would jabber like a crow, and Cauvin wouldn't get a day's work done."

Cauvin could have done with a better defense. He could have done with the wits to do something more than smash stone all day. He could have done with lots of things, but he made do without. "Tough cess, pud," he advised Bec, tousling the boy's hair as he spoke and nudging Bec's scowl into a bit of a smile.

"Sweet Sabellia! How many times to I have to tell you—mind your tongue around Becvar. Bad enough you run like a sewer around us who shelter you. Think of his future? What master'll have him if he runs off like you?"

"Don't worry, Mama. I remember what you've told me about talking to masters and lords and ladies. 'Yes, my lord' and 'as you wish, my lady.' Cauvin knows I'm no lord or lady—same as you when you call him 'sheep-shite' or 'turd-head' or when you and Batty get talking about—"

"That's *Mistress* Dol to you, young man!" Mina snapped at Bec who rarely heard the edge in his mother's voice. Then Mina turned on Cauvin. "You've got your orders for the day. Go harness the mule and get gone. You're naught but a bad influence around here."

"Fine!" he snarled on his way to the door. "I'm leaving! Leaving for good and forever. Got that? Find someone else to smash out your red bricks, someone with a priest's tongue in his head!"

Cauvin hated her just then, hated her as much as he hated the Hand and everyone else who'd ever pushed him around with fists or words. He had a bad temper—that was no secret—and he had the scars to remind him what happened when he lost it. He was through the door and letting it slam when Bec caught the wood.

"You'll be back for supper?"

Gods knew where Bec had gotten those huge dark eyes—not from his parents, for froggin' sure. He could charm a snake out of its scales and have it hissing thanks in the bargain. Bec's soft-eyed smile wouldn't last the night on the Hill or in the Maze—and that was another reason the boy could get whatever he wanted from Cauvin.

"I'll be back by sundown," he promised, and tousled the dark hair again.

"I'll help you harness Flower?"

"Nah—" Cauvin whispered.

"I'll tell you a story . . . a *new* story—"

"Later, Bec. There's no time now. Get back to the table and make your mother happy."

"How come *I* have to do all the hard work around here?"

"*Sh-h-sh,* and get your ass back in there."

Cauvin led Flower in her harness out to the wagon and began attaching the traces. Bec waved to him from the far corner of the work shed, where he was practicing his letters on a loose slab of slate. No shortage of writing material in a froggin' stoneyard.

The boy had shown Cauvin how to write his name in both Imperial and Ilsigi characters. Mina wouldn't have approved, but Mina didn't know. She didn't know that sheep-shite Cauvin could read numbers and a few Ilsigi words—the sort merchants and mongers wrote on the slates tacked to their market stalls. The stoneyard's account book, which Mina kept in the language she knew best, was safe. Cauvin couldn't read a froggin' Imperial word—except the name Bec had taught him. But Mina was only fooling herself if she thought she was going to stay in charge of her son's life for very much longer. The boy was froggin' clever, cleverer than his parents put together, not to mention a sheep-shite stone-smasher named Cauvin.

The previous spring, when it had rained so much they'd thought they'd all drown, Bec had come up with an idea to channel the roof runoff into a covered cistern. It had taken Cauvin three tries to get the cistern built right—the boy didn't understand that wood bent and swelled when it got wet until Cauvin explained it to him—but the whole idea had been Bec's, and they'd been froggin' sure glad of the cistern's clean water a month before, when the well went rank.

Cauvin went to get his tools. Grabar intercepted him in the shed, where neither Mina nor Bec would witness their conversation.

"Don't go taking the wife to heart, son."

"I'm not your son, Grabar; your *wife* froggin' sure never lets me forget that."

"She frets over the boy, but she don't mean no harm by it. Those bodies in the crossing this morning. She fancies she should've known the sparker. You know how it is: We all got things we don't talk about, don't think about neither—'til something up and grabs your balls."

Cauvin shouldered out of the shed with an armload of chisels. "Now Mina's got froggin' *balls*?"

"Cauvin." Grabar's tone pled for peace. "Cauvin, the stoneyard's yours after I go. I said you were my son when I brought you home from the palace. I meant it then, and nothing's changed since. You're the eldest, Cauvin—the burden falls on you because you're the one who's strong enough to bear it. Bec's your brother. If I'm not here, you'll see to it that he's set up someplace that suits him . . . *and* you'll take care of the wife—because the wife's your mother, too, not just the boy's. You're my son. The wife's your mother. The boy's your brother."

The clatter of wood and metal as Cauvin dumped the tools in the cart served as his reply.

"You're family, Cauvin. The wife knows it. There'd be no talk of jewelers and apothecaries but for what you've done these last ten years. You'll inherit the yard, Cauvin, I swear it. The quarter knows; they'll stand up for you . . . all the way to the palace."

Cauvin took the mule's lead rope and got the cart moving toward the yard gate.

"I'm an old man now, Cauvin. I can't run the yard without you. You go now, and it won't be just the wife and me who'll suffer. The boy'll suffer. You know he's not made for smashing stone and brick. He'll break early. You don't want that, Cauvin. I know you don't."

There was a desperate edge to Grabar's voice that burrowed

under Cauvin's skin. "You want me to smash out those froggin' redwall bricks or you gonna stand in front of the froggin' gate all day?"

"I'm trying to ease your mind."

"Froggin' sure, I'm family, Grabar. If you weren't passing me off as your sheep-shite son, you'd have to pay me wages, and that'd put a froggin' quick end to Bec's apprenticeship. No froggin' goldsmith or 'pothecary's gonna take him for less than a fistful of soldats—old-fashioned, froggin' sweet on the tongue, *silver* soldats. Or some nice gold coronations from an emperor who didn't cut his coins with copper. If you had 'em, you wouldn't be sending me out to smash bricks froggin' nobody wants. An' if the palace knew you were hoarding coins 'stead of paying your froggin' taxes, they'd be down here digging up the garden and knocking on the rafters."

Grabar's mouth worked, but no sounds came out. They'd never talked about where he kept his little hoard. Maybe he thought Cauvin didn't know. Froggin' sure, if he'd chosen better hiding places, Cauvin wouldn't.

"Froggin' sure, I'm family," Cauvin repeated. "Up to my froggin' neck I'm family."

He reached for the bar across the gate, and Grabar, at last, got out of his way. At an arm's length, people usually got out of Cauvin's way. They usually got hurt if they didn't. His temper made life simple, not good. Time and froggin' time again, Cauvin found himself too far gone and looking for a way back.

"I'll be home for froggin' supper," he snarled over Flower's withers as he led the mule out of the yard.

Grabar got the last words, but they were lost in the scraping of wood against dirt as the gate closed. Alone on Pyrtanis Street, Cauvin endured pangs of regret and echoes of the things he could have said to calm his foster parents. They were both good people—better than a sheep-shite like him deserved, better than he'd have had if his blood-kin *had* shown up at the palace to claim him ten years before.

Lost in mulling thoughts as he walked, Cauvin was blind to the street around him. He didn't notice the city guards until he was between the pair of them in the crossing where the bodies had been found.

"Hey, Cauvin! Where you headed?"

The men of both the guard and the watch knew Cauvin by name, and he knew them by type. No matter who sat in the palace, order got maintained by city-bred bruisers—big men, mostly, tough, and just enough older than Cauvin that they'd stayed clear of the pits even if they hadn't always stayed clear of the Hand.

"Takin' the mule for a walk," Cauvin replied as the more grizzled of the pair reached into the cart to peel the canvas back from his smashing tools. "It's too nice to keep her in the yard all day."

Steel gray clouds were scudding in off the ocean, driven by a raw, southwesterly wind. It didn't take froggin' sorcery to know that the warm days of autumn were giving way to the storms of winter. Like as not Cauvin would be warming his blankets tonight with coals cadged from Mina's hearth.

"Mind your own business, pud."

"Always do, same as you. So, who got killed here last night? Mina says you sheep-shites hauled off two bodies."

"Not us," the second guard grumbled. "We're lookin' for the bits that might've got left behind."

"Find any?"

"Not yet," the grizzled guard said. "Pork all. We'll be here the whole porkin' day."

Cauvin thought he looked familiar; if he was, then his name was Gorge and he was honest, for the guard. He didn't know the second man from a shadow.

"Somebody important, then?"

"Atredan Larris Serripines," not-Gorge spat, as if the name said everything that needed saying.

And, in a way, it did. Mina was right—a Land's End sparker had come to his final grief a few hundred paces from Grabar's stoneyard. The Enders were squirrelly. Most of them never set foot in Sanctuary. They let their gold speak for them, their gold and the Irrune.

"Good cess to you, then," Cauvin gibed. "You're froggin' sure going to need it. City's got to suffer if the Enders do. What about the other corpse? Don't suppose the sparker slew the pud who slew him?"

"Not a porkin' chance. The other body was one of ours," Gorge said, throwing the canvas back over Cauvin's tools. "Believe it or not, someone finally killed the froggin' Torch."

"Froggin' shite!" Cauvin exclaimed with genuine surprise. "I figured him for dead years ago."

Gorge shook his head. "Don't get out much, do you pud? He was stuck to Nadalya like her porkin' shadow an' he stuck to Arizak the same way once he came back to Sanctuary. Can't figure what him and a shite-face sparker were doing in this porkin' quarter middle of last night."

"Going to the palace," Cauvin replied and wished he hadn't, by the way both guards stopped cold to stare at him. "Any *dog* knows the fastest way from the East Gate to the palace is up the Stairs and across the Promise to the Gods' Gate. How much do *you* get out?"

Gorge and not-Gorge exchanged heavy glances.

"I was sleeping alone in my froggin' little bed last night," Cauvin insisted honestly. "Talk to Grabar. Shalpa's eyes—I've got no cause against the Torch."

"You said you thought he was dead," not-Gorge reminded Cauvin.

"Lay off him, Ustic," Gorge commanded, then speared Cauvin with a stare. "Killer wasn't you, not unless you've taken to throwing Imperial steel."

"Shite, no!" He carried a knife—just about everyone did—but it wasn't his weapon of choice. When Cauvin got into a fight—which was more often than either he or Grabar would have preferred—he relied on his fists. "Imperial steel—that's too rich for my blood. You're looking for Enders, or one of your own." He wished he'd swallowed that remark, too.

"Maybe. Maybe not," Gorge snapped. "Maybe you and your she-mule better keep on walking now."

Ustic added, "Don't go picking up anything that's not yours."

"Never do," Cauvin promised with a grin as he got Flower moving again.

It was an open secret that Grabar sold scavenged stone and brick. Grabar froggin' sure sold new goods when he could get them, but the nearest stone quarries were deep in Ilsigi territory, and the local clay pits were flooded three seasons out of four, so Grabar froggin' sure sent Cauvin out scavenging three days out of four.

Long before Cauvin's mother ran afoul of his froggin' father, Grabar had worked for the Imperials scavenging stone from Sanctuary's old Ilsigi-built wall for reuse in the higher, longer new wall that was supposed to keep the city safe from the hazards that had laid Imperial Ranke low. Froggin' sure, the new wall hadn't protected Sanctuary from sea storms, plague, or Dyareela's Bloody Hand.

Grabar said Sanctuary had shrunk by half since he'd been a boy; and by all the empty, gutted buildings Cauvin saw, Grabar was overly generous. Whole quarters were abandoned and ripe for scavenging—if they'd ever held anything worth scavenging. The best pickings were outside the froggin' walls, where the rich folk once lived. Their sheep-shite gold hadn't protected them any better than walls had protected Sanctuary.

The Irrune—gods rot them—understood scavenging. Shite for sure, they *were* raiders—horse-riding brawlers who looked at a city the way farmers looked at a field ripe for harvest or fisherfolk looked at schooling fish. The Irrune had laws—and punishments that would've made the Hand blink—but scavenging wasn't a crime unless someone complained. Only once in Cauvin's memory had some sheep-shite Ender made his way to the palace waving a dusty old scroll and forced Grabar to make restitution.

Grabar had been more careful since then, asking his wife what she knew about each of the estates they plundered. Mina swore the old, red-walled estate had been empty before she got born. She said it was haunted—something about betrayal, massacre, and divine retribution. Cauvin didn't pay much attention to Mina's froggin' stories; and so long as he was home by sundown, sheep-shite ghosts didn't worry him either.

Cauvin could have led Flower down any of the crossing's streets and gotten her to the red-walled ruins, but the easiest route, and the quickest, was across the Promise of Heaven then down the Hill to one of several gaps in Sanctuary's defenses. Cauvin would froggin' sure come home the regular way, through the East Gate. No way Flower could pull a loaded cart up the Hill, but in the morning, the Hill's haphazard streets were safe enough for a man, a mule, and an empty cart.

The Promise was empty, save for a boy grazing a flock of goats on the weeds. Goats didn't care that the dirt here was rusty with blood. Goats didn't care about mules or carts, either, but Flower didn't like goats. She blew and balked until Cauvin gave in. He led her away from the goats, along the broken, stained marble slabs fronting the ruined temples.

The Irrune worshiped their own god and wouldn't share him with anyone not born to their tribe. They didn't much care who or what other people worshiped—excepting Dyareela, of course—but they didn't want any priests underfoot. After the Troubles, pretty much everyone in froggin' Sanctuary agreed with them. The temples were in pretty bad shape by then, anyway. The Hand *had* cared; the Bloody Mother was a damned jealous bitch. Her priests had burnt or broken every statue and priest they could seize.

If you needed a god or a priest these days, you went outside the west wall between the old cemetery and the froggin' brothels on the Street of Red Lanterns. Cauvin didn't need any froggin' gods or priests. He'd had his fill of them even before he'd fallen into the pits. As for women, he had Leorin to think about, and so long he did, there was no froggin' way any extra padpol that flowed between his fingers was going to wind up in some whore's treasure chest.

Cauvin was brooding about the future when he heard scuffling in the temple shadows. *Froggin' dogs hunting rats,* he told himself, and tugged on Flower's lead. But rats didn't groan . . .

Any man who put himself in the middle of someone else's fight froggin' sure deserved all the trouble he got; still, Cauvin left Flower's lead dangling. On his way up the uneven steps of the soot-streaked Imperial temple, he reached inside his shirt and tugged on the lump of bronze he wore suspended around his neck. The slip-knot loosened, the way it was supposed to. He closed his fist around the only token he'd kept from his days among the Bloody Hand of Dyareela.

By then Cauvin could see a bravo from the hillside quarter behind the temples deep in dead-end shadows rousting someone who wasn't putting up a fight. The Hiller sensed Cauvin's approach. Hunched over his victim like a wolf, he raised his head and snarled a warning: "Back your froggin' arse out of here, pud."

There was enough light to assure Cauvin that he didn't know

the Hiller and, more significantly, to reveal the knife in the Hiller's hand. With two corpses in the crossing and the murderer still loose, a prudent man might have gone looking for Gorge and Ustic, but a clever man thought of the reward Lord Serripines' would froggin' surely give to whoever caught his froggin' son's killer. Cauvin figured he could put those coins to better use than any sheep-shite guard.

"Froggin' after you," Cauvin snarled back, and came closer.

Cauvin didn't much care if the Hiller bolted. One Hillside pud was as good as another as far as the Serripines' reward was concerned. If he couldn't have the Hiller, Cauvin would happily drag the Hiller's victim back to Gorge and Ustic as his first stride toward riches.

At least Cauvin hadn't cared who ran and who remained until he got a better look at what was lying in the temple rubble. The Hiller's victim had to be the froggin' *oldest* man in Sanctuary. His head looked like a parchment-covered skull. But he wasn't dead, and he wasn't done. With the Hiller distracted, the old geezer actually made a grab for the froggin' knife.

The geezer didn't have a sheep-shite prayer of getting anything away from the Hiller, and he was froggin' sure lucky that he didn't get his wrinkly throat slit for his efforts; but two things became clear to Cauvin. First, the geezer wasn't a murderer. Second, if he wanted a reward from Land's End, he'd have to best the Hiller.

When Cauvin had halved the distance between them, the Hiller got to his feet and made a threatening pass with his knife. Cauvin just shook his head. They were about the same size, and his weighted fist had gotten the better of bigger men, bigger knives.

The geezer—gods rot him—didn't have the sense to lie still but tried to crawl away. The Hiller booted him in the ribs and something snapped inside Cauvin. He might have shouted as he surged toward the Hiller; he sometimes did when his temper got the better of him, or so he'd been told. Once his rage had boiled over, Cauvin's thoughts were in his fists.

Warding the Hiller's knife with his empty hand, Cauvin delivered two quick, bronze-filled punches to the Hiller's gut and a third to his chin that sent him reeling backward. The Hiller spit blood at Cauvin's face, squared his shoulders, and surged forward, leading with the knife. Cauvin dodged; he caught the Hiller's wrist as it passed and gave it a vicious twist. The knife landed in the rubble. The Hiller landed on his knees with a wide-eyed, worried look on his face. He eyed the corridor and the weeds of the Promise of Heaven, but Cauvin straight-armed him against the moldy wall before he could make his escape.

Cauvin didn't count his punches, but when he let go, the wall couldn't keep the Hiller upright.

"Take the damn thing," the Hiller wheezed, tossing a nut-sized object into the rubble.

It rang like metal before it disappeared, but Cauvin wasn't interested in some trinket the Hiller had lifted from his victim; he had his heart set on a Land's End reward. The geezer, though, heard the sound and came crawling like a groaning, moaning skeleton. Cauvin's legs took him backward before his head could stop them, and the Hiller got a head start toward the Promise.

Froggin' sure, Cauvin could have caught the Hiller and, froggin' sure, he would have, if the skeleton hadn't rasped—"Help me!" at just that moment. Cauvin wanted that reward. Gods rot him, he wanted it bad, but not bad enough. He let the Hiller get away and sifted the debris instead until he found a signet ring with a black stone set in a golden band.

Cauvin couldn't make out the symbol carved into the stone, but that didn't matter much. He knew his stones, both the common ones and the precious. He didn't know anyone important to have an onyx signet stone, much less a gold band to set it in. The ring alone had to be worth quite a bit, but the geezer himself might be worth more.

"You got a name?" Cauvin asked as he pressed the ring into the old man's grasping hand.

With movements that were scarcely human, the geezer twisted the ring onto a bleeding, probably broken, finger. "Staff?" he asked. "I had a staff."

"Don't see it," Cauvin said after a quick glance at the nearby debris. "You got a name, old man?"

"Black wood—old and polished, topped with a piece of black amber as big as your fist. Look for it!"

Cauvin took orders from Grabar and stoneyard customers, not from some sheep-shite old man. "It's not here! You got a name, pud? A home? People who give a froggin' damn whether you're dead or alive?" He was thinking about a reward again.

The geezer latched onto Cauvin's sleeve and tried to pull himself upright but didn't have the strength. Cauvin got an arm beneath him and began to lift. Bec would have weighed more. The old man was nothing but skin and bones inside a well-made, way-too-large robe. Cauvin had his shoulders up and was starting to raise his hips when the geezer let out a groan, and Cauvin eased him quickly back to the floor.

"Where does it hurt?"

"Where doesn't it?" he snapped back. "Find my staff!"

"Listen to me, you sheep-shite pud. I could take that froggin' ring of yours and leave you here to die, but I'm trying to help you instead, so act grateful."

"If you want to help me, pud, find my froggin' blackwood staff."

For someone who couldn't stand or sit on his own, the old geezer was froggin' feisty—and not from Sanctuary, though he cursed like a native. Cauvin had begun to feel like a fisherman who'd hooked a fish that was bigger than his boat.

He tried bargaining: "You'll tell me your name, right, if I look for your froggin' staff?"

"If you find it."

Cauvin got up and walked toward the Promise, dragging his feet through the rubble and finding nothing until he was out on the steps. Flower was nibbling weeds alongside the pavement and there, not two froggin' paces from the cart's rear wheels, was the sort of black staff an old man with a gold-and-onyx signet ring might lean on. Leaving Flower to enjoy her midmorning meal, Cauvin returned the staff to the old man, who smiled a death's-head grin when he saw it.

"So, what's your name?"

"You can call me Lord Torchholder."

"And you can call me the froggin' Emperor of Sanctuary."

"I very much doubt that."

The man calling himself Lord Torchholder struggled to brace the staff against the wall and himself against the staff. Cauvin saw that the effort was a froggin' sure lost cause, but the geezer wouldn't give up until he was flat on the floor again and moaning like the winter wind. Having a better idea what the old man could endure, Cauvin scooped him up and carried him toward the cart.

"I'll take you home. Just tell me where you live, and I'll take you there."

The old man squirmed in Cauvin's arms. "My staff! Don't leave my staff!"

"Gods rot you, pud—you're one ungrateful bastard," Cauvin groused as he settled the old man in the cart, but that didn't stop him from brushing dead leaves and worse from the bastard's thick silvery gray hair or cushioning his bones with folded canvas or noticing, as he did, that the lower half of the old man's robe was stiff with dried blood.

The pieces didn't fit. The geezer was so thin, so frail; he couldn't have bled that stain and survived. He was wealthy enough to have a gold ring and a polished staff, but his fine-woven wool robe hung around him like rags. And his eyes— All the old men Cauvin knew—and admittedly he didn't know many—had cloudy, weak eyes. Not this one. This old pud's eyes were bright and sharp as a hawk's. Froggin' sure he wasn't just anybody's grandfather—but Lord Torchholder? Maybe, if the guards hadn't just said that the Torch had been killed in the crossing . . .

Or maybe Gorge was wrong about the corpse they'd carted up to the palace? Were those the eyes Cauvin had met behind a table inside the liberated palace? Was that the voice, the accent that had ordered him to follow a stranger to a tiny room where he'd sat, cold and terrified, while the Hand's other orphans died?

"Don't stand there gaping—go fetch my staff. You're a disappointment, pud, no doubt you are. I prayed for better, but you're what I got."

Without a word, Cauvin returned to the dead-end shadows. The staff was where they'd left it, but he took another moment to search for the Hiller's knife. The blade was rusty and brittle, not a weapon an emperor would give his name to.

Which meant froggin' what?

Froggin' nothing.

Cauvin slipped the knife inside his boot and put the staff in the cart beside the old man.

"If you're Lord Torchholder, then I guess I better take you up to the palace."

"You'll do nothing of the kind. It's too late for that. Too late or too soon. I can't tell. You've got a home somewhere; take me there. I need time—" The old man winced and pressed a hand against his hip. "Time. So little time. Listen, pud—listen close, and you'll hear the gods laughing."

"I'll take you to the palace, Lord Torchholder," Cauvin decided. "They'll know what to do—"

"The hell they will, pud. By now, they think I'm dead, and this is no time to contradict them. I'm staying with you; you're all I've got—the Emperor of Sanctuary, or do you have another name?"

"Cauvin," Cauvin replied, stalling for time because the pieces were starting to fit, and he didn't like the shape they were forming. "They call me Cauvin. You called me Cauvin once, if you're really the Torch."

"Oh, I am, Cauvin, or I was until last night. But you've got me at a disadvantage. I've known too many people to remember them all."

"The day Arizak led the Irrune into the palace. You talked to all of us, one at a time—"

The old man's eyes widened. "Ah, Vashanka," he whispered, almost in prayer. "How our deeds come back to haunt us. I tried to build Him a temple, right here on the Promise of Heaven. It was a mistake—the biggest mistake I made . . . until last night. Listen to the wind, Cauvin. My god is laughing. After all these years, Vashanka has avenged Himself upon me."

There wasn't a breeze stirring so much as a leaf on the Promise of Heaven.

"I'll take you to the palace, Lord Torchholder."

"Not there," the old man insisted. "Think of a better place. Where do *you* live, Cauvin?"

"Grabar's stoneyard," Cauvin answered before he could stop himself. He imagined Lord Torchholder at the stoneyard. There was Mina squawking to all the neighbors that she had the froggin' *Hero of Sanctuary,* in her kitchen. Grabar would complain about the cost of keeping him and Bec—! Froggin' sure Bec would be telling stories about the froggin' chickens until the Torchholder's froggin' eyes rolled back in his head. "No froggin' way I can take you there."

The palace was simple. The palace was where Lord Torchholder belonged, and the palace was close by; Cauvin could see the Gods' Gate from the cart, and there wasn't anything the old man could do to stop from leading Flower in that direction. Yet their argument continued until the goat boy was staring at them, and three women with nothing better to do were walking toward them.

"You can't stay here—" Cauvin pled desperately.

The old man—the legendary Torch—grabbed his staff and pointed its amber end at Cauvin's chin. "Therefore, Cauvin, you will take me with you. Wherever you were going, we will go there *now*!"

Cauvin stared at the amber and shivered. "The old red-walled ruins?" The place was a roofless ruin with trees growing in the empty rooms. But, the outbuildings were in better shape—or they had been, the last time Cauvin had scavenged bricks. "Froggin' sure you'll sing a different song before the day's done."

Cauvin got Flower moving, and the old man let the staff fall to the bottom of the cart. His eyes closed. For a moment Cauvin thought the geezer had froggin' died, then his chest began to move, slowly, steadily. Sure as shite, he'd wind up bringing the old man back into the city. Grabar would be frothing pissed because the cart would be empty when he got back to the stoneyard, but Grabar had been frothing pissed before.

# Chapter Three

The feather mattress had seen better days. Its cover was stained with the gods froggin' knew what, and the feathers had molded. The only good that could be said of it was that it didn't move by itself when Cauvin shook it onto the bed frame.

Cauvin could have afforded better—the purse the Torch had given him was heavy with froggin' silver soldats, bright soldats minted years ago in froggin' Ranke itself—but bedding wasn't like eggs or oil: You couldn't just walk onto a market square and find someone selling it. Folk didn't need a froggin' bed all of a sudden. They planned. They went to a chandler and ordered something for delivery in a week or two or they made do and slept on froggin' straw the way Cauvin slept in the stoneyard loft.

Except the Torch was too frail to sleep hard and, though he'd surprised Cauvin by looking better by the time they got to the red-walled ruins than he had when they left the Promise of Heaven, it still didn't seem likely that he had more than a couple days left to his life. The bruises he'd gotten in his struggles with the Hiller weren't serious, even for him, but there was a weeping hole at the point of the old man's hip. The wound didn't bleed much, but it went down to the bone.

So Cauvin had walked the Spine path through the Hillside quarter, begging for bedding.

"I wish you'd let me take you to the froggin' palace," Cauvin said, and not for the first time. "So the guards made a mistake identifying your body. It's not like it's the first time they've made a froggin' mistake, and Arizak will send for a priest to heal you—maybe even that wild-man brother of his."

"I *am* a priest, pud, and I know the limits of prayer. The limits of prayer, magic, and witchcraft together. None of them will help. I'm dying, pud, and I'm more aware of it than you can imagine, but I'm not dead yet."

Having seen the wound, Cauvin was inclined to agree. "Arizak will see that you're kept warm. He'll have someone sit beside you to tend your fire and bring you food—"

"I have more food than I can possibly eat—" the Torch swept a hand toward the bread, fruit, and greasy sausage Cauvin had brought back from the Hill. "And you've laid the fire."

"You can't tend it yourself. You'll fall if you try to rise from the bed, and if you froggin' fall, you'll froggin' lay on the froggin' cold ground until you're froggin' dead."

"I can reach everything I'll need with my staff. I have everything I need—well, everything that you could scrounge up. You've done well, Cauvin—better than I'd hoped. Go home. I can take care of myself—"

"Froggin' *hell* you can take care of yourself! You're old, you're injured, and you're outside the walls! If the froggin' cold doesn't kill you, something else will."

"A ghost perhaps?" the Torch asked, wrinkling his battered forehead and raising a single eyebrow.

"Maybe. The women say this place is haunted. I've never stuck around after sunset to see if they're right."

"Then you'd better get moving. The sun's sinking, and the sky's turning red."

Cauvin opened his mouth, but before he could utter his familiar protest, the Torch cut him off.

"Has it occurred to you, yet, to use that lump of unshaped stone you're hauling around at the top of your neck and ask yourself—If Molin Torchholder is alive, then *who* was that second body the guards found? No? I didn't think so. Understand this, Cauvin: I've made enemies, and I haven't outlived them all—although I outlived the one I met last night. Right now my enemies—the ones that tried to kill me last night—think they've won the battle and the war. They're not going to be looking for me in a rat warren outside the walls. I can handle cold, lad, and I can handle any stray dog or wolf that might come wandering through the door after midnight. I could even handle a ghost, but I can't handle my enemies right now. Maybe by tomorrow I'll have thought of a way—"

"Maybe you'll be dead," Cauvin countered, though once he considered the Torch's question he could appreciate the old man's caution.

"And if I am, then you'll bury me and get on with your life—but if I'm not dead, then I expect you to be here with leaves of parchment, good black ink, and three goose quills—good quills, from a white gander."

Cauvin raked his hair. "When I get home and Grabar sees that there's practically nothing in the cart he's going to ream me out for froggin' sure. I'll be out here tomorrow smashing stone as if my sheep-shite life depended on it—if I'm not singing for my supper at the Lucky Well."

"I've already told you what to tell Grabar: On your way to the wall a merchant persuaded you to use your cart and mule to help him relocate his shop. You've got the coins to prove you were well paid for your labor. If by some chance the remains of my purse don't soothe your foster father's temper, then don't waste your time trying to sing for your supper, lad—I can tell you don't have the throat for it. Come back here with the parchment, ink, and quills; I'll have work for you to do."

"If I hold out enough money to buy your froggin' parchment, there's no way Grabar's going to think I was froggin' well paid for my labor."

The Torch scowled. "So it's more money that you're looking for?"

Cauvin was too embarrassed to answer the question honestly, but his silence was enough for the Torch.

"I may have enemies, Cauvin, but I'm not completely without friends in Sanctuary . . . or resources."

"So, I'm to go to the palace after all?"

"Forget the palace, pud. I do have friends at the palace—friends who are no doubt mourning my death and putting men in the streets looking for my murderer. You show up there laying claim to my property, and you're going to find yourself in parts of the palace you've never imagined."

"I froggin' sure doubt that," Cauvin shot back defiantly. "Your froggin' friends or your enemies can't show me anything I haven't seen before. Or have you froggin' forgotten where you froggin' found me the first time?"

It seemed to Cauvin, as he met the Torch's sharp, black eyes without flinching, that the old pud did, finally, remember their previous meeting.

Then those eyes narrowed like a thief's, and the Torch murmured: "You'll do. I believe you'll do just fine," before continuing in a more normal voice: "Fortunately for you, Cauvin—for both of us—I've never been one to keep all my resources in one place. My late, unlamented wife taught me that trick. There's a tavern—the Broken Mast—along the wharf, past the Processional, near the docks where the fishermen tie up their boats—but it's a seaman's place, not for fishermen. The owner's name is Sinjon. Give him this—" The Torch fussed with his robe and came up with a bit of green stone, from where Cauvin couldn't have said. "Tell him that there was blood on the moon last night—"

"Blood on the moon? The moon was plain as white—"

The Torch sighed. "It's a password, Cauvin. Tell Sinjon that there was blood on the moon last night—exactly those words—and he'll give you a box that should ease your mind for a week or two."

Cauvin took the token. It was a tiny ship, and the stone was apple green jade, worth its weight in pure silver. "Is it ensorcelled?" he asked, turning it over and looking for a carver's mark.

"No. There's no sorcery more potent than a man's conscience. Take your mule and cart. Go home, eat your supper, visit the Broken Mast, get the box, push the leaves apart, and come here tomorrow morning with my quills, ink, and parchment. I'll know what we're going to do by then."

"Unless you're dead."

"Then you'll bury me—and Sinjon's box will be yours. But don't get your hopes too high, Cauvin. I may have set myself adrift, but I'm nowhere near ready to drown—and you've taken my token. I've marked you for a man of conscience. I'm never wrong about such things."

The old man's confidence worried Cauvin. Froggin' truth to tell, everything about Lord Molin Torchholder worried Cauvin, and the tiny ship, which he'd tucked into his boot along with a single silver soldat from the Torch's purse, worried him most of all. He wasn't a man of conscience, no more than he was a dreamer because, like dreams, conscience brought back memories he'd rather not remember.

The jade ship pressed against his calf like a hot coal. He thought about tossing it away, but that wouldn't help. He couldn't abandon the Torch or pretend that nothing had happened—even if he'd wanted to. Grabar wanted bricks to tempt Tobus the tailor, and the old red-walled estate was the only place to scavenge them. Cauvin would have to come back tomorrow, and he'd have to go to the Broken Mast tonight.

Clouds had piled up in the west to block the sunset and bring an early twilight to Sanctuary. The night watch was on duty at the East Gate when Cauvin arrived at the wall, but the gate itself was still open. He and Flower got in line behind a mountainous hay wagon and a trader's string of five overburdened donkeys. The watch challenged the trader and demanded that he unpack his lead donkey; they passed Cauvin through while the man was still untying the pack ropes.

Pyrtanis Street was dark by the time Cauvin reached it. Grabar was waiting for him with fire in his eyes and the stink of wine on his breath. He'd spent the day at the Well. Grabar didn't drink himself drunk often, but when he did, there were sure to be arguments.

"You're damned late! The boy's in tears. The wife's been waiting on you since the first-watch bells! Been two murders—" Grabar began, then he noticed the nearly empty cart. "What's this?" he demanded. "What were you doin' all day?"

Cauvin told him, "A merchant hailed me before I left the city. He had stock to move, and his own mule was lame." Cauvin dug out the Torch's purse. He tossed it gently in Grabar's direction. "He offered a fair price for my labor, so I sold it to him."

Grabar spilled the purse into his palm. He wasn't so drunk that he couldn't count coins. "Damn sure you don't work this hard around here," he commented, but his temper had cooled, and his tone was largely admiration.

"Tell Mina I'm going out to celebrate," Cauvin said, careful not to make his words a question or a request. He nudged Flower toward her stall at the back of the yard.

Grabar hurried after them. "You held some back!" he complained.

"I earned it—an honest day's work." That much, at least, was true. Cauvin hadn't broken any laws, but there was an edge on his voice. "What difference does it make if I held out a sheep-shite soldat or two? You were froggin' tickled a moment ago when you thought you had it all."

Grabar took a long step back and raised his hands, palms outward, not in fists. "It's fair. It's fair. Keep what you've kept. No need to be tellin' me how much you got—but you be the one to tell the wife that you won't be eating her supper. I told her you're needed around here; she made up a peace offering: mutton stew, just the way you like it. And you be tellin' the boy that you're back. You scared him for froggin' fair this morning."

Cauvin let loosening Flower's harness serve as a reason to hide his face. He didn't care if Mina and Grabar had taken his threats seriously, but Bec? He'd thought he'd set that to rights before he left.

"Froggin' forget it," Cauvin said, lifting the harness from Flower's back and hanging it on the wall. The mule let out a jackass bray of relief and trotted into her stall. "Tell Mina I'm not going anywhere until I've had a bowl of her froggin' mutton stew. I won't go any-damn-where, now or ever. You've nailed my froggin' feet to the floor."

"No one's begrudgin' you a bit o' celebration," Grabar insisted.

He got to the feed bucket first and poured grain into Flower's manger, then he pushed the cart into its proper corner of the shed. Cauvin tried to remember the last time Grabar had done his chores for him. He was too irritated to be certain, but it had been a year if it had been a day.

"Go see that woman of yours. A man's got silver, a man's got to see his woman."

Leorin's face floated into Cauvin's thoughts, a cool breeze at the end of a hot summer's day. With silver in his boot, he didn't have to settle for the Well's sour wine or Mina's froggin' mutton stew. He could walk into the Vulgar Unicorn, order a mug of their best ale with a plate of sweetmeats beside it, and Leorin would sit in his lap as he ate. She knew how he'd gotten out of the palace by mistake and the Torch's grace; she'd appreciate the tale he could tell.

"Just you be careful," Grabar continued. "The Unicorn's no place for an honest man. You got yourself overpaid for an honest day's work. Don't think it'll be a habit. There's not so many fools in Sanctuary."

Trust Grabar to douse him with froggin' ice-cold water, but Cauvin shook off the warning. "Any more about the corpses in the crossing?" he asked innocently.

"The talk at the Well was that the young man was a Serripines from Land's End and the other, some old bastard from the palace. Digger said it was Lord Torchholder, then Honald said the Torch's been dead for years, so it couldn't have been him. But the bells were ringin' all afternoon, so maybe it was—or maybe they were puttin' on a show for the Serripines. Gotta keep the Enders happy. No one's owned up to killing the pair o' them. You be careful tonight. The Dragon's still loose in the town—don't get into trouble that's not your own. Wouldn't surprise me none if 'twere the Dragon what kilt the Torch—if'n it were the Torch that got kilt."

*The Dragon!,* Cauvin thought, then excused himself to get his spare shirt from the loft and clean himself up at the stoneyard's trough. If the Torch had killed the froggin' Dragon— Or more likely, if the Torch had killed one of the Dragon's froggin' cronies, then no wonder he didn't want to go back to the palace. But if one of the wild Irrune had attacked the Torch, would he have used an Imperial knife? Wouldn't the Dragon's men use a sword? Or an arrow? The Irrune were froggin' fierce archers, shooting better from the saddle than the guard could shoot while standing on their froggin' feet.

Could the Torch have ravaged a corpse to make arrow holes look like they'd been made by a froggin' knife?

Did the froggin' sun come up in the froggin' east?

Grabar shattered Cauvin's wandering thoughts. "Remember, got to eat your supper first, or there'll be no peace around here for weeks."

Mina's peace offering was a thick, tasty stew that Cauvin ate faster than he knew he should. He kissed her on the cheek to make up for his haste. She wasn't fooled. Leorin's name had come up while they were eating. Mina hadn't offered up her opinion of women who served in taverns or lived in rented rooms above them—and that was a blessing for which Cauvin was duly grateful.

He'd stripped to the waist and was sluicing dried sweat with icy water and a rag when Bec asked—

"You want to hear a story? A new story. I thought it up just for you."

The rag leapt from Cauvin's hand to the dirt, and his heart damned near leapt out of his chest. The boy could be as quiet as a cat when he wanted to be.

"You made me a story?"

"I said so, remember? This morning, before you left? I made one up about Honald. Scratch and Honey get tired of him strutting and crowing—"

When Grabar mentioned Honald, he meant the blowhard potter who lived at the other end of Pyrtanis Street. When Bec mentioned Honald, he meant the stoneyard rooster who was every bit as loud and preening. Scratch and Honey were Bec's favorites among the hens.

"Not now, Bec."

"But you said that this morning. You said 'later.' It's later. I spent all day making it the best story ever!"

Cauvin pulled his other shirt on and tried to tousle the boy's hair, but Bec eluded him.

"You *said,*" Bec complained in a nasal whine that was already halfway to tears.

"I've got to go out—"

"You're going to see *Leorin.*"

The boy had met Leorin a handful of times. Leorin hardly spoke to Bec at all. Boys, she said, were noisy, dirty, and boring. In return, Bec disliked her with all the intensity he could muster.

"If I can," Cauvin admitted. Leorin wasn't expecting him and might not be at the Unicorn. She had her own life and guarded it zealously.

"She's mean. She doesn't love you at all, Cauvin. She treats you like her dog. Worse than a dog. No dog would have anything to do with her. The yard dog said—"

"Lay off, Bec. Stick to stories about chickens."

Cauvin was joking, but his sheep-shite tongue put an edge on his words. Bec's eyes widened, and his jaw dropped. He turned tail and darted away. Cauvin couldn't see where the boy had gone, but he could hear him sniveling.

"Gods all be froggin' sure damned!" Cauvin fished his sweated-up shirt out of the trough. "Bec! Come back here!" He beat the wet shirt against the outside of the trough. "Tell me how your story starts. You can finish telling it tomorrow. Bec! Becvar!"

Nothing—except froggin' sniffles and sobs that he didn't have time for. Cauvin wanted to see Leorin at the Unicorn, but he had to find the Broken Mast first, and he didn't want to be late on the streets of Sanctuary. Two men had died last night in his own quarter. Maybe the Torch had the froggin' truth of it: The killer had been hunting particular prey, and the rest of the city was safe. Or maybe not. Cauvin might have sheep-shite in his head, but even he wasn't dumb enough to think he could best the Torch's enemies with a fistful of bronze.

He draped the damp shirt over a fence, where it might dry by morning.

"Bec! Bec, you hear me? I *want* to hear your froggin' story about Honald and the hens. All right? I *want* to hear it, I just can't listen now. I've got to go. It'll be too late for you when I get home. I'll listen in the morning. I swear it. I'll get up early. You can tell me before breakfast? All right?"

The boy didn't answer, and Cauvin was twitchy with guilt when he opened the stoneyard gate. By Arizak's law, every household kept a torch or lantern burning beside its gate or door from sunset until midnight, and those who kept a sheaf of torches available for the public good paid a smaller hearth-tax. The townsfolk said it was because the froggin' Irrune were afraid of the dark, but the abundant torches had gone a long way toward making the city safer after the Troubles.

Cauvin didn't usually bother with a sheep-shite torch when he left the stoneyard for a night on his own, but usually he wasn't going someplace unfamiliar, and tonight the clouds of sunset were settling in for a night of fog. Sanctuary's cats would be blind by midnight, so Cauvin grabbed a torch from the stoneyard's bucket.

If worse came to worst, the shaft made a decent weapon.

Cauvin made his way down the Processional to the wharf—always best to stick to the widest streets after dark. The wild Irrune were still in town. If the babble of their froggin' language didn't give them away, the telltale scent of horse dung did. Cauvin tried to stay on the other side of the street whenever he passed a clot of them. It was one thing to get drunk every froggin' night—he'd do it himself, probably, if he weren't trying to save money, but the Irrune didn't believe in paying for what they drank or for anything else.

The sitting Irrune in the palace were supposed to make good on their wilder cousins' debts, but that was like paying your froggin' right hand with coins from your left, so there were fights whenever the wild Irrune came to town, especially when the Dragon led them. And Cauvin, who seldom shirked a brawl, had learned the hard way that when you threw a punch at one of the Dragon's own, five other Irrune returned it. If he'd traveled in a pack himself, it wouldn't have been so bad, but Cauvin was a loner, start to froggin' finish.

Someone hailed Cauvin by name a few paces short of the Wideway and the wharf. It was a city voice—not garbled by an Irrune or Imperial accent—but he pretended not to hear and headed west along Sanctuary's waterfront. By the smell of things, something large and rotting had come in with the tide. Cauvin found himself breathing shallow and wishing he'd brought a lump of camphor. At least he had the froggin' Wideway to himself.

The Broken Mast was right where the old man said it would be: dark, imposing, and hanging out over the water's edge. Its doors were closed—no great surprise. Cauvin gave the latch a tug, expecting to find the doors locked as well. Gods be damned, not even froggin' fishermen could eat or drink with that stench in the air. But the latch lifted easily and after planting his torch in the sand bucket beside the door, Cauvin stepped into a quiet, dim commons.

His presence lifted heads at the handful of occupied tables.

Strangers gave Cauvin the froggin' once-over, and he returned the favor. They were a strange lot—seamen with dressed hair and jewelry dangling from their ears and elsewhere. One sported a jeweled eye patch that glowed in candlelight. Several were drawing down on small-bowled pipes. Cauvin sniffed. The dominant smell inside the Broken Mast wasn't rot, nor even incense to disguise it; it was *krrf,* the dreamer's drug from northern Caronne.

*What have you froggin' sure gotten me into, Torchholder?* Cauvin demanded of the absent geezer.

A tall young man, pale-eyed and maybe a year or two older than Cauvin himself, ghosted out of the shadows.

"You be looking for someone, eh?" The ghost's Wrigglie was colored by an accent Cauvin couldn't place. He carried his left arm bent and close to his side. The hand was withered and curled like a chicken's foot.

"I've come to see Sinjon."

"Captain Sinjon?"

"Could be he's a froggin' captain. Could be he's not. I'm here to speak for another . . . *privately.*"

The maimed man grinned, revealing a shiny gold tooth in his upper jaw. "How privately?"

"You Sinjon?"

"No."

"Then you don't froggin' need to know, do you, pud? Is Sinjon here?"

"And who's here to speak *privately* with Captain Sinjon?"

Cauvin gave his own name and knew at once he'd said the wrong thing. He considered the passwords Molin had given him, but that was for Sinjon and this wasn't Sinjon, so he gave Molin's name instead. The maimed man recoiled as if he'd just gotten a mouthful of something foul. In the edgy silence, Cauvin produced the carved jade token.

"Tell Sinjon I've got this."

The ghost attempted to conceal his froggin' astonishment and failed utterly. "W-wait here," he stammered, and ran two-at-a-time up a crooked flight of stairs.

Cauvin had enough time to regret every word he and Molin

Torchholder had exchanged before the ghost reappeared. He hadn't come down the stairs and didn't lead Cauvin up them either.

"Froggin' fantastic smell around here," Cauvin snarled as they stepped out onto a balcony ringing the second floor of the Mast. "Is it coming from your sheep-shite kitchen?"

"Blackfish," the guide said with a soft chuckle. "As big as a boat. Washed in last night. Have you ever seen the hagfish?"

"Blackfish, hagfish, what's the difference? A froggin' fish with an old shrew's sheep-shite head?"

The ghost chuckled again. "The hagfish, she's a fair lover and not no shrew. She always knows when a body's drownded. She glides up to him, all soft and gentle, 'til she finds his arse, then she slips herself inside, like a greased witch, and reams him from the gizzard out—"

Cauvin hesitated with one foot poised to follow the ghost down a different flight of stairs. He had no difficulty imagining the ghost's hagfish or guessing where those pale eyes would go in a crowded room. There hadn't been much room for innocence growing up in his mother's shadow, and less in the pits. He thanked his froggin' father that he'd never been the sort to attract a boy-eater's eye and wondered how loud the froggin' ghost would scream if his chicken-y fingers were forced straight.

"I was on the *Queen of the Waves,*" the ghost continued, drawing farther ahead of Cauvin, who cursed Molin Torchholder earnestly and silently, then followed him into the Broken Mast's depths. "We came upon jetsam and grappled it on deck. There was a man in the wrack, naked pink as the morning he was born and not a mark on him. The cook's mate, he gives it a shove with his toe—as to waken it up. Burst like a ripe carbuncle, it did and there was hagfish all over the *Queen*'s deck, writhing like snakes. We shoveled like the damned getting them back to the deep, and when we were done, there was only the hide of a man left on the wrack, not a speck of bone or blood. The hags'd eaten him up, stem to stern."

Between the still air, the stench, and the ghost's story, Cauvin wiped cold sweat from his forehead. "This the way you usually welcome new customers?"

"The fools on the shore . . . they touched the blackfish, same as the cook's mate, he touched that corpse. That's why the stink."

"Froggin' fantastic."

The ghost knocked on a door. From the inside a man's deep voice said, "Send him in, Anst."

"The captain will see you now."

# Chapter Four

Cauvin entered a low-ceiling room heated by a brazier smoking in a sandbox atop one of the barrels. The room was cluttered with crates and barrels that might contain the Broken Mast's stock of brandy. Captain Sinjon—a bald, gray-bearded man—sat behind a checkered table that had been cleared of its counters. A brass lamp of unfamiliar design cast shadowy light on the captain's lean, weathered face and an intricately, but obscurely, carved and painted box.

When Cauvin had closed the door, Captain Sinjon asked to see the token. The room was considerably warmer than the commons or the streets had been. Cauvin felt himself beginning to sweat before he stood the little ship in the center of one of the black squares.

The captain examined the jade by lamplight. "How'd you come by this?"

There was only one chair in the chamber, and Sinjon was sitting in it, which left Cauvin standing and feeling awkward. He nudged one of the crates with his boot and, judging it solid, sat down on the corner.

"I got it from an old man with the instructions to tell you that there was blood on the moon last night."

From his crate-corner perch, Cauvin could meet the captain's stare directly, which quickly proved a mistake. The man didn't blink. One eye—his left—bore straight on, like a snake's, while the other wandered slowly: up, down, inward, outward. Cauvin had seen more than his share of strange sights, but Sinjon's roving eye made him anxious. He had a predictable response to anxiety.

"My old man," he snarled angrily, "says you're supposed to give me a froggin' box. *That* froggin' box."

After an overly long hesitation, the captain sighed. He folded his hands over the carved box and pushed it toward Cauvin without releasing it.

"Just today I'd begun to hope it was mine to keep . . . and open. Considering who he was . . . *what* he was, Lord Torchholder understood the sea. So long as he was up in the palace, the captains could be sure of a fair hearing for their grievances—no telling what's to happen now. The Irrune—they'd never seen the sea, didn't have a porking word for it in their jabber. Most of the Rankans, they weren't much better than that stinking silty port of theirs. The Ilsigi—now they understand the sea. You can sail an Ilsig ship through any water, any weather, but as She rules, you'll pay and pay forever for the privilege. The Ilsigi—they understand gold and silver best of all. The Torch, he knew that, so when Her folk came to Sanctuary, he saw the advantage straightaway."

Captain Sinjon said a word—a name, perhaps—in a language that Cauvin had never heard before. It sounded like "bey-sib" or "bey-sah"; or maybe it was two different words. The captain must have seen the confusion on his face.

"You're too young," he said. "You couldn't remember, even if you wanted to—and who wants to remember nowadays, eh? Better tuck your head under your wing. No one here saw them coming—a fleet as big as the harbor, and it sailed in all unannounced carrying the hope of the Empire: the bey-sah herself, her court and all they'd need to sustain them until Mother Bey made rights of the home they'd left behind. Bow down, She says; sail away to the north and east, She says. Sail away and wait, for there's nothing She can do to right the wrongs with the righteous bey-sah still about and apt to suffer. So the bey-sah shipped out with her court, north and east, came to Sanctuary, and *waited.*"

The captain stroked his beard. His left eye stared at a point past Cauvin's shoulder while the right wandered a while before he sighed, and said:

"A life in exile's too long and twice as bitter—that's what my mother told me. They never belonged here, never meant to stay past the first tide home. She was a sailor, born on her ship—died there, too, if the Mother was willing. The sea's the same for every sailor; they got on all right with Sanctuary's sailors. Not like the court.

There was blood in the street every night—gods' blood and worse—until the ships started coming again.

"My own eyes were open then. I saw them myself. Big and graceful. They sailed closer to the wind than any ship before or since, but they shipped oars, too. Old Lord Torchholder, he never set foot on a bey-sib ship that I saw, but he took one look at 'em and knew what they were meant for. When pirates from Scavengers Island took to harrying our ships, he sent those ships after them. When the tide went out, it took the pirates with it. When it came back in, Scavengers Island was Inception Island—because Sanctuary was going to grow greater than Ranke or Ilsig together—"

"That'll be the froggin' day," Cauvin interrupted, though the captain's tale held his attention. The only mother-goddess he knew was Dyareela, and no one ever spoke of *Her* with the reverence in Sinjon's voice.

Cauvin knew the hell he'd lived through, but folk who'd survived the Troubles didn't talk much about what had gone before. Ashamed, he figured, because he'd smashed apart too many well-built walls not to realize that there must have been a time when Sanctuary wasn't a froggin' wreck of a city. He wanted to know what had happened—no froggin' good reason, except the same sheep-shite curiosity that got him whipped in the pits and kept him coming back for Bec's gods-all-be-damned tales about the stoneyard chickens.

Captain Sinjon leaned forward. "You hear," he whispered, "if you hear anything at all—that it was the sack of Ranke that did in Sanctuary's hopes. Even Old Lord Torchholder, he can't see past his great Empire, his great city, but nothing born on land can rule the sea, my friend. Sacrifice—that's the only way the sea can understand. 'Twas pride—lubber's pride—that laid Sanctuary low. Tell me, my friend, tell me the sea-god's name!"

Startled by the shouted demand, Cauvin nearly unbalanced himself. "How in froggin' hell should I know? Do I look like a sheep-shite priest?"

The captain sat back, nodding smugly, as if Cauvin's blurted answer had settled everything. "You live cheek by jowl with the sea, but do you worship? No, of course not. Temples aplenty alongside the whorehouse. Two for the sky and the storm, two for women, and others for the land, wine, and lesser things, but for the sea, only the little altars to Larlerosh in the well of every ship. You can catch fish with Larlerosh. You can run grain up and down the coast, timber and even stone—"

Cauvin's ears pricked at the mention of stone.

"But rule the sea with Larlerosh? Not from the back of a boat!" Sinjon pounded the checked table with his fist. The Torch's token and his box both jumped and landed on different-colored squares.

"After the usurper fell in the Beysib Empire and her influence was purged from the land, my mother's ships took the bey-sah and her people home; took Mother Bey with them. No sooner was the fleet gone when the sea and sky together turned black. We prayed, but Mother Bey was gone, and there was none to take Her place. We suffered winds so strong they'd lift a man clean off his feet and tides that carried ships to the very gates of the palace. Five storms like that we suffered in ten years and when they ended, Sanctuary was wracked and alone on the edge of the sea.

"Oh, I've got me a cog or two that'll carry grain and such out to Inception—but it's Ilsigi ships that keep the pirates away, not ours. And the bey-sib? Even if I had me one of my mother's sleek ships, I wouldn't know how to sail it, or where. It's all lost, lad—lost forever, and not all Lord Torchholder's gold will bring it back again. Damned shame. We paddle the shores now, like children, never out of sight of the shore. And we shun the seas where we once sailed like men."

Sinjon stared across the table, both eyes together and watching something that wasn't in the room with them. Then he blinked—only not with his froggin' eyelids, but with something clear and shiny that flicked out of the inside corner of his eyes.

"Shipri's tits!" Cauvin shouted. He was on his feet before he knew he was moving. "You—You're—!"

Word failed Cauvin because the only words he knew to describe what he'd seen were too crude, too insulting to say to any man's face without starting a brawl. Indeed, he'd never actually *seen* anyone blink without moving their eyelids.

"You're a froggin' *fish,*" he sputtered, settling on the word Mina used to describe the invaders who'd ruled and left Sanctuary before she'd been old enough to remember anything, because Mina truly did try not to curse. By what Cauvin had heard, the fish-folk were worse than the froggin' Dyareelans, which was—for him, anyway—froggin' hard to imagine.

Captain Sinjon hadn't exactly *denied* his race. He'd spoken of his mother and her departed kin; the phrases swam in Cauvin's freshest memories.

"B-B-But they *left*. They *all* left . . . didn't they? Packed up and went home as if they'd never been?"

There were some on Pyrtanis Street who swore they hadn't—that the fish were just froggin' stories made up to frighten children when tales of the froggin' Hand weren't enough. Sheep-shite Batty Dol—*she* swore the fish were real, that she'd seen their froggin' staring eyes for herself and stood on the Wideway with her children beside her to watch them sail away for good . . . But, frog all, Batty Dol talked to the ghosts every night and swore up and down that the dead could come back to life. A man had to be froggin' moon-touched if he believed Batty Dol.

Then Sinjon *blinked* again, and said, "The ones who came, left. And the ones who'd been born here with clan rights through their mothers and fathers. But not the others, not the ones born to the bey-sib *and* Sanctuary. It wasn't a matter for questions. I wouldn't have gone; I'd visited the land—maybe—I could have passed. I knew the language, then"—the captain made noises that froggin' might have been words—"and I have the look. But the Beysib Empire's no place for a man without a clan to back him. The Torch made me an offer. He thought the trade would continue—Damned shame," the captain said, and blinked again, as if he were holding back tears.

The remains of Mina's mutton stew heaved in Cauvin's gut. Gods-all-be-damned knew that the Hands with their worship of pain, blood, and chaos were worse than the fish. The fish *stared* . . . and their women did *things* with snakes. They had snakes between their legs, so did their men—according to Batty Dol, who said a man-fish could see where he pissed and what he fucked. If he believed Batty Dol . . .

Cauvin found it getting harder not to believe Batty Dol.

*Damn your froggin' eyes to froggin' hell,* Cauvin sent a heartfelt curse toward the old man in the redwall henhouse.

"Gimme the froggin' box and let me out of here." He held out his hand.

"You're too young," the captain countered, his hands still resting on the box. "You don't know what it means to watch your dreams disappear."

"Gods damn your dreams—there was blood on the froggin' moon last night. That box belonged to the Torch, now he says it belongs to me."

Sinjon slowly lifted his hand from the box, leaving it where Cauvin could reach it without moving closer. The carvings were all leaves and froggin' serpents with forked tongues and fangs. Cauvin guessed that the box had probably been carved by one of Sinjon's mother's snake-y, staring relatives and realized, a few heartbeats later, that there was no obvious way to open it—although he could hear, as he turned it this way and that, sounds that could easily be coins sliding against one another.

"Where's the froggin' clasp? The froggin' key?"

The captain shrugged. "You'll have to break it—unless Lord Torchholder taught you the trick?"

Tricks. Suddenly Cauvin imagined a welter of tricks—poisoned needles, deadly insects . . . froggin' *snakes*—that opening the box improperly might release. To froggin' hell with the old man's quills and parchment. On the spot, Cauvin decided that he'd take the box, unopened, to Molin Torchholder. The old man could open it himself. Froggin' bad cess, if it killed him—at least it wouldn't kill Cauvin.

And if the old man died before dawn?

Fleetingly, Cauvin considered marching down the Hill, through a breach— He stopped cold before his imagination took him all the way back to the ruined estate.

If the old man died, then he'd prop the box against a wall and heave stones at it until it cracked apart.

"Did he?" Sinjon asked while Cauvin tossed imaginary stones.

"He froggin' sure told me not to froggin' open it in front of witnesses." Cauvin forced himself to meet the captain's eyes but, of course, he couldn't break the older man's stare. "It's too shiny to carry at night; attract too much attention. Give me a scrap of cloth to wrap around it?"

Sinjon cocked a thumb toward a pile of rags in a corner. "Two padpols."

Cauvin had bright soldats and an uncut shaboozh, fresh from the palace mint and not yet tarnished, in a pouch tied to his belt. He could bite off a corner of the shaboozh and still have enough silver for a feast at the Unicorn, but the notion of buying rags offended him. He snatched a piece of tight-woven, reddish cloth that looked large enough to tie around the box. "The Torch would've wanted his box kept safe for free."

Trailing a knotted, filthy cord, the cloth proved to be a vermin-chewed sack, and though the box was larger than any individual hole, Cauvin wasn't about to test the sack's strength by slinging it over his shoulder. He loosened his shirt instead and tucked the stiff cloth against his gut.

"I'm leaving. I better not have any froggin' trouble getting out," Cauvin said with his hand on the latch.

Sinjon watched Cauvin. His left eye was wandering again, but they both *stared*. The effect was unnerving.

"He must have been desperate," the captain said, still *staring*.

"Who?"

"The Torch, boy—Lord Torchholder—if he's made you his heir."

"I'm not his froggin', sheep-shite heir. I'm just collecting a debt."

The captain shook his head the same way Mina did when she thought he was too sheep-shite stupid to understand her insults. It was a look that got under Cauvin's skin in an instant.

He lifted the latch, and snarled, "Have a froggin' good life," as he opened the door.

Sinjon said something that Cauvin's ears couldn't untangle. He didn't want a second hearing. Anst, the ghost, was waiting at the top of the stairs—out of earshot, *if* he'd been there the whole time. And if he hadn't? Well, Cauvin didn't give a froggin' damn. The Torch's box was safe inside his shirt, and he could take any one-handed ghost who disagreed.

The fog had gotten heavier while Cauvin was inside the Broken Mast, the blackfish stench, too. He still didn't know what a hagfish looked like, but he imagined they stared. The air on the Processional was almost clean-smelling by the time Cauvin reached the street called Lizard's Way, which was the best—though far from the only—path into the warren known to one and all as the Maze. The Maze had its own smells, stronger and older than dead fish.

Cauvin didn't know the Maze well. As a child he'd lived with his mother on the Hill until she ran afoul of the Hand, for what, he'd never known. Maybe for nothing. The Hand didn't need a reason to make a sacrifice out of someone, and the Hillers were too poor, too weary to fight back.

Moments of flames, screams, and sheer horror exploded in Cauvin's mind when he thought of the last time he'd seen his mother, like bumping a sore he'd had so long he'd forgotten it was there, forgotten how froggin' much it could still hurt. She'd been stripped of her clothes and tied to a post on the Promise of Heaven before the Hand bled her out by stripping away her skin—

Cauvin hadn't loved his mother, not the way Bec loved Mina—all trust and devotion. She hadn't loved him, either, but it could have been froggin' worse. Everything except the pits could have been froggin' worse. He didn't truly remember her death. Just as the Hand put their knives to her face, some man Cauvin had never seen before spun him around and conked him cold. When he thought about her dying, Cauvin filled in the empty moments with the sights and sounds of the uncounted sacrifices he witnessed later.

When Cauvin had come back to consciousness, he'd been in a dark, sweat-smelling room with a naked, snoring man pressed up against him. He had lit out of there like a greased cat. He knew what went on in rooms like that. Whenever she got angry with him, Cauvin's mother had threatened to sell him to dark, sweaty men who collected unruly, sheep-shite boys. He'd run to the Maze . . .

After all the years, Cauvin still couldn't decide if he'd made the biggest mistake of his sheep-shite life that night. Not that it mattered. The Hand followed him into the Maze. They caught him in an alley more than a month—caught Leorin, too—less than a year after they'd caught his mother. The years of his childhood were blurred in Cauvin's head—he couldn't have been more than eight when they'd ended.

A whole froggin' lifetime had passed since then, and the Maze changed every storm or season. Unless he were there every day, a man stuck to the Serpentine, the oldest and widest of the quarter's streets.

Cauvin passed a knot of Irrune betting shells-and-nuts with a smooth-talking Mazer. Waste of time on both sides: the Maze-rat wouldn't let the Irrune win; the Irrune wouldn't pay if they lost. In the right-side shadows, someone puked his guts. Another sheep-shite drunk was doing the same across the Unicorn's threshold. Cauvin stepped over the mess.

Inside, the Unicorn was brighter than the Broken Mast had been and untainted by the sweet-rotting tang of *krrf.* Newcomers—including Cauvin when he'd begun meeting Leorin here—expected a darker, far-more-menacing lair but, as Leorin had explained, the Unicorn wasn't a place where solitary patrons came to swill themselves into a stupor. Drunks were rare, brawls, rarer, because the Vulgar Unicorn truly was a covered market where services were bought and sold, no different than the stone in Grabar's froggin' yard.

Most of the light came from an old wheel—once part of a wagon or a froggin' ship, Cauvin couldn't tell which through the soot—suspended from the massive center beam. The wheel supported a half score of oil lamps, each of them hooded with polished copper to cast the light downward. The rest of the light came from clay lamps centered on most tables.

If he wanted to, a man could find a shadow deep enough to hide him and a few friends in the corners or beneath the stairs, but most patrons preferred to keep an eye on their closest drinking companions. Or, they saw no reason to pay extra for shadows. Whoever owned the Unicorn these days—and it wasn't the lean, surly Stick who minded the coin box whenever Cauvin dropped in—had decreed that the drinks cost more at the tucked-away tables. Never one to pay a padpol more than necessary, Cauvin found himself a stool at one of the long tables beneath the wheel. The Torch's box pinched Cauvin's gut when he leaned forward. He set it, still wrapped in Sinjon's ratty cloth, on the table between his elbows.

His nearest neighbor was an arm's length away: a greasy-haired fellow who drank with his eyes closed. Farther along on the other side, a quartet of men younger than Cauvin were arguing about the

Dragon, his father, and the Irrune in general. It was the same froggin' bitterness Cauvin could hear anywhere on Pyrtanis Street, and he ignored it until one of them mentioned Molin Torchholder's murder.

—"Shalpa's cloak—it was the Dragon who did it," another voice insisted. "The froggin' Dragon or someone close to him."

Cauvin didn't try to connect the voice with a face. He might be sheep-shite stupid, but he knew better to look where he listened.

"Or a score of others," a third, slightly softer and soberer, voice suggested. "That Torch—he's been collecting enemies since Grandpa was a pup. Enemies, secrets, and *gold*. My pa says it's a froggin' wonder no one got him before this."

" 'Cause the Torch's a frog-rotting sorcerer, that's why," the quartet's fourth and loudest voice weighed in.

"He's a froggin' priest!"

"Of a froggin' *dead* god," Loudmouth added. "And he'd've died, too, right with the Stormbringer, if he wasn't a frog-rotting sorcerer. He says the Torch's been sucking souls for years. About time somebody got rid of him."

"Someone paid by Ilsig," the soft-voiced man suggested.

"No . . ." two men chorused, and Cauvin, in silence, was inclined to agree—not merely because the Torch wasn't dead, but because if there was one thing the Wrigglies of Sanctuary could take pride in it was that their ancestors had refused to remain slaves and prisoners of the Ilsigi kings. Froggin' sure the Ilsigi kings were on the rise. It was their armies, and not the Rankan emperor's, that broke the backs of the Nisibisi, the northern witches. And it was their warships that kept the sea-lanes clear between Sanctuary and Inception Island. But a royal assassin stalking the Torch near Pyrtanis Street? A royal assassin with an Imperial knife? That was froggin' impossible.

Cauvin had no sooner reached his judgment than he began to have doubts. If King Sepheris the Fourth of Ilsig had offered him a chest of golden royals to kill the Torch—not that Cauvin would have taken the money—but wouldn't it have made sense to kill the froggin' geezer with an *Imperial* knife, a knife that wouldn't ever be associated with an Ilsigi assassin or with a Wrigglie, either . . . ?

The Torch had admitted he had enemies, but that was all. The froggin' geezer hadn't said a word about the man who'd attacked him, the man he'd killed. Of course, Cauvin hadn't actually asked any questions. He'd thought about it. Sitting in the common room at the Vulgar Unicorn, Cauvin clearly remembered questions forming, but each time the froggin' geezer opened his mouth first and Cauvin's questions—questions that needed answering—went unasked.

He'd have to do better tomorrow . . . somehow.

As if a sheep-shite stupid stone-smasher could outwit the froggin' *Hero of Sanctuary*!

"You've come at a bad time—"

Cauvin leapt off the stool, fists at the ready, startling the woman who'd startled him. "Mimise! Sorry," he sputtered, realizing his mistake. Every head in the room had turned toward them. Cauvin felt like a froggin' fool and wished the floor would melt beneath his feet.

Mimise closed her eyes with a sigh. "Reenie's already gone upstairs."

"For the night?"

Whatever the Vulgar Unicorn had been in the past—and it had been around longer than even Lord Molin Torchholder—these days it was more than a tavern. The wenches who wandered among the tables were freelancers who bought every drink before they served it and picked up extra soldats and shaboozh in upstairs rooms.

Mimise wrinkled her nose. "Don't think so. Except for his silver, he wasn't her type. Want I should send a boy up to scratch her door?"

Cauvin shook his head. "I'll take a chance and wait."

"Gotta drink, if you're planning to wait."

"Which is better tonight, the wine or the ale?"

"Wouldn't touch the wine 'til the Stick taps a new barrel."

"Get me a mug of ale, then." He scooped the silver coin out of his boot.

Mimise dug a fistful of blackened padpols from the crack between her less-than-plump breasts. She took Cauvin's uncut coin and offered him five irregularly shaped bits in exchange. Three of Mimise's padpols were larger than the others. They could have been split once, but not twice.

Cauvin grimaced. "You're rooking me."

He took the padpols Mimise offered and kept his hand out for more. She laid three more of the smaller bits in his hand. Cauvin dug his fingernail into each padpol. None crumbled—meaning they were at least metal, not charred bone or pottery. He slapped them onto the table.

"A *full* mug," he reminded Mimise's back.

Leorin herself brought Cauvin an overflowing pewter tankard. With the scent of another man hanging heavily around her, Leorin kissed Cauvin chastely on the forehead. Her golden hair fell loose about her face; her cheeks were flushed; and the bodice of her gown was twisted around her waist.

"I wasn't expecting you until Anensday." She spun onto the stool on the opposite side of the table.

Cauvin patted the rag-covered box. "I've had some luck."

"What kind?" Leorin attacked the knotted cords without further invitation. "What's inside?"

"Not here." Cauvin pulled the still-tied cords out of her hands. "Let's go upstairs."

Leorin pouted—not the seductive pout she flashed at paying customers, but a sharp-eyed scowl. "Can't. That bastard shorted me. He promised me three shaboozh, then tried to give me soldats instead—as if I wouldn't know the difference!" She stared into the distance. Cauvin then pulled into a faint, but satisfied smile; Cauvin could feel the air grow cold behind him. "He won't be climbing anyone's stairs anytime soon." He wouldn't have asked what his beloved had done, even had she given him the chance. "That doesn't help me with the Stick. I've got room rent to pay. Nothing's free tonight, love, not even for you." She stroked Cauvin's hands, then caught sight of the padpols on the table. "You can't call a box of them *luck,* Cauv."

"That's not my luck, love." He peeled back the cloth just enough to give her a peek at the carved wood. A pawnbroker would offer a few decent shaboozh for the box once Cauvin got the coins out—assuming he didn't have to break it open. "I met a man today. I think he's going to change my life."

"How much did he give you?"

"I'll tell you that when we're alone upstairs."

Cauvin couldn't answer that until he opened the box, and he

wouldn't do that with strangers around. He trusted Leorin utterly, but no one else in the taproom. Instead, he told her where he'd gotten the box.

"The Broken Mast!" she exclaimed. "That's a bugger's haven! You never— You didn't, did you?"

"Not froggin' close," Cauvin assured her. Never mind what the infamous vulgar unicorn was doing to itself on the weatherworn signboard above the front door—Leorin would have nothing to do with men who shunned women. "I collected a debt for an old pud outside the walls, that's all. There's bound to be something left off after the quills and parchment. And this is just the beginning. The old pud's got more stashed away; he's said as much. He won't begrudge me; wouldn't dare. He's old and he's dying—got a froggin' evil wound atop his leg. I'm all he's got."

Leorin sat back. Gods knew how she'd come by it, but Leorin had all the fragile Imperial beauty Mina lacked. Her eyes were the color of warm, golden honey. Her complexion glowed like the finest porcelain, even beneath the Unicorn's froggin' soot-covered wheel. Her hands were delicate, her waist, willowy, and her breasts were perfect. When Leorin swept across the taproom, a bouquet of beer mugs clutched in her hands, conversations had been known to stop between words. She could have commanded the best rooms, the highest prices on the Street of Red Lanterns—she might even have found a Land's End sparker who'd marry her—but Leorin had lived inside the palace, the same as Cauvin. She chose the sort of freedom that couldn't be found behind walls—the kind of freedom—and risks—that the Unicorn offered night after night.

She chose Cauvin, too, because he'd been there, and her memories couldn't frighten him. The nights he stayed with his beloved in her cramped upstairs room weren't filled with passion; they were filled with tears and shudders while his arms protected her from the horrors in her memory.

Possibilities and calculations narrowed Leorin's eyes. She looked like a cat pretending not to notice the mouse that had wandered into her pouncing range. As well as he knew her, Cauvin couldn't move fast enough to keep her from seizing the box and giving it a shake. The clinking rattle of coins brought a new smile to her face.

Clutching the box tight, she unwound from the stool. "There better be enough in here to buy off the Stick."

Leorin led the way up the stairs past the day-or-night rooms and up again to the dormers where she rented a chamber little larger than a cot and three clothes baskets. It had a door, though, and a string latch that could be drawn up and knotted around the bolt. A determined intruder could get in, no trouble at all—just slice the string and pull it through. But honest folk would knock or go away altogether and—sure as sheep-shite on market day—most folk were honest most of the time.

Cauvin lit the oil lamp with a taper he'd carried up from the taproom while Leorin secured the door. He was stirring the embers in her tiny charcoal brazier, hoping to find a live one, when her arms circled him from behind. With their bodies close together there was no need for a brazier, nor even a lamp, though he liked to see his lover's face when her eyes were closed and her mouth was open, searching for his.

It was *time,* he thought. His fortunes *had* changed today. There were coins in the carved box and more to follow. Grabar had sworn that the stoneyard would become his and Mina had made peace with his favorite stew on a night when they usually made do with beans, bread, and fatback.

After two years of waiting, of clenching his jaw until his teeth hurt, it was froggin' sure *time*.

Cauvin freed a breast from its bodice and, caressing it, lifted his beloved off her feet. He took the short step toward her cot and was astonished beyond words when Leorin wriggled free.

"Open it. Open it now. I want to see what's inside."

Just then the coins inside of Molin Torchholder's carved box were not the top thoughts in Cauvin's mind. He reached for Leorin, and though his arms were long enough to span the walls of her dormer, she eluded him. For a heartbeat, Cauvin's fingers formed into fists.

"I can't," he whispered.

"Use this," Leorin replied, offering him a whiplike bit of metal as long as a rat's tail and supple as a green-willow branch.

Cauvin had no notion where she'd hidden it, though he was

froggin' sure that she had pulled it out of her garments. The Hands had taught sheep-shite fools like him to kill with their fists, but they taught other things to other children. Leorin had told him some of the lessons the Hands had taught her; she'd never mentioned the sharp little tail. He was careful as he took it from her. Its tip was sharp enough to pierce flesh, and it might well be envenomed. Without a froggin' word Cauvin stabbed it into the wall.

He retrieved it, though, a little bit later when he'd found the catch—at least he thought he had. A swirling loop of scrollwork had shifted ever so slightly when Cauvin had nudged it with his thumb. If he could get the sharp end of the tail wedged beneath the carving, something useful might happen. Or it might not. The scrollwork was carved from a separate piece of wood, but it wasn't the catch, and when he pushed a little too hard, it snapped, bounced once on the floor, and vanished beneath the cot.

"Damn the froggin' gods."

"Let me try," Leorin demanded, and took the box from Cauvin's hands.

She shook it and pinched it and shook it some more before hurling it onto the mattress. Patience had never been Leorin's game. Cauvin could be patient when he needed to be, when he needed time for his wits to work.

"The old pud wants me to froggin' *buy* parchment and quills for him," he said, as if in listening to himself he might learn something he didn't already know—which sometimes happened. "That's why he told me about the Broken Mast, the password, and the sheepshite box. So, I'm froggin' *supposed to* use what's in the froggin' box to buy his froggin' parchment and quills. But he didn't give me a key, and he didn't tell me a froggin' trick for opening it—"

Or had he?

*. . . Visit the Broken Mast, get the box, push the leaves apart . . .*

Cauvin snatched the box and brought it closer to the lamp. In addition to the broken scrollwork there were clusters of leaves on what he'd taken for the box's bottom. He prodded them gingerly, in various combinations. On the fourth try the box sprang apart. There were pieces of wood falling to the floor, coins bouncing everywhere, and a sharp pain at the root of Cauvin's right forefinger. He stood transfixed, watching a bead of blood well up from his flesh.

---

*"Ki-thus, I must return home—to the land of my mothers. My people need me; and I need you."*

The woman who spoke in Cauvin's mind was a soft, tiny creature—no taller than Bec—wearing a snug gown that widened her hips threefold and bared a woman's ample breasts. For a moment, there was nothing in Cauvin's mind save those breasts, then he managed to look at her face. Fortunately, he'd seen a fish before, else he might have dropped to his knees when the glistening membrane flicked across her eyes.

*"And that is precisely the reason I cannot sail with you, Shu-sea. We could be together while we dwelt in Sanctuary, but nowhere else. We were each born with obligations we cannot avoid—and now those obligations are calling us, both of us and at the same time. You must return to your Empire and I to mine."*

The man who held the woman's hands between his own had bright gold hair and guileless eyes.

Cauvin blinked. He looked past the embracing couple and recognized—barely—the angles of the palace roofs. The man, his memory told him—though Cauvin couldn't understand how it could be *his* memory—was Prince Kadakithis, last of Sanctuary's Imperial governors, who'd left Sanctuary for Ranke seven years after its sack in the faint, futile hope of saving the Empire from anarchy—

Seven years! In his own life Cauvin had listened to old Bilibot and the charlatan-hazard Eprazian tell the tales of the Rankan Empire's collapse and how the Kitty-Kat prince had vanished one day, never to be seen again, but the details—where the prince had gone or when or why— None of that was part of Cauvin's memory.

And what, exactly, was "anarchy"?

Suddenly—as if the pair had heard Cauvin asking his sheepshite questions—they unwound and looked his way. The woman—her name was Shupansea and she was the ruler-in-exile of the fish people—ran toward him, rouged breasts bouncing. She embraced him. Cauvin felt the surprising strength in her arms and smelled her perfume, familiar in memory though he'd never smelled its like before.

*"Lord Molin—Thank you for coming so quickly. Can you speak sense to him?"*

Cauvin gasped. He wasn't himself; he'd become Lord Molin Torchholder, or a few of his memories.

*"What's wrong?" the prince asked.*

*"It's too late," Molin replied.*

Or Cauvin replied; or it didn't matter because the words all flowed out of memories that had been old and meaningless long before Cauvin had gotten his froggin' self born.

*"What's too late?" the woman asked.*

Cauvin felt a sense of relief as strong as his anxiety had been a moment earlier. Molin had always gotten along well with the Beysa. She understood expediency better than her naive husband ever would or could. If she'd been a man, not a fish, he—Molin, not Cauvin—would have backed her all the way to the Imperial throne in Ranke.

*"A messenger just arrived from the capital. Your cousin was deposed five days after he was made emperor. He did not survive."*

There was more in the scroll the golden prince took from his hands. Molin had already read it through. Cauvin recalled the details: a battle in the streets around the Imperial Palace, a new emperor proclaimed—the third since the year began, a ten-year-old boy hacked apart for the crime of being his father's last surviving son.

Cauvin had his froggin' answer. He'd learned the meaning of anarchy—it was just a sparker word for his own childhood and adolescence.

*"Go with your wife, my prince, or stay here in this gods-forsaken city, but set aside all thoughts of returning to Ranke. Your presence there will not bring peace. The capital has gone mad. The mob will hail you one day and tear you apart the next."*

*"Ki-thus, come with me. My people will welcome you—"*

*"Your people need their Beysa; they do not need a foreigner as her consort."*

The prince wasn't the fool people thought he was. He was merely a man who'd been born at the wrong time—a man of grace and wit and justice trapped in a moment when those admirable qualities were worthless.

*"I must return to Ranke. That is where I belong, no matter what fate awaits me there."*

Molin—Cauvin—watched the tide change in the Beysa's glistening eyes.

*"What of our children, Ki-thus? Our daughters? What will become of them?"*

The prince's face became a mask that could not hide his anguish as he said the little girls would be safer far away in the Beysib Empire than they'd ever be in Sanctuary.

The two should never have jumped the broom together, Cauvin judged, and in the echo of memories not his own, the old man—Molin Torchholder—agreed.

"Cauvin! Cauvin! What's wrong with you!"

Cauvin looked into the eyes of Prince Kadakithis, who'd left Sanctuary but never arrived in Ranke—

No, he wasn't looking at a prince's face, he was looking at Leorin, who could have passed for the prince. Or his daughter? No. No. The years were wrong. Kadakithis had vanished more than thirty years ago. His daughters would be Mina's age, not Leorin's, and decades gone from Sanctuary. Still, the resemblance—

"Sweet Sabellia."

"Since when do *you* swear by Imperial gods?" Leorin demanded.

Cauvin shuddered from his feet all the way to the top of his head. A ghost had touched his soul—that's what Batty Dol would say. And this time, maybe she'd be right. The ghost of the old pud he'd left in roofless ruins outside the walls? The ghost of Prince Kadakithis? Or the ghost of his daughter?

Whatever it had been—Whatever had possessed Cauvin's life for a moment and stirred its memories into his, it was gone. He was alone with Leorin in a room above the Vulgar Unicorn.

"Look at these!" She held her cupped hands where Cauvin could not help but see them and the shiny coins they contained. "Look at them! Not a mark on them. There's fifteen silver soldats—I don't even recognize the face on the—and a gold coronation! A coronation, Cauvin— Look at it! Have you ever seen a coin so big and bright? And more tumbled under the bed!"

Leorin emptied her hands into his and dropped immediately to her knees. Cauvin couldn't explain what had happened to him, but coins—uncut and as shiny as the day they'd come from the mint—needed no explanation.

"I can't take these to a scribe asking for quills and parchment." Cauvin's mind stumbled from one consequence to the next. "He'll say one soldat's as good as another and rob me blind. I'll have to go to a changer first. With one soldat. I'll get a better price for one good soldat than twenty—"

Clutching more coins in her hands, Leorin looked up from the floor. "Forget the old pud! We're rich, Cauvin. Rich enough to leave Sanctuary and start over somewhere else. Mother's blood, let's leave! There's a merchant downstairs; he's leaving for Ilsig city tomorrow morning. We could travel with him. Oh, Cauvin." She spilled the coins onto her bed before wrapping her arms around Cauvin. "Please, love, please? Let's run away from Sanctuary before it's too late. Come. Let's go downstairs and talk to him. Right now. There's nothing keeping us here. Grabar's no more to you than the Stick is to me."

Leorin tugged Cauvin's sleeve. He took one step toward the door and became unmovable. "I left an old man alone outside the froggin' walls. Easy money says he's dead by morning—I've never seen anyone as old and frail as him. I've got to see to him, Leorin. I've got to know that he's dead, if he's dead, and bury him, if he is. I can't leave him to rot. I'm done with that. My—" Cauvin's stomach sank. The old geezer was right: "My sheep-shite conscience won't let me."

"Sheep-shite is right. What's one more, Cauv? Do you think almighty Ils is keeping count after what you've done? What we did? You can buy a new conscience when we get to Ilsig city. Cauv—"

She tugged again. The coins spilled between his fingers.

"One day—one morning, that's all. I swear it. I'll go to the red-walled ruins—"

"And if the froggin' pud's alive—what then? Mother's blood, Cauvin—listen to me: If I don't run away tonight, I won't have the strength to run in the morning. I swear *that*."

"You'll have the strength," Cauvin assured her. "It's just one night—one *last* froggin' night in Sanctuary. Summer's over. Autumn, too. I felt it in the air this afternoon. There'll be froggin' frost on everything by morning. Everything, including the old man." He hugged her close, but there was a stiffness in Leorin's spine that hadn't been there before. "One night, love. What's one more night after all the others?"

There was only one law in Sanctuary: Stay out of the past, and they'd both broken it. They were even, but the price was high.

Cauvin hugged Leorin tighter than she wanted to be held and caressed her wavy golden hair. "I'm sorry. I'm sorry."

"It's too late." Leorin wrestled free. She collected coins from the mattress and the floor. "Visit your old man. Buy him parchment and ink. We're never getting out of Sanctuary, Cauv. Never."

Leorin stuffed the box pieces into the sack, then dribbled the coins atop it. She wrapped the bulging cloth and string around Cauvin's hands like manacles. There were tears in her eyes. Cauvin couldn't be sure—there was so much he didn't remember—but he didn't think he'd ever seen Leorin cry before, at least not when she was awake.

"We'll go," he assured her. He would have given her a hug, but he could not untangle the cloth.

"It's too late."

"It can't be. It's just one more night."

"One too many. One week too many. One month, one year. Mother's blood, it's always been too late. Go, Cauvin. Go, now."

"One night, Leorin. Even if the geezer's not froggin' dead, I'll make arrangements, find someone else to dig his grave."

Leorin shoved him toward the door. "You're blind, Cauvin. You always were. You're strong because you can't see what's there."

"I'll be back tomorrow night. We'll find another—"

"Come if you want, or not. It was a dream. Now I'm awake, and it's gone."

"I don't—"

"Just *go,* Cauvin."

He was powerless to fight her, powerless to remain in the room to comfort her.

The air was past chilly when Cauvin left the Unicorn. The fog had been transformed into ice crystals that glistened in torchlight. The yard dog barked once as he came through the gate, then slunk away before Cauvin got the bar down. It wouldn't come when Cauvin whistled; it just hunkered in the shadows, whining.

Who would have thought that he—froggin' nobody Cauvin—could have more gold and silver than he could measure and be miserable, too?

# Chapter Five

Five piles of four coins or four piles of five coins, either way they added up to more soldats than Cauvin had called his own before. And froggin' *bright* silver soldats, as shiny as gold by the light of the little clay lamp he'd set on the floor beside his pallet. They must have been sealed tight in the wooden box since they'd been struck. There wasn't a mark on them, not even a speck of black tarnish. The emperor's profile was sharp, and Cauvin could have read the man's name in the ring of letters around his portrait, if his name had been Cauvin.

The stoneyard didn't encourage payment in bright, uncut coins. Grabar couldn't give them to Mina because the honest merchants on Pyrtanis Street wouldn't take them, and the rest insisted on exchanging them for face value—which was a froggin' bad joke. So when an Ender paid in bright silver, Grabar hied himself down to his changer in the Shambles—an honest man, they hoped, who'd barter anything on the counter of his cavernous shop. For a price, Bezul would convert bright soldats or shaboozh into purses of Sanctuary's greasy, clipped coins that turned black the day they were minted.

But the treasure in the Torch's box went beyond silver. Cauvin had spread three froggin' *gold* coronations beside the silver piles. They were bigger than the soldats, nearly the size of an uncut, sixteen-padpol shaboozh. Froggin' sure even one of them was worth more than all his soldats. The three of them together might be worth more than the froggin' stoneyard. Cauvin didn't know how froggin' much more. He'd never actually *seen* a gold coin before.

Froggin' sure, Cauvin thought he'd seen more than three coronations tumble to the floor of Leorin's dormer, which meant—probably—that she'd froggin' palmed one for herself. Shipri's tits—he didn't hold the theft against her. Probably, he'd have palmed one of the froggin' huge coins himself, had their positions been reversed. Froggin' sure, he could buy a year's worth of Mina's affection with a coronation, maybe two, or make her think twice before selling the stoneyard out from under him.

Leorin had wanted to use the coins to run away from Sanctuary . . .

Cauvin had thought he knew the woman he'd decided to marry, thought he'd come face-to-face with all her moods and demons, but he'd never guessed she wanted to leave Sanctuary. Froggin' sure, *he* threatened to leave all the time—leave the stoneyard, anyway. In his froggin' heart of hearts, Cauvin couldn't imagine out-and-out leaving Sanctuary. Miserable though it was, Sanctuary was home: not loved, but familiar.

When strangers moved into Sanctuary—and froggin' odd enough, there was always a steady stream of strangers moving into Sanctuary—they sooner or later came to the stoneyard to resurrect whichever ruin they'd claimed for their own. While he and Grabar figured out how much and what kind of stone the reconstruction required, the newcomers would complain about the city's flaws: the rank smell of its sea air, the bitter taste of its water, the grating sound of the Wrigglie language he and Grabar spoke as they worked, the coarseness of their clothes.

Cauvin had no desire to live where everything would be as unpleasant to his senses as Sanctuary was to its newcomers. No, all Cauvin wanted from his froggin' life was Grabar's stoneyard when Grabar no longer needed it. But if Leorin wanted to leave—

"Cauvin! What are you doing?"

Cauvin was a spark in dry tinder when taken unawares. He was on his feet with his fists clenched in front of him before his thick wits found anything familiar in the face peeking up through the ladder hole in the floor and needed a good long moment before he could trust himself to speak to Bec. By then the boy was in the loft and had gotten a glimpse of silver and gold.

"Furzy feathers!" Bec exclaimed, and fell on the treasure. "Where'd you get these? Did you find them out at the red-walled ruins or did you *steal* them from that merchant you said you helped today?"

(Cauvin didn't know what a furzy feather was; no one did. They—him, Grabar, and Mina together—didn't want the boy cursing, so he made up oaths of his own.)

"I froggin' sure didn't steal them," Cauvin snarled, and seized Bec's wrist for good measure. The boy yelped and shed the coins onto the floor.

"So, you held out on him! You gave Poppa a pittance to keep him happy and held out the rest for yourself. That must have been some load of moving you did this afternoon."

"It was," Cauvin agreed, gathering the coins.

"Bet *he* was stealing—the merchant you helped, that is. I'll bet everything you helped him move was stolen fresh from the palace, from Arizak and his ladies—or maybe from the Dragon. I'll bet he stole what the Dragon stole first. I'll bet you half of these coins—"

"Don't go making bets you're going to lose, Bec."

The boy's imagination and his recklessness worried Cauvin. He foresaw Bec falling in with men who'd squeeze him dry.

"How, then? Poppa would bust his froggin' gut if he knew you had this much silver—and *gold,* too!"

"Mind your mouth. You'll have Mina down on me, if she ever hears you talking like that."

Bec rolled his lower lip. "Momma will come down on you twice as heavy if she thinks you're holding out on her and Poppa. Poppa, too, if I tell them you're hoarding a hundred shaboozh."

"They're soldats, not shaboozh," Cauvin corrected as he grabbed Bec's ear. "And you'll keep your froggin' mouth shut."

The boy howled and Cauvin released him, lest he draw his parents to the loft.

"Froggin' froggin' froggin'—I will if you tell me how you *really* got them. Wasn't any merchant, was there?"

Cauvin shook his head. "There wasn't—"

"So you *did* steal them!"

"No, gods all be damned, I didn't steal anything. There was—there *is* an old man—"

Cauvin's mind raced. Did he dare tell his foster brother the truth? Did he dare tell the boy anything less? The boy was too froggin' clever by half. He'd picked up the scattered pieces of the carved box and started putting them back together again, as sure as if he'd done it every froggin' day of his life. Could a sheep-shite stone-smasher possibly put together just enough of the truth to satisfy Bec's demanding curiosity?

"This is what they came in?" Bec concluded, as the box grew in his hands. "You found it, maybe? Found it so you can say you didn't steal it, but you found it with the merchant's goods—or left behind in the place where you were moving them—"

"I didn't steal anything! It's complicated, Bec. I don't hardly understand what's happened today myself, but you've got to swear you'll keep your mouth shut—"

Bec mimed placing a strip of cloth over his mouth and tying it tight behind his ears.

"There is an old man. He lives in the palace; and he's an important man there. He'd gone to the old temples and got himself attacked."

"He gave you the coins for saving his life while he was praying to the old gods?"

"No," Cauvin corrected and cursed himself a heartbeat later: Bec's conclusion was simpler—better—than the truth he'd condemned himself to tell. "The old pud wasn't praying. He was—He'd been looking for whoever killed those two puds at the crossing, but he got himself froggin' set upon and robbed. He was beat-up pretty bad when I found him. I would've taken him to the froggin' palace, but nothing would satisfy him, except I took him out to the froggin' red-walled ruins—"

"But you said you never went to the red-walled ruins. I heard Poppa say you didn't bring back any bricks!"

"Look, Bec, I'm telling you the truth, so froggin' keep quiet! You want to listen or you want to, maybe, *stumble* on your way down the ladder?"

The boy blanched and didn't say another word until Cauvin had cobbled together a version of his misadventures in the ruins and at the Broken Mast. He left out his meeting with Leorin at the Vulgar Unicorn.

"It's a good thing it's turning cold—" Cauvin concluded, "or we'd be smelling that rotten blackfish up here. Probably will be anyway when the sun comes up."

"You went to the Broken Mast?" Bec asked with wide-eyed astonishment. "That's a bugger's den."

"Who told you that?" Cauvin couldn't hide his surprise. "Who tells you sheep-shite nonsense like that?"

"Nobody *tells* me. I keep quiet and listen whenever people come to buy stone, and especially when Momma has me go to market with her. Teera the baker says that Cervinish would rather spend his nights at the Broken Mast with the seamen than with his new wife—"

It was Cauvin's turn to gape. When he'd been Bec's age there wasn't anything he didn't know about the things men did alone, with women, with other men, and sometimes with boys who weren't strong enough to defend themselves. But Bec wasn't living in the streets or under the Hand. There was no reason, Cauvin hoped, to think he understood the rumors he'd repeated. There better not be. Cauvin didn't care what Cervinish did or didn't do with his wife, but if that froggin' little man had laid a *finger* on Bec!

Some of Cauvin's anger got into his voice. "Don't go repeating sheep-shite stories you froggin' don't understand. You hear me?" he snarled.

"But I *do* understand," the boy protested. "There's never any women at the Broken Mast, just like there's never any women on a ship. Seamen and sailors, they've got no use—" The boy's words caught in his throat and when he spoke again it was in a whisper. "You're not a seaman, are you, Cauvin? You and Leorin—you'd make babies with her if she'd let you?"

Cauvin couldn't think of a way to answer that question without backing himself into a froggin' deep, dark corner. "Froggin' gods all be damned, Bec, the—" Cauvin barely kept himself from blurting out the geezer's name. "The old man told me to go to the Broken Mast to redeem a box—that box, the one you've put back together—so I'd have the coins to buy him froggin' parchment, ink, and quills tomorrow morning before I go out to the red-walled ruins."

"The old man, he's a seaman?"

"Froggin' gods—he's an old man, the oldest I've ever seen. His pizzle shriveled up years ago."

"You saw it?"

"No!" Cauvin raked his hair in frustration. "Look, he gave me a token, I took it to the tavern, and redeemed the box. That's froggin' it. There's nothing more to tell."

"You were gone a *long* time."

"I stopped at the Unicorn on my way home. To see Leorin."

"Did you make babies?"

The ale Cauvin had drunk at the Unicorn was souring in his gut. He covered his eyes and shook his head repeatedly. "That's not a question you ask someone, Bec. Not anyone, not froggin' ever. It's late, too late. Mina will have our froggin' hides if she finds out you're outside the house."

"Did you?"

"Are you listening to me? That's no froggin' concern of yours."

"She's mean, Cauvin. Reenie's real mean. I bet you told her about the old man, though, and getting the box from the Mast and the coins."

Cauvin lowered his hand. "Yes, I told Leorin about the old man. I showed her the box. We've pledged to each other. We don't keep secrets."

"And she *still* didn't let you make babies with her? Even after she'd seen silver and *gold* together?"

If it hadn't been his nine-year-old foster brother asking outrageous and barbed questions, Cauvin would have been pounding his questioner's skull against the nearest wall. As it was, Cauvin could barely keep his hands at his sides. "All right—since you're so froggin' determined—when Leorin saw how much was in the box, she wanted us to leave Sanctuary right away—tonight, in fact."

The boy was at an age where words could hurt more than blows. He shrank in his skin, and whispered, "What did you tell her?"

"That I had to come back to the froggin' stoneyard."

Bec's mouth worked, but moments passed before he made a sound. "You're leaving, Cauvin? You're really leaving and not coming back forever?"

By the way Bec glanced around the loft, a stranger might have thought he was a cat cornered and looking for a way to escape. Cauvin knew better: The boy was checking the whereabouts of the few possessions Cauvin called his own. They were few enough in number and less in value. Had Cauvin meant to leave Sanctuary, he'd never have bothered to collect them, but for the boy's sake, he made a different excuse—

"I gave my froggin' word to that old pud. I told him I'd be back in the morning with his froggin' parchment and quills. Gods all be damned, Bec—he's an *old* pud. Got no business spending a night like this in a roofless ruin. I left him with fire and wood for the night, but sure as shite, he's wounded in the leg and can't stand to tend it—" In his mind's eye Cauvin saw the Torch sprawled helpless and dying on the cold ground. "I should've taken him to the palace. He wouldn't go but, frog all the rotted gods, I should've just drug him; he couldn't have froggin' *stopped* me."

"You should've gotten him blankets and a flask of brandy to keep himself warm if you were gonna leave him out in the ruins all night."

Cauvin nodded absently. He owed the Torch an armload of the best blankets and brandy in Sanctuary along with the best parchment, best quills, and ink. The old pud had made him a rich man.

"What did Reenie say when you told her about the old man?"

"She didn't think I needed to come back here, Bec. Sure as shite she didn't tell me to check on the geezer," Cauvin conceded.

He could purchase brandy at any tavern, but Mina made their blankets, and he couldn't very well ask her for help.

"I'll bet she did. I'll bet she asked if he had any more boxes filled with gold and silver."

Cauvin recalled a blind man south of the market who bought and sold secondhand clothing.

"She did, didn't she? I'll bet she got mad at you when you wouldn't do what she wanted, and she wouldn't let you make babies with her, would she? But if someone—not you—offered her one of those silver coins—"

Cauvin made a fist. The boy gaped, and after a moment of silence it was Cauvin who felt ashamed.

"Leorin didn't get mad. It wasn't like that. When she saw the coins, she wanted to leave Sanctuary tonight. And when I said that I couldn't just up and leave, she froggin' started to cry."

"I'll bet that's not all she did."

"Stop betting. You don't have any money. You can't ever afford to lose money you don't have."

Bec was unimpressed by Cauvin's pearls of wisdom. "You've given your word to Poppa and Momma, too—you promised to be their son and to take care of *me* no matter what else. You *can't* leave Sanctuary."

Cauvin met Bec's eyes and saw not just a nine-year-old boy, but Leorin and all the countless others—including the froggin' Torch—whose wits were quicker and sharper than his. He swept the coins up and squeezed them so tight his fingers hurt. "I said I wasn't going anywhere, not tonight, not tomorrow, not froggin' ever!"

" 'Cept out to the old red-walled ruins to see the old man . . . *after* you buy him his parchment and quills *and* blankets and brandy and anything else he might need."

"Yeah," Cauvin conceded in defeat.

"And me. You'll take me with you."

"Hell no."

"Hell *yes,*" Bec insisted, his mood shifting like quicksilver. "What do you know about buying parchment, eh? Momma buys a full skin every season—for the yard accounts. I go with her, so I know what to look for. You don't. You'll get cheated. They'll offer you the cheap stuff—goat hides with splits and cracks. That's all right for doing accounts, but not for someone from the *palace*. And quills! You don't know anything about quills. You've got to be careful. The best quills come from a *white* goose, but the scriveners, they'll try to cheat you with *bleached* feathers. A buyer's got to know what he's looking for . . . you *don't,* but *I* do."

Bec was right: Cauvin didn't know about quills, but he did remember that the Torch had given him similar instructions. "What froggin' difference can it make what froggin' color the froggin' bird was?"

The boy gave him a withering stare. "It makes *all* the froggin' difference."

"Don't curse."

"The white-goose feathers are thicker and stronger. They squeeze up a lot more ink. You didn't know that, did you, Cauvin?

I know you didn't. Take me with you tomorrow. I can help. Honest. I know where all the good stuff is. Momma takes me *everywhere*. I watch. I listen. I *remember*." Bec tapped the side of his head.

"Name me a good 'changer, then, on this side of the Processional—someone we don't usually go to. Someone who'll give me a fair exchange on all these bright silver soldats, and won't go running to Grabar the moment I walk out of his shop."

The boy's shoulders sagged, as Cauvin had anticipated, but not for long. "Swift the blacksmith, he couldn't change all of them at once, and not the golden ones at all, but he could change a few soldats." An' he won't tell Father, 'cause Father says he still owes for the wall behind his forge."

It was a good suggestion, though Cauvin thought he would have remembered that Swift would sometimes melt small amounts of silver in his forge and take the purified metal to the palace for reminting. "Thanks, I'll pay my friend a visit. I was only going to change one soldat tomorrow anyway."

"Two," Bec corrected. "You'll need one for the parchment, quills, and *ink*. You gotta have ink, less you think he's going to use his own blood. And for Batty Dol, too, for blankets. She's got piles and piles of old cloth in her pantry—collects it from the Enders, fixes what she can, makes candle wicks and stuff from the rest. Some of it stinks a little, but we can air it out at the red-walled ruins. The other soldat's for the brandy—can't be pouring the Well's rotgut down his throat, not if he's an old man used to the palace. And for food, too. If the old man's not dead, you've got to feed him, and you can't snitch from Momma. She'll spot it right away."

Bec was right about Mina and maybe the brandy, but not Batty Dol. "Batty'll tell everyone, starting with your mother."

"Not if we tell her it's a surprise. She'll stay quiet for a day, then she'll forget."

"Not 'we.' "

"Then I'll tell. I'll tell Poppa everything—about the old man and his treasure, and how you set him up out at the red-walled ruins instead of smashing bricks. And how you went to the Broken Mast and what goes on there and that you're planning to run out on him and Momma and me."

"You'd be telling lies, Bec. The fish—" He started to say the fish would get him while he slept, but he knew too much for those old threats.

The boy stuck out his tongue before Cauvin thought up a new threat.

"It's your word against mine, an' I can tell a better lie than you can tell the truth. But I won't, if you take me with you. Please, Cauvin. *Please?* I won't make any trouble; I swear it. I'll swear anything you ask. Just take me out to the red-walled ruins? Let me meet the old man who gave you the box? Momma never lets me do anything exciting."

Cauvin weighed the trouble the boy would be against the froggin' trouble his tales could make at the stoneyard. Bec *could* tell a damned lie better than Cauvin could tell the froggin' truth. And if the geezer were still alive, then the boy could tote and fetch for him while Cauvin smashed bricks out of the wall. It wasn't as if a few coins, even a few gold coins, meant he didn't have to work for his living. "All right. You can come—"

The boy whooped. Cauvin quieted him with an upraised finger.

"You can come *if* Mina and Grabar agree. I'm not stealing you out there, and you froggin' remember what they said this morning. If either one of them says no, you're staying here, and it's not my fault. You understand that, Bec: It's not my froggin' fault, so you keep quiet with your froggin' lies."

Unfazed by Cauvin's conditions, Bec declared, "You leave Momma and Poppa to me!" before he leapt at his foster brother's waist—half hug, half wrestle, all enthusiasm.

It was no contest, or it shouldn't have been, but Cauvin let the boy back him across the loft. He remembered himself at Bec's age: alone on the streets, ripe for the Hands to pluck. Bec wouldn't have gotten caught by the Hands; he was too clever, too charming. He'd have found his way into one of the houses that kept their children close.

Cauvin wrapped his hands beneath Bec's armpits and hoisted him up into the rafters. He could feel the boy's scrawny ribs beneath his palms. A little effort—or even an accident—and those bones would break like kindling sticks. Mina worried about her son, and rightly so. Without the love and strength of his family, Bec wouldn't make it through a hard winter. He wasn't built for hard times.

Cauvin lowered Bec to the floor again. "Now—get out of here! Sure as shite, it's hours past midnight and you've got work to do tomorrow! Get back to your own froggin' bed and for gods' sake don't get froggin' caught!"

The boy was all smiles and confidences as he disappeared down the loft ladder. Cauvin kept an ear out for sounds of trouble, but there was only silence. He blew out the lamp and crawled into his nest of straw and cloth, expecting to lie there, wide-awake, until dawn. But sleep caught Cauvin from behind, and the next thing he knew one of the roosters had crowed, and the loft was filled with gray dawnlight.

An ice scum had formed overnight in the trough. Cauvin broke it with his fist. He shook like a wet dog while he washed the night from his face and mouth. Old Hazard Eprazian up at the Well, they told stories about Sanctuary before the Hand seized it, when there was a mage's guild south of the palace. There were so many hazard-mages at the guild and they were so powerful that Sanctuary's winters were warm.

Ice never thickened on open water, and snow never fell.

Cauvin believed those tales about as much as he believed Batty Dol's tales about her dead husband sitting at the foot of her bed each night. In his experience, dead was dead, and Sanctuary's winters were froggin' cold enough to turn whole men into shivering eunuchs.

Grabar was already up and keeping warm by squaring stone. No bitter water for him on mornings like this. If the stoneyard's master washed between now and spring, he'd do it from buckets his wife heated at her hearth or down at the public baths in the Tween. He chuckled when a shivering Cauvin joined him beside a heap of unsquared stone.

"Cold enough for you yet, lad?"

Cauvin ignored the gibe. Let Grabar have his memories of mild winters; he remembered the Hands and the pits. For ten years he'd never washed except in the rain. Shivering was a small enough price to pay to feel clean every morning.

"Thought I'd go out to the red-walled ruins this morning—" He'd almost said *back out to the red-walled ruins.* "I'll smash out the bricks I didn't get yesterday—unless you've got plans for Flower and the cart?"

"You take the mule and the cart and go about yesterday's business. That'll be fine. I'm not going to be making deliveries across the Processional 'til that damned Dragon leaves town. No deliveries, no business, no money neither. You run into some merchant who wants you to do a day's work for him, that'll be fine, too."

Cauvin didn't mention Bec. He was counting on Mina to crush the boy's dreams. But Bec was grinning ear to ear when Cauvin came into the kitchen, and Mina was packing a basket with food.

Froggin' truth to tell, the boy came in useful throughout that morning, though not at the forge. Swift was the closest Cauvin came to a friend on Pyrtanis Street. They were a lot alike—wary young men who got by on hard work rather than cleverness—though Swift hadn't fallen into the Hands' grip. Swift held three of the Torch's soldats between fingers that were half again as thick as Cauvin's. He set them gently in one pan of a swing scale and dribbled pellets of iron into the other pan until both pans were level beside each other.

"Where'd you say you got these?" Swift asked, swirling the pellets back into a sack."

"I didn't. How many padpols?"

Swift scowled. "If they're as pure as they look, there's as much silver in each of them as there is in one of Arizak's shaboozh. Course, I'd have to melt them and measure them again to know if they're that pure."

"Go ahead, but give me an advance—how about twenty padpols?" It was a generous exchange, though merely fair if Swift were right about the coins' purity.

Swift was a fair man and a friend. He gave Cauvin twenty-five padpols with a promise of more once he'd melted and measured the purified soldats. They sealed their bargain with a handshake, and Cauvin left Swift's forge with a fistful of gritty coins thumping against his thigh and Bec yanking on his sleeve.

"You should've held out for more. If he was willing to give you twenty-five he'd've been willing to give you thirty."

"You sound like your mother," Cauvin groused, and freed himself. The boy was probably right, but haggling left a bad taste in Cauvin's mouth. His clearest memories of the woman he'd truly called Mother were of her haggling wine from barman upon barman. He'd had a strong back, even then, and often found himself cleaning stables or pushing barrels while she drank.

Bec proved his usefulness in merely finding the scriptorium where Mina bought the stoneyard's parchment. The shop was logically tucked behind a tanner's yard deep in the Tween, but Cauvin never would have found it on his own. There were grades of parchment, grades of quills, and grades of ink as well; and none of them were meaningful to a man who smashed and squared stone for his livelihood. Bec told a charming tale about practicing his letters and writing a perfect copy of some old Imperial poem for his beloved mother's birthday and got the best of everything at dirt-cheap prices. They left the scriptorium with a ribbon-tied roll of parchment the same pale, creamy color of Leorin's cheeks, four "perfect" quills (that looked no froggin' different from feathers their roosters shed daily, except for their size and colors), and a greasy lump of lampblack.

"If your geezer's really from the palace," Bec said once he was back inside the stone cart, "then we should get wine, too: aged, red wine. That's what they use in the palace to make their ink."

"Bad enough I had to *buy* soot! The old geezer can mix his froggin' ink with water— Can't he?"

"Wine's better. Wine or piss."

"That's sheep-shite nonsense."

"Is not," Bec insisted, and went on at length about ink-making . . . as if Cauvin were going to believe someone who made up tales about chickens and birthday presents.

Cauvin guided Flower toward the Promise of Heaven and the Hill behind it. He was grimly eager to get to the abandoned estate until Bec reminded him of Batty Dol and the old man's blankets. Reluctantly, Cauvin turned the cart back toward Pyrtanis Street.

The addled woman greeted them with a taste of her fresh-baked bread. That was the odd thing about Batty—one of them, anyway—what she did, she did well. She was a froggin' witch with a threaded needle, and the bread she baked was good enough to sell to taverns and houses in the better parts of town. Batty was harmless, everyone said, but she gave Cauvin the chills whenever she looked at him like she'd known him *before* because, sometimes, like this morning, damned if she didn't look familiar, too.

Batty never stopped talking about neighbors only she knew about. Bec spun his lies, Batty shook out enough threadbare cloaks to carpet the floor, and Cauvin paid a fair price for three of the best.

"She won't tell," Bec said as he made himself a woolly nest in the cart. "Come noon, she won't even remember it was us and not ghosts."

Cauvin grunted. He led Flower away from the tumbledown house. The boy was right, of course, and there was no reason to pity Batty Dol: She might be addled, but she never dreamt. Still, Bec didn't know *why* Batty talked to ghosts, and, not knowing why, he couldn't possibly care.

The boy wouldn't care, either, if the day's adventure ended with Cauvin digging a grave. He'd turn it into story about chickens and roosters. Death, madness, and the Hand weren't real to Bec, not the way they were to Cauvin. Cauvin envied his foster brother, who didn't know the darkest meanings of terror or loneliness, but the boy's carefree confidence irritated him, too. A voice deep in his mind would mutter: *You'll learn,* Bec, *and the older you are when you do, the worse it'll hurt.*

Cauvin choked that voice before it got to his tongue, but he was prepared for the worst—the Torch not merely dead but torn apart by dogs or wolves, his limbs scattered, his eyes wide-open, and smeared with blood. Cauvin didn't need a sheep-shite imagination when it came to violent death.

"Stay here," he said when another ten steps would have taken them into the ruined room where he'd left the Torch.

Grabbing one of the blankets, Cauvin crossed the threshold alone.

"So you decided to come after all."

The Torch was very much alive and reclining on his makeshift bed. His face had made a remarkable recovery from the previous day. What had been purple was now a pale yellowish gray. What had been swollen smooth was now sunken, wrinkled, and terribly old. If the Torch's recovery were miraculous, his persistence was twice that, which led Cauvin toward thoughts of gods and magic. Those thoughts and the sight of the heavy blackwood staff in the Torch's hand stopped him cold in his tracks.

Bec wriggled between Cauvin and the doorframe.

"Who is that?" the Torch asked in a tone that changed "who" to "what."

"My foster brother, Becvar—we call him Bec."

"I seem to recall asking for parchment, quills, and ink. What possessed you to think I wanted a *boy*?"

The worst scars Cauvin had carried away from the Hand came from insults that couldn't be evened with a well-thrown punch and words that cut deeper than the sharpest knives. Without effort, the Torch had reopened the worst of them. Cauvin stayed put, speechless and seething, but Bec—Bec, who didn't know any better—strode forward.

"That's where you're wrong, old man. I'm the one who picked out your parchment and quills, an' I'll make your ink, too. Cauvin wouldn't buy any wine, and you don't look like you could piss up a spit bowl."

The Torch gave a frigid smile. "Charming. Remind me not to come calling on your parents."

"They're *my* parents. Cauvin's are dead," Bec corrected, pulling himself up to his full, scrawny height. "And you've got no right to insult his or mine. You've got no right to be anything but grateful that me and Cauvin came out here to take care of an old geezer like you."

To Cauvin's surprise, the Torch said nothing at first, merely narrowed his eyes and gave them both the once-over before asking, "Did all go well with Sinjon at the Broken Mast?"

Cauvin had a score of answers for that question, but before he could utter even one of them Bec asked—

"Are you a seaman?"

Cauvin clamped a hand on Bec's collarbone and hauled him backward as he hissed, "Froggin' shite, Bec, don't go asking him questions like *that*!"

The warning came too late. Lord Molin Torchholder gave another of his icy smiles. "I'm naught but a dying, old man. Once I was a priest of a great god, a builder of great temples, and a friend of emperors, but I was never a sailor."

"Then why did you send Cauvin to the Broken Mast? They're all seamen—"

Bec couldn't finish through the shaking Cauvin gave his shoulder.

"Let me guess: You procured the box without difficulty, brought it home, opened it, and attracted the attention of the *boy*? One thing led to another, and you brought him here because it was that or he'd tell his tales to his father?"

"Something like that," Cauvin admitted. He pinched Bec's shoulder hard, then released him. "He talks a lot. Mostly he lies."

"That's not true! I don't *lie.* You know I don't."

"The *boy's* right," the Torch purred. "On both counts I imagine, else you wouldn't have brought him out here."

# Chapter Six

"Cauvin?" Bec whispered as his brother headed for the door. He put himself in Cauvin's path, and though Cauvin never seemed to see him standing there, he very carefully avoided him just the same. "Cauv . . . ?"

Bec raised a hand while Cauvin was still in reach. His fingers got within a handspan of Cauvin's shirt, then his arm dropped back to his side. When his brother's chin was down and his shoulders were up around his ears, it really was wiser to leave him alone, even if that left Bec by himself with a scary-looking old man.

"Follow him," the raspy voice commanded. "Make yourself useful. Tell that young man to get himself back in here. There's work to do. I haven't got all the time in the world. I need someplace to write, someplace to sit. Follow him, boy!"

Bec stayed put when he heard Cauvin unharnessing the mule. Then, satisfied that his brother wasn't going to abandon him entirely, he swallowed the dry lump in his throat and turned to face the old man. "My name's Becvar; you can call me Bec. I'll call you Grandfather 'cause you're too old to be anything else. Cauvin's angry, and when Cauvin's angry, he gets stubborn, just like the mule, an' he's bigger than both of us together—even if you could walk—so, there's no changing his mind." The ruins rang with the sound of an iron-headed mallet striking stone. "He's angry at both of us, anyway, for talking faster than he could listen. If you're going to talk that fast, you'd better talk to me."

"Nonsense. Cauvin's the one they sent, their best answer to my prayers. There's work to do . . . and money for his efforts at the end of it. Ten times what he earns in that stoneyard. Run along and tell him that."

There were insults lurking in the old man's words, insults directed at him, at the stoneyard, and maybe even at Cauvin. Bec wouldn't stand for insults. He folded his arms across his chest. "Run along and tell him yourself."

When stubbornness was the lesson, he'd had very good teachers.

The old man raised his staff and pointed it in Bec's direction. It was a thick, blackened thing with a big lump of honey-colored stone stuck on top and ashes clinging to its bottom.

"Do as you're told!"

There wasn't much sorcery on Old Pyrtanis Street. Sure, everyone *talked* about the big, empty lot at the western end of the street where nothing but nothing grew. Anytime she lost something in the kitchen, Momma blamed the ghost of Enas Yorl, whose magic house had vanished from the empty lot years before Bec was born. But that was just talk and Momma's carelessness. When it came to sorcery seen with his own eyes, there were the midsummer bonfires that changed color and shape when Hazard Eprazian waved his arms in the air and old Bilibot, who lived in a shed behind the Lucky Well and claimed he could see the future in a handful of ashes cast against the wind.

Neither of those prepared Bec for the sight of that shiny-bright stone pointed toward his heart. Before it could belch fire or lightning, he leapt sideways and pled for his life.

"Don't hurt me! Please. I swear—I swear, honest—when Cauvin's angry, it's better to leave him alone. Lots better. I can do anything he can . . . almost. I'll find what you need: a table, chair, whatever you want. Just don't point that *thing* at me!"

The old man lowered his staff, and Bec tried to live up to his promises. He emptied the cart—food from the stoneyard, blankets from Batty Dol, ink and parchment from the scriptorium—then went on a quest for wood for furniture, wood for a fire, and water for tea.

Grandfather wasn't the first person to hole up in the abandoned estate. After gathering wind-fallen branches for the fire and filling two waterskins from a shrunken but clear-flowing stream, Bec found the remains of someone else's weather-beaten lair stashed in what might have been a storeroom or servants' quarters. There were enough planks for a crude worktable and a serviceable stool—if he could put together something to replace its two missing legs. Right-sized chunks of masonry would have done the job, but Cauvin had ignored Bec every time he came near the wall where he was smashing bricks, and the boy judged it wise to lie low a while longer.

He made do with stones from the stream. The final result wasn't pretty, but he thought it would support a skinny old man. And it would have, maybe, if the old man hadn't had a nasty wound at the top of his right leg. The old man could stand and hobble a bit with his staff for support, but he couldn't sit upright without the wound paining him badly after a few moments. They tried padding the stool with Batty's blankets; that only made it tippy and harder for the old man altogether. Grandfather was wheezing and shiny before Bec managed to get him back into what passed for his bed.

"You shouldn't be out here, Grandfather," Bec said, using his extracourteous voice—the one that sometimes worked with grown-ups when they were wrong. "You need to see a healer."

"There's nothing a healer can do for me, boy. I've taken my death wound. It's only a matter of time 'til I'm gone. Fetch one of those planks and lay it here, across my lap."

But that was worse than the blankets. The old man fainted clean away. Bec made strong tea with half-heated water and held the cup close to the old man's face so the fragrant steam could work its way inside.

"Get your brother," were the first words out of Grandfather's mouth once his eyes were open again. He'd said them in Imperial Rankene.

Gamely, Bec replied, "Won't do any good. He's still angry," in the same language.

The old man propped himself against the wall, halfway between sit-up and lie-down. "Wouldn't."

"Wouldn't what?" Bec asked, lapsing into Wrigglie, the language he knew best despite Momma's efforts otherwise.

"Wouldn't, not won't. Say, 'It wouldn't do any good to approach Cauvin,'" Grandfather continued in Rankene. "You haven't done anything yet, and you don't know for certain that no good will come of approaching your brother, so the proper form is 'Wouldn't do any good.' "

Bec knotted his brows and stared through his eyelashes. "If you say so. Wouldn't. Won't. Means the same to me."

"Perhaps it does when you've got your mouth rooted in Sanctuary's streets, but if you're going to speak Rankene, you should do it properly. Who taught you what you already know?"

"My mother."

"Who is not . . . Cauvin's mother."

Slowly Bec nodded, even though he'd missed a few words between who and mother. "Want your tea?" he asked, swirling the cup so a few drops splattered onto Batty's blankets.

The old man clutched the cup between long, bony fingers. Bec expected him to make disgusting noises as he sipped the way Poppa and even Cauvin did when Momma served soup for supper. But Grandfather had Momma's manners, *aristocrat* manners. He drank quietly, and his lips were dry when he lowered the cup.

For several long moments, Grandfather stared at nothing.

"You need me to do something?"

Grandfather blinked. "There's so little time left, but there's nothing to do. Your bullheaded brother won't talk to me, and I can't put pen to parchment without seizing up from pain."

"I could write for you, Grandfather."

It seemed to Bec that the old man looked at him, really looked at him, for the first time. "What I have to say is more difficult than 'wouldn't' or 'won't,' boy. I've gone through a score of scribes in my time—twoscore. Trained men, well versed in the subtleties of our language, and I've driven all but a few of them to drink. I have no liking for children, but you've done nothing to deserve that from me."

"I can write for you—if you go slow and spell out the hard words."

"No. It's beyond question."

"Then my brother and me better take all that writing stuff back to the scriptorium, 'cause it's not going to get used. Cauvin can't read but maybe ten Imperial words, and the only one he can write is his name—'cause *I* taught him how to make the letters."

The faraway look returned to Grandfather's eyes. "There is justice, boy," he said softly. "Cold, bitter justice. Very well, get the parchment. What's left to lose, eh?"

Bec got to work. This was more to his liking, more what he had in mind when he'd surprised Cauvin in the loft the night before. He scavenged a curved bit of crockery, wiped it off on his breeches, and set it against the wall.

"That won't be necessary," Grandfather advised him.

"But we don't have any wine—"

"Water will do."

Muttering, Bec doused the crockery with water from the skins. He set about mixing ink for only the fourth time in his literate career. Usually he wrote with chalk chips on a piece of slate. Momma didn't trust him with ink, much less with parchment. The feather quill felt awkward in his hand and was damnably difficult to fill with ink.

"I'm ready," Bec announced at last. He'd seated himself cross-legged on the hard ground with the parchment flat in front of his knees. Looking at Grandfather from that angle, all he saw was a wrinkled face hovering above the drab blankets.

"You've done this before, have you?" Grandfather asked.

Bec nodded emphatically and a great dollop of black ink landed on the parchment. He swiped it quickly with his sleeve.

"And which language do you write best, boy? Rankene or Ilsigi?"

"Imperial. My mother wouldn't teach me Ilsigi letters, and my father can't. I've picked up a few—some of them are the same as Imperial letters, only the sounds are different. It's confusing," Bec admitted. "But if you speak slow, I can sound it out and write it down. If I can't do that, I'll ask you to spell it out for me, if you can. What am I going to be writing about? When Momma dictates, I do better if I know what the words are about."

Grandfather spat out a mouthful of syllables. Imperial was like that, leading bits and trailing bits attached to a center word that might not mean what it sounded like it meant when the word was finished. Bec heard the sounds for "man" and "right" and—maybe—"blood"; he got no meaning at all.

After a deep sigh, he warned, "Maybe you better start off spelling."

"Well, you tried—"

"I can do it! All you've got to do is tell me what I'm writing about and spell me the hard words!"

"All right, boy . . . Bec. Our story begins more than two hundred years ago, in the city of Ilsig, which gave its name to a kingdom and a language." He paused until Bec finished writing the words. "The Ilsigi called the mountains well west of their city the Queen's Mountains because they were harder to climb than— No, never mind why they called them the Queen's Mountains—"

"Should I write that—'never mind about the mountains'?"

"No, write what's important. In Ranke—which was a kingdom itself, then; the Empire hadn't been founded yet—we called those same mountains the World's End Mountains or the Spine, which is exactly what the Irrune called them when they first saw them some twenty years ago, though the folk they drove from the mountains—the folk who've lived in these parts longer than any of us—called the mountains Gunderpah, for the clouds that hide their peaks—"

"Gunderpah!" Bec complained. "You better spell me that one. What kind of word is Gunderpah?"

"The same kind as Bec or Cauvin or Molin Torchholder. It's a name, boy; the name the mountain folk gave to hills where they lived. The Ilsigi king said to the mountain folk: Defend us from the king of Ranke and his armies! The tribes did, or tried. In those days, when Vashanka's star was rising, we Rankans never lost a battle, not even a skirmish. The mountain tribes were no match for a well-led disciplined army. And when the Ilsigi army finally came down to the World's End, they faced not only the Rankan army, but the mountain tribes as well—for it's a truth, boy, that such folk will fight for gold and for whoever gives them the most gold."

Bec laid down the quill. "Is any of this important?" He'd missed most of that last part anyway.

"I'm telling you the history of Sanctuary, boy—*your* history, and it's a damn fool who isn't interested in his own history. While that Ilsigi army was losing ground in the Spine, the Ilsigi king was taxing his people to the breaking point. There were uprisings throughout the Ilsigi kingdom. Their army had a choice—stand and fight, and lose everything; or make peace with Ranke, pay tribute, and hightail it home before the king's own city was in flames."

"So, what's that got to do with Sanctuary?" Bec held the quill over the puddled ink. He squeezed the vane gently and drew up a column of the black liquid.

"This miserable city was founded by Ilsigi rabble—slaves, whores, gladiators, and all the rest who struck out on their own rather than stay in Ilsig once its king and army were humbled. And humbled they were, boy—"

"My *name* is *Bec*!"

"And humbled they were, *boy,* because the rabble got away, and the rest—the good folk who carry any kingdom or empire on their shoulders—saw their king's weakness and lost heart—"

"The way the Enders have lost heart?" Bec met Grandfather's eyes and held them a moment before looking away.

"Just so, Bec. Just so. A king can hold his people together after they are defeated by a worthy enemy, but when the enemy is unworthy or—worse—if the enemy is *inside* the kingdom, only the greatest kings or emperors will prevail. Our Empire had no great emperor when it needed him most. Men like Serripines retreated to Sanctuary, hoping a great man would emerge to lead the Empire back to glory. What he found here, of course, was worse than what he'd left behind."

"What happened here, Grandfather? What *really* happened here that was worse than anywhere else?"

"Our gods abandoned us, and we abandoned our gods."

Bec shook his head. "Dyareela," he said solemnly. "What happened with Dyareela? Everybody remembers. Everybody tells me, 'be glad you weren't born yet,' but nobody says why. Momma cries sometimes, and Poppa drinks. Batty Dol talks to ghosts, old Bilibot, too. And Cauvin—you made Cauvin remember Dyareela when you mocked him; that's why he got all dark and scary. You know he's got a great big scar on his chest? Two scars, like a crossroads . . . I asked him, and he wouldn't talk for a week, so I asked Poppa, and he said the 'Reelans would sometimes cut through a man's chest and take out his heart so quick that he was still alive and screaming.

But they couldn't have done that to Cauvin, could they have? If they'd cut through his chest, he'd be dead, wouldn't he, whether or not they took out his heart?"

It was the wrong question to ask. It was always the wrong question. Bec lived in one world while everyone else he knew lived in another. They thought he was lucky, but how could anyone be lucky when there were secrets everywhere and even a dying old man went white around the eyes when Bec asked his wrong question?

The nightmare began in earnest one balmy summer morning, eighty-one years after the founding of the Empire. No one guessed, then, what lay ahead, not even Molin Torchholder, whose lifework had changed from building temples for the god of war and storms to the gathering of information and the detection of omens. He'd had reason to think the worst was over. Twenty years had passed since, on his orders, the Imperial city of Sanctuary had last sent its collected taxes to Ranke. Life hadn't been easy—between storms and droughts, fires and floods, a priest might think all the gods in paradise had turned against him and the city whose course he guided—or tried to guide—from deep within the palace shadows. But lately, life had been better. The city's defenses were solid, its fields were green, its treasury, if not overflowing with gold, was at least bright with silver.

They'd gone a year without a riot or plague.

Molin had been sipping flower-scented tea on the balcony of his palace apartment when Hoxa, by far the best of the amanuenses who'd served him over the years, arrived with the news:

"The S'danzo, Lord Torchholder, they've gone . . . pulled up stakes and disappeared during the night. The women have left their shacks in the bazaar, and the men are gone from the taverns, leaving only their debts behind. There's not a one to be found. The word is they've all headed south—"

"South, Hoxa? How? All that lies south of Sanctuary is days upon days of empty ocean. Did they set sails in the middle of their wagons? Put oars in the hooves of their mules and oxen?"

"No, not directly south, Lord Torchholder. They've headed east first, east, then south—beyond the Empire. They said there's a land far to the south, beyond the ice, where horses have wings and chickens lay eggs of pure gold."

"That's nonsense, Hoxa. Don't believe a word of it."

"No, Lord Torchholder, but the S'danzo *are* gone. Every last one of them. I looked for myself."

There was at least one S'danzo left, of course, a half-breed woman living in the bazaar who saw the future more clearly than many men saw the past and who, sometimes, could be persuaded to share her visions with a disenfranchised priest.

Molin visited her that very afternoon.

"Last week, three women saw the same vision," Illyra explained while they sat in a shadow-filled chamber behind her husband's forge. "It was a warning: Bad times are coming. Very bad times."

"Worse than we've already seen?" Molin remembered asking in a bantering tone. "Wetter storms? Hotter fires? A plague with spots? Or are the dead coming back again?"

Illyra folded her hands on her table and stared at them. "No," she replied so softly Molin had leaned over the table to hear her.

"What then? Surely you were one of the three . . . ?"

She shook her head in denial before Molin could finish. "The Ancient One will return . . . to Sanctuary."

"The Ancient One?" Molin asked.

He prided himself in his knowledge of the world's pantheons. Off the top of his memory, he could recall two Ancient Ones. His palace library would undoubtedly contain references to more, but none of them would make mention of the S'danzo. The S'danzo did not acknowledge any gods; they'd lose their gift of timeless sight if they did.

Illyra was visibly anxious. She glanced about and twined her fingers, looking more like the young woman she'd been when Molin first arrived in Sanctuary than the gray-streaked seeress she'd become.

"An elder god," she whispered. "To speak Her name is to invite Her across the threshold."

"A goddess, then?"

Illyra watched her husband through the open door. Dubro remained a mighty man, but the years had taken their toll, and a pair of journeymen—adopted sons—did the heaviest work now.

"A goddess," Illyra conceded. "A goddess with the parts of a man as well hidden beneath Her skirts."

"Ah—" Molin began triumphantly, "The Bloody Bitch, the Mother—"

Illyra's eyes and mouth widened. "My lord!" she pled. "Do not speak further, lest your voice be heard."

Courteously, Molin complied, though he was confident that he'd linked Illyra's *Ancient One* with Dyareela, a cesspool goddess with a reputation for savagery and androgyny. Dyareela was rightly outlawed throughout the civilized world, though Her cult had proved stubbornly impossible to eradicate. Molin could well imagine that respectable folk—and artisans like the smith and his wife were among those folk most concerned with respectability—would go out of their way not to speak Dyareela's name, but She was not a particularly *ancient* goddess, nor had Molin ever linked Her name for good or evil to the S'danzo.

"Why the *Ancient One*?" he asked, all diplomatic innocence and curiosity.

Illyra explained, "The S'danzo were not always wanderers living in tents and wagon, my lord. Once they had homes like any other people until the Ancient One came to their lands. She offered many fine things if the S'danzo would worship only Her. Some of the S'danzo—the menfolk—were tempted, but the women used their gift of timeless sight to foresee that the Ancient One would steal their eyes to work great horror upon the innocent. There was much argument between husbands and wives, but the women prevailed. They preserved their vision and the world, but they paid a price: leaving their homes because the Ancient One had become their eternal enemy.

"Even since, the S'danzo have used their sight to stay free of the Ancient One. When Her shadow falls across a particular time or place, they pack their wagons and move on. The Ancient One's shadow has fallen on Sanctuary."

Molin nodded. He didn't debate mythology with true believers, though he did observe, "You're still here, Illyra. You didn't go with the others. What did *you* see?"

The S'danzo touched the deck of cards that were never far from her hands. Reversed, they were ordinary rectangles of painted paper, but faceup, that was another matter. With his own eyes Molin had watched the images change from one of Illyra's readings to the next.

"I saw nothing, Lord Torchholder. This dreamer was not one of those who dreamt the dream. The warning did not come to me. The S'danzo have no homes; they make none, so, when the time comes, they can leave without hesitation or regret. I have a home—here, in Sanctuary, with a husband and children. I am not S'danzo, not when it matters."

Molin had misunderstood Illyra that afternoon, or perhaps the seeress, herself, had misunderstood. She was S'danzo, when it mattered, although two years had passed by then.

There'd been drought the previous summer, and the little rain they'd gotten had fallen at the wrong time. The grain harvest was meager. Come autumn, the remains of Sanctuary's aristocracy sent envoys to the man who, that year, called himself the Emperor of the Rankan Empire while a deputation of Ils-worshiping priests and peers offered their city to the Ilsigi king in exchange for food.

The Rankan emperor sent Sanctuary's envoys away without hearing their pleas. The Ilsigi king wanted no part of a legendarily troublesome city; not when his own granaries were less than half-full.

By Moruthus, the month of midwinter, death stalked Sanctuary's streets.

The new plague struck fast, taking forms no healer had seen before and which none could cure. Men who were healthy and working in the morning fell into screaming agony by dusk and were dead by midnight. Their bodies bloated almost beyond recognition. Corpses turned black within hours and were apt to burst, leaking bile and contagion before the takers came to collect them.

Someone, somewhere in Sanctuary bitterly dubbed this new nightmare the "Quickening"; the name stuck.

With physicians helpless and charnel fires belching putrid smoke by day and night, the living began to whisper that the Quickening was not a disease at all but a curse sent by anonymous gods. They turned to Sanctuary's varied temples for absolution and release. No known god went unapproached, unappeased.

Molin Torchholder put on the heavy Vashankan robes he had

ignored for a decade. He chanted prayers of desperation, alone at first, then in alliance with other Imperial priests, and finally with the massed clergy of the city, be they Rankan, Ilsigi, or completely foreign. They even prayed to Mother Bey, the venomous goddess of the departed people of the sea.

And all their prayers were utterly without effect.

In many ways the Quickening was more a curse than a disease. It struck one street in one quarter, but not another. One house, but not its neighbors. One person, but not always his closest kin. Those who survived an initial brush with death learned not to count their fortunes: Like a marketplace thief, the Quickening returned to steal again and again.

The full moon of Moruthus shone over the trembling city when a small band of preachers appeared at the western gate. With white robes and red-stained hands, they proceeded from the bazaar to the wharves to the Processional, the palace, and the temple-ridden Promise of Heaven itself, warning one and all that judgment awaited Sanctuary. They called themselves the Servants, without saying whom or what they served.

People listened; they would have listened to anyone by then. Molin Torchholder worried. He had only his own memories to guide him—the annals of Vashanka had been lost when Ranke burnt—but it seemed to him that there was only one god beneath the sun—one goddess—who bid Her priests to stain their hands with crimson dye: the Bloody Bitch, Dyareela, Mother of Chaos.

The Red Mother's cult was banned throughout the Empire, in the Ilsig Kingdom, and anywhere that men sought to hold themselves higher than beasts. Even in the north, among his mother's people, the witches forbade the worship of Dyareela. Molin Torchholder had never encountered a chaos worshiper; he'd been taught the cult was a fraud and Dyareela's so-called priests were never more than a criminal gang.

By dint of meditation, Molin recalled that the Dyareelan cult prophesied that the primal paradise would be reborn in the mortal world once everything raised by man and woman were destroyed. To hasten that rebirth, the Bloody Bitch's priests practiced arson, murder, kidnapping, and—especially—deceit. He recalled, as well, his conversation with the seeress Illyra two years earlier after the S'danzo had disappeared.

If in those days of Moruthus Molin could have proved that the red-handed Servants were worshipers of the forbidden cult of Dyareela—if he'd summoned the city's noblest and wealthiest residents to the Hall of Justice and told them what Illyra had told him about her Ancient One—who could guess how different these last two decades might have been? If Sanctuary's peers had seen the danger as he saw it—as the S'danzo had foreseen it—might they not have helped him drive the Servants out of Sanctuary rather than invite them into their marble-walled homes?

But Molin had had only his suspicions, and in the bitterly cold waning days of Moruthus with the Quickening loose on the ice-slick streets of Sanctuary he kept his suspicions to himself because his gouty toe had swollen to the size of a pig's bladder. The pain held him confined to a massive chair in his palace apartment, where he huddled beneath thick fur robes waiting for spring and for Hoxa to bring him another goblet of mulled wine. It was there beside a crackling fire that the city's peers—its noble-blooded exiles from wherever and its boldest sea traders—trickled into his presence, each bearing a variation of the same message: The Servants had discovered the root of the Quickening. The S'danzo harbored a contagion in their godless, filthy souls, then they breathed that contagion into the faces of their enemies, causing them to die a Quickening death.

Summon the council, each whispering peer demanded, because with no prince of Ranke or Ilsig resident in Sanctuary, Molin Torchholder was all the government Sanctuary acknowledged. Send out guard, they urged, because Molin paid the city's troops, often from his personal treasury. Rid Sanctuary of the S'danzo, they begged, none wanting to bear the burden of command. Sacrifice the godless outsiders to the Servants' god and save the city from the Quickening!

Reluctantly—because there were dire risks each time he summoned the witch-y talents he'd inherited from his mother—Molin quenched the fire in his toe and stirred from his chair. He summoned the peers of Sanctuary to the Hall of Justice for the first time in five years. He settled himself gingerly on a bench in front of the prince-governor's empty throne, the slender Savankh, symbol of

Imperial authority, in his hands, but he did not give in.

"Rot and rubbish," he lectured the silk-wrapped peers. Had they all forgotten what had happened two years earlier? The S'danzo had vanished overnight. There weren't any left in Sanctuary to breathe contagion or anything else on anyone. Frightening as it was, the Quickening was no different than any other plague. It would relax its grip on the town once people—led by Sanctuary's peers—began enforcing a traditional quarantine. A week—two or three at the most—of strict isolation *throughout the city* and the Quickening would be just another of Sanctuary's countless nightmares.

The peers weren't interested in tradition. The Quickening, they insisted, *was* different—the Servants had told them so. Moreover, it had slipped over *their* doorsills (borne, they were certain, by sly tradesmen and flighty maidservants) as easily as it had slithered through the Maze. And while no one would object to burning a few plague-infested buildings in the Maze, it was unthinkable—quite unthinkable—that the peers might find their mansion windows sealed with foul-smelling pitch.

Far easier, Lord Mioklas insisted—far *better*—to take advantage of an opportunity to rid Sanctuary of its undesirables. "You know they're still here," the old man simpered. "Those women and their shiftless kin. They only pretended to disappear. The Servants have a sacred cloth that darkens when the contagion's breathed across it. Let the guard carry it quarter to quarter, door to door—"

Molin lost his temper—a rare occurrence and possibly the price of the witchcraft he'd used to rise from his chair. He scolded the peers, calling them craven and greedy and swore he would never send the men he commanded—the heirs of the Hell-Hounds, the Stepsons, and all the other legendary units of the Imperial Rankan army—to do the bidding of the Mother of Chaos or Her red-handed priests.

The peers were aghast, made speechless not because they had taken Dyareelans into their marble-walled homes but because Lord Molin Torchholder, upon whom they had truly come to depend for such government as they found convenient, had suddenly gone mad. One had only to look at the Servants in their bleached white robes or listen to their piety to know that they were not—could not possibly be—chaos worshipers. Which raised questions none dared ask aloud in the Hall of Justice: Had Lord Torchholder fallen victim to the S'danzo curse? Was it *safe* to remain in his presence?

"Go home," Molin ordered the peers as though they were naughty children. "And stay there. Seal your windows and hang a black flag above your door so everyone will know you're observing quarantine. The guards will enforce it, and that's *all* they will enforce!"

Grateful for any excuse, the peers fled the palace. Hoxa appeared, as he was wont to do, offering his arm to his footsore lord.

"If you ask me," Hoxa said, though Molin rarely asked his opinion, "it's the Servants brought the Quickening on us. Them and their chaos god."

"Nonsense." Molin sighed as he stood. "Savankala himself couldn't piss up a plague in Sanctuary. The power's gone. We used it up a generation ago. These days, whatever befalls Sanctuary is pure chance, fetched up here because there's no god strong enough—or interested enough—to keep it away."

Molin took a tentative step. His foot might have been carved from wood or stone for all he could flex it, but there was no pain. Releasing Hoxa's arm, he began the limping journey to his apartments.

Hoxa walked beside him. "They're fools, Lord Torchholder, and—wait and see—the common folk will tell them so. They won't listen to the Servants; they're outsiders. And we all know the common folk of Sanctuary don't listen to outsiders. They know there's only one S'danzo seeress left in Sanctuary, and she was born here. They've known her all their lives. They'd sooner point their fingers at each other than ask Illyra to breathe on some raggedy cloth—"

Suddenly Molin saw the truth between himself and his amanuensis. He gasped, "Light from above—" and seized Hoxa's arm. "Run to the stables," he ordered. "Tell them to saddle my horse and as many others as they've got, then go to the barracks. Find Walegrin, if you can, but find an officer no matter what. Tell him to gather his best men and meet me in the stables."

"For what, Lord Torchholder? Should they arm themselves? And how?"

"For butchery," Molin replied with his eyes closed. He prayed to his god; there was only the familiar emptiness. He opened himself to witchcraft's power and it flowed into him from the earth, from the sky, and from the man at his side.

Hoxa's face was white and glassy-eyed when Molin released him. He blinked blindly until Molin gave him a shove toward the stables.

Molin's chamber servants were equally stunned when he stormed through the door calling for his long-unused weapons and armor. He'd been an old man, a limping invalid when last they'd seen him. They whispered Vashanka's name, assuming that their priest had finally relocated his god. They didn't know about his witchcraft talents, and he saw no reason to enlighten them.

Young men came forward to lace Molin quickly into layers of quilted wool and studded leather. A young woman approached with the ceremonial sword he wore whenever he needed to appear more warrior than priest.

"Not that one. Not today. Get me the sword beneath my bed." The young woman stood as blank as a whitewashed wall. "Under my bed!" he shouted at her. "In the chest under the bed!"

They were all young enough to be the children of Molin's own children, his children who hadn't lived, who hadn't survived. He'd never noticed before, but he'd always avoided the company of older people, even now that he'd become an old man himself.

The young woman opened the dusty oblong chest she'd dragged from beneath Molin's bed. The scabbard it held was as long as Molin's arm and, once wiped of its greasy protection, faintly green, as though the steel had been adulterated with brass or bronze.

"Surely, Lord Torchholder . . . ?" she asked, eyeing the newly cleaned blade with careful disdain.

"Behold, the fabled steel of Enlibar," Molin replied, taking the weapon from her hands.

It was lighter than common steel and it was adulterated with bronze. At least *this* blade was, bronze from the Necklace of Harmony, which had once adorned the marble statue of Ils in His temple on the Promise of Heaven. The crippled bellmaker who'd forged the blade had said only that the formula called for a relic of sanctity and power. Molin could have commandeered a medallion or weapon from his own god, but he and Vashanka weren't on good terms that season, so he'd sent his thief to Sanctuary's rival pantheon.

The thief had succeeded; likewise the bellmaker. While his servants watched, Molin plucked fruit from a bowl and let it drop an arm's length to the blade. There was silence as the fruit split and fell in halves to the floor, then the young woman gasped.

"Stay here," Molin told her and the others. "Listen to Hoxa after he returns. His voice is my voice in my absence. Whatever he tells you to do, do it."

Panic returned to his servants' eyes. Molin didn't waste time allaying it. If his assumptions proved correct, even the fabled steel of Enlibar might not be enough to see him safely to sunrise.

He met Hoxa on the stairs.

"Did you find Walegrin?"

Hoxa nodded. "He came to me in the stables, my lord, while the hostlers were readying the horses. They're waiting for you below, at the gate. I don't understand, my lord. The city is quiet. You sent the peers home to prepare for quarantine, yet now you've armed the guard—"

Molin pushed past his faithful servant, not answering any of his questions. He descended the remaining stairs as rapidly as weapons and armor allowed. The vast palace courtyard was gray with winter's early twilight. The scent of ice sharpened the air. Walegrin himself held the reins of Molin's horse and cupped his hands to boost the older man into the saddle.

Walegrin's lifelong dream had been escape from Sanctuary, and he'd succeeded once or twice in putting the city's walls behind him. He'd fought well in Ranke's northern wars and led the clandestine expedition that rediscovered the ancient formula for Enlibar steel. But fate had always dragged him back to the city of his birth.

Though he was only in in his fifties, Walegrin's shaggy, parched-straw hair was streaked with wintry gray. His face was creased like last year's leaves. He limped when he walked, thanks to a fractious horse. Three fingers had disappeared from his off-weapon hand after the Maze ran riot. Molin hadn't seen Walegrin smile since his wife had died of the sweats five years earlier. Still, there was no man in Sanctuary—no man in the whole benighted Empire—that Molin would rather have beside him in a close-quarter skirmish.

"Have you heard the tales the Servants have sprouted about the Quickening's source?"

Walegrin nodded his answer.

"Pray we're not too late."

"Two years ago was too late," the green-eyed man countered. "I told her to go, her and Dubro both. But they wouldn't listen. Dubro couldn't imagine any other place, and she said because she was my half sister, the S'danzo wouldn't have her. Damn the S'danzo, says I, the Empire's gone to ruin and Sanctuary's Wrigglies wouldn't treat her any better, push come to shove. They were stubborn, both of them. Break their backs before they'd take my advice . . . anyone's advice."

He put his hands on his horse's withers, raised himself up on his arms, and balanced there. For a breathless moment it seemed Walegrin lacked the suppleness or strength to swing his weight across the animal's back, then he and the horse grunted from deep in their guts. His leg arced over the saddle, and he settled lightly onto the blanketed leather.

"Say 'they are stubborn' instead," Molin suggested. "There's hope yet—"

"Say we're after vengeance and be done with it."

With a minimum of motion, Walegrin wheeled his horse toward the city. They took torches from the guards at the palace gate.

"Lower the bar behind us," Molin ordered, "and keep it down 'til it's light. We'll come back through the postern."

"*If* we come back," Walegrin added, though neither he nor the six men riding behind him hesitated to follow Molin onto Sanctuary's streets.

Along Governor's Walk they met a gang coming up from the slums on the hillside behind the Promise of Heaven. Armed with torches, shovels, and other tools, they were looking for someone to lead them against the S'danzo.

When Molin asked why, a lean, sour-faced man snarled, "The gods will." His Ilsigi grammar was as bad as his teeth.

"Not *your* gods," Molin snarled back, matching the churl's tone. "Thousand-eyed Ils never wages war on women. He watches you now, and He'll smite you a thousand times for every blow you take without His blessing. Go home, and quickly, lest you be marked for heresy, or worse."

A dark-haired lout bearing an ax shaft in each hand objected to Molin's advice by raising his weapons, but—no matter that Molin

Torchholder was a Rankan priest or that his god had been vanquished years earlier—he couldn't endure Molin's glower for long. Once the lout's arm dropped, the gang melted away.

"They'll change their minds before they're halfway home," Walegrin muttered.

Molin agreed before adding, "But they'll do their hunting in the uptown quarters, not the bazaar. That's the best we can hope for tonight."

They weren't halfway from the palace to the bazaar when Molin first smelled smoke. Walegrin was right, he realized, and the best they'd achieved would be vengeance. But the men riding with him said nothing, and neither did he. Closer to the stone-arch entrance to the bazaar, the bitter scent and twilight merged into a thick fog.

A handful of watchmen met them at the bazaar gate. Poorly armored for a winter night much less a riot, they said they'd sent a runner to the palace when the first gang appeared.

"Were there Servants with them?" Molin asked.

"No white robes, Lord Torchholder," a watchman replied.

"None that we saw, anyway."

"They was plain-dressed folk, my lords, not even from the Maze," a watchman whose baldric and sword marked him as the night's commander said, partly defending his men, partly defending the mob. " 'Tweren't nothing we'd do to stop 'em."

" 'Twas let them pass or be killed ourselves."

"Said they'd come to stop the Quickening. Said the Servants told 'em how with a patch of bleached cloth," said the man who hadn't seen a white robe pass near him.

Molin ordered the watchmen to take up their spears and torches before Walegrin could cut them down with his own Enlibar sword.

"They're filthy cowards," Walegrin hissed. "*Wrigglie* cowards!"

Walegrin had been born in Sanctuary and spoke Rankene with an outlander's accent, but he was an Imperial citizen, as his father and grandfather had been before him. He bore his prejudices proudly, without repentance.

Molin's ancestry wasn't nearly so pure. "Let them redeem themselves," he told his companion, "if they can. They didn't join the mob."

Grumbling, Walegrin allowed the watchmen to form up between the mounted guards.

Sanctuary's bazaar was forbidding on a pleasant, moonlit night; on a frigid, smoke-filled night it was confusion incarnate. Walegrin, Molin, and the other guards had given their torches to the watchmen. The light barely reached beyond the moving ring of horses and was nowhere near as bright as the flames they glimpsed to the south.

"They live against the northern wall," Walegrin reminded Molin, and took the lead.

It was just as well the riders had surrendered their torches. They needed both hands on their horses' reins when the animals balked at the first overturned vendor's cart they encountered. Betraying his own anxiety, Walegrin brought his gelding up short and berated it with heavy heels until a watchman shouted:

"There's a body down here!"

"A woman?" Molin asked before Walegrin could.

"No, my lord—a man. Throat's been slit ear to ear."

Walegrin kneed his gelding to the north. "Keep moving!"

The smoke thickened with every stride the horses took, but worse than the smoke in their eyes were the sounds of chaos—shouts, screams, timbers snapping in flames as livelihoods were put to the torch. Molin's consolation—small and bitter though it was—was that the riot seemed worst in the southern quarter of the bazaar. The northern quarter was quiet, perhaps untouched or, better, empty because those who dwelt there—Illyra and Dubro among them—had heard their neighbors screaming and slipped away before the noose was tightened around their own necks.

Molin's conscience—that useless relic of his priestly education—prickled and reminded him that no good came of fortune seized from another's tragedy. He hastily corrected his hopes, but not hastily enough. A woman clutching a torn and bloodied bodice over her breasts erupted from the smoke and ran toward them. Between shrieks of terror she pleaded for protection. Her hair was Imperial yellow, meaning she couldn't possibly be Illyra, but the ruffian trio chasing her had murder in their eyes.

"They killed my son!" she wailed when she was still farther from

Walegrin than the ruffians were from her. "Killed him before my very eyes!"

"Go on!" Molin shouted to Walegrin. He unsheathed his green-tinged sword. "These puds are mine."

It wasn't an empty boast; Molin Torchholder had always been a better warrior than he'd been a priest. Aided by a battle-hardened horse, twenty years prior—even a decade earlier—he would have sliced through the ruffians like so much rotten cheese and caught up with the others before they'd disappeared from sight. Except it wasn't twenty years ago, nor even a decade. The horse was steady, but Molin's arm was not. He missed his mark on the knife-wielding ruffian nearest the woman, giving the man a wound that would kill him, but not nearly soon enough, and—worse—unbalancing himself in the saddle.

Molin needed two heartbeats to get himself righted and that was one heartbeat too many. The flat blade of a workman's shovel slammed into his shin. His armor kept his leg in one piece, but it was numb from the knee down and left him with a deadly choice—finish off the ruffian he'd cut or protect himself from the shoveler. He had a better angle on the bloody ruffian, though as a man who'd breached a fortress rampant armed with nothing more than a flaming torch, Molin knew better than to underestimate a shovel.

So Molin bore down on the shoveler, Enlibar sword held high. The horse beneath him screamed and shied—this was no formal battle where the animals were sacrosanct. He corrected his aim at the last instant and struck true. The uncanny sword threw off a shower of spring green sparks as it sliced clean through the shovel's shaft, no greater challenge to its temper and edge than the fruit in Molin's bedchamber.

One down, two—no three . . . *five* to go.

The rioters had swarmed to the sounds of carnage. In a lucid flash worthy of a S'danzo seeress, Molin saw himself brought down by the least of Sanctuary, by ignorant men swinging tools and scraps of formerly white cloth. It would be an ignominious death, but so was every other death. He hauled on the horse's reins until its mouth hurt more than the wound in its hindquarters and it charged at one man who'd die before Molin Torchholder did.

Naked hands fastened to Molin's armor even before he delivered his killing stroke. He felt himself slipping sideways in the saddle, headed for the ground where his sword and armor would be useless. The first prayer he'd learned—*Into Your mighty hands, O Vashanka, I consign my soul. Lift me up to paradise*—passed through his mind.

A heavy weight struck his chest. Molin closed his eyes. Another weight fell. He couldn't feel, couldn't breathe, couldn't think . . .

And then he could.

Sensation returned with a jolt that began in his wrist and ended in his battered leg.

"Can you mount?" a voice Molin almost recognized demanded.

His vision blurred from smoke and shock. He didn't know where he was or why.

"Can you walk? Stand? Can you *fight*?"

Walegrin. Walegrin had come back for him, or never left. Walegrin had chosen Ranke and duty over his half sister.

Molin found his balance. "Can't mount," he admitted. "Can stand. Can walk. Can fight."

On foot himself, the bigger man dragged Molin forward, northward, through the bone-chilling panic. They marched with the torch-bearing watchmen, with the riders slightly ahead. Past the Settle Stone in the middle of the bazaar, impossibly rumored to be the first stone raised in Sanctuary; the northern wall, the oldest and thickest of the city's walls, became a boundary they could sense but not see.

"Illyra!" Walegrin shouted, leaving Molin at last. "Answer me, damn you!"

He loved his sister, but he did not always like her.

Molin seized a torch from one of the watchmen and, true to his name, carried it forward.

"Sweet Sabellia—"

The northern quarter of the bazaar was indeed quiet, but it wasn't empty. The mob had visited. Perhaps they'd begun their savagery right here, at Dubro's forge. He'd put up a fight, that much could be seen by the light of the torch Molin held. There were three corpses . . . four . . . sprawled in the dirt around the dead blacksmith. A man who forged iron needed wood for his fire. Dubro had been almost as good with an ax as he'd been with a hammer.

He'd died with his eyes open, the ax still clenched in his hands. By the looks of things he'd fallen backward—tripped, perhaps, or struck low and from behind and landed slumped against the anvil post. Bits of skull and scalp clotted on the anvil itself. The prime symbol of Dubro's trade had slain him.

You'd think his seeress wife would have seen that coming.

Absently, Walegrin kicked over one of the corpses, then cursed and kicked it again, lifting it completely off the ground.

"Illyra! Illyra!"

Molin hobbled over with the torch. He thought he recognized the face of one of Dubro's journeymen through the blood and swelling. The man might have stood beside Dubro, fighting the mob to the end. More likely, Walegrin judged right, and he'd led the mob against his master.

"No use," Molin whispered, tugging on Walegrin's arm. "It's done."

"Illyra!" Walegrin's speech had been reduced to a single, anguished word.

The tiny home where Illyra and Dubro had lived all these years stood unburnt, but the shutters had been broken, and the door had been wrenched from its hinges. Lengths of curtain cloth in Illyra's bright, beloved colors flapped outward, into the smoke. Molin knew what he would see when he thrust the torch through the gaping doorway, but he did it all the same and blocked Walegrin's view and entrance with his body.

They'd killed her. Slit her throat and plunged a knife at her heart where it remained. By firelight the metal glinted redder than the stains across her breasts.

"She's been dead since sunset," Molin assured Illyra's brother. "At least since sunset." Although it was hard to mark the time of death in winter. He'd learned that as a young man fighting the northern witches.

"Let me pass."

Walegrin laid hands on Molin's shoulders. He tried to shove the older man completely out of the ruined home, but Molin sidestepped. He wedged himself into a corner and wondered—pointlessly—how Dubro had fit into his own home. The flames from his torch licked the flimsy roof. Painfully, Molin got down on his knees.

Walegrin knelt, too, misunderstanding Molin's gesture, waiting for a prayer.

"Into Your mighty hands, O Vashanka, I consign our sister's soul. Lift her up to paradise."

The Tenslayer was not by any measure a woman's god, but He'd take care of Illyra, if He knew what was good for Him.

Walegrin found his sister's hand buried in the folds of her many-layered skirt. A rectangle of stiff paper slipped from her fingers before he lifted them to his lips. In charity—not wanting to witness a warrior's tears—Molin looked away . . . at the painted paper.

It was a sign Molin had seen many times upturned on the cloth-covered table where Illyra scryed the future. A single face formed from the shards of many other faces, all of them anguished and deformed. She called it the Face of Chaos, and he almost fed it to the torch, then thought better of the sacrifice. He collected the rest of Illyra's scrying cards and, though Molin had been careful as he searched, a flame leapt from the torch to the curtain cloth.

Walegrin snarled like a wolf when Molin shoved him at the door.

"Let it burn," Molin countered. "She's past pain or caring. Let it *all* burn."

Bec laid down the white quill. He whispered, "Grandfather?" but wasn't sure if he wanted to hear an answer or not. The old man had been talking all morning, and while keeping up with him, Bec had covered half a sheet of parchment with the tiniest script he could manage. Then Grandfather had started talking about a woman named Illyra (Bec had asked how it was spelled). He'd begun to mumble and wouldn't speak clearly when Bec asked him to. Furzy feathers! The old man didn't even seem to hear him ask the question.

And now he was *crying*! Tears were streaming down his cheeks, same as they streamed down Batty Dol's cheeks when she got going about the Troubles. Or Momma's cheeks, when she told him about the fine, fine house with twenty rooms that used to stand in the middle of the stoneyard.

Bec had never seen a *man* cry before.

"Grandfather?" he asked, his loudest effort yet. "Grandfather, are you dying? Should I get Cauvin?"

Bec stood up, but he'd been sitting crosswise too long, and his legs had gone to sleep. He hopped noisily, foot to foot, waiting for the burning and prickling to end. *That* finally got Grandfather's attention.

"Stop dancing, boy!" the old man snapped. "Take up your quill. Where were we? Read back the last words you've written."

The prickling was terrible when Bec folded his legs beneath him again, but Grandfather wasn't the sort of man a boy argued with. He cleared his throat and read cautiously, because he hadn't caught all the words: "It began to snow. The fires turned the ice flakes into raindrops . . ."

Molin continued, "But there wasn't enough water in that winter night to keep the bazaar from burning to the ground. We beat a retreat to the Governor's Walk and cut through the mob when it tried to follow us. Twenty men and women there on the walk. Good riddance! The gods alone know how many more died in the bazaar. They spread, you realize. The fires and the mob, they both spread through the city. It was two days, I swear, before we returned to the palace. Two days of fighting fires and damned fools. But damn us all, when the smoke cleared, the Quickening was gone, and the Servants of Dyareela took the credit."

# Chapter Seven

Bec blew across the cup of tea, not because it was steaming hot but because if he blew hard enough, Grandfather might think the tea had indeed once been steaming hot. Momma made the stoneyard's tea. She went outside the walls to collect the leaves and flowers. She dried them and crushed them and, most important, she tended the hearth fire that heated the water that became the tea Bec drank with every meal. Bec watched his mother coax the embers back to life every morning. She made it look so simple, Bec had never imagined it wasn't something he could do.

"Here," he said, offering the cup. "I was afraid it might be too hot, so I blew on it for you."

Grandfather extended a trembling hand. Bec tried to make the exchange without actually touching the old man's fingers. It was impossible, and Grandfather's flesh felt like— Well, it felt like nothing Bec could describe, except that it wasn't *right* and sent shivers down his backbone. He took a backward step and then another before attempting to meet Grandfather's eyes.

"Next time, boy—if there is a next time—don't bother blowing."

Bec opened his mouth to protest and shut it quickly. Grandfather was the most frightening man he'd encountered. Far worse than Poppa when Poppa was angry, or Cauvin, who got angrier and got that way more often. The old man was scarier than the Irrune who lived in the palace and took whatever they wanted from any shop in any quarter of the city—

Thank Shalpa (Bec's favorite among Sanctuary's gods, despite his mother's Imperial disapproval, because Shalpa was quick and clever and He never, ever got caught) that the Irrune had no use for stone!

Bec had slipped into an Irrune daydream when Grandfather's raspy voice brought him back to the ruins. "Did that stone-headed brother of yours buy more parchment, or is that the only skin you've got?"

Should he tell Grandfather that it had been *his* idea to buy a single skin? Momma could get a whole year's worth of writing onto a single sheepskin. Or should he let Cauvin take the blame? Cauvin could take it. Cauvin could take anything because he'd walked out of the palace alive.

At least that's what Cauvin said.

Giving the question a second heartbeat's thought, Bec decided that he shouldn't make things worse between Cauvin and Grandfather. Grandfather had an edge against Cauvin the likes of which Bec had never seen. It had something to do with the Troubles . . .

"That night when your friends died in the bazaar," Bec asked boldly, determined to get his answers, "was that when the Troubles began . . . with the Servants? Cauvin says the Hand caught him, and that's all he'll say. Was the Hand the same as the Servants, or were they something different?"

Grandfather glared over the lip of the teacup. His eyes seemed to glow with a light of their own, and Bec regretted to the soles of his feet that he'd dared to ask any questions at all. Then Grandfather began talking again in a voice so soft that Bec ignored the ink, the quill, and the parchment. He sat on the floor beside Grandfather instead, with his chin resting resting on the mattress and his eyes closed to remember every word.

The shape of the future should have been clear to anyone with the wit to see beyond the tip of his own nose, but the men and women Molin summoned to the dilapidated Hall of Justice in the wake of the fires that had leveled the bazaar and most of the Shambles, too, thought otherwise.

"I say it's an excellent idea!" old Lord Mioklas declared, brandishing a white badge—a proof of purity given to him by the Servants he continued to house in his Processional mansion. It was not the only twisted bit of white cloth visible in the Hall. "A simple proof of one's virtue and better than anything *you've* come up with in years, Lord Torchholder."

"These Servants are doing what your precious garrison full of *expensive* guards never could do," another peer continued. "In less than a week, they've rid Sanctuary of its most worthless elements *and* put a stop to the Quickening! My house has lost no one since we took the badge."

"Hear, hear!" a third man shouted. He had the golden hair of an Imperial family and the crimson nose of a man who drank too much wine. "Why keep the garrison at all?" he demanded. "For five soldats—and not one of them pure silver—I've got a Servant sitting at my high door, sniffing everyone who comes or goes. And it's not just moral contamination he can scent. He says he can smell a thief at ten paces—and I believe him. He pointed a finger at my wife's maid and we found a gold necklace hiding in her skirts! Tell me your precious garrison could have done that—and caught the thief before she left my home! You're wrong about the Servants, Lord Torchholder, as wrong as a man can be. This nonsense about Dyareela—you can't expect us to believe your superstitions. Face it, Lord Torchholder: The Servants are the best thing that's happened to this city since you stopped sending our taxes on to Ranke."

Molin looked at the men and women arrayed before him. They were men—women—his own age or older, meaning they'd all lived through the tumultuous years when Prince Kadakithis had been Sanctuary's governor and the city had become a battlefield for gods and distant wars. They knew what happened when gangs turned the city's quarters into rival kingdoms. They knew that the purest silver, the whitest badge was no guarantor of safety—or they should have.

"Start packing," Molin told Hoxa after the council had told him his services as acting governor were no longer needed. "We leave at dawn."

"For where, my lord?" the loyal Hoxa asked.

"Anywhere. Anywhere but here. I've wasted my last breath on these fools. They deserve whatever the Servants do to them."

No sooner were the words out of Molin's mouth than the air chilled. By sundown, Sanctuary shivered in a bitter north wind. By midnight, sparkling white powder fell thick from a black sky. It buried the city to a finger's depth with the promise of much more by dawn.

"Snow," Hoxa observed. "Do you suppose anyone will notice it's the same color as the Servants' badges?"

Molin would not dignify the question with an answer. In his youth winters throughout the Rankan Empire might have been raw, but water rarely froze. Snow was yet another indignity that had befallen Imperial lands since the capital fell.

"Will we wait until this storm blows over, Lord Torchholder, or shall I continue packing?"

"What do you think?" Molin's temper reached its breaking point. "Of course we wait!" he shouted at Hoxa. "I may be damned never to escape from this gods-forsaken town, but I'm not suicidal. Why die in a snowdrift tomorrow when we can sit tight and wait for Dyareela's Servants to slit our throats!" He slammed the door hard enough to splinter the wood.

The sound was fresh and sharp in Molin's mind, more real—more shocking—than anything that followed, because there was a limit to shock, a threshold which, when crossed, opened into numbness. He'd counseled emperors and princes and led armies to victory, but, once again, Sanctuary had gotten the best of Molin Torchholder. He knew who and what the Servants were, but knowledge was useless against their seductive weapons. He could anticipate the Servants' moves—the escalation of their sermons from the simple scapegoating of the S'danzo and anyone else suspected of "contamination" and "impurity" to the trickier bits of Dyareelan theology: confession, mutilation, and execution disguised as sacrifice.

Molin had one weapon to wield against his red-handed enemies, at least in the early days. He paid the guards in Sanctuary's garrison, and they repaid him with loyalty. Walegrin and the others would have carried out any orders he gave them, no questions asked, but not even the Architect of Vashanka dared send armed men into the courtyards of Sanctuary's elite houses, and that was where the Servants laired once they'd gotten hold of aristocratic ears.

Loath as Molin was to admit it, then or now—Dyareela's Servants were clever and subtle, and they were one step ahead of him from the start. They'd looked at the palace and realized that neither he nor his garrison could pose a threat to their plans, even after the bloodshed started, so long as they catered to the fears of the wealthy and self-righteous.

Two types of people met their deaths at the Servants' hands. There were those who sacrificed themselves willingly—hysterics who swallowed the Servants' theological clabber whole. They believed that their deaths would hasten the mortal paradise the Servants promised at the end of every sermon. There was no saving a man or woman from sheer stupidity. The other early victims were those who, like Molin Torchholder, saw through the Servants' plans and opposed them. Unfortunately for Molin, these natural allies were also the heart and soul of Sanctuary's underbelly—the gangs that ran its rackets, traded its drugs, and hosted the least savory houses on the Street of Red Lanterns.

Molin was a practical man, but he drew the line at joining forces with the likes of Basho Quarl, even though Quarl had the right measure of the Servants. The king of beggars and lord of thieves sent his minions to the palace offering gold and information in exchange for protection as the Servants closed in on him. Molin said no, he wouldn't trade the stewpot for the fire. He watched from his palace balcony when white-robed justice dragged Quarl, naked, bruised, and pleading for his life, into the palace courtyard, where a platform built from charred wood had replaced the Hall of Justice. The Servants accused Quarl of every crime he'd committed and more besides. They judged him, then bled him out slowly, to the cheering satisfaction of the crowd.

Despite the false accusations, Quarl deserved every cut he got; but on his balcony, Molin couldn't help wondering if he hadn't been outfoxed again.

After Quarl's "sacrifice" the peers eagerly paid tithes to the Servants rather than taxes to the palace. Molin saw how the wind blew. He released the garrison and told them to leave Sanctuary, *fast.* He made plans to travel with Walegrin to the city of Lirt, about as far to the north and west as a man could go and remain in what could still be called the Rankan Empire. He got as far as converting all his property into gold and jewels, then his gout flared up. His big toe swelled to the size of a melon, and despite his best efforts with mineral soaks and witchcraft combined, it stayed that way until an early winter put an end to all thoughts of following Walegrin to Lirt.

That winter, the eighty-fourth winter of the Imperial calendar, Dyareela's Servants insinuated themselves into every temple ringing the Promise of Heaven. They wanted the palace, too—for an orphanage, they said. Dyareela was a mother-goddess, they said. She couldn't bear to see a child's tears, they said. Molin knew better; there wasn't a priest in the world who didn't know better: Innocent children were ever the easiest to shape for good . . . or evil. He sent messages to his remaining friends among Sanctuary's peers; with his grossly swollen toe, travel, even across town, was out of the question. A few replied, but none was in the mood to listen.

Molin told Hoxa to find them a place outside the palace, a place where they could disappear until spring when—gods willing—his toe would have shrunk and they could set out for Lirt. Hoxa hunted up an abandoned wreck of a building deep in the Maze. It had three usable rooms: one for himself, one for Molin, and the largest for the eight wooden chests they smuggled out of the palace. They settled in for a cold, quiet, and, for Molin, a painful winter.

Spring came and brought with it a long caravan of Imperial refugees. They carried good news and bad. The good news was that the Empire's longtime enemy, Molin's people—the Nisibisi witches of the north—had been beaten, crushed, vanquished, shattered into a thousand pieces the previous summer. The bad news was that the Nisi hadn't been humbled by Rankan might. A horde of demon-worshipers from the far east had crushed the witches, then demanded tribute—or else—from the Empire.

The horde's numbers were great beyond counting. They'd formed a solid ring around the Imperial city of Lirt and when it refused their demands they burnt it to the ground. Not one soul, the refugees insisted, had survived. They weren't Lirters; they were from the city of Sihan, south of Lirt. When the horde hove across Sihan's landward horizon, the pragmatic Sihanites had simply abandoned their port city. Their fleet had sailed south, expecting a warm welcome in the capital.

Instead, they learned that there'd been another coup in the capital and a new usurper was sitting on the emperor's throne. He called himself Vengestis the Magnificent and swore that he'd lead the army to victory over the Dark Horde, but until then the refugees could fend for themselves, west of the capital. He sent his soldiers to the wharves and threatened the Sihanites with death if they set so much as one foot off their ships.

"Lord Serripines says the last month has been hell, and this place is truly *Sanctuary* to his eyes," Hoxa said while slowly shaking his head. "He means to settle his whole clan outside the walls. They're going to grow grain for export, same as they did in Sihan!"

Molin lowered his foot from the cushion. His toe had shrunk. He could think of riding again without leaking tears, but there was nowhere to go if Lirt was gone. Lirt and Walegrin and the rest. He shivered—not from cold—and considered that except for Hoxa, there was no one left who shared his memories, certainly not this Lord Serripines from Sihan.

"The man thinks *this* is *Sanctuary*?" Molin murmured. "And he thinks he's going to grow grain *here*? The man's either a fool or a green-thumb genius."

"And us, Lord Torchholder? What do you make of this Vengestis the Magnificent?"

"Get your cloak, Hoxa. We're leaving." Molin stood up and immediately stubbed the wrong toe. He gritted his teeth against the pain, then stamped into his softest boots.

"For Ranke, Lord Torchholder?"

He sighed as he thumped one of the chests with his fist. "It's time to forget Ranke, Hoxa." The chest groaned and opened. Molin took a handful of soldats and coronations from the wealth of coins, gems, plate, and weaponry. He poured the coins into a plain leather scrip and let the chest lid slam.

"If we don't go to Ranke, Lord Torchholder, where shall will go?" The little man glanced about the dingy room. "We can't stay *here*."

"I absolutely agree." Molin tore a length of brick red cloth from one of his court robes. He wound it intricately around his head, covering his steel gray hair, and let the loose ends fall against his face. With his profile thus obscured he could pass for anything but an Imperial lord.

"Come, Hoxa. By sundown we shall be shopkeepers—"

"Lord Torchholder?"

"Forget 'Lord,' Hoxa— Forget Hoxa, too. Call yourself . . . call yourself Venges, for our new emperor. Call me Boss. By sundown we shall be the new proprietors of a respectable wine shop—or an apothecary. An apothecary would be best. I have some small knowledge of mixing potions, you know."

And by sundown they were proprietors of a run-down apothecary that had been clinging barely to life in what, twenty years earlier, had been the jewelers' quarter.

Compared to the ashes of Lirt or Sihan, or the convulsions of Ranke itself as the Imperial city digested Vengestis and his successor, life as an apothecary in Sanctuary wasn't unbearable. An honest apothecary could make a living in Sanctuary no matter who held power. People ached, they couldn't sleep, they couldn't stay awake, they got indigestion, they looked for an apothecary to solve their problems. Word got around quickly that the shop in the old jewelers' quarter had a new owner whose syrups and powders worked most of the time and whose prices were fair.

Life as a grain exporter wasn't impossible, either. Lord Serripines *was* a fool when it came to his home, his family, and his undying belief that Imperial glory would be restored no later than next year. But he was a genius in the ground. He bought up land that had lain fallow since the Imperial families of Prince Kadakithis's reign had abandoned the city. Then he went to the villages ringing Sanctuary and made himself useful to the villagers that Molin Torchholder, like other city-dwelling men, preferred to ignore. Serripines had added the treasury of Sihan to his own before he left the city and he spread his coins like autumn manure, convincing the villagers to work his fields before they worked their own. Two years after his arrival, there was more land under the plow and scythe than there'd ever been, and big-bellied argosies were sailing high into Sanctuary's harbor, sailing low in the water when they left.

But life that wasn't unbearable or impossible wasn't necessarily good. Slowly, inexorably, the Servants of Dyareela squeezed the priests of Ranke and Ilsig out of their Promise of Heaven temples. The High Priest of Ils got himself flayed for preaching against Dyareela's plans, but most of the city's clergy either changed their allegiance—the Servants were accommodating that way—or slipped out through the walls. Dyareela's justice was swift, and few were tempted to take up the underbelly life once they'd seen a man bled out or a woman peeled of her skin.

Molin Torchholder's little apothecary shop bought more than herbs, of course, and it sold more than syrups and powders. Though Molin had become inconspicuous, he hadn't disappeared, and the secrets of Sanctuary—even the secrets of the Servants of Dyareela—made tracks through his shop, especially its back room.

There wasn't a large market for knowledge within Sanctuary while the Servants gripped it, but the city's harbor was the last deep-water anchorage between Ranke and the Hammer's Tail at the southern tip of the Spine Mountains—or the first, if the ship had sailed around from the Ilsigi side of the Spine. Strangers floated frequently into Sanctuary. Some were drawn there by the grain Lord Vion Serripines grew on the hills above the city, some by misfortune or accident. All strangers, though, eventually made their way to the unassuming shop in the old jewelers' quarter.

Lord Vion Larris Serripines got wind that there was an officer of the old Imperial court—an archpriest of the old Imperial storm-god—selling potions in Sanctuary. Scarcely a day went by when someone from that lord's new Land's End estate didn't cross the apothecary shop's threshold. Those habits would have tragic consequences eventually, but in the Empire's eighty-fifth year, it was simply good business for both the Serripines and Molin Torchholder, so long as the Rankan exiles kept their youngsters safe at home.

"Don't be deceived," Molin warned Lord Serripines. "The Servants are like an arrow wound—you think it's healing, then one day your leg's swollen purple and the next you're lying on your deathbed. I can't get an eye inside the palace anymore—no one can, including the Servants who've set up housekeeping in Savankala's temple. They're not there for worship, Vion, they've been tossed out by their brethren. That alone would be a bad omen, but I know for a fact, the Servants still in the palace have snatched many a child from its parents to keep their so-called orphanage filled. Had I a son or daughter, I'd never let them out of my sight."

The golden-haired Rankan aristocrat straightened the sleeves of his impeccably Imperial robe. "I've sent word of the Servants to Emperor Vengestis. I've told him what must be done, and he agrees.

Any day now, we'll be seeing a contingent of *real* soldiers arrive to put these heretics in their place."

Vengestis had regained the Imperial throne twice since his initial usurpation, each time less magnificently than before. The man had a positive genius for manipulating aristocrats like Serripines, who should have known better but chose pipe dreams of resurrected Imperial glory over the truths held in their own memories. Lord Serripines wasn't an utter fool. Though he kept his absurd faith in the Rankan Empire's promise and had sited his Land's End villa where it could be easily seen by ships sailing down the coast from Ranke, he took Molin's advice and kept his sons and daughters under close watch.

Lord Serripines never got his Imperial ships or soldiers, but he and all Sanctuary did get the Irrune. Traveling under a cloud of dust as tall as a thunderstorm, the city-sized tribe advanced on Sanctuary's ill-guarded walls in the autumn of the Empire's eighty-sixth year. They'd come from the north and east, fleeing the same barbarian hordes that destroyed Lirt and drove the Serripines clan out of Sihan—which, considering the manners and appearance of the Irrune, painted a truly nightmarish picture of the barbarians.

The Irrune had taken a less direct route to Sanctuary than the Serripines. For a generation the tribe had wandered the north, offering their services now to the Nisi witches and next to the Imperial generals in exchange for a new homeland. Both the witches and generals had found it easy to make promises to the Irrune and easier to forget them until outriders of the Black-toothed Beasts—the Irrune name for the barbarians who'd driven them from the lands of their ancestors—reappeared on the eastern horizon.

As soon as he saw the banners of the Beasts, Arizak per-Mizhur, chief of the Irrune, rode west to the Spine, then south in search of empty land for his people and their herds. Their quest finally brought them to the gates of Sanctuary and into sight of more water than their language could describe.

Arizak's demands were simple: food, land, and all the wealth of the city or he'd do to Sanctuary what the Beasts had done to Lirt. He shouted the demands himself from the back of a lean, mettlesome stallion and in the midst of two hundred similarly tempered warriors. The chief Servant of Dyareela, a Maze-bred pimp who'd changed his name to Retribution, scurried to Her altar in what had been Savankala's temple. He asked his goddess for guidance and She, remarkably, sent him to an apothecary's shop in the old jewelers' quarter.

Less remarkably, perhaps, Molin was dressed in a soldier's leather armor when Retribution arrived. For Sanctuary's sake—for the sake of all those whose worst crime was ignorance—he proposed a plan that took him into the Irrune encampment as sole negotiator. Molin expected the worst from the ragged nomads and got Arizak's second wife instead.

Nadalya was a handsome woman and young enough to be the chief's daughter. Molin met Verrezza, Arizak's first wife, at the same moment he met Nadalya. Glancing from matron to maiden, he thought he had the full measure of the chief's domestic disharmony. It was an honest mistake. The Irrune were a sturdy, light-haired, fair-skinned people. Cleaned up and properly attired, not one of them would have attracted attention on the capital's streets—not the way Molin had, growing up swarthy and black-haired in Vashanka's Temple.

Then Nadalya opened her mouth.

"My husband asks me to speak for him, Lord High Architect," she said, using Molin's god-bestowed title, which she shouldn't have known because Molin hadn't used it in her lifetime. "Though Arizak per-Mizhur understands Rankene as well as you or I, it is not the language of his inner thoughts. On his behalf and for all the Irrune, I bid you welcome, Lord High Architect. We are honored to meet you—me, most of all. To his dying day, my father spoke highly of you, Lord High Architect, and often. I heard how you led the charge at Phorixas on Wizardwall so many times, I sometimes think I was there myself." Her smile was cultured, her Imperial grammar, flawless, her accent marred only slightly by a northern twang. Clearly her father, whoever he'd been, had spared no expense for Nadalya's education.

Molin strained his memory and recalled her father's chosen battle. If he'd had moments of greatness in the northern wars—and Molin humbly believed that he had—Phorixas hadn't been one of them. A warrior cherished the victories he hadn't earned but, if he were a wise man, he never bragged about them. The Rankan center, led by a commander's vainglorious nephew, had collapsed when the young man panicked and got himself killed. Molin had led a desperate cross-field charge against the Nisi flank because it was attack or be cut down where they stood.

"Was your father an officer?" he asked Nadalya tactfully.

"Chief purveyor, Lord High Architect," she replied with a blush.

"Ah," Molin sighed.

Purveyors were the necessary evil that followed every army, keeping it supplied with food and fuel, weapons and armor, and everything else it required. There'd never been an Imperial commander who wouldn't rather face the enemy naked than a cranky purveyor. Molin had been grateful that as a priest he'd never had to deal with the breed—until now.

"Where do we begin?" he asked cautiously.

They began with food. Molin gave away the grain Lord Serripines had hoped to sell for a tidy profit. Lord Serripines wouldn't dare complain, not since he'd chosen to live in an undefendable villa far beyond the city walls. To satisfy the Irrune appetite for gold, Molin gave away some of the treasure the Servants had appropriated when they took over the temples. Retribution wouldn't dare complain, either.

Then he and Nadalya got down to the hard bargaining: After a generation of wandering, the world-weary Irrune had come to the end of their road. They needed land for themselves and their herds of sheep and horses, and they expected Sanctuary to provide it.

Though Molin habitually thought of Sanctuary as a carbuncle plunked down in the middle of nowhere, it was, in fact, one of the thirty-seven Imperial cities. It did not sit in reeking isolation beside the sea; instead, it was surrounded—quite thoroughly surrounded—by a broad ring of homesteads, hamlets, and villages. No matter that most of the people living in the Sanctuary's purview regarded the city with the same suspicions and low opinion that Sanctuary itself held for the Rankan capital, the fact remained that there were easily four times as many people living *around* Sanctuary as lived within its walls—and if Molin had settled the Irrune among them, he'd have doomed them all.

The nearest empty land lay southwest of Sanctuary, and it was empty for a good reason. Between Sanctuary and the Hammer there wasn't enough high ground to forage a pig. What wasn't saltwater marsh was bracken fen or blackwater swamp. The natives of Sanctuary called it simply—accurately—the Great Morass, and if Molin had tried to settle the Irrune there, they'd have returned in a month with blood in their eyes.

What Molin and the Irrune needed was grass-covered land which, if not empty, was at least not occupied by Imperial citizens. There was such an expanse in the foothills of the World's End Mountains, about four days' ride to the north and west.

"Follow the White Foal River to its source," Molin advised, omitting any mention of the Gunderpah brigands as he went on to describe a nomads' paradise.

If the brigands and the Irrune couldn't stand the sight of each other—and Molin doubted they could—they'd resolve their differences with the brutal efficiency of their kinds. If the Irrune wiped out the brigands—well, the foothills *were* a veritable paradise for horse herders. And if the brigands drove out the Irrune? Sanctuary had little to fear from a tribe that ran from the Gunderpah brigands with their tails between their legs.

Arizak per-Mizhur had heard too many hollow promises to take Molin's word for land that lay over the horizon. He dispensed with Nadalya's interpretations and took charge of the negotiations himself. Molin would never have gotten rid of the tribe without the help of a sea squall that roared out of a blue-sky afternoon. The wind-whipped, salty rain panicked the herds, flattened half of the Irrune tents, and convinced Arizak per-Mizhur that he would not spend another night near water that spanned the horizon.

The haste with which the Irrune departed for Gunderpah was enough to make an old priest think that his god was taking an interest in the mortal world again.

Molin went back to reciting his prayers when he returned to the city, and it seemed for a few years thereafter that Vashanka was indeed listening—though Lord Serripines and his fellow Land's End exiles stopped listening or visiting the apothecary shop after Molin gave away their profits, and the Servants were no happier to surrender even a small portion of the treasure they'd looted from Sanctuary's temples and palaces. Still, the apothecary business prospered, and so did Molin's back-room trade in information.

The Irrune found their way to the Spine foothills, where the Gunderpah brigands took one look at their new enemy and high-tailed themselves into Ilsig territory without so much as a skirmish—at least that was how the Irrune told the tale whenever they returned to Sanctuary for bribes or barrels of beer. The Servants, having killed or intimidated their opposition, turned inward and, in the way of all those who placed paramount value on purity and prophecy, accusations of heresy began to fly between the Servants tending Dyareela's altars on the Promise of Heaven and those who tended Her orphanage in the palace.

By the winter of the Empire's eighty-seventh year, there were two Dyareelan sects within the city: the Servants of Mother Chaos along the Promise of Heaven and the Bloody Hand of Dyareela in the palace. The Servants had the numbers and the freedom of Sanctuary's streets, but the Hands were utterly self-righteous and utterly ruthless. Anyone unlucky enough to get caught between the two sects could count the remainder of his life in agonizing hours, but the ordinary denizens of Sanctuary were as adept at avoiding Dyareela's authority as they'd been at ignoring the laws of both Ranke and Ilsig.

Sanctuary's reputation as an outpost of stability—provided one could tolerate the occasional public flaying—seeped through the crumbling Empire. The city's population rebounded, and the talk in the back room of Molin's apothecary was that the Servants were on the verge of victory in their religious war with the Hands. Compared to the Hands or the new emperor (who, after slaying Vengestis in his mistress's bed, had, reportedly, raped, then married her himself), the Servants were rulers with whom a prudent man could live.

Then the spring rains failed and became a brutal summer drought. What little grain sprouted, withered and died before it was knee high. Land's End feared for their granaries filled with last year's harvest while Servants and Hands spilled blood on their altars. In the palace, Dyareela told the Hands that Sanctuary was home to too many strangers, too many newcomers whose purity was suspect. The Servants, after listening to the same goddess, prayed for rain.

The Hands were wrong outright, but the Servants were city-bred fools who knew how to rob a second-story bedroom but nothing about the ways of grain.

Ending the drought with slow, steady rains wouldn't have harmed Sanctuary, though they wouldn't have prevented famine, either. Only the Serripines could do that, with the keys to their granaries. But the rain the Servants prayed into Sanctuary was a wind-whipped sea storm. The worst weather surged ashore beneath a new-moon midnight when the tide was already rising. It sucked off roofs, collapsed entire quarters, and undermined another section of the city's walls. In the villages beyond Sanctuary, the storm wrote a different story. Torrential rains recarved the hillsides and flooded fields with ominous, muddy lakes. Then, before the rain had ended, the White and Red Foal Rivers burst out of their banks. Swirling currents swept up toppled trees, drowned livestock, and ruined lives. All flowed downstream, to helpless Sanctuary.

Plague was loose again before the rivers crested.

Someone got the notion that flames would stop the plague and set blazes between the Maze and the harbor. Against all expectation, the fires took root in sodden wood. Molin and Hoxa were throwing buckets of water at their shop's walls when the Bloody Hand emerged from the palace looking for vengeance. When the last flame died, there was only one Dyareelan sect in the city, and it wasn't the Mother's Servants.

Flush with the blood of victory, the Hands spread a new message through Sanctuary's swampy streets. Drought and famine, storm and flood, plague and fire were each and all a clear message from the Mother of Chaos: The end of the old age was upon the world, the time of final purification had begun. The people of Sanctuary had been honored above all others because Dyareela had appointed Her Bloody Hand to lead them against the rest of the world.

But before the people of Sanctuary could wield the Bloody Mother's cleansing swords, they had to become the purest of the pure.

Molin was a veteran of the Wizardwall campaigns. He'd dwelt thirty years in Sanctuary. He'd have sworn he'd seen the deepest depths of darkness, then Hoxa fell afoul of the Hands. With all his spies and contacts, Molin could never learn who had denounced his faithful amanuensis. Probably they'd both been denounced, but the Hands had drawn the line at cracking Vashanka's Architect. The Hands extended no such professional courtesy to Hoxa. The poor man was mad and mutilated by the time Molin bribed his way into the palace chamber where a corpulent thug calling himself the Fist of the Bloody Hand presumed to do a goddess's bidding.

In his heart of hearts, Molin had convinced himself that the Bloody Hands of Dyareela and the Servants of the Chaos Mother before them were frauds. The atrocities the Hands committed—the eyes they'd gouged from Hoxa's skull, the nerves they'd laid bare in the stumps of his arms and legs—were evil, to be sure, but the offspring of mortal imagination rather than divine inspiration. Gods—Vashanka foremost among them—could be inscrutable, capricious, and unspeakably cruel, but evil was a mortal vice.

That day in the dungeon chamber beneath Sanctuary's familiar palace, Molin learned how wrong he was. Though his features were hidden by a robe and the red silk swathed around his head, the Fist of Dyareela's Bloody Hand was, by his voice and movements, a grown man, not so the two responsible for Hoxa's suffering. They were children—a girl on the verge of maidenhood and a boy no older than seven. Their hands were red with fresh blood, not tattoos, and they giggled as they went about their ghastly work.

Molin's heart shuddered with shock when the girl recognized him.

"Lord Torchholder!" she trilled, and ran to him, waving her bloody knife.

Her breath was icy despite the heat of a roaring hearth and two physicians' braziers. It invaded Molin's lungs and burnt the pores of his flesh. He shuddered involuntarily and the girl's trill became laughter. Then the cold was gone, leaving the sense that it had spat him out rather than the other way around.

Had Vashanka bestirred Himself? Or was his maternal witch-blood somehow incompatible with the essence of evil? Either way, Molin was properly—silently—grateful for the divine rejection.

The Fist's breath was no colder than his own, though the man was certainly filled with mortal evil. The children, nurtured for who knew how long in the orphanage, were different. They teased each other like any two children playing a game in the sun, except that this game was the dissection of a living man. Molin begged the Fist to give the order that would end both Hoxa's life and the children's hideous game.

"He is past telling you anything you want to hear—past any hope of recovery. What's the use of prolonging agony?"

"Have you ever had a kitten, Lord Torchholder?" the Dyareelan asked, his red-swathed face pointed at the children.

"Every house has its cats," Molin admitted cautiously, unsure where the conversation was headed, and all the more uncomfortable.

"Then you know that the mother cats teach their kittens to toy with their prey before they kill it. They know that the livelier the prey, the more nourishing the meal."

There were easily a thousand philosophical, ethical, and religious reasons to argue with the Dyareelan priest. Molin chose not to utter any of them. He left the palace knowing it would be too long before his friend escaped into eternity and that he couldn't allow the Bloody Hand of Dyareela to endure.

The next year was a grim one.

The Hands' quest for ultimate purity forbade the inhibitions of alcohol unless it was mixed with blood and drunk with Dyareela's blessing. They shuttered the taverns and breweries and turned executions into festivals. Men and women continued to drink and drink too much. Molin mixed more of his morning-after remedies than anything else, but people drank alone behind locked doors, mourning private losses, and increasingly wary of sharing confidences with anyone. It was an open secret that the only way to escape once the Hands' suspicion had fallen on your shoulders was to point an accusing finger at someone else.

Everyone knew Molin Torchholder and nearly everyone offered him up to save themselves. Each time he talked or bought his way out of suspicion, and each time it was a little more difficult, a little more expensive. Like as not, he'd run out of luck before any of his nemesis schemes could be brought to fruition. A wise man might have swallowed his conscience and slunk out of town, but there was another new emperor in Ranke, a madman by the name of Ferrex, who'd slaughtered the Imperial commanders and replaced them with birds trained to recite his favorite orders. Compared to Ferrex and his birds, Molin chose the pain of his conscience.

One crisp autumn day, after a two-year absence, a handful of Irrune rode into Sanctuary, looking for a barrel or two of beer. The Irrune didn't know the shifts of power inside Sanctuary, couldn't have understood, and probably wouldn't have cared if they had. Arizak's young wife and his son's wife had both given birth on the same auspicious day. He'd called for a celebration and, for a young Irrune rider, there were few honors greater than fetching their chief's beer from the nearest, hapless settlement.

When no one would give them a barrel (the Irrune rejected any notion of payment), they went looking for unguarded barrels to steal. They found the Bloody Hands instead. Three of the Irrune—Arizak's youngest brother and two companions—wound up upside down, skinless and bleeding on the black platform in front of the palace, but one was held back as a witness and sent home to tell Arizak that the Irrune would be the first to feel Dyareela's wrath if they defiled Sanctuary again.

It was the wrong message sent to the wrong man.

The Irrune were raiders at heart. They would have raided Sanctuary eventually. The Hands gave them a good reason to come raid with vengeance in the spring of '91. Sanctuary's walls were weak and patched with rubble, but they were enough to ward off less than a hundred hell-bent horsemen. Sanctuary's outlying settlements weren't so fortunate. Those villagers and farmers who could run, ran to Land's End for protection. Lord Serripines, who fancied that the gold his grain trade brought to Sanctuary bought him protection from the Bloody Hand of Dyareela as well, descended on the palace demanding protection for his family and the refugees cluttering his courtyard.

No apothecaries were consulted before or invited to Lord Serripines' meeting with the Fist. Molin knew about it, of course; his ears were still the sharpest in Sanctuary. And he knew that the lord of Land's End was doomed to dissatisfaction, but he didn't guess that the Bloody Hands would send the same message to Lord Serripines that they'd sent to Arizak. The very next time Lady Serripines entered the city they were waiting for her. She was dead before Lord Serripines knew she was missing.

The terror that was part of common life finally invaded the great houses. They bestirred themselves against the Bloody Hands, but it was too late for stout men in silk robes to reclaim their city. Since Lord Serripines' natural allies within Sanctuary bowed to Dyareelan intimidation, he turned to a neglected apothecary.

"The Hands are madmen!" the Rankan lord raged. His eyes were red. He hadn't slept well since his wife's death.

Molin helped himself to a goblet of the nobleman's wine. "I told you that years ago."

"They must be stopped—driven from the city!"

"I told you that, too."

"And the Irrune! I thought you'd gotten rid of the barbarians!"

"I thought I had, Lord Serripines, no thanks from you. I've heard they're quite happy up there along the Spine."

"They're ravaging my fields!" Lord Serripines sputtered. "They're attacking *me,* as if *I* were their enemy. They're madmen, too—I am not their enemy!"

"The Irrune are not mad, Lord Serripines—they've simply made a mistake. The Irrune believe the Bloody Hands cherish the same things they themselves cherish. The Fist of the Bloody Hand of Dyareela executed Arizak's brother. The Irrune would execute the Fist's brother, if he had one or Arizak could touch him. But they can't, so they ravage the villages, instead. As the Irrune see it, the villages are the herds of Sanctuary, and if the Fist were Irrune, he and the rest of the Bloody Hand would have to come out from behind the walls to protect or avenge them. You and I, Lord Serripines, we both know that the Hands are not the Irrune. The Irrune cannot goad or outrage the Hand. The Hand's only weapon is terror. It is more effective with some than with others."

Molin sipped his wine while Lord Serripines grew dangerously pale and quiet. A knotted vein on his forehead throbbed as if it might burst, but when the nobleman spoke his voice was soft and calm.

"I've appealed to the emperor—"

"Pork all," Molin interrupted, resorting to vulgarity. "Ferrex is madder than the Hands . . . and he won't lend you one of his bird-brained armies."

"I know," Serripines replied, perhaps the most painful admission he'd ever uttered. "I'd hoped . . . *you* . . . You were quite the soldier in your day, quite the hero. And you sent the barbarians away before. . . ."

"So, you think I'm the one to send them away again. Explain to them that the farmers they're killing, the fields they're burning have nothing to do with the boys who got skinned last autumn? Would you listen to such tripe, Lord Serripines?"

"I'd hoped there was something you could do, because you have proven yourself wiser than all of us—wiser than I—time and time before. I'd hoped you could see a way to rid Sanctuary of the Irrune and the Hand together. To turn them against each other, the way you turned the Irrune against the Gunderpah brigands."

The man had audacity, Molin would grant him that. He set the goblet down; it was a prime Caronne vintage, as old as he was himself, and it would be a sin to waste one drop. "The Irrune are raiders, Vion, not an army. The Irrune live in tents. Their idea of a wall is something you can cut with a knife. Sanctuary's wall stopped them. If you want to *drive* the Hands out of Sanctuary, you've got to get into the palace, then you've got to drive them out. Gods, Vion—do you have any idea what that place is like on the inside? I'll take the damned Maze any day over the palace storerooms. And the Irrune—they'd be chasing their tails after the first step."

"I was hoping—and I'm not the only one holding hope—that you'd lead them. You're Vashanka's Architect. The way I always heard that, Vashanka's Architect doesn't spend all his time drawing up the plans for the next temple, his true calling is battle plans."

"You're mad, Vion." Molin deflected the flattery. "Madder than the emperor. Madder than the Hands themselves."

But the back of his mind was already churning. It wouldn't be easy, but it could be done.

It would be done.

The next day, Molin took what he needed from his locked treasure chests, then covered them with dusty canvas and shuttered the apothecary. He slipped out of the city and claimed a stallion—the best in the Serripines stable. Two weeks after he rode into the raiders' camp, he led them back to the World's End Mountains. By the time they arrived there, Molin had mastered enough of the Irrune language—its grammar was similar to the Rankene of the oldest prayers—to get him into Arizak's tent without Nadalya's help.

Molin's schemes would never succeed if he relied on the chief's second wife to present his arguments. An outsider with young sons, Nadalya stood on shaky ground with her husband's people and—remarkably—she knew the limits of her influence. She was shrewd enough to stay out of Molin's way; wise enough to send him messages that warned him of tribal rivalries before he inflamed them.

Nadalya's messenger was her son's nursemaid, who showed up in Molin's appointed tent every night. She was a comely enough woman—if you liked your women stout and strong enough to carry a horse on her own back. Molin preferred his women lean—not that it would have mattered. He was in his seventies, decades too old for passionate affairs or wintering in a tent with only a few furs for warmth and a layer of autumn grass for a mattress. Night after night, Terzi knelt over him, kneading the aches from his old muscles, imparting her mistress's wisdom.

Molin won the Irrune one by one, like a man spinning fleece into yarn. Arizak's first wife, the redoubtable Verrezza, was the hardest. She distrusted him and hated Nadalya not because she was younger or more beautiful—though Nadalya was both of those things—but because Nadalya was change incarnate for Irrune traditions and Verrezza, a handful of years older than her husband, remembered the colors, sounds, and smells of the Irrune homeland. She'd suffered too many changes since her girlhood to embrace any more.

"Think on this, dear lady," Molin suggested to Verrezza in her own language. He'd learned more of the language in three months than Nadalya had learned in ten years. "Sanctuary is small and gods-forsaken, but it *is* Rankan. There is a bathing pool within the palace—"

"*Feh!* Such things do not impress me."

Molin ignored the interruption—"Where the water runs cool in summer and hot in winter; there are three of them, in fact. One of them is lined with black marble and ringed with alabaster statues of naked women cavorting with unicorns."

The redoubtable's eyebrows formed a disapproving angle. Her chin receded into the soft flesh of her neck.

"Think on this as *she* will think on it. Do you think that *she* will choose to live in a tent when she can live in such a palace? Do you think that *she* will expose those boys of hers to the sun when she can surround them with thick walls and whisper-soft silk?"

Verrezza at last cracked a smile. "My husband is Irrune. He could not bear to live between walls that cannot be moved. He will leave her there and her sons with her. His heart will be mended toward me and mine."

Once Molin had the voice of tradition on his side, the remaining holdouts and doubters fell quickly in line. After that he had until the snows melted and the ground hardened to mold a passel of raiders into a force that would follow him through the distractions of Sanctuary's streets to the palace, where the fighting would be done afoot, not astride, against fanatics who worshiped destruction.

Two hundred men and twice as many horses thundered away from the Spine. From a distance, they could pass for Rankan cavalry. Closer, they were raw and rowdy. The oaths Molin had collected from the lot of them wouldn't have held through the first night, but Arizak per-Mizhur was a rarity among barbarians—a leader who could see beyond tomorrow. He craved vengeance for his brother's death, and he'd been sincerely appalled by Molin's tales of Sanctuary's recent, desperate history; but mostly Arizak had grasped the advantages of separating his wives before Molin explained them.

With Arizak firmly in command of his clans, the journey south was as smooth and swift as the White Foal River flowing beside them.

The Sanctuary Molin had left behind had been under Dyareelan control for nine years. Its people despaired, but they were accustomed to despair. The executions of Arizak's brother and Lady Serripines had inflamed the Irrune and the Rankans at Land's End, but in the minds of the common folk in the quarters, they were merely two more links in a long chain of outrage. Molin had no reason to think that the Sanctuary to which he returned would be any different, but it was.

For a start, the outlying settlements were empty. There wasn't a person, a chicken, a pot, or a bucket to be found in any of the deserted settlements the riders passed. Some time after the Irrune abandoned their raiding, the people had packed up their belongings and disappeared. The Irrune congratulated themselves on the fear they'd struck in the dirt-eaters' hearts, but Molin suspected a less sanguine cause. He persuaded Arizak to circle the Irrune eastward, to Land's End.

Lord Serripines greeted Molin without enthusiasm. He'd lost weight, his eyes were redder than ever, and his villa overflowed with quiet, gaunt men, most of them from nearby Sanctuary rather than some other benighted corner of Ranke's once-thriving empire.

"You're too late," Lord Serripines explained. "No sooner had you left for the Spine, than their bloody goddess made some unholy appearance to her Bloody Hand priests. Next we knew, they were hauling everyone out of their homes—inside the city and out, too. The ones you see here, they're the ones who got out before they shut the gates. We've got food, for now, but they've shut down the harbor." Serripines squeezed his eyes shut—remembering, perhaps, a scene he couldn't share, or was trying to forget. When his eyes reopened, he stared out the window a moment before picking up the fabric of his thought a few strands distant from where he'd dropped it. "They've got *power,* Molin . . . prayer, sorcery, call it what you will, but it's not madmen anymore. They've got a god in there, the footprints of one. The stories— Stragglers got out for a while, a few at a time. No one since midwinter. It's hell in there. Monsters. Demons. Dyareela's got Her army. She's packed Sanctuary's wounds with poison; the Hands are waiting for it to burst open. We can hear the chanting. They're coming, Torchholder. When those gates open again, it'll be the end of us. I've sent the women and children away with all the horses, all the wagons I could muster. I pray they reach safety, but who's listening?"

Vashanka listened, for all the good a disenfranchised storm-god could do. Wreathed in moonlight, incense, and memory, Molin recalled the days when Sanctuary had been a divine playground, swarming with gods, heroes, magicians, witches, priests, not to mention whole neighborhoods populated with the living dead. He'd thought *that* was hell. He'd never thought to see the day when he'd have welcomed the likes of Tempus, Ischade, or his own overly troublesome niece, Chenaya, with open arms.

If a man lived long enough, he'd get the chance to relearn all his lessons from the back side.

Tempus and Chenaya were with Vashanka on the far side of legend, and Ischade had followed her deadly little curse into oblivion. Vashanka was *there* for His priest when Molin prayed, but *there* was a long, long way from Land's End. He was on his own when he went down the Ridge Road to spy on the city he'd always hoped to leave behind.

Collecting a lifetime of debts, Molin made his way through Sanctuary's grim streets. He saw no evidence of Lord Serripines' monsters and demons, but more than enough guilt and shame. Of course, once brothers betrayed their sisters or parents betrayed their children to save themselves, they became monsters in the eyes of those around them, and in their own eyes, too. The only people who looked straight ahead when they walked were those who'd willingly surrendered what was left of their souls to the Bloody Hands of the palace.

Still, Sanctuary was a city of survivors, and Molin knew where in the Maze to look to find a handful of resilient optimists willing to risk their lives unbarring the eastern gate that very night, assuming Molin could deliver a fog dense enough to blind the Hands to the Irrune riding down from Land's End.

Vashanka, god of storms, warmed Molin's heart: He could do that much for His old priest. There was a chill in the air and clouds seeping off the harbor waters before Molin got back to Land's End to make the final preparations.

"The gates were open when we got there," Grandfather droned. "We were halfway to the palace before the Hands knew we were inside the city. They prayed Dyareela against us. If one of our men went down, the mob tore him apart, flesh from bone. We hung tight. I feared we'd have to kill them all, and even that might not be enough. She's a soul-stealer, the Mother of Chaos. Our deaths strengthened Her. We dismounted and drove the horses ahead of us—O Vashanka, may His name be praised, the noise and the stench! It was pure butchery until we got to the palace. We lost every man on the ram, twice, and twenty more when we cracked the gate. Then the Hand lifted our fog; I thought for sure we were finished . . ." He shook his head. "Dyareela, She feeds on death and chaos, but She's no battle goddess. Doesn't have the belly for it. Her chanters couldn't hold Her, and She fled with the fog. *We* fed on chaos—"

"Furzy feathers!" Bec interrupted. "All that, and you *don't* know! You froggin' don't *know* what happened. You weren't there. I know what happened *after* the Irrune got to the palace. That's no secret. What I want to know is what happened *before* they got there!"

Grandfather got that owl-y look grown-ups got when Bec caught them cheating. "I've spent all afternoon telling you what happened *before* we swept out the palace."

"Says you. I say you weren't there and you don't know what hell was like, no more than me. Momma and Pa were there and Cauvin was *in* the palace, in the palace for years, in that *orphanage* you talked about. But he won't talk about it. No one will. Not one word, except by accident, kind of, or craziness, like Batty Dol. You said you'd tell me what really happened. You lied, Grandfather. You *lied.*"

Grandfather reached for his black staff again, and Bec scrambled for dear life. The crockery inkpot and the parchment both went flying.

"You didn't write down a word I said!" Grandfather complained, as the parchment floated in a late-afternoon breeze. He lowered the staff and rubbed his wrinkly forehead.

"You were answering me. You didn't say I should write down what you said when you were answering me." Bec retrieved the crockery. The ink had dried. He spat on the thick stain and reached for the quill. "All right. You can start over; I'm ready. But who's going to care if you don't know what really happened that winter?"

"Your brother—"

"Cauvin can't read . . . *and* he was there. He already knows."

"What do I already froggin' know?" a familiar voice asked from the doorway at Bec's back.

Grandfather might be old and dying, but his tongue was quicker than Bec's. "He says you already know what it was like in the palace that last winter. He wasn't satisfied with my version."

"Shalpa's froggin' shite!" Cauvin snarled.

For Cauvin, cursing was as natural as breathing and about as serious, but sometimes he meant it, and this was one of those times.

His eyes fairly disappeared as his face got red in spots, pale in others. He charged across the rubble and kicked Bec's improvised inkpot into a wall. The crockery shattered to dust. Then he ground the parchment beneath his boot. Through it all, Cauvin never took his eyes off Grandfather.

"You don't go talking shite to my brother, you hear me? He's got no need for it! No froggin' need! That's over. Over! Sooner it's forgotten, the better."

The parchment was holes and tatters. Cauvin advanced on Grandfather, who pulled his staff up, two-fisted across his chest.

"I haven't told the boy what he wants to hear, Cauvin. I can't. That's for you; as he says, you were there, I wasn't."

Bec prayed to Mother Sabellia. She was the peacemaker among the gods his mother had taught him, and he needed a big dose of peace to come falling out of the sky. Cauvin wouldn't back down for anything when he was blind angry, not even a staff topped with a stone that shone like fire. Bec closed his eyes. A *whump* of a breeze shot past his ears, then Grandfather said:

"You can't make anything go away by hiding from it, Cauvin."

"Shite if I can't."

Once again, Cauvin's voice came from behind Bec, who turned toward the sound and opened his eyes. Cauvin was one stride out from the wall. There was dust in his hair and all over his back, but his face wasn't all twisted up with anger anymore. Bec dared a glance in the other direction. Grandfather still gripped the staff crosswise. He didn't look like he was an old man close to dying.

"If no one remembers, Cauvin, if everyone's silent, then who's going to stop them next time? They're not gone, Cauvin. Not all of them. The man who murdered me, he had blood-red hands and red silk wound around his face."

Bec swiveled in his brother's direction.

"Froggin' hell— *You're* the one said they were gone. I heard you. Froggin' sure you didn't say anything about the Bloody Hand yesterday."

"And I'm saying I'm wrong, Cauvin. I was wrong ten years ago, wrong two night ago, and yesterday, too. I'm dying of mistakes, Cauvin. The next move falls to you."

Cauvin's eyes got small, and for a heartbeat Bec thought his brother was going to fly off in another rage, but he didn't get red or pale, just very still, like something had hurt him bad inside. When he talked again, his voice was soft.

"This has gone too froggin' far. I'm not having any-damn-thing to do with the froggin' Hand. I'm *movin'* you to the palace. Let your high-and-mighty friends take care of you . . . of them."

"Out of the question."

"Don't froggin' think you can froggin' stop me."

Bec didn't dare look Grandfather's way. He had all he could do to keep his eyes open as Cauvin took a deep breath and held it a long time, then let it go.

"You froggin' swear you won't froggin' tell my brother *anything* about the palace, or the Hand, or any other sheep-shite. He starts spouting off at home, his froggin' mother'll hang my froggin' skin on the wall."

"I wasn't there, Cauvin," Grandfather said, all sweet and nasty together.

"Swear, you sheep-shite pud!"

"In Vashanka's sacred name and for the good of all, the boy's ignorance is safe with me. What you won't tell him, neither will I."

The oath had to be a cheat. It sounded good, but Grandfather had used too many words for it to be simple-honest. Cauvin didn't hear the holes. Bec could have warned him, but Bec wanted the holes, the tales his brother wouldn't tell.

Cauvin was satisfied with Grandfather's promise and ready to move on. "I'm ready to load the wagon, Bec. It's not a full load. I'm telling Grabar that the mortar's hard as steel, and I've got to come back tomorrow. I'm counting on you to back me." He looked at Grandfather. "One more day, that's all, then—" He shrugged. "Think about it, pud—you can't stay out here. You've got to go to the palace—"

Grandfather waved Cauvin off. "I have a plan."

"For what?"

"For teaching your brother his letters, for saving Sanctuary from Dyareela's Bloody Hand. What does it matter? I need papers from my chambers in the palace. There's an ironbound chest beneath my bed—"

"Froggin' shite, I'm no thief! You need something at the palace,

I'll take you there. You can sleep on your own froggin' bed. That's where you belong."

"You're not stealing anything, Cauvin—and you won't get caught, even if you were. I can promise you that. I've often needed to meet with people who couldn't walk through the palace gates. Listen—"

Cauvin didn't listen, not until they'd had another argument and Grandfather had shaken that blackwood staff. Bec was *sure* the staff was a wizard's weapon—or a priest's—though it didn't belch fire or lightning or anything like that. Grandfather just held it in front of him and, little by little, Cauvin backed down and listened to Grandfather's instructions. It had to be sorcery; Cauvin *never* backed down.

"So, can I go with you to the palace?" Bec asked when he was in the cart and the cart was headed back to Pyrtanis Street.

"Who said anything about going to the froggin' palace?"

"You did—you told Grandfather you'd get his papers: the scrolls, the picture of gods—the one used to be painted on the temple walls—"

"He's not your froggin' grandfather, Bec, and I'm not risking my neck breaking into the froggin', sheep-shite palace!"

"But you *said*—"

"I froggin' lied, all right? Same as he froggin' lied when he gave me that froggin' worthless oath of his. Forget it, Bec. I'm coming out here alone tomorrow and I'm hauling that pud's froggin' ass down to the palace—where it belongs—unless I'm froggin' burying it instead."

Bec protested until Cauvin knuckled him across the back of his head. Not hard—but hard enough that Bec sidled around the piled-up bricks in the cart and stayed out of reach until they got home.

# Chapter Eight

Supper at Grabar's stoneyard was fish soup thickened with all the leftovers on Mina's sideboard, including last night's mutton stew, because, as she announced with the ladle in her hand—

"Hearth's going to be cold tomorrow."

Arizak was sending his friend Molin Torchholder to his god with full Irrune ceremony: pitch-soaked shroud wrapped around him, wagon beneath him, wood piled high above him, wailing women, pounding drums, and enough animals sacrificed to serve a feast to the whole city. The Irrune didn't care who came—they didn't let outsiders worship their god, Irrunega—but the residents of Sanctuary had never been known to pass up a free meal, no matter who was serving it or why.

"There was a cart came down the street this afternoon, collecting wood for his pyre," Mina explained as she handed Cauvin his bowl. "I gave up the slats from an old wine barrel—that'll please the gods—for the good he did for all of us. But you, Cauvin, you owe him more. I set that aside—" She pointed at a length of ornately carved wood propped by the door. " 'Twas the top of the stairs outside my grandmother's room. Can't get wood like that these days. Can't find a carver, even if you found the wood. Show some respect for your good fortune. Take it down to the palace and put it on the pyre. Shove it in deep, where it'll burn hot."

Cauvin agreed without saying a word. He didn't want a froggin' fight with Mina, not where it might concern the froggin' Lord Molin Torchholder and especially not with Bec sitting at the froggin' table, big sheep-shite grin across his face. He didn't want to talk about Molin Torchholder at all, but Grabar had already paid a visit to the

Lucky Well and gotten a leg up on tomorrow's holiday.

"Damn shame," Grabar decided, then repeated his judgment: "Damn shame a man like that couldn't die in his bed—"

"Mind your language," Mina hissed.

"Well it is, and damn the man or woman who says otherwise. He was a hard and proper bastard, but he always came in right-side up after a storm. Never raised a finger or did a favor except there was something in it for him. But a fair bastard just the same—"

"*Husband!*"

Grabar wasn't listening. "Waste o' wood," he continued, "building that pyre. The gods won't need smoke and flame to find the Torch; he's drinking with them already, I'll wager. Better to put men in the streets to find the bastards who murdered him."

"There's a reward—ten gold coronations from the reign of Abakithis," Mina added. There was, after all, no offense in calling a murderer a bastard and money was money.

Bec whistled through his teeth. "Furzy feathers! Ten coronations! *Everybody's* going to be looking everywhere for ten coronations. *I'm* going to look."

Cauvin caught his brother's eye and made a dire face. Ten coronations, though, gold coronations from the days when there was froggin' silver in a soldat—that was enough to set a man up for life if he weren't too particular about his work. Bec was right: There'd be folks poking into every froggin' corner of the city and outside it, too. Somebody was sure to march through the old redwall ruins. No one would mistake the wounded old man for a murderer, but it would be one shite-sure mess—

Or, maybe not.

Maybe the froggin' smartest thing Cauvin could do was hope that someone *did* stumble into the redwall ruins. Then someone else could tote and haul for the old man, or haul him back to the palace—

A wad of meat stuck in the back of Cauvin's throat when he tried to imagine telling the palace Irrune that the froggin' Torch was still alive. He tried to swallow the meat and the image, but neither budged. Tears streamed down his face by the time Grabar pounded him between the shoulders.

"You've got the graces of a dog," Mina complained.

"It's a shock to him, Mina." Grabar pounded Cauvin again. "The Torch saved his life. Hadn't've been for him separating a few lads from the rest, the Hand would've killed our Cauvin."

Cauvin took shelter where he could find it, but his appetite was gone. He pushed the bowl away. "I'm done."

Mina sniped, "Finish your food!" and Cauvin felt his temper starting to fray, then Bec came to his rescue.

" 'Hadn't've been.' That means something that would have happened—could have and should have happened, but didn't. Tell me, Momma, how would I say hadn't've been in Imperial?"

Mina couldn't resist an appeal like that. She started singing away in Imperial, shutting Cauvin and Grabar out. Grabar went back to his eating, but Cauvin's appetite was truly gone. He poured his soup dregs into Grabar's bowl and started for the door. Grabar caught his wrist.

"Stay atop the Stairs," Grabar advised his foster son. "Word at the Well was that the Dragon's fired up about the honors his father means to heap on the Torch. They say he's taking his men and that hell-spawned mother of his out of town tonight, before they light the fire, but your friend Swift says he heard from the palace smiths that they've been grinding swords all day—for the Dragon. I'm not thinking the Dragon's fool enough to fight in his father's forecourt, but the rest of Sanctuary's fair for mischief, especially the Maze. Tonight's no night to go visiting your lady friend."

Cauvin hadn't intended to visit the Vulgar Unicorn. He hadn't intended to leave the stoneyard at all. A piece of Flower's harness had come loose on the way home from the ruins. It needed mending, and the rest of the harness needed close inspection. When one strap worked loose others would soon follow, and they couldn't risk injury to the mule. But Grabar had put the notion in his head where it clung like a barnacle. He gave his word that he'd stay on Pyrtanis Street and made his way to the Lucky Well, where the wine was as cheap as it was sour.

His friend Swift held down one end of the center table along with the potter whose daughter he hoped to marry. Swift spotted Cauvin before Cauvin's eyes had adjusted to the smoke-shadow light and made room for him on the bench. A good man, Swift was; and damned well aware that he was froggin' lucky to have avoided the Hand and their pits while he was growing up. They'd been closer years ago, when Swift's father was still alive to work the forge day in, day out and Cauvin struggled to change the habits he'd learned in the pits and on the streets.

The smith repeated the tale he'd heard from his metal-pounding peers at the palace. "The Dragon's fit to set the world alight. Him an' his mother, they thought it was the Torch pulling strings and that once he was gone, Arizak would go back to the old ways, *their* ways. Now Arizak's giving the Torch an Irrune send-off, and they're talking *abomination*. You know where *that* can lead."

Cauvin did. There wasn't enough wine in froggin' Sanctuary to blot those memories from his mind. He poured dark liquid from Swift's pitcher and lost himself in those memories. Grabar came in after a while. They acknowledged each other, but sat with different men at different tables until the keeper's boy, Dinnas, shouted last call. Grabar wasn't interested in a final mug of wine and took his leave, but Cauvin held on until a drudge cleared the table. He wasn't nearly drunk—it took a braver man than Cauvin to get drunk on the Well's wine—but Swift walked him to the stoneyard.

"See you at the feast tomorrow?" Swift asked when they reached the stoneyard gate.

Cauvin hesitated, then nodded. No reason not to go, even if the man in the pyre wasn't Molin Torchholder. He bid Swift a good night, then closed the gate. One of the iron straps that held the bar in place against the door was loose. It pulled out of the wood planks entirely when Cauvin tried to tighten it. There were two other straps; the bar wasn't going anyplace tonight, but he'd have another froggin' chore tomorrow morning, along with Flower's harness.

A raw wind blew off the harbor and through Cauvin's loft. He could have used another layer of fleece above and below, but the winter bedclothes were still hanging from the rafters . . . Another froggin' chore for the morning. Cauvin pulled off his boots, nothing more, and huddled beneath the blankets. He had no trouble falling asleep. A man who couldn't fall asleep whenever the opportunity presented itself wasn't working hard enough, and a man who couldn't sleep 'til dawn was a fool.

Cauvin proved himself a sheep-shite fool a few hours later when he found himself sitting bolt upright. His nerves were jangled, and every sense strained to its utmost, trying to absorb the quiet darkness. He didn't know what had awakened him, not a nightmare, maybe a noise. Cauvin held his breath, listening, hoping whatever had awakened him would repeat itself.

Most night noises did repeat, and most thieves eventually got caught because they didn't know how long to remain quiet after making a noise. The best thieves knew that while an unexpected noise might awaken an entire household, honest people would stay put in their beds if no further noise stoked their suspicions. Cauvin knew what the best thieves knew—the froggin' Bloody Hand of the froggin' Mother of Chaos had beaten the lessons across his shoulders—but he had no talent for thieving. He'd gotten himself caught and locked in the crypt every froggin' time they'd tested him.

Silence had been no protection in the froggin' dank and stinking crypt, and it didn't reassure Cauvin now.

His boots were where he'd left them, and the pitchfork he used to muck out Flower's stall was a decent weapon so long as no one was shooting arrows. Cauvin might not have been good enough to steal for the Hand, but he slipped out of the work shed without disturbing Flower, the dog, or the chickens. The moon was past full and sinking, but bright enough for shadows and wouldn't set until after sunrise. With the pitchfork angled in front of him, Cauvin prowled the stoneyard.

He started with the house, where Grabar, Mina, and Bec slept. Nothing appeared wrong: The door was shut, the windows were dark, and the place was quiet as a tomb. Farther on, the yard dog had its glowing red eyes on Cauvin, same as Cauvin was watching it. And beyond the dog—

The damned froggin' gate was open—not wide-open, but cracked a handspan or two, and the heavy bar lay on the ground.

Forgetting caution, Cauvin dropped the pitchfork and raced to the gate. Rich folks put their faith in fancy locks and winched gates, but a froggin' bar anchored on the hinge side of a door was every bit as good at keeping trouble out. A barred gated could be scaled, of course, but that's what the dog was for; or it could be battered down, but that would splinter the bar and wake the sheep-shite dead. The yard dog wasn't barking, and the bar wasn't broken.

Cauvin had a pretty good idea what had happened before he got to the gate.

"Bec? Becvar!" If the boy had made the noise that awakened Cauvin, then he wasn't out of earshot yet. Cauvin didn't shout, but his hoarse whisper would carry all the way down to the empty lot where Enas Yorl's house had stood. "Becvar Grabar's son—if you can hear me, get your froggin' ass back here!"

Silence, utter and complete.

Cauvin shut the gate without barring it and tried the house a second time. The door was unlatched, but that was nothing out of the ordinary. Once inside, Grabar's snoring echoed from the walls and rafters. The man made one froggin' racket once he closed his eyes for the night. Cauvin had moved into the loft just to get away from the noise. He didn't understand how Mina or Bec ever got to sleep, but they managed. Listening between the honks and blasts, Cauvin heard his foster mother's softer sounds.

Bec's part of the room was quiet, as it should have been; healthy children didn't snore. Cauvin eased himself in that direction. His feet found blankets on floor; they put an end to the story. Grabbing a torch from the rack outside the gate, Cauvin took off down Pyrtanis Street without lighting it.

The thought of Bec—scrawny little Bec—roaming the froggin' streets of Sanctuary in the dead hours between midnight and dawn struck fear in Cauvin's gut. He couldn't bring himself to *think* about what might go wrong, so he blamed Molin Torchholder instead. If the froggin' damned old man hadn't put ideas about stealing treasure from the palace into the boy's fool head, Bec would be safe in bed.

And Cauvin wouldn't be standing in the froggin' middle of the old Money Path wondering which way to turn next. He'd made up his mind the moment the Torch opened his mouth that he wasn't going to *steal* into the damned palace for froggin' love nor money, so he hadn't paid attention to the sheep-shite's instructions. The best Cauvin could remember was something about a tunnel beneath a run-down house in Silk Corner.

Froggin' hell—every house in Silk Corner was run-down. Every froggin' house in Sanctuary needed repairs; that's what kept Grabar's stoneyard in business. Cauvin would be all night and most of tomorrow if he had to check the cellar of every house in Silk Corner, and he'd have cheerfully wrung the last breath from the Torch's froggin' neck—or anyone else's neck, if there'd been a neck nearby to wring.

But there wasn't. Cauvin was alone, and he had to choose one end or the other of the doglegged street. He chose the south end, farthest from the palace, because his first thought was to choose the north end, and Cauvin's life was the history of making the wrong froggin' choice whenever it counted. That's how the froggin' Hand had caught him— He'd run left when he should've run to the froggin' right.

Cauvin marched up the street, scarcely able to tell the abandoned houses from the occupied ones. Halfway along, he heard a scuffle seething in an atrium's depths.

*Not my froggin' concern,* he thought, *not this froggin' night.*

He kept going until his ears caught a single word, thin and desperate—

"Feathers—!"

There couldn't be two souls in Sanctuary who made up their own curses. Cauvin surged into the atrium without pausing to plan his attack, except to switch the torch to his left hand and move the bronze-weighted thong from his neck to his hand.

The first Hiller never knew what was coming at him. Cauvin broke the torch over his head, then booted him in the face as he fell. He grabbed the second from behind—one handful of hair, the other twisting up the Hiller's belt—and hurled him at the nearest solid-seeming wall. While the Hiller spun and groaned, Cauvin loaded his fist with bronze and broke the bastard's jaw with a single punch. He landed a kick at the second Hiller's crotch before he collapsed.

The other Hillers—there were at least three more—knew Cauvin had waded in by then. Two of them shifted their attention to the new target. Cauvin dodged fists aimed at his face, but endured punches to his gut and flank before locking his left arm around a set of shoulders and pummeling a face with his metal-loaded fist until the froggin' Hiller's arms were dangling. Cauvin finished that Hiller off by running him headlong into a stone pillar. Both the pillar and the Hiller collapsed.

A sheep-shite Hiller who'd missed Cauvin's head each time he'd swung must have decided his chances weren't going to get any better now that he had the lion's share of Cauvin's attention. He backed out of reach, then ran away like a froggin' rabbit.

That left one Hiller in the atrium—a short and scrawny bastard who held Bec in front of him as a living shield. When Cauvin advanced, the Hiller wrapped his hands around Bec's chin and scalp and began to twist. Bec gave out a terrified squawk. Cauvin stopped in his tracks. He *knew* that maneuver, how quickly it could kill a man, woman, or brother. He'd learned it from the same red-handed trainer who'd taught him to ignore pain and fight with a lump of metal weighting his fist. A shiver of fear that was not for Bec's survival shook Cauvin's spine. Holding his breath, he circled right to get a better view of the bastard's face.

There was only darkness in the shadowy moonlight, but if there'd been sunlight Cauvin knew with cold, sinking certainty, the patch of darkness behind Bec's shoulder would have turned blood-red. Cauvin wasn't fighting the froggin' Irrune or Wrigglie street scum; he was squared off with his own past.

Cauvin's every instinct was to cut and run, and if it weren't his brother between him and the Hand, his froggin' instincts would have seized control of his feet. But it was Bec with a face as bright as the moon and rigid with terror. Cauvin mastered his fear and, meeting eyes he couldn't see, strode forward.

His sheep-shite life wouldn't be worth living if the Hand finished what he'd started, but he had a chance. If the Hand wanted Bec dead, the boy would have been dead before Cauvin set foot in the atrium. He raised his weighted fist.

"Let him go, or I'll rip your froggin' guts out," Cauvin snarled, and, to his astonishment, the Hand gave Bec a shove forward, then took off for the street.

Bec gasped and staggered to his knees. Without hesitation, Cauvin caught the boy before he fell completely. The Hiller Cauvin had smashed into the pillar wasn't moving, but the others were. Probably they wouldn't be interested in continuing the fight now that their Bloody Hand leader had fled, but Cauvin wouldn't take that chance. He hoisted Bec onto his shoulder and lit out for Pyrtanis Street.

Halfway down an alley shortcut, Bec, who'd started wiggling the moment they'd cleared Silk Corner, slipped free.

"Leave me alone!" the boy protested. "I'm not hurt."

A little voice at the back of his sheep-shite mind told Cauvin to ignore the wide, woefully ineffective punches Bec promptly threw at his gut, but no froggin' little voice stood a chance against the aftermath of a four-against-one brawl with the Bloody Hand of Dyareela. Before he could stop himself, Cauvin had clamped his hands over the boy's shoulders and shoved him against a wall.

"Not froggin' hurt? You could've been froggin' killed, Bec! Froggin' *killed.* Eshi's tits! You'd be dead now, if I hadn't come along. Froggin' worse than dead—"

Undeterred by earlier defeat, the little voice shot another notion through Cauvin's mind: When he'd left the stoneyard he'd thought Bec was just ahead of him, but the boy had been long gone by then. Still, if Cauvin had awakened later, he'd have missed the scuffle; he'd have missed it, too, if he'd awakened much earlier. Froggin' sure—it couldn't have been any froggin' *accident* that he'd woken up exactly when he had.

Maybe he should hie himself out beyond the west gate and say a prayer or two at Sweet Lady Eshi's altar—a thankful, respectful prayer that didn't mention Her most obvious attributes. Or, maybe he should start asking questions about the Torch's god, Vashanka.

Shaken and sobered, Cauvin released his brother. "Frog all, what's the froggin' matter with you, Bec? Didn't I tell you the Torch's damned games were too froggin' dangerous? Didn't I tell you I wasn't going to the palace? Did you think that was a froggin' invitation for *you* to go instead?"

Bec wrapped his arms tight around his chest. "*Somebody* had to. If you wouldn't, then it had to be me. I remembered everything Grandfather'd said about getting into the palace and getting out again, so I did what he said. I got the picture right here—" He patted his shirt above his heart. "I got it, and I kept it."

"He's *not* your froggin' grandfather, Bec. He's the froggin' Torch. Maybe he's a froggin' hero in this town, but he's a froggin' hero because he doesn't care who froggin' lives or dies—not him and not you or me, either."

"That's not true!" Bec protested loudly. "He said there'd be no trouble getting into the palace, and there wasn't. All the trouble came on my way home. You can't blame Grandfather for that. My fault. Get mad at me, if you've got to get mad at someone."

Cauvin shook his head. Bec was slippery in ways he couldn't fathom; he could feel his anger slipping away. He would have let it go altogether, but for one thing— "Frog all, Bec, that wasn't some sheep-shite drunk from the Hill with his hands around your head— that was a priest of the froggin' Mother of Chaos. A *Bloody Hand* priest, Bec. You're so froggin' clever, Bec—the froggin' Hand was froggin' *waiting* for you!"

"If I'd've turned right, instead of left, when I came out, nothing would have happened," Bec protested. "Nothing. You'll see—" He pulled folded-up parchment from the waist of his breeches.

"You'll see when I give this to Grandfather tomorrow."

Cauvin snatched the parchment out of Bec's hand, doing what the Hand had failed to do, if he and not Bec were right about the Hand. He held it above Bec's desperate reach. In the moonlight, the sheepskin didn't look worth killing or dying for.

"It's *mine,* Cauvin! I went and got it, not you. Give it back, so I can give it to Grandfather tomorrow."

"Froggin' *hell.*"

Cauvin shoved the wad into his boot and, when Bec lunged for it, shoved the boy away.

"I'll tell!" Bec shouted his threat. "I'll tell Momma and Poppa what you've been doing out at the redwall ruins. How you've got the Torch holed up out there and that you've held out on the silver and gold he gave you. I'll tell them that you *made* me—"

"You do that," Cauvin shouted back. "You tell your sheep-shite parents whatever the froggin' hell you want to tell them. Go ahead, get me thrown out of the stoneyard— Then what, Bec? Then what? Weren't you paying attention? I'm talking about the Bloody Hand. A priest of the Bloody Hand of Dyareela had his hands on your neck, Bec—even if it were a froggin' *complete* accident. Don't you froggin' forget that the Torch says—in so many froggin' words— that him and the sparker got ambushed by the Hand two nights ago. Was that another froggin' accident? Two froggin' *accidents* involving the froggin' Hand? Do you think anything Lord-High-and-Mighty Molin Torchholder does is a froggin' *accident*? You think Dyareela's froggin' Hand believes in *accidents*?"

"Quiet down there!" a faceless stranger shouted from the upper story of one of the buildings surrounding the brothers.

They said shame couldn't kill, but the froggin' shame of knowing that he and Bec had been sharing their anger—and their secrets—with strangers hurt Cauvin worse than the bruises he'd gotten in the atrium. Shame or something similar took the wind out of Bec's sails, too. The boy began to shiver violently, then threw himself against Cauvin.

"I was *scared,*" Bec whispered, "scared like I've never been before."

"So was I."

Bec's arms tightened into an unexpectedly strong hug, and his head pressed against one of Cauvin's growing bruises, but Cauvin didn't care. He wrapped his arms around the boy.

"You're safe now. C'mon, let's get home."

He unwound the boy and got them moving toward Pyrtanis Street.

"Cauvin . . . ?" Bec asked softly after what was, for him, a lengthy silence.

"What?"

"Cauvin, that one, that one that you said was a Bloody Hand priest. I'm not so sure. He never said anything, but the way he was holding me—what I could feel against him—well, I think he was a woman."

"Man or woman, it was still a Hand."

"But how could a priest be a *woman,* Cauvin? Women are priestesses. And I've never heard of priests *and* priestesses serving the same god. Even yesterday, when Grandfather told me his tale and you an' he were arguing, you said priests, not priestesses."

Cauvin sighed and dropped an arm around Bec, pulling him close so they walked side against side and could talk with whispers. "There were women among the Hand," he admitted. "Dyareela is a goddess, but She's a froggin' *god,* too. A herm-something. Every time they initiated a priest, they made a priestess, too, to be—"

His voice broke on a reef of memories. If it had only been beatings, Pendy might not have killed herself and Leorin might not have chosen to make her home above the Vulgar Unicorn; but Dyareela was a froggin' *love* goddess—and god—as well as the Mother of

Chaos. There was nothing Dyareela craved more than the raw power of sex, especially if somebody wound up hurting afterward.

"To be like seamen?" Bec asked eagerly.

The question jolted Cauvin. "Seamen? What have froggin' seamen . . . ?" Then he remembered the boy's curiosity and disdain the night before after he'd visited the Broken Mast. "No. She's got—*Dyareela's* got the private parts of men and women. A herm-something."

Bec pulled away, shaking his head and his shoulders, too. "No—that can't be. Either there is one, or there isn't, right?" The boy waited futilely for Cauvin to say something. "I'm right, aren't I? I've got to be right—you've either got one or you don't."

"Gods and goddesses are different."

"Not *that* different. There's a statue of Father Ils at the fane. He's all naked and he's got one and that's all he's got. He's got no titty-bits."

"That's Father Ils, Bec, not Dyareela. Dyareela didn't need any sort of lover. She could *do* for Herself."

"Furzy feathers! Does Grandfather know?"

The danger with answering any one of Bec's questions was that there'd always be a second, worse than the first.

"I don't know if Grandfather knows, I don't care, and you don't either." Cauvin realized he'd said "Grandfather" and groaned.

"Grandfather should know, if he doesn't. Something like that's *got* to be important. Do Momma and Poppa know? Should we tell them?"

"Froggin' *no!*" Cauvin snarled back, loud enough to draw more unwanted attention. "Can't you get it into your sheep-shite skull"—he cuffed the boy behind the ear for emphasis—"the *Hand's* on the streets again and you've got to keep your froggin' mouth shut 'cause if you don't, there's no telling who's going to overhear you—"

Bec just stood there, an arm's reach away, rubbing the spot Cauvin had slapped.

Cauvin felt small and shamed by his outburst. "Froggin' *gods,* Bec, I didn't mean to hurt you, but we've got to be careful, both of us—so careful it froggin' hurts."

"My head's sore . . . sorer than it was. I've got a lump."

Cauvin hauled Bec closer. He probed the lump gently and turned the boy so his face caught what was left of the moonlight. There were shadows where shadows shouldn't be.

"You're raising bruises— Mina. Shite. Froggin' sheep-shite— your mother's going to take one look at you come morning and start asking questions—"

"Don't worry, Cauvin."

"Don't worry!" he sputtered. "What am I going to tell her? Can't be the truth . . . but it's got to cover the froggin' bruises—"

Bec extracted himself from Cauvin's embrace and pulled himself up to his full height near the middle of Cauvin's breastbone. "I'll think of something."

"What can you say to your mother—"

"I don't know yet, but I've got until after dawn, don't I . . . ? Wait! Furzy feathers—I know what I'll tell her! I'll wake myself up before she does, and get myself out of bed—but I'll *fall.* Get it . . . ? I'll make like I get tangled in my blankets, then I'll pretend to trip, then I'll pretend to *fall* and—furzy feathers—I've got bruises! You watch—I won't have to tell Momma a word about what's really happened—"

Cauvin saw holes in that froggin' bucket. It wouldn't hold water if he were the sheep-shite carrying it, but with Bec. When it came to telling stories, only a froggin' fool would bet against Bec.

"Can I have my picture?"

They were near the empty lot at the head of Pyrtanis Street. If the sun were shining, they could have seen the stoneyard.

"You did a sheep-shite stupid thing, Bec, going to the palace like that. If the Torch isn't froggin' dead when I go out there later, he's going to wish he was. I'm taking the cart and putting him in it. He can interrupt his own froggin' funeral. We're done with him, Bec; I froggin' sure swear it. Say your prayers before you fall out of bed. Pray that once the Hand knows that froggin' Lord Molin Torchholder's back in the palace, they'll look for him there and they'll forget they ever saw your face or mine."

Bec said nothing until they were inside the stoneyard. "I'm sorry, Cauvin. I wanted to help Grandfather—I wanted him to be my grandfather. I'd be in real trouble now, wouldn't I, if you hadn't followed me."

Never mind that Cauvin hadn't actually followed his brother or that "real trouble" didn't begin to describe the danger Bec had gotten himself into. "You want 'real trouble,' sprout, you try sneaking out of here again. Now—off with you. Get back to your bed!"

Cauvin sped the boy on with a swat across the rump. The eastern sky was brightening, but it was too early to smash stone. Up in the loft, Cauvin lit an oil lamp. Bec's stolen parchment was grimy on the outside and stiffer than the sheepskin they'd bought at the scriptorium—not the stuff an important man like the Torch would use for writing an important message.

Cauvin unfolded the parchment, even though he couldn't read more than a few Wrigglie words, just to see what words worth dying for looked like.

"Gods!" he swore softly. "Froggin' *gods,*" because that's what the parchment revealed: an unfinished drawing of Father Ils and Allmother Shipri holding court in some black-ink garden behind a tavern that could have been the Lucky Well.

The artist had drawn a stout Lord Anen, a goblet dangling between his fingers. A broad and drunken grin slit the wine-god's face as he watched a barely gowned and not particularly beautiful Lady Eshi dance. Lord Shalpa skulked in the garden shadows, young, sullen, easy to recognize, even without His telltale shadowcloak. The other figures were probably Ilsigi gods, too, though Cauvin couldn't put names to Their incomplete faces.

He'd had his fill of religion in the palace. The froggin' gods were real; Cauvin didn't doubt that for a heartbeat. Life in the pits wouldn't have been half so oppressive if he hadn't been sheep-shite sure that the Mother of Chaos *was* real and *was* watching. And if one goddess was real, then so, probably, were the rest, but neither Father Ils nor any of his froggin' family had lifted a froggin' immortal finger to help the orphans.

In Cauvin's mind, no god was worth dying for and dying for a froggin' *drawing* of feckless gods was an outrage. Cauvin had already made up his mind what he'd do with Molin Torchholder, the gods-all-be-damned drawing only hardened his resolve. He refolded the thick parchment, rasping his thick, blunt fingernails along the creases, and blew out the lamp. The faintest dawnlight seeped through the loose boards around the loft's solitary window. Cauvin pulled the blanket over his head.

Maybe he could convince himself that a whole night's sleeping still lay before him.

Maybe, with the Torch's funeral occupying Sanctuary for a day, Grabar would let him sleep away the morning.

Maybe the froggin' Torch would get worried, thinking his servant wasn't coming out to the redwall ruins, and have second thoughts about the sheep-shite errand he'd sent them on.

It would serve the old pud right well if he worried himself to death.

On the cusp between dreams and thoughts, Cauvin imagined himself walking into the redwall ruins. The Torch hadn't died, but he'd stopped moving. His forehead was all twisted up and his mouth wide-open, with no sounds coming out. Cauvin could have taken the old man to the palace and added him, like a log, to his funeral pyre, but anger had him and he decided to leave the Torch where he lay, for vermin to devour. He imagined leaving . . .

The door was gone, the red walls, too. White marble walls rose in their place while, behind Cauvin, men and women engaged in lively conversations. He turned again, knowing in a small way that he'd begun dreaming, yet caught up all the same and unsurprised to find that the voices belonged to the gods he'd seen on the parchment painting.

Lady Shipri beckoned Cauvin closer. She was a large woman, strong and soft, together with arms that could hold a baby or swing a hammer with equal ease. Cauvin drifted toward Her, but stopped when She offered him an apple so bright and perfect that it glowed. He knew better than to eat anything in a dream, especially if it rested in the palm of a goddess.

"*What brings you here?*" She asked.

What good were gods if They had questions, not answers?

"*You're troubled.*" The goddess measured Cauvin with eyes he couldn't meet. "*You're looking for someone. Something.*"

Cauvin shook his head. His feet, which were all he could see, weren't his feet—not the feet under his blankets. They were the feet he'd had the winter after the Hand got his mother—dirty, wrapped in rags, aching from cold. He'd prayed for boots, for a cloak, for someplace warm and safe. Lady Shipri hadn't listened.

"*It's never too late,*" the goddess whispered.

Cauvin found the strength to raise his head. Froggin' hell it wasn't too late. Cauvin didn't need boots anymore. He was a grown man with a past he couldn't quite forget. There wasn't anything Lady Shipri could do. The goddess disappeared, taking the other gods with Her. He should have been alone in his bed in the stoneyard, or at the very least returned to his own dream in the redwall ruins. But the white marble walls remained and instead of gods or an old man's withered corpse, Cauvin found himself drifting toward a little man with sparse ginger-colored hair and the stained fingers of an artist.

The little man was hard a-work on a drawing. The drawing was the one Cauvin had folded and tucked beneath the boots beside his bed. He was still dreaming.

"*You've got work to do, pud,*" the artist said without looking up from his work. "*You're not finished. You've scarcely begun.*"

Against his will, Cauvin thought of red walls and bloody hands.

A voice that belonged to neither Cauvin's nor the ginger-haired artist echoed among the marble walls. "*You're a disappointment, pud, no doubt you are. I prayed for better, but you're what I got. Rise to it, pud. Surprise us all.*"

Molin Torchholder had said some of those very words moments after Cauvin had rescued him. Who wouldn't have prayed for a rescuer . . . and who wouldn't have been disappointed by the sight of froggin' Cauvin not-quite-Grabar's son, whose fists were so much quicker than his wits? But had Molin been praying for a rescuer . . . *just* a simple rescuer?

"*Go now,*" the little artist suggested. "*There's only so much a man can give to Sanctuary. Do what I did—find another life, another city. The door's open.*"

It was, along with the walls. Cauvin had fallen out of paradise during the ginger man's speech. He'd returned to his own dream, to the redwall ruins and the corpse of Molin Torchholder which shone with a gentle, golden light.

"*Run away, Cauvin. I did.*" The artist rose from the rubble. Cauvin saw his face for the first time: a froggin' plain face, except for its sadness. "*You're a free man. No one will blame you. No one blamed me.*"

Darkness as black as the pits on a moonless night surrounded the ruins. Cauvin could run . . . but he'd be lost in the froggin' dark if he did. Then the Torch's light-shrouded corpse began to move. It sat up, stood up, extended its arms, and began walking toward them.

"*Run away!*" the artist urged, blocking Cauvin's view of the Torch's face. "*You've been lost before. You've been lost all your life. Lost is your home.*"

Cauvin decided to run, only to discover that his froggin' body was nailed to the ground, frozen like stone. He couldn't so much as close his damn eyes.

"*Move it, Cauvin.*"

He tried and felt a sharp pain in his side.

"Move it, Cauvin—There's chores to be done no matter who's laid on a pyre at the palace."

Cauvin blinked awake. Grabar was in the froggin' loft—never a good sign—and there was sunlight streaming through the shutter slats. With an angry sigh, Cauvin got his arms under his shoulders and pushed himself off the mattress. He was still half in his dream—his froggin' *dreams*—and wondering what it all had meant. The pain in his side, though, that hadn't been part of the dream. Cauvin ached from the punches he'd taken in the Silk Court atrium and from the toe of his foster father's boot.

"Froggin' hell," Cauvin snarled. He swung his arm in Grabar's direction.

"Been calling you for a donkey's age and pounding on the floor. None of it was doing me any good, so I had to climb the ladder—and you know how I hate to climb that ladder, what with my knees and back and all."

Cauvin started shivering before he was standing. He pulled a thick wool tunic over his head. That helped, or it would once his body warmed it. There was nothing he could do for his bare feet. If he touched his boots, Grabar would see the parchment. Better to froggin' freeze than have *that* discussion.

"I'm awake, all right? I'll be down. There's no froggin' need to stand here watching me."

Grabar hesitated. He truly did move like an old man—older than the Torch—when the weather got cold: the price of a lifetime working stone. Cauvin watched him creak down the ladder and wondered how he'd feel in another twenty years. Wouldn't be any froggin' worse than he did this morning with bruises the size and shape of a froggin' cat curled up on his flank.

Somewhere, though, three red-handed puds felt a froggin' lot worse.

Cauvin stamped into his boots and slid the creased parchment between the leather and his shin. He shoved past Grabar, who crowded the foot of the ladder. This wasn't like his foster father; the man usually knew better than to froggin' hound him. The whole sheep-shite city knew Cauvin had a temper and woke up cross-grained.

"Where are you off to today?" Grabar asked while Cauvin put his fist through the ice in the trough and splashed frigid water on his face.

The question caught him off guard. He answered, "The froggin' redwall ruins," without thinking.

Grabar responded with another froggin' question: "Why?"

Cauvin's hands fell to the trough rim. "Why?" he muttered. Bec was the family storyteller. Words failed Cauvin when he had to answer a question with an excuse. He stood there a moment, sheep-shite foolish, with water dribbling off his beard onto his shirt.

"Yes, why? We've got enough brick until Tobus shows up for business. For all I know, he won't show up until the spring."

" 'Til spring." Cauvin wracked his mind while he chafed feeling back into his cheeks. " 'Til the froggin' spring. Well, the mortar's gone rotten in some of those walls out there. We get froggin' freezes and heaves this winter and sure as shite if we wait until spring to smash the rest of the bricks out, the froggin' walls'll be down and everything'll be froggin' cracked to bits. Figured I'd smash all the bricks out now and cover them up with straw . . ."

It was a good plan . . . if the mortar were flaking away. And maybe the mortar was; Cauvin hadn't paid much attention while he was smashing yesterday. He'd had other thoughts churning through his head.

Grabar clapped him soundly on the back. "Good. Good! You're

thinking ahead. That's good. I've got half a mind to give you a hand myself. Not going to be anything worth doing here today."

Cauvin's sheep-shite gut turned over. He stood flat-footed and staring at the ice floating in the trough.

"Got plans, eh?" Grabar clapped him again. "A mite cold, but that doesn't so matter much when you're young and making your own fires."

"What?"

"You and that woman of yours from the Unicorn—Leorin? How often does a young man get a chance to pass the time with his woman and no one's in earshot, eh? Smash out a few bricks . . ."

Grabar let the rest go unsaid. Cauvin did the same.

"Never could have gotten out of here anyway," Grabar said into the silence. "The wife's beside herself. There's no breakfast—we'll all be going hungry 'til the funeral feast."

"She said she wasn't going to light the fire," Cauvin said, eager to talk about something else.

"Oh, she never meant that, but this morning, the boy ups and trips over himself getting out of bed—must've been growing while he slept. Me—I didn't hear a sound, and more's the pity: Somehow that makes me to blame for the boy's bruises. Sweet Shipri! You'd think he'd lost a fight with his own fists by the look of him. And the wailing when the wife tries to tend to them! Not since he was cutting his first tooth. The wife's got him back in bed. She's talking apothecary—if there's one willing to work on the Torch's holiday—and you know that's going to cost."

Cauvin tucked his chin against his breastbone. Bec had done it; he'd covered their froggin' tracks and then some. The boy had clever to spare. A sheep-shite stone-smasher could only bite his tongue to keep from grinning. He had to stay out of the froggin' house—no way he could have faced Bec without undoing the boy's good work—but Cauvin's heart was still laughing when he led Flower out of the stoneyard.

The Torch had propped himself up against the wall. He had parchment strewn across his lap and a white-feather quill dangling loosely from a motionless hand. Cauvin thought—hoped—the old pud had died, but his eyelids fluttered and he coughed himself awake as Cauvin crossed the threshold to his refuge.

"Did you get it?"

Not *good morning* nor *it's good to see you* nor *did all go well last night?* but the froggin' greeting of a gods-all-be-damned sparker to the least of his froggin' servants. Any reluctance Cauvin might have felt about arguing with a man on his deathbed was gone in a heartbeat.

"Shite for sure we got it." Cauvin removed the parchment from his boot and brandished it beyond the Torch's reach. "We damn near *died,* too. Your friends were waiting for us. Your *friends* with red hands and faces," he snarled and went on to describe the skirmish in Silk Corner, leaving out only one froggin' detail: that Bec had done the deed alone.

The Torch—gods rot his sheep-shite soul—wasn't fooled.

"Send a boy on a man's errand, and what else would you expect? He'd have stayed snug in his bed if *you* hadn't shirked your obligations."

"My froggin' obligations? I saved your froggin' damned life, you old pud—I don't owe you sheep-shite. What about *your* obligations? Go here. Go there. Get me this and that. You froggin' well knew the Hand would be watching—"

"I know precious little about what the Bloody Hand of Dyareela knows right now, pud. Until three days ago, I thought they were dead. Stop waving that parchment about. Give it here."

The Torch held out his hand. Cauvin hesitated, then slapped it into the old man's palm.

"There—it's yours, if Bec snatched the right one. It's a froggin' *picture*! A froggin' picture of the froggin' Wrigglie gods in a froggin' tavern garden."

"Then it's the right one," the Torch said mildly, and began unfolding it.

"A *picture,* you damned pud—you risked our lives for a froggin' picture!"

The mildness vanished, replaced by a hiss of contempt that rocked Cauvin back a pace.

"Pay attention, pud, and you might learn something. It's not what's *on* the parchment—though I could tell you a tale or two about the man who drew it: Laylo . . . no, Lalo . . . Lalo the Limner he called himself. He had the gift of his gods whenever he picked up a brush or pen—"

Cauvin watched with gape-jawed astonishment as the Torch held the drawing at one corner and began to carefully split it into two thinner sheepskin sheets. He started to ask a foolish question, but clamped his mouth shut before it escaped.

"Lalo painted the truth of a thing . . . or a person. Damnably inconvenient for a portraitist who'd hoped to support himself painting the nobility, as you can imagine. He painted a picture of my wife . . . no surprises; I'd known her for what she was from the start—but frightening all the same—the features of a pig draped in pearls . . ."

"What happened when this Lalo painted *your* portrait?"

"I've been many things in my life, pud, and none of them a fool. I never sat for our little ginger-haired artist, and if he ever sketched me, he had the wit to keep the lines to himself. Painting the truth wasn't enough; his gods gave him the gift of life. Those brightly colored flies the women catch with honey and grind up for dyes . . . ? They're his. Them and less savory beasts, but we got rid of those . . . or they followed him when he cut his strings. Damn shame. Sanctuary was his city, and he ran away when it needed him most. Ran from his family, too—damned if I can remember her name, but she posed for Shipri—Eshi, too, as I recall."

There was a sheet of parchment in each of the Torch's hands. He flapped the sheet that didn't bear the Limner's drawing at Cauvin.

"Stoke up the fire and hold this in the smoke a moment."

"I'm not your froggin' slave, pud. You can't order me around."

"By all means, pud—humor an old man and *please* hold this above the fire, high enough for heat, but careful not to singe your dainty fingers."

Cauvin seized the parchment and knelt by the ashes.

"You remind me of Lalo, pud," the Torch gibed, while Cauvin fed fresh tinder to the embers. "You want a thing bad enough that you can taste it, but you spit it out as soon as it's in your mouth."

Cauvin swallowed the insult whole. When the fire was as big as a dinner plate and crackling nicely, he picked up the parchment. His froggin' hands were the froggin' opposite of dainty. He and Swift used to play a betting game—who could hold a live coal longer. He could hold one for ten count and had every intention of holding the parchment in the flames until it was utterly consumed, but when row upon row of tiny black marks appeared suddenly on the sheepskin, he tossed it away from himself and the fire both.

"Froggin' shite—what's *that?*"

"Writing, pud. My notes about the Bloody Hand of Dyareela."

"But—But—That parchment was *blank*! Sorcery . . . you're working sorcery, damn you. I want no part of sorcery."

"No sorcery. Best fetch them before the wind carries them away."

Cauvin stayed put.

"My word, Cauvin, there's not the least bit of sorcery involved, only a few drops of lemon juice. Now, fetch them. I am an old man; I forget. I need my notes if we're to beat back the challenge the Bloody Hand has thrown at us."

"Froggin' thrown at *us*? I don't have anything to do with the Hand." Cauvin held his hands between himself and the old man, as if to ward away the whole froggin' idea.

"Come now, Cauvin. Remember what you just told me—they attacked your brother in Silk Corner. Surely you, above all others, know what would have happened to him—"

"Bec was there because of *you!*"

The Torch dismissed Cauvin's objection with a wave. "Because of a dead man? Did you tell them I'd sent you? Did you tell them I'm still alive? Do they think *I* sent you or your brother? They had him, then they saw you. That skull of yours can't be so thick that you don't grasp the implications. Even if they didn't recognize you, Cauvin—and I doubt that they did—they'll remember you now, and they'll be looking for you and your brother."

Cauvin shook with shock and rage. "All the more froggin' reason to go to ground. I'm done with you, pud—you're getting into the cart and going to the palace or you're staying out here—*alone*—'til you froggin' die."

"Nonsense, boy—you want revenge! I saw it in your eyes yesterday when you realized what your brother and I were talking about. You don't want him to know what happened to you in the pits because the wounds are still raw. Revenge will heal you, Cauvin; nothing heals like vengeance. And you want it so bad your hands are shaking."

Cauvin looked down and saw that the Torch's accusation was true, as far as it went. "The only revenge I want is against *you*."

For the first time, he seemed to have surprised the old man. The Torch's lips disappeared in a scowl, and the ruins were quiet until he said: "Against me? I saved your porking life. You'd have died in the pits like all those others if I hadn't seen a spark of conscience in you. Talk about obligations! Look at me, Cauvin. Look at me and tell me you'd rather have died that day. I gave you your life."

Cauvin could stop his hands from trembling by clasping them behind his back, but he couldn't meet the Torch's stare, and his response, when he got it out, was whispered, not snarled: "What life?"

His memories had broken free. They ran riot behind his eyes, more real than the ruins.

It hadn't been so bad at first. Life with his mother had never been froggin' *settled*. Life after the Hand flayed her had been shadow to shadow with an empty gut. He'd lived off what he and Leorin found in the gutters—which wasn't much—and what they stole. They were bound to get caught sooner or later. With the Hand there was a roof to keep him dry, a fire to keep him warm, and a full bowl every day, even if it was gritty bread and froggin' fish-head chowder. Besides, they taught him how to use his froggin' fists.

For froggin' sure, the pits were brutal, and he'd never froggin' get over the first time he'd seen the Hand kill. Not *execute,* the way they'd *executed* his mother, but just *kill* with a backhand clout to a girl's head. Without trying, Cauvin could still hear the sound of her skull cracking. She never knew.

*Honor to the Great Mother,* the Hand said, and carried her body to the altar.

*Waste not, want not,* Cauvin's own mother had said when she fed him scrapings from her clients' plates.

He'd gagged at the altar and again at supper, but—the froggin' truth be told—anything was better than froggin' fish-head chowder.

The palace gates were barred and guarded by Hands who'd kill you as soon as look at you, but the Hands were teaching Cauvin how to fight, too, and he'd never had any trouble obeying froggin' rules—provided he and they were pointed in the same direction. He liked to fight and didn't shirk his lessons.

Bigger, smaller, willing or not, Cauvin fought. The Hand took him out on the streets. When there was froggin' trouble, he helped take care of it. Froggin' truth be told, it wasn't unpleasant, especially when the Hand pointed Cauvin at a merchant who'd used to make his mother's life miserable.

He'd killed the man. He supposed he'd froggin' killed more than a few men. He couldn't be sure. The Hand told him when to start fighting and when to stop, too. They always left their victims behind.

He learned how the Hand had killed the girl with a weighted fist, but except for dogs and a few goats for practice, they'd never asked him to kill with an unsuspected blow—that was an honor reserved for priests. If he'd been thinking straight then, Cauvin might have realized where he was headed when they taught him the trick. He hadn't been. He liked fighting, and being a brawler served him well in the froggin' pits when the Hand wasn't watching close. Weaker sprouts looked to him for protection. They served him like slaves; he'd been as comfortable as you could be in the pits.

Cauvin got used to his life. He didn't expect it to change, then it did: The Hand introduced him to Dyareela. They gave him wine—more than wine. There was nothing in wine to make the world glow and shimmer the way it did after he'd drank Dyareela's warm, bloodred wine.

They'd led Cauvin into the palace where he saw the Mother's statue without its black robes, cock and cunt together. When Chaos came and Dyareela reshaped the world in Her image, they'd all be like that—so said the Hand. Until then, the priests and priestesses did what they could with what lesser gods had given them. There were others at the altar, men and women, naked except for the red silk over their faces, all writhing together. *Take off your clothes,* they told him. *Join your brothers and sisters.*

Froggin' hell—there wasn't wine enough to get Cauvin *that* drunk.

He'd said no thanks. Leaving a body in the street, not knowing if it were dead or alive, Cauvin didn't have froggin' problems with that, but he wanted no froggin' part of what was happening around

Dyareela's altar. He'd thought saying no would be enough. As usual, he was froggin' wrong when it mattered.

Cauvin didn't know why he hadn't froggin' broken. Imprisoned alone in the utter dark for who knew how froggin' long was bad enough, but it wasn't the worst. The froggin' worst came when they dragged him back to Dyareela's froggin' altar—not the black-stone fornication altar but another one, far below the palace. He was blindfolded when they slashed his chest; he figured he was going to die without his froggin' skin, same as his sheep-shite mother. Then they took the blindfold off.

Some *thing* hung there above him: some *thing* with too many glowing eyes, too many shimmering teeth, too many everything. It wrapped around him like a snake . . . or a lover . . .

"Cauvin!"

Cauvin came back to himself with a shudder. He'd survived—the gods knew why or how. He was alive, in the redwall ruins, with Molin Torchholder.

"Cauvin, you're here and now, not there and then. Do you hear me, Cauvin?"

Memories couldn't harm him. Even so, he was dripping sweat and shaking. There was a froggin' black staff pointed at his chest again. Cauvin tried to convince himself it was only the old pud stirring his memories.

"You need vengeance, Cauvin. You wish for vengeance."

"I wish I'd died with the others. It froggin' ended for them. No froggin' memories. No froggin' dreams. The ones you separated—the ones that the Hand didn't manage to kill—do you know how many are still alive?" Cauvin began to tick off the names of those who weren't.

"Spare me, Cauvin, I'm years past guilt. They had the same chance you had, and you're still here—I count that victory enough, but you take me back to the palace, and I'll be dead in a day. I can't fight the Hand any longer, and I have no sons alive, none to finish what I've started. Let me make you my heir, Cauvin. My wisdom, my cunning; your eyes, your ears, your strength. My vengeance and yours together—the Bloody Hand of Dyareela will know the fear that you knew in the pits."

Cauvin shook his head. "You've got froggin' nothing I froggin' want," he swore, because there was nothing that would set him free of his memories.

"Not for you, Cauvin, for your brother."

Cauvin snarled a fast rejection, but the damage was done. "Can you swear it by your god-all-be-damned Vashanka—Bec stays safe from the Hand forever?"

The Torch grinned; his face looked like parchment stretched over bone. He lowered his staff. "Swear by my god—is that what you want me to do? Very well, then: For little Bec and the future of Sanctuary, I swear by Vashanka that I'm offering the noblest vengeance a mortal can taste. Open your mind, Cauvin—you've got a lot to learn and precious little time for learning it. We'll start with the lessons you'll welcome—you need to become a fighter. You were lucky once, but luck isn't enough when you're confronting the gods—"

"I can fight. That's the one thing I *can* do; it's what the froggin' Hand taught me."

"Dyareela has no use for a man who can think. They have no use for *men*. Why do you think they steal children? The Hands take boys and make them brawlers, little more than trained beasts. You'll never best them with the weapons they gave you. Be honest with yourself: You *were* lucky last night, and you won't likely be that lucky again, not after they've seen your face."

Cauvin opened his mouth to protest. The Torch's flicking hand warned him to silence. He could grow to hate that froggin' gesture as much as he'd ever hated anything in the pits.

"Obviously, I cannot teach you, but I'll second you to the best armsmaster in Sanctuary—in lands far beyond Sanctuary. He'll teach you now and when I'm gone. He'll keep you alive until you can carry that burden for yourself. You'll find him in a place you already know—the Vulgar Unicorn. He'll recognize you by the token you'll be carrying—a mask, not red silk, but leather, boiled hard and dyed blue. You need not wear it—just expose a bit of it as you sit and drink. Listen close; I'm going to tell you where I've left a cache of them."

The cache was in the Maze, and the Torch's directions were as tangled as that quarter's streets. Cauvin recited them back after the Torch finished laying them out, then endured a froggin' oration—

"A man who wishes to revenge himself on the Bloody Hand of Dyareela can rely on neither steel nor sorcery. He must be a master of both—and a quiet master at that. Let no one suspect the depth of your skills, once you've acquired them. It's always best to lull your enemies into underestimating you. I speak from experience. For that matter, Cauvin, it's never a bad idea to have your friends underestimate you a bit, too. Make it look too simple, and they'll take you for granted. They'll fail to show up when you need them—"

Cauvin wondered how many of Torch's experiences might have led to that froggin' conclusion. He was still wondering when the old pud surprised him with a question:

"Now, recite those instructions I gave you again."

With his eyes closed tight, Cauvin reconstructed the Torch's words in his mind. He stumbled a few times, but in the end, he put them together correctly and knew, as he finished, that it would be a good long time—if ever—before he forgot them.

"Good, lad. I see it in your eyes—you're cleverer than I thought, cleverer than you give yourself credit for. Run along and enjoy my funeral before you hie yourself into the Maze."

"I've got work to do." Cauvin pointed at the empty cart.

"On the day of *my* funeral?" the Torch asked with a rare hint of humor.

"Frog all," Cauvin replied in the same tone. "I know you're not dead—" He paused. "How do *you* know today's your funeral?"

"You told me. Something about Arizak declaring a feast day and why you were late."

Cauvin thought a moment. "I didn't say that. I didn't say anything about a feast or a funeral." But maybe he had. He was sheepshite stupid and couldn't remember half the gods-all-be-damned words he'd said to the Torch today, but he'd swear on his mother's name that the Torch was toying with him.

"Well, then, call it wishful thinking. I've been dead two days, haven't I? By Irrune custom, they burn their dead at the second sunset. My old friend Arizak swore he'd send me off with an Irrune funeral."

"He is," Cauvin admitted. "The pyre's built . . . and your froggin' corpse is atop it. I guess. Somebody's corpse is. I haven't seen it; others have."

"How many horses are they going to roast? How many oxen, and pigs?"

"Don't know," Cauvin shrugged. "Mina said, but I wasn't paying attention. No froggin' reason to. Look, I've got to smash some froggin' bricks out of these walls or Grabar'll have my sheep-shite hide—" He headed for the cart and his mallet. As soon as he crossed the threshold, he saw the flaws in everything he and Molin had been discussing.

"It's froggin' useless, old pud. Grabar's not going to give me the froggin' time to become some froggin' hero warrior. I used up all my froggin' excuses this morning, coming out here to tell you that I'm hauling your sheep-shite butt down to the palace. The only froggin' reason I've been coming out here at all is because the Dragon and his men have kept honest folk off the streets—an' he's leaving—doesn't want to be around when his froggin' father lights your froggin' pyre. Come tomorrow, I'll be down at the waterfront, standing in mud all day, piling stone around the piers. I won't be coming back out here until froggin' Tobus hires us to get the stone for a dower house. There's no telling when that's going to happen. Maybe spring. Maybe never.

"You're going back to the palace, old pud, going to die in your own froggin' bed—"

"Tobus?" the Torch asked. "Tobus the wool dyer? Little man with big eyes? Afraid of his own shadow?"

Cauvin nodded. "He faced the house he's got now with bricks from this place. He'll want the dower house to match, but he and Grabar haven't come to terms . . . haven't froggin' started. It's not going to work. I smash stone, Lord Torchholder; that's all I froggin' do. Anything else is dreams . . . nightmares. Get yourself ready. I'm taking you to the palace."

"Smash your stone, Cauvin, if that will keep the peace at the stoneyard. Let me worry about Tobus and Grabar and the rest. The only thing you need to worry about is how crowded the Unicorn's likely to be while my bones are burning."

"No," Cauvin said with patience that surprised him. "It's *over,* Lord Torchholder."

As Cauvin advanced across the rubbled floor the Torch reached for his staff. The old pud didn't have the strength to ward off a froggin' lapdog, but Cauvin stopped short of manhandling him.

"You asked me to swear an oath by my god, Cauvin, and I did. Now you've got to trust me and listen to me and do what I say."

Another time and Cauvin would have slipped into a stubborn rage. This time his temper failed to kindle. He smashed a few bricks, then noticed that clouds were piling up above the ocean. Sanctuary had gone four days without rain; at this season, the city couldn't count on a fifth. He tried one more time to get the Torch into his cart, but the old man wouldn't listen to reason. The best Cauvin could do was waste the rest of the day shoring up the walls of a half-collapsed root cellar and rebuilding the Torch's bed there.

He and the old man were both drained by the time the job was done. Cauvin surveyed his efforts from the foot of the stairs. The cellar was dark and dusty and reeked of decay.

It was like a froggin' tomb.

It was likely to *be* a froggin' tomb.

"Bring me a lamp tomorrow. Better, bring several. And a brazier."

Cauvin didn't bother arguing.

"And give this to the boy." The Torch produced a lump of what appeared to be hardened tree sap from the depths of his robe. "Tell him to suck on it. He'll feel better."

Cauvin tucked the lump in his boot and left. With no anger to sustain him, he was hollow inside, convinced he'd as good as buried the Torch and convinced the froggin' old pud had left him no other choice.

# Chapter Nine

The storm clouds looming on Sanctuary's horizon collapsed as Cauvin led the mule home to the stoneyard. Mina said the improving weather was a good omen, an omen that Savankala and Sabellia had welcomed Lord Torchholder and that he'd continue to befriend the city from the lofty heights of paradise. Cauvin agreed with her. Froggin' sure he couldn't tell his Imperial foster mother that her gods had to be sheep-shite fools if they were wasting good omens on the corpse of a man who was a murderer, not a priest.

Come to froggin' think on it: Molin's god, Vashanka, was the Imperial god of storms. Maybe a break in the clouds wasn't a good omen at all.

Cauvin worried that he'd get trapped into escorting his brother to the froggin' funeral. He'd assumed the boy had been working on Mina all day and with that kind of time, Bec usually got what he wanted. The boy wanted to go to the funeral. He wanted to see a corpse burn, no matter whose it was. But Bec was hurting still. One eye was swollen nearly shut, his lower lip was the size of a chicken sausage, and everything in between was angry purple. He sat slumped over his right side, favoring ribs that the Hand had probably broken.

For mercy's sake, Cauvin heard himself suggest that he'd stay with Bec on Pyrtanis Street while Grabar and Mina went to the feast, but Mina would have none of that. Her precious son was moving slow, and she wasn't about to let anyone else take credit for his recovery. It was a froggin' trial to steal a moment's privacy to press the lump of tree sap into the boy's hand.

"He says to suck on it and you'll feel better," Cauvin whispered.

He wanted to muss Bec's hair the way he usually did, but didn't dare.

"Who says?" the boy demanded with a wince.

"Your froggin' grandfather, that's who."

"Is it sorcery?"

The question hadn't entered Cauvin's mind until Bec asked it.

"He didn't say. Better not be. I'll wring his froggin' neck."

Bec popped it in his mouth and immediately made a demon-face. "It's *sour*. I'm going to shrivel up like dried fruit!"

"You could do with a little shriveling, sprout." Cauvin patted Bec's hair lightly and stood up. "I'll see you later."

"Later tonight?"

"Not tonight. Tomorrow. You go to bed tonight and you stay there."

"You're going to see *her,* aren't you?" The boy stuck out his lower lip. With the swelling, it was an impressive sight.

"Maybe."

"You're going to make babies?"

Cauvin hadn't given a thought to that possibility, either. "Tomorrow, Bec, I'll tell you everything tomorrow."

"You're not going to that other place, are you? That seaman's place . . . ?"

Cauvin didn't answer.

When Grabar suggested they walk down the Stairs together, he said he'd rather go alone and left immediately. There were still swatches of clear sky overhead, but clouds were back. They'd swallowed the sun, and there'd be no saying for certain when sunset became evening. Arizak's shaman would have to guess when to light the froggin' pyre. He'd figure it out; priests always found a way to do what their princes, if not their gods, wanted them to do.

Grabbing a torch from the bucket outside the stoneyard's gate—he'd need it later—Cauvin hustled toward the palace.

Whether for the funeral or the feast, Sanctuary turned out to say farewell to Molin Torchholder. Most of Pyrtanis Street was there: Swift, with his arm around the woman he meant to marry someday; Honald, the potter; Teera the baker and her whole froggin' household down to its squalling infants; Bilibot, of course—that geezer could smell free food clear across the horizon. Cauvin nodded at them all and kept to himself.

The stoneyard's customers were scattered through the crowd in the forecourt. They gave Cauvin the nod as he passed; at least the ones who weren't owing nodded. The dodgers pretended they didn't know him, and maybe they didn't. Maybe Cauvin was mistaken about whom he recognized and whom he didn't. The Torch's funeral—the funeral of the man everyone thought was the Torch—had drawn the largest crowd of Cauvin's memory.

Wealthy Wrigglie merchants from the Processional mansions stuck together behind their spear-toting bodyguards upwind of the pyre. Froggin' sparkers, they looked uncomfortable in their embroidered silks and fluffed-up furs, but they had good reason to mourn an Imperial geezer. With the Torch gone, who'd plead their froggin' cases to the Irrune? There was a throng from Land's End, too, keeping an arm's length or more between them and the common folk. Every one of them was dressed in garments that might have been the proper style in Ranke—a generation ago—but looked sheep-shite foolish here in Sanctuary. Shite for sure, they'd rather be tucking the Torch's corpse in a Land's End grave, but Arizak wanted to give his friend an Irrune send-off, and the Irrune ran Sanctuary, no matter the Wrigglie merchants or the Enders.

The sky was darkening gray when some twenty Irrune men marched out of the palace, ten of them bent double by the drums they carried on their backs, another ten banging away, and one leftover Irrune waving horse-head rattles in each hand.

"Zarzakhan," Cauvin's neighbor in the crowd said, or something similar.

When people spoke Imperial, Cauvin heard words he couldn't understand, but when he overheard Irrune jabber, he might have been listening to a drunkard sneezing.

Zarzakhan—if that was the shaman's name—was a froggin' unholy sight to behold wrapped in a cloak of froggin' tied-together, raw pelts. He'd worked a black paste into his hair so it whipped around his face like so many dead snakes. The wild man was a blur of paws and tails, serpents and skulls as he danced away from the palace doors.

Cauvin's sheep-shite luck put him between Zarzakhan and the pyre. A line of garrison guards locked spears and shoved the commoners aside. Cauvin got an elbow in his already bruised ribs, and elsewhere, too, but he got a good look at Zarzakhan as he passed by, a good whiff, too. He could have done without either. The shaman froggin' reeked of rotting fish, and the muck from his hair clumped on his lips, eyebrows, and beard. Cauvin didn't need to understand a word of Irrune jabber to know that Zarzakhan represented death come to collect a mortal soul.

The Irrune swarmed behind their shaman, more of them than Cauvin had ever seen in one place. They'd matted their forelocks with red clay and drawn greasy black rings around their eyes. Arizak rode a sedan chair borne on the shoulders of four men who weren't accustomed to the work. There was no hiding his concern as his heavily bandaged leg swung from one near collision to the next. But Arizak wasn't nearly as grim-looking as the woman who stood behind his right shoulder once the chair was set down.

Cauvin hadn't seen Verrezza, Arizak's first wife, before. She was a tall woman with steel gray hair and the eyes of an angry hawk. Age had clawed countless lines across her face, and by the lay of them, Verrezza wasn't a woman who smiled much, though maybe she was just unhappy that the Dragon, her son, wasn't on hand. Cauvin didn't pretend to understand the power struggles of Sanctuary's rulers, but he had an inkling of what an elder son might feel when he got pushed aside by a younger one.

Arizak's second wife Nadalya stood behind Arizak's left shoulder. She was oh-so-froggin'-careful not to touch Verrezza and didn't seem a match for her hardened rival, though maybe that was because Nadalya looked enough like Mina to be her sister. Nadalya acted like Mina, too—her mouth and hands were never still, and she fussed over her youngest son, the red-haired Raith, already head and shoulders taller than she, but not yet as tall as Verrezza.

Of all the folk gathered upwind of the pyre, only Raith and Arizak had the hollow look of men in mourning. There were streaks on Raith's face where his tears had sluiced through the black grease. Nadalya swiped at them with a bit of cloth that would never be clean again. Raith didn't seem to notice his mother's efforts—the froggin' sure sign of a boy whose mind was in another place. Apparently,

Bec wasn't the only boy to fall under the Torch's froggin' "Grandfather" spell.

Naimun, eldest son of Arizak and Nadalya, arrived late and stood apart from his kin. No streaks in the grease around his eyes, Naimun appeared as sullen as Verrezza, but not nearly so strong. He whispered something to a sparker companion and brought a smirk to that man's face.

The drumming stopped, and Zarzakhan leapt onto the pyre, which creaked but didn't tumble. For the first time since he'd arrived, Cauvin found himself looking closely at the corpse that wasn't Molin Torchholder's. Tightly wrapped in dark, wrinkled cloth, it resembled a log more than a man, which was froggin' fine with Cauvin. Despite all the death he'd seen, he wasn't comfortable with cremation. There was something about the notion of rendering a man down to froggin' ashes that left him weak in the gut.

Zarzakhan exchanged his horse-head rattles for burning torches, which, after a jabbering speech, he pointed at Arizak. After a moment's hesitation—and a froggin' nudge from his father—Raith made his way to the pyre. The boy said a few words no one but Zarzakhan and the corpse could have heard before taking the torches and shoving them between the logs.

In a heartbeat the pyre was engulfed in searing flame. Sorcery, Cauvin suspected, or pitch, or a combination of the two. The shrouded corpse was briefly visible, a dark shadow within the fire, then it burst into flames. Cauvin felt the heat where he stood. He held his breath as long as he could, let it out, and inhaled reluctantly. The difference between a roast on the hearth and a corpse on a pyre was in the mind, not the nose. But—Sweet Shipri's mercy—the only smells in the evening air were wood, bitter pitch, and the froggin' muck in Zarzakhan's hair.

"Look at him," a nearby stranger complained.

Cauvin followed the woman's eyes and guessed she was speaking about Raith. The boy had returned to his father's side with unmanly tears running down his cheeks.

"The Torch won't see justice," another stranger, a man, added.

Cauvin realized they were watching Naimun, still joking with his Wrigglie companion.

"Sure as shite," the first stranger agreed. With her round, chinless face and frayed, blue shawl, she could have been any one of the middle-aged women Cauvin saw in the doorways and market stalls once he'd strayed from Pyrtanis Street. "Arizak's not going to look inside his own house."

"Nor outside it neither," another shapeless woman added.

"Aye," said the man. "Frog-all sure, the Dragon's taken off—and look at his mother's face. *She* knows who killed the Torch. Frog-all sure."

"Strange beds for stranger times. Those two—the old bat and Naimun—had just one thing in common: hating the Torch," the blue-shawled woman said.

"No wonder there," the man explained, showing off for the women. "The Dragon wants his father's people, Naimun wants Sanctuary—no need to fight between them. But Raith—the Torch raised *him* to want both—and take both, if he'd lived long enough."

The second woman sucked loudly on her teeth. "Poor lad—he'll be lucky to see midwinter now that his protector's gone; Arizak, too. See those wrappings? My neighbor's brother says that his cousin's wife does the palace laundry and *she* says Arizak's linen stinks of death. A week ago they cut away the last of his toes on that foot. Says she saw them burn the bits on the roof."

"Eyes of Ils have mercy," the other two chanted together.

"Eyes of *Savankala,*" the man corrected. "We're at the Enders' mercy already."

Cauvin edged away from the man and his audience. He sought a better view of the clumped-together Enders. Which one of those white-robed men was Lord Serripines? And what was in *his* mind? What little Cauvin knew about the Enders he learned from Mina, and the harder she tried to build them up, the more they seemed like sheep-shite fools, but sheep-shite fools who owned frog-all everything worth owning in Sanctuary: the fields, the ships . . . the land beneath the stoneyard.

What were they thinking as Zarzakhan continued his wild dance around the blazing pyre?

—"If there's an emperor in Ranke who'll give them the gold, he'll swear whatever he's got to swear to get it."

Cauvin's attention slewed back to the nearby conversation. He'd been thinking about Lord Serripines and the rest of the Enders, but—no froggin' surprise—he was froggin' wrong.

"You've got it wrong, Dardis," the blue-shawled woman said with exaggerated patience. "If the Dragon bends a knee, he'll bend it toward King Sepheris in Ilsig. He'll get the same gold; and after he takes off to conquer the old Irrune lands, he'll be on the far side of the Empire, where he can ignore his oaths."

"And we'll have Sepheris all over our backs—"

"Better an Ilsigi king who speaks our language than the Rankan Empire and Rankan taxes."

The man called Dardis expressed his opinion of Sanctuary's ancestral home with a loud hawk and louder spit. "Pox on Sepheris. The Empire," he declared, "can levy all the taxes it wants on Sanctuary, seeing as it can't collect a rusty soldat."

"Wherever the Dragon goes," another man, a stranger to the others as he was to Cauvin, chimed in, "he'll bleed us all white before he leaves. He thinks the only good city is a sacked city. Naimun's the man for us. Does what he's told."

Dardis hawked and spat again. "Frog all—Naimun does what Naimun wishes . . . and Naimun wishes for gold, women, and wine!"

"Then we'll give him women and wine until he forgets about the gold," the other man argued.

A fourth voice—*Cauvin's* voice—entered the conversation. "I think we'd be better off with Raith."

Strangers turned and stared as if a froggin' dog had reared up on its froggin' hind legs and started to talk.

"You're young yet," Dardis explained. "Take it from a man who's seen it all. The last man Sanctuary needs for prince-governor is a froggin' clever man who learned his lessons from the froggin' Torch."

The others grumbled their agreement while the blue-shawled woman muttered, "Raith's still a boy. Once Arizak's gone, his older brothers will dispose of him quick enough."

"Arizak or no, Raith'll be dead by midwinter, mark my words," Dardis swore, repeating the words Cauvin had heard when the conversation began. "The Dragon won't wait until Arizak's dead to bring that one down; his froggin' mother will boil his balls if he doesn't do it by then."

"If the Torch taught Raith," Cauvin scarcely believed he was hearing his own froggin' voice. A sheep-shite stone-smasher didn't care who ruled Sanctuary. "He won't be easy to kill."

"If the Torch taught him everything," the second man agreed with a cackling laugh, "but what boy learns all his lessons, eh? Did you, lad? Put your money on the Dragon, if you want to see the future of Sanctuary."

Dardis cleared his throat; they all stepped back, but the man didn't spit this time. He stared straight into Cauvin's eyes, and said: "If Raith's brothers can't kill him, then froggin' Ils have mercy on our shite-baked souls, 'cause he'll be ours for-froggin'-ever, just like the Torch."

For a moment, Cauvin thought he recognized Dardis after all. A stoneyard customer? The wheelwright who'd mended the mule cart three years back when the axle split? Or maybe someone from the older depths of his memory? The palace? Dardis was too old to have been in the pits but could he have been a Hand? His weren't stained red, but was that proof? Or was he only another hard-eyed wary man come to say farewell to the one thing in Sanctuary that hadn't changed in a lifetime?

Before Cauvin could make up his sheep-shite mind, the Irrune started pounding their drums again. The aroma of roast meat wove through the funeral crowd as oxcarts emerged from the palace kitchens. Servants bore a platter of delicacies to Arizak and his close companions. The Irrune tossed fatty morsels onto the pyre, where they burst into sorcerously bright flames: The false Molin Torchholder's funeral feast had begun.

The women of Sanctuary had the foresight to bring bowls and knives. They and whoever stood beside them devoured generous portions of meat and bread. Cauvin, who'd come to the funeral feast without a woman or a bowl, pierced a stringy slab of ox shoulder with his boot knife. He burnt his fingers, got stains on his shirt, and savored each juicy mouthful.

Street musicians roamed the forecourt with their instruments and leather cups. They sang new songs that celebrated the Torch's life and the traditional dirges of Ilsig. Neither withstood the onslaught of the Irrune drums. Nothing could compete with that pounding; nothing could resist it, either, not after the casks were breached and the ale began to flow.

Ordinary folk who wouldn't froggin' *dream* of dancing like a Red Lanterns whore clapped and whirled about. Swift's face was as red as his forge fire when he and his ladylove spun into Cauvin's view. They called Cauvin's name, inviting him into their celebration. He'd sooner leap blind off the froggin' highest wall in the city and beat a retreat to the crowd's fringes. There he spotted Batty Dol arm-in-arm with Bilibot. Once he'd seen that gods-forsaken sight, Cauvin was ready to look for a blue leather mask.

The Maze was quiet, nearly deserted, which made it all the more froggin' dangerous. Cauvin loaded his fist with bronze and, with the torch he'd carried down from Pyrtanis Street in his off-weapon hand, straddle-walked the gutters that ran down the middle of the quarter's twisted, narrow streets. His directions were precise, including the number of paces between turns as well as the corner turns themselves, but Cauvin didn't entirely trust them.

The Maze was riddled with tunnels, sewers, and other hidden passageways that were apt to collapse without warning, taking a house or two with them. New buildings sprang up almost immediately, but never in quite the old location. Season to season, the streets of the Maze moved like a flooded stream, finding new courses between familiar places or disappearing altogether. Since he'd started seeing Leorin, Cauvin had made it a point to visit the Maze at least once a week, lest he lose the Vulgar Unicorn.

The Torch was far too old for carousing in taverns or chasing wenches. Froggin' sure it had been more than a week since he'd visited the Maze. A man following the old geezer's directions put himself at risk for getting lost or worse. Cauvin's shoulder muscles were aching knots as he counted another eight paces, turned a tight corner, and found himself unexpectedly staring at the lantern-lit doors of the Vulgar Unicorn.

Like the rest of the quarter, the Unicorn was uncommonly quiet. Through an open window, Cauvin saw two of the wenches sitting at a table, deep in their own conversation. Neither of them was Leorin, but she was surely working. She hadn't been at the funeral. Crowds spurred her nightmares—not the rowdy crowds that frequented the Unicorn, but open-air crowds. She said they reminded her of executions. She'd never have gone back to the palace to see a man burn, even a dead hero.

Two nights ago, Leorin had wanted to run away from Sanctuary forever. Last night Cauvin had gone home to bed, not to the Unicorn. They didn't see each other every night, or every other night for that matter. Theirs wasn't the sort of love that left the lovers red-faced and spinning like Swift and his lady, but it wouldn't hurt to walk through the doors.

And tell her about last night? Tell her about the Torch, the Hand, and the froggin' blue mask that was supposed to connect him with an armsmaster?

Cauvin pounded his head against an imaginary wall. Shalpa's froggin' cloak! If he'd had half the wits Father Ils had given the shited sheep, he'd have insisting on meeting the mysterious armsmaster somewhere other than the Vulgar Unicorn. Gods all be damned, the froggin' Broken Mast would have been a better meetplace than the Unicorn!

Froggin' sure he was going to regret going into the Unicorn tonight, so Cauvin resolved to put it off a bit longer. Following the Torch's directions, he went left down a passage that was too wide to be called an alley but too narrow to be called a street anywhere except the Maze. Thieves could have jumped from black doorways on either side and from above as well.

A man needed a strong gut when he went exploring in the Maze; and if he were a smart man, too, he brought a froggin' hat. In the froggin' Maze, the buildings leaned out over the street. At noon the only sunlight to reach the pavement landed in the gutter along with the slops from upstairs. Bareheaded as he was, Cauvin barely avoided a honey-pot dousing as he plodded deeper into the dark.

The Torch's directions ended precisely in a rubbish-strewn emptiness that the Imperials would call an atrium and a Wrigglie like Cauvin called a death trap: The only way out lay behind him, but there were froggin' windows and roofs aplenty where an archer, or even a decent knife-man, could make short work of a sheep-shite fool with a glaring-bright torch blooming in his hand.

*Gods damn your sheep-shite eyes, Lord Molin Torchholder, if this gets me killed,* Cauvin swore silently.

Yet, aside from the predictable dangers of clambering over charred wood, crumbling brick, and broken pottery, the atrium felt as safe as his loft. Glancing at the gaping windows, Cauvin had the uncanny sense he was invisible, at least to anyone who might be lurking in those black holes. Froggin' sure, a magician could hide a man. Back on Pyrtanis Street, the old-timers said that Enas Yorl had hidden his big house, with him still in it, in the middle of a big storm and kept it there all the years since.

Cauvin didn't pay much attention to the old-timers. Hidden wasn't the same as gone, and Yorl's house was *gone.* A man could walk across the corner where it had once stood, if he had a reason to. Cauvin had run across on a ten-padpol dare. It was a spooky place, full of shadows and sounds that couldn't be heard from the street. He was head-to-toe gooseflesh before he'd reached the other side, but he'd gotten across and gotten his padpols.

The Hand could hide things, or Dyareela could hide things for the Hand. Priests prayed and gods worked miracles that froggin' *seemed* like magic, but weren't because priests weren't mages and you could get in trouble if you said otherwise. The Hands, gods rot them all, were consecrated priests—

Molin Torchholder was a consecrated priest, too.

Cauvin thought about that staff the Torch kept beside him. Froggin' sure it was more than a stick of black wood, and that lump of amber had the look of sorcery. And why hadn't the old pud died? The Torch swore that he was dying, but though that wound on his hip went down to the bone, he froggin' sure wasn't fading away.

Questions hung at the back of Cauvin's mind, thoughts like midnight after a supper of cabbage and onions when it was down the ladder or lie there with a gut-ache until dawn. They kept him anxious as he rammed the torch into a crack in the wall and began clearing rubble.

He was still working up his sweat when he uncovered the edge of the trapdoor the Torch had said he'd find: a paving stone remarkable for its perfectly square shape and nothing more. There was no lifting it, but the geezer had given Cauvin an answer for that, too. He took the torch to another corner where, right as froggin' rain, there was a perfectly square brick sitting shoulder high in the wall. Pull it out, the Torch had said, then pull the lever at the back of the hole.

Cauvin had gotten his fingers wedged around the brick when sensations that were both hot and cold shot up his arms. His hands shook so badly he couldn't keep them pressed into the mortar. Then the sensations passed from his shoulders to his neck. He opened his mouth and would have been horrified, but not froggin' surprised, if a hive of bees had swarmed out of his throat, except—suddenly—the sensations ended as if they'd never begun.

Warding, he told himself. Cauvin knew a bit about warding, the expensive sorcery that rich people bought for their treasure chests and real thieves bought amulets to counter. He'd have wagered his last froggin' padpol that there wasn't anything in Sanctuary worth warding—out at Land's End, perhaps, but nothing inside Sanctuary's walls.

Needless to say, the froggin' geezer hadn't mentioned warding. Cauvin stared at the froggin' square brick a good long time before touching it gingerly with the fourth finger of his left hand.

Nothing. No chills, no sweats, no tingling. Nothing at all.

Cauvin dug deep into his stock of oaths and insults. There wasn't one that satisfied. The froggin' brick hadn't been warded; warding strong enough to numb a man's flesh didn't disappear after a single touch—he'd learned *that* from the Hand. No, someone—the froggin' Torch—had anchored a one-time spell on the brick, a spell which had gone to ground in Cauvin's flesh.

"You better froggin' well be *dead* tomorrow morning, you froggin' bastard!" Cauvin hoped the old pud could hear him; he didn't care who else did. " 'Cause I'm going to smash every froggin' bone in your froggin' body."

Cauvin yanked the brick from the wall—his own choice, at least he thought it was. He'd come too far, risked too froggin' much to turn back without the gods-all-be-damned blue mask. The lever took two hands and all his strength before it budged. In his mind's eye, Cauvin saw the atrium transformed into a vast chamber with smoky lamps and pillars and Lord Molin Torchholder waiting for him atop a massive throne, but in the Maze nothing changed.

The paving stone remained as Cauvin had left it. From his knees, he pried it loose, revealing not the mask-filled cache he'd hoped for, but the rising end of a steep, ladderlike stairway. The Torch hadn't mentioned that either. Muttering and cursing himself for froggin' foolishness as heartily as he cursed Molin Torchholder for deception, Cauvin dragged the paving stone to the center of the atrium and covered it with rubbish—little as he liked the prospect of leaving the froggin' hole open behind him, he liked the notion of someone else closing it even less.

With a stone-worker's professional eye, Cauvin admired the stairway. Each of the steps was steep and narrow, befitting the paving-stone entry, but they were made from shaped stone and bore his weight without shifting. The tunnel at the foot of the stairs was stone-faced, solid, and drier than the atrium above it. There wasn't a froggin' cobweb or slime streak to be seen. The air was stale, but not foul, which reassured Cauvin as he made his way toward what he thought was a dead end but proved to be a dogleg turn to the right.

Once he'd turned the corner Cauvin conceded that the Torch hadn't sent him on a fool's errand and almost forgave him for the warded brick. In front of him the tunnel widened into a chamber large enough that the light from Cauvin's torch didn't reach the walls. What the torch did reveal was racks of armor and benches covered with weapons, all bright and shimmering beneath layers of protective oil.

Drawn by curiosity too strong to resist, Cauvin entered the chamber. It wasn't occupied—at least not by anything larger than a mouse or lizard. He thought the torch flared when he raised it toward the chamber's higher ceiling; more likely, it wasn't the torch, but his eyes going wide with awe. Off to one side, in an alcove fit for a froggin' god, a suit of armor like nothing Cauvin had seen before hung on a stone torso. The breastplate was burnished bronze and shaped in a style that was neither Imperial nor Ilsigi. Over one shoulder the torso wore a battle cape of boldly speckled fur from an animal Cauvin couldn't name. A crested helmet rested on the floor beneath the torso along with bracers, greaves, and a sword that was remarkable for its plainness in comparison to the armor around it.

Stories said the Torch had been a warrior in his younger days, but he'd never been man enough to fill that bronze armor, which begged the question: Who had worn it, and how had it wound up beneath the Maze?

Cauvin looked for a bracket in which to set his torch. There was one beside the doorway but there was also a glass lamp—he was starting to expect the froggin' unexpected—with a bellyful of oil hanging from the ceiling. He lit the lamp, waited a moment for the froggin'-gods-only-knew-what, then returned to the alcove.

The air turned red the instant his fingertips touched the bronze. Cauvin had a moment to realize that the armor was leather, not metal, and to curse his curiosity before a voice surrounded him. It spoke in his mind and filled his ears.

*At last, you have*—it began.

A whirlwind circled Cauvin where he stood. It threatened to tear his clothes from his body but did not disturb either his torch or the lamp.

*You are not My chosen minion. I do not know you. You are no one. You do not belong here. Close your eyes, mortal; you have seen all that you will ever see.*

Cauvin was too sheep-shite frightened to move even his eyelids, but not too frightened to invoke another silent curse that touched the froggin' Torch by name.

*You know him.*

The words weren't a question, and Cauvin didn't need to answer.

*He sent you. He lives?*

Cauvin croaked a single word: "Yes," and the wind around him eased. "Your minion sent me, Holy Vashanka—" He guessed he was trapped in the presence of the Torch's god. "He did not warn me—"

*The man was My priest, never My minion, and ever a source of doubt and stubbornness. Though Tempus was that, too, and more. I have been too long without a minion in the mortal world.*

Another wind wrapped around Cauvin; no longer indignant, it had the feel of Mina's eyes when she looked for bargains in the market.

Frightened as he was, Cauvin was that much more repelled by the god's curiosity. He'd refused Dyareela; he'd refuse Vashanka, too, disregarding the risks. "I am not for sale."

Vashanka chuckled. *And I do not BUY My chosen ones. Even in Sanctuary. I have come back to Sanctuary—*

The chamber went dark. It went more than dark; it froggin' disappeared like Enas Yorl's froggin' house and took Cauvin's body with it. His awareness was limited to his eyes, and his eyes were bird high above a transformed Sanctuary.

A man wearing the bronzed leather armor and a bloody red glow rode a troublesome gray horse along a cleaner, busier Wideway. Cauvin thought of himself as a brawny man able to overpower any sheep-shite fool who challenged him, but not the bronzed rider. Measured against recognizable landmarks, the pale-haired man had to be at least a head taller and stronger not so much in muscle as manner. He exhaled power and contempt. People kept their heads down and got out of his way without—Vashanka agreed—knowing who the warrior was or why he'd ridden into their city.

A bold youth—or simply a froggin' careless and unlucky one—darted in front of the gray horse. The animal attacked with a ferocity Cauvin associated with wild dogs, not horses. No one on the Wideway dared come to the youth's aid. They cowered behind paltry shelters and watched as the armored rider let the attack continue until the youth was past dead and little more than bloody pulp beneath iron-shod hooves. He rode on in silence, his and theirs.

The warrior's name was Tempus Thales, and he was used to being watched; he'd been Vashanka's minion for nearly three centuries before he rode toward the palace.

*The omens were favorable . . . a city, isolated on the edge of the world, filled with ambition, with pride and hatred; and more wealth than showed on the surface . . . I sent My best and expected nothing less than perfection.*

Destruction followed the man called Tempus. Cauvin saw it all in an explosion of sparks each of which was too fleeting for consciousness but hot enough to burn memory. Within days of arriving in Sanctuary, Tempus slew a man who wore Imperial armor similar to his own and many whose protection was limited to a blue-leather mask. He brought sorcery and uncanny weapons to the Maze and terror to the Street of Red Lanterns because for Vashanka's minion it was either rape or celibacy, and he was never a celibate man.

Sanctuary cowered and Vashanka was pleased, then Sanctuary took vengeance. The Wrigglies ambushed Tempus as he lay in a drug-laced stupor. They dragged him beyond the walls and sold him to a man obsessed with pain. Tempus lost his tongue, an arm, a foot, and other parts besides. A mortal man would have died; Vashanka's minion merely suffered and suffered and suffered.

*He never once called upon Me; therefore, I could not allow him to die.*

Recklessly—because he was not used to having a god in his head—Cauvin thought—*How could Tempus call anyone without a tongue?* And, *How could he die, if a god had made him immortal?*

The red wind licked Cauvin's throat. *If I'd made Tempus immortal, I could unmake him . . . or save him.*

Like a froggin' starfish, Tempus grew back his missing parts once he was freed from the vivisectionist's lair, with nary a scar on his flesh to betray his suffering. But the minion's mind, his spirit . . . Cauvin's mind filled with weariness that was neither his nor Vashanka's.

*He was never the same. He'd looked at death and seen that it would not take him. I thought it would make him bold . . . inventive— But he grew jaded instead. The game was over before it fairly began.*

No one in Sanctuary guessed that Tempus was a changed man, a hollow minion. Dizzying scenes of carnage and miscalculation passed before Cauvin's eyes. Except for one, they were no different than the earlier visions. And that one vision, which lingered in Cauvin's mind's eye long after Vashanka had moved to other memories, revealed not Tempus, but merely a man known to him, a man who'd stumbled into the power of a witch who was more raven than woman.

The witch had staked the man flat over a hole in the ground. She commanded her servants to start a greenwood fire, then bid them fan the smoke underground. Not even a god could forget the screams as a badger clawed its escape through the man's gut.

*The omens changed.* Vashanka conceded. *Doom could have been seen, perhaps; I was distracted.*

Cauvin saw a woman—a goddess, perhaps—with snakes draped around her body and the same staring eyes Cauvin had seen on Captain Sinjon's face in the Broken Mast. The snake-y woman did more than distract Vashanka, she destroyed Him and Sanctuary with Him. Tempus and the Torch worked together—a froggin' odd and frightening pair they made—to pull their god out of the snake woman's embrace, but failed.

Darkness clouded Vashanka's vision. The raven witch brought her war with all things Imperial and Tempus Thales in particular to Sanctuary. Gangs, not armies, waged nasty war in every quarter, even on Pyrtanis Street, where Cauvin glimpsed the mansion that meant so much to Mina and was now the stoneyard. He watched in astonishment as dead men and women were raised by a handful of rival witches and turned loose to ravage the city. Cauvin knew he looked down upon the dead because he saw the spread-eagled man moving among them, a froggin' badger-sized hole, raw but not bleeding, right through his gut.

*Do not blame Me.* Was the storm-god sulking? Embarrassed? Ashamed? *They blamed Me. Blasted My temple. Broke My minion and My priest. I had done nothing Savankala had not done a hundred times before and Ils, a thousand. If the dead did not stay dead, why blame Me? The dead were never My concern. Great Father Ils of the Ilsigi claimed the city. Its dead belonged to Him, too. His problem, not Mine. He solved it by banishing Me . . . Me! Ils thought to banish war; He banished victory instead. Did he think His gray daughter, Sivini, could grant Him victory?*" Vashanka answered His own question with a clash of thunder and bolts of lightning. *Sanctuary fell to the dead. To the dead, to thieves, and children.*

When Cauvin first came to the stoneyard, ignorant of everything except the streets and the pits, Grabar had told him tales of the days of children, thieves, and living corpses—the days of *his* childhood, when a man couldn't leave home without a braid of colored strings and ribbons tied around his arm to grant him safe passage from one quarter to the next. He said the night the dead finally, truly died a pillar of fire rose from the Hill all the way to the stars.

Cauvin knew the Hand was real because he'd lived through it . . . but living corpses, fiery pillars, and ribbons? Cauvin had listened, because after the streets and the pits he'd do anything to stay at the stoneyard, but listening wasn't froggin' *believing.*

*Believe, mortal. The dead did walk and a pillar of fire did burn all the way to paradise. It took the dead, the witches, the mages, and the priests with it. When the sun rose, there wasn't a sorcerer left who could make water in the rain. And the gods of Sanctuary—the gods who'd banished Me for meddling!—They couldn't make rain. They couldn't undo what They'd done, so They went away. They forgot.*

Tempus couldn't forget. He led what was left of his men, of Vashanka's men, to fight the northern witches. His bronze armor shone, his gray horse pranced, but the minion left Sanctuary without his god. There would be no more victories, not for the Rankan Empire and not for Tempus Thales. He was immortal. No bleeding wound could kill him, but despair?

The burnished armor had returned to Sanctuary while the Hand held the palace. A woman with silver-streaked hair had brought it. She'd dumped it on the floor of an apothecary shop and left without saying a word once-mighty Vashanka could overhear.

Thunder became rain.

*Do not weep for Ranke or its gods. Sanctuary did not destroy the Empire. The Empire did that to itself. Sanctuary did not destroy Me. I did that to Myself. Now I wait, the only god in Sanctuary. Are you the one? Do you think you are?*

The red wind raised a shiver on Cauvin's spine before it spun away to nothing. Cauvin shook sense back into his head. He was on the floor, underground in the Maze and staring up at a lamp. It seemed wise to stay there a moment longer, making certain everything still worked and getting clear of the images Vashanka had burnt into his memory.

When Cauvin did move the first thing he saw was a rack of armor: four tunics made from squares of dull metal and worn leather laced together. They'd meant nothing to him when he'd walked through the door, now they froggin' shouted Hell Hounds, and in his mind's eye Cauvin could see the men who'd worn them: sour-faced veterans with their backs to the golden prince, Kadakithis, protecting him from Sanctuary.

They'd have given the froggin' Bloody Hand a hard time if they'd still been in Sanctuary when the city needed them. But Vashanka's visions revealed the last Hell Hounds had left with the prince. They were buried in unmarked graves, except for one who'd been planted in an herb garden on Red Lantern Street.

Cauvin shut his eyes to end the flow of unbidden knowledge and cursed an old man—

"Gods all damn you and froggin' damned god—"

There wasn't room left for a doubt in his sheep-shite mind: He'd fallen into a god's power—a froggin' *Imperial* god—and he wasn't half the man that Tempus Thales had been.

Cauvin couldn't lie blind on the floor forever. He had to open his eyes again. That meant more armor—lacquered black, trimmed and laced with leather so dark Cauvin had to squint to realize it was wine-colored rather than black. A face-concealing helmet lay on the floor beneath the armor. It sported a crest of red feathers so bright and fresh it seemed likely the bird was still alive. Words came to Cauvin's mind: Abarsis, another priest of Vashanka; he'd died not long after he arrived, but the men he brought with him, the Stepsons—the Stepsons of the rapist Tempus Thales—remained behind.

The Stepsons got along well with each other, too froggin' well, Cauvin decided when the full nature of their sword-side, shield-side pairs burst into his mind. No froggin' surprise then, that no one else did. If there was one thing Wrigglies and Imperials had in common it was a distrust of men who had no interest in women. But, with Vashanka's minion leading them, the Stepsons were meaner than the Hell Hounds and better trained than all the sheep-shite brawlers in Sanctuary, especially the gang that called itself the Hawkmasks—

At last Cauvin's gaze fell upon the object he'd come to retrieve. On the floor like he was and out of sight near the corner, the Torch had collected the blue leather masks that protected the wearers with a fringe of fake feathers and his nose with a sharp, downturned beak.

Cauvin crawled to the heap, reached out, then pulled his hand back before his fingers met the leather. First the brick in the atrium, next the armor. Was he froggin' foolish enough to touch something else in this hole?

He was, because the mask was what he'd come for. It was stiff, yet supple, in his grasp, like the best boot leather, the kind no one on Pyrtanis Street could afford. One eyehole was damaged; a crusty stain thickened the inside leather and coarsened its texture. As one of the thongs that would have held in place around its wearer's head fell apart in his hands, Cauvin realized it had been removed from the corpse of a man who'd died from a head wound—decades, probably, before he'd been born.

"Too many men with froggin' swords and grudges," he whispered, fighting off another deluge of a god's bitter memories. "Too many froggin' rivals who'd rather fight one another than a common foe. They pissed it away."

Sadness and regret filled the chamber. Cauvin breathed it in and made it his own. Retrieving an undamaged mask from the pile, he held it to his face and braced himself for an onslaught of visions in blue.

There was nothing but a loss of sidewise vision. The sheep-shite men who'd worn the blue masks couldn't see what was coming toward them, unless it came from straight ahead—unless it was froggin' exactly what they were expecting. If this was the sort of thing the Torch's armsmaster relied upon, he'd say no to the lessons. Frog all—the Hand had taught him better than that: You were only as good as what your eyes and ears revealed.

As he reached to untie the mask's thongs, Cauvin got his vision, not as dramatic as the visions he'd gotten from Vashanka, but froggin' powerful all the same. The men—and women—who'd worn these masks were brawlers, not warriors like those who'd worn the room's armor. They were like the Hand who'd taught Cauvin to fight, and they'd worn masks for the same reason the Hand wrapped their heads in red silk—not to protect their faces, but to hide them. The Hawkmasks collected debts and marketed slaves on behalf of their gang's leader, a man named . . .

The name hovered just out of reach in the shadows, then it strode forward: a bull-necked man of a ghost with a blue mask across his face and skin as dark as the shadow behind him. Cauvin lowered his borrowed mask. The ghost remained. It wasn't merely that the ghost's skin was a dark, shiny brown—that could have been a mark of death—everything about him was different: the jut of his nose and chin, the angle of his eyes, the shape of his mouth.

"Spare me your judgments," the ghost said with a voice that was deeper than Vashanka's and almost as weary. "Men have bought and sold one another since men began. It's an old business, and it will last as long as a few men are strong while the rest are weak. Ask a beggar which he would rather have: a bowl of food or his freedom, and you'll get the same answer every time. Strong men will not protect the weak unless they are property."

"I'd choose freedom," Cauvin responded without hesitation.

The ghost's throaty laughter echoed off the walls. "Then you've never been a beggar."

No, Cauvin had been a thief, and a sheep-shite unlucky one at that. He hadn't been a slave, either, not officially. The Hand didn't keep *slaves*; slavery was against the froggin' law. They tended orphans instead, raised them up for the glory of the froggin' Mother of Chaos.

"What use is freedom to a beggar?" the ghost persisted. "The freedom to starve and shiver? When a mighty king conquers his enemies, which is better—that he kill them all or make them his property? The poor man with a beautiful daughter—what use is *freedom* to either of them? A well-run slave market offers hope all around—to the *buyer* and seller, and the slaves."

"Froggin' hell it does." Cauvin threw the ghost's words back at him: "You've never been a slave."

The ghost erupted with hollow laughter. "Not a slave? I was born a slave in a land so far from the Empire that it's been forgotten ten times over. My father called himself a king—of what, I never knew, but he was afraid of his sons, even the sons of his slaves. He had them killed, except for me. Me, he sold to a friend or an enemy; it scarcely mattered to me. The world had become my enemy. I fought, not for freedom—what use was freedom? I fought to avenge my own shame. Whipped, branded, and whipped again, I was chained and sold a dozen times. Each time I was pulled farther from my birthplace, closer to the Rankan Empire until—when I was about your age—I had a master who brought me to Ranke itself.

"He wasn't a poor man, my new Rankan master, but he owed more money than he could hope to beg from his rich father. In me—a man who hated everyone and lived for rage—he saw the solution to his problems. They had a special sort of slave in Ranke—they have them elsewhere, too—slaves who fight to the death in public arenas while unwashed crowds cheer and a lucky few grow rich by betting on the winners. My owner promised me freedom if I'd make him rich. He lied, but I made him rich all the same, then

I bought my own freedom and slit his throat on my way out of the capital.

"I made my way to Sanctuary to practice what I'd learned from my many masters. This city was mine and I cared for it until that golden-haired Kadakithis showed up at the palace with his priests and his Hounds. In the name of freedom and *justice,* they hunted my hawks like vermin. They broke me and used the home I'd built to quarter their animals—but did they protect the weak? Did they care for Sanctuary? Look around you—is Sanctuary better without slaves, without Jubal and his hawks? Answer honestly, if you dare."

Cauvin turned the challenge over in his mind. Only a sheepshite fool would think life in Sanctuary had improved since Prince Kadakithis left the palace, but Vashanka had just refused to take credit for the city's fall. "You take too much for yourself, Jubal," he said, sinking into the stubbornness that got him into trouble more often than not. "Sanctuary's not a froggin' cesspool because of you, and if it's going to change, freedom's a better place to start than slavery."

"Are you the one to make those changes? Do you think you are?" Jubal asked, an eerie repetition of Vashanka's words before the ghost, like the god, vanished.

If there'd been either a ghost or a god. If the damned brick and its damned spell weren't to blame for everything he'd seen and heard since entering the chamber. And if Lord Molin Torchholder weren't to blame for the froggin' brick.

"The geezer's going to die," Cauvin swore when he was alone. "That froggin' pud's going to die." But he folded the mask along well-worn creases and tucked it beneath his shirt.

Cauvin was tempted to take the torch and hike out to the red-wall ruin to settle things between him and Lord Molin froggin' Torchholder, then his eyes fell on the weapons. He was angry enough to murder the Torch with his fists, but a froggin' sword, though, would be more satisfying. Hadn't the Torch said he'd needed to learn to fight with steel? And he'd spotted just the sword, resting beside its scabbard on a black-lacquered rack in the place of honor among the weapons.

It was an odd-looking sword: half again as long as the swords Sanctuary's guards carried and faintly green, as if mold had gotten into the metal. If it weren't sitting alone on the rack, Cauvin would have figured it for junk. There were at least twenty swords in the chamber, most of them standing in a point-to-point cone on a knee-high table. Any one of them could have sliced through the neck of a treacherous old man—not that Cauvin was any great judge of swords or the steel that made them. Until he closed his fingers on the green sword's leather-bound hilt, he'd never so much as touched a froggin' sword. They weren't much use for smashing stone.

Cauvin expected the weapon to pull his arm down the way a mallet did, but the sword's weight was in its hilt, not its tip and it was pleasantly light in his grasp. Length, of course, exaggerated his movements: a wrist flick arched the tip from one end of the weapons table to the other. He flicked it again and sensed the weapon's power. If he swung it the way he swung his mallet—especially if he cramped both hands onto the hilt to put all his strength into the effort—the Torch's head would fly for yards before it landed.

At the Lucky Well, Bilibot said a man's eyes went on seeing a while. Cauvin knew better than to believe a froggin' word Bilibot said, but just this once he hoped the old sot was right, and the Torch got to see his body standing headless before it fell.

He took a practice stroke, a double-handed swing that started above his right shoulder and ended a heartbeat after the green sword smashed into the sheaf of upright swords. The sheep-shite collision raised a racket that could be heard in the middle of next week and brought a burning flush to Cauvin's face. He dropped the sword. It bounced tip first, then hilt, then tip again against the stone floor. The chamber froggin' rang like the inside of a great bell.

Cauvin clapped his hands over his ears and dropped to his knees, wishing that the froggin' ground would open up to swallow him and praying that no lingering god or ghost would grant his sheep-shite wish. He wrestled with the fallen swords. There had to be some froggin' trick to leaning them together but Cauvin hadn't a froggin' clue what it might be. After several failures he spread the weapons neatly on the table. Then he reached for the green-steel sword, dreading the damage he'd probably done to the weapon. It wasn't a fancy sword—no froggin' gemstones to knock loose or golden knotwork to untie—and the blade was neither nicked nor bent. Cauvin returned the weapon to its lacquered stand.

With his fists braced on the table and his head hanging low, he thought about the change three days and one dying old man had made to his life. Maybe he'd seen a god and a ghost—or maybe not; he'd been spelled by froggin' sorcery. Nothing but sorcery could have made him handle the froggin' things in this chamber. Bec would have mauled every weapon, every piece of armor, but not him, not the sheep-shite stone-smasher.

He knew better. He should have, anyway.

Cauvin drew a stuttering breath and raised his head. There was a shield propped against the wall behind the table. No, not a shield, merely a shield-shaped slab of wood with a painting of a one-horned beast that could only be a froggin' unicorn caught in a froggin' vulgar—and a froggin' impossible for a four-legged animal—act of self-gratification.

Swords, masks, and a suit of armor fit for a god's minion stored in the same froggin' room as a signboard from some long-gone ancestor of the Vulgar Unicorn. Cauvin had to laugh: the great Lord Torchholder's treasures hidden in a tavern's cellar—and not any tavern, but the Vulgar Unicorn! Froggin' sure, Grabar said the tavern had burnt twice in his lifetime; Cauvin hadn't figured that meant it had moved as well. Buildings burnt and buildings got rebuilt in the same place because the land was still there and, usually, so were the froggin' walls.

Cauvin wondered if the Torch even knew he'd stashed his froggin' treasures in the old Unicorn's cellar—it was hard to imagine a *priest,* for gods' sakes, walking through a door with that signboard hanging over it. But if there was one thing Cauvin had learned in the past three days, it was that Molin Torchholder was no ordinary priest.

Amid the charred wood, dented tankards, and the rusted iron that might have been a hanging lamp holding the shield upright against the wall, there was one chunk that seemed straighter and less damaged than the rest. Closer examination—Cauvin hadn't shaken himself free of the froggin' spell that drove him to *touch* whatever caught his sheep-shite eye—revealed a sheath of dark, scaly leather and, within, a long-bladed dagger quite unlike the tool he kept in his boot cuff. Both edges had been honed and a middle groove from hilt to sharp tip made the blade ideal for stabbing. The hilt was wire-wrapped wood, sweat polished, and the right size for Cauvin's palm and fingers.

When they were in their cups and talking about the days before the Irrune, before the Hand, the Lucky Well regulars insisted that there was a perfect weapon for every hand. To the extent that Cauvin listened—which was no froggin' great extent—he presumed his perfect weapon was his right fist closed over a lump of bronze. Not so. A vulgar unicorn had been guarding Cauvin's perfect weapon for gods knew how long.

Once he'd held the long-bladed dagger in his hand, Cauvin knew he'd want it nearby always.

Thongs trailed from the sheath. Cauvin could attach them to his belt or around his leg, but the weapon would rest comfortably against his thigh only after he'd loosened his belt to a dangerous extent. He'd need a froggin' second belt, or a single belt, long enough to wrap once around his waist and again over one hip. He could see the long belt in his mind's eye. Thanks to the Torch's box, he had the coins to purchase it, if any cobbler could match the sheath leather.

Or perhaps he'd sling the sheath inside his breeches . . . or up his sleeve, or tucked in at the small of his back. As natural as the dagger felt in Cauvin's hand, it was awkward everywhere else. Except for the bronze slug, which hid inside his shirt, Cauvin never carried a weapon. He left the dagger tied to his thigh, though it got in the way climbing the stairs to the atrium. While walking the Maze to the Vulgar Unicorn—Leorin's Unicorn as opposed to the one below the atrium basement—Cauvin was froggin' sure the knife was drawing attention from everyone who saw it.

Leorin was working, or trying to. Business hadn't improved. She spotted Cauvin as he came through the door and pointed toward one of the empty tables along the walls. Privacy cost at the Unicorn, and though Cauvin had the coins to buy it for one night, he didn't want to develop either the taste or the habit. He took a seat at one end of a long, common table with a view of the front door. The knife, he realized, was the first thing anyone entering the tavern would see.

Maybe he should sit on the other side of the table? Or, maybe he should bind the knife to his other leg? Cauvin was right-handed;

he carried his boot knife in his right boot; he'd naturally slung the knife on his right side, but the men who wore swords—and there were several in the Unicorn—wore them on their off-weapon hip. Was his long-bladed dagger a froggin' knife or a froggin' sword? And what would the Torch's froggin' armsmaster think if the man saw Cauvin with a weapon worn the wrong way around?

The unanswerable question reminded Cauvin that he needed to display the froggin' mask. Where? Froggin' sure not tied over his face. He settled on his belt, folded over the knife's hilt. It was a clumsy solution, but the best he could do before Leorin arrived.

She greeted him with a mug of beer and "Welcome, stranger. Missed you last night."

Leorin's moods were never easy to follow—his weren't either—but neither anger nor disappointment seemed to dominate her voice.

"Things ran late at the stoneyard." He decided he'd stick to that. Leorin dreamt. She'd work herself up to a sleepless week if she knew the Hand was loose again and he'd tangled with them last night.

Leorin nodded and took a solid swig of his beer. "The old pud dead yet?"

"Not yet."

"He give you any more silver or gold?"

Cauvin shook his head.

"Maybe the gods will take him tonight, now that everything's done with the Torch." There was a bitter edge to Leorin's voice when she spoke the name.

"What's he got to do with anything?" Cauvin asked cautiously.

"You know the gods have to be celebrating. He's cheated Them for years. Afraid to die—and with good reason."

"A lot of folk call him a hero for what he did to bring the Hand down. You should have seen the crowd at the funeral."

Leorin took another swig of Cauvin's beer. "Don't go to funerals. Don't like crowds. The Torch was never *my* hero."

Cauvin shrugged. "Mine, neither, but you know where we'd be if he hadn't led Arizak and the Irrune through the gates—where I'd be, anyway. I think about it sometimes, when I can't stop myself: They wanted me to make vows to the Mother—

"Sacrifice," Leorin corrected.

"Yeah, that's what they called it. I said no and thought it was over, but it wasn't. They said they'd give me another chance, another month. The Irrune come first. I don't know if I could have said no a second time. If I'd said yes, I'd be dead."

Leorin reached across the table. She seized Cauvin's wrists and squeezed them tight, digging her fingernails into his flesh. "No, Cauvin, you would have survived." Their eyes met, and Leorin explained herself: "I *need* you, Cauvin; I need you that much. You would have survived. Somehow you would have survived, just so I could find you when I needed you most." She relaxed her grip.

"Then you've got to give the Torch some credit—he's the one locked me up by myself the night the rest of us died. Shite for sure, I'd've gone up in flames like everyone else." Cauvin freed his hands and closed them over hers. "The old geezer's not going to live much longer, love. He'll leave me something, maybe not enough to get us out of Sanctuary, but enough to set us up. I'm about ready to jump that broom and tell Grabar I've done it."

"We can go upstairs and jump it tonight with the gods as our witnesses. The Stick won't care—there's nobody here. Can't compete with roast meat and free wine. Even the regulars are out there, filling their guts for nothing. You could've taken a side table . . . we could go upstairs."

She was right about the regulars. Not one of the handful of men sitting in small groups or utterly alone was known to Cauvin. One of them looked an utter foreigner with a stiff-necked cloak and a hood that hid his face in shadows. The armsmaster? He'd looked Cauvin's way more than once, looked his way and looked at his leg where the mask—and the dagger—were on display.

Of course, he'd shot more looks at Leorin. Most men did. A score of women toted the Unicorn's beer and wine, but only one of them was beautiful, and since no one had ever suggested that Cauvin was handsome, most men would wonder why a drop-dead gorgeous woman like Leorin gave him a special smile.

"C'mon, Cauvin—let's go upstairs and celebrate the Torch's death our own way."

He was tempted—froggin' gods, he was tempted to finally bed the woman he loved, but his head still rang with ghosts and gods. When push came to shove, this wasn't the night he'd been waiting for.

Leorin pulled her hands free of his. "What's froggin' wrong, Cauv? You just said you were ready. What's ready, if not tonight? You think Grabar or the Stick's going to parade us through the streets with musicians and goats?"

"No." A loud, wedding parade was nothing either of them wanted. "No, just not tonight. Maybe he wasn't a hero, love, but he was there. As long as you and I have been alive, as long as our parents and grandparents the Torch has been pulling the strings behind Sanctuary. Who's going to replace him?" Cauvin was hiding the truth about the Torch, but his questions weren't lies.

"What difference is it to you or me? What did he do, anyway? The Irrune, you see them, but the Torch. If you'd come around here last Ilsday and asked if the Torch was even alive, I'll give you odds that three people out of four thought he'd been dead for years. People who didn't know he was alive won't care that he's dead now."

"I can't explain it, love, but it matters who takes his place. The whole city's going to change when he's gone. I feel it." That told the simple truth. Even if he told Leorin everything that had happened in the past few days, he couldn't explain an hour of it.

"Well, you keep on feeling it, then." Leorin stood up. "I've got customers to tend."

She didn't—at least not beer- or wine-drinking customers. Leorin put a sway in her hips and strode over to a wall-hung table where two men—neither of them the man in the stiff-necked cloak—were deep in conversation. In no time she was sitting in one man's lap, toying with his beard.

Another reason for Cauvin to be angry with Molin Torchholder: The froggin' old pud had come between him and Leorin. Cauvin sipped his beer. He didn't want to think about the changes barreling into his life with the Torch not yet dead, so he listened to the conversations around him.

The men with Leorin were the loudest and talking about how the new emperor in Ranke didn't look half as Imperial as she did. He heard her laugh and say something that included the words "gown" and "upstairs." When Cauvin glanced over his shoulder again, there was only one man sitting at the table.

It wasn't jealousy. Leorin had been taking men upstairs since before they'd found each other two years earlier. She might stop after they jumped the broom; she might not. Cauvin never worried because Leorin didn't care about any of the men she bedded, any more than she cared about her Imperial beauty. But until tonight, she'd never taken a man upstairs to spite him.

Slowly Cauvin finished his beer. He'd given the Torch's arms-master ample time to see him. If he gave any more, Leorin would be coming downstairs. That was a froggin' moment Cauvin wanted to avoid. He dropped a chipped and blackened soldat on the table and left the Unicorn.

The funeral feasting had been cut short by a cold rain that numbed Cauvin's bones before he'd escaped the Maze. Even so, he took the long way home, up the Processional and along Governor's Walk, passing close to the palace. The gates were barred; the smell of smoke seeped through cracks in the wood. The stoneyard gate was closed, too, but not barred. Cauvin bribed the yard dog with affection, then carefully stowed his new knife behind the grain barrel. Grabar and Mina would ask questions if they saw it, so would Bec, and though the froggin' questions would be different, Cauvin didn't want to be answering either batch.

# Chapter Ten

A storm descended in full fury not long after Cauvin wrapped himself in blankets. It hammered Sanctuary with mighty peals of thunder and lightning bright enough to see through closed eyes. Rain pounded the loft's wooden walls, rattling the shutters and flicking cold water onto Cauvin's face. There was a board beside the window. He could have propped it against the shutters—he'd nail it over them before the month ended—but getting out of bed was more work than he cared to do after midnight.

Wild storms were common visitors in spring and summer. This one was late, but Cauvin would have slept through it if he hadn't been burdened with a storm-god's memories. The skies were quiet before he slipped into restless sleep.

Hours later, aching cold shoulders awakened Cauvin from a dream about Leorin. He'd tossed and turned himself out of the blankets and nearly out of his shirt. Straightening them quickly, he tried to recapture the dream-stuff before it fled. He was partially successful and could have lain in the straw a while longer, imagining the pleasure he'd denied himself last night, but he'd opened his eyes while rearranging the blankets and knew that dawn was in the froggin' loft.

If shirking could solve problems, Cauvin was more than willing to give it a try; and this time maybe shirking could. If he didn't go back to the red-walled ruins, then the Torch would die. Eleven years ago Cauvin could have lived with leaving a man to die—he wouldn't be alive if he couldn't—but he'd put all that behind. Cauvin didn't believe he owed the froggin' Torch life for life, but he couldn't let a froggin' root cellar become any man's tomb.

He blinked Leorin out of his mind and found his boots.

The stoneyard stood on high ground, along with the rest of Pyrtanis Street, so it didn't froggin' flood out like most of Sanctuary, and for thirty-odd years Grabar had been thickening its dirt with stone chips. Even so, after a nightlong rain, the yard was a quagmire. Cauvin stuck to the paving-stone paths. Several stones shifted beneath his weight; he knew what he'd be doing as soon as the ground dried.

Grabar said as much while Cauvin splashed trough water on his face.

"Got to reset those stones before the wife or the boy gets hurt."

Cauvin grunted. Grabar never worried that Cauvin might get hurt, or himself, for that matter; it was always Mina and Bec.

"Saw you at the feast," Grabar went on. "By yourself—where was that woman of yours? Don't tell me she was working. The Well shut itself down. Nobody paying for what they could get free at the funeral."

"The Unicorn doesn't close for funerals." Cauvin dried his face on his sleeve.

Grabar snorted his opinion of taverns that didn't respect the dead. "Back to work for us: The Torch's gone to his gods, and the Dragon's gone, too. There's an archway that wants building along the wharf. Figured we'd pull stone and lay it out."

"Today?" Cauvin asked incredulously. The stoneyard built everything twice—laid flat in the yard where they selected and shaped the stones and again upright with mortar. Cauvin's favorite part of any job was fitting the stones together, but not when the yard was ankle deep in mud.

"Got to get it done," Grabar countered. " 'Less you're giving up food for the winter. If you noticed, we haven't been busy around here, and there's no assurance Tobus is going to buy those bricks you've been hauling each by each."

"He will," Cauvin muttered. The Torch had said he'd take care of it. Cauvin didn't trust Molin, but after last night, he froggin' sure believed him. "I'll wager you Tobus comes round today to see what we've got. Just wait."

"Meanin' you plan to go back out there?"

"If I have to drag the froggin' cart myself, yes. Face it, Grabar—

winter's coming, we're between jobs, and there's too much mud to pull stone. It's go out there and smash us some bricks or sit here and carve."

In deep winter, when building was impossible, Cauvin and Grabar sat beside an open hearth adding value to their stock by carving it. Grabar could do passable faces, male or female. Cauvin had a knack for birds—sharp-beaked hawks, mostly—and hands. He could turn a rock into a fist in an afternoon. There was a merchant whose warehouse door was framed with Cauvin's fists.

"Sure you're not taking your woman out to those ruins? You seem damned determined to get there day after day."

Cauvin shook his head. "Not froggin' likely." He asked, "How's Bec this morning?" to steer the conversation away from tender subjects.

"Haven't seen him, but the swelling was down last night. He should be sprightly. Boys heal fast, even spindly ones. The wife's got the fire up. Breakfast's cold, but there'll be hot supper. I stuck around last night, helped the cooks with the pots and got us a leftover boar's head. The wife had it in the pot before sunup. Now, that's something to look forward to."

Cauvin nodded—red meat three froggin' days in a row—but Mina's cold breakfasts were nothing to celebrate. "I'll be behind you," he told Grabar. "Flower needs her grain."

And Cauvin needed to move his new knife from its hiding place to the back of the cart, where he wrapped it in canvas and tucked it beneath his tools. He felt sheep-shite foolish for hiding the weapon; he *intended* to wear it openly, proudly . . . but not until he felt froggin' confident that he wore it properly. When Mina or Grabar asked where he'd gotten it, he'd tell them—the idea came to him like lightning—he'd froggin' tell them that he'd found it while smashing stone out at the redwall ruins.

Pleased with his uncommon cleverness, Cauvin entered the kitchen. Mina stood guard over the hearth. Grabar and Bec were eating through a cold breakfast of stale bread slopped in a buttery mixture of stewpot dregs and raw eggs. Cauvin had gone hungry often enough that he'd eat whatever was in front of him, even dregs and eggs. The trick was to hold his breath and gulp as fast as possible, bypassing the meal's taste, if not its texture.

Bec hadn't learned Cauvin's trick. The boy took small bites, chewed them endlessly, and stared at Cauvin the whole froggin' time. Cauvin dodged the boy's eyes, though not before noting that his bruises had faded and the swelling was almost unnoticeable. Grabar was right: Boys healed fast, a little too fast. Cauvin knew if he gave Bec the chance, he'd have froggin' company out at redwalls. That was reason enough to gag down his dregs and eggs before Bec was halfway through his.

This late in the year, fogs didn't lift, they sank into the froggin' ground, in lungs and guts. A fog like the one hanging over the stoneyard took Cauvin back to the palace and coughing memories. It wasn't sacrifice that claimed most of the orphans, but cold and raw fogs. The Hand said he was blessed because he never got sick; blessed meant he dug the graves.

Cauvin tossed the harness across Flower's back with a vigor that made the mule swipe sideways with a hind hoof. He took time to reassure her with a handful of oats. Mules were froggin' clever beasts. They knew what they deserved. A man could whip a mule bloody and it still wouldn't do what it shouldn't. The Hand didn't keep mules, not when they had sheep-shite orphans to do their work.

Cauvin was squatted down, attaching Flower's harness to the cart, when he saw Bec's feet and legs in front of him. "No," he said, answering the boy's questions before they were asked.

"I've got our lunch. Momma's made bear's-head stew to keep the cold from our bones."

"Boar's head," Cauvin corrected. "What makes you think 'our bones' are going somewhere?"

"Grandfather's got to eat." He set a cloth-wrapped crock into the cart and climbed in after it.

"Shalpa's cloak! You *told* Mina?"

"Never! I asked, since breakfast was cold, if we couldn't have hot lunch. She said we could have some skimmings, so I filled a pot. She said I should bring it out quick."

Skimmings were a vast improvement over breakfast, but Cauvin wouldn't let his stomach get the better of his head. "She didn't say anything about letting you go out to the ruins in a fog, did she?"

Bec didn't answer.

Cauvin gave the last harness strap a hard yank, stood up, and targeted his foster brother. "Frog all, Bec— How much trouble are you trying to land me in? Get back inside before your mother comes out here looking for you."

The boy braced himself into a corner. "Froggin' no. I'm working for Grandfather, writing for him. I missed yesterday. I'm froggin' not going to miss today, too."

"Watch your mouth. Mina'll have *my* hide when she hears you talking like that."

"Then I froggin' won't let her."

Cauvin steadied himself. "Get out, Bec. Thanks for the pot; I'll share it with him, if the rain and fog haven't done him in, but you're not going anywhere except back into the kitchen—"

"Froggin' no."

"Bec—"

"I'm going with you, and we better get going before Momma comes looking."

The boy had always been persistent, but flat-footed defiance was something new.

Cauvin wasn't pleased. "I'm warning you—"

"And I'm warning *you*: I'm telling Momma and Poppa that when you came back from seeing *her* you had a great big knife tied around your leg."

"You've been dreaming."

"Yeah? Then why's it all wrapped up here in the cart?"

Bec held up the wrapped weapon. He unwound the canvas and drew a finger's length of sharpened steel from the sheath.

"Put that down . . . now!"

Bec shed the sheath and the canvas. He pointed the knife at Cauvin's chest. The boy wasn't serious—at least Cauvin didn't think he was—but that didn't make the moment less dangerous.

"*Now,* Bec. Now . . . and get out of the froggin' cart."

"I'll tell them what happened night before last . . . what *really* happened, how you dragged me with you and left me alone and how I got lost and beaten up."

"That's a froggin' damned *lie,*" Cauvin snarled, and brought his fists up.

The boy had earned the thrashing of his life, and Cauvin was ready to give it to him, though new bruises would only make Bec's lies more believable. If Cauvin gave in to his rage, he'd need the gods' own luck to sleep in the loft another night. For that—and because in his gut he'd regret pounding the snot out of the boy no matter his lies—Cauvin relaxed.

The boy crowed, "I won't say a *word* . . . if we get going quick." He sheathed the knife and tucked the canvas around it.

Cauvin didn't trust himself to say a word as he led Flower from the stoneyard. They weren't clear of Pyrtanis Street when Bec started talking as if there hadn't been an arm's length of steel between them moments earlier.

"Poppa said he saw you leaving the feast last night, alone and walking toward the Maze. Did you see *her*?"

Sweet Eshi! "Yes," Cauvin growled.

"Did you jump the broom and make babies?"

"No."

"But you will, won't you?"

"Leave it be, Bec. It doesn't concern you."

The cart was quiet, but not for long. "It doesn't matter, does it? if you jump the broom? Or if you've got a real bed with a feather mattress? You don't have a feather mattress, but *she* does, doesn't she? at the Unicorn? The feathers aren't important, are they? Except for the chickens and the rooster. Dogs don't need feathers, and feathers wouldn't turn Flower into a momma mule, would they? So, if it's not the broom and it's not the feathers, what is it?"

Cauvin brought Flower to a halt. He faced his brother. "What in the froggin' frozen hells of Hecath are you talking about?"

"Momma," the boy admitted, staring at the planks he sat on. "Poppa's face was all red when he came home last night. Momma said he'd had too much wine and blew out the candle, but he and Momma didn't go to sleep—and I couldn't, either, 'cause of the bed. *Creak-creak. Creak-creak*. I snuck outside—watched *you* come home. This morning, I asked Momma if they'd made a baby—'cause I'm ready to be older. She said the feathers were wore out. I don't understand what feathers have to do with it. Or brooms. I heard Batty Dol say that Honald's daughter Syleen jumps the broom with a different man every night, but Syleen's got no babies. She doesn't have a feather bed, either—I looked, she sleeps in straw, same as you. So, what about *her*—about Reenie—*she's* got a feather mattress and *she* jumps the broom same as Syleen—just not with you. Why doesn't *she* have babies?"

"Leorin's *not* like Syleen!" Cauvin sputtered before he could stop himself.

"Maybe not every night, but some nights."

"You don't know that—"

"She lives above the froggin' *Unicorn,* Cauvin—everybody knows."

"Everybody doesn't know what he's talking about."

"Momma does. Momma says—" Bec cleared his throat and launched a dead-on imitation of his mother's voice. "It's a shame, a god's own shame. We took him in, raised him as our own, and what does he do? Chases a whore in the Maze. Gods forgive me, but *they* knew what they were about when they plucked him up. Him and his whore. Alike as peas. No surprise they found each other in that cess of a tavern. Blood will out. It always does. I bar the door every night. No telling when they'll come to slaughter us—"

Mina thought Cauvin had a foul tongue in his mouth; Grabar, too. They thought his language was a bad influence on their precious son, but they'd never heard him use the words he used to quiet his foster brother. Bec certainly didn't know them, except by tone. His face paled, and he wedged himself into the farthest corner of the cart.

Cauvin covered his eyes in shame. It wasn't Bec's fault he listened to his mother. Frog all, most of what Bec heard was the froggin' truth, or froggin' close enough that, angry as he was, Cauvin couldn't call Mina a liar.

"It's not true, is it?" Bec managed, little more than a whisper. "You and Reenie, you're not really alike?"

"I've known her since I was younger than you, sprout. We remember the same things, all of them; but froggin' shite, Bec—you *know* we don't agree about everything."

The boy blushed but sobered quickly to ask, in a quivering whisper, "The Hand marked both of you for sacrifice, and you both survived?"

"Who told you that?" Cauvin demanded because he knew for froggin' sure *he* hadn't.

"Pendy. Right before . . . before she *died.* She said you and Reenie were sweet on each other *before* and when she disappeared, you thought they'd killed her. It made you moon-mad, and you got yourself in trouble just so they'd sacrifice you, too. And you *did* disappear, just like *her,* but you came back. Pendy said once you saw *her* again, you wouldn't look at another girl. She said it was sorcery."

"Pendy?" Cauvin mumbled.

He would have burst out swearing again if he could have gotten the words past the memory of Pendy's face. Gods all be damned, Cauvin had never thought of Pendy as anything but a tagalong, a little sister who'd landed in the pits years after him. Pendy was one of the lucky ones: The Torch had locked her up, too, and her parents—her gods-all-be-damned real parents—showed up at the palace before the smoke had settled. Pendy had nightmares, though, and for years she showed up at the stoneyard once or twice a week to tell Cauvin about them. She'd weep and tremble, and he'd wrap his arms around her, rocking her gently until the shaking stopped. But not the way he held Leorin. Frog all, Cauvin hadn't stopped looking at Pendy because Leorin had come back; he'd *never* looked at her as a woman, and he'd never asked himself why she'd stopped coming to the stoneyard or why she'd cut her own throat not long after that.

Froggin' gods—how could he have been so froggin' *blind*?

The Hand had known him best. They put bronze slugs in his fists because he was too sheep-shite stupid for anything else. He couldn't see anything he didn't expect—just like Jubal's sheep-shite fools wearing their hawk masks. No froggin' wonder that the Torch had told him to pick up a mask, not a sword.

Froggin' Lord Molin Torchholder used Cauvin the same as the Hand had used him: strong back, hard fists, sheep-shite head. He was no match for them, simple as that. But Cauvin was still bigger than Bec, still able to cower the boy with a scowl.

"You keep your mouth shut about me and Leorin, you hear? And don't go spouting words like 'sorcery' when you don't know what in froggin' hell you're talking about. You especially keep your mouth shut when we get to the ruins. I don't want the froggin' Torch hearing *anything* about me that he doesn't already know—if there's anything that froggin' pud doesn't already know. The Torch plays games with men, Bec, and he's been doing it since before we were born . . . before Grabar was froggin' born. You listening?"

Bec nodded, but he didn't agree. "Grandfather needs you more than you need him, so if he's playing games, you're going to win, Cauvin."

Cauvin snorted. Froggin' sure, the boy knew how to get himself out of trouble. "I wish I had your faith." He slipped a hand beneath Flower's bridle and got her moving again.

"It's not faith, Cauvin. Grandfather's old and dying. You and me, we're his last chance, and he's too full of himself to admit he's made a mistake with us. But, Cauv—*she's* different. Pendy was afraid of her, ice-water scared. She—when the Hand cut her—you know—to take out her heart, they couldn't find one."

The stiffening of Cauvin's back was all the response Bec got to that froggin' remark. Three times the boy said he was sorry and three times Cauvin didn't so much as froggin' twitch. He threaded Flower through the tangled Hillside streets, pausing only to buy a skewer of roasted fish from a peddler—anything to get the tastes out of his mouth. There was enough meat to share with Bec, if Cauvin had wanted to. He didn't.

When they were clear of the city, Cauvin stopped the mule long enough to retrieve his new knife and bind it to his leg, his left leg this time, instead of his right. Bec watched him with wide, anxious eyes. If he'd said something, Cauvin would have responded, but the boy hadn't recovered his spirits—Cauvin didn't doubt that he would—and Cauvin wasn't ready to break the ice.

The fog thinned as they approached the ruins. By the time Flower was splashing along what was left of the graveled paths, they were bathed in sunshine. Bec said "Where . . . ?" when the cart didn't stop where it had two days before, but he didn't finish his question, so Cauvin said nothing until they were on the far side of what had been the main house, in sight of the root cellar and in sight of the Torch.

Somehow—Cauvin didn't want to know how—the geezer had dragged himself to the light. He'd propped himself against the wooden uprights of the cellar entrance. The black staff lay across his legs, which were sticking out straight in front of him. His head was cocked back, soaking up sunlight and not moving so much as an eyelid as the cart crunched to a stop.

"He's dead," Cauvin said softly, for himself.

Bec beat Cauvin to the cellar. The boy seized a withered hand and the old pud awakened with a jolt that must have hurt. He studied them, eyes black as midnight, yet burning. No froggin' wonder he was known as the Torch. But the Torch was ancient, despite his fire, and needed several moments to get his words flowing.

"I wasn't expecting you today."

"I'll wager that's true," Cauvin agreed. He gave Bec a swat across the shoulders. The boy got out of the way. "I went to your froggin' funeral, then I followed your froggin' directions." He unwound the blue mask from his belt and shook it. "I went to the froggin' Unicorn. I waited there 'til past midnight. Your armsmaster never showed up, Lord Torchholder. You made a sheep-shite fool out of me . . . and you owe me for two mugs of ale."

The Torch's gaze fell to Cauvin's thigh, which was square in front of his face. No way the old pud wasn't looking at the froggin' dagger.

"Seems you helped yourself to more than a mask. Sell the knife, if you need to get yourself drunk. It's Ilbarsi. You should be able to get thirty soldats for it, even in Sanctuary."

Never mind that the Torch couldn't stand, that there was mud on his black woolen robe, or that his skin, wherever it wasn't still dark with bruises, was so thin that Cauvin could see through it. Never mind any of that, because the Torch's tongue remained sharper than any knife.

"You used me. You sent me down to the Maze and you knew what would happen—"

"Couldn't keep your hands to yourself, could you?" the pud asked with a froggin' grin.

"Why?" Cauvin countered. "Why play me with sorcery, then leave me sitting in the Unicorn waiting for a man who froggin' sure doesn't exist."

"Oh, he exists all right, pud," the Torch said an instant before Cauvin heard footfalls that weren't Bec's or the mule's.

A stranger emerged from the bushes that grew around the cellar entrance. His clothing was a study in shades of black: tunic, breeches, high boots, and a leather cloak rolled back from his left shoulder. His hair was a bit lighter and worn long with braids to control it near his face. Not a Wrigglie style, nor Imperial, nor Irrune. The braids were touched with a few strands of gray. Cauvin guessed the man was maybe ten or fifteen years older than he was, but it was only a guess.

For adornment, the stranger wore a chain hung around his neck and wide bracelets over his wrists. They were black and shiny and not like any familiar metal. Cauvin looked for weapons—if the man was an armsmaster, there should have been some, but except for a knobbed pommel rising out of the stranger's right boot, Cauvin saw none. Which didn't mean Cauvin was reassured; when their eyes finally met, the stranger looked through him like a froggin' ghost.

The stranger and the Torch exchanged words that weren't any sort of Ilsigi dialect Cauvin recognized and weren't—judging from the confusion he gleaned from a quick glance in Bec's direction—Imperial either. When Cauvin heard his own name tossed about, he'd had enough.

"If you're going to froggin' talk about me, froggin' talk about me so I can froggin' understand what you're saying."

The Torch swiveled his head around, as slow as Flower on a hot day in summer. "Soldt says you are the man with the hawkmask that he saw at the Unicorn last night."

"Froggin' *hell* he did. I looked the commons over when I got there, and I kept an eye on the door the whole time I was there—and he wasn't there."

"I was there when you came in, lad, and there when you left. I would have joined you, had I trusted the company you kept."

The stranger had an accent Cauvin couldn't place and a smile he didn't like. Feeling cockier than he had a right to feel, Cauvin restated his claim. "The Unicorn was dead-quiet last night. I could see who sat at every froggin' table, and you weren't there, or you'd know that I came alone, I wasn't keeping company with anyone."

"Except a woman. Which is why, although I saw you clearly—You tucked the mask over your belt and you bore your knife on the right last night. Is it your habit to rearrange your weapons each day?—I chose not to reveal myself."

"He's young yet," the Torch said, coming unexpectedly to Cauvin's defense and giving him a chance to scrutinize the stranger again. "And full of himself. Succumbing to the charms of a Unicorn wench is an accident that befalls most young men in this town once or twice."

"Begging your pardon, Lord Torchholder"—Soldt gave the Torch his title—"but, upon inquiry, I find it is not once or twice, and this wench is not the Unicorn's common breed."

"What breed, then?"

Soldt shrugged. His cloak slipped. As he rearranged it Cauvin caught sight of a collar and hood. With that, he recognized the faceless man who'd watched him—and Leorin—the previous evening. That made the stranger a froggin' spy, which to Cauvin's mind was worse than a froggin' liar. He didn't take a swing at Soldt—armed or not, the stranger had a fighter's aspect—but he got close enough to smell his breath as he shouted—

"Leorin's not a froggin' whore! She works at the Unicorn because there's good money to be made there . . . *honest* money. When we've got enough between us, we'll marry, but until then she's got nothing to be ashamed of. I won't listen to you talk about her as if she were a whore, and I won't stand for being spied on."

"Trouble doubled, Lord Torchholder," Soldt said calmly, turning away from a threat he obviously didn't consider serious. "You can't lean on a man who's burdened by love; and the girl herself, my lord, you'd tremble to see her by candlelight."

"Would I?" the Torch asked, as arrogant with Soldt as he was with Cauvin. "At my age, I'd count it a god's boon to tremble at the sight of a woman."

"It's not her beauty, though that is considerable—"

"Say it straight," Cauvin snarled, getting in Soldt's face again, now that he could froggin' see where this was headed. "I've heard it before and so has she—as far back as she can froggin' remember. Leorin's the froggin' image of Sanctuary's last sheep-shite prince, Kadakithis. She's got Imperial hair and Imperial eyes. If she showed up on their doorstep, the Enders would have to take her in, and if she approached a madam on the Street of Red Lanterns, she'd be rich in a week. But she stays at the Unicorn because once he's paid, the Stick sees that she's left alone."

The Torch's eyes narrowed. "How old is this woman?"

"Too young to be legitimate," Soldt answered before Cauvin. "Too young by half, but the resemblance is uncanny. I can think of a few notables in Ranke who'd claim her in a heartbeat, just to start rumors. One would like to glimpse her parents—"

"One froggin' sure would!" Cauvin returned Soldt's words with a snarl. "You aren't listening—the damned Hand scooped Leorin up and dumped her in the pits, same as me—"

"Impossible," the Torch insisted. He seized his staff and tried, with no success, to stand up. "Nonsense and impossible. I misplaced your face, pud, but a youth who resembled Prince Kadakithis, girl or boy, *that* I would have remembered."

Cauvin would have liked to call the froggin' old pud a liar, but that would have made him the liar instead. "You never saw her," he admitted. "They'd pulled Leorin out of the pits before the Irrune got there. A couple winters before. There was one—" he lost his voice as a Hand's face floated up from memory. Lean, scarred, and the cruelest of the cruel, the Hand he and the other orphans called the Whip had taken an interest in Leorin from the beginning. She seldom spoke of him, but Cauvin was certain that he was the reason her sleep was broken and haunted. "He took her behind the walls, and took her out of Sanctuary, too, just before you arrived with the Irrune."

The man who couldn't stand on his own two feet managed to give Cauvin a look that hurt. " 'Behind the walls,' you say? So this man initiated her into the Bloody Mother's priesthood?"

The palace orphans had their own way of talking. It wasn't a separate language—the words were ordinary Wrigglie—but the meanings changed . . . doubled or even tripled. "Behind the walls" meant inside the palace, but the phrase also described someone who was doing favors for the Hand or who'd become one of them. Cauvin hadn't expected the froggin' Torch to know the hidden meanings.

"Don't gape like a gaffed fish, boy. You were there; you know what I'm talking about."

"They took favorites," Cauvin admitted, shamed by the shakiness in his voice. "Women, mostly—*girls,* but boys, if they were the pretty kind—" He stole a glance at Bec who, thank the froggin' gods, seemed not to be paying attention.

"Leorin, from what you tell me, was very pretty. You, I imagine, were not. She was taken behind the walls; you weren't. You were in the pits when the Irrune stormed the palace; she wasn't. What should that tell me about your ladylove, Cauvin?"

"Nothing!" Cauvin shouted, suddenly on the verge of blind rage . . . blind panic. "Nothing. It doesn't mean what you're saying it means. People went behind the froggin' walls, people came out—" He tugged at his hair and stared at the sky because he couldn't hold the Torch's stare. "Frog all, Torchholder—they took *me* behind their froggin' walls, into the room where they kept their froggin' statue of *Her*. Gave me a choice, and when I said no, next thing I knew I was bent over backward on the froggin' altar with a black knife cutting into my chest. I thought—I thought I was done for, but I walked out, Torchholder, same as I walked in. I got the scars to say it was no froggin' dream—" Cauvin peeled back the neck of his shirt to reveal the bronze slug and a handspan's length of the knotted, pale lines that crossed his chest. "I kept my heart."

"I know you did," the Torch said softly.

Cauvin heard, but wasn't listening. "I didn't change, and Leorin didn't either. We both knew everything they told us was lies. How we'd been chosen to do the Mother's work. How we wouldn't need tattoos because the Mother would stain our hands with real blood. How we were going to carry the Mother along the coast to Ranke. The sea would turn red for us, the sky black. Our army would grow until nothing could stop us, and the Mother would come down to remake the world. It was all lies, and even if it wasn't, it still wasn't the truth 'cause we weren't an army, just sheep-shite and sweat. If we were the vanguard, then either the Mother didn't plan to win Her wars, or She sure-as-shite didn't need an army. No matter what they told us, we knew froggin' better than to believe."

The Torch nodded. "You and a handful of others. You kept more than your hearts, Cauvin, you kept your lives. Arizak, Zarzakhan, and I questioned every orphan we pulled out of those filthy pens. We saved the ones who hadn't forgotten what it meant to be human, and they were the only ones we saved. Are *you* listening to me now, Cauvin? *We* scoured the palace, Arizak, Zarzakhan, and I. We put out the poisoned meat and we set the fire afterward. Except for you and a handful of others, we spared no one. No one, Cauvin, not a priest, not a slave, not an orphan, no matter how young.

"The Bloody Hand was a plague on the soul of man. If we had the slightest doubt about an orphan, we did not send him—or her—to the safe rooms. We judged them, and we killed them. *All* of them."

"Not quite all," Soldt corrected. The stranger had been so quiet, Cauvin had forgotten him.

The Torch sighed. "No, not all of them. Some got away and stayed hidden for ten years. Damn. That's a long time for a man with red hands to wear gloves and plot vengeance. Or a young woman with those particular features, for that matter. Someone should have noticed. Where's she been?"

"Hiding in the Vulgar Unicorn," Soldt answered.

Soldt was a foreigner, so he probably thought that was explanation enough. When sheep-shite foreigners came to Sanctuary, they didn't know which way to the froggin' ocean, but they'd heard of the Vulgar Unicorn. Cauvin could think of several Hillside taverns whose reputations were so unsavory he wouldn't cross their froggin' thresholds on a gold-coin bet, but from sunrise to sunset, the Vulgar Unicorn was the stuff of froggin' legend.

The Torch was a foreigner, too, but he didn't think like one. "Not for ten years, Soldt. No woman works the Unicorn for ten years—not without my knowing that she's got Imperial looks. She wouldn't survive."

"Leorin survived the pits. She survived the Whip. There's nothing at the Unicorn she can't handle. And I didn't say she'd been there for ten years."

"That's true, you didn't. Where did she hide herself?"

"Not in Sanctuary. I told you, the Whip pulled out right before you arrived, and took Leorin with him. As soon as they were clear of Sanctuary, she killed the Whip with his own knife, then took his plan, his disguise, his money for herself. She wound up north of Ilsig city, but the dreams followed her, and when she ran out of road, she turned around and came back. Our paths crossed two years ago—a little more than two years. She said she'd been back since winter."

"It fits, Lord Torchholder—some of it. I made inquiries. The woman calling herself Leorin showed up about three years ago. She told a story about Ranke, kidnapping, and a family that wouldn't take her back. With her looks, it was believable enough."

"So, what doesn't fit, Soldt?" the Torch asked. "What did you see that you didn't like?"

"It's not the way she looks. Leorin's got a Rankan face, yes—but Kadakithis was before my time. His face means nothing to me. It wasn't who she looks like that caught my attention; I learned that afterward. It's how she acts. She carries a shadow, Lord Torchholder, a cold shadow. She looks at a person and sees a thing. Even Cauvin. She took another man upstairs while he still sat watching her."

"Jealousy," the Torch said. "Women think it's an aphrodisiac, men, too."

"Jealousy without passion, Lord Torchholder? She led him past me. I looked into her eyes and felt her shadow. Leorin has no heart, my lord. Her soul's burnt down to ashes—"

Before Cauvin could call them both liars, the ruins echoed with the sound of Bec's small feet slapping across mud and gravel, headed gods-knew-where.

—"It is not for me to question," Soldt continued. "But whatever the truth of this woman's past, she's trouble doubled and not to be trusted—"

"You don't know!" Cauvin found his voice. "You weren't there. You think you know what went on in the pits, Torchholder, but you don't know the froggin' half of it. Shite for sure, Leorin's not like other women. The Whip didn't choose another woman, the froggin' bastard chose her. You think you sent me and the others to sheep-shite safe rooms. You think you did us some great froggin' favor. Do you know how many are left? I can tell you how they died. Harl hung himself not two months later. Canissi, the next spring. It goes on—Pendy gave up and slit her own throat last winter. Not counting the five who left town, there's three of us left, and since I met you, pud, now *I'm* having nightmares!"

"That's the point, Cauvin. Everything I see and hear from you tells me I was right to separate you. Everything I hear about Leorin tells me I'd have sent her back where they found her for her final meal."

Cauvin turned his back on the two men. Bec had gone to ground beside Flower and was feeding the mule frost-dried weeds. Their eyes met, then Bec darted out of sight on the far side of the cart.

"All right," he conceded, returning to the men. "All right. Leorin's cold. She doesn't get happy, but she doesn't get angry, either. Life's all the same to her, and only money matters. She can count money and lock it in a box—" A thought crossed Cauvin's mind, "and it's hard and cold, too. You, Soldt, you watched her go upstairs last night—you think that doesn't stick in my froggin' gut? But Leorin doesn't care about them, and she does care about me. When we're together, it's different; and if we weren't together, we'd both be alone.

"You must think I'm one great sheep-shite fool, too stupid to come out of the rain. I froggin' damn sure knew Leorin didn't walk out of the palace. I figured she was dead, but I didn't *know* that, any more than I froggin' knew what happened to the Whip, or Baldy, or the rest of those Hand bastards. I hoped they were dead, and I'll go on hoping as long as I live. So, listen close, Torchholder—when I spotted Leorin one afternoon and I hadn't seen her for eight froggin' years, the first thing I did was ask her how she'd gotten away when practically no one else had and where she'd been hiding.

"That's when she told me about gutting the Whip and lighting north on her own. She said she came back 'cause here at least she knows why she has the nightmares."

The Torch gave Cauvin a chance to catch his breath before saying, with his sharp tongue: "I think I'd have nightmares, too, if I'd given my heart and soul to Dyareela."

"She didn't!"

"She'd hardly tell you if she had, now, would she, pud? You wear your heart for all to see. What would you have done if she'd told you she'd decided to take the Whip's place along with his disguise?"

Cauvin had wrestled with the question two years ago. "I believe what she told me," he said after a moment, and realized his belief wasn't as strong as it had been an hour ago. "What else could I do? She can't *prove* anything. Shite for sure, I can't froggin' *prove* that I'm not in league with the Hand right this very moment."

"He's got a point," Soldt commented. "You can demonstrate that something is, but how do you demonstrate that it isn't?"

"The Savankh," the Torch replied quickly, as though he'd been interrupted.

"Which is?" Soldt asked, betraying his foreign roots.

Even Cauvin knew what the Savankh was—a slender bone rod that stood for Imperial power in the hands of a prince or governor. The rod would fry the hand of any sheep-shite fool who told a lie while holding it, at least it would, if Savankala were paying attention. But that wasn't all Cauvin knew about the Savankh. "Nobody's seen a Savankh in Sanctuary since last prince lit out."

The Torch nodded, lost in his thoughts.

"All gods can hear the truth, can't They? And whatever a god can do, so can His froggin' priest, right? So, Torchholder, can't you say a froggin' prayer to prove her and me right?"

"In a temple with an altar, an acolyte beside me, and a bowl of flaming unguents, assuming I had an altar, an acolyte, and unguents that haven't been seen in Sanctuary since before the Savankh disappeared. *And* assuming your Leorin isn't sitting snug under *her* goddess's protection. The gods aren't active in Sanctuary these days, especially when it comes to meddling with the devout—which is a good thing, pud, until you need justice or information. I'd do better with holding a rod of red-hot iron under your ladylove's bare feet than I'd do with a prayer—but I don't suppose you'd stand for that."

Cauvin blinked. "You can't be froggin' serious—"

"No," the Torch assured him. "Torture's not perfect. Most people say what they think will end the pain, and of the rest, you can't be sure if they're telling the simple truth or they're simply true believers."

"We're back where we started," Soldt said. "Strong suspicions but no way to get past them."

"You could believe me," Cauvin shouted. "I'm telling you: I know Leorin, I know the Hand— Frog all, I'd know if she was one of them!"

Cauvin would never know if it was his shouting or something else, but Flower chose that moment to get ornery. With an echoing bray, she kicked the cart with her hooves then reared up in the traces. Bec—who was the likelier cause of the mule's outburst—dangled from the bridle.

There were no questions in Cauvin's mind. His feet were moving as soon as his eyes perceived the danger. It was his own sheep-shite fault: Once he'd seen the Torch fallen against the cellar way, he'd abandoned Flower—left the mule harnessed and standing in mud. Flower didn't like mud and with good reason, considering the froggin' damage it could do to her hooves. She could have hauled the cart ten steps to drier ground, but Flower was a mule; she'd take care of herself, if she froggin' had to, but it was Cauvin's job to take care of her and she had ways to see that he did.

"I was just trying to lead her to grass," Bec insisted, once his two feet and Flower's four were planted.

The mule was giving Cauvin the evil eye. Her left rear hoof flashed out when he unbuckled the harness. Another finger's breadth and he could have hired out on Red Lantern Street. But *that* would have been an accident. In the ten years Cauvin had known her, Flower's hooves had never struck his flesh, except by accident.

She stood patiently while Cauvin undid the other buckles.

"You've got to unharness her first," he explained to Bec.

The boy was staring at him.

"You heard everything?" Cauvin asked.

"Not everything. Almost."

"You're doing a good job of keeping your froggin' mouth shut. Don't change."

"I don't like her, Cauvin. I try real hard, but I don't. She's mean, Cauvin. She treats you mean."

"I'm mean, too. Comes from how I grew up."

"You're not mean, Cauvin, but you're in trouble, aren't you?"

"You stay here with Flower," Cauvin replied, not answering the question.

Soldt and the Torch were talking deep until Soldt saw Cauvin coming closer.

"There is a way to settle this about Leorin," the Torch began. "If you're game."

"Tell me how, first."

"None of the paths of sorcery are available—not prayer or magic, and witchcraft would require Leorin's presence in some form, if not her cooperation—"

*Witchcraft,* Cauvin thought. Wrigglies and Imperials could agree on at least one thing: no witches in Sanctuary. It was froggin' odd that the Torch would even say the word aloud.

"And we've ruled out torture. That leaves the S'danzo."

"Fortune-tellers!" Cauvin sputtered. If witchcraft was forbidden, then the S'danzo and their froggin' painted cards were fit only for sheep-shite fools. "You won't believe me, but you'd believe some greasy-hair, fat, and addled woman sitting in the dark?"

"If you could find her," Soldt said, as froggin' surprised by the notion as Cauvin had been. "The fortune-tellers in this city's bazaar may be calling themselves S'danzo, but I'm not taking their word for it. According to the S'danzo up and down the coast, Sanctuary's still cursed as far as they're concerned, and they're not coming back until the children of their enemies, and their children's children are dead and gone."

That was a revelation about Soldt, and while he was trying to make sense of it, Cauvin nearly missed the Torch's reply.

"—will they know that?—Unless they've got eyes and ears in place."

Soldt hissed through his teeth, which meant Cauvin didn't have to.

"The Sight's real," the Torch insisted. "There's not many who've got it, and few of those can use it, but the Sight's a gift the gods Themselves envy— The S'danzo won't worship a god. Clever women. They take their money up front and won't leave a debt owing past sundown, either. Beyond their cards, there's nothing they need. No tokens. No powders or spirits. Just ask the question and wait for the answer. I knew a seeress—" he stopped talking suddenly and stared at the ruins. There was nothing there that Cauvin could see. Then, just as suddenly, the old pud started talking again. "She said a question and its answer were twins, born together and inseparable. She heard the question, then looked at her cards and saw the answer."

"Where can we find this woman?" Soldt asked.

"She died, but there's another. She won't scry for gold or silver, but I've got a gift that will tempt her. I've kept it hidden, waiting for the right time."

"Where will we find it?" Another question from Soldt.

"Buried in a box beneath the bazaar—"

"Frog all, not *another* sheep-shite box!"

The Torch paid no attention to Cauvin's outburst.

"Get me parchment—the boy brought a sheet the other day. I'll draw you a map . . . and how to find Elemi. She won't be glad to see you, but you'll manage . . ." The Torch leaned back against the cellar wall. "You'll manage."

His eyes fluttered and closed.

"Froggin' shite—"

They opened.

"You want the truth, don't you, pud? Get me parchment."

# Chapter Eleven

There was a game Bec had made up at home in the stoneyard when he was left to himself—

In truth, all of Bec's games were games he'd made up for himself and games he played by himself. His momma didn't approve of the other youngsters on Pyrtanis Street. She didn't let him out the gate unless he was with her, or Poppa, or Cauvin. And she would never let him go out with Cauvin if she knew half the places Cauvin took him. The only reason Bec knew anyone his own age was because of Cauvin. Cauvin knew people in every quarter of the city and let Bec roam while he visited with them.

Sure, sometimes Bec broke the rules and sneaked out of the stoneyard when Momma was distracted, but the Pyrtanis youngsters called him a momma's boy. They teased him with words and sticks. So, mostly, he was a momma's boy, keeping her happy, waiting for the chance to tag along after Cauvin, and making up games like Are you the one?

The object of the game was simple: pick who among the men and women who visited the stoneyard actually bought stone. Since Bec both made the rules and kept the score, it was easy, but not challenging, to be the champion. To keep himself amused, Bec made the game tougher and tougher until Poppa started asking him, after a potential customer departed—

*Is he coming back? Is she going to buy?*

Bec hadn't been wrong in over a year. He'd learned that watching Poppa was as important as watching the strangers. It wasn't just what people said, it was how they reacted—how close they stood, who leaned forward and who backed away, who told jokes, who laughed, and how. One man's laugh might sound the same as another's but mean the opposite because of how the man moved while laughing, or how Poppa stood while listening. Above all, an Are-you-the-one? champion had to pay attention to the little things and keep an open mind. An Are-you-the-one? champion also learned that the game would answer questions that had nothing to do with selling salvaged stone.

At the beginning—before Bec decided he really didn't *want* to hear the conversation—Cauvin, Grandfather, and the stranger named Soldt stood so far apart that they couldn't have touched fingertips if they'd tried. After Flower got ornery and Cauvin had returned from calming her, the men were, if anything, farther apart than they'd been when Bec ran, but gradually, as their conversation got quieter, they closed ranks. Before long, Cauvin and Soldt were practically rubbing shoulders, as if the two of them made common cause as they talked with Grandfather, who pressed himself against the root-cellar doorway until the very end, when he leaned forward and backed the younger men off.

No surprise, then, that when Grandfather settled back against the doorway as if for a nap, Soldt and Cauvin peeled off together. They headed straight for Bec.

"Get in the cart," Cauvin ordered when he was close enough for conversation.

Bec leapt to his feet. "Where're we going?"

"You're going home."

"Home?" Bec protested. "I didn't do anything wrong. I was just trying to help when Flower acted up; you said so yourself. It wasn't my fault!"

"I didn't say anything was. We're not staying out here today, and you're going back to the stoneyard."

"That's not fair! I want to come with you!"

"Forget it."

"Then, let me stay here— If I go home now, Momma and Poppa will wonder where *you're* going when you should be working. Let me stay here, and we can pretend we were all together." Cauvin didn't answer immediately, and that got Bec's curiosity burning. "Where are you going? You're not going to miss supper, are you? You wouldn't leave Sanctuary, would you?"

"The boy made a good point," the stranger said. He had a deep, yet soft, voice, an accent Bec couldn't place, and a manner unlike any he'd encountered before.

"Which point?" Bec demanded.

Cauvin had yet to answer Bec's first questions and didn't get the chance to answer his last either because Soldt did.

"There's no keeping secrets around sprouts," Soldt said. "Send him—"

"I can *so* keep a secret! Tell me anything and, pain of death, I won't tell anyone what you've said."

"No need to attract attention. I've used Lord Torchholder's maps before. They're good. We'll be done before sunset. Let the boy stay here—unless he's the wandering type."

"I'm not!" Bec insisted. He would have given the toes on his left foot to unravel the mysteries of Grandfather's map with Cauvin and Soldt, but he knew the difference between possible and impossible. He met Cauvin's eyes with a silent plea that all his past misadventures be forgotten.

"It would be simplest to leave the boy here, if you trust him," Soldt said, acknowledging Cauvin's authority where Bec was concerned, but clearly inviting Cauvin to agree with him.

"If all goes well," Cauvin said with a tone that was far from agreeable. "And if it doesn't, he's a boy outside the walls with an old man who should have died yesterday."

Soldt scowled at Cauvin. "Best for you, lad, that you shed the habit of borrowing trouble. If the boy's not safe here, then he's not safe anywhere."

Bec held his breath, fearing an outbreak of Cauvin's legendary temper. All the signs were there: shoulders rising, neck thickening, lips going thin and pale, eyes, too. But Cauvin didn't shout. He cupped his hand beneath Bec's chin and made sure that their eyes were locked as he said—

"Count yourself lucky, sprout, and don't do anything to shame us."

"Not a single thing," Bec agreed, nodding free of Cauvin's callused hand. "I'll get the ink and parchment and write down more of Grandfather's stories."

"Grandfather?" Soldt laughed.

If Poppa had asked about Soldt, Bec would have said, No, he's not the one, he won't buy stone, but stone wasn't the question. Soldt had flanked Cauvin's temper, he'd gotten Bec a day of freedom, and he thought it was funny that Bec had called the great Lord Torchholder "Grandfather." No doubt about it, Soldt was a man to be reckoned with—a man who created changes. Bec felt it when he led them to the weathered cupboard where he'd stowed the parchment and ink.

Sometimes grown-ups talked in names and places, as though their words couldn't be heard by anyone whose head stopped short of their eyes and sometimes they talked with "he's" and "she's," "there's" and "later's" that had no meanings by themselves. Bec endured both of those times while Grandfather sketched a map. It wouldn't have been so bad if he'd been able to get a glimpse of the words Grandfather wrote between the lines.

Cauvin couldn't make head nor tail of a map no matter what was written on it; he'd never have thought to block Bec's view. Soldt, on the other hand—Soldt who'd been so helpful a few moments earlier—kept himself between Bec and the map like a dog guarding its bone. Bec sidled right; Soldt did the same. Bec sidled left, so did Soldt. Then he snatched up the parchment before the ink could possibly be dry.

With the map hidden from Bec's curiosity in the inside flap of Soldt's fancy leather scrip, the two able-bodied men linked arms to carry Grandfather away from the cellar. They didn't reconstruct Grandfather's wooden bed, but arranged blankets on the remains of a broad-sill window overlooking the city and the sea, then set Grandfather atop them.

"The boy will serve until we get back," Soldt assured Grandfather without asking Bec. "Is there anything we can bring you?"

Grandfather winced as wrapping the blankets tight around his legs though the day had warmed, and Bec planned to shed at least one of his three tunics soon. "A new body? One without holes."

Soldt laughed, but Bec didn't think the joke—if it had been a joke—was funny, and neither did Cauvin. Cauvin spun on his heel, crunching hard through the gravel toward Sanctuary. Soldt had to break into a run to catch up.

It took that long, no longer, for Grandfather's eyes to close and his hand to lose its grip on the blanket wound over his hips. Bec called "Grandfather" just loud enough for a waking man to hear. When Grandfather didn't rouse, Bec tiptoed closer. The sounds of breath reassured him, though he'd hoped for better. Yesterday, when he'd lain in bed pretending to hurt worse than he did, Bec had set himself to recalling every word of Grandfather's long, rambling tale of Sanctuary's history. He thought he had made the story his. He'd hoped to show off a bit and get a second chance to learn the passages where his attention had slipped.

There wasn't a lot of time. One look at Grandfather, and Bec knew that even if the old man survived through tomorrow or the next day, he wasn't going to last out the winter, especially if they didn't find some place warm and civil for him to live.

That was Cauvin's problem, or maybe Soldt's. Bec's problem was to keep trouble from finding him the way it usually did. (Bec never *looked* for trouble, no matter what Momma, Poppa, or Cauvin said.) He checked Flower's hobbles, approaching her cautiously lest she decide to get ornery when Cauvin wasn't around to calm her. The mule nibbled a handful of grass Bec offered her, even though it was no different from the grass between her feet. He scrounged windfalls and tinder for a fire, which caught on the second attempt.

When he'd finished settling Momma's stewpot where it would heat but (hopefully) not boil over—and a pot of water, too, for tea—Bec had done all the chores he knew to do. He thought about smashing bricks, but a few practice swings convinced him that, today, trouble had set itself up in Cauvin's big hammer. That left him with the ruins themselves, a sprawling tangle of cracked walls and rubble several times the size of the stoneyard.

Bec didn't know how old the ruins were, but its bones had been picked clean. A few bits of bright paint clung to some of the inside walls, and there was one room where, beneath the leafy bits and dirt, the floor was made from tiny stones—each no bigger than his thumbnail—that formed portraits of the Ilsigi gods. Bec knew They were the Ilsigi gods because Their names were written—with Imperial letters—in bright, stone chips beside each portrait.

Father Ils had two eyes, not a thousand, and looked like Grandfather; all old men looked like one another. The god pointed at the largest, almost intact wall. Having nothing better to do (and hoping that trouble was content to stay with Cauvin's mallet), Bec set about examining every exposed brick and swath of plaster he could reach. He found nothing of interest on the wall, but the hollow sound and sinking feeling he got when he stood on a particular section of the floor captured his attention.

On hands and knees, the boy soon marked out a hollow square. Moments later he'd retrieved a chisel from the cart and not long after that he'd pried up a board covering the hollow. The wood crumbled in his hands and crawly bugs scrambled away from the sudden light Bec brought into their world. A true son of his mother, the first shapes Bec identified were black, round and flat . . . coins! He tapped one with the chisel to satisfy himself that beneath the crust the coins were . . . silver shaboozh!

Bec was rich with ten shaboozh, each larger than the Rankan soldats Cauvin had brought back from the seamen's place. He couldn't wait to see the look on Swift's face when he brought the coins to be cleaned and changed.

The coins weren't the only treasure in the foot-deep hollow, though Bec judged them the only part that would interest adults. Also in the hollow was a snake's shed skin. The snake had been thick as Bec's wrist and longer than he was tall. Beneath the snake skin, Bec found a goblet, now broken, that had been blown from astonishingly blue glass; and a string of glass beads—each different from all the others. The string was in worse shape than the wood. It disintegrated as soon as Bec touched it.

The coins were more valuable—too valuable to keep. Swift would turn them into padpols which would disappear, too. If Bec wanted a token to remember this day, the bead would be the best choice, better than the sharp glass fragments. He tucked one of the beads—a pretty white one marked with blue-green swirls—in his sleeve hem where it would be safe until he got home.

Poppa was proud that they never went hungry or cold, but Bec's clothes were all sewn from drab homespun, and the stoneyard house was drab, too. Color was precious. Bec snatched up a whole handful of glass beads.

There were other things in the hollow, though even Bec wouldn't call them treasures: a lamp that looked more like a shallow bowl than a proper lamp, or maybe call it a shallow bowl with an oil lamp bulging out of it. At the very bottom, Bec found a handful of clay-wrapped tubes.

Points of polished stone protruded from the tubes. Bec knew his stones; Poppa had taught him. Most of them were agates, one was dark and shiny obsidian, and one was green, greener than springtime apples or any stone Bec could name.

*Odd,* Bec thought. Odd that anyone would have rolled a pretty green stone in clay before stashing it in the hollow. He found a flat spot on the fallen wall, picked up a handy smashing stone from the ground, and began pounding at the clay—which proved harder to chip than he'd expected, almost as if it had been hard-baked in a kiln.

Determination was the key. Bit by bit, the brown clay flaked and revealed that the green stone was a signet stone, cut with shapes that might prove to be letters once the rest of the clay was gone. Bec pounded carefully, satisfying his curiosity.

Poppa had a signet stone—not a tube, more like a half-opened flower carved from a bit of soft marble. The three Ilsigi letters cut into the broad part of Poppa's seal didn't fully spell a word or have any meaning that Bec had been able to unravel; still the seal was precious. Whenever a wealthy patron came to purchase stone, Poppa would melt a great puddle of red wax onto parchment, then he, the patron, and witnesses called from the street would all slap their signets down on the puddle before it cooled to make a contract.

Momma, of course, wrote the contract—in Rankene, unless the patron insisted on Ilsigi. She could write Ilsigi, though she didn't like to. She could have used the signet, too. Poppa kept it hidden atop one of the rafters, where thieves wouldn't find it, but Momma knew where it was, and so did Bec.

Someday, she said, it would be his.

Or, maybe, Bec would make his mark with the apple green stone, now further exposed and revealing the beginnings of the head of what might be a horse, or even a *dragon*! A dragon was better than three Wrigglie letters that weren't part of his name.

Bec brought down his smashing stone and loosened a large clay chip. It *was* a dragon—he'd uncovered a wing!

"Boy! Boy, what have you found in there?" Grandfather's shout struck the back of Bec's head.

Bec turned around. He was alone in the room—alone as far as he could see. There was at least one wall, maybe three, between him and the ledge where Cauvin and Soldt had settled Grandfather. No way that Grandfather could have seen him open the hollow. For that matter, it didn't seem right that the old man could hear him pounding clay off the seal or that he could yell loud enough for Bec to hear him. Which meant he'd been imagining things again. That happened; when trouble didn't trip Bec up, his imagination did.

He resumed pounding.

"Boy! Bec! What are you doing? Come here!"

Bec spun around. He was still alone, still convinced that Grandfather couldn't possibly see him or shout loud enough to be heard, but his curiosity had a new target. Leaving the signet behind, he wandered toward the window ledge.

Grandfather was wide-awake and waiting. "Don't you come when you're called?" he demanded, using a tone that would have set Cauvin on a tirade and didn't please Bec much, either. "What have you found?"

Bec had questions of his own. "How do you know I found anything?"

"When a boy wanders off and isn't heard from for a respectable length of time, then I safely surmise that the boy has found something that holds his interest."

Bec wasn't sure what a safe surmise was, but it might explain why Momma seemed to come looking for him whenever he least wanted to be found. He vowed to remember Grandfather's wisdom—and to make noise from time to time. In return for the wisdom, he said, "I can show you. I found some stones. I'll go get them. Wait here."

He scampered off, chiding himself: *Where else is Grandfather going to wait?* He can't *walk*! . . .

Bec had snatched up the green stone, the obsidian, and two agates from the hollow when he heard a thump and a following noise that could have been a moan. Breaking into a run, Bec found Grandfather sprawled on the ground. He dropped the stones and raced to the old man's side.

It wasn't easy—Grandfather might be little more than skin and bones, but he was still bigger and heavier than Bec, and though he tried to hide it, Grandfather was in a lot of pain. His breath rasped and caught when Bec, hunched on his hands and knees, tried to lift him from below—the way he'd lever a stone out of mud.

"My staff . . . boy—" Grandfather wheezed. "Hand me . . . my staff."

Bec obeyed and between his efforts and Grandfather's grasp on the staff, they got him back onto the blankets and the windowsill.

"I've made fire. There's water heating, and stew. I can make tea," Bec offered.

Grandfather went to shake his head that he didn't want tea and nearly fell off the sill again. Not wanting to take chances, Bec stood himself at Grandfather's shoulder, ready in a heartbeat—in less than a heartbeat—to catch the old man before he fell.

"I'm sorry," he confessed, finger-combing dust and leaf bits from Grandfather's wispy hair. "They told me to watch you, and I didn't. I'm sorry—and I'm sorry that you hurt. I've got a coin—a shaboozh; I'll take it to Mother Sabellia's fane—Cauvin will. Her priests will accept it, even though it's an Ilsigi coin. They'll say prayers for you."

"A kind thought, boy—but save your shaboozh for yourself. I'm dying—putting it off as long as I can, but there's only so much a man can do when he's sucked himself full of Dyareelan poison."

"Poison!" That was a detail Cauvin had neglected to share. "Does it hurt?"

"Mercifully, no. The dead feel no pain, Bec, take comfort from that when your time comes. But the poison consumes me, nerve by muscle. Each time it takes a bite, I feel the loss. Each time I strain myself, I pay the price."

"When you shouted for me to come here, was that a strain? I should've been here. I shouldn't have wandered off. I'm sorry."

"I didn't shout, boy, and shouting's no worse than talking or breathing or eating. I died five days ago."

Without thinking, Bec retreated, leaving Grandfather to support his own weight against the wall. "I—I don't understand. You're alive." He could see Grandfather breathing, blinking, "You've got to be alive; you can't be dead. Dead people don't—don't breathe. They can't eat or drink."

Grandfather grinned. "They shouldn't, should they? But they used to. Your father's old enough. Ask him about the seasons when dead men held the Shambles."

"Dead men?" Bec couldn't help himself; he put his longest stride between himself and Grandfather.

"Don't be frightened, boy, those days will never return. I will lose my battle with death, but not before I've finished what I've started."

"What've you started?"

"Nothing that concerns you. Show me those stones you dropped."

Warily, Bec retrieved them, never turning his back on the old man. "I found them in a hole next to a wall. I'm cleaning them off. I'll keep the green one and maybe sell the others," he proudly told Grandfather as he dribbled the stones into a large, gnarled hand, which immediately closed over them.

"Would you desecrate a tomb and sell the bones you found within?"

Bec replied, "Not ever!" Without hesitation.

"Then you must put these back where you found them."

"*Whoa!*" Bec complained. "It was just a little hole, not big enough for burying anything in. And, anyway, these're *stones*—" He'd decided that Grandfather's eyes must not be seeing clearly. "Not bones. Stones that weren't ever alive."

"True, but the family who put them in that hole are almost certainly dead. You have dug up the bones of their tradition, young Bec; put them back."

Grandfather reached out with his hand, but Bec refused to meet him halfway.

"What *kind* of tradition?" he demanded. "A good kind, or a bad kind, like with the 'Reelan's?"

"A good kind, the kind that holds families together."

Bec took the signet stones onto his palm and studied them skeptically. "How?"

"In the old days—the very old days when I was young—it was the custom—and had been since Emperor Naihikaris decreed it at the Founding—to bury the dead in open fields far outside the city walls. Those with fortune, prestige, and the proper inclination built small, open galleries over their graves which they visited once a year, on the new moon of the vernal equinox (and gods help them all if the ground had not hardened from the winter thaw by then!).

"One supper a year, Naihikaris thought, was more than enough time spent with ancestors. But Naihikaris was an orphan, and his four sons outlived him; he knew nothing about grief or mourning. The citizens loved him as the font of glory; they obeyed him, and they defied him. They buried their dead in the open fields, but they dug reliquaries inside their homes: small pits about so big—" Grandfather framed a familiar shape with his hands. "When a woman dies, a piece of her jewelry is interred—not the precious kind—*that* gets passed along—but the everyday sort; or some domestic item more cherished than valued. When a man dies, they wrap his personal seal in clay. For a child, a favorite toy—unless the child were so young that its name hadn't yet been written in the rolls; those they bury inside their houses. You can be sure that several times a year the cache you've found was opened and everything within was passed from hand to hand through the family. When you hold the signet your father once held, it is very much like having a piece of him in your hand—"

"Inside?" Bec gasped. He'd stopped listening when Grandfather described the fate of infants. "They buried the babies *inside* their houses? I didn't see any bones, I swear. I wouldn't have touched any baby's bones."

"I'm sure you didn't. Babies are buried beneath the kitchen hearth, where they'll stay warm forever. Do you know that the Irrune do very much the same thing—burying children beneath a fire rather than immolating them within its flames?"

The boy shook his head. "Momma's never told me any of this." He folded his arms over his heart. "There aren't any babies buried in *her* kitchen. No relic holes, neither."

Grandfather took a breath for words, then didn't say them. He took a second breath. "I said the traditions had died. Perhaps your mother didn't know where her family's reliquaries were kept, or perhaps there came a day when she no longer wanted to hold the past in the palm of her hand."

"Like the family that lived here?"

"Perhaps—more likely, they all died in one of the plagues that swept through Sanctuary long before you were born, and there was no one left to remember or forget." Grandfather plucked the green signet from Bec's hand. "I should remember them. I must have been here, but the memories are gone, washed clean like the sand after the tide. I think I remember a woman—tall, with a slight limp . . ." He shook his head. His eyes brightened, but he wasn't looking at Bec. "No. *Her* family packed everything up and left in Ninety. The last thing they'd have done would have been to empty the reliquary. She'd have carried the box on her lap—

"What was their name? The Monnesi?" Grandfather asked himself questions and answered them. "No, not Monnesi. The Serripines received the Monnesi relics when the last son died. The Tetrites! No . . . no . . . Serripines have theirs, too. You should see it, boy—your mother should—the reliquary at Land's End! It is big enough to bury someone in. Say what you will about Lord Vion Serripines, he honors the ancestors. He's got the relics of a score of families, treats them the same as he treats his own—"

Bec interrupted: "So it would be all right if we took all this to Land's End? Do you think Lord Serripines really would let me see the other relics? Maybe he's got the signets and such from my great-grandfather. Momma says they were rich. Their house on Pyrtanis Street had *twenty* rooms. My great-grandfather was an important man. Momma didn't know him; he was dead before she was born—but you're old, did you know him?"

"Possibly—what was his name?"

"Coricos," Bec replied and it seemed that Grandfather's eyes widened a bit. Momma had warned him against bragging about his Imperial ancestry. The folk on Pyrtanis Street didn't understand how important lineage was to Imperials, to Momma. They made jokes about the family's fallen fortunes. But surely Momma would have told Grandfather herself, considering who Grandfather was. "Coricos Cordion Coric—Corsic—Coricsicidos?" That wasn't it. Too many sounds. Bec's tongue frequently got tangled around all the sounds of Momma's family name.

"Coricos Cordion Coricidius," Grandfather supplied helpfully. "I would never have guessed. In his day, Coricidius was the face of the Empire in Sanctuary—the emperor's vizier. A bit of irony, that. Vizier is an Ilsigi office, left over from the old days when the kingdom ruled this place. Only in Sanctuary were there Imperial viziers."

"Great-grandfather wasn't a Wrig—" Bec caught himself. Cauvin could call himself a Wrigglie, because he was, and so could Bec. Anybody who'd been born in Sanctuary or spoke the language of its streets could call himself a Wrigglie. But someone speaking Rankene or claiming Imperial lineage, he *couldn't* call anyone a Wrigglie without it being a bitter insult. "Great-grandfather wasn't Ilsigi; he was Imperial, the best Imperial—Momma said."

"And what does your poppa say about that?" Grandfather asked, still speaking Rankene but sounding stern.

"Poppa knows," Bec answered. There weren't words in either language for the subjects that weren't ever discussed at the stoneyard. "I put some water by the fire. I can make tea. Or stew. If you're hungry."

"Tea might be pleasant. No stew. I'm sure it's delightful, but a dead man has no need of stew."

Bec retreated, leaving Molin alone. The priest had lied about his pain, which was considerable, though not entirely physical—call it a consciousness of loss as his soul faded from his body; or regret for missed opportunities. Molin had bungled as many opportunities as he'd seized. He could have handled Bec better just now, and regretted that he'd mocked the boy's ancestors. Molin knew the ache of inglorious ancestors.

Wrigglies weren't the only reason Molin Torchholder despised the city where he was doomed to die. The native breed of Rankan aristocrat was worse than any son or daughter of Ilsigi slaves. The old vizier Coricos Cordion Coricidius had been among the worst of the worst.

To be sure, there were fouler specimens of mankind to be found in Ranke, but they left smaller marks on a vastly larger city. In Sanctuary, the Imperial vizier, Coricidius, had been the greatest fish in a tiny pond, proudly dominating the stolid Wrigglies, never guessing that he was great simply because in Sanctuary he had no competition. No competition, that was, until Emperor Abakithis had sent his young half brother into exile.

Prince Kadakithis, normally a man of the mildest temperament, had marked Coricidius for elimination within days of his arrival in the city. It wasn't that the feast the vizier served that first night in Sanctuary was so poorly prepared that sixty years later Molin could still taste every miserable course—but the man had been fool enough to think that he could bribe the prince with glass jewels and doctored gold! The prince had wanted to pronounce judgment immediately; Molin had said no, give him rein, see where he goes and with whom.

If Molin had been attentive—not prescient, but merely clear-headed—he would have realized right then that he'd been bitten by Sanctuary and was doomed to die from its poison.

When he closed his eyes, Molin's memories cleared. The crumbled brick walls reassembled themselves and became the villa once known in Rankene as High Harbor View. Only the Ilsigi gods knew what the Ilsigis had called it when they ruled the city; it had been built in their era. For his life—what was left of it—Molin couldn't recall the name or face of the patriarch who'd called it home. It hadn't been Coricidius, that would have been too bitter, even for Sanctuary. Coricidius had been a High Harbor View visitor, though. Coricidius and everyone else who'd mattered in those early days.

Thanks to its mongrel population, Sanctuary eagerly observed the festivals of the Rankan and Ilsigi gods, and a handful of other pantheons as well. The rabble would seize any opportunity to indulge their indolence. The nobility wasn't much better. For them the festivals were an excuse to entertain—and observe—one another. For a hindmost city—the smallest of the Imperial cities—Sanctuary had been blessed—or cursed—with an abundance of aristocrats. No real mystery there—generations of kings and emperors had been exiling their malcontents to this armpit by the ocean.

A man of status and good conversation need not dine at home above one night in four.

Molin's status and conversation in both Rankene and the Wriggle dialect were beyond reproach, and the peace of his household had depended on his regular absences. Moreover, Kadakithis, who was every bit as clever as his half brother–the-emperor's advisors had feared, ordered his own advisors to get to know the locals not in the palace, but in their own homes.

Now that he was thinking about it, Molin could see the face of the man who'd lived at High Harbor View. A dipsomaniac Wriggle, wed to the daughter of a Rankan exiled in a prior reign. He still couldn't remember the family's name, but they were great entertainers. The various feasts and festivals of High Harbor View were firmly painted on Molin's memory, not as individual events, but blended into one . . .

In the corner where the public and private rooms came together, Molin spotted a heavyset man, a Wrigglie by his swarthiness. His garments were the best the local cutters could concoct, silk brocades carefully fitted to his barrel chest and thick arms. Despite the cutters' efforts, the Wrigglie seemed uncomfortable. His timing was off—his laughter a heartbeat late for the jest, his greeting a shade shy of sincere. Women avoided him entirely, and men did not linger in his company.

Molin had sought him out, plied him with the subtlest interrogations, and learned little more than his name: Lastel. He was a broker, a middleman, but he resisted Molin's every effort to draw him into conversation that might reveal something of his character. Resisted, but did not completely evade. Morsel by morsel, Molin learned that Lastel worked the darker shadows. He'd begun to piece together a network of drugs, whores, gambling debts, and disappearances that centered, somehow, on that notorious tavern in Maze's heart: the Vulgar Unicorn.

He'd never guessed—not until it was much too late for profit—that Lastel lived a second life as One-Thumb, the tavern's owner, and a third as a silent partner in a Red Lanterns brothel. By then Lastel himself had vanished, only to reappear more than a year later, a cowed shadow of his former self.

Even Molin had pitied Lastel in his later years, sitting in a corner of his own tavern, talking to his wine. Lastel survived only because Sanctuary *needed* the Vulgar Unicorn. Where else could men—or women—go to conduct business that could be conducted nowhere else? And who else would continue to run the place, except One-Thumb, a man with three pasts and no future?

The last time Molin had seen One-Thumb—not long before the Servants of Dyareela shuttered each and every one of Sanctuary's taverns—the man had been missing more than a single thumb. His eyes were white with cataracts, and, with each step, he dragged one leg behind the other. Perhaps one of the Unicorn's wealthier patrons—of which there'd always been more than a handful—had sheltered One-Thumb through his last days. Molin doubted it—One-Thumb had never cultivated friendship or bothered to sire the children a man needed to see him to death's door.

For that matter, neither had Molin Torchholder, which was why he found himself on a ruined window ledge, tended by other men's sons.

That was never the fate of Shkeedur sha-Mizle who scuttled through Molin's memory, following his High Harbor View host, whose name remained elusive. Stop a Rankan nobleman, ask him to describe his Ilsigi counterpart, and he'd describe Shkeedur sha-Mizle: soft of flesh and discipline, superstitious, but faithless; given to worry, but untrustworthy; blessed with all the wits of a rabbit and the same strategy for survival: When sha-Mizle died his bed-chamber had been too small to contain his numerous children. By reliable count, there'd been twenty; twice that many, if one counted the sons and daughters sha-Mizle had gotten on his slaves.

The sons had kept up their father's traditions, and so, on a smaller scale, had the daughters. Another clan might have suffered for carving up the patrimony into so many pieces, but the sha-Mizle estate straddled the Red Foal River at its most fertile point. Then the great drought of '82 turned the river into a stream of dust and the lesser branches of the clan scattered on the dry wind. Those who'd remained guessed wrong when the Dyareelans seized the town. No few ended their days on the bloody sands of the palace courtyard, and their fertile estate lay abandoned until Lord Serripines plowed it into Land's End.

Rabbits were timid, rabbits ran, and at the end of the day, rabbits were harder to get rid of than rats. Surely, there must be a few of Shkeedur sha-Mizle's great-grandchildren tucked away in Sanctuary.

In Sanctuary, Wrigglie rabbits chronically outnumbered the Rankans. Despite the efforts of Bec's mother, Rankene was a dying language on the city's streets. The very name was disappearing; they were *Imperials* now, not Rankans. Molin asked himself when that had happened and realized the change had probably begun within months of the Imperial takeover. Change a few sounds and the word—in Ilsigi—implied irregularities in both parentage and partnership.

Wrigglie or perverse-bastard Imperial—what did it matter when they were all trapped in Sanctuary?

With his eyes still closed, Molin looked up and recognized a man he hadn't seen in over thirty years, hadn't thought of in at least twenty. When he couldn't recall the name, the shade reintroduced himself—

"*Lan-co-this-s-s, Tasfalen Lancothis.*"

Molin's eyes popped open and he reached for his staff. Straining his weakened senses, he took the measure of his surroundings: a warming day, a bald sky, a boy making tea, a leg that was dead-numb from the hip down, but nothing of Rankan nobleman, Tasfalen Lancothis, though he, too, frequented High Harbor View.

Molin loosed a sigh and let his eyes fall shut again. Before the Servants of Dyareela brought terror to Sanctuary, there'd been witches—his mother's people, though the Nisi weren't the only ones wreaking chaos and living death on the city.

For a heartbeat Molin imagined Sanctuary if the Servants of Dyareela and the witches had been in town at the same time. Between the Hands' preferred methods of execution and the witches' love of corpses . . . He shook the image of flayed and charred drunks ordering ale in the Vulgar Unicorn from his mind and concentrated on Tasfalen Lancothis instead.

A heavy-lidded man—his eyes were ever-shadowed, his moods impossible to gauge—and inclined to indulgence, particularly in the bedroom, Tasfalen Lancothis had the wealth, the connections, and even the wits to escape Sanctuary. Molin had never been able to determine why he remained in residence, except that his roots were sunk deep. The few times they'd talked—the few times when Lancothis hadn't been drunk on wine or in the grip of some other drug—Lancothis had hinted about loves gone awry in the capital. If true, Lancothis wouldn't have been the first man to ruin his life for a woman, but, surely, few men born since the dawn of time had ruined it so completely.

Half a lifetime later and approaching his own death, Molin still winced when he recalled Tasfalen's fate. The man had wound up an unwelcome guest in his own body after a witch—Roxanne, *the* witch of the north, by some reckoning, and quite possibly one of Molin's unacknowledged aunts or cousins—claimed it for herself. It had taken a handful of magicians, an equal number of gods, and more mortal lives than Molin cared to recall to ward what remained of Tasfalen's body and Roxanne's mind inside the walls of Tasfalen's house not far from Bec's stoneyard home on Pyrtanis Street.

Twice a month—new moon and full—Molin had inspected the wards himself, visiting that near-deserted neighborhood where wisps of angry, blue light sometimes flickered in the gaping windows. Alone, he nursed them through Sanctuary's first great fire and, a few years after that, the second and third. When glints of rotten green began to seep through the roof tiles, Molin donned a blindfold and paid a visit to the basilisk-guarded home of Tasfalen's erstwhile neighbor, Enas Yorl.

Yorl had no need of the gold which, even then, Molin had accumulated in such embarrassing quantities. All the shape-shifting mage wanted was death. On his best day and with the might of his god behind him, Molin was no match for Enas Yorl's curse, but the decaying wards were another matter— At least that had been Molin's argument and there was a chance—an outside chance—that he was correct.

When next the moon was dark, Molin and the dregs of Sanctuary's mageguild witnessed Enas Yorl enter the very haunted home of Tasfalen Lancothis. The mage did not come out again, but some days later Tasfalen's house crumbled into a layer of dust no thicker than a baby's knuckle. A few nights later Yorl's forbidding home disappeared as well, leaving not even a layer of dust behind.

For years, Molin allowed himself to believe that Yorl's dearest wish had been granted. Certainly the mage never again proclaimed his presence in Sanctuary—nor anywhere else that Molin had determined—but a man who rarely looked the same two days running could hide in plain sight more readily than most. There'd been times when a message that crackled with Yorl's bitterly dry wit would reach Molin's ears. He suspected—but would never prove, not with the time that remained—that the shape-shifter had been transformed by what he'd found inside Tasfalen's home, that he had transcended his curse, but that when confronted with the choice of death and freedom or the curse of endless life in Sanctuary, Yorl had chosen Sanctuary.

It was a choice Molin Torchholder could at last understand—a choice he might make himself, if it came to him on the hard bricks of High Harbor View. He loathed Sanctuary—the city was beneath him in every respect, yet there was no denying that he'd lived a better life in Sanctuary than he would have lived in Ranke. Not an easier or more comfortable life, but a life that made a greater difference.

Sometimes it took the worst to bring out the best . . . More often there were no such fortuitous symmetries, and the worst was best forgotten.

Of all the memories of Sanctuary Molin had striven to forget, none was more inglorious than the fate of his wife. Oh, he'd counted himself in the ranks of the most fortunate when, as a young hero freshly returned from the northern campaigns, his superior in Vashanka's hierarchy had suggested that he pay court to one of his own cousins: Rosanda, the youngest of Lord Uralde's four daughters, the eldest of which was the emperor's much-beloved second wife and mother of Prince Kadakithis.

Lord Uralde had resisted the notion. Molin's heroics notwithstanding, his god was a rapist and his mother had been a temple slave and a foreigner, to boot. A less determined man might have folded his tent, but determination had been Molin's strongest armor, his sharpest weapon . . . plus he'd been utterly beguiled by Rosanda's perfection. Her eyes were brightest amber, hair was the color of sunrise gold, her laughter could teach the birds to sing, and if her wit was limited to worshiping the men in her life, well, what more could any husband want?

The poet-sage Eudorian had laid down the rules of domestic bliss at the Empire's founding: A good wife was a delicate bird. She was not meant to fly wild among the brambles. A wise husband kept her safe inside his home, listening to the songs she sang only for him.

Molin wed his delicate bird on a warm summer's day. He brought Rosanda home and within a week she'd taken over his life, replacing all of his servants, most of his wardrobe, and many of his campaign-days friends. Before she was finished, Rosanda had transformed her young husband from a battlefield priest into an Imperial confidant.

Rosanda asked only one thing in return for her labor: sons. Molin hadn't objected—he was as adaptable as he'd been ambitious and truly grateful for the doors his wife had opened, doors no slave-born priest of Vashanka could have opened on his own. He performed his duty and gave his wife four babies in the first five years of their marriage, three sons and a daughter, each born with a shock of jet black hair and every one buried by the kitchen hearth before a month was out.

Molin's lady wife took to her bed after they buried their fourth child. The best physicians in Ranke opined that if Rosanda's fever didn't kill her, a broken heart or another unfulfilled pregnancy would. They suggested a change of surroundings . . . and separate bedchambers. Lord Uralde went a step further: He spread the tale that his daughter's misery was the tragic—but not surprising—consequence of a slave's son marrying into the oldest, purest bloodline in the Empire.

Privately Molin agreed with his father-in-law's conclusions, if not the logic behind them. The bloom was off Rosanda's flower by then. She echoed her father's prejudice, and blamed Molin for the pregnancies that had taken her beauty without leaving anything in return. Rosanda consoled herself with sweetmeats and gossip which, more than once, threatened to get both of them banished to the eastern provinces.

Hoping to end the hostilities, Molin offered to petition his brother-in-law, the emperor, for a divorce, a privilege the Empire granted husbands, not wives. He'd thought Rosanda would leap at a chance to return to her father's household. He'd forgotten—or, more accurately, failed to consider until Rosanda, in full shriek, pointed out to him—that only men were freed by divorce. Divorced wives went home in shame, without hope of remarriage. It wasn't unheard of for a divorced woman to live out her life as a servant to her brothers' wives or, worse, to die in a "kitchen accident."

Rosanda made it clear that sole hope for freedom was widowhood, and she'd made it very clear that she intended to live in her lawful husband's home until he was tucked away in a crypt. Then she planned to live precisely as she wished, with no father, husband, brother, or son to stand in her way.

Siege became the way of life for Molin and his wife until the newly enthroned Emperor Abakithis had the notion to send his troublesome half brother to Sanctuary. Molin and Rosanda were natural choices to accompany the young prince. Molin had accepted not out of loyalty to Abakithis or love for his nephew, but to deprive his wife of the capital life she loved.

He should have been more suspicious when Rosanda agreed to exile without a single complaint, should have guessed she'd fallen into someone's plot, should have known it would be abortive. As it turned out, she'd thrown in with disgruntled army commanders in a plot to disgrace Kadakithis and—not coincidentally—get her husband hung as a traitor. The prince himself had unraveled the plot before damage was done and properly doomed all save one of the conspirators.

Molin interceded to spare his wife's neck. Lord Uralde never guessed the disgrace with which his daughter had almost burdened the oldest, purest bloodline in the Empire. Rosanda interpreted the reprieve as a warning that she'd never again have the upper hand in her household. The shrew became a mouse who catered to her husband's every whim, real or imagined.

A man could live with an enemy. An enemy kept his wits sharp. Indulgence softened him, left him vulnerable to passion. When he'd least expected it—when Rosanda had most nearly transformed herself into one of her favorite cream-filled pastries—Molin succumbed to a second love even more inappropriate than his first had been. Not only was Kama young enough to be his daughter, she was, in fact, Tempus Thales's sole acknowledged child and a fully initiated member of a mercenary band—the Third Commando—so renowned for its ruthlessness that even Thales steered clear of it.

Rebellion had no doubt played a role in Kama's choices—if her father couldn't appreciate her talents, then, by the god they all shared, she'd find someone who would. And in those days—the same days when witches, gangs, and cognizant corpses ran riot on the streets of Sanctuary—Molin had needed all the talent he could get. A set of eyes and ears inside the Third Commando was a gift he could never have purchased and couldn't refuse when Kama offered to provide them.

He didn't ask questions when Kama began visiting his palace chambers at midnight, slipping in through a window, never the door. If she stayed until daybreak, that was because they shared a fascination with intrigue and a need for uncensored conversation.

Kama took Molin completely by surprise when she suggested they share his bed for "curiosity's sake." Vashanka have mercy! Molin enjoyed Kama's company, her friendship; she could take a joke at a time when jokes were scarce. He knew who and what she was, of course, and that she made a ritual out of sleeping with each of Commando's new recruits. When she sat cross-legged on Molin's worktable, bantering politics and philosophy, her hair hacked short, and her woman's body encased in a mercenary's scuffed leathers, it had been remarkably easy to forget that she *was* a woman. And even if Molin *had* seen the woman in her, Kama was Tempus Thales's daughter, and no man who knew the Riddler wanted him for a father-in-law.

But wine had flowed freely that night and once she'd raised the flag, Molin discovered that he, too, was, curious. Kama proved adventurous between the sheets and he—he'd only recently begun to explore the gifts his witchblooded mother had left him. There'd been a moment, as the sun rose, when they could have laughed and declared their curiosities sated, but that moment passed in silence.

Fate facilitated their passions. The situation in Sanctuary went from bad to worse—the fish-eyed Beysibs, the Nisi witches, a host of mages, Kama's fellow mercenaries, her father's Stepsons, a Wriggle revolt, a usurper on the Imperial throne, and a necromancer or two all conspired to reduce the city to chaos. As the first among Prince Kadakithis's advisors, Molin *needed* to meet with Kama almost every night. They were discreet but happy, and those who knew them best sensed the change.

Tempus Thales took his daughter's choice of lovers in stride. If anything, the revelation eased the tension between the two men. But Rosanda, who hadn't graced Molin's bed in a decade, judged herself betrayed—all her tightly cherished dreams of a prosperous widowhood were doomed if Kama bore Molin a son. Rosanda was not bold enough to confront Molin directly, instead she found a man—several of them—to advance her cause.

After the assassination of Emperor Abakithis, and under the aegis of Lowan Vigeles, husband of yet another of Lord Uralde's daughters, Sanctuary became a true sanctuary for what remained of the Imperial family. Their Land's End estate, though closer to the city walls than the similarly named Serripines estate, served the same purpose—a bastion of false hopes as the Empire crumbled. Armed with her version of events, Rosanda appealed to her brother-in-law. More to the point, she appealed to her niece, Chenaya.

If by some chance Molin Torchholder lived a thousand years, he'd never fathom why Savankala had chosen to imbue Chenaya with a measure of immortality. The girl couldn't lose a contest whether it was a simple coin toss or a fight to the death on the hot sands of the gladiatorial arena. Perhaps all the Rankan gods were mad, or at the very least self-destructive.

Children needed the taste of a defeat or two if they were to mature into useful citizens of the Empire. Chenaya had grown bored with winning bloodless games while yet a child and picked up steel instead. If Tempus, Vashanka's minion, was the ultimate Rankan warrior, then Chenaya, Savankala's misbegotten daughter, longed to be the Empire's ultimate gladiator.

Chenaya had help in that quest. Her father had a passion for vicarious combat and the wealth to indulge it. He'd endowed one of the most successful gladiatorial gymnasiums in the Empire and, with her father's blithe indulgence, Chenaya had started her training while still a child. Thanks in no small measure to Savankala's blessing, she was as good with steel as she thought she was. Another thing Molin wouldn't live to understand was *why* those, like Tempus and Chenaya, to whom the gods had granted a measure of immortality, felt the burning need to test that gift time and time again.

When Lowan Vigeles relocated to Sanctuary, he brought his gymnasium with him. Just what the city had needed: another cadre of hotheaded fighters!

Chenaya's attitude and exploits had inspired her aunt Rosanda to take up swordwork—Molin had imagined why, though he'd never taken the threat seriously. Prince Kadakithis's estranged wife, Daphne, who they'd all believed had died in an unfortunate caravan raid on her way from Sanctuary to the capital, was another matter. Obviously, Daphne hadn't died, and by the time Chenaya rescued her from slavery, the traumatized woman harbored an understandable grudge against the prince and his advisors, who had never, it was true, searched for her. Worse, during her absence—when he'd believed himself a widower—Kadakithis had made an alliance a few steps short of marriage with the exiled queen of Sanctuary's fish-eyed invaders.

If Molin's northern features had made him a mongrel in aristocratic Rankan eyes, what must Daphne have seen when she first beheld the Beysa Shupansea with her bared and painted breasts and her wide, staring eyes?

Indulged utterly by Lowan Vigeles, Chenaya and her spear-carriers, Rosanda and Daphne, pursued their dreams of redress and retribution. Of the three, only Chenaya understood the consequences, but obscenely blessed as she was by Savankala, Chenaya didn't need to worry about consequences.

Chenaya collected men—not that she'd ever have admitted it. She especially collected men who had no interest in women, because they spared her any need to consider the absurdity of the path she'd chosen for herself. She collected enemies, too, in a far more haphazard way and very nearly accomplished the impossible: uniting all Sanctuary's irreconcilable rivals in common cause against her. The need to get the self-styled Daughter of the Sun *out* of Sanctuary before she brought the wrath of every god in creation down around their heads had been one of the few things Molin and Tempus had agreed upon without negotiation.

If only they'd had the ear of a god worthy of their combined prayers . . .

If only Vashanka hadn't sunk into obsession with the Beysib mother-goddess, so many things might have turned out different. No soldiers, sorcerers, or Bloody Hands of Dyareela fighting their private battles on Sanctuary's streets. The city might have made something of itself. Molin might have died in his prime rather than on a crumbling window ledge overlooking equally crumbling walls. So many things that might have been, but one thing was certain—

When Chenaya's massed enemies finally paid a call at Land's End, it had been Rosanda who had paid the price. Kama swore that neither she nor anyone else of the Third Commando had been along for the raid that night, and Molin chose to believe her, even though the men they did catch and charge with the crime—a home-bred gang that didn't know the difference between freedom and anarchy—owed their tactics and weapons if not their viciousness to the Third in general and Kama in particular.

It was Kama's opinion—voiced the night of Rosanda's funeral, which Molin had not attended—that Sanctuary owed the gutter rats a pardon. They had, after all, demonstrated to Chenaya Vigeles—in no uncertain terms—that *her* invulnerability did not extend to those around her and that she didn't have to fight in the contest in order to lose it.

Kama was right. Chenaya's overlong childhood ended the night Rosanda died. She didn't exactly repent, but she chose her enemies with greater care thereafter and brokered a reconciliation of sorts between the prince and Daphne. Molin even got some leverage on the gutter rats after Kama persuaded him to release their leader with his limbs and manhood intact.

Rosanda Uralde had not accomplished half so much in life as she did by the simple act of getting in the way of a man with a sword. And for that reason alone, Molin Torchholder sank into a morass of guilt from which Kama could not lift him. She left him and Sanctuary.

Molin never saw her again, or took another lover.

Chenaya stayed. So long as the city was gods-ridden, it held her interest. But when the stuff of sorcery began to dry up, when the witches left, the Beysib, and all the warriors, too, she was left with only her father's gladiators for company. When her cousin Kadakithis announced his intention to return to Ranke and stake his claim to the Imperial throne, she buckled on her weapons and armor and went with him.

Two years passed, two endless, silent years without word from either of them nor about them. Lowan Vigeles swallowed his pride and came to the palace, begging for information, believing Molin still had influence with Vashanka and the Imperial court. Nothing could have been further from the truth; Vashanka was utterly vanquished at that point, and Molin survived in Sanctuary because his enemies in Ranke assumed he was dead.

Molin had no desire to attract attention by reawakening his web of spies, but a father's desperation was difficult to ignore. After months of alternating pleas and threats, he betook himself to the bazaar, to a blacksmith's stall and the little home that stood behind it. The S'danzo still dwelt in Sanctuary—it would be another nine years before they pulled up stakes—and Molin was on good terms with the best of them. He'd gotten Illyra's boy out of Sanctuary before either the witches or the gods could lay their hands on the gifted, fated boy. Arton had grown to near manhood on the distant Bandaran Islands, and though Illyra had confessed that she did not expect to see him again in her lifetime, she welcomed the messages Molin brought her two or three times a year.

Her first words were about her son. "Have you had word from the Isles?"

"No," he'd admitted. "The ship I sent isn't due back until autumn. I've come to beg a favor. I'm looking for my niece. You remember Chenaya . . . ?"

When Molin thought of Illyra, he always saw a girlish face framed by dark chestnut curls in his mind's eye, but the truth was that Illyra had been young no longer when he went to the bazaar to ask his brother-in-law's questions. Her hair had dulled and the skin around her eyes was wrinkled from too many hours spent squinting at her cards, looking for trouble. The look she gave him when Molin mentioned Chenaya's name was both ancient and bitter.

Chenaya might have mended her ways after Rosanda's death, but she hadn't changed anyone's opinion.

"Two years have passed since she left Sanctuary with Prince Kadakithis and no word from either of them—"

"They rode to their doom. It was no secret. He should have sailed off with the Beysa and she . . . She should have stayed away from Sanctuary," Illyra replied.

The moment that followed had been of the few times Molin Torchholder had been at an utter loss for words. He knew more about Sanctuary's hidden lives than anyone else, but he had no notion what Chenaya had done to earn Ilyra's coldest disdain. They'd sat there on opposite sides of Illyra's scrying table, staring at each other like the fish.

*Clang, tap!* each time the hammer struck the anvil then rested while Dubro worked his trade nearby. *Clang, tap! Clang, tap!* There was a face burnt into the metal, a face reflected in a mirror as it shattered. The same face—the Face of Chaos—stared up from the deck of cards at Illyra's elbow, mocking Molin as his heart sped up to the hammer's rhythm.

"It's not for her," he'd said at last. "But for her father. If there's anything you can tell Lowan Vigeles about his daughter's fate . . . ? You know that pain."

She took up her cards. Age had crept into the seeress's hands, but it had not robbed them of their grace. She fanned the cards before Molin.

"Choose three."

He'd reached, hesitated, then dropped his hand on the cloth-covered table. "It's not me who asks." The cards were tricky, like gods. Sometimes they revealed fates unconnected to the querant's question, fates a man might not want to know.

Illyra loosened her grasp; a single card fell facedown on the table. She straightened the rest and set them aside. When Molin would not touch that card either, she sighed and turned it over herself.

The painted scene was a study in grays, greens, and the pale, terrified face of a man drowning in sight of the shore.

"Six of Ships," Illyra announced. Molin had seen many of her cards over the years, but he'd not seen that one before and did not know its name or guess its meaning until she whispered: "Undertow."

Long before, when a very young Chenaya had first come to her uncle, seeking an explanation of her uncanny knack for winning, Molin had done some scrying of his own. He'd had the power then, when some said it was Vashanka, not Savankala, who ruled in paradise; perhaps he'd had it still. He *knew* what the card revealed without Illyra's help.

The was a catch to the gift Savankala had bestowed upon Chenaya. Had there ever been a god's gift that didn't have a catch as sharp and deadly as a serpent's fang? The Daughter of the Sun was vulnerable to water, to drowning.

"She's gone? Drowned in the ocean?" he'd asked, unable to maintain silence.

"There are worse deaths in water than drowning," Illyra replied, as cryptic as she was honest.

Molin, who could be as cryptic and honest as any seer when the need arose, had trekked out to Land's End and told Lowan Vigeles that his daughter had crossed water and was not likely to return in his lifetime. Rather than take what Molin offered, Vigeles promptly sank all his money in a ship and sailed off in search of her.

That autumn, the seas off Sanctuary boiled with storms that leveled stone houses and wrecked every boat in Sanctuary's harbor. Lowan Vigeles's ship was last seen racing the black winds off Inception Island, and the ship Molin had sent to the Bandaran Isles never made it home to port. With the loss of its captain and navigator, the Isles themselves were lost, along with the Beysib Empire. Like Chenaya, Illyra's son had crossed water, never to return in his parents' lifetime.

Undertow, indeed—

"Grandfather?" Bec asked. His eyes were squeezed shut, and there were tears dribbling down his cheeks. "Grandfather, are you awake?"

Eyelids parted suddenly. Bec found himself nailed by the old man's black, birdlike eyes. He defended himself with a mug of steaming fragrant water.

"Here—I made tea. Are you well, Grandfather? You were—you were—" Bec couldn't bring himself to put words to what he'd seen.

"Well enough, boy, considering what I've seen. Settle yourself beside me here. I'll tell you a story—"

"Wait! I'll get the inks and parchment."

Grandfather caught Bec's sleeve before he got away. "No need. This isn't a story others need to hear, it's just for you."

"What's it about?"

"Call it the 'Women of Sanctuary.' "

# Chapter Twelve

The bazaar wasn't one of Cauvin's haunts. Its walls—broad-based, tapering, dirt-filled relics of Sanctuary's earliest years—had withstood the worst that gods and man could hurl at them. They didn't require a stonemason's constant attention, unlike the froggin' royal and Imperial walls that crumbled whenever wind or rain touched them. The bazaar's residents in their wooden homes, many of them built on the hulks of foundered ships and wagons, weren't among the stoneyard's regular customers, either.

But more than the tapered walls or the odd-shaped homes, it was the people of the bazaar themselves who kept Cauvin from feeling comfortable in their midst. Bazaar-folk looked on outsiders as prey, and anyone whose parents and grandparents hadn't lived within the old walls was an outsider—even a sheep-shite stone-smasher from up on Pyrtanis Street. Besides, Cauvin never had enough money to take advantage of what the bazaar offered those who visited it.

The bazaar was *not* the market for purchasing a cooking pot or a pair of boots. New or secondhand, ordinary goods could be gotten for less in other quarters, particularly in the Shambles, south of the bazaar, where a handful of merchants sold a steady stream of cast-offs. Food was more expensive in the bazaar, too—unless you were an insider or were looking for delicacies.

Bilibot and Eprazian at the Well spoke of hundred-camel caravans and a wharf crowded with merchant ships from ports whose names they couldn't remember. These days a ten-mule caravan was the start of rumors, and the wharves might stand empty for weeks at a time. Still, when foreign goods arrived—exotic delicacies and luxuries—the bazaar was the place to find them.

Just inside the open arch that funneled traffic from Governor's Walk into the cobblestone alley that led into the bazaar proper, Cauvin spotted vendors selling dark green eggs that stank of brine, sweet oranges with bloodred pulp, a purple powder from Aurvesh that was so pungent it made his eyes water, and dried lizard feet. Cauvin would sooner catch himself a mangy rat than pay a single padpol for a froggin' green egg or a lizard foot, but rich folk were different.

And there were rich folk in Sanctuary.

A litter-borne woman in gaudy brocades—almost certainly purchased elsewhere in the bazaar—directed her flock of servants and bearers to shove everyone else aside so *she* could sample the gods-forsaken eggs.

"Ten padpols each," the vendor chirped as she ladled up a selection from a bucket at her feet.

"How much for the lot?" The eager woman licked her fingers like a snake.

"Fifty soldats."

"Pay the man," she told her purse-bearer.

Fifty soldats, just like that—without even a token round of haggling. Fifty soldats for a sloshing bucket of delicacies a froggin' *dog* wouldn't eat! Give Mina fifty soldats and she could put festival meat on the table every meal for a month.

Cauvin wanted to spit in the bucket as it passed from the vendor to one of the servants, but that would have bought him more than fifty soldats' worth of trouble with the guards—and separated him from Soldt, who'd taken the opportunity to study the Torch's map. The dark-dressed man was already off the cobblestones and striding deeper into the bare-dirt bazaar.

Point of fact—Cauvin didn't need to follow Soldt. The Torch's stranger had let on that they were looking for a blacksmith's anvil. There were five blacksmiths in and around Sanctuary. They all knew one another, and Cauvin was close friends with one of them, which meant that Davar's forge, tucked up against the bazaar's northern wall, was one of the few places Cauvin could find with ease. He could have taken the lead, or struck out on his own (and gotten to Davar's forge first, judging from the direction in which

Soldt was headed), but it served Cauvin best to stay a half step behind the Torch's stranger, trying to measure the man.

Soldt was a mystery. Sanctuary was large enough that Cauvin didn't claim to froggin' recognize, much less know, everyone he passed, yet between the Hill and the bazaar arch, he'd been hailed several times by familiar faces. Soldt spoke Wrigglie well enough that he couldn't be a complete stranger to the city's streets, yet no one had hailed him. No one had even seemed to notice Soldt, which struck Cauvin as froggin' odd since Soldt was a memorable sort with his brushed-leather cloak and fancy boots.

No point in stealing those froggin' fancy boots. With their steel studs and catgut laces to keep them snug, they'd clearly been made to fit Soldt and Soldt alone. Cauvin, who'd never worn a boot that wasn't worn before he got it or didn't bind somewhere, envied those boots. Someday before he died, he swore he'd own a pair of boots cut to fit his froggin' huge feet.

Guided by the Torch's map, Soldt made their way to the man-high Settle Stone in the middle of the bazaar where he paused to consult the parchment a second time. The Settle Stone had been carved from local rock, which meant it had weathered so badly that Cauvin could scarcely have read the inscriptions, even if he'd known how to read. The legend was that it had been raised by the Ilsigi slaves who'd founded Sanctuary. Fitting, then, that in Cauvin's experience it was the daytime home of beggars displaying their misfortunes.

Cauvin had lived on the streets long enough to know a few beggars' tricks—a leather harness to bind a healthy leg from sight, a few grains of pepper to bloody an eye and make it weep all day. He knew, too, that a bound leg eventually withered and soon enough a peppered eye would bleed and weep itself to true blindness. He'd rather break his froggin' back smashing stone every day than cripple himself beside the Settle Stone.

Some of the beggars didn't resort to tricks. They exposed twisted feet, fingerless hands, and faces fit for nightmares. Cauvin dug into his belt pouch and tossed a black padpol to a girl about Bec's age who'd been cursed with a lopsided, wine-colored face and moon eyes.

Soldt folded the parchment. He'd watched gods knew how much

of Cauvin's charity. His eyes were utterly without pity when he sneered: "They're all frauds."

"Not all of them. That girl—she couldn't fake that."

"And she won't keep your measly padpol, either. She's got a keeper, Cauvin, someone who tends her, same as you tend your mule. He—or maybe she—will get your charity while that girl gets gruel."

Soldt was right—and he wasn't telling Cauvin a truth he didn't, in his head if not his heart, already know. He'd tossed the padpol because cheap charity felt good, but Soldt left him feeling foolish and, worse, soft around the heart. He hated feeling soft around the heart. "At least she gets something!" he snapped in his own defense.

The Torch's stranger gave Cauvin a once-over stare, then set off in the general direction of Davar's forge. Cauvin almost let him get away. Yes, the conversation in the ruins had rekindled all his froggin' questions about Leorin, and when the Torch had said he could get the answers, Cauvin went along willingly to get them; that didn't mean he trusted the Torch's stranger. But, not trusting Soldt was all the more reason to stay on his sheep-shite tail. After a final glance at the beggar girl—whose silvery eyes were looking for new targets—Cauvin caught up with the dark-dressed man.

"According to what Lord Torchholder's written, about fifty paces on, we should be coming to a perfumer's stall. If we turn left there, the blacksmith's should lie straight ahead—"

"Depends," Cauvin shot back. "How long do you think it's been since the old pud bought perfume? The bazaar changes, you know, like the Maze."

"Fifty paces, whether there's a perfumer's stall there or not."

Soldt wasn't Grabar. Cauvin couldn't get the better of him, and they'd have to turn left—turn north—in about fifty paces, if they were going to Davar's. He swallowed all the sheep-shite clever replies that came into his mind and followed Soldt when he turned left . . . at a perfumer's aromatic stall.

Cauvin would have recognized Davar anywhere. His arms were longer than his legs, giving him the look of a tall man squeezed short. There was more gray in his hair than Cauvin remembered, but his beard was still black and confined in three stiff braids. Davar didn't look pleased to see them, reminding Cauvin that his friendship with Swift didn't count for shite in the bazaar.

"Come to get an edge from a master?" Davar asked, flicking a thumb toward Cauvin's new weapon.

Cauvin shook his head. When the knife needed honing, he'd take it to Swift.

"What then?"

Before Cauvin could answer, Soldt announced. "We're looking for a box. We expect to dig for it. Right about there—under your anvil, I presume there's a mark on the metal? A kind of face gone to pieces?"

Davar nodded slowly. His face was pale above his beard. Cauvin figured they were headed for trouble when Davar asked—

"Who sent you?"

"Lord Molin Torchholder."

"He's dead."

"He wasn't when he told me to dig it up," Soldt countered with froggin' honesty that wasn't honest. "Don't worry. We'll set it back down once we've got what we're looking for."

"Frog all, we can't do that—" Cauvin corrected his partner of inconvenience. "An anvil's got to sit on ground that's ten years' settled." Swift had told him that. Maybe Swift wasn't the best blacksmith in Sanctuary, but he had the best forge: high up on Pyrtanis Street, where floodwaters never lingered.

"Then we'll move it to settled ground."

"There's work to be done." Davar pointed to a tangle of iron that froggin' sure looked like a scrap hoard to Cauvin. "Man's got to keep food on his family's table. Five soldats."

Trust the bazaar-folk to cheat outsiders every chance they got. Five soldats was robbery, froggin' plain and simple, but Soldt—who wouldn't give a froggin' padpol to a beggar girl—didn't balk at the smith's request.

"Seven—if we can use your shovel."

"Davar doesn't *need* seven froggin' soldats if we're doing the froggin' digging!" Cauvin muttered, while the smith rummaged behind the gap-planked shanty he called home. "This ground's hard as stone."

"Then you should be well suited to dig through it."

Cauvin clenched his fists without thinking, then unclenched

them again when Davar returned with a decent shovel and a pick with a crooked arm and a broken shaft.

"We'll set the anvil here—" the smith said, scratching a mark in the dirt a foot closer to the fire.

Cauvin didn't expect Soldt to help with the anvil. The sheep-shite thing was heavy as sin and whatever Soldt did to keep himself in boots and cloaks, it wasn't hard labor. Besides, there was scarcely room for him and Davar to get their arms around the froggin' iron without knocking heads. He was sweat-drenched from holding up one side of the anvil after the other while Davar added pebbles to the pad.

When the anvil was leveled to Davar's satisfaction, Cauvin thrust his arms into the slaking barrel. He splashed the bitter water against his face, swallowed some, and spat out the rest. Not by accident, the stream barely missed Soldt's fine, black boots. Soldt gave Cauvin a one-sided grin and never budged. Then Davar pulled a length of red-hot metal from the fire where it had been since before they arrived and started hammering as though he always had a froggin' audience when he worked.

Shite for sure, If they'd been shouting, the two men couldn't have made their froggin' thoughts clearer: There was hard work to be done, and he was the sheep-shite fool who had to do it. With a silent snarl, Cauvin grabbed the pick. The froggin' shaft was so short Cauvin had to hunch over to swing it, and the crooked arm made it buck and twist. If his luck ran true to form, he'd have blisters under his calluses before he was through . . .

"Back a bit to the right," Soldt advised. "You're starting to drift."

Cauvin adjusted his swing.

"*My* right," Soldt corrected.

Froggin' hells of Hecath! Cauvin corrected his mistake. He slammed the pick into the packed, brown dirt so hard the metal nearly separated from the shaft, then he raised it up and slammed it down again.

"Good, good—you'll find it soon enough," Soldt said, ladling out the kind of mealy-mouthed praise no man wanted to hear.

Cauvin didn't raise his head until there was enough loosened dirt about to warrant the shovel. The froggin' shovel was where he'd left it, but the Torch's froggin' stranger had made himself scarce. Davar shrugged with his hammer and heated metal.

Shalpa knew what he'd do with the box—if there were a box, if the damned gods weren't determined to show up him up as a great, sheep-shite fool in front of bazaar rats. The Torch had told them to take it to some S'danzo woman. Any sheep-shite fool with dark eyes and a moustache could call his froggin' self S'danzo; likewise any woman with a taste for clinking jewelry and gossip, but *real* S'danzo—the ones who'd cursed Sanctuary on their froggin' way out of town—knew froggin' better than to parade around Sanctuary. If there were any S'danzo left in the city, they were hiding deep, which meant that, without Soldt and the Torch's froggin' map, Cauvin had no notion where to take the damn buried treasure, *if* he found it.

Cauvin put his foot to the shovel and removed the loosened dirt from his hole. He enlarged the hole to shin depth, striking up a crop of rocks and broken crockery and an arm's length of rusted iron that Davar claimed for his hoard. He had the pick in hand and was chipping out another littered layer when he and Davar both heard a sound hollow enough to be a box. Before Cauvin could get down on his knees and clear the rubble, Soldt had reappeared, doling out unnecessary advice.

"Careful now. The box itself is apt to be valuable. Use your hands—"

Cauvin had half a mind to splinter the damn thing, just for froggin' spite. He could feel it by then beneath the rubble: one hand by two . . . wooden . . . carved . . .

A froggin' big brother to the one he'd gotten from Sinjon at the Broken Mast! The Torch must have bought out a froggin' peddler!

"Give it here," Soldt commanded.

Cauvin tucked it under one arm and clambered to his feet.

"Give it here. I'll hold it while you repair the damage you've done to this man's yard."

Both Davar and Soldt were giving Cauvin a scowl with edges and, reluctantly, he surrendered the froggin' box for the froggin' shovel.

"Are you certain you don't want the anvil replaced," Soldt politely asked Davar once Cauvin had the hole refilled.

Shite for sure, Soldt wasn't planning to move it if Davar did but, sensing another defeat, Cauvin walked behind the anvil, ready to heave it on his forearms. He got his first good look at the mark Soldt had mentioned; he'd been on the other side when they'd moved it before. A shattered face, that was true, as far as it went. It didn't describe how the face seemed to bleed off each of the jagged shards or how the whole thing seemed to froggin' *shimmer* the longer Cauvin stared at it.

"No—'s'like I told you—it's better here, closer to the fire." Davar held out his hand, and not for froggin' courtesy.

For one of the rare times in his sheep-shite life, Cauvin had the seven soldats Soldt had promised the smith, but he froggin' sure wasn't going to part with them. "You made the deal," he said over his shoulder in Soldt's direction. "You pay the man."

He didn't know what he'd do if Soldt didn't fork over the soldats, but it would involve fists, blood, and lots of trouble afterward. Soldt took his own damn time figuring out the obvious before he dug out two of the weightier Ilsigi shaboozh coins that passed for four soldats in most parts of Sanctuary. Not in the bazaar. Davar dropped the coins into a pouch he wore around his neck and gave no hint that he'd considered returning a soldat or even a padpol.

"He'd have accepted less from you," Soldt argued when they were clear of the smithy. "And, either way, you had more than enough left from Lord Torchholder's treasure."

"I'm not carrying it with me," Cauvin lied, while wondering if Soldt were guessing about the contents of the Broken Mast box or if he'd been spying from the start. "You made the deal. You owed the money." Spying was a good bet. Hero or not, the whole of Sanctuary knew that the Torch was a damned spider with a web full of spies. "If you're pinched, you shouldn't have offered Davar the extra soldats. And give me the froggin' box."

"I paid for it. I should think that it's *my* froggin' box."

"Fine—then you talk to the froggin' S'danzo when we find her."

They'd reached the perfumer's stall. Soldt pulled right, Cauvin to the left.

"We turn this way," Soldt said.

"Only if you want to go the long way back to the arch. My way, and we'll be out in half the time."

Soldt stopped and studied Cauvin. "You knew another way?"

"I know more than you think I do," Cauvin shot back, figuring that Soldt didn't credit him with sense of a stinkbug.

Soldt stopped short, spread his arms, and bowed. "You're the one knows the way, you carry the box." Soldt's leather cloak rippled as he extended his arms, the carved wooden box balanced in his right hand.

Ignoring the insults and mockery, Cauvin snatched the froggin' box, tucked it tight under his sopping armpit, and set off at the longest pace his legs could manage. He didn't truly expect to lose the Torch's froggin' spy. Soldt had an air of strength and wiliness around him; he'd keep up without breaking a froggin' sweat. Besides, Soldt had the Torch's froggin' map. But, threading through the throng—shouldering between a matron and her maid and *knowing* that Soldt would be the one to catch froggin' hell from their body servants when he followed—soothed Cauvin's temper.

The archway alley to Governor's Walk was more crowded and noisier than usual. Another time, Cauvin would have hung back, waiting for the traffic to sort itself out, but today—with Soldt a few steps behind him—Cauvin strode into the thick of it.

Suddenly there was shouting and screaming up ahead, and in a heartbeat the crowd was thick as Batty Dol's sour jam. Another heartbeat and there were elbows froggin' everywhere. Slowly a sickening stench wove its way out of the arch.

"What froggin' *died?*" Cauvin muttered to himself—because that was the smell. Some froggin' pud's gut had burst and dumped his last meal between his ankles. Some froggin' *huge* pud, or maybe a froggin' horse. A burst horse could account for the screams and the way the crowd had frozen in the alley. The stench was that froggin' bad.

The crowd parted for a heartbeat. Cauvin saw all the way to Governor's Walk and saw the source of their stench before the crowd congealed again. A cart had tipped over dead center beneath the arch and dumped barrels of night swill on the cobblestones. The west side of Sanctuary wasn't as steep-sloped as the east side Stairs or the Hill or froggin' Pyrtanis Street itself, but it wasn't froggin' flat, either. The swill was gushing into the bazaar, and the people in its path—the people between Cauvin and Governor's Walk—were desperate for high ground.

Before Cauvin got himself turned around, a woman lost her balance. She lurched against Cauvin's chest and together they staggered into a third person, too small to be Soldt. They all would have fallen, if there'd been enough room to fall or if the palace wall hadn't been directly behind the body behind Cauvin. That body grunted rather than screamed. It didn't have the froggin' strength to free itself.

Cauvin wasted a heartbeat feeling thankful that they'd left Bec behind—what was merely froggin' uncomfortable for him could be death for a sprout. In his mind's eye Cauvin saw the boy slipping down to the froggin' cobblestones. He was imagining boots tromping on Bec's chest as he braced himself and *shoved*. The woman against his chest yelped like a stepped-on dog, but Cauvin had made a hole large enough for them both to turn around in. He shoved again, this time against the bald runt who'd been behind him.

The dug-up box shifted beneath Cauvin's arm. He put his free hand over the clasp and shoved again. The runt and several others stumbled out of Cauvin's way and onto one of the bazaar's uncrowded dirt paths. Cauvin had saved the runt's life, but the little man didn't see it that way. From one knee in the dirt he cursed Cauvin up one side, down the froggin' other. Cauvin looked around for Soldt, who'd made his own escape from the throng, and strode on without saying a word.

There was another way out of the bazaar— There were two, actually, but the second was back over by Davar's: the old Common Gate that opened *outside,* to the graveyard, the rebuilt temples, and the whorehouses on the Street of Red Lanterns. The second way between the city and the bazaar was south, down where the big caravans used to tie up. It wasn't so much a gate as a whole froggin' missing wall, but, as the crush at the arch had shown, not many went that way unless they had to.

Storms before Cauvin's birth had whipped up the placid White Foal River into a torrent, and the river had carved itself a new channel to the sea. The change had transformed a fishermen's village into a bracken marsh, good for hunting crabs and birds, but little more, and gouged a treacherous cove into the middle of what had once been Caravan Square. The fishermen had rebuilt their stilt-y homes on what was left of the square. What was left of the caravan trade came through the East Gate near Pyrtanis Street because there was a man-deep ditch connecting the cove and the eroded wall.

The ditch wasn't empty, and it wasn't really a ditch, but the remains of a tunnel meant to transfer water and waste from Sanctuary's west side to the sea. It still did; it just didn't do it very well. The stream at the bottom of the ditch was low or high, fast or stagnant, depending on rainfall and the season. This time of year, the stream should be nearly pure swill, knee deep and rank as froggin' hell.

Some families from the Shambles had built a footbridge from their quarter on the eastern side of the ditch to the bazaar on the western side. They'd set gates at both ends of the bridge and hired bruisers too froggin' stupid to join the watch to sit beside them, charging every man, woman, or child a padpol to keep his feet dry.

Froggin' sure, no one *had* to use the Shambles bridge. People could slide down the ditch bank, jump across whatever happened to be flowing at the bottom, and climb up again on the other side, but if a person misjudged the breadth of the swill or lost his footing, which was damned easy to do, then that person was going to be out boots, breeches, and a tub of coarse soap from the gluemaker. If Cauvin had wanted to take chances with his boots, he could have braved the arch to Governor's Walk. Instead, he extracted the smallest padpol from his belt pouch and advised Soldt to do the same.

Five people had beaten them from the arch to the bridge—or maybe they were froggin' rich enough that they regularly paid to enter or leave the bazaar. A handful of others stood on the Shambles side. Though the bridge looked sturdy enough for a horse, the padpol collectors didn't allow but one person at a time on its planks. Someone left the bazaar or someone entered. Cauvin and Soldt waited their turn.

Cauvin let his mind wander. He'd returned to the gray fog of his palace years, thinking of nothing at all, when he got rocked from the right. As fast as Cauvin's hand dropped to his belt, he knew his coin pouch was gone before it touched. The thief, a sprout Bec's size, was already out of reach, three strides from the ditch. The man to Cauvin's right—not Soldt—had seen it all and shouted an alarm—

"Thief! Thief! Catch him before he gets away!"

But no sheep-shite fool was going to follow the sprout into the ditch, not for the size of Cauvin's purse. No sheep-shite fool except for Cauvin himself. Arms and legs pumping, he took one stride where the sprout took two and caught the thief halfway down the bank. With one hand on a scrawny neck and the other on a pair of ragged britches, Cauvin threw the little bastard clear across the swill stream.

The sprout landed hard, but had shaken off the shock before Cauvin had bounded the stream himself. The child turned and showed a face that was softer, even, than Bec's. A girl—a froggin' *girl*—Cauvin realized—had thieved him! Embarrassment pushed Cauvin to the limits of restraint. The girl saw the change. She brandished the leather pouch she'd sliced from Cauvin's belt, tossed it downstream into the sludge, and clawed her way, hand over foot, up the Shambles bank.

Cauvin had a choice to make: vengeance or his money. No way he'd have both. Turn his back on the pouch, and some other thief would claim it. Take the moment to retrieve it, and the sprout would get away. Cauvin chose his froggin' money, but there was no way to retrieve it without letting one foot sink ankle deep in swill. Gritting his teeth, Cauvin took the step and plucked the pouch off a slick brownish lump he hoped to the gods was rotting wood and not a froggin' dead cat.

Then he heard applause . . . and laughter coming from both ends of the bridge. Worse, he saw Soldt at the bazaar side of the ditch, laughing and clapping along with the rest, the gods-all-be-damned wooden box tucked under his arm. The froggin' spy waggled a finger and pointed to the ground at his feet.

A man wasn't a froggin' dog. A man deserved to be asked, not told, but standing at the bottom of the bazaar ditch with swill clinging to his only pair of boots, Cauvin didn't feel much like a man. He stuck his hand up in the air and accepted Soldt's help climbing up to level ground.

Soldt greeted him with: "That was well done. Do you think you could have made a greater spectacle of yourself?"

"I'm not as rich as you. When some froggin' thief steals my froggin' coin pouch, I need to get it back."

"You could have lost this—" Soldt offered the wooden box.

Cauvin hadn't expected to get it back. He eyed it and Soldt a moment, then tucked it under his arm again.

"Let's just get out of here and go back to the ruins. I can't listen to some froggin' S'danzo lie about my betrothed until I've scraped myself raw. Maybe the arch is clear by now—"

"That way's not possible now."

"Froggin' sure why not?"

"Thanks to you, we're being watched, so we're not going anywhere that we want to go. We'll take a walk along the river instead. Lure them out or lose them."

Soldt started walking away from the footbridge. Cauvin scuffed his boots brutally against the nearest rocks before catching up with him.

"All right, they laughed at me. I made a froggin' fool of myself. People in Sanctuary have better things to do than watch fools crawl away in shame."

"How do you know? You don't know that we're being watched right now."

They were back in the bazaar with Soldt leading at a steady pace, not headed for the arch or Davar's or the center, and not consulting Molin's map, either.

"Frog all, no one's watching us. This is Sanctuary, Soldt, home to the world's greatest fools. Safest way to hide in this froggin' city is to act like a sheep-shite fool."

Soldt sighed from somewhere below his navel as he confronted Cauvin with—"We are not being watched because you made a fool of yourself chasing a child into a sewer. We're being watched because we have secrets, and secrets attract a certain type of man the way sewers attract flies, children, and sheep-shite fools."

"What secrets?"

Soldt raised a finger to his lips. "We'll just go for a little walk along the river. Lure or lose—follow me."

Cauvin had no intention of following Soldt one step farther. "Damn you to Hecath's hells, you've been baiting me like a fish since you walked out of the froggin' shadows up at—"

Soldt blew across his finger. "Take advantage of opportunity and try to control yourself."

"You're not as clever as you froggin' think you are, Soldt. I've got all the control I need to put my fist between your eyes."

That almighty smile spread across Soldt's face again. "Have you? Lord Torchholder said I was to teach you. I know a secluded spot along the White Foal where you can *try* to put your fist where it doesn't belong."

Cauvin liked the idea of battering Soldt's froggin' face. He'd have liked it more if Soldt had liked it less. The man was a froggin' spy and, for all intents, unarmed. If he were the Torch's froggin' armsmaster, Cauvin didn't expect to do much learning.

Anger and resentment made Cauvin cocky. "Since I've got the box and you're not going to feel like showing your black-and-blue face anywhere tomorrow, you mind telling me where I'm supposed to find this froggin' S'danzo?"

Soldt held out the parchment scrap. The writing didn't look Wrigglie; Cauvin guessed it was Imperial. Too shamed to admit that he couldn't read much more than his own name in either language, Cauvin said, "Can't read it here—we're being watched," and stuffed the scrap into the pouch he'd retied to his belt.

"Can't read it at all," Soldt corrected. "Can't read a word of your own language, can you? and certainly not Imperial Rankene."

Gods all be damned, Soldt grated on Cauvin's nerves—grated so much that he retrieved the parchment and unfolded it. The Torch had drawn a map, after all, not written an edict. Cauvin knew about maps, and he knew the lay of Sanctuary. There was a chance—a froggin' small chance—that he'd be able to make sense of the map, but his froggin' luck didn't change. The Torch's map consisted of four lines, three dots, and a froggin' waste of words. Cauvin rotated the parchment, as if that would help. His eyes burnt the way they did when he was on the brink of a froggin' rage. Sweet Eshi's mercy, Cauvin wanted to hit Soldt a thousand times, in a thousand places, he wanted to hit himself, too, for being a sheep-shite idiot who couldn't read a word that wasn't his own name—which, froggin' come to notice, the Torch had written above one of the dots on the parchment:

"Cauvin," followed by another word, "home."

And "blacksmith" above another dot, which, froggin' come to

notice, was at one end of a crooked line that had "Settle Stone" at its beginning. Above the third dot the Torch had written "Elemi's home" and in a column beside it, a series of street names: "Wideway," "Stink Street," "Shambles Cross," "Shadow Street," "Dippin Lane," and "Paddling Duck" . . .

Dippin Lane. Dippin Lane. Cauvin knew Dippin Lane. It was one of those froggin' Shambles' dodges off the street they called Shadow because it was so narrow and the roofs so high that sunlight never got down to the ground . . .

The parchment slipped through Cauvin's suddenly lax fingers. His vision blurred. If someone had asked—and froggin' held his head underwater until he'd answered honestly—Cauvin would have admitted he was crying. Crying because he was reading—reading froggin' Imperial Rankene. He didn't know why he was reading or weeping.

It had to be the Torch meddling with him again. The box had to be like the brick in the Maze atrium—larded with sorcery and set to trap him. Cauvin tried to be angry, but his tears washed away anger. He wanted to go home, to the stoneyard where Bec practiced his letters on a slab of slate. Froggin' sure *writing* had to be easier if you could *read.*

Soldt picked up the parchment. "Careless is as careless does."

Cauvin's anger returned.

Cauvin was froggin' sure Soldt was the Torch's cat's-paw, but, just as sure, he hadn't caught the sorcery passing between Cauvin and the parchment. At least Cauvin didn't think Soldt had, because Soldt had that sheep-shite smirking grin glued on his face when he put the parchment into the scrip he wore folded over his belt. Cauvin smiled back. He no longer needed Soldt to lead him to Dippin Lane. He could follow Soldt to the White Foal, pound the froggin' snot out of him, and leave him there to rot.

Froggin' sure the Torch would have questions, of course, when Cauvin showed up to reclaim Bec and the mule without the spy behind him. The Torch could believe whatever lies Cauvin concocted between now and then; or not believe them. It didn't much matter. Cauvin had the box, he knew where to find the froggin' S'danzo, and those questions the Torch had asked about Leorin—

Cauvin froggin' sure had asked them himself and he'd froggin' sure sleep better when he had the answers he wanted from the S'danzo . . . from *Elemi.*

Cauvin knew the S'danzo's name now; he'd froggin' *read* it.

With Soldt in the lead and Cauvin seething behind, they dog-legged around Davar's forge and left the bazaar through the old Common Gate with a single word weathered on the lintel. Today, for the first time, he read it—"Sanctuary."

They passed the fane of Shipri All-Mother, the finest of the rebuilt temples, though it, like all the others, was small and built more from wood and brick, than stone. Through the open door Cauvin saw Shipri's painted statue atop the altar. It seemed the goddess was looking straight at him, smiling at him, too—the soft, proud mother's smile that Bec got from Mina all the froggin' time.

Cauvin knew he should thank the goddess, but Cauvin had never been one for visiting temples. Except for the time when he'd walked out of the palace behind Grabar, he'd never felt the need to *thank* a god for anything. Even then it hadn't seemed froggin' right to thank a goddess when it was Grabar who'd just paid good silver to feed and clothe him and give him a home. And now—why thank Shipri when it was the Torch's froggin' sorcery that opened his eyes?

Besides, if Cauvin went into the fane, he'd have to tell Soldt what had happened, and that would give away a froggin' precious secret. Cauvin decided the All-Mother would understand that he couldn't pay such a high price for good fortune.

There were only two roads that meant anything around Sanctuary: the East Ridge Road to Ranke and the General's Road that flowed out of the Street of Red Lanterns, across the distant Queen's Mountains, and on to the Ilsig Kingdom. Cauvin didn't know what general had named the road, and there weren't any signposts for him to read, or time to read them. Soldt had settled into a long-legged stride—easy in *his* froggin' supple boots—that was likely to have them in the kingdom before sunset.

Soldt slowed once they were beyond easy sight of the city walls. He led Cauvin off the road, and for a moment Cauvin thought they were taking the very long way to the ruins, but—no, Soldt headed into rows of trees that must have been an orchard. There was a walled and gated yard in the midst of the trees. Within the wall the grass was cropped short, as though animals were usually penned there. Outside the pen stood a little square building, about the size of Flower's stall, but with no telltale traces of manure and straw to give it away. Cauvin guessed they'd come to one of Soldt's haunts, if not his outright home.

Not bothering with the gate, Soldt threw a leg over the waist-high wall. "Well, let's get on with it."

"On with what?"

"The fighting, Cauvin, the fighting. You're nursing a grudge; I promised Lord Torchholder I'd test your mettle. Let's see what you can do. Draw that Ilbarsi knife you've been carrying."

Cauvin reached awkwardly across his body for the hilt. The weapon was, as Soldt had just named it, a knife, not a sword, and it belonged on his right hip, not his left. He'd look the sheep-shite fool fumbling it out of its froggin' sheath, and Soldt had seen enough of Cauvin's foolishness for one day.

"I'm not a knife fighter," he admitted, releasing the hilt. "I fight with my fists. I'm good with my fists."

"If you say so. Come at me with your fists."

Never mind that pounding bruises into Soldt's face had been foremost in Cauvin's sheep-shite mind a moment earlier, he couldn't simply lay into a man, any man. "It wouldn't be right," he explained. "The Torch—I don't know what he told you, but I was in the palace when he led the Irrune against it. The Bloody Hand, they taught me; I was one of their warriors. If I fight you, I'll hurt you. I don't want that on my conscience."

"Don't insult me, Cauvin. If the Bloody Hand taught you to fight with your fists, then you were a thug, Cauvin, not a warrior, not even Dyareela's. You went out at night, marching behind a red-handed priest, and when he told you to hurt someone, you did—exactly the way you'd been taught. You'd kill, if that's what you'd been told to do, and not just in Sanctuary's dark streets. You'd killed in the pits, too—when they told you to make an example of someone. You weren't even a thug, just a big dog, trained to obey its masters' commands."

Cauvin swallowed hard. The Torch's spy had described the essence of his life in the Hand's fist, except for one important detail. "Not the pits. I looked out for the little ones. Protected—"

Soldt cut him off with a sneer. "Better be damned for killer than a liar, Cauvin. If the Hand taught you anything, it was because they trusted you wherever, whenever, and against whomever they chose. What did you do to earn their trust?"

Sweat seeped on Cauvin's forehead. He wiped it off on his sleeve, then ran his hand across the back of his neck, slipping the knot and drawing the bronze slug into his palm. Those memories were buried; he wouldn't dig them up. "Not the pits," he repeated.

Soldt wouldn't back down. "How many did you kill?" he taunted. "How many others exactly like yourself before the Hand taught you?"

"None!" Cauvin shouted. He'd never beaten another orphan to death—except . . . except . . . But those times didn't froggin' count. Those froggin' times had been froggin' kill or be killed. He'd done what he'd had to do to stay alive, and if the Hand had watched—If the Hand had liked what it froggin' saw—

"Don't lie to me, Cauvin. Were they bigger than you? Older? Or did you take the easy way and brain the little ones while they slept?"

For his answer to that accusation, Cauvin vaulted the wall, using his unweighted hand for balance. He closed fast, getting inside Soldt's reach before the spy knew what was coming. He chose his target—the point under the man's chin where his tongue was rooted. A solid blow there could kill a big man . . . a bigger orphan.

After ten years of smashing stone and regular meals, Cauvin figured he was a bit heavier, a shade slower, and a froggin' lot stronger than he'd been in the pits. When he surged in close and unwound a punch at Soldt's jaw, he expected the man to froggin' drop like a poleaxed pig and—maybe—not get up again. He figured, too, that he could live with his guilt. Froggin' sure, he'd had lots of practice.

Cauvin missed. Everything had gone the way he'd expected it to, but suddenly there was his froggin' fist clean to the right of Soldt's smirking face. He pulled his fist back and unloaded it a second time in less than a heartbeat. No way could Cauvin miss a second time but, gods all be froggin' damned, Soldt twitched left and Cauvin's punch didn't so much as ruffle the man's sheep-shite hair.

Shame, embarrassment, frustration—each was more than Cauvin could froggin' bear. He attacked without thought or plan and found himself facedown in the mud before he'd known he was falling.

"That was your best?"

Froggin' sure, it had been, but Cauvin tried again. If there'd been a froggin' tree to pin Soldt against, Cauvin knew he could have bloodied the man's face for fair, or if the stone wall had been more than waist high in the corners . . . If, if, and froggin' more ifs. There wasn't a froggin' tree, the wall was only waist high, and Soldt dodged each of Cauvin's punches, all the while tapping Cauvin on his chest and shoulders, even his sheep-shite chin. Taunting taps that said *if* I'd *wanted,* I *could hurt you* here *and* here *and* HERE.

Rage made Cauvin reckless, careless. After he'd landed in the muddy grass a third time, he growled and leapt at Soldt like a froggin' mad dog. He saw the moves that dropped him—sweeping arms and countersweeping legs—but had no defense against them. The way the Hand taught fighting— The puds he'd fought against, there'd never been much need for froggin' defense.

He got up, eyeing Soldt's legs. Maybe he could kick out the man's froggin' knee . . .

Or not. It froggin' sure seemed that as soon as Cauvin was upright and thinking about kicking, he was on his back again, hurting this time because he'd landed wrong. His knee buckled when he tested it, but he managed to stand with most of his weight on the other leg. Cauvin had the strength and wind for another go, what he lacked—suddenly, unexpectedly—was the will.

"I'm beat," he conceded. "Compared to you, I'm no froggin' fighter."

"Compared to me, I wouldn't expect you to be. You *like* to fight, Cauvin; I like to *win.* Center yourself. Stand so your weight can go down either leg in a heartbeat. In less than a heartbeat. You'll find it easier to keep your balance."

Cauvin had had enough of playing Soldt's sheep-shite fool. He said, "Swallow your froggin' suggestions and froggin' choke on them. It's over, I'm beat," adding a suggestion that Soldt lie with his mother and a few yard animals.

Soldt responded with a sigh. "That won't work, Cauvin. You

can't goad me the way I've been goading you all day. Lord Torchholder's chosen you and chosen me to ready you."

Captain Sinjon had spoken similar words three nights past. Cauvin hadn't liked hearing them in the *krrf*-scented Broken Mast and liked them no better in the cold, wet grass. "Hear me on this: The froggin' Torch didn't *choose* anything. He was getting the snot beat out when I found him in the froggin' old Temple of Ils. If there was any *choosing* done, it was me choosing to save his sheep-shite life . . . and, froggin' sure, I wish I hadn't."

The black cloak rippled with another shrug. "You know, he might agree with you. Lord Torchholder didn't say that *he'd* chosen you, only that you *had* been chosen. He blames you on the gods, on Sanctuary itself, claiming vengeance against him. But, you and I, we're not priests, are we? We don't believe in gods or cities with a conscience. We're just men doing our jobs.

"Listen, Cauvin— Whatever you did while you were in the palace, I don't know anything about it and I don't want to. What I just said—I was making it up, one word to the next, by watching the guilt cross your face. You got out alive; that's what matters. All that matters. Don't let memories get you killed."

The sudden change in Soldt's tone rattled Cauvin. He wracked his imagination for understanding and cursed himself for finding none. "How . . . ?" he began, but he couldn't ask all his questions at once. He chose one, not the hottest in his mind. "Were you spying on me when I found the Torch—Lord Torchholder—in the temple?"

Soldt shook his head. "Not even in Sanctuary. The Irrune women were wrapping his body by the time I got to the palace. At the start, I wasn't looking for Lord Torchholder. I was looking for his murderers and for vengeance. First place I looked was the Broken Mast, not that I thought I'd find a murderer there, but Sinjon keeps his eyes open—" Soldt smiled briefly. "You'd met Sinjon by then; he told me about your visit. That's when I knew I wasn't looking for vengeance but for Lord Torchholder alive but not well . . . and for you. For all I knew, you were the one who'd attacked him. Sinjon had you marked as a journeyman laborer who'd just happened by. I started at the crossing where the guards found the bodies. You know how close that is to your stoneyard. Once I'd found you, I followed you . . . You truly have no notion when you're being watched, Cauvin—that's got to be corrected. Day before yesterday, you led me to the old estate. I waited until you'd left."

Soldt clapped unseen dust and dirt from his gloves.

"Enough of that. What do you say? Can you balance on both feet, or is your knee shot? We don't have time, Cauvin. Lord Torchholder is dying— He's been saying that for years, but this time the shadow's fallen. You'll inherit his enemies—"

"I'm not the Torch's froggin' heir—" Cauvin complained until he recalled Bec risking death in a Copper Corner alley. It didn't matter what *he* thought; if the Torch's enemies thought he was their man, then everyone he knew—Bec, Grabar, Mina . . . Leorin!—was in danger.

"Sweet Shipri," Cauvin whispered as the realization sank through his mind. He stared into Soldt's eyes. He meant to ask: *Can you teach me to fight well enough to protect my brother?* but the honest question, "Can I trust you?" slipped out instead.

"That's a question you must answer for yourself, Cauvin. I can tell you that Lord Torchholder trusts me. He wants me to prepare you for the battles he won't be here to fight, and I will, but I'll give you choices, if I can, choices he might not. Are you ready for a lesson?"

Cauvin eyed the ground where he'd landed too many times already. "Who are you? What are you?"

"A bit of a stranger, not born here or any other nation, for that matter."

"Froggin' riddles."

"No—I was found newborn on a ship two days out of Caronne. I'd seen the world before I turned ten. Your weight's on your right foot. Stand between your legs, or you'll wind up on the ground again."

It didn't matter where or how Cauvin stood, he wound up in the mud. But a heartbeat before his fifth fall, he'd felt a moment of perfect balance. Somewhere around the twelfth attempt to stay on his feet, Cauvin moved with the other man, resisting, retreating, and returning like grass in the wind until he made the sheep-shite mistake of thinking he knew what he was doing.

Cauvin skidded across the froggin' grass an instant later.

Soldt extended a hand. "I'd go slower, if we had the time, but he's dying, hour by hour."

They clasped wrists. Cauvin groaned as Soldt jerked him upright. Shite for sure, he'd be aching all over come tomorrow morning.

"The Torch—he's a froggin' old man, right?"

"Eighty, at least."

"Then he couldn't have been much of a fighter before he got that wound."

Soldt shrugged. "He killed whoever attacked him."

"Frog all. I rescued him, remember? The Torch was game, but that made no difference to the Hiller pounding him."

"There were two bodies in the crossing. No question one was a Land's End sparker. But who was the other, the one they burnt, and who killed him? The sparker? He went down running with a knife in his back."

Cauvin hadn't known that, hadn't thought much about the second corpse, except he knew it couldn't have been the Torch. "Must've been another old pud, if the Torch managed to kill him and get mistaken for him. Wouldn't take a lot, really, to kill an old pud."

"Maybe not, but the corpse they burnt had been beaten to death. Its leg was broke and its nose had been hammered so far into its skull that its brains had leaked onto what was left of its chin. That's a lot of work for an old pud, as you say. My guess is that Lord Torchholder transformed whoever attacked him."

"*Transformed?* Froggin' shite. The old pud could do that?"

"The old pud's Lord Molin Torchholder, Archpriest and Architect of Vashanka. With the right prayer, he could do anything his god could do."

Cauvin didn't have time to think about that as Soldt came after him again, without warning.

They balanced, forearm to forearm. Someone sitting on the wall—if there'd been someone sitting on the wall—would have seen two men standing still, scarcely touching. But inside his skin, Cauvin felt constantly changing pressure and adapted to it. Moments passed. Cauvin kept his balance through several breaths and might have kept it longer, except he got bold and tried to do to Soldt what Soldt was doing to him. Staggering toward the wall, Cauvin imagined the pain he'd feel when he landed and, desperate to avoid it, managed to get his feet under him again before he fell.

"Better! Much better. You're quick."

Cauvin disagreed with a snort. He swiped sweat off his forehead. "The Torch—why pray for Vashanka to transform a froggin' corpse? Why not pray for a bolt of lightning *before* he had a hole in his hip?"

"Ask him, if you dare. Something went wrong, he won't say more than that. You're what's left: his heir. He says Vashanka and all the other gods are laughing. Gods." Soldt spat the word.

Cauvin remembered soaring above Sanctuary with a god's laughter ringing in his ears.

No froggin' surprise—he wasn't paying attention when Soldt closed against him. He never saw the move that flipped him ass over heels into the froggin' grass. But that was the last time Soldt caught him unprepared, and while Cauvin couldn't flatten the spy, he did knock him to his knees . . . once. After that, Soldt changed the exercise. He wanted to tie a strip of cloth over Cauvin's eyes.

There wasn't enough trust within the low, stone walls for Cauvin to agree to that Bloody Hand trick. He expected trouble when he said no. Soldt surprised him.

"We've done enough for one day, then, and whoever was watching, lost interest or nerve—or is too smart to leave cover. It's past time to rescue Lord Torchholder from your young brother."

"The S'danzo?" Cauvin gestured toward the box and the town, which were both in the same direction.

"Not today. You stink of swill and sweat, Cauvin—no way to visit a lady, even if she is S'danzo. Have you got enough money to get those boots dipped in sweet oil? Do you own a shirt that isn't frayed, or breeches that aren't patched on their patches?"

"My clothes are good enough for an honest man," Cauvin snarled. "They were froggin' clean when I left the stoneyard this morning. I'll rinse 'em off in the trough and they'll be clean again tomorrow."

"You need better than that. There's a laundress at the Inn of Six Ravens—you know the place?"

Cauvin swallowed and nodded. He and Grabar had once delivered stone there, but other men had done the wall-building. It was that kind of inn, maybe the only Sanctuary inn where a husband needn't worry about his wife's virtue if she stayed there alone.

"Her name's Galya—she'll stitch you up a white-linen shirt for a soldat—maybe less, if she likes your smile."

Cauvin grimaced.

"You must have a spare soldat? *I* paid the blacksmith."

"Not to spare. What am I going to do with a froggin' white-linen shirt?"

"Tuck it into a pair of woolen breeches."

Soldt did a one-handed vault over the wall. In the whirl of cloak and cloth Cauvin caught sight of a dark pole hung straight along Soldt's spine and what looked to be a froggin' sword hilt hanging out the bottom end.

Come winter, when the nights were long and even Mina's kitchen was too cold for working, Grabar would lead the whole household to the Lucky Well. Neighbors who didn't speak the rest of the year would crowd the common room until it was toasty warm. While the innkeeper's idiot son stirred a simmering kettle of watered wine—a dip for a padpol—Bilibot and Eprazian took turns telling tales. A night didn't go by without a tale about a man who wore his sword upside down along his spine. Not quite a villain, but never a hero, such a man showed up to do what no one else could do. Sometimes he carried a message across enemy lines, or rescued a prince and averted a war. More often, though, he stepped out of the shadows, sword in hand, for a fight to the death that wasn't his. If he was on the hero's side, he was called a duelist. When he was paid by the villain, Bilibot and Eprazian called him *assassin.*

It made sense—perfect sense—that the Torch was on close terms with a duelist . . . an assassin. But for Cauvin . . . ? Could a sheep-shite stone-smasher have been more foolish than to confront such a man with a lump of bronze in his fist? Cauvin wanted to run and hide for a month—it would be that long before his cheeks ceased burning; but he retrieved the wooden box instead and followed Soldt wherever he led.

# Chapter Thirteen

"Cauvin, do you know what Inception Island used to be called?" Bec asked from atop Flower's back.

They were headed back to the stoneyard well ahead of the sunset.

Cauvin would have preferred to linger at the ruins. Well, not exactly linger. Froggin' sure, there hadn't been a reason to *linger.* The Torch and his assassin had made it clear that they wanted to be alone. No matter what Cauvin or Bec suggested, the Torch froggin' twisted it into a reason for them to leave the ruins. He even let himself be stowed in the cellar again, just so Cauvin could get Bec home "before the boy's mother begins worrying about him." Frog all, the Torch didn't worry about anyone except his sheep-shite self.

Cauvin found it impossible to ignore the old pud's direct orders, but he would have dearly loved to creep up close to the two men and eavesdrop on their conversation which, shite for sure, be all about him. He could sneak back to the ruins after supper. Cauvin knew where there were gaps in the city walls, and he wasn't afraid to go outside them after dark—though he rarely did. But they knew languages he didn't froggin' recognize, much less understand, and were canny enough to use them whether they were alone or not.

Besides, he was aching from more froggin' bruises than he cared to count and—despite his best efforts with sand and water—his swill-doused boot had ripened to a fine stench. There'd be no sneaking up on anyone until he soaked the leather in sweet oil.

So he'd loaded the wooden box and his Ilbarsi knife into the back of the otherwise empty cart, plopped Bec on Flower's back—the boy was a gentle rider and light enough that the mule didn't mind carrying him when the cart was empty. They'd taken the roundabout, easy route home along the Eastern Ridge Road.

"Scav-something," Cauvin answered Bec's question. "Scavenge Island. Something like that. It was long before me. Long before your parents, too."

"Scavengers Island and forty years ago—exactly. Same year as the Dark Horde sacked the Imperial city."

Cauvin grunted. Had he been alone, the history of Sanctuary would have been the farthest thought from his mind. His body ached, but his head ached worse, maybe from the stench his boots released each time he took a stride or maybe from the sorcery that had made him literate. But most likely Cauvin's head ached from a froggin' stubborn refusal to think about Soldt when the duelist—the *assassin*—was everywhere in his mind. Froggin' forget the Torch and Soldt, *Cauvin* wanted to be alone.

But Cauvin wasn't alone and he couldn't be for hours, so he took refuge in whatever distraction Bec could provide. Fortunately, his little brother was a master of distraction.

Since leaving the red-walled ruins, they'd watched an Ilsigi galley make its way into Sanctuary harbor. The galley dwarfed everything else on the water. Its mast was taller than any wharf-side building, and its immense sail, furled now, had been like a cloud branded with the pointed crown of the Ilsigi king, Sepheris. Centipede oars arranged in two ranks that ran the length of the ship had brought the galley into the Wideway wharf. He'd heard that the lower rank of an Ilsigi galley was manned by condemned criminals—four to each froggin' oar, chained to their benches until they died or drowned.

Maybe the tale was true, maybe not. Cauvin's path had never taken him into a galley's hold and neither had the path of anyone he knew. What he did know was that the galley had rowed and sailed its way to Sanctuary from Inception Island, whose dark hilltops could be seen hovering, as if by sorcery, above the ocean on the hottest days of summer.

Once, the island had belonged to Sanctuary, then the Hand came to power and lost it to the Ilsigi Kingdom. Of all the things Sanctuary had lost to the Bloody Hand of Dyareela, Inception Island was among the least valuable. The island itself was barren—not fit for farming or living. The water, Cauvin had heard, was brackish. If men wanted to live there, they drank the rain, or sent galleys to Sanctuary, across the strait, for barrels of water as well as food.

That kept the population down.

Then, a few years back, the Ilsigis had crowned themselves a new king, a froggin' *ambitious* king who'd plunked a full-blown garrison on the island. Since then, two or three times a month—more often if the rains were sparse—a big Ilsigi galley hove into Sanctuary's harbor. Its officers paid whatever the Sanctuary merchants charged to resupply their garrison—and why not? They were spending Sepheris's money, not their own. They and the crews spent their own money almost as freely in the taverns and markets.

Thieves waxed their fingers when the galley breached the horizon. Merchants laid out their best and brightest wares; whores did much the same. Few complained that everything cost more when the galley sat in the harbor.

Well—Mina minded, but Mina had the tightest fist on Pyrtanis Street. Padpols flowed through her hands like glue. And, on balance, the stoneyard benefitted from the Inception trade. Wary of storms that could roil the strait without warning, the galleys set sail with island rock ballasted in their cargo holds. They threw a goodly portion of that ballast overboard as they laded up for the return voyage. Grabar paid a padpol for every barrow of island rock the low-tide gleaners pulled out of the mud.

"You want to hear a story about Scavengers Island?" the boy asked, pulling Cauvin's thoughts back from the piles of Inception rock he'd be sorting a few days from now.

"Is it about Honald the scavenger chicken?" Cauvin teased.

"No-o-o-o . . . *pirates*! It's a story about pirates!"

"Our chickens and their rooster have turned pirate?"

"No! It's not a made-up story, it's lived-through. Grandfather lived through it—"

Cauvin lost the rest of Bec's explanation. A sheep-shite like himself might not have expected to see a galley this particular day or any other, but the Enders clearly had. They'd sent a string of carts onto the spur road between Land's End and the East Ridge Road when the galley had furled its sail. The carts looked to be weighed down with grain, and Cauvin had figured empty-carted Flower could clear the watch gate before they were anywhere near. And she would have, but that's not how the froggin' Enders saw it.

An Ender steward thundered up to them.

"You there!" he shouted through a thick Imperial accent. "You there! Clear the way, pud!" His horse stamped and shook, spraying Cauvin with horse sweat.

"We'll be through before your—"

The steward cut him off. "Don't argue with me! Pull this porking rig off the road here and wait until we've passed. We've got trade with that ship in the harbor and can't be waiting while you fix a wheel or harness."

Cauvin wondered if the Ender would have been so froggin' cocksure if it had been someone else—Soldt with his cloak and boots—walking beside the cart and not a Wrigglie like him in ratty homespun and stinking boots.

"You hear me, pud? Move it! It's Lord Serripines' money that maintains this road and Lord Serripines' carts that use it first."

"You don't look like you're froggin' Lord Serripines," Cauvin muttered. He imagined that Soldt or the Torch might have said something similar . . . of course, they'd have spoken Imperial and the froggin' steward would have whored himself with apologies.

"What? What did you say to me, pud?"

"Nothing." He wrapped an arm around Flower's head and shoved her gently sideways.

The mule went easily. She knew when not to argue and, sometimes, so did Cauvin. A steward was always worse than a lord, no matter whether the lord was an Imperial sparker, home-grown Wrigglie, or the kingdom-captain on that galley. Lords never had to prove themselves; stewards did, stewards and stoneyard foster sons sent to collect debts from their betters. Froggin' sure Lord Mioklas would settle his stoneyard accounts in a hurry if an assassin showed up to collect their debts.

"It's not *his* road!" Bec grumbled, distracting Cauvin from vengeful thoughts once the cart was off the road and the steward had spurred his horse back to the sparker caravan.

Cauvin hissed the boy quiet. "Froggin' Enders . . . Shalpa's luck, give them a broken axle on every cart— Tell me your story. We've got the time."

"It's not my story; it's Grandfather's."

"Just tell it, Bec."

"It starts at the very beginning, with the gods. Grandfather says that every story has to start with the gods—"

"He's a froggin' priest. What else would a froggin' priest say?"

The boy said nothing for a moment, as if he'd taken Cauvin's gibe for a serious question, then began his tale in earnest: "The gods love to laugh. They gave Sanctuary a good harbor, then put the best harbor in all the world on an island just over our horizon. To amuse themselves further, they scraped most of the dirt off the island and sucked up its streams. Then they waited and waited for fools to find it—"

Cauvin caught himself staring. Bec, despite his squeaky, short-winded child's voice, had pretty much nailed the Torch's style. The boy sat stiff on Flower's back, except for his arms and hands, which stabbed the important words. The words had come from the old geezer, too—Honald and the chickens didn't care about gods or laughter.

"It's possible to earn an honest living in Sanctuary, not easy, but possible—" The boy's arms dropped to his sides, and he spoke with his own voice. "You and Poppa do, and Swift, and Momma says Teera never shorts the loaves she bakes. Grandfather said an honest life couldn't be lived at all on Scavengers Island. Only smugglers, thieves, sorcerers, and mis- mis- *miscreants*!"

The boy struggled to get the word past his teeth. He needn't have bothered. It was one of the Torch's fancy, Imperial words, and Cauvin didn't know the meaning except by tone.

"Don't ever forget," he advised Bec, "that pud you're calling Grandfather's a froggin' sparker lord. We're all nothing but Wrigglies to him."

"But the Scavengers were worse. It was them who ruled Sanctuary before the Imperials came. When Emperor—Emperor . . . ? Furzy feathers! I can't remember his name, and Grandfather even spelled it out for me!"

"And I *won't* remember it, so don't bother. One emperor's the same as another, or a king."

"Well, the emperor's army chased the pirates out of the palace and sent them sailing out to Scavengers Island. The people of Sanctuary welcomed him—"

"That's what Sanctuary does best: welcome its froggin' conquerors, from the Ilsigis to the froggin' Irrune. We *are* sheep-shite Wrigglies."

The Land's End steward rode past, a hundred or so paces ahead of the carts. He wouldn't so much as look at them, and neither would his sweated-up horse, so Flower loosed a bray worthy of her she-ass mother. She spooked the steward's horse and the teams pulling two nearby carts. The steward put brutal strength on the reins, bloodying the horse's mouth and flanks while he kept it in froggin' order.

The drovers had a harder struggle. One drover won, the other didn't. The inside rear wheel of his cart skidded off the road, struck a stone, and popped off its axle. The loose wheel missed Flower by less than an arm's length an instant before the unbalanced cart overturned, dumping sacks of grain directly at Cauvin's feet.

By rights, Cauvin should have helped get the cart righted and repaired—if only because the accident had Flower trapped, too. And he would have helped—the pounding he'd taken from Soldt had left him aching, not injured—if the sheep-shite steward had bothered to ask. The Ender looked through Cauvin as if he weren't there, so Cauvin told Bec to continue with his story.

"The emperor's governor was a fair man. He didn't go looking for trouble. He proclaimed a pardon for any pirate who laid down his trade. Those that could lay it down sailed back to Sanctuary. The rest hid on Scavengers Island. Woe betide the ship that ran aground on Scavengers Island!" Bec dragged a finger across his throat. "If not enough ships ran aground, then the pirates would scavenge each other, or lurk near Sanctuary's harbor. The pirates raided merchant ships as they sailed in or out, and there wasn't a lot that Sanctuary could do to stop it, until the fish-folk arrived. If their ships couldn't run a pirate down, they'd *stare* him down instead—"

Bec had his thumbs and forefingers against his eyes, holding them unnaturally wide open. Froggin' sure the Torch hadn't done that.

"Between the fish-folk, Tempus and his Stepsons, the witches, the gods and demigods, the hazards," Bec counted the threats on his fingers, concluding with—"and all the resur- resur- resurrected dead in the streets, the pirates decided that Sanctuary was too dangerous for them and stayed away. Then the witches got rid of the gods, and the gods got rid of the witches. The dead people disappeared . . . so did Tempus and his Stepsons. The pirates thought the time was ripe for raiding.

"They stole people off the streets at night and stuffed them in barrels bound for the island. The stolen people, they were mostly lowlifes, thieves and troublemakers. Some other people thought the pirates were doing Sanctuary a favor, but not Grandfather. Grandfather said that stealing thieves was worse than stealing honest folk because honest people always came through the front doors. No matter how much they got tortured, they couldn't tell the pirates anything about the holes in Sanctuary's defenses. Stealing honest people was a moral outrage and demanded retrib- retribution, but stealing thieves was worse. Thieves could be bought without torture. Thieves knew where Sanctuary was weak. Thieves could lead the pirates in—"

Cauvin interrupted. "*Grandfather* said that That froggin' pud knows more about sneaking in and out of Sanctuary than any froggin' thief. The froggin' pirates should've stolen *him*."

Bec started to protest. Cauvin waved him down. The drovers had righted their cart, and the steward was shouting orders to get the caravan moving again. By chance, Cauvin snagged the Ender's attention. No good would come from arguing with the mounted man in a froggin' sour mood, so Cauvin bent his neck and studied his feet.

Froggin' sure, Cauvin knew his place. He was a sheep-shite orphan who'd walked out of the palace alive through no froggin' fault or plan of his own, a stone-smasher with no prospects, a Wrigglie to the core. No moral outrage or retribution if pirates stole *him*!

The steward yanked the reins and clapped his spurred heels against already bloodied flanks. His driven horse took off down toward the East Gate.

"He doesn't like you," Bec observed. "Good thing he doesn't know your name."

The string of carts was moving again. Cauvin distracted Flower with an ear scratch, lest she let out another froggin' bray. "Just let him come looking for me."

"You'll get in trouble for fighting."

"Not if he starts it."

Bec shrank. The boy wasn't a fighter. Even in the cradle he'd been all smiles—pick him up, put him down, feed him, or ignore him, as a baby Bec had taken it all in stride. As a result, the world was easier for him than it had ever been for Cauvin. That bothered Bec far more than it bothered Cauvin.

"Finish your story," Cauvin suggested when the Enders had all passed and the boy's mood hadn't lifted.

"It's not a very good story. Grandfather talked to people—the prince and his wife, she was one of the fish-folk. I can't remember their names—"

"The prince was Kadakithis. Her name was Shupansea."

"How do you know? Did Grandfather tell you the story already?"

"I know, that's all." Cauvin didn't want to get tangled up in the truth. "I must've heard the names somewhere."

"They called him Kittycat, did you know that, too?"

"No," Cauvin lied. "Never heard that before."

"He took Grandfather's advice and sent the fish-folk's ships out to Scavengers Island to clear off the pirates. When they were done, they changed the island's name to Inception, 'cause it's the first land between here and wherever the fish-folk came from—and went back to—and because it was supposed to be the start of Sanctuary's glory. With the pirates gone and the Empire losing its war in the north—nobody was paying attention to the kingdom—Grandfather thought that Sanctuary could grow into a mighty place, maybe a kingdom of its own, because the fish-folk were rich, and they'd only sail into Sanctuary's harbor, on account of their queen being the prince's wife."

"He got that froggin' wrong." Cauvin laughed. "It's been downhill for Sanctuary since the fish."

"That wasn't Grandfather's fault! Sanctuary would have become a mighty place if the gods had let it. But the gods wouldn't let Grandfather finish what he'd started. The prince disappeared on the road to Ranke, and his wife went home with the fish. Then the storms came and wrecked all the big ships; and plague killed all the captains and sailors and navigators who knew where the fish-folk lived. Then, just when Grandfather had rebuilt the ships and was ready to send them out looking for the fish-folk, the Bloody Hand took over the palace. Grandfather sent the ships to Inception, 'cause he thought they'd be safer there, but he said he couldn't watch the horizon and his back at the same time and no ships wanted to come to Sanctuary once the Hand was in charge—"

The boy hesitated . . . wary of Cauvin's reaction and with good reason. Froggin' sure, Cauvin usually walked away whenever the Hand got mentioned, but he let it slide this time, and Bec continued.

"Grandfather said he knew the Ilsigi king had put men on Inception Island, but there wasn't anything he could do about it, and the Irrune . . . they won't set foot in a boat, not even Arizak. So, now it's still Inception Island, but it belongs to the Ilsigi king. The king's ships control the strait between here and there. They keep pirates away from Inception and us, both—but they keep closer watch over ships that put in at Inception Island. The galleys come here for supplies, but everything else goes there. It'd be better for us if we held Inception Island again. Better for the Ilsig king if he held Sanctuary, instead. Grandfather doesn't think the Ilsigis will try anything while Arizak's alive, but he won't live forever. His sons will have a choice to make . . . his sons and Sanctuary: the Empire or the kingdom."

Cauvin had his eye on the gate where the Ender steward was arguing with the watchmen at the East Gate. "Froggin' puds," he said without looking at Bec. "If it comes to choosing, you know which way this place'll swing."

A silent moment passed before Bec said softly, "Everybody hates the Imperials. Maybe they're right to. Momma talks, but I wouldn't want to live at Land's End, even if I could. I don't think they're *nice*."

Bec's hair was darker than Cauvin's. So was his mother's, where it grew out of her head. Mina would rather look like a heap of straw at the end of summer than a Wrigglie. She bought bleach from the dyers and daubed it on her scalp until it bled and made froggin' sure Bec wasn't proud of anything he'd gotten from his Wrigglie father.

Cauvin wasn't proud of his ancestors, either. On the whole, his people—the sons of thieves and daughters of slaves—weren't as clever or brave or honest as other people. But Cauvin never liked to see Bec with a frown on his face. He dropped a hug around the boy's scrawny shoulders.

"If *nice* mattered, sprout, we'd put Batty Dol in the Governor's Palace—she's just about the *nicest* person I know, but look out afterward, 'cause she's mad as a magpie. I hate the Imperials because they sit out at Land's End, proud as peacocks, getting richer every day even without their froggin' Empire to back them up, and there's not a froggin' thing we can do about it. But the Ilsigis—the *real* Ilsigis from the kingdom, not us bastard Wrigglies—would be froggin' worse in the palace. To Imperials, we're barbarians, but, shite for sure, they think everyone who's not a citizen is a barbarian—"

"I'm a citizen. Momma made Poppa pay to put my name on the rolls at the palace. She keeps a copy behind a hearthstone, all sealed in wax to protect it."

"Then you could live at Land's End. That's the way the Imperials are: They'll treat you like a froggin' turd, but show up with the right piece of parchment, and you're one of them . . . well, maybe not quite—you'll wind up like that steward, always having to make yourself important. I'm telling you, though—it's different with the Ilsigis. We look like them, pretty much; we speak the same language, almost; and when some sparking Ilsigi comes to Sanctuary the only thing he sees is escaped slaves. A turd's got use in this life—leave it alone and plants grow better; but a runaway slave means somewhere there's a master who's frogged himself. If we bow down to King Sepheris, we'll stand up in chains with hot brands on our backs."

"It's been over *two hundred years,* Cauvin. All those slaves who ran away from their masters are dead and their grandchildren and their grandchildren's children, too. Nobody could come into Sanctuary and say—you, your great-great-grandfather was a runaway slave. Nobody remembers who their great-great-grandfather was."

"The Ilsigis won't care. Far as their kingdom's concerned, Sanctuary's worse than a mistake, it's shame, and there's nothing worse than shame. It's all smiles and shaboozh now, but if Sanctuary goes to bed with Sepheris, that parchment over the hearth won't mean froggin' shite."

Cauvin had surprised himself with his passion. He'd surprised Bec, too. The boy squirmed free.

"Furzy feathers!"

Embarrassed, Cauvin mumbled, "I don't *know*—I never froggin' thought about it much, but everything just came clear in my mind all of a sudden." He didn't like the way that sounded, almost as if the thoughts hadn't been his, the way reading hadn't been his yesterday. "If it comes to choosing— If anyone asks me, I'd say Sanctuary should stick with the froggin' Empire. The worst they'll do to Sanctuary is start collecting taxes again."

"Furzy feathers!"

Young as he was, Bec was the stoneyard's clever one. When Bec's mouth hung open with disbelief, Cauvin could be certain he'd made a fool of himself . . . again.

"I—"

"Furzy feathers! Grandfather said almost the *same* words. He even told me that the palace rolls wouldn't count for anything with the Ilsigis, and that's why Raith's got to succeed his father, not Naimun or the Dragon. Did Grandfather tell you what to think?"

Stunned, Cauvin snapped, "The froggin' Torch doesn't tell me what to think!" though that was his precise fear. "You want to write down his froggin' nonsense, that's fine, but you shouldn't pay attention to what he says. The Torch's got one foot in his grave . . . and your stories about Honald and the hens are better than anything he's told you. Forget about Inception Island. It's all past and over. He's crowding your skull with froggin' ideas you don't need 'cause no one's ever going to care what you know or think."

Bec's eyes stayed wide, but his mouth closed, and he wrapped his arms tightly over his chest. "You don't mean that, Cauvin." The boy's voice was soft. He took after his father when it came to anger: slow and stubborn, not at all like Mina, who raged like a summer storm, or Cauvin himself. "You're angry because I said that you and Grandfather see Sanctuary the same way, and you don't want that to be possible."

"He's a froggin' Imperial *priest*! Froggin' sure, if the Torch says something's good for him, it's not going to be good for me. Can't be."

"Not good for you or Grandfather. Good for Sanctuary. That's different. You agree on what's good for Sanctuary, whether or not it's good for you."

"If something's not good for me, I don't care how good it is for froggin' Sanctuary."

The Ender steward and the watchmen had settled their differences. Carts were rolling forward. Looping Flower's lead over his wrist, Cauvin guided her onto the Ridge Road.

He didn't care about Sanctuary, Cauvin assured himself. He cared about himself, about Bec and Leorin, maybe about Grabar and Mina—on a good day. But suppose the Ilsigi did take over Sanctuary and they did just what he'd predicted? Would he let the Ilsigi burn their mark into Bec's cheek? Or Leorin's? Could he do anything to stop them?

*Don't think,* Cauvin reminded himself. *You're not made for thinking. You're sheep-shite stupid and made for doing what you're told.*

In desperation, Cauvin sought gray fog to quiet his mind, but the fog was impossible to find late of an autumn afternoon. Instead, he stared straight ahead and up a bit, at the carved-stone plaque above the open gate. He'd seen it countless times before—two heads in profile facing each other over a symbol made from two swords crossed over a spear, all of them pointed at the ground. The profiles were better than Grabar's work, but not by much. They both looked alike, and neither looked like a real man.

Cauvin had looked at the plaque countless times. Today he read the inscription—

AT THIS PLACE
AT THE 60TH COMMEMORATION OF
THE FOUNDING OF THE GREAT EMPIRE
KADAKITHIS—PRINCE & THERON IV—EMPEROR
DID DECREE SANCTUARY
A CITY OF THE EMPIRE
BY THE GRACE OF SAVANKALA, HIS LIGHT AND HIS LAW

The words, Cauvin realized with a start, were Imperial, which made sense, considering what they meant, but it was froggin' odd to read meaning from words he couldn't froggin' pronounce.

The watchmen beckoned Cauvin forward. They'd seen him often enough in the last few days to know him and Flower by sight, if not by name, and passed him through with only a few gibes about the aroma clinging to his boots.

Flower sensed that her stall and her grain weren't far away. She would have picked up a trot if Cauvin had let her, but a trot would have brought them up against the slow Ender carts. So he kept a firm hand on her lead, which the mule protested by swinging her head hard against his arm. If he'd been in a good mood, Flower's behavior would have soured it, but his mood wasn't good and got worse with every stride, every head butt.

When Bec announced, "Grandfather won't be surprised when I tell him that you think Sanctuary shouldn't throw in with the Ilsigis. He says he owes you an apology. He says he was right about you the first time and wrong the second, whatever that means. And the only one who thinks you're a sheep-shite fool is you," Cauvin had all he could do to keep from striking the boy down.

"I don't care a frog-sucking damn what the froggin' Torch says about anything, especially me. I didn't ask him to haul my froggin' ass out of the pits, and I never should have hauled his out of the temple. He doesn't owe me anything except his death. The sooner he dies, the better. Tonight! Good riddance!"

Bec blanched and knotted his fingers in Flower's skimpy mane. The mule responded by straining against the traces and giving Cauvin her hardest butt yet. He snapped the lead against her nose—which was a froggin' foolish thing to do. The world didn't know from stubborn until the first mule got born. Flower bared her flat, yellow teeth and brayed up enough racket to draw a man down from the gate.

Cauvin made peace with the watchman and the mule while Bec sat on her back, white as winter snow, his eyes shiny with unshed tears. Bec's obvious misery shamed Cauvin, and he hid deep in his own thoughts to escape its weight. The boy slipped off Flower's back as soon as they were through the stoneyard gate. He ran straight to the kitchen. Cauvin didn't think Bec would tell Mina the true reason he was on the verge of tears, but Mina would notice, and she'd blame Cauvin.

Supper was going to be froggin' unpleasant. Cauvin would have climbed the ladder to his loft if he hadn't gone hungry since breakfast. He could have gone to the Lucky Well for supper, or to the Unicorn, but he'd still have to face his foster mother, and the way he ached from top to bottom, he wasn't eager to hike for supper. He tended Flower, hid the wooden box with the Ilbarsi knife, and after coating his boots with sweet oil walked barefoot through the sunset into Mina's kitchen.

Everyone on Pyrtanis Street knew there was an Ilsigi ship in the harbor—they need only walk to the end of the street to see its mast rising above the wharf. The first words out of Mina's mouth weren't about Bec's tears or Cauvin's feet—as he'd feared. They were a warning that supper would be long on grain, short on fish.

"Someone thinks they're worth a feast and sucked half the fish out of the damned market. Drove up the prices up on what was left. Hecath's fires will burn cold before I spend *four* padpols on scrod."

Mina had added extra grain to the pot to make up for the missing fish. It was tasty, though—Mina knew her spices and, more importantly, her spice-sellers the way sots knew the town's froggin' taverns. But food couldn't lighten Cauvin's thoughts. Nor could conversation.

The night's good news—if it could be called that—was that late in the afternoon Tobus the dyer had shown up at the stoneyard to talk about rebuilding an adjoining house for his soon-to-wed son. Tobus wanted the fronts to match—to show his prosperity, now stretching into a second generation, to anyone walking down Sendakis Way.

"More than bricks, Cauvin, Tobus wants new lintels across *both* houses, with carvings, no less. I warned him the Irrune won't abide gods in the city, Imperial or otherwise. He's settled for fish, a row of them above each door and window. Tobus the dyer lives in a house crowned by *tobutt* fish—clever? We'll cross the fish like this—" Grabar made an X with his forearms. "We've agreed on forty coronations paid in soldats—soldats minted in Ranke and not cut since they got here."

"Forty! You should have gotten sixty!" Mina carped from the hearth. "Even a good soldat's not the same as a damned shaboozh, you know." It bothered her that shaboozh were worth more than soldats, never mind that a shaboozh was almost four times the weight.

"Wife! Enough! We'll see a good profit. And before we're done, I'll tempt Tobus with columns, great thick columns faced with brick, to frame his two front doors. Meantime, I've got to order red-veined marble for the lintels all the way from Mrsevada. Tobus gave me the name of a ship's broker—Sinjin, Minjin, something like that. The three of us will meet Ilsday to make the necessary arrangements—"

"Forty!" Mina repeated, "If Tobus can afford foreign marble, then he's got enough to pay you another forty coronations for your labor. Think of the boy, Husband! Another forty coronations would see him apprenticed to a master apothecary in *Ranke*."

"Enough! Forty coronations it is and will be!"

Mina's spoon clanged against the pot, but she said nothing more. Cauvin said nothing either, though his mind swirled with memories of the Torch assuring him that smashing red bricks wouldn't prove a froggin' waste of time. He wasn't surprised. After sorcery and assassins, why would he be surprised that Tobus—a Wrigglie through and through despite his Imperial name—was suddenly reckoning his accounts in coronations and soldats or that Grabar was headed for a meeting at the frog-all Broken Mast?

Even tucked away in a root cellar, the froggin' Torch had the power to shape a sheep-shite stone-smasher's life.

Then conversation turned to the day's bad news—not the appearance of an Ilsigi galley or the surge in prices at the market, but runners who'd appeared at the stoneyard not long after Cauvin had taken off in the morning. A building had collapsed in a quarter south of the palace and as Sanctuary's only master stonemason it fell to Grabar to decide where men could safely dig for survivors.

"That rain we had last night must've done for the walls," Grabar muttered. "The corner gave at the bottom and everything above collapsed. We pulled one lucky fellow out—he'd been asleep in the attic when it fell; he'll live. The poor bastards below—"

"Husband!" Mina snapped with a sidelong glance at Bec, who was all ears listening.

"Damned miserable morning. Could've used you and the cart," Grabar said in Cauvin's direction.

"You knew where I froggin' was," Cauvin said, which wasn't a complete lie—not for the morning, and he was covered for the afternoon: Bec would have said if runners had come to the ruins after he and Soldt had taken off. Shite for sure, the runners would have noticed the froggin' Torch sitting on the window ledge, and that's the story the city would be serving with supper, instead of a collapsed building or an Ilsigi galley.

Damned gods knew, Cauvin had been as lucky as the fellow Grabar had pulled out of the rubble. He couldn't resist the relief, or the shame. Pushing the empty bowl aside, Cauvin left the kitchen for the loft. With no lamp or candle to break the gloom, Cauvin threw himself down on the straw, wishing he could unlive the last five days or, failing that, fall asleep.

As far back as he could remember, Cauvin's best and surest defense had been sleep. No matter what had happened with his mother or with the Hand, once he was alone in the dark, Cauvin could retreat into the gray, hide in dreamless sleep, and wake up with an armor of emptiness between himself and his memories. Day or night, rested or exhausted, he'd been able to will himself into dreamless sleep, so it came as a froggin' unpleasant surprise to find himself wide-awake and staring up at the shades-of-black rafters.

They were all there, whirling in Cauvin's mind: the Torch with his glowing staff and parchment skin; Sinjon and his mismatched staring eyes from the Broken Mast; the guards, the watchmen, the Hiller from Ils's temple, and the Ender steward on his sweating horse; the would-be killers who'd laid their red hands on Bec in Copper Corner; and—looming larger than Lord Molin Torch-holder—the froggin'-sure killer, the assassin, Soldt. A crumbled home Cauvin hadn't seen with his own eyes filled the center of Cauvin's confusion. In his mind, it was a froggin' redbrick ruin.

Cauvin's friends were in there, his loved ones: Bec and Leorin, Grabar and Mina, Swift and his Pyrtanis Street neighbors; Pendy, Jess, and everyone who'd ever died. Even his ghostly mother was trapped beneath red bricks. He had to get them out, with a mallet, not a shovel—*his* mallet with a shiny bronze head. It was more than comfortable in his hands, and Cauvin swung it with confidence, certain that he could smash the bricks aside in time.

The ruins shuddered each time Cauvin struck them, loosening

more bricks, piling them higher and higher. Between heartbeats the ruins swelled like waves before a gale. Growing faster than they crumbled, the brick walls towered over Cauvin's head. He staggered backward, defeated, looking desperately for Grabar, who could read the strength of a wall and tell him which bricks could be removed and which must remain.

But his foster father was in the ruins, under the bricks with all the others. The Torch moved in Grabar's place, squatting down on his haunches, measuring the jagged walls with his blackwood staff. The priest noticed Cauvin. He stood and pointed the staff at Cauvin's scarred chest. His mouth opened and words came out, ribbons of written words—commands Cauvin couldn't obey because he'd forgotten how to read. In a blind, frustrated rage, Cauvin swung his mallet, striking whatever stood in its path.

Arms reached into Cauvin's madness. The arms became thick ropes that bound Cauvin against hard stone and held him prisoner. The bronze-headed mallet fell from his hands. Cauvin screamed from his gut, and the ropes were gone. He searched for his mallet. The ruins had swallowed it, as they'd swallowed everything else he cared about. Cauvin dropped to his knees. He attacked the rubble with his bare hands.

He was no longer alone. On either side, rows of men knelt and dug with their hands. They all looked alike. They all looked like the assassin, Soldt.

*We're just men doing our jobs . . . just men doing our jobs.*

The sounds of suffering seeped up through the bricks. Cauvin dug frantically until burning pain made him stop. He looked down at his hands.

His hands were red, bloodred from fingertips to wrists.

His hands had turned red.

The stain was spreading from wrists to arms, arms to heart.

Cauvin screamed again and found himself alone in darkness, gasping for air, and unable to hear a sound above the pounding of his heart. For a moment, Cauvin didn't know where he was, then the wood at his back, the mule smells, and stone smells became familiar. He was in the loft—wedged into a corner beneath the eaves with no notion how he'd gotten there, but home all the same. His heart slowed. His breathing steadied.

He'd had a dream, a nightmare, and it was over. Yes, a building had collapsed in Sanctuary, but not the building Cauvin had dreamt about. Yes, people had died—crushed and broken, but not the people Cauvin cherished. Nightmares weren't the truth—that's what Cauvin told Leorin, Pendy, and the other orphan dreamers. The twisted memories nightmares left behind could be banished because they were lies.

Cauvin crawled back to his pallet and clutched the blankets tight. He had no intention of falling asleep—one nightmare was more than enough—then a fine rain began to beat on the walls around him . . .

The rain had ended when Cauvin awoke, blissfully empty-headed. With little effort, he remembered his nightmare, but sleep had put an arm's length of peace between him and it. He was calmer than he'd been since rescuing the Torch. The nightmare had been just the froggin' dose Cauvin had needed to see the events of the last five—now six—days for what they were.

Frog all, Cauvin still didn't know what he'd done to deserve it, but the Torch had singled him out—drawn him to the Temple of Ils, tricked him with froggin' sorcery time and time again, battered him with gods and assassins, then—finally—invaded his dreams. Shite for sure, the old pud had sent him a nightmare message: Work with Soldt if you want your little brother, your beloved, or your foster parents to be safe.

Cauvin had heard that message before—from the Hand. He'd listened. What else could he have done? Froggin' Lord Molin Torch-holder had made a froggin' mistake when he'd seized the strings on Cauvin's soul. He was still a sheep-shite fool, not made for thinking, but it didn't take much froggin' thinking to see that there wasn't a big difference between the Torch and the Hand, except that the Torch was dying.

The treacherous old pud had said it himself: He didn't have much froggin' time. All Cauvin had to do was stay away from the red-walled ruins for a few days, and the Torch would be dead. Shite for sure, he might have another run-in with Soldt, and no man wanted a froggin' assassin on his back, but Cauvin thought he could endure that . . . and the Bloody Hand of Dyareela, too.

Damn the Bloody Hand, but Sanctuary knew the Mother of

Chaos now. They wouldn't make the same mistake again. If red-handed preachers started showing up in the streets, the city would rise up to exterminate them. Cauvin didn't have to do it alone—if it needed doing at all, if the froggin' Torch wasn't responsible for his own ambush, or the Copper Corner attack on Bec. Keeping Bec safe *was* Cauvin's responsibility. Bec, Grabar, and Mina, too.

And Leorin.

Cauvin paused with his oil-dripping boots in his hands. Damn the Torch to Hecath's coldest hell, but Cauvin had had doubt about Leorin when she reappeared in his life and, no froggin' thanks to the Torch, he had them again. He had the means to extinguish those suspicions forever—if he were willing to believe a S'danzo seeress or tempt her into answering *his* questions with the Torch's second wooden box.

He pondered his dilemma through an uneventful breakfast, then, confident that he was clever enough to outwit a froggin' S'danzo, followed Grabar into the work shed.

"Has Mioklas paid what he owes us?" he asked, laying the groundwork for another day away from the stoneyard.

Grabar shook his head. "Haven't seen hide nor hair of him—and the wife would have said if he'd sent someone else to pay."

"I'm off, then. I'll be back with what he owes us by sunset." Cauvin tried to hold Grabar's narrow-eyed stare, but his foster father knew him too well, and he looked away first.

"Your back's up; you're looking for a fight again. Father Ils knows why—"

"Because Tobus won't pay us a padpol if Mioklas doesn't settle up."

"Tobus has already left ten of his soldats for earnest and showed me the others. He wants those houses, Cauvin; he'll pay. Lord Mioklas pays slow, the whole city knows that; but he's good for his debts over time. Settle yourself. I'll tell you when—and if—it's time to knock on his high door."

"It's time. He said autumn, and it's froggin' autumn. He froggin' *owes* us." Cauvin made a fist and held it between his face and Grabar's. "I'm not asking for anything that's not already ours, anything that he doesn't froggin' already have in his froggin' chamber."

"You're looking for a fight."

"I'm not," Cauvin insisted. "I ask. He pays. No fights. Froggin' simple." He met his foster father's eyes.

"What's come over you these last few days, Cauvin?" Grabar asked, conceding defeat without admitting it. "You're not yourself. Are you in trouble? Of your own or someone else's?"

Cauvin couldn't answer that. "I'm not looking for a fight, Grabar. I swear to you. I've got things to do—not trouble. Tell Mina not to cook supper for me; I'll eat at the Unicorn."

"The Unicorn! Where are you getting the money to eat at the Unicorn?" Grabar demanded. "What kind of trouble are you tangled in?"

But Cauvin was already headed out the gate. He walked fast until he was past the emptiness where Enas Yorl's home had stood, then headed for the Stairs. Every few steps, he glanced back, cursing Grabar, yet hoping to see him.

*Tangled is right,* he thought, pounding through the Tween. *I'm so tangled. I'm going to bribe a S'danzo to learn if I can trust the woman I love. I've got a man who should be dead working sorcery on me and a froggin' gods-be-damned* assassin *telling me how to fight and dress—*

"Whoa! Cauvin, where're you headed so fast?"

An unfamiliar voice hailed Cauvin from behind. Spinning, he saw an older, careworn woman coming toward him with her arms wide-open. Cauvin needed a moment before he recognized dead Jess's mother. He hadn't spoken to her since Jess threw himself in the froggin' harbor. For Jess's memory, she had to wrap her arms around him and tell him how *good* it was to see him, never mind that there were tears leaking from her eyes; and Cauvin had to endure the embrace, even return it. He'd patted her shoulder and was wondering if meeting her counted as a good omen or a bad one when flickering movement snagged his attention. He turned quickly, but not quickly enough, and was left with only the sense that he'd seen something black disappear into a shop, or an alley, or thin air itself.

If it had been Soldt, then he knew what kind of omen held him in her trembling arms.

"You come by the shop." She wept. "There's always candles for you and little Pendy."

He couldn't tell her that Pendy was dead, too, or that nothing would lure him to the chandlery where Jess had seemed so froggin' happy, right up to the day he killed himself. Jess's mother must have guessed. She stretched an arm's length between them and gave Cauvin a strange look. Then she hid the lower half of her face behind her scarf and took off running.

*Froggin' gods all be damned,* Cauvin swore, but he made his way toward the Shambles more carefully after that, not drawing attention and keeping an eye out for Soldt's black cape, which didn't reappear.

What Cauvin did see were words. Words painted on open shutters, above doorways, on barrels and crates, even fluttering on banners hung from upper-story windows. Most of them added nothing to his understanding. (What use was the written word for bakery in Wrigglie or Imperial—rarely both—when a man's nose could find the shop faster than his eyes?) But a few unmasked mysteries Cauvin had never suspected.

A banner above one fish stall proclaimed that the owner sold only today's catch while his nearest competitor claimed only his fish were good enough for Land's End. Given a choice, Cauvin would prefer today's catch over what was left after the Enders took theirs—assuming both sellers were completely honest, which sellers almost never were. They lied easily enough to a customer's face; froggin' sure, they'd lie even more easily with a pen.

Someone had chalked ENDOSH CHEATS AT DICE on the wall of an abandoned warehouse and, as if to challenge that claim, a different hand had written MANAKIM OWES ENDOSH 5 SHABOOZH right below it. ERLIBURT'S SCRIPTORIUM had work for anyone who could read and write Ilsigi, Rankene, or two other languages employing letters Cauvin still couldn't make sense of. The SISTERS OF SHIPRI ALL-MOTHER would offer prayers of thanksgiving at the goddess's fane beneath the full moon of Esharia, which was one month away.

A message so fresh that its white paint glistened in the morning light advised that the bodies pulled from the ruins of PELCHER'S TAVERN had been taken to the charnel house on Shambles Cross, where, for a fine of five padpols, they could be claimed until sundown by relatives.

Cauvin's path of discovery took him past the Broken Mast, where a good-sized signboard he hadn't noticed during his first visit hung between two upper-story windows. Its words were arranged in two columns, the first of which was ships' names and the second was dates, some in red, others in white. The red dates were past and gone; those ships, he realized, were overdue. The EMPEROR OF THE SEAS was nearly a year overdue, but the KABEEBER was due the same day the Sisters of Shipri would be offering their prayers.

The comings and goings of ships was of no froggin' concern to a stone-smasher, unless he were waiting for a load of fancy marble to arrive from Mrsevada. Cauvin wondered if such a ship would be listed on the Broken Mast's signboard. It might be useful to know when their ship was due; more useful to have read it off the Broken Mast's roof rather than depend on Captain Sinjon's honesty, and most useful of all if the captain never suspected a stone-smasher could read.

No wonder that Mina spent so much time teaching Bec how to read and write. No froggin' wonder, either, that she'd never offered the same lessons to Cauvin: a lettered man had the same advantage day in and out that Cauvin had when he weighted his fist before a fight.

Cauvin found himself glad that he hadn't mentioned his sudden mastery to Bec—froggin' glad and froggin' ashamed, too. But the boy would eventually tell his mother, and Cauvin felt no shame about keeping secrets from Mina.

Beyond the Broken Mast, Cauvin followed his nose up Stinking Street and into the Shambles. Written words were rare in a quarter that was, on the whole, less prosperous than Pyrtanis Street. The words Cauvin did see were etched rather than painted or chalked onto the walls. Most of the etchings weren't truly words at all, just letters—the same Ilsigi letters scratched over and over until Cauvin passed an old warehouse whose lintels proclaimed that: THE EYES OF ILS WATCH SHARP. THE DEAD WALK PAST. Taken in order, the first letters of each word on the lintels matched the letters he saw repeated on less substantial walls. Cauvin realized that the mysteries of writing went as deep as sorcery.

Cauvin hadn't heard the stories of dead men walking the streets of froggin' Sanctuary until after Grabar brought him home to Pyrtanis Street. Old Bilibot had cornered Cauvin outside the Lucky Well and told him, with breath so foul it had turned his stomach—

that neither the Hand nor the Troubles were the worst Sanctuary had endured. The worst—if a man were sheep-shite foolish enough to believe Bilibot—had been the witches and hazard-mages who'd invaded the town during the northern wars and the living-dead corpses they'd raised. The living dead had been men, mostly, but some women and a few animals, too—their death wounds gaping for all to see and their minds so frogged they didn't remember dying.

Even fresh out of the froggin' palace, Cauvin wasn't sheep-shite stupid enough to take Bilibot's word for anything. He'd asked his new foster father if the sot's memory was as rotten as his breath.

Grabar had replied that though he'd been born after the witches and hazards left Sanctuary, he'd grown up with a neighbor man who claimed he'd been dead once—

*"He had an eye as white as the moon but, other than that, there weren't no differences from other men that I saw—'til he slipped on the Wideway and got himself crushed beneath an oxcart. Swelled up like the pox straightaway, then burst and shriveled, all before they could get the cart off him. Weren't nothing left 'cept the bones they took to his widow. Didn't see it myself, mind you—I weren't no older than Bec when it happened—but that's what I heard. Saw one of his rib bones, though, years later—they said was his bone—black as night and all shiny, like it had been glazed and baked in a potter's kiln. Some say that's the witches' mark, but he wasn't no witch, so maybe the old hags put it on him, if they'd raised him—*

*"Or maybe not. His widow, she was young and Sumese. Could be she did him in. She sold his tools for cheap soon enough and took off with a sea captain not long after."*

The Sumese were renowned for treachery . . . and poisons. It was easier to believe an unhappy wife had gotten away with murder than it was to accept walking corpses. Cauvin had taken the easy way and never given the matter another serious thought, until he read those words on the warehouse lintel. According to Bilibot, the Shambles had gotten its name from the corpses wandering its streets.

If that, the most unbelievable of the old sot's tales were true, could the rest still be lies? Had there ever been a crab the size of a man terrorizing the harbor? A pillar of fire reaching up to the stars? A horned beast lurking in the alleys, skewering drunks in the Maze?

Had the mystery of words and reading ever been so widespread that ordinary neighbors in an ordinary quarter of Sanctuary had not only protected their homes with written charms, but assumed the dead could read them?

Before Cauvin could answer any of his private questions, his thoughts—and the thoughts of those near him on Shadow Street—were shattered by a woman's scream. Cauvin's ears placed the sound at his back and well above his head. He'd be looking at second-story windows once he'd turned himself around, but while he spun, his gaze stayed low, on the crowded street, because bad things happened in Sanctuary when people got distracted.

At the corner of Cauvin's vision two men collided. One continued to run *away* from the scream, which had not been repeated. The other became a sudden statue, clutching its tunic. Letters and words were new to Cauvin, but he'd been reading the language of Sanctuary's streets since he'd learned to walk. A crime had been committed: a theft of property or possibly life, and the thief was getting away. Let others attend the victim; by instinct, Cauvin went after the thief.

Chasing down one of Shadow Street's innumerable dodges, Cauvin gained strides on the thief. The thief was aware of Cauvin's pursuit, casting desperate glances over his shoulder as he shoved his way past stalls along the narrow passage. Cauvin shoved back, flattening vendors and their customers alike against the walls and dropping a customer to the ground. They cursed him and the thief with equal venom.

A roving sausage-seller with his wares hung from poles like battle pennants heard the commotion and chose to block the dodge against them both. The thief crashed hard against him. Sausages flew and, for a heartbeat, Cauvin clutched the thief's tunic. Then, the thief back-slashed with a bloody knife. Cauvin released the cloth and they were running again.

The thief cried, "Father!" and crashed through a flimsy gate, exposing another passageway. Cauvin, bigger, heavier, and unfamiliar with the lay of the street, barely kept his balance as he cornered. He was still reeling when the passage opened into a courtyard. Skidding to a two-stride halt, Cauvin saw mounds of pottery: raw and baked; a pair of shimmering kilns; and a handful of men, each armed with heavy kneading sticks and the will to use them.

For the moment, the strangers held their ground, and so did Cauvin. He spotted his quarry, the thief, in the shadow of a stranger, much as he might have taken shelter in Grabar's shadow during his first years on Pyrtanis Street.

"Who are you?" the thief's protector demanded.

Cauvin swallowed an honest answer. The potters' faces were unfamiliar but not entirely unknown. The man to his extreme left—a rangy sort, his face ringed with wild, black hair, his club thumping against an open palm, and his eyes so narrowed they didn't glint in the sun—that man's name hung just out of reach in Cauvin's memory. If he waited another moment, he might remember these men.

"He robbed a man on Shadow Street—" Cauvin pointed at the thief. "Maybe killed him. A woman screamed first."

The protector seemed unsurprised, undisturbed. "That's no concern of yours."

The leftmost potter strode forward. Forget the wild hair and change the thumping club into a five-tailed whip—one blistering braid for each finger—drawn again and again through a cupped hand, and you'd have one of the pit guardians of the Bloody Hand. It seemed impossible that Cauvin could forget the men who'd tormented him, but ten years was a long time. The guardians' faces were nearly as faded as his mother's now, and the potters' hands were stained with brown clay, not red-as-blood tattoos.

"You're not part of this, boy," the protector warned. "Get out before you are."

Boy? Bec was a boy; Cauvin never was. The thief, now there was a froggin' boy, with nary a whisker on his chin but a fresh bloodstain smeared across the front of his shirt. His chest heaved from the chase—so did Cauvin's—but he wasn't afraid. Cauvin hadn't been afraid when he'd walked behind the Hand.

Cauvin wasn't behind or ahead of the Hand any longer, so he did what men and women had done when the Hand owned Sanctuary: He ran. His feet kicked up dust and grit, but there was no pursuit. The potters were as good as their word. Besides, they knew Cauvin wouldn't take his tale of blood and theft to the guard . . . He was an outsider in the Shambles; the guard wouldn't believe a word he said.

After leaping over the broken gate, Cauvin slowed down. No

one took note of him leaving the dodge; the street's attention was still fixed at its other end, where a flash of sunlight off metal showed that the city guard had finally arrived to investigate a murder. Guards might wander down the dodge, talk to the people he and the thief had shoved aside, even find the broken gate and visit the pottery. The potters would deny everything. They'd have their boy hidden by now and wouldn't set the guards on Cauvin's trail.

Cauvin thought he could count on that, the same way they'd counted on him. The stoneyard wouldn't set the guard on a stranger's trail, not without reason; and Cauvin hadn't given them reason. Enough reason. It might be a froggin' clever idea to get his sheep-shite arse out of the Shambles—

Then Cauvin spotted a banner tied to the side of a corner-front cooking oil stall. "Jaires," it read—Wrigglie letters for a Wrigglie name—and "best quality" and "Dippin Lane." He'd come this far; he took the chance of walking down what might be Dippin Lane. He hadn't gone far when he saw a green-headed duck surrounded by rippling lines in faded paint on a signboard: the Paddling Duck tavern behind which lived a woman who could tell him the truth about Leorin.

Neither the potters nor the guard were likely to look for him—if they were looking for him at all—in a S'danzo's sitting room.

"I've got a message for a woman, name of Elemi," Cauvin said to the old woman sweeping the tavern's steps. "I was told she lived around the Paddling Duck."

She stared at Cauvin long enough that he'd begun silently cursing the Torch for sending him on another sheep-shite fool's errand.

"There's a woman above goes by that name. Around back. Take the stairs." She shaped fingers into a crescent and pressed them against her temple, a warding against the evil eye. "Mind the dog."

Cauvin minded. He avoided eye contact with the mastiff—larger and fiercer than the stoneyard's dog—which growled ominously but let him climb the detached stairs. His butt scraped the rough-planked wall until he'd reached the narrow porch with a single door at its far end. One gentle tap on the wood, and a woman opened the door.

The S'danzo was roughly Cauvin's age, dark-haired, thin, and sun-starved as though she rarely left her curtained chamber. Her clothes were drab, nothing like the legendary layers of color that came to Cauvin's mind whenever he heard the word "S'danzo" spoken—but, then, the legendary S'danzo had vanished from Sanctuary long before he'd been born, vanished on their own or massacred by the Hand.

Not to contradict Soldt, at least not to his froggin' face, but to Cauvin's understanding, the reason there weren't any S'danzo in Sanctuary had nothing to do with any curses laid on the S'danzo or the city. Shite for sure, the fortune-tellers simply weren't welcome. Thirty-odd years earlier, long before the Mother of Chaos stuck Her bloody Hand in Sanctuary, why hadn't any of them warned their neighbors what was coming? Maybe they couldn't have saved everyone or stopped anything, but a few families might have gotten away. Instead, the S'danzo had taken the cowards' way, saving their own necks—most of them, anyway—leaving everyone else to suffer.

As men and women, most of Sanctuary would have lit out, same as the S'danzo, but as a community, the city had a long, unforgiving memory.

Elemi said, "I've been expecting a stranger since yesterday—you, I suppose." She spoke Wrigglie, but not like someone born in Sanctuary.

Cauvin waited until she'd closed the door and bolted it before saying—"I'm not a stranger, Elemi. My name is—"

"I don't want to know your name. It is enough that you know mine."

The room was stifling, but it might have been a windy winter day on the wharf for all the warmth in Elemi's voice. Cauvin removed the carved box from a sack he'd tied to his belt.

"I've brought you a gift."

Elemi refused to take the box from Cauvin's hands. Awkwardly, he put it down on a cloth-covered table. The S'danzo's home got its light from a pair of oil lamps. Their flickering transformed the carved vines into writhing serpents. No wonder Elemi didn't want to touch it; Cauvin didn't either, once he'd set it down.

"It's from the Torch—Lord Molin Torchholder. He asked me to give it to you."

Beyond froggin' doubt, Elemi recognized that name. With her arms behind her back, she retreated from her own table, watching the box as though it might burst into flames.

"I'm sorry," Cauvin muttered, renewing his silent curses. "The old pud didn't tell me anything, except where to find it—I dug it out of the froggin' ground in the bazaar. And that I should give it to you. Sheep-shite fool that I am, I thought it would be something you'd want. I'll take it back and shove it down his froggin' throat, if that will please you more. Just what is it, anyway?"

Her eyes widened. The S'danzo didn't approve of his language, or his intentions, or maybe the box had moved.

"I can guess," she said.

"Guess? Do you people *guess*?" Cauvin asked, and wished that he'd bitten off his tongue instead.

"Many times," Elemi admitted. "The Sight is dimmest at arm's length. It's easier to see what might happen next year in the Imperial cities than what awaits me this afternoon."

Cauvin guessed that Elemi had told him something significant, but he couldn't froggin' unravel the clue. "I could open the box for you," he offered. "If you don't want to touch it. If it's cursed or something—I don't care. I wouldn't notice another froggin' curse."

Elemi smiled a sad, weary smile. "Open it, if you wish. You're here now; the damage is done."

When Cauvin pressed his thumbs on the carved leaves and pried them apart, the lock opened with a metallic *ping*. He lifted the lid—a tighter fit than the lid of Sinjon's box. The Torch had long ago sealed this treasure in wax-soaked silk. Cauvin sought Elemi's eyes. She nodded, and he unsheathed his boot knife.

Within the waxed silk Cauvin found a layer of rust-colored flakes that powdered and released a scent of summer and roses into the room as he touched them. Elemi's hands flew to her mouth, not quite stifling a sob, but she nodded again, and Cauvin unwound silk so sheer beneath the outer waxed layer that he could see the S'danzo's tear-streaked face through several thicknesses of it. She lowered herself into a high-backed wooden chair.

When he'd finished with the silk, Cauvin fanned a deck of painted cards between his hands. "I've seen these before."

"Do you always open another man's gifts before you give them away?"

"No. I saw these in a dream—something like a dream. They were laid out on a table—"

The S'danzo sighed. "Illyra. She Saw the world, but not her own fate . . ."

"I didn't dream of a woman. I dreamt of a man—the artist who painted these. He told me to leave Sanctuary, that no one would blame me."

Cauvin's statement didn't get a reaction from the distracted S'danzo. Idly, he arrayed the cards around the empty box. The pictures were unmistakable, though their colors were not so bright as they'd been in Mother Shipri's garden.

Elemi stretched a trembling finger toward one of the simpler designs—a bush bearing five flowers, each a different kind and color—but stopped a handspan short of touching it. "Between life and fate, there can be no blame." She folded her fingers into fists and held them against her breast. Froggin' sure, Cauvin didn't know if the S'danzo was talking to herself or to him. "We thought these were lost; those who believed they existed at all. Illyra's cards. So powerful . . . so useless."

Elemi's eyes shone with reflected candlelight. She didn't blink, and whatever she watched, it wasn't in the room. Cauvin had heard how the Hand led a mob against the last of Sanctuary's S'danzo. Compared to what came later, the seeresses had died quickly, painlessly.

"You need to watch out for one another, since you can't see what lies ahead for yourselves." Cauvin thought that was a reasonable conclusion, but as with so many things he thought were reasonable, all it earned him was a *you've-stepped-in-shite* stare.

"Illyra didn't need the Sight to see the fate awaiting her. She knew what she was and what she did. Half-breed that she was, Illyra treated with priests and *gods*. It takes no Sight to scry what happens to a S'danzo who does that."

"Half-breed S'danzo," Cauvin corrected.

Effortlessly and passionately, Elemi nailed Cauvin to the floor with a stare. He'd thought she was frail and timid, and couldn't have been more wrong.

"When Illyra's S'danzo half met its fate, it took her other half with it, and everyone around her for good measure. If she thought it be otherwise, then she was the sheep-shite fool. S'danzo don't treat with priests or gods."

"The world needs fools and sheep-shite," Cauvin replied, wondering how he'd stumbled into a game of wits with a seeress—with an attractive woman who set his blood afire. He hadn't come to Dippin Lane looking for another woman. He had Leorin—the only woman he'd ever wanted . . . if he could trust her. The Torch had said Elemi could answer his questions. "How did Molin Torchholder know where you live, if you don't treat with priests?"

Elemi looked away. "I don't. Lord Torchholder was the last man I expected. I should have turned around and walked through the gates when I learned he was still alive. There's precious little in Sanctuary that old man doesn't uncover sooner or later, and there's no use probing *his* secrets. If he weren't a man, we'd say he had the Sight. I've known he'd send someone after me. I've waited for three years—every day dreading a knock on my door. Now you're here . . . with Illyra's cards. My sisters would kill for the chance to spread those cards across their tables."

"Better not let them know you've got them. The Torch said you answer questions. I've got one—"

Before Cauvin could say another word, Elemi swept up the painted cards, showing none of her previous reluctance. Without shuffling them, she snapped them down one after another, making a serpentine pattern until there were more cards faceup on the table than remained in her hand. She came to one card—he couldn't see the image—that gave her pause. Wrinkling her lips, she drummed the stiffened parchment against her teeth.

"I could ask my question, that might help," Cauvin suggested.

"*Suvesh!* You think it's questions and answers!" She grinned and said—"Cauvin. Your name is Cauvin. Cauvin, I was born with the True Sight. I see the truth as stars shining on the sea of time. Tomorrow's truth, yesterday's, and today's, they're all the same and all revealed to the True Sight. No questions or answers, tricks or slights. You're *here*—" The S'danzo snapped her troublesome card down atop another card in the middle of the serpent pattern. "That tells me all I need to know."

Cauvin shook his head. "You'll have to do better than that. There's a madwoman on my street who says the same thing and tells fortunes by blowing ashes onto bowl of rainwater—" He imitated Batty Dol's singsong: "You'll meet a stranger. Your life is changing. A challenge awaits—"

"You have," Elemi said, looking at the cards. "It already has. The challenge lies ahead, very soon. You came here with a woman on your mind. Her name is Leorin. She loves you as she loves no other man—that will *not* change. The Mother of Chaos has wound a web of darkness around her—"

Cauvin clenched his teeth a moment then confessed, "Around us both. We were orphans together in the palace. People don't talk about it much, but you've probably heard—"

The S'danzo silenced him with a glower. She studied the cards on the table. "I See that you have known each other since early childhood and that you have suffered much together—suffering is the bond of your love, isn't it? But I See no darkness or shadows where you stand. It is all around the woman, Leorin. You are the only light that falls upon her."

Cauvin felt a sickening twinge of guilt. He should never have suspected Leorin, he should have helped her. "The Torch—"

"Is a man," Elemi interrupted. "Worse, he's a priest, blinded by gods and power. The S'danzo have no gods, no power. No divine intervention stands between us and the truth. We watch. We wait. Do you think we have no better use for our Sight than to answer your *suvesh* questions?"

Cauvin didn't know what *suvesh* meant but, shite for sure, it wasn't a compliment.

"We had a home, once, a blessed land of tall grass and flowers. Then *She* came. Our land withered. Worship me, *She* commanded, and all that was yours will be returned. Some bent their knees and became *Her* servants but the rest, the S'danzo, vowed that we would live without a land and without a goddess until we could undo what *She* had done. At the end of time, we will take back what was given to us at the dawn."

The S'danzo leaned toward Cauvin, teeth bared, the froggin' image of ferocity and vengeance.

"You told the Torch that?" Cauvin asked incredulously.

The S'danzo answered with a laugh. "I told him nothing he did not already know. I told him what he wanted to hear."

"Would you . . . ? Can you tell me if I can free Leorin from the Hand?"

Elemi gave the cards to Cauvin. "Shuffle them."

Poor men gamed with dice. Only sparkers played with painted cards. Cauvin had seen card-shuffling sparkers in the Unicorn shadows, but when he tried to imitate them, the parchment rectangles flew from his fingers. Grimly, he collected them from the carpeted floor and neatened them against the table.

Elemi placed her hands over his. "Never mind," she whispered. "I'll help you. It's not your fault."

Somehow, that sounded like a curse.

The S'danzo's fingers were no bigger than Bec's and cool despite the room's heat. She caressed Cauvin's hand as a lover might and, as he held his breath, half the deck dropped to the table. She took the remaining cards from his hand and set them aside before turning the topmost card of the dropped stack faceup.

The painting was simple: a muscular forearm brandishing a flaming spear. "Lance of Flames, reversed," Elemi said and, from Cauvin's view, the card was indeed upside down.

"Is that bad?" he asked, unable to restrain himself.

Elemi scowled. She retrieved the bottom card from among those that hadn't dropped—the card that had rested atop the Lance of Flames—and said, "That which is farthest away, denied, ignored, or forgotten," as she placed it faceup upon the burning spear. From Cauvin's view, the blond woman and dark-haired man were standing right-side up.

"No," he protested. "Pick another card. That's Leorin and me. You weren't listening. There's nothing denied or forgotten about Leorin and me. When the time's right, we're jumping the broom—"

"When the time's right," Elemi repeated, a hint of mockery in her voice. "I *See* a hard choice before you, hard because no matter how righteous your choice, the outcome will not change." She raised her head. There was surprise and sadness in her eyes. "You can choose where you will bear your scars, Cauvin, the rest is fate. You think you have no innocence left to lose—that you had none—"

The S'danzo folded both of her hands over his and squeezed them tight. "It's too late, Cauvin. I'm sorry, so sorry."

Cauvin pulled free. "No, I won't accept it. We'll leave Sanctuary . . . tonight." He paced the length of the room. "The two of us—we'll find a place where no one's ever heard of Molin Torchholder, or Sanctuary, or the froggin' damned Bloody Mother of Chaos!"

"You can try." Elemi traced the flaming lance with a forefinger. "You could go alone. *That* dream was true. The path from Sanctuary is open. No shame will follow you, if you take it . . . alone."

"No froggin' shame in giving up—froggin' sure, that's what my dream told me. Leave froggin' Sanctuary behind, and no one will blame me. But what about Leorin? Leave her behind, too? You tell me she's caught in the Hand's web. How can there be no shame, if I leave the woman I love behind. I'd sooner cut off my arm."

"Then cut it off," Elemi agreed coldly. "You can choose your scars."

In two strides Cauvin returned to the table. He loomed over Elemi. "What about Leorin? What do you see for her? Find me a path that gets us both safely *out* of this gods-forsaken city!"

Elemi swept up all the cards. "You will not thank me for this," she warned, and began tossing them onto the table. "Imagine yourself alone in the midst of a vast, empty field. There are no paths; each step you take is a new choice. Now imagine another field, equally vast, but there is one difference: a single path, clearly marked. You could choose not to follow it, but do you have that strength, *suvesh*? Without True Sight's vision, the future is like the first field." The S'danzo squared the cards and set them aside. She'd laid out less than half the number she'd laid out before. "Last chance, *suvesh,* do you want to See the path?"

"Yes," Cauvin replied without hesitation.

"Your beloved has made her choices—the Archway stands behind her." Elemi tapped the card portraying a stone arch between sunlight and darkness.

"Reversed," Cauvin observed.

She smiled with her teeth. "The path beneath the Archway can no longer be walked. Your beloved has done more than make a choice. She has chosen to make it irrevocable."

"No," Cauvin said softly, retreating to the farthest, darkest corner. "No. No, I don't believe that. You don't understand— What Leorin did, she did years ago. She did it to survive. There's a world of difference between surviving and . . . and what you're saying."

"There is darkness woven around your beloved, Dyareela's darkness. Sight cannot penetrate that darkness. I See because I See you. Your love for her reaches into that darkness. She loves you—"

"Then there's a chance. I can set Leorin free. If I can get her away from Sanctuary. I know Leorin. I love her. I—" Cauvin hesitated, then finished his statement: "I *trust* her."

Elemi collected the cards, swirled the sheer silk about them, and stuffed them into the wooden box. "Of course you trust her," she said as she squeezed the lid into place. "She doesn't change, Cauvin; she's *constant*. You can always trust someone who's constant; they're predictable. You know what Leorin will do."

"She'll leave Sanctuary with me. She *is* trapped here. I've heard her say so. I'm the one who hasn't wanted to leave . . ." Cauvin thought of Bec. Saying farewell to Bec—never seeing the boy again—that would leave deep and lasting scars. "I can do it. I *will*."

"Choose carefully, *suvesh*. Yes, for you, many choices are possible—You may choose to pull your beloved from the darkness, but she may choose to pull you *in*. The one clear path does not always lead to safety."

"I have to try."

The S'danzo took a deep breath, as if to lecture him, then made her own choice against it. She held out the wooden box instead. "Take these with you."

"The Torch told me to give them to you."

"And I don't want them. They shine too brightly. I would rather not See what they reveal. Take them with you."

"They're no use to me."

"All the more reason for you to keep them."

Cauvin was in a hurry now, bursting with plans and eager to visit the Maze and the Unicorn. The door beckoned. He put his hand on the latch— "No."

"I'll burn them if you leave them here!"

"No, you won't," Cauvin decided. "You're right . . . about the path. Once you know it's there, you've got to take it. You've shown me a path, but you've seen one for yourself, too. You *want* Illyra's cards."

The box crashed against the door as Cauvin closed it behind him.

# Chapter Fourteen

Cauvin's thoughts were behind him on the Paddling Duck's rickety stairs, expecting the S'danzo to burst out her door and hurl the box at his back. He'd forgotten about the watchdog until it lunged up the stairway, teeth bared and snarling.

"Down," he commanded it, and, "Go away!"

The second was a sheep-shite stupid mistake. He'd been the one to teach the stoneyard dog to attack when it heard those words. Cauvin found himself trapped on the stairs long enough to conjure up another handful of questions for the S'danzo. But she'd been right about answers: The more answers he had, the less freedom, too. He made his choices based on the answers he had and, as the dog went back to its shaded den beneath the stairs, Cauvin resolved to get Leorin out of Sanctuary, even if it meant confronting the Hand, or the Bloody Mother of Chaos Herself.

Stinking Street marked the west-side border between the Shambles and the Maze, and though Cauvin knew his way to the Unicorn best from the east, midmorning was a fairly safe time of day for wanderers, even in the Maze.

He was tempted to revisit the Torch's atrium armory. If he and Leorin were leaving Sanctuary, they'd need money, particularly if they followed another decision he'd made while waiting out the watchdog. Rather than walk out of the city—which committed them to a long, footsore journey and left open the possibility that they could always turn around, and walk back—they would buy passage on the next ship to Ilsig. There'd be no turning around once a ship left the harbor and, from what Cauvin had heard, they'd be in the kingdom's capital a week later.

The cost of an Ilsig passage was measured in shaboozh, not padpols. Cauvin had three gold coronations from Captain Sinjon's box. Three coronations was a fortune on Pyrtanis Street, but was it enough to get one person to the kingdom's capital, let alone two? He'd feel better with a purse filled with heavy Ilsigi silver to go with his Imperial coins, and the best source of shaboozh lay in the cellar of a ruined Vulgar Unicorn. The preserved armor of Tempus Thales should get him and Leorin to Ilsig and keep them on their feet until they found livelihoods. Cauvin had gotten as far as imagining to whom he could trade the armor, when the voice of his conscience shouted—

*For the love of Shipri—talk to Leorin first! Tell her what's happened—* all *of what's happened—and get her advice. She's no sheep-shite fool; she's made for thinking—*

A shiver ran down Cauvin's back. The people who'd said that Leorin was made for thinking were the same as said he'd never be more than a sheep-shite fool. Cauvin knew what the Hand had taught him; he didn't know what they'd taught Leorin after they'd taken her behind the walls . . .

Cauvin caught himself on the verge of suspicion. *She loves me. The S'danzo said that Leorin loves me and nothing, nothing at all, changes that. Love is enough . . . It's got to be.*

He turned toward the Unicorn—the new Unicorn.

The tavern looked smaller by daylight, just one more warped doorway, framed with unfinished wood, opening onto an alley with a slippery gutter running down its middle. The door stood open; anyone could wander inside where, without its lamps and candles, the common room was darker by daylight than it was at night. Abandoned mugs scattered across the tables scented the air with stale beer and sour wine.

A solitary wench—an unbudded girl with long, braided brown hair—collected the mugs. She looked Cauvin up and down once he'd cleared the threshold and, judging him no concern of hers, went back to work. A fresh keg had been rolled up to the bar; the tools to tap it lay on the floor, as though the keeper had gone off in search of an assistant.

The upper-room stairs beckoned, but Cauvin resisted their invitation. No matter that Cauvin knew exactly which room was Leorin's or his determination to get his beloved out of Sanctuary, he wasn't about to knock unexpected on her door. He sat at a table, waiting for the keeper or a familiar wench to appear, and was still waiting when the girl headed out of the commons with the last of the dirty mugs.

Realizing that he could be sitting alone until midafternoon, he called: "Have you seen Leorin this morning?"

The girl set her mug-filled bowl down with a clanking *thud*. "Who's asking?" She might be too young to serve customers, but she knew how the Unicorn worked.

"A friend," Cauvin replied; he didn't give his name to Unicorn strangers either.

"She's gone."

Cauvin's heart skipped a beat. "Gone? Gone where?"

The girl shrugged. "How should I know? I heard Mimise say she left last night." She put one arm on her hip and cocked her body around it, imitating the wenches at work. "Why're you looking for Leorin?"

"I was in the quarter and wanted to see her. We're friends."

"She left with a *man,*" the girl said with a voice both childish and seductive.

A bad taste rose in Cauvin's mouth. Once they were gone, he'd froggin' sure find a way to earn enough money that his wife didn't go off with other men. "I'll come back later . . . She'll be working tonight?"

"Maybe . . . maybe not." The girl twirled the tip of one braid against her lips, then caught it with her teeth.

"I'll take my chances." Cauvin made a hasty retreat into the clear light of morning.

There was another way to gather up enough money for passage out of Sanctuary, an easier way than trading the Torch's treasures, at least for Cauvin's mood as he stalked out of the Maze. It would mean keeping money that was owed to the stoneyard, something he'd never considered doing before, but the moment Cauvin began to think of abandoning Grabar, Mina, and Bec—the only true family he'd known—other previously unthinkable thoughts became possible.

Jerbrah Mioklas—*Lord* Mioklas to the likes of Cauvin—owed the stoneyard a froggin' pile of money because Mioklas's father had been one of the first sheep-shite stupid Wrigglies to invite the Servants of Dyareela into his home on the Processional. The old patriarch had met the same flayed fate as Cauvin's mother. The family would have fled to Land's End, had they been golden-eyed Imperials, but being Wrigglies, they'd gone to ground in a farm village north of Sanctuary.

Lord Mioklas had reclaimed the family mansion at about the same time as Grabar claimed a foster son from the palace. A reasonable man would have realized that his childhood home was beyond salvage. A reasonable man would have torn the whole place down and maybe moved to another froggin' city.

Lord Mioklas wasn't a reasonable man. He was determined to have his home back, better than memory, if it was the last thing he or Grabar did. Grabar or Cauvin. Half of what Cauvin knew about stone he'd learned at the Mioklas mansion. Last spring, when Mioklas was ready to repair the perfume garden, Cauvin had done the work himself, shaping hundreds of stones by hand, then fitting them into a swirling wall that stood sturdy without a dollop of mortar between its stones and whispered gently when rain trickled between its stones. It was the best stonework Cauvin had done—his masterpiece, if he'd been a proper apprentice or if Sanctuary needed two stone masters.

Come high summer when the wall was finished, Mioklas had hosted a feast to celebrate the rebirth of his perfume garden. He'd invited every Wrigglie who mattered, the Irrune from the palace, and all the froggin' Imperials from Land's End. Mina complained the markets were empty for a week. Then Mioklas sent his housekeeper to Pyrtanis Street, pleading poverty and saying it would be autumn before he could even begin to pay his debt for the wall.

Grabar hadn't argued. Shite for sure, they knew the man's ways, and there would always be more stonework to be done at his mansion. When Mioklas decided what he wanted done next—and not one day sooner—his housekeeper would show up with enough silver to soothe even Mina's easily ruffled feathers. Until then, they'd let it ride. It wasn't as though Grabar had money tied up in the stone

Cauvin had used—they'd scavenged the rock from another ruined garden. The debt in Mina's eyes was labor only—Cauvin's sheep-shite labor, day after froggin' day.

Promises were promises. They were well into Esharia, the second full month of autumn and past time for Lord Mioklas to lay down his debts—or as much would buy two passages to Ilsig.

One block from the Processional, Cauvin came to an alley that led, even here in the wealthiest quarter of Sanctuary, to a courtyard where the scars of fire, storm, and the Bloody Hand of Dyareela were still clear on the abandoned buildings. Cauvin scaled a naked wall and picked his way carefully across a balcony that was more gap than wood. Next autumn, it might be gone altogether, but this year it still provided the best view of Mioklas's perfume garden and Cauvin's winding wall within it.

Cauvin stood in silence a moment, admiring his own craft. The mansion bustled with the servants a rich man needed to keep himself happy. One was a grizzle-bearded bodyguard with whom Cauvin had tangled before. He carried a sword and knew how to use it, but his presence assured Cauvin that Mioklas was at home and working as rich men worked: clean clothes, clean hands, and seated on cushions before a polished table.

After just one of Soldt's lessons, Cauvin wasn't sheep-shite stupid enough to think he'd win any challenge with a rich man's bodyguard, but the guard had removed his sword belt, the better to hide under the gold-and-amber trees with a woman. Cauvin could have had his hands on Lord Mioklas's neck before the guard knew there was an extra man in the garden, if that had been what Cauvin had wanted to do. It wasn't. The only reason he'd climbed to the balcony was to see his stonework. If he got what he wanted, he'd never see it again.

There were two doors to a rich man's home—the high door where his family and peers made their entrances and the low door near the storerooms for servants and tradesmen. When Cauvin worked on the wall, he'd come and gone without complaint through the low door, but when he came to settle debts he climbed the stone steps to the brightly painted high door and let the bronze ring strike hard against the plate beneath it. Within moments a woman's face appeared at a barred round window and quickly vanished.

He could imagine the messages whispered from one servant to the next: *He's here again—That sheep-shite stone-smasher from Pyrtanis Street— You tell the master— No, you tell him—*

Just when Cauvin was about to hammer the door a second time, it creaked and cracked open.

"We receive tradesmen below," the housekeeper snarled, as though he'd never laid a sheepshite eye on Cauvin before.

"Tell Lord Mioklas that Cauvin, Grabar's son, is here on business."

"Lord Mioklas is not at home—"

The housekeeper tried to shut the door. He wasn't quick enough, or strong enough. Cauvin slapped his palm against the wood and effortlessly held the door open against the housekeeper's best efforts.

"I know the pud's here, in his workroom, counting his coins."

"He's not expecting you—"

"That's his froggin' problem, not mine and not yours either, unless you don't take me to see him."

Though the housekeeper sported a tuft of black beard on his chin, the rest of his face bore the soft, unfinished features of a lifelong eunuch—not someone who was likely to stand his ground against a stone-smasher. In fact, he hadn't on the other occasions when Cauvin had come to collect a debt. Cauvin put his strength into his arm and, straightening his elbow, moved the door—and the housekeeper with it—far enough to get across the threshold.

"You won't cause trouble, will you?" the housekeeper pleaded.

"Not if you get your ass turned around and take me to Mioklas. Or, I could take myself. I know the froggin' way. I've been here how many times before? Your froggin' lord doesn't pay his debts. He's froggin' greedy, and he's froggin' cheap. I'll wager he doesn't pay you on time, either; does he?"

The housekeeper shot Cauvin a look sharp enough to draw blood but didn't deny the accusation. He led Cauvin down a corridor and stairway each painted with murals of Ilsig's gods and Ilsig's glory. Cauvin counted three braziers, each piled high with charcoal and ready for the flame, ready to heat the froggin' corridor.

Mioklas's bodyguard, his sword now properly belted below his waist, blocked the workroom door. "You're here to make trouble?"

"Lord Mioklas said autumn. It's been froggin' autumn for weeks now. We were expecting him at the yard. He should've been expecting me."

"Let him in, Brevis," the froggin' lord himself called from behind Brevis's back.

Brevis—Cauvin had forgotten the man's name until he'd heard it again—stepped back, putting himself inside the workroom before Cauvin entered it. They exchanged keep-your-froggin'-hands-to-your-froggin'-self glances as Mioklas rose from his chair. He was a few years younger than Grabar and in better shape than either Grabar or most rich men nearing the end of their prime. His eyes were sharp, his handshake firm and freely given—even to a man who might make trouble.

"How's the garden?" Cauvin asked, freeing his hand.

"A delight. Would you care to see it?" Mioklas beckoned Cauvin toward the door behind his table, the door through which Cauvin had watched him moments earlier. "I've planted evergreens and gathered driftwood ornaments for the winter—"

Cauvin stayed put. "Up on Pyrtanis Street, we're gathering driftwood for the froggin' hearth. You know what I'm here for, Lord Mioklas." He hadn't meant to swear, not this early in the conversation, but oaths and curses were part of him, like breathing.

"It has been an unsettled season, Cauvin—I wouldn't expect you to fully understand. With Arizak dwelling in the palace now, our Irrune are preoccupied with their own affairs. The customs we'd cobbled together—who does what, when, and how between them and us—have unraveled." The man winced dramatically. "Not *unraveled*; I wouldn't want you to leave here thinking that the peace and security of Sanctuary are in any way jeopardized. It's merely that Arizak is as much a stranger to Sanctuary today as he was the day he came through the gates we'd left open for him. More so, perhaps, because we'd come to so many *arrangements* with his wife and Lord Naimun, so many *accommodations* for their comfort and ours—"

Cauvin cut him off. "That the last thing you wanted was *Lord* Naimun's froggin' father back in Sanctuary, poking his nose into your accommodations *and* trailing his full-grown Dragon-son in behind him. Sorting out the palace is your problem, I just want my money—*our* money—so we can keep warm this winter."

Another slip of the tongue. He wasn't a good liar, especially when he was wrestling a guilty conscience.

Mioklas stood tall and silent, his hands folded calmly, intricately beneath his chin while his eyes all but disappeared. "The welfare of Sanctuary is not a shadow play with puppets dancing behind a sheet. Lives and livelihoods are at stake here—your own and your father's. You'll do a lot worse than shiver up on Pyrtanis Street if that wound kills Arizak this winter and the wrong son inherits."

Cauvin considered saying something snide: *When there's no froggin' wood in winter on Pyrtanis Street it doesn't matter who's in sheepshite palace,* or: *Froggin' sure, I've already done worse than shiver*. Then he considered what the Torch might say, or black-cloaked Soldt. He kept his mouth shut, sensing that silence, along with quickly raised eyebrows, was more powerful than words.

"I've known you since your father pulled you out of the palace," Mioklas informed Cauvin. "You've got a strong back, and you're good with your hands, but you haven't the least notion what's good for you or Sanctuary—"

Cauvin pointed at Mioklas's nose. "I know which one of Arizak's sons is right for Sanctuary—" He folded his fingers into a brawny fist. "And his name isn't Naimun per-Arizak."

"Brevis!"

The bodyguard approached Cauvin's back. The man could kill him, no questions asked: It was a crime to attack a nobleman, but neither the trial nor the punishment occurred in Hall of Justice at the palace. And if Brevis didn't kill him, Grabar would likely toss Cauvin out the door when word got back to Pyrtanis Street. Cauvin lowered his arm, yet didn't unmake his fist. Brevis stopped, waiting for his master's next words—

"You and every other pigheaded Wrigglie in Sanctuary. The lot of you haven't got the sense Great Ils gave a single ant. Young Arizak—the Dragon—do you think he's going to build *walls* with stone from your precious stoneyard? The Dragon and his *sikkintair* of a mother won't—"

"This pigheaded Wrigglie's tired of listening to some other pigheaded Wrigglie tell me what I'm thinking. I wasn't thinking about the froggin' Dragon!" Cauvin wasn't thinking at all. He'd burnt his bridges with Mioklas, with Grabar, with Sanctuary itself. He was free—and reeling, as though he'd drunk three mugs of beer without pausing to breathe. "There's a better brother for Sanctuary!"

"Nonsense—"

"Raith," Cauvin spat back.

"Raith? He's a boy—" Mioklas paused with his mouth open. When he spoke again, it was with the slow, falsely patient tone strangers used with children or idiots. "Ah, you think the city would thrive best with an unbearded child for its prince? Do you think the city would govern itself? Good idea, Cauvin, but you're not as clever as you think you are. What Sanctuary needs is a prince who relies on his advisors to govern for him."

"And you'd be one of the advisors?" It was the obvious question for Cauvin to ask, though a sheep-shite stupid one, with a bodyguard standing behind him.

"Not alone, I assure you. I am neither so ambitious nor so bold as Lord Torchholder was."

This time Cauvin's silence wasn't deliberate.

"Don't get me wrong—Lord Torchholder was a great man," Mioklas went on. "Absolutely fearless. Never a thought for his own safety. That's why we sent him out to negotiate with the Irrune; they respect that sort of courage. Afterward, in the palace—he was beyond control. I'll tell you, now that he's dead, the Torch had something on everyone. Almost everyone. Nothing on me. Lord Torchholder was ever my friend. But there were a few men—more than a few—who breathed easier through their tears as the word went round—"

Their eyes locked by chance. Cauvin's mind was spinning like a dog in pursuit of its flea-bitten tail. He needed to say something, but only one word came out of his mouth: "You . . . you . . . you . . ." He'd never felt so slow or sheep-shite stupid.

"Ah—forgive me. The Torch was your personal hero, no doubt. Leading the charge into the palace, returning you to your family. Yes. That's why you mentioned Raith. You'd heard that Lord Torchholder favored him. You saw the lad at the funeral? I'm sorry, Cauvin—but Lord Torchholder was an old man, a very old man. One might say *unnaturally* old. There were rumors—no need sharing them now. Young Raith's grieving, but he's better off without Lord Torchholder whispering in his ear, putting dangerous thoughts in his head. There'll be a place for Raith—a place for *you,* Cauvin. A city needs its master stone-workers. Indeed. How much do you need? Did you say twenty shaboozh now, the rest—oh, say after midwinter?"

Cauvin's tongue remained thick and lifeless.

"Thirty, then? As Ils watches, I don't have it all! Not before midwinter. How about forty? Will forty shaboozh suffice to keep you warm on Pyrtanis Street?"

With some effort, Cauvin dipped his chin and raised it again.

"Wait here. Brevis?"

The rich man and his bodyguard exchanged glances before Mioklas left the room. Cauvin found himself face-to-face with a man fondling the hilt of his sword. He had his long knife, and one steel-fighting lesson from Soldt. That wasn't going to help Cauvin, not if Brevis had been given orders to skewer him.

When moments had passed and the sword hadn't moved, Cauvin allowed himself a question: What in the froggin' frozen hells of Hecath had just happened? Had his ears heard Lord Mioklas admitting to the murder of Lord Torchholder? Had he—the sheep-shite stone-smasher of Pyrtanis Street—glimpsed Lord Mioklas's secret guilt? Did Lord Mioklas *believe* Cauvin had guessed that secret? Was Mioklas offering Cauvin forty shaboozh in payment for his work on the garden wall? Was Mioklas in his privy chamber gathering coins from his strongbox, or was he summoning more bodyguards?

Brevis grinned when Cauvin dared a glance at the doorway. Cauvin quickly lowered his eyes. He looked at the worktable and several sheets of parchment. Without trying he could make out the Ilsigi words, even though they were reversed, as the S'danzo's cards Lance of Flames and Archway had been.

> To My esteemed lord. The matter which concerned you has been resolved. The captain who brings you this message will accept . . .

Words could mean anything, especially an unfinished message. Cauvin turned away from the parchment, toward a round, oddly bright and blurry painting. Moments later he realized that it wasn't a painting at all but a silvered mirror.

Leorin owned a palm-sized square of polished brass she called a mirror. She used it to guide her hand as she drew a black, cosmetic line around her golden eyes. Whenever Cauvin had tried the mirror's sorcery, he saw blobs and scratches, nothing at all like a face, let alone his face. Mioklas's froggin' mirror was better than Leorin's; good enough that Cauvin believed he was looking at sorcery.

The silver mirror reflected images Cauvin couldn't see with his own eyes: Brevis leaning against the doorjamb, still grinning. Cauvin scowled and jumped when his reflection scowled back. Brevis laughed aloud. Cauvin shook his head; the reflection did likewise, but *backward*. Warily, Cauvin raised his right hand to his cheek; the reflection raised its left. He closed his left eye; the reflection closed its right. He closed his right eye—

That was froggin' stupid.

He strode closer to the mirror. The reflection got larger, clearer. If it was him, only *backward,* Cauvin didn't like the view. His shirt—the better of the two he owned—was stained and shabby. Raw threads sprouted around his neck, and the thong holding his bronze slug looked like a noose tightened around his neck. Cauvin knew the color of his hair—Mina told him often enough that it was the color of the yard after a rain. He lopped it off with a knife whenever it got in his eyes. The result, according to the mirror, was a dirty brown fringe around his face, longer on top, and noticeably longer over the reflection's right ear—*his* left. Cauvin's beard was almost as ragged as his hair. He shaved once or twice a month during the warmer seasons and not at all now that the weather was cooler.

Cauvin's nose pulled toward the right because the punch that had broken it had been a right-handed punch; the reflection's nose pulled to the left. Cauvin couldn't see the reflection's eyes; they were too dark and set too deep in its head. He didn't trust people if he couldn't see their froggin' eyes. If his eyes were truly as dark and deep as the reflection's and set that close together, then he could almost understand why Mina didn't trust him.

Worst was the reflection's mouth—his mouth. It was small compared to the rest of his face, thin-lipped and so pale it almost wasn't there. Leorin joked that he had a maiden girl's mouth. Hers was womanly: wide, lush, and soft. When Cauvin tightened his lips and lowered his eyebrows, the reflection looked mean and ready for a fight. Truly, Cauvin looked no friendlier when he relaxed or smiled.

No matter how Cauvin stretched or shaped his face, his reflection remained sullen, angry, and sheep-shite stupid. Nothing added Bec's charm to his reflection, and Grabar's weathered honesty was every froggin' bit as elusive.

"Enjoying yourself?"

Lord Mioklas's voice caught Cauvin unaware. He blinked hard and saw the rich man's reflection before spinning around to face him.

"Sorcery?" he asked about the mirror.

"A bit of magic, but not where it counts. The face you see there is the face you wear on the street at noontime, no more or less. Have you never seen your own reflection clearly? Were you surprised? Disappointed?"

Cauvin tried another silent answer.

"Don't be," Mioklas continued. "Not everyone can be handsome. A face like yours has its uses. Master Grabar saw that from the start. I hear you're plenty good with your fists and not reluctant to use them. He's wise to send you to collect the stoneyard's debts."

"I suppose," Cauvin replied. Froggin' sure, the rich man knew too much about him.

"I could find a place for you where you wouldn't be looking at stone all day."

"I like looking at stone."

Mioklas went to his table. He untied a cloth and spilled a mass of silvery shaboozh onto the polished wood. The silver wasn't the best Cauvin had seen—that froggin' honor went to the Torch's soldats—but a sea captain wouldn't ask questions.

"Forty," Mioklas said. "And two extras. Forty-two, in total. Don't take my word for it—count them."

With a grimace, Cauvin complied. In his slow, sheep-shite way—the only way he knew: The Torch's magic had taught him reading, not arithmetic—he made piles of five until there were two single coins left over. Then he counted the piles on his fingers until there were two fingers left over. Forty-two.

He unslung his coin pouch. No way would it hold forty-two

shaboozh, even if he threw away every chipped padpol.

"Keep the cloth," Mioklas offered, pushing it across the table.

For reasons Cauvin couldn't untangle, taking the cloth was worse than taking the shaboozh, but he needed something to carry the coins. He knotted them securely, creating an extra loop in the cloth to feed his belt through. The pouch was secure from a casual dip, should he bump into one on his way home—

Home. Cauvin had never felt so frog-all far from home. He threaded the knotted sack onto his belt. Looking up, he realized that Mioklas had been watching him like a hawk.

"Not taking chances, eh?"

"No, my lord."

"An interesting combination: quick fists and a cautious nature. Very interesting. Don't forget what I've told you. I could find you a place where you'd do what you do best."

Cauvin had heard that before from the Hand. "I'm grateful, my lord, but no thanks, I do my best with stone and a hammer."

Mioklas shook his head with exaggerated sadness. "Think about it, Cauvin—talents like yours, they don't last forever. You don't want to waste them building walls, do you?"

"No, my lord—I mean, yes, my lord." Omen or daydream, Cauvin imagined himself in the Ilsigi capital, hungry and looking for work—looking for a stoneyard but finding only a man who needed an obedient man with a mean face and hard fists.

"Think about it . . . and come back when you're ready. I see great things on Sanctuary's horizon. You could be a part of them. I've watched you become a man, Cauvin, working for the stoneyard. Why, you're almost as much like family here as you are on Pyrtanis Street. There's not a wall in this house that doesn't have a bit of your sweat, maybe even a bit of your flesh and blood worked into it."

"If you need another wall, my lord, or anything built from stone—"

"I'll come looking for you, Cauvin. I know where to find you, don't I? Now, I have work to do before the tide changes and my ship sails. Brevis will show you out. Brevis?"

The bodyguard led Cauvin to the high door.

"Mind where you're walking," Brevis advised as Cauvin descended the steps to the Processional. "You might step in something that clings."

Cauvin nodded. He walked toward the harbor, paying no attention to where he put his feet. When the water was in front of him, he sat down on a piling. His breathing steadied, but not his mind. He leaned forward, elbows on his knees and head between his hands, trying to make sense of the forty-two shaboozh hanging heavy at his waist.

The Torch had been so certain that he'd been attacked by a Bloody Hand survivor. Whatever else Mioklas might do, he wouldn't go near the Hand, not after what the Hand had done to his father. People didn't forgive things like that, not even rich people. Yet when Cauvin had spoken the Torch's name, Mioklas betrayed all the signs of a man with something to hide. What? Could the Torch have been wrong about the attack? Could Mioklas truly have plotted murder but not known the would-be murderer?

Froggin' gods all be damned—Cauvin knew the Hand and its way better than any Imperial lord or Wrigglie magnate, but could he have misread the Copper Corner ambush?

Confusion became a throbbing pain behind Cauvin's eyes. A sheep-shite stone-smasher wasn't half clever enough to put these pieces together. He needed to talk to someone older and wiser—

No, he put that thought out of his mind. The Torch was the source of his misery.

Soldt? Frog all, Soldt was the Torch's man, the Torch's assassin. Bilibot's winter tales were froggin' full of assassins who betrayed the men who'd hired them. Froggin' sure Soldt had had ample opportunity to correct any mistakes he might have made six nights ago, but—what was it that the S'danzo had said: Cauvin could trust Leorin because she was predictable. Shite for sure, Cauvin couldn't predict Soldt.

Leorin herself? Because Cauvin had already given her his love and his trust and because, from the moment Mioklas had spread those forty-two shaboozh across the table, broadening his suspicions, Cauvin had seen Leorin in a brighter light. If it weren't for the S'danzo's cards—

No, Cauvin's worries about his betrothed went deeper than paintings on stiffened parchment, deeper than the attack on the

Torch. The seeds had been planted when she'd reappeared in his life two years earlier, and they grew—damn every god and goddess—each time she disappeared with another man. Shite for sure, Cauvin wanted to talk to Leorin. He wanted to get her out of the Unicorn, out of Sanctuary . . . Then, and only then, he'd tell her about the last few days. He wouldn't—couldn't—turn to her for advice while his own mind was a sucking mire.

"Move it, pud!"

A harsh voice and a sharp pain above his right ankle jolted Cauvin out of his thoughts. He blinked up at a burly man whose face was obscured by the sun. Before Cauvin could determine if this was a threat to be taken seriously, different hands clamped on his neck and shoulders. With a jerk, some unseen stranger tried to drag Cauvin off the piling.

He was Wrigglie; he endured insults, but once Cauvin had gotten away from the Hand, he'd sworn that he would not suffer manhandling. The oath had gotten him into more brawls than all his other bad habits combined. This time, after Cauvin swung wide, it not only got him clouted hard above his ear, it cost him his best shirt. The cloth tore when two men contested for the privilege of slamming him to his knees on the wharf planks. His left sleeve dangled around his wrist.

With an animal growl, Cauvin surged to his feet and renewed the fight. He grabbed one tormentor by *his* shirt, yanked the man close, and locked an arm around his head. Then Cauvin pounded the man's face a few times before they were pulled apart. He wound up breaking a fall on the knee he'd bruised fighting Soldt the previous day. The pain cleared his mind; he stayed put, sniffing and panting.

"Azyuna's mercy! I know this one. Pork all, Cauvin. What are you doing down here? Drunk out of your mind at this hour? Spiked on *krrf* or kleetel?"

Cauvin recognized Gorge, who usually prowled the Stairs, the Tween, and Pyrtanis Street, with two other guards whom he didn't recognize, one with a very bloody nose. There was a bit of satisfaction in knowing he'd bloodied a city guard when there'd been three of them against one. "I wasn't doing anything I shouldn't. What are *you* doing down here? Couldn't find anyone to roust up in the Tween?"

"We got visitors"—Gorge hooked a thumb toward the Ilsigi galley—"and they don't like garbage around their property, or sitting on it, either—if you catch my meaning."

"Froggin' shite," Cauvin replied, and tasted the blood dribbling down from his nose. He lifted his left arm to wipe his face with his dangling sleeve—

One of Gorge's companions didn't approve. They'd have been into it again if Gorge and the third guard hadn't scrambled to keep them apart. Cauvin's shirtsleeve lay on the ground. He reached for the cloth and thought better of it. The way his luck ran and with his shirt coming apart, it was a froggin' miracle the guards hadn't spotted the pouch on his belt or the Ilbarsi knife.

There wasn't a law against a free man carrying a weapon in Sanctuary, but froggin' sure, it wasn't against the law to sit on the froggin' pilings, either, and look what that had gotten Cauvin. He stayed on his aching knees while Gorge berated him, then got slowly to his feet.

"Stay off the wharf, Cauvin," Gorge advised. "The captain there"—he hooked his thumb again, this time in the direction of a black-bearded man, head-and-shoulders taller than his mates and dressed in the dark blue breeches and leathers of the Ilsig king—"says he doesn't like the look of you so close to the king's ship."

Cauvin couldn't help it—he rolled his eyes in froggin' disbelief.

"Yeah. Must be he's mistaken you for someone else, but I don't argue with him, and you don't argue with me— Clear your pork butt out off the Wideway."

"Right," Cauvin agreed, retreating a long stride away from the water.

Then he remembered his torn-off sleeve. He only owned two shirts and couldn't afford to walk away from the cloth. Gorge guessed Cauvin's intent. The guard tossed the ratty sleeve into Cauvin's hands before either of his companions objected.

"Keep going, Cauv—"

Cauvin did, but there *had* to be some mistake. He'd recognize the captain again—a man that size wasn't easy to forget—but there was no reason for a galley captain to know him, even less for a royal Ilsigi to be wary of a sheep-shite Wriggle stone-smasher. No reason at all—or none that Cauvin wanted to imagine. He added the sleeve to the clutter at his waist and kept going.

There was a second reason for leaving the Wideway. A cloud had swallowed the sun while the watch was hassling him. Not just any cloud, but the leading fingers of a horizon-covering ridge of dark gray clouds. The wind had picked up, and it was warm for Esharia. Cauvin didn't know storms the way seamen did, but warm winds off the sea in autumn usually meant the city was in for heavy weather. The galley captain and his crew were stuck in Sanctuary for another night. Lord Mioklas could wait another day to finish writing his letter. And outside the city walls, a dying old man was going to have to choke down his pride: an abandoned root cellar was no place to ride out an Esharia gale.

That was Soldt's problem; Cauvin wasn't going out to the ruins. If the assassin solved it—if he dragged the Torch from the ruins, then Cauvin would be at a loss for finding the old pud again, no matter what—

*Good riddance! I can leave this froggin' city with a clear conscience—*

But as soon as Cauvin had that self-congratulatory thought, it began to slip away. He'd never know if the Torch were truly responsible for his sudden literacy. He'd never know what the old pud thought of the forty-two shaboozh Lord Mioklas had given him or whether the rich Wrigglie could possibly be in league with the Bloody Hand. And if he were . . . ? Or if he weren't . . . ? Or he was in league with someone, but he didn't know that someone was in league with the Bloody Hand?

*I don't care. He's an old man—unnaturally old, just like Mioklas said—and I'm leaving Sanctuary forever. Leorin and I. Together. We're getting out. Going to Ilsig and never looking back. If the Hand's here— If Mioklas set the Torch up— It's a lot of froggin' nothing to me. I don't care!*

Cauvin did care. His conscience whispered that he cared in so many ways that his gut knew he'd never leave the city if he counted them. If Cauvin listened to his conscience, he'd make his way to the ruins. To quiet his conscience, Cauvin needed a middle course—and found it when two girls hurried past, their hands covering their mouths, as though their fingers could keep their shrill, giggling laughter from his ears.

No wonder they'd laughed. Children laughed at Bilibot when he passed out on the street, and, froggin' sure, Cauvin looked worse than Bilibot. His face was bloody. His shirt was in tatters. A torn sleeve dangled from his belt. Cauvin had one other shirt . . . folded beside his pallet in the stoneyard loft. The odds that he could swap shirts without Bec or Grabar or Mina taking notice of him weren't good.

He also had forty-two shaboozh beating against his thigh and the name of a laundress at the Inn of Six Ravens who, according to Soldt, would fit him with a white-linen shirt for a soldat or less, if she liked his smile. Cauvin couldn't count on his smile for water on a rainy day, and he had no idea how long it took to make a white-linen shirt, but maybe the laundress could repair the one he was wearing if he tempted her with a shiny shaboozh.

More to the froggin' point, the six black birds huddled on a single branch signboard were visible from where Cauvin stood.

The Inn of Six Ravens was a quiet place where a rich man could lodge his wife, daughter, or favorite mistress. It had its own stable, a fountain courtyard, and a closed iron gate. A man in green livery sat inside the gate. He wasn't drunk, and he wasn't going to let Cauvin inside. He wasn't even going to stand up until Cauvin mentioned Soldt's name.

"Master Soldt told you to come here?" the guard asked on his way to the gate.

"He told me the laundress named Galya lives here . . . works here. He said she'd make me a shirt—" Cauvin shrugged a naked shoulder. "I need a shirt."

"She's around back. Follow the path around the stable."

As easy as that, Cauvin was through the gate and on his way to meet a laundress whose visitors were admitted if they mentioned an assassin's name. He tried to be ready for anything at the back end of the stone-paved path but he wasn't ready for the inn's cramped, rear courtyard: A huge wooden tub dominated the yard with a short, stocky woman standing on a stool beside it.

The laundress sang up a storm as she pounded the tub's contents with a beater that looked a lot like the shaft of a stone-smashing mallet. Galya's face was smooth and pale for a Wrigglie. Wisps of coppery hair stuck out from her kerchief. Cauvin guessed she was Mina's age, but might be wrong either way.

Galya's senses were sharp. She spotted Cauvin before he'd cleared the shadows between the path and the yard. An instant later, the loudest sounds were birds chirping in the eaves.

"Galya—" Cauvin began, then remembered his manners. "Mistress Galya? I'm Cauvin. Soldt said I should come here. He said you could fit me with a white-linen shirt. I need a shirt."

"I can see that, lad." She beckoned him closer. "You could do with a bath, too, a haircut, and some bitter-root paste before that nose swells. Looks like you lost a fight, lad. Against whom, if you don't mind my asking?"

Anyone else had asked that question and there'd have been another fight, but Galya disarmed Cauvin before with a grin.

He grinned back as he answered: "The city guard—but it took three of them."

"You bloody any of them?"

"Mashed a man's nose and split his upper lip."

"Well then, you're a mighty brawler, aren't you. No wonder that shirt's done for. You've given it a hard life." The laundress climbed down from her stool. "Follow me."

The top of Galya's head didn't clear the paps on Cauvin's chest, but her arms, after a lifetime of pounding dirt out of cloth, were nearly as thick as his. Cauvin followed her into a room where jug-laden shelves hid the walls, and every beam or rafter was hung with damp linens. Ignoring the linen maze, Galya pointed Cauvin toward the wooden box, while she rummaged among the shelves.

"How do you know Soldt?" she asked with her back to Cauvin.

He sat on the box and thought a moment before answering. "An old, old man sent me to him to learn how to fight."

"Looks to me as though you'd be better served learning how *not* to fight!" The laundress found what she was looking for and advanced on Cauvin clutching lengths of frayed, knotted string. "Stand up, lad. Stand tall and strip off what's left. You can't expect me to measure you with you slumped over and hung with rags."

Cauvin went shirtless when he worked, and he'd long since discovered that a few women enjoyed watching him build a wall or smash it down, but they didn't look at him the way Galya did. She circled him like a cat hunting mice, then hopped up on the box. Her stubby fingers pressed one string end into the base of his neck. She ran her thumb and the string down Cauvin's spine, clicking her tongue as she went past his waist. He was too surprised to dodge or protest when she knotted in another piece of string and circled it around his hips.

"If your arms were just a little shorter," Galya said when she was finished knotting, "or your shoulders narrower, then we could do the job simply with four ells of cloth, but you see where skimping's gotten you." She lifted the knotwork over Cauvin's head and pointed at his discarded shirt. "No, you'll need five lengths, at least. I've got the cloth and nothing better to do with my time. I'll have a shirt for you this time tomorrow, but—sorry, lad—I'll have to charge you a whole soldat."

"I hoped—I need—"

"Ah! You've somewhere to go before then," Galya guessed with a grin. "Someone to see? Someone important? Someone beautiful? Well, you might be in luck." She beckoned Cauvin to follow her through the linen maze at the center of the drying room. "All manner of things get left behind at an inn, you know. Most of 'em wind up down here. I bundle it up now and again and send it down to the Shambles, but it's been a while—"

They came to a doorway and dim room cluttered with waist-high—for Galya—heaps of cloth. Cauvin took it for a storage room until he spotted a neatly made bed in one corner. The bed, Cauvin noted, was a marriage bed, big enough for two. His mind began to wander, and he looked for traces of a husband—or maybe a lover—who favored black clothing while Galya attacked the heaps.

"Here," she said, flinging a wad of pale cloth his way without looking up. "And here." A wad of dark cloth followed. "Let's see how you look in those."

Cauvin shook out the linen shirt and pulled it on. He had no intention of stripping off his breeches in Galya's bedchamber.

He thought he'd put an end to conversation by asking, "Does Soldt send a lot a of men here?"

Galya laughed as she said: "Not at all, Cauvin. You're the first. The Sweet Mother knows what he was thinking. Now, put on those breeches. They might be short; and I'm not sending a man out with his knees showing."

She left the room, and Cauvin did as he'd been told. Far from being too short, the finely woven breeches were long enough to tuck into the tops of his boots. Cauvin thought himself quite improved until he caught sight of Galya scowling.

"It's a start, but starting's never enough, is it? You'll be wanting new boots—I can't help you there—but you're wanting that hair neatened more. Who's been cutting it for you, lad? Not Nerisis on the Wideway?"

"I cut it myself, when it gets in my eyes."

"Take off that shirt and sit," Galya ordered, and went to the shelves. She returned with a set of shears. "If you don't tell, I won't either."

Cauvin grimaced. He didn't care that there was a law against women cutting men's hair. What worried him was sharp metal close to his head but not in his hands. He flinched each time the blades ground against each other. Clumps of hair as long as his thumb lay in his lap and on the floor. Shorter wisps clung to his skin. They itched mercilessly and worse after Galya flicked at them with a rag.

"Go, jump in the tub and scrub yourself off."

He met Galya's eyes and realized she was serious.

"I've raised two sons to manhood, lad, and buried their fathers along the way."

"But—"

"Go on with you. I'll stay in here folding linen."

After exchanging his boots and belt for a knot of soapweed, Cauvin carefully closed the drying room door on the laundress, stripped, and climbed into the laundry tub.

There was a bathhouse in the Tween, not far from the stoneyard. For three padpols a man could scrub himself with soapweed, then rinse down beneath a hand-cranked waterwheel. The cost went down to two padpols if he took a turn or two cranking the wheel before he soaped up. If he forked over ten padpols, he could stand neck deep in a steaming pool next to anyone else who'd paid for the privilege—provided he was male. Women had their own bathhouses, run by the Sisters of Eshi and absolutely forbidden to men.

Come winter, Grabar would pay for the pool a couple times a week; he said it was cheaper than an apothecary's powder for his aching joints and just as soothing. Cauvin's first few winters on Pyrtanis Street, he'd gone to the bathhouse with his foster father, even earned a few padpols cranking the wheel. But once Bec was old enough to walk that had changed. Bec went with his father, and Cauvin kept himself clean at the stoneyard trough.

It had been years since he'd sunk himself into water—even the shallow, lukewarm water of a tub filled with unfinished laundry. He'd forgotten how good it felt to be clean everywhere at once and lingered until his fingertips were wrinkled like raisins. By then gray clouds had spread across the last patch of blue sky over the Inn of Six Ravens. Cauvin wrapped a strip of linen around his waist and returned to the drying room carrying his new clothes.

"We're headed for a storm," he explained. "I'd better wear my own clothes out of here. I wouldn't want to ruin these."

"Is that the way you ask if I've got a woolen cloak stashed away?"

"No—"

Before Cauvin could finish, Galya offered him folded layers of wool.

"I can't afford that," he whispered, though it was likely that Galya knew how much money he was carrying—he'd left Mioklas's cloth-bound payment looped around his belt and laid across the box.

"And I'm not selling it. The man who last wore it, didn't take it with him when he left the Ravens. I told you, lad, what guests leave, comes to me."

Cauvin set the shirt and breeches down. He shook out the cloak. It wasn't new; close up he could see several places where the cloth had been rewoven. There was a generous hood attached to the collar and a leather martingale dangling from the back seam. A loop for holding an assassin's sword? Cauvin could imagine Soldt wearing this cloak—if the black-leather one were unavailable.

"Why me?" he asked, scarcely aware he'd spoken aloud.

"Why not?"

"Because I don't have answers. Because I don't even know where to look for answers. Because the—" Cauvin caught himself before he slipped and mentioned the Torch by name. "Because if I'm what they're looking for, then it can't be very important, or they don't really care."

"Who are they?"

Cauvin hesitated, then said, "Soldt."

The laundress blinked but said nothing.

"Tell me, Mistress Galya—what does Soldt want with me?"

"Get dressed, Cauvin."

He did, quickly and relying on the maze of drying linen to shield him. The laundress was pouring thick blue liquid from one of the jars into one of the basins when he confronted her again.

"Do I get an answer?"

Galya corked the jug. "Why ask me what Soldt wants? Ask him yourself. He'll tell you—if it suits him."

"He must have told you something. You said I was the first he'd sent here. What does an assassin want with a sheep-shite stone-smasher like me?"

"Duelist," Galya corrected.

"Assassin. Duelist. No froggin' difference." Cauvin shot back—though there was some difference, if the tavern stories were true and not that one was a villain and the other a hero. An assassin killed without warning and not necessarily with a sword. A duelist made his intentions known and gave his victims a chance—whatever chance an ordinary man could manage against a master like Soldt. "What does a froggin' *duelist* want from me?"

"Your attention, I imagine." Galya folded her arms beneath her breasts. "He's been hired to do a job: teach you to fight, that's what you said, isn't it? He won't be happy to hear that you tangled with the guards . . . and lost."

"Will you tell him?"

"No, you will—if you're clever. Aren't you going to ask me who hired him?"

"Do you know?"

She shook her head. "But whoever it was didn't tell him to send you to the Ravens, lad. That's what I meant when I said you're the first. You must be very important—to Soldt, and not only the man who hired him."

A twinge of guilt crawled down Cauvin's back. "You can give Soldt a message?"

The laundress didn't answer.

"Tell him— Tell him I went to look at a wall today on the Processional—a perfume-garden wall. Tell him that while I was there the man who owns the garden seemed to know things he shouldn't know about the death of a man who isn't dead. He'll understand."

Galya closed her eyes as she nodded. "And should I tell him where you're running off to?"

"I'm not running off."

"Of course not. A what—a sheep-shite stone-smasher?—always carries a sackful of silver tied to his belt while he's losing a fight with the guards on the Wideway."

Cauvin studied the floor, feeling very much the sheep-shite stone-smasher.

"It's no concern to me, but a knotted cloth's no way to carry silver in Sanctuary. There's a broker's baldric there on the box. Wear it under your shirt."

He picked it up. The leather was thick but supple, and there was a substantial pouch where the ends overlapped. Galya restrained Cauvin's wrist as he reached for the flap.

"Let me show you how—"

The broker who had made or owned the baldric didn't want to share his wealth accidentally. The flap was edged with quills that might not pierce a pickpocket's fingertips but would almost certainly throw him off stride. They'd give an unwary owner a nasty surprise, too, until he learned where to grasp the leather safely. It would take some getting used to, but Galya was right: A knotted cloth was no way to carry forty-two shaboozh through Sanctuary. Less than forty-two shaboozh.

"How much do I owe you?" Cauvin paid his debts . . . at least he froggin' tried to . . . usually.

"A soldat for the shirt tomorrow, when you come for it. The rest is mine to give."

He didn't argue, but left the small courtyard behind the Inn of Six Ravens under a cloud of guilt as vast and dark as the clouds over Sanctuary. If Galya passed the message along to Soldt, Cauvin told himself, that would be payment enough . . . in the long run . . . maybe.

Gusty winds were clearing the streets of Sanctuary. Half the shops and stalls had pulled their shutters, and the rest would be closed soon. Three decades after the first great storms tore through the city, the people of Sanctuary recognized a bad storm while it was still on the water. Nobody, though, not even the best of Sanctuary's priests, regardless of their devotion, could accurately predict how bad "bad" would be. Cauvin went to the nearly empty Wideway to make his own prediction.

Every ship in the harbor was bobbing to its own rhythm. If there were oarsmen chained on board the Ilsigi galley, they were wishing their mothers had never screwed their fathers. The open waves were rough and whitecapped but they were breaking well below the wharf, and the tide was coming on high. Storms were worst on an incoming tide. The sky to the south and west was a horizon-to-horizon expanse of dirty, seething gray, but it was darkest to the south, while the wind blew mostly from the west. The worst storms were darkest on the east, and their winds came straight up from the south.

Cauvin's prediction, with gusty winds lifting his new cloak aloft, was that "bad" would be miserable, but short of disastrous. He returned to the dilemma he'd dodged all day: go to the ruins or avoid them. The Torch had hired Soldt—that seemed a reasonable conclusion after meeting Galya. Soldt would take good care of the man who'd hired him. Cauvin could go to the Unicorn, maybe spend the whole night there. If they were going to leave with the first tide after the storm, then surely it was time to jump the broom with Leorin.

How much of the doubts eating his mind were true suspicion and how much the growth of willful frustration? Shite for sure, caution had been the right choice, but he wanted Leorin so much it hurt each time he left the Unicorn. Leorin wanted him just as bad, though she didn't sleep alone in a drafty loft. The only reason the two of them hadn't had each other in the pits was lack of opportunity. In a general way, the Hand encouraged screwing; the Mother of Chaos loved nothing better than newborn blood. The girls got better treatment, usually, until they delivered, and the lads got what lads had always wanted.

The worst fights in the pits had nothing to do with the Hand.

Leorin, though, had that Imperial beauty. No beardless kisses for her. The Hand fought amongst themselves for the privilege of taking Leorin to their beds. The wonder wasn't that she was different from other women, the wonder was that Leorin had any use for men at all. Tonight all that would change. He and Leorin would make their vows, with or without a broom lying on the floor in front of them, and while the gale broke around them, they'd start a new life together.

Cauvin headed west down the Wideway, wind swirling the dark cloak around him as though he were Soldt, the duelist, the assassin.

# Chapter Fifteen

Rain began as Cauvin entered the Maze, pebble-sized drops that stung bare skin and left craters in the muck when they hit the streets. Growing up beside the sea, Cauvin knew the worst was yet to come. He ran along the Serpentine and reached the Unicorn's doorway a heartbeat before the sky ripped open with deafening thunder and sheets of rain as dark as night.

The Unicorn's signboard had been lowered and its door pulled shut against the weather, but the tavern was open for business. There were empty tables along the walls, but Cauvin ignored them. Even if he'd visited the place more often, he had the wrong attitude for a shadowed table, an east-side attitude, a Pyrtanis Street attitude, where men sweated when they worked. The Vulgar Unicorn regulars were rogues and schemers for whom breaking a sweat was the greatest sin of all. They might give Cauvin a glance as he came through the door, but not a second—he wasn't rich enough to rob, nor tough enough to recruit.

But this night was different. Despite rain drumming the walls, Cauvin heard the commons fall quiet around him and watched heads turn his way. Hardened eyes asked silent questions. He held off a stare or two, because he'd learned the price of weakness before the Hand caught him. Once Cauvin had backed a regular down, though, there was no way in Hecath's hells that he could sit at a community table. He chose the nearest empty wall-side table and settled into a chair that gave him a good view of both the door and the other patrons, even though that also gave them a better view of him.

By then, Cauvin's heart beat so furiously that his hands shook.

He kept the cloak around his shoulders. Froggin' sure he wouldn't let the regulars catch him fumbling the knots holding it closed.

Mimise, the tall, rangy wench who slept in the room beside Leorin's, reached Cauvin first. She plunked a brimming mug of ale on the table and stayed to stare.

"Reenie's stone-smasher. As Ils will be my judge, I didn't believe my eyes," she declared with her slow, Twandan drawl. "*What* happened to you?"

Cauvin took a deep breath, and said, "I lost a fight with the city guard."

Mimise propped a hand on her hip and leaned away from it. "If that's what comes of losing to the guard, then we've all been playing this game wrong. Reenie's out back. You want me to get her—or has that changed along with the rest of you?"

"It hasn't," Cauvin answered. He broke Mimise's stare by adding: "And it won't, either."

He was calmer after the Twandan left and shed his cloak confidently. Two other wenches found reasons to walk toward his table. They hadn't cared when their sister in service was less than faithful to a sheep-shite stone-smasher, but let him show up in a pale linen shirt and a substantial cloak— Suddenly they were ready to freshen his mug before he'd taken a sip from it. Each offered to fetch Leorin, but only after telling him that she'd been with another man earlier in the day.

Still, flattery was pleasant, and Cauvin was listening to the second wench—her name was Rose or Rosa or Rosy, and she couldn't be a day over fourteen—talk about her life at the Unicorn when Leorin emerged from the storeroom. She raked the commons with her eyes and smiled when she found Cauvin. Then she saw Rose, and the smile vanished. Cauvin could have warned Rose that the storm outside was nothing compared to the one marching across the commons, but that would only get him in trouble with his beloved, and no warning was going to spare Rose. The girl yelped and overturned an empty mug when Leorin's hands clamped down on her shoulders like eagles' claws.

Besides, there was no flattery to compare with Leorin crushing a rival.

"They're looking for someone to clean up out back."

Leorin's voice was cold as winter, and her fingers were white. She wasn't at all gentle shoving Rose toward the storeroom, then she flowed into the empty chair like a cat. With a changer's narrowed eyes, Leorin sized up Cauvin's new shirt, his freshly trimmed hair, the heavy cloak draped over the third chair.

Shite for sure, Leorin looked worried, and worry was not one of Leorin's usual expressions. Cauvin could have repeated what he'd told Mimise and would eventually have told Rose—he wasn't interested in other women—but silence had served him well lately, and there was no reason to change tactics in a froggin' storm.

"Are you going to tell me what's happened?" Leorin demanded, sobering Cauvin in a heartbeat.

He nodded. "A lot's happened. We need to talk—"

"I can see that. Did they all die up on Pyrtanis Street?"

The question caught Cauvin by surprise, though it would be the simplest way to explain his change in fortune. "No, Grabar's fine," he mumbled. "They're all fine."

"The old man—the one that gave you the box— Did he give you more silver? Gold? Did he finally die?"

"No, nothing like that." He and Leorin had become the center of uncomfortable attention. "Can we go upstairs? I don't want to talk about it down here."

"I've got customers to tend—regulars." Which meant they expected good service from their favorite wench, and she expected extra padpols each time she visited their tables.

Cauvin took a deep breath before saying, "Let them wait. Rose can tend them, or Mimise—"

"That Twandan witch! If she thinks she can take what's mine—"

Leorin spun around, looking for the tall wench. Mimise tended a table near the stairs, laughing heartily and tucking something into her bodice. It was Leorin's tables, her regulars, and she didn't take kindly to the invasion. She was half out of her chair before Cauvin caught her arm. Their eyes locked across the table lamp.

He was supposed to know better than to touch her in public. Strangers grabbed at Leorin nightly, and she encouraged the regulars because a caress loosened their purse strings, but Cauvin was neither a stranger nor a regular.

"Please, Leorin," he pleaded, their eyes still locked. "Let it go. Just this once—I need to be alone with you." He released her.

As suddenly as it had arisen, the tension departed. Leorin was all smiles, brushing her fingers lightly across Cauvin's wrist, gliding around the table to stand with her body against him while she toyed with his fresh-cut hair.

"You're sure?" she asked.

Cauvin nodded. He couldn't see Leorin's face for her breasts, and what he was sure of had nothing to do with leaving Sanctuary. The storm, the lewd chuckling from the wenches and regulars, none of that mattered as he followed Leorin up the stairs. He found the tortoiseshell clasp that tamed her golden hair and removed it as she unlatched the door to her room. He'd dropped his cloak on the floor and started on her bodice laces before she'd closed the door.

Neither of them needed lamplight to find the bed.

The long knife clattered to the floor, followed by belts, boots, and shoes. Cauvin wrestled with Leorin's bodice until the braided laces were hopelessly tangled. He solved that problem by yanking them hard enough to tear the cloth. Her breasts moved freely then within her gown, but the gown itself was securely laced in back.

Men's clothing was simpler. Two slipknots kept Cauvin's breeches snug at his waist, or loosened them entirely. While Leorin used one hand to untie those knots and peeled his new shirt over his head, Cauvin grappled blindly with her gown. Leorin moved on to the leather baldric, which was snared in the remains of her bodice and couldn't be lifted over his head.

Her fingers sought the clasp and her shriek of pained, enraged surprise almost certainly echoed through the commons despite the storm.

Too late Cauvin recalled the quills worked into the broker's purse. Meant to stymie a thief; they'd gotten Leorin instead. He located her stung fingers.

"Sorry," he murmured, pressing her fingertips to his lips.

"Don't touch me!"

Leorin exploded out of his arms, raking his cheek with her nails and elbowing his gut for good measure.

Cauvin caught a handful of gown. "I said I'm sorry."

He attempted to lure Leorin back to the bed, but she'd have

none of that, lashing out with her fists and snarling, "Leave me alone! Don't touch me!"

The blows didn't hurt, but Cauvin had to let her go. She threw herself through the dark room, striking first the bedpost, then the floor on her way to the corner where the ceiling came closest to the floor. A stray thunderbolt brightened the room, showing Cauvin the anguish he couldn't otherwise hear: Leorin with her knees tucked under her chin, clawing her own flesh until it bled. Before darkness returned, he was off the bed and fumbling with the lamp on her dressing table.

Thank the froggin' gods the lamp was full—Leorin was usually careful about such things—and there was a flint-and-steel striker dangling from its handle. Cauvin struck a flame and left the lamp on the dresser, where it shed flickering light into Leorin's corner.

"Leorin?" Cauvin approached cautiously, on his knees. "Leorin—I didn't mean to hurt you." He spoke softly, calmly. "The person who gave me the baldric showed me how it was rigged against snatchers, but I forgot. Sheep-shite stupid me forgot what she showed me—"

Leorin lifted her head. Cauvin held his breath, half-expecting her to surge for his eyes the way an injured animal might its rescuer. But the face she showed him, shiny with tears, wasn't masked with anger, nor even fear. It was empty, achingly empty, as if she'd never seen Cauvin before and, perhaps, didn't see him now.

"Leorin? Leorin, it's all right. Come back—"

Cauvin reached for her arm. She cringed and he froze, waited, then reached closer. With his third reach Cauvin's hand circled hers.

"Come back, Leorin. It's only dreams and memories." The dreams and memories and the darkness Cauvin had escaped.

An inch at a time, Cauvin drew Leorin into his arms. The storm peaked with howling winds, crashing shutters, and bright-as-day thunderbolts. He flinched when they fell close enough to shake the walls, but he kept hold of Leorin and she, lost within herself, was blind to the storm. A few moments passed, or maybe a few hours—Cauvin had let his mind go gray and lost track of time. The rain had gentled when Leorin began to shiver. Cauvin wrapped her in blankets pulled from the bed.

"Storm's over," he suggested, and Leorin began to cry in earnest.

Leorin cried until tears had washed away whatever memories had risen earlier. First one arm, then the other emerged from the blanket cocoon. She caressed his shoulders, his back. She pulled his face to hers and gave him a kiss fit for waking the dead; but it was a wasted effort. Cauvin never loved Leorin more than when she needed him, but it was a chaste love at cross-purposes with passion or lust.

"No." He pushed her away. "Not now. That was a bad one, Leorin. I wasn't sure where you were, or who you thought I was, or if you were coming back."

"You worry too much."

"And you don't worry enough. Sanctuary's not a good place for you—or me either. Too many memories. We've got to get out of here. I collected forty shaboozh today. With them and the coronations I got the other day—it's enough, Leorin. We can pay a ship's captain. We can go to Ilsig in style—"

"A ship to Ilsig?" Leorin's eyebrows arched. Her voice was acid. "Frog all, Cauvin, Ilsig's the *last* place I'd go. You haven't made any promises to some froggin' sea captain, have you?"

"No," Cauvin confessed. "I just got the shaboozh." He found the broker's purse and showed her its secrets. "What's so bad about going to Ilsig? Just the other night, you wanted to follow a merchant to the kingdom."

Leorin paused in her coin counting. "Look at me, Cauvin. Do I look like I belong in froggin' Ilsig? If I'm leaving Sanctuary, I'm not going where I look like the froggin' down-on-her-luck, Imperial whore. Ten days with that merchant, and everything he owned would have been mine—*ours*. We wouldn't have *stayed* in Ilsig, not one day longer than necessary."

"I want to take care of us, Leorin. I can earn enough that no one would ever think you're a whore, Imperial or otherwise, here or in the heart of Ilsig," Cauvin proclaimed before he could stop himself.

"No." Leorin stroked Cauvin's cheek. "But, if I'm leaving, I'd sooner go to Ranke. Froggin' sure I could turn heads there. You know I could."

Cauvin clenched his jaw.

"Oh, Cauvin, don't sulk. It's business . . . opportunity there for the taking. You'll have me long after I've lost my looks, but until then, I can make us *rich*!"

"You may look Imperial, but inside you're just another Wrigglie. What chance have we got in a city where we don't speak the froggin' language?"

She called him a child and a fool, but she did it in Imperial, using the gutter words every Wrigglie understood, then she went on with words he didn't understand in his ears, but—perhaps—could have read, if she'd written them out.

"Enough!" he snarled. "You've made your point. I don't want to argue with you, Leorin, I just want to get you out of Sanctuary before something bad happens."

"What 'bad'? We've been through the worst, haven't we?" She shook out the last of the shaboozh. "Froggin' gods, Cauvin—you've got forty-two shaboozh here. Forty-two froggin' shaboozh on top of four coronations and twenty-three soldats. That old pud you're working for must be made of gold and silver. What's his froggin' name, anyway?"

"It's not the same pud. I got the shaboozh from Lord Mioklas on the Processional. You remember I built a wall in his perfume garden last spring?"

"Forty-two—that's just a start, just for your labor. He still owes for the stone, doesn't he? You're finally taking your share first?"

"Something like that," Cauvin confessed. "I want to get us out of Sanctuary."

"The Ender, can you tap him again?"

"What Ender?"

"The froggin' Ender pud who gave you the coronations and soldats! Is he good for more?"

Cauvin squirmed uncomfortably. "I never said I got those coins from an Ender."

"Frog all—who but an Ender has bright, shiny coronations and soldats in this city?"

*The Torch,* Cauvin thought, but didn't say. Having held Leorin in his arms and kept her safe as she wandered through her waking nightmare, he'd convinced himself that the only path for him and Leorin was the path out of Sanctuary, to Ranke or Ilsig, by land or sea, the sooner the better.

"Forget more coronations or soldats or shaboozh. We've got the money to leave, and once we're out of Sanctuary none of this will matter . . ." Cauvin was hoping out loud and cringing inside because if he let his guard down, then all his suspicions came roaring back to life.

"We can never have too much gold and silver, Cauvin. Never. If there's silver to be had, then let's have it. If there's gold, so much the better."

Cauvin answered by scooping up pile after pile of shaboozh from the planks between them. Leorin reached for his wrists.

"What troubles you, Cauvin? If you'd rather stay here in Sanctuary—If you're doing all this just for me—?"

"No. No, I want to leave Sanctuary."

"You never did before. You didn't when I told you about the merchant."

Cauvin tucked the closed purse within the heap of his cloak. "All this had barely started then. I didn't know where it was leading."

"Where all what was starting and leading?"

He shook his head. "I can't talk about it. I want to—that's why I wanted to come up here—but I can't. I can't separate the good from the bad, even in my own mind."

"Don't try." Leorin slid her arm around Cauvin's shoulder, more friend than lover. "If you're in trouble— If it's more than collecting what you're owed—"

"No—that's the easy part, the good part, the part I can believe happened, because the rest of what's happened to me this week, I don't believe it myself. It started the morning when they found the bodies at a Pyrtanis Street crossing."

"The bodies? Oh—the Torch and the Ender—the old pud's spare son? Nothing hard to believe about that. A sparking Ender cut down on the streets. A froggin' old pud. Only bit that's hard to believe is that the Torch was alive to murder. That was one *unnaturally* old pud."

"He didn't die, Leorin," Cauvin whispered. "The Torch didn't die on Pyrtanis Street. I found him the next morning. He was getting the snot stomped out of him on the Promise of Heaven—"

"Where on the Promise?" Leorin demanded.

"Inside the old Temple of Ils. All I saw at first was a Hiller pounding an old man—"

"Did you recognize him?"

"Not hardly. I couldn't tell if it was a man or a woman getting pounded—"

"No, the other one—you said a Hiller. Did you recognize him?"

Cauvin shook his head. "Some rat from the Hill. He couldn't fight me and knew it. I'd've followed him when he ran, but the old pud—the Torch—he was in bad shape."

"He was *in* the temple of Ils?" Leorin demanded.

Froggin' sure, the Torch was an Imperial priest with no business in an Ilsigi temple, but froggin' sure Great Father Ils hadn't been seen on the Promise of Heaven lately. "He must have gotten himself lost. I said he was in bad shape and so old you'd froggin' swear a good sneeze would blow him apart."

"And you stayed with him until he died, then you took what he had on him?"

"The Torch didn't die, Leorin. He's still alive. I wanted to take him to the palace. Shite for sure that's where he belongs, right? But, no, he won't go to the palace. We're arguing and suddenly he says: 'Where were you going when you found me?' And me—the sheep-shite idiot—the next thing I know, I'm on my way with him in the gods-all-be-damned mule cart."

Leorin drummed her fingers against the leg of her dressing table. The rapid movements made the lamp tremble and filled the room with flickering light.

"The Irrune," Cauvin continued, "who knows who they burnt on that pyre. But the Torch won't go back to the palace. He *is* dying; he's just taking his own froggin' sweet time about it."

"Where were you going? You weren't working on Mioklas's perfume garden—"

"No—Grabar heard that a dyer over on Sendakis Way was going to be marrying off his son. We put new bricks on the front of the dyer's house, so Grabar figured that when he set his son up, he'd want the fronts—"

"Where, Cauvin? I don't care about bricks or dyers. Where did you take the froggin' Torch?"

"Outside the walls, up into the hills, to the old estate where we got the bricks to do the first front."

"Sweet Mother, there must be twenty old estates in the hills out there. Which one? What's its name?"

"How should I know? Nobody lives there. Nobody's lived there since before Grabar and Mina were born—that's what she says. She recognized the place from our description, but she didn't know the name—never had, I guess."

"To the east? The west? Near the Red Foal? The White?"

"What's the difference? Pretty much in the middle, then. It's brick-built but the bricks were imported. You can't make red bricks with Sanctuary sand, Sanctuary clay. I tell Grabar I'm going out to the red-walled ruins, and he thinks I'm out there smashing bricks out of the walls, not waiting on a man too stubborn to die."

"The Torch is still alive? Still alive in an abandoned estate built from red bricks?"

"Well—" Cauvin thought about the storm. It had packed a punch, but the winds had pretty much died down. Sanctuary got worse from afternoon squalls in summer. A few roof tiles might have blown loose, a few shutters unhinged themselves, nothing more. He'd have no trouble getting back to Pyrtanis Street, but outside the walls, in a crumbling ruin of red bricks? "He was alive when I left yesterday. Today's the first day I didn't go outside the walls. He's had me running errands. That first night . . . it was the Torch who sent me to the Broken Mast after that box."

"You were fetching for Lord Froggin' High-and-Mighty Torchholder and you didn't tell me? Just some old pud! All Sanctuary's buzzing about who killed the froggin' Torch, who killed the sparker from Land's End, and you sit right here on my bed keeping secrets?"

Cauvin couldn't hold Leorin's glower. He looked at his naked feet. "I didn't tell anyone. I wanted to. I wanted to go to the palace and get the old pud out of my life, but that's not what he wanted—and I'm here to tell you, that withered old pud that he is, there's no winning an argument with Molin Torchholder. *He* says that his enemies think they killed him there at the end of Pyrtanis Street and that there's no froggin' point to letting enemies know when they're wrong. I didn't even tell Grabar. He sends me out every morning with the mule, thinking I'm breaking my back smashing bricks and I'm running ragged for Lord Molin Torchholder! You know how Mina would be if she thought she could get her hands on an *Imperial lord*." He almost mentioned how Bec had gotten the secret out of him and was calling the Torch "Grandfather" as he wrote down the old pud's memorial—but he already felt sheep-shite foolish enough.

"So, who does the froggin' Torch think murdered him?"

Cauvin continued to stare at his toes. "That's one of the reasons I didn't tell you—I didn't want to get you frightened, but—according to him—it was the Hand, a red-handed Servant of the Bloody Mother. If he's right, they're back in Sanctuary . . . and all the more reason for us to get out, Leorin. We got out alive; there's no way we could be lucky a second time."

He reached out to take Leorin in his arms, but she eluded him. She threw off the blanket, stood up, and said, "Please, Cauvin, have mercy." Her tone was anything but merciful. "The Hand returned to Sanctuary? Do you think they're sheep-shite fools? Molin Torchholder broke the Hand into a thousand pieces, then burnt the pieces, and scattered the ashes to the winds. Shite for sure there's a Mother's priest somewhere who'd love nothing better than to lay the bastard's beating heart on the Mother's altar, if only he'd set foot *outside* Sanctuary. There's nothing left of the Hand inside Sanctuary except bad memories and nightmares."

"They nearly got Bec," Cauvin informed her, lifting his head. "The boy followed me"—that was a lie, but it would stand—"and wound himself tight with the old pud and decided to do him a froggin' favor—after I told not to. The froggin' sprout got jumped coming home. Froggin' sure it was the grace of the damn gods I got there in time. I dreamt the boy was in trouble—"

Leorin scowled. She said, "You've always said you don't dream," as though this were the most potent lie Cauvin had ever told.

"I've been dreaming a lot since the Torch didn't die—"

"You should have told me."

"It's just dreams, not nightmares or terrors. The important thing is, I dreamt Bec needed rescuing, and I went out after him. I wound up fighting the Hand in an old courtyard off Copper Corner."

"How do you know it was the Hand?"

"The bastard getting ready to twist Bec's head around wore red silk over his face."

"Sweet Mother, Cauvin—that doesn't prove anything. Why did you wear the red silk in the first place? It was as much to frighten people as to hide your faces. So, what better way to wait in an alley or courtyard than with some red silk wound over your face? Froggin' gods—you fell for it quick enough."

"All right—it was more than the silk, it was the way he fought, the way he had his hands around the boy's head, all set to snap his neck. I know what the Hand taught me, Leorin. I know it when I see it. If that bastard wasn't consecrated Hand, then he was froggin' taught by them."

"Maybe not everybody who walked out of the palace decided to live like a sheep-shite dog smashing stone for stewed meat twice a week."

"I know every one the Torch set aside, every orphan who walked out of the palace the day after . . . everybody who's left." Cauvin was on his feet. His right hand had become a fist. He didn't remember either act.

"You didn't see me walk out, did you, Cauvin? The froggin' Torch never did anything for me."

Leorin's words were fists in Cauvin's gut. It wasn't merely that she was right; Leorin usually was. But he'd never considered that Leorin might not be the only orphan who'd survived the Hand's collapse without the Torch's help.

"We've got to leave Sanctuary," Cauvin said. His fist fell open to his side. "Anyone who doesn't want to meet the Hand again has to leave—" Grabar and Mina, Swift, Batty Dol, and everyone else on Pyrtanis Street marched past his mind's eye. Even rich Lord Mioklas on the Processional and Gorge of the city guard, who wasn't a bad sort. And Bec. Mostly Bec. "They've got to be warned. I've got to tell them!"

"You haven't told anyone what happened? The brat hasn't?"

Cauvin shook his head. "He came up with his own lies."

"But you've told Grabar and Mina about the Torch?"

Another headshake. "He doesn't want anyone to know. The old pud's clever. He'd have my liver if he knew I was telling you."

"Me, in particular?"

"No, any—" Cauvin's breath caught on that lie.

"What did you tell him about me?" Leorin demanded. "You're keeping secrets. Gods all damn you, if you're keeping secrets!"

Secrets! Cauvin was drowning in them, froggin' secrets and lies. He wanted to tell her everything, just to be free again—"When I came here to the Unicorn, what—two nights ago, three?" Time blurred for Cauvin with Leorin glaring at him. "It was because the Torch sent me to meet someone." The colder Leorin's eyes got, the more Cauvin realized there were worse fates than drowning in secrets. "I didn't see him, but he saw me . . . and you."

"And wondered why I was here, not out at Land's End?"

Suddenly there was a branch within a drowning man's grasp. Seize it and he'd be safe, with another lie, another secret hanging over him. "That, and other things, too. I told him that we'd known each other a long time—before the pits and in them. You know, he didn't recognize me. The froggin' pud didn't remember locking me in a room after the Irrune took the palace, but he swore he'd have remembered you . . . if he'd seen you."

"So?"

"So, you're right—the Torch didn't help you get free of the Hand. So he thinks— He thinks you must have had the Hand's help."

"I told you!" she snapped. "The Whip dragged me along until I got the drop on him. One slit clean across his froggin' belly. His guts fell out, and I was alone . . . days away from Sanctuary."

"That's what I said, but he didn't believe me. The Torch believes you left with the Hand and came back the same way."

"Sweet froggin' Mother, Cauvin! You sound as though *you* believe it, too."

"Where *do* you go when you're not here?"

Leorin seized the water jug with both hands. "So *that's* the froggin' bone!" She raised the jug shoulder high. Water sloshed over her hair and gown. "It's not the flea-shite Torch and it's not the Hand—it's *you*! Have you forgotten that the froggin' Stick doesn't pay us wages? I *buy* every froggin' mug I serve, and the froggin' Stick charges rent for this flea-shite room on top. If it's been a slow week—and between the damn froggin' Dragon and a froggin' funeral for a corpse that wasn't the frog-all Torch, this has been one froggin' slow week—and I need the rent, or padpols for the Sisters of Eshi or, Sweet Mother forbid, I've torn a hole in my shoes, the froggin' gods know I can't turn to you. 'Til this week, you've been poorer than dirt, but don't hear me complaining, do you? I do what I have to do and get what I need from my regulars. It's what I know how to do, Cauvin. I don't froggin' enjoy it, but I do it because I've eaten dirt, and it doesn't froggin' fill your stomach."

Ashamed, Cauvin said, "I didn't mean that."

"What did you mean, then?"

"I meant— I froggin' meant that you were so close to them. You can think like them, and sometimes you're as froggin' cold. It's hard not to wonder, that's all. The Torch had me take his doubts to a S'danzo—"

Leorin's arms trembled. It seemed she would heave the jug, but she set it down hard on the dressing table instead. "There's a froggin' poor joke. I'd sooner be Hand than S'danzo. Why don't you jump *her* broom?"

"Because, frog all, you're the woman I love, Leorin. I want to get us out before the darkness closes in over both our heads. You couldn't see yourself during the storm—the look in your eyes, the way you turn cold as death. I don't want to lose you to the Hand! They're back, Leorin. What do you think they'll do if they find out you slit the froggin' Whip?"

In silence, Leorin wrapped her arms around herself so tight it seemed she'd break. She didn't blink, didn't breathe. Cauvin caught her just as she began to topple.

"I ran once," she whispered, squeezing his ribs, now, rather than her own. "And no matter how far I went, the dreams were already there, so I came back." Leorin looked up at Cauvin, her amber eyes shining in the lamplight. "It was better here."

"Because I hold you when you dream. Think how much better it will be when we're in Ranke."

"Ilsig."

"But?"

"I'll go wherever you go, Cauvin. Give me a day to get ready, to sell what I can; and one other thing: We've got to be married before we leave. No priests, no processions or feasts—just you and me. Tomorrow, at sunset, we'll make our vows, just to each other.

We'll have one night, together and alone, together in Sanctuary. The day after tomorrow, lead me onto whatever ship, bound for whatever port."

"We don't have to wait until tomorrow," Cauvin whispered in Leorin's ear. Anger could become lust faster than any mage could cast a spell.

"I want wine, Cauvin—good wine from Caronne, perfumed oil for the lamp . . . and *elsewhere*." With a kiss-moistened fingertip, she drew a swirling shapes down Cauvin's chest that took his breath away. "I'll have it all here before sunset tomorrow—" Leorin paused, then grinned. "*Today!* Froggin' sure, it's hours after midnight."

Cauvin let go slowly. He'd been caught in the undertow once already tonight; twice was almost more than a man could endure without getting drunk on sour wine.

"You find the ship," Leorin purred. "I'll get the wine and the oil."

Cauvin stood beneath a streaming gargoyle on Stink Street. The storm had scoured the roofs. He let the water splash against his face without fear and marveled that he'd walked away from Leorin again. Overhead there were stars shining through high, shredded clouds. The Irrune torches were all soaked and useless, but with every puddle turned into a mirror by the starlight, Cauvin could see his way to the Processional.

He hadn't planned to go back to the stoneyard, but short of the ruins, there wasn't anywhere else to go. Cauvin turned left on the Processional, toward the palace, and had the avenue to himself—or he'd thought he did. He'd passed Mioklas's darkened mansion before he realized he wasn't hearing the echo of his own footsteps following him.

Cauvin's shadow raised a lantern, revealing a face—Soldt's face. They met in the middle of the avenue.

"You've been following me?"

"I was at the Vulgar Unicorn waiting for you when you came downstairs. I thought we'd share a pitcher of mulled wine, but I couldn't catch your eye."

This was a different Soldt. If Cauvin had joined him at the Unicorn, there wouldn't have been much wine left in his pitcher.

The assassin was short of drunk, but not by much. Cauvin asked himself: Why would the Torch's man drink himself tipsy?

"He's dead." Cauvin answered his own question. "The Torch is dead."

Soldt shook his head. "Not to my knowledge, though my knowledge stops with the storm. First thing this morning I told him there was a gale-storm coming. I'd found a quiet room inside the walls—"

Cauvin guessed that he knew where.

—"But there's no moving Lord Torchholder when his mind's set. I could have forced him, one way or another; no doubt, that would have killed him sure as the gale. I hauled extra blankets for his bed and oilcloths to nail over the cellar way. I'd have stayed with him, damn him, but he'd have none of me. He was worried about you and what sort of trouble you'd gotten yourself into. Said I needed to keep an eye on you. And your imp of a brother."

"Bec? What's happened to my brother?"

"He's home in the stoneyard, asleep in his bed—or plaguing his parents. The little demon showed up while I was collecting supplies . . ." Soldt laughed—a small heave at the shoulders, marking unshared humor. "At first, I was glad to see him. If anyone could move Lord Torchholder, I thought he might be the one. There's not many beautiful women who can wheedle half so well as that boy. But Lord Torchholder was adamant, so the imp started in on *me*! If Lord Torchholder wouldn't leave, then we should stay with him . . . telling ghost stories, no doubt. Lord Torchholder wouldn't hear of that. He gave the boy a good scolding for insolence and said to take him home. I thought we were done, but the imp scampered. He's got the makings of a spy in him. By the time I dug out his bolt-hole, I thought we'd be caught in the storm. The weather held—Lord Torchholder's a storm priest. I got Bec to the stoneyard before they closed the gate." Another shoulder heave. "You're not truly collecting eggs from talking chickens?"

Cauvin chuckled. "Who knows? They play dumb when I'm around. Too bad Bec couldn't persuade the Torch to move. He's going to die alone out there—"

"That's what he wants. He's down to pride and fear. I tried to clean that wound— It's hopeless. His leg's turned black. Any other man and the flesh would have gone putrid, but Lord Torchholder's a priest. One morning, soon, he'll be gone but for his bones; maybe them, too. He's a believer again, saying his prayers, making the signs. Lord Torchholder knows Vashanka's waiting for him. I think that frightens him more than death itself. Can't say as I disagree. If I can't die quick, then let me die alone. Pride's stronger than fear."

The wind behind the gale blew cold. Cauvin shuddered. He thought about the thousandth eye of Father Ils, the eye that saw the deeds of a lifetime and weighed the soul accordingly. He'd survived the Hand by doing what he'd been told. If that didn't appease Father Ils when it came time, then Cauvin knew exactly how the Torch felt. Cauvin shuddered again—he couldn't change the past, but, maybe the future . . . ?

"Did you get a message from me? I went to see that laundress at the Inn of Six Ravens . . ."

"I can see that," Soldt agreed, and added, without directly answering Cauvin's question, "It's no secret that he and Lord Torchholder walk in different circles, but I'll take a look at who Lord Mioklas has been talking to lately. I'm not known through the palace, lad. The good there is, no one recognizes me; the bad is that I've got few connections there other than Lord Torchholder. None at all near Naimun, and that—I'll wager—is where I'd need to look."

With his conscience acting up, Cauvin felt obligated to add, "The Hand killed Mioklas's father—peeled him right here, in front of his own home."

"Meaning, he wouldn't knowingly plot Lord Torchholder's murder with the Hand?"

"Something like that. If he knew— If the right person proved it to him, he'd be the first looking for revenge."

"Nothing better than a rich man's vengeance!" Soldt laughed. "The poor man knows the gods of fortune aren't smiling on him, but a rich man takes it personally."

Rich men took sea gales personally, too, sending their servants out to check for damage. At Mioklas's mansion, the keeper barked the orders while his master made a noble silhouette in front of the high door.

"Time to move on," Soldt suggested.

Cauvin agreed. The men walked together toward the palace,

which was out of the way for a man returning to the Inn of Six Ravens. Cauvin braced himself for questions and when they hadn't been asked by the time they turned eastward on Governor's Walk, he asked them himself.

"Don't you want to know what happened when I went to visit Elemi? She knew my name, but she wasn't glad to see me or the Torch's froggin' box. It was full of cards, S'danzo cards."

"Women," Soldt muttered. "I'd be more interested in knowing why you suddenly felt the need to visit Lord Mioklas on the Processional to collect the stoneyard's debts."

"That's what I do. I smash stone, I build walls, and I make sure we get paid for the work we do. Last spring, Mioklas had us—me—build a wall in his perfume garden. About time he paid for it."

"With everything else that's happening, I wouldn't think you'd be worrying about walls or gardens or unpaid debts. Unless you needed money. Let's see—new cloak, new shirt—new to you anyway. Got your hair cut—"

"I'm leaving Sanctuary!" Cauvin waited for Soldt's reaction, which was, predictably, silence. "Frog all," he exploded. "I'm going to buy ship passage for Leorin and me. I've been thinking about it almost since I found the Torch, but I made up my mind today. That S'danzo, she said I was the only light in Leorin's darkness. If I can get us away from Sanctuary, we'll be free. Maybe Ranke, maybe the kingdom. We'll ride that froggin' galley out to Inception, then buy onto any ship that promises to take us far, far from the Hand."

"You're Lord Torchholder's heir, Cauvin. You can't leave Sanctuary."

"Froggin' watch me. I don't care how much gold and silver he's got hidden away. I can't be bought, Soldt. I'm *not* his froggin' heir."

"You won't get away, lad."

"What, are you going to stop me?" Cauvin reached inside the cloak and withdrew the Ilbarsi knife.

"Put that away. I'm trying to help you."

"Froggin' hells of Hecath you are. You're his man—"

"Put it *away,* Cauvin. You've been chosen."

"Froggin' forget 'chosen.' The old pud can choose any sheepshite fool he wants but, shite for sure, I'm not choosing back."

"Lord Torchholder didn't choose you! He wouldn't wish his

curse on his worst enemy—not that he hasn't considered it."

"Curse? Damn him to Hecath's coldest hell—*What curse?*" Frog all, a curse could explain everything: the dreams, the veil of sparks in the old Unicorn's basement, even the sudden ability to read languages he couldn't speak. "I should've left him there. I should've let that froggin' damn Hiller kick his froggin' brains out his froggin' nose."

"A figure of speech, only. I don't mean a true curse . . . no drinking blood or turning into a wyre. Only Lord Torchholder considers it a curse—the curse that keeps him tied to Sanctuary. He speaks of the city as though it were a living creature that can't be mastered or taught; it requires a keeper—for its secrets, if nothing more. Lord Torchholder would say that Sanctuary chose him, and now that he's dying, it's chosen you to replace him."

"Froggin' sure, the Torch *and* froggin' Sanctuary can just forget about me replacing him. Sanctuary can keep its own froggin' secrets . . ."

Cauvin's voice trailed as he recalled the dreams and visions of the last week. Had the Torch gone through similar turmoil? Were they adversaries or kindred victims? Hard to believe— Impossible to believe that anyone or anything—including Sanctuary—could make a victim of the Torch. The old pud was pulling the strings. He had to be.

"I can read," Cauvin declared.

"The city's not going to offer you a written—"

"No, that's not what I meant. Yesterday, when you handed me that map of the bazaar, I could read it. I never learned letters, never needed them. Before I was supposed to meet you, the Torch sent me after that froggin' blue-leather mask. To get it, I went digging in the Maze—digging in the froggin' cellar of what used to be the Vulgar Unicorn. I tripped something—"

"Defensive wards—Sanctuary's a desert where sorcery's concerned. Takes a lot of pull to set them. Not so in other cities. You'd have them at your stoneyard, in addition to a dog."

Cauvin disagreed. "Not defensive. The froggin' Torch wanted me to touch that froggin' brick *before* I went into the cellar. It wasn't enough that I got the froggin' mask; I froggin' had to meet the froggin' black ghost who'd worn it. Then, yesterday, you handed me that map. Soldt—" Cauvin met the assassin's eyes—"Soldt, I can *read* a language I can't froggin' speak except for cursing."

He hadn't considered what reaction he'd get for his confession, but it wasn't the dead-stop, slack-jawed concern plastered on Soldt's moonlit face.

"What?" he demanded. "What's going through your mind, Soldt?"

"Nothing."

"Froggin' sure that's not 'nothing' on your face. Shalpa's mercy, if you know something, *tell* me."

"I said to him once, 'How do you keep all that treasure safe?' He said it was in caches throughout the city and warded. The wards were tough enough to turn an unlucky rat into a turnip, subtle enough to pass him through, him—Lord Torchholder—alone."

"So, if these wards were so tough, how did I get through? It felt like there were froggin' fireflies inside my skin, but no froggin' turnips."

"It recognized you, Cauvin. Lord Torchholder's warding recognized you, which means in some essential way you and Lord Torchholder are one and the same. I wonder if you can read Caronni or the northern script, Nisi."

"Froggin' shite. I'll kill that old pud. If he's not dead already, I swear I'm going to froggin tear him limb from bony limb."

"I couldn't let you do that, lad."

They'd come to Sendakis Street, where Tobus the dyer had a redbrick house and wanted another beside it; and where a man headed for the Inn of Six Ravens had to turn south.

"You'd kill me?" Cauvin asked before they separated.

"I'd stop you. While Lord Torchholder lives, I'll protect him."

"You weren't there last week."

Soldt shrugged. "I didn't expect to be here now." He hesitated, choosing his words, or his lies. "My work in Caronne finished sooner than I'd expected, and the winds were highly favorable."

"Not highly. If the winds had been *highly* favorable, you'd have taken care of the Hand, or died trying, like any good bodyguard."

"I'm not Lord Torchholder's bodyguard. I'm not beholden to him, nor he to me. I'm not Rankan, either. I don't attend Lord Serripines' Foundation Day festivities."

"What are you and he, then?"

"Say we've become useful friends."

Cauvin asked a question with his eyes alone.

"Ten years ago— No, more nearly fifteen. Time flies. I accepted a goodly number of coronations from nameless faces, with the promise of more later—much more—if I'd pay a short visit to Sanctuary and put an end to the life of a most troublesome man. Lord Torchholder was an old man even then and I—I was no older than you. A newly made master of my craft and far too confident to wonder why they'd come to me when more experienced duelists could have been found.

"Needless to say, I stalked and plotted myself straightaway into Lord Torchholder's trap. He offered two choices; I negotiated a third. We've done well by each other, and Sanctuary's become the place where I am when I'm not somewhere else. The city's been good to me, whatever it's been to Lord Torchholder. Most of those who think they want to hire my services hesitate before venturing into a city where the stuff of sorcery's scarce as hen's teeth. But messengers *do* come. I might leave tomorrow, or the next day, for Ranke or the kingdom, or wherever else vengeance calls. I was born on a ship, Cauvin; I have no roots. I'm not the man to serve the soul of this city."

"Neither am I," Cauvin agreed. "Maybe we'll be on the same froggin' ship. You wouldn't get in my way, would you?"

Soldt shook his head. "Far from it, lad—but I'd try to be on a different ship. Any captain who takes money from you is likely to watch his ship founder before it casts its last mooring rope."

"Thanks for the warning." Cauvin took a backward stride toward Pyrtanis Street. A stray thought crossed his mind. He dug into the broker's purse and flipped a shaboozh at Soldt. "For Galya. Tell her, thanks, but I won't be needing that shirt she's making for me. And, thanks, too, for passing my message to you. Maybe Mioklas is Sanctuary's man. He's got the wealth and the ambition . . . and he'll be looking for vengeance once he finds out the Hand's back. You can work for him."

"Not a chance. A man's got to have someplace where he can be seen by his neighbors. For me, that's Sanctuary. I don't work here—

except to teach a few youngsters how to stay alive: you, Raith at the palace—"

"I'm not the Torch's heir," Cauvin insisted. "I appreciate the lesson you gave me, and the advice, even about changing my shirt. But this is good-bye. Leorin and I are leaving Sanctuary."

He held out his hand. Soldt's remained at his side.

"I'll wish you good luck, Cauvin; you'll need it, but I'll hold my good-byes until I see you standing on a ship's deck."

"Suit yourself," Cauvin said and walked away.

# Chapter Sixteen

The gate was barred when Cauvin arrived at the stoneyard. He could have put his shoulder against the planks, raised a racket, roused the dog, and awakened his foster parents—not to mention everyone else on Pyrtanis Street. He'd done that once, about a month after Grabar led him out of the palace. Once had been enough. After that, Cauvin had hammered out a set of footholds near the east corner.

He hauled himself to the top of the wall, waited for the dog to recognize his scent, then dropped onto a heap of broken bricks and scree. A few stones rolled and clattered, but not enough to awaken the lightest sleeper—and considering the way Grabar snored, a light sleeper would never rest at the stoneyard.

Flower whickered when Cauvin passed her stall. He bribed her with oats and clambered up the ladder to his loft. The roof had leaked, the way roofs did when the thatch was starting to rot and gale-force winds drove rain deep into the straw. Cauvin's pallet was against the northern wall, the coldest wall in winter, the hottest in summer, but leeward during sea storms. His blankets were dry.

Cauvin shed his new clothes without lighting a lamp. He spread the cloak over the blankets for extra warmth and crawled between the lowest layers. He'd had a long and troubling day, but was satisfied with how talking to Soldt had ended it. His mind was drifting toward sleep before his eyes closed—

*Swish! Bang!*

The lower door opened and crashed against the wall. Cauvin cursed himself for forgetting to latch it. He'd have to climb down the ladder . . . butt naked. He could get dressed . . . At the very least he'd have to pull on his boots . . .

"Cauvin! Cauvin!"

That was Grabar shouting, and not from anger. There was an edge on the stone master's voice that Cauvin had never heard before and couldn't deny.

"Coming!" he called, and groped for the clothes he'd shed only a few moments before. His breeches were still warm when he grasped them.

Grabar couldn't wait. "Where's Bec?" The ladder creaked as he climbed. "Where's the boy? We thought—*prayed*—he was with you."

The fabric of Cauvin's breeches fell through his fingers. "No. I haven't seen Bec all day. He was—" Cauvin couldn't finish.

"He was what?"

Cauvin found his breeches and cinched them tight. "He wasn't with me." Painfully tight.

"He's *gone*— After you left, I thought he went to market with the wife; the wife thought he was with me, but he'd run off . . . run off without telling either of us."

In his mind's eye, Cauvin saw what must have happened: Soldt and Bec at the stoneyard gate after his day at the ruins. Bec saying farewell, going inside. Soldt believing Bec was where he belonged, where he'd be safe for the storm. And Bec slipping out again as soon as no one was watching.

Damn Bec's puppy-dog eyes. His parents loved him so much, they couldn't see that he was a practiced liar. Cauvin had to tell the truth even though—shite for sure—the blame for everything was going to twist around *his* neck, not Bec's. Good thing he'd already planned to leave the stoneyard.

He stamped into one boot, and said, "The boy's out at the ruins—where we've been smashing brick."

"How . . . ?" Grabar snarled, but relief got the better of him. "Are you certain?"

"Fairly. Coming back from the Unicorn, I met a man who'd seen him. Thought he'd walked him home, too."

There wasn't enough light in the loft for Cauvin to see the boot he held in his hand if he held it in front of his face, but it didn't take light to sense the change in Grabar's mood.

"What man? Who? What was *he* doing out there? What was Bec doing? What's going on, Cauvin? If something's happened to the boy—" Grabar let the threat hang unfinished; it was more potent that way.

"Husband! Where are you?" Mina's shrill question was followed by the wildly flickering light of a lamp held in a trembling hand. "Where have you *gone*?"

Cauvin and Grabar's eyes met in the faint light. Cauvin saw his foster father standing halfway up the ladder, nightshirt loose on his shoulders, nightcap lopsided on his head. Worried shadows played across Grabar's face. A moment ago Cauvin's thoughts were about blame, injustice, and his own future. Those selfish thoughts disappeared, replaced by a single, burning need: Find Bec.

Grabbing his shirt on the way, he stamped into the second boot as he strode toward the ladder. Grabar retreated ahead of him.

"Has he got Becvar?" Mina demanded, then, when she saw Cauvin: "What have you done with our boy?"

Cauvin dropped down, barely touching the rungs. "Nothing—but I know where he went."

If Cauvin hadn't recognized Mina's voice, he wouldn't have recognized her. The tears streaming from her eyes had aged her face twenty years since morning.

"Where? Where did you take him?"

"I didn't *take* him anywhere. I was in the city all day. Bec went by himself to the ruins to visit—"

Cauvin paused for breath before admitting who was holed up in the abandoned estate. Mina didn't give him the chance to finish.

"The ruins? What ruins? Where? Did he go to Land's End? We'll go there— The good lord Serripines will help us."

Cauvin was speechless: Trust Mina to find an Imperial opportunity in her beloved son's disappearance. Thank the damn gods that Grabar could answer Mina.

"The ruined estate where Cauvin's been collecting bricks for the front of Tobus's new house."

Mina's mouth worked but no sounds came out. When the dam of silence burst, her rage was directed equally at her husband and her foster son. "Fools! Both of you! Fools! Put the Savankh in my hands! Let it burn my soul to ashes, if I'm wrong. I've tried, Sweet Sabellia, I've tried to protect him from both of you. You wouldn't be satisfied until he was out in the sun, breaking his back, ruining his hands? I can see him— I can see him in front of me—" She blinked and focused on Cauvin. "I can see my son struggling with that hammer, trying to do the work *you* were too lazy to do. In the city all day— In the city whoring with your Unicorn bitch while your poor brother worked himself to exhaustion. Too tired to come home, he was, I'm sure of it. Too tired, he lay down to rest and— Sweet Sabellia! The storm! He's drowned! Blown away and *drowned*! You've killed him!"

Froggin' sure, it was clear where Bec had gotten the gift for spinning tales.

"He wasn't trying to smash stone—"

"Hecath's hells!" Mina interrupted. "How would you know? *You* haven't worked all week. You may have fooled my husband, but you haven't fooled me. I've seen the cart. Empty! You've been idling. It's gotten to be a habit. A bad habit—Sweet Sabellia—look at you! New *breeches*! And your hair cut like some Red Lantern fancy-boy. Where'd you get the money?" She gasped. "What have you done with my boy?"

Cauvin tried to dodge his foster mother's lunge for his throat, but she wouldn't be thrown off. In self-defense, he seized her wrists and shook her hard.

"Frog all, woman! Bec's not smashing stone or bricks. He's out at the ruins because the Torch is out there—*Imperial* Lord Molin Torchholder—and the old pud wouldn't come inside the city, not even with a gale blown up."

Mina was too wrought to listen, but Grabar heard and separated his wife and foster son with his hands. "What's this you say, Cauvin? Don't tell us lies, son. Bad as it may be, you'll make it worse with lies. The gods all know Lord Torchholder's dead. We saw his funeral three days past."

"The Torch isn't dead. I don't know who roasted on the pyre the other day, but it wasn't him because I found him, still alive, inside the Temple of Ils, on my way to the ruins the morning Batty said the guards found the bodies at the crossing—"

"The Temple of Ils?" Grabar sputtered, "The Torch was an Imperial pr—" He fell silent. "From the beginning, Cauvin—what leaves you thinking that the Torch isn't dead?"

Mina wasn't interested. "He lies, husband! Ask him what he's done with our son! Make him answer!"

"Quiet, wife!"

Grabar rarely shouted. When he did, only a sheep-shite fool would fail to listen. Mina was many things, but not *that* foolish. She bit her lip white, but said nothing as Cauvin began with the guards at the Pyrtanis Street crossing. It was a long tale, too long and cold for a man and woman in the nightclothes to hear without shivering. Grabar led them all back to the house. Mina reluctantly kindled the hearth.

"Waste of wood," she muttered. "He's lying. All he does is lie. He's killed our boy for money." But even Mina realized that made no sense—who would pay Cauvin to kill Bec? So Mina found an accusation she, at least, found more believable. "He's *sold* our boy . . . sold him to the brothels on Red Lantern Street."

Cauvin had to defend himself against *that.* "Frog all—"

Grabar held up his hand. "That night, after the bodies were found, I went up to the Well. Teera told a tale—how the guard had caught a Hiller lighting out of the Thunderer's old temple. Said he'd been sleeping off a drunk when he got attacked. The guard wouldn't have that. They'd marked him for a thief, and soon enough he confessed he'd waylaid an old man but swore up, down, and sideways that it was a trap—the old man's son showed up out of nowhere and pounded the Hiller, who had the bruises to show he'd lost a fight. The guard wouldn't have that, either—except they couldn't find the old man or his son and the Hiller had no swag—"

"Damn all liars," Mina complained. "Our boy is missing, this one's telling lies, and now you're repeating lies about Hillers and ghosts."

"Because, wife, I'm thinking that Cauvin did walk the Promise that morning, and the Torch, he's an old man by anyone's reckoning."

"Lies. He tells lies!"

"Sometimes," Grabar agreed, "but mostly he gets into fights." He shot a sidelong glance Cauvin's way.

"I marked the man for a Hiller. I'd've chased him home, except the Torch was wounded—wounded bad—but not dead. I wanted to take him to the palace, but he made me take him outside the walls instead."

"An old man?" Mina hooted. "An old *wounded* man, and he bent *you* to his will?"

Cauvin had an answer for that one: "An Imperial lord. A froggin' priest of Vashanka. Who was I to argue with him? He said, where are you going? I said out to smash bricks, and he said, take me with you."

"The merchant who hired you to help him move his stock?" Grabar asked.

"A lie," Cauvin admitted, then added quickly: "The Torch didn't want anyone to know he was still alive—especially his enemies. He wanted them to think they'd killed him."

"Did he know who attacked him? Not some damned Hiller, I'll venture."

It was time for another deep breath. "The Hand. The Bloody Hand of Dyareela."

Mina let out a shriek that was sure to wake the length of Pyrtanis Street, Grabar turned pale as his nightshirt. As he confessed the rest, Cauvin learned—to his astonishment and horror—that the suspicions he held against Leorin could be held against him.

"Nobody's clean," Grabar admitted, after Cauvin had related his meeting with Mioklas for a second time. "If it came down to you or your neighbor, your cousin, or your brother, the choice was so clear it wasn't rightly a choice at all—"

"Speak for yourself!" Mina snapped.

"Sahpanura," Grabar replied, equally quick.

It was a name, a woman's name, that meant nothing to Cauvin but, sure as froggin' sorcery, it froze Mina's tongue to the roof of her mouth. In the silence that followed, Cauvin repeated something he'd said many times already—

"I'm sorry."

"I brought you home to be our son," Grabar said to the wall behind Cauvin's head. "I knew what you'd done, but Lord Torchholder said, not to worry. He trusted you and so could we, because the Hand was gone. I can't say I'm surprised the Torch was wrong about the Hand—vengeance has a long memory. But you, Cauvin—how could you not tell us? If not when you found the Torch, then—by the mercy of Ils—after you saved the boy in Copper Corner? I don't know whether to thank you for that or curse you to Hecath's deepest hell."

Mina said, "I know."

"Frog all, I didn't *plan* this!" Cauvin snarled in her direction. "I didn't ask Bec to follow me like a lonesome puppy. I didn't tell him to sneak into the palace in the middle of the night. I didn't tell him to go out to the ruins today, or sneak out again after Soldt walked him home. I've done wrong, and I'm sorry—but it's not all my froggin' fault. Blame the Torch, why don't you? His froggin' Lordship needed someone who knew Imperial to write down his froggin' testament and, shite for sure, that wasn't me, was it, Mina? You're the one taught Bec that an Imperial man was a better man. And, what about Bec . . . when it comes to lying—"

Cauvin didn't finish his rant. Grabar's right fist rounded out of nowhere and knocked him out of his chair. He sprang up, fists cocked and ready for a brawl . . . but not with Grabar. The pain in his cheek wasn't Grabar's fault. He'd have wept for pain or grief or fear or aching disappointment, if he hadn't cried all his tears long ago.

Mina flung herself on the bed, sobbing loudly and dramatically. Grabar stood on the far side of the table, the look of vengeance on his face. Cauvin held his ground; bad as the moment was, he'd endured worse. Grabar cracked first, stomping out of the house. Cauvin listened for the sound of the gate swinging open, but wherever Grabar went, it wasn't out the gate.

He waited a few moments. A tear might have leaked down his cheek, or maybe it was cold sweat. Honald the rooster gave his first crow of dawn. Mina's sobs had quieted; Cauvin was careful not to disturb her on the way out. Grabar was below the loft, tightening the buckles of Flower's harness.

"I'm coming with you," Cauvin said.

Grabar didn't respond, which was a better reaction than Cauvin had feared he might get. He bounded up the ladder to get his new cloak, which drew a sour glance, nothing more from Grabar. They walked down Pyrtanis Street with the mule between them, not saying a word. No matter what they found outside Sanctuary's walls, it was suddenly easier to imagine leaving the stoneyard than staying.

Shite for sure, Cauvin would have preferred a scolding, even a beating once they'd cleared the eastern gate. (Without conversation they'd agreed that the boy would have come and gone through the gate rather than the Hillside gaps in the wall.) It was bad enough being worried sick over Bec without wondering when Grabar would finally explode.

Flower gave them their first hint of trouble halfway up the tree-lined avenue to the brick-walled ruin. She planted her hooves and let loose with one of her "I'm *here*" brays which was answered by a horse on the far side of the trees. Cauvin struck off and found a brown gelding grazing the frosted grass. The animal wore a saddle and bridle; neither was wet enough to have weathered last night's gale.

Horses were notoriously skittish and not Cauvin's favorite beasts. He approached it cautiously and counted himself lucky to grab the trailing reins without sending it galloping across the meadow in panic.

"Soldt's?" Grabar asked—his first word since knocking Cauvin off the chair.

"Maybe," Cauvin replied. He didn't doubt the assassin could ride as well as he handled a sword. But Soldt wouldn't have left a sword lying out in the rain, and it didn't seem likely that he would have left a horse out either. "Don't think so."

Grabar grunted and, holding on to Flower's lead, indicated that Cauvin and the gelding should go first into the ruins. Inside the wall, they took turns calling Bec's name.

"This is where I set the Torch up first." Cauvin gestured toward the roofless bedchamber and noticed a body sprawled on the ground within it. "Frog all," he swore, and looked for a place to tie the horse.

Grabar did the same with Flower. They met on either side of the body. It was a man in worker's clothes, facedown on what had been a springtime mosaic. His nose was buried in storm-soaked leaves and muck. Cauvin's best guess was that he'd been dead before he hit the ground, but his hands were beneath his gut and he could have been cheating. If there'd been a stout stick nearby, Cauvin would have used it to nudge the body; instead, he shoved a foot under the body's shoulder and booted it over.

"Eyes of the Thunderer!" Grabar exclaimed, leaping clear as the body flopped toward him.

Froggin' sure, the body was a corpse, a stranger to Cauvin, with a skull-sized hole in its gut. There was gore on the mosaic tiles, but not enough—in Cauvin's experience—to account for all the missing flesh. He got closer and noticed how the dead man's clothing was charred around at the edges and that the hole itself had the look—and odor—of seared meat. He prodded with his finger—

"Eyes of the Thunderer! Don't do that!"

Cauvin straightened. "I wonder what killed him?"

"Wolves!" Grabar decided, then shouted Bec's name four times, once to each quarter. "You said there's a cellar. Show me!"

"Couldn't be wolves," Cauvin argued on the way to the root cellar. "Wolves bite and tear. That man's gut burst and burnt—from the *inside*! There's no animal that could do that. No weapon, neither."

"Gods could."

Of course! Without warning Grabar, Cauvin ran back to look at the corpse's hands. One was charred, the other was missing along with half a forearm. No way to tell if he'd been Hand—

"Cauvin! Where's that cellar?"

They found another corpse near the cellar entrance. The pud had lasted long enough to curl into a ball, as if that would have smothered the fire or kept his guts where they'd belonged. He'd died with his eyes open and sheer terror shaping his face. Cauvin glanced at the corpse's hands as they passed: The palms were burnt bloody, but the backs were pale.

"Hurry up!" Grabar scolded, making it clear that he wanted Cauvin to enter the cellar first.

Cauvin didn't object, though his eyes took a moment longer than he'd expected to adjust to the dim light, and he stumbled over a third corpse. It was so thoroughly blasted that its bones were nothing but charcoal and collapsed beneath Cauvin's boots. There was a fourth corpse just beyond the third and the dark shadow of a fifth beyond that.

"Bec! Becvar!"

Grabar shoved Cauvin aside, not noticing or, perhaps, not caring what he stepped on as he searched frantically for his son. Cauvin let him go. He'd already seen that none of the dead was child-sized and was looking for the Torch. The pallet Cauvin and Soldt had put together for him was disordered, but empty. The fifth corpse was dark because, unlike the others, it wore a black robe.

Cauvin circled the body, getting out of his own shadow. Like the first corpse, the Torch had fallen forward, but he'd gotten his left hand up to cushion his chin before he hit. His head lay naturally in profile. His eyes were closed and Cauvin dared to hope that the old pud was merely asleep. He wanted to finish the killing himself.

"Hey, pud— Wake up—" He nudged a shoulder. There was no warmth, no resistance, no chance that the Hero of Sanctuary had survived to fight another day. "This time they got him."

"What? Who?" Grabar didn't recognize the black-robed Torch.

"His enemies. This time the Torch's enemies got him." Cauvin slid his hands beneath the black cloth. He wasn't surprised to bump his fingers against the old pud's hardwood staff. "He went down fighting—"

"The boy, Cauvin! Where's Bec? If the Torch is dead, we can't help him, and he can't help us. Help me look for the boy."

Cauvin didn't argue, but he couldn't take vengeance on a corpse. He lifted the staff and the Torch, intending to carry both to the pallet, but he'd barely raised his hands above the ground when the black wood warmed against his flesh. Before he could free himself, the Torch's eyes—scarcely a handspan from his own—opened. Gods forbid, but the old pud's eyes shone silvery white and streaked with shimmering flame.

Yelping like a stepped-on dog, Cauvin dropped his burden and scrambled backward until his shoulders struck the earthen walls.

"Enough of that—" Grabar shouted, then he saw what Cauvin had seen and prayed aloud as he, too, retreated: "Ils, Father of Life, take me in Your hands, lift me up!"

But the only lifting in the root cellar was done by the Torch himself as he braced that blackwood staff and hauled himself upward, hand over hand, like some skeleton come to life. When he'd risen to his knees, the amber atop the staff began to glow. Froggin' sure, Cauvin knew exactly how the other men had died.

"Lord Torch! It's me! Cauvin—the sheep-shite idiot who saved your froggin' life! Frog all, don't kill me!"

The Torch didn't seem to hear or care, or maybe there was nothing left of the old priest except a ghost bent on burning anything, anyone, that got close.

"Lord Torch, it's *me*—Cauvin. We're looking for Bec, my brother. You remember my little brother? He called you 'Grandfather.' "

"Bec?" The Torch's voice was raspy and seemed to come from somewhere other than his throat, somewhere other than the root cellar. "Cauvin? Is that you, Cauvin?" With each word, his voice grew more anchored in time and place.

"It is, old pud. What . . . ?"

"You're not alone. Who's with you?"

"My father— My *foster* father, Grabar. We're looking for Bec. He didn't come home. We thought— I thought he might have come back out here, to be with you during the storm. Was he here?"

Despite all that he'd said in the stoneyard, Cauvin hoped the Torch's answer would be no, but the skull-like head bobbed up and down.

"I sent him away. Twice I sent him away." The Torch's eyes burnt brighter. "Once, with Soldt, but the boy got loose from his parents. The sky was black when he showed up again. First thing he said: too late to send him home. Oh, the boy thought he was so very clever. Offered to make tea and keep the fire burning so I could tell him stories of Sanctuary. I told him he could make tea and tend the fire, but there'd be no stories, no rewards for a boy who didn't listen to his elders and deceived his parents."

Cauvin stole a glance at Grabar. His foster father knew the truth now, but the price was much too high.

The Torch continued, "When the gale began in earnest the boy knew he'd made a mistake—a hole in the ground is no pleasant place when the rain's falling sideways and the lightning's struck so close your hairs stood on end. I told him we'd be safe, and we were . . . from the storm. It was over and the stars were fading when I felt men nearby. I woke the boy and told him to hide himself in the bushes and keep still no matter what. They were after me, not him, and they'd find me, but they'd never look for a boy."

"We called and called his name," Grabar said, taking a step toward the entry. "He didn't answer."

"That boy does not do as he's told," the Torch said, staring at Grabar with those odd, odd eyes. "A leather strap would have gotten him to safety, but I had none to hand."

"What happened?" Cauvin asked.

"I have some skill with sorcery," the Torch admitted—and, shite for sure, it was heresy for a *priest* to speak of sorcery, not prayer. Might as well confess that his god had abandoned him. "Enough that I knew the Hand had come looking for me and that I could attack them before they attacked me. I spared nothing, save my life—and I would have given that, had I been certain I could annihilate them all in a single burst. I took down four of them before my fire burnt out, but there were more than that. How many more, I can't say. It is bitter morning to find myself yet alive and the boy gone."

Grabar took off, shouting his son's name and flailing the bushes that surrounded the root cellar. Cauvin faced the Torch alone. The Torch spoke first.

"The Hand knew where I was—*exactly* where I was. Not merely this estate, but here, hidden in a cellar. How did they know?" the Torch asked. "Arizak burnt a body. I was dead to the world, but they knew where to find me."

The old man's strength failed; his knees buckled. Without thinking, Cauvin lunged forward, catching him before he collapsed completely. The Torch had been light as a child when Cauvin carried him out of the Temple of Ils and lighter still whenever he and Soldt had carried him through the ruins, but now it seemed that the damned black staff weighed more than he did.

The Torch squeezed his wrist. The old pud's fingers were as fleshless—and strong—as a hawk's talons. "How did they know?"

"Frog all if I know."

"They came straightaway to the root cellar, Cauvin. They knew where to find me, and they took the boy. He's not outside. Your father will not find him; he's gone. Why take the boy?"

Cauvin twisted free of the Torch's grasp. "Because they're the

Bloody Hand of Dyareela!" He snapped, a swirl of emotion and memory getting the better of his tongue. "That's what they do—they collect children!"

"From the streets, not abandoned root cellars!"

"Maybe they thought you were already dead and they didn't want to leave empty-handed. Gods all be damned, why blame me?" Cauvin protested. "Why does it always have to be my froggin' fault? Soldt found his way here without my help. He could have been followed. Froggin' sure, Bec could have been followed. Blame some other sheep-shite fool for a change!"

There was no other sheep-shite fool. There was only the memory of last night at the Vulgar Unicorn. Cauvin had told Leorin that the Torch wasn't dead and she'd asked—she'd *specifically* asked—where he was. She'd been angry when Cauvin could only describe the ruins, not give them their proper name.

The Torch read Cauvin's mind, "You told her," he accused sadly. "You went to her, and you told her."

"No. No—there's no connection. There can't be." Cauvin's hands shook. He clenched them into fists, but that only made the shaking worse. "There wasn't time. Whatever I did, it didn't matter. Couldn't."

"Not any longer," the Torch conceded. "The damage has been done, hasn't it? The Hand has your brother. They took him and left me behind. I'm the one they wanted, if they wanted vengeance . . . I was alive—I must have been alive—but they took the boy instead." The Torch fell silent a moment, then said. "I understand. Four died. But there were more than four. Survivors. This close to my body. Saved by luck—by the grace of their goddess. They saw me, no different than a corpse, and they saw the boy. What would they think? A boy standing beside a body— A boy finally making a run for freedom. What would I have thought?"

While the Torch pondered his own question the loudest sounds came from outside the cellar, from Grabar still searching for his son.

"They're not me, they're the Bloody Hand of Dyareela. They *collect* children because children love and children fear more freely than men. They *collect* children because children can be molded by their love or fear. Children adapt. They remake themselves and become whatever they're expected to be, whatever they're taught to be. If a Servant of Dyareela were dying . . . ? If that Servant had learned the secrets of transformation—the poor man's immortality . . . ? Wouldn't he have used his last prayer to summon an heir? Better a child heir than a man. Men are willful, but a child is willing."

The Torch caught Cauvin's eye. "The greatest trap, lad, is assuming that your enemy thinks the way you do. The Hand has fallen into that trap: They have assumed your brother is the heir of Molin Torchholder."

Cauvin had no response. He was still reassuring himself that he couldn't have said anything to Leorin about Bec being with the Torch. He'd blundered badly when he'd revealed the old pud's existence, his location, but when he'd been with Leorin at the Unicorn, he'd assumed the boy was tucked in safe at the stoneyard. Then Cauvin recalled telling Leorin that Bec had written the Torch's testament. Unable to hold the Torch's eerie eyes another moment, Cauvin turned away.

"The Hand believes they've found the perfect vengeance," the Torch whispered. "Stealing my heir, adapting him to Dyareela. And perhaps they would be right . . . if Bec were my heir. But you and I, Cauvin, we know he's not."

There was a limit to the guilt Cauvin could bear while standing still. With one parting word, "No," Cauvin burst out of the root cellar. He ran to the horse, saddled and bridled and already tossing its head as Cauvin approached.

Grabar had always kept a mule to do the stoneyard's hauling; Cauvin had ridden both Flower and her predecessor, but never with a saddle or the determination to return to Sanctuary as fast as a horse could carry him. Cauvin had seen the Irrune run to their horses and vault cleanly onto the animals' backs without missing a stride; and he'd watched lesser horsemen make sheep-shite fools of themselves trying to match the feat. Caution advised leading the horse to a wall and easing himself into the unfamiliar saddle from there. If Cauvin were cautious, Bec wouldn't be missing, and he wouldn't desperately need to find Leorin. He gauged the vault blindly and wound up with his belly on the saddle, his arms and legs flailing air.

But Cauvin held on. He righted himself and instantly understood why the Irrune prized their high-backed saddles almost as much as their horses. Seizing the reins, he pounded the gelding's flanks and was nearly left behind when it bolted—thanks to the damned gods—toward the city rather than away from it. With a bit of luck and a strong right arm, Cauvin got the animal pointed down a narrow path to one of the Hillside breaches.

A galloping horse attracted attention. There were a handful of men studying Cauvin as the gelding picked its way through the breach rubble. Any one of them looked criminal enough to steal the horse out from under Cauvin. For a moment, he seriously considered just letting them have it, but a mounted man—even an awkwardly mounted man—commanded respect. The Hillers kept their greed to themselves.

Cauvin rode until the street traffic was more than he could handle, then he dismounted. If he'd led the horse to the Unicorn, froggin' sure it would get stolen moments after he dismounted, so he took it the stoneyard, instead. Mina came racing out of the kitchen, Batty Dol a half stride behind her, when she heard the gate scraping. Both women stopped short: Cauvin and a sweated-up horse weren't what they'd been praying for. Cauvin didn't have anything to say to his foster mother. He let go of the horse's reins, trusting that Mina's deep understanding of *value* would compel her to take care of it rather than follow him across Sanctuary.

Cauvin took the Unicorn stairs two at a time, no matter that he heard Mimise calling, "She's not up there."

Leorin's door was latched. Cauvin knocked once, then put his fist to the planks while shouting her name. The walls shook and three other doors opened, but not Leorin's.

"She's not there!"

Stopped by the sound of a man's stern voice, Cauvin turned and saw the Stick standing at the top of the stairway, an ax handle in his hand.

"Where's Leorin?"

"Don't know."

"When did she leave?"

"Don't know that, either. Do know you're leaving now and not coming back." The Unicorn's barkeep thumped the handle against his open palm. "You don't want trouble, now—do you?"

In the right hands, a length of hardwood, cut on the grain and baked in a kiln, was as deadly as the sharpest sword and, by everything Cauvin had heard, the Stick had the right hands.

"I've got to find her."

"I'll tell her you're looking for her when she gets back . . . right after I tell her to clear out."

The Stick stood aside, motioning Cauvin toward the stairs. Reluctant, but without another choice, Cauvin eased past the barkeep. Downstairs, he would have struck up a conversation with Mimise—she might have some idea where Leorin went when she left the Unicorn. Froggin' sure, Cauvin didn't; other than that first time, two years ago, when he'd spotted her on the Wideway, Cauvin hadn't seen Leorin except at the Unicorn. With the Stick in a froggin' foul mood, Mimise wasn't about to follow Cauvin onto the street for small talk.

The alleys near the Vulgar Unicorn were no place to wait for his betraying beloved. In the Maze, an unlucky man could die of boredom, and with Bec caught up by the Hand, Cauvin wasn't feeling lucky—until Soldt's name crossed his mind. He set off for the Inn of Six Ravens.

The same guard as before sat on the bench inside the inn's gate. He recognized Cauvin and let him in. Cauvin found the inner courtyard deserted and the door and windows of Galya's quarters still battened down from the storm. He pounded on the door and called the laundress's name until he heard the bar scraping in its brackets.

"I need your help Galya," Cauvin said as the door cracked open. "I've got to get word to Soldt—"

Rather than invite Cauvin in, Galya came out into sunlit courtyard, pulling the door shut behind her.

"The Torch was attacked last night at Red Walls right after the storm. My sheep-shite brother was with him. He's been kidnapped by the Bloody Hand of Dyareela—"

Words poured out of Cauvin's mouth and would have kept coming if Galya hadn't held up her hand.

"Slow down, Cauvin. What happened last night?"

"The Torch was attacked—Lord Molin Torchholder—" This time Cauvin paused, waiting for her to say that the Torch was dead, but Galya simply nodded. "He killed four of them—four of the

Bloody Hand—before he collapsed. But four wasn't enough, and the ones the Torch didn't kill, they left him for dead. He's not, not yet, not when I left him a little bit ago, but the Hand just left him lying there in the root cellar. They took my brother instead. He's only a boy. I've got to find my brother, Galya. I've got to find Soldt because I—he—" Cauvin couldn't finish. He didn't want to admit the roles he or the assassin had played in the catastrophe.

Galya led Cauvin to an overturned tub.

"Soldt will understand," Cauvin explained, watching the laundry door and refusing to sit down.

"What will he understand?"

"He'll understand that Bec's got to be rescued, even if it's mostly my fault that the Hand's got him. And the Torch, too—somebody's got to protect the Torch, in case the Hand realizes they don't have what they think they have."

"And what does the Bloody Hand of Dyareela think it has?"

The voice asking that question was Soldt's voice, and it came from behind. Cauvin spun around to see Soldt in plain clothes, no cloak, no weapons. He had a brindle dog beside him and, wherever he'd come from, he hadn't made a sound getting to within striking distance of Cauvin's back. The dog was massive across the chest. If it had stood on its hind legs, it could have straddled Cauvin's shoulders with its forepaws. But with its huge, droopy eyes, droopy ears, and jowls that hung well below its jaw, it clearly wasn't a fighting dog, even though it wore a wide, spiked collar around its neck. It wasn't any kind of dog Cauvin had met before, and when it stretched forward—nostrils flared, jowls quivering—he retreated without a moment's thought.

"He's just getting your scent," Soldt explained, then added a sound, maybe a word from some other language, and the dog sat. "So, tell me, what happened in the ruins?"

Cauvin went through his story again, including his failed attempt to confront Leorin at the Vulgar Unicorn. "The Stick said he didn't know when she'd left. Shite for sure, she must've gone looking for the Hand last night while you and I talked. You and the Torch were right all along—"

"Cold comfort in that. I thought— Lord Torchholder thought,

too—that your loyalties might be tried, that's all. I didn't see her sending the Hand out after Lord Torchholder. What exactly did he say about the boy being his heir?"

"Frog all—Bec's *not* the Torch's heir. That's me . . . supposed to be me. Damn it."

"But the Hand would think otherwise?"

Cauvin gave a halfhearted nod. "The Hand would've chosen Bec, 'cause of his age. It doesn't matter who inherits the Torch's gold. We've talked too much when we should be looking for Bec."

"No, it's not just talk. As I understand it, when a sorcerer—and damn me for saying this, but Lord Torchholder's more sorcerer than pure priest—chooses an heir, it means he's found someone who'll carry his memories—a foothold in the future. If the Hand thinks they've got Lord Torchholder's heir then, trouble doubled, they think they've got Lord Torchholder himself. They'll treat him accordingly."

Cauvin shuddered. "Frog all," he swore more sincerely than usual. "We've got to find Bec before they kill him."

"Killing Bec is the last thing the Hand wants to do," Soldt said grimly.

"We've— We've got to start looking!" Cauvin started toward the tunnel to the inn's main courtyard and the city streets beyond it.

"Not so fast. It's not as if the Bloody Mother's got a Hand-filled fane sitting outside the walls. Maybe your ladylove could tell us where they hide, but even if we could persuade her to help us, she's gone missing."

"Copper Corner," Cauvin said. "We could start there. It's close by, and that's where the Hand tried to grab Bec the first time—"

Soldt interrupted his good idea, "What first time?"

Cauvin explained and Soldt shook his head. "The next time something like that happens—assuming we live to see a next time—*tell* someone! It's too late to find anything there now; last night's storm will have washed away whatever scent was left. My thought is to take Vex out to the ruins, see what his nose can turn up around the bodies, and see to Lord Torchholder while I'm there. He's got to come in now."

By the way the dog raised its head when Soldt said "Vex," that was its name; and by the way Galya walked away after Soldt said "he's got to come in," Soldt's plan to stash the old pud amid her laundry was going to meet strong opposition.

"Shite for sure, he's in already. Grabar wouldn't stay out there, not once he'd convinced himself that Bec was gone, but he wouldn't leave the Torch alone and, froggin' sure, the old pud wouldn't get anywhere arguing with Grabar."

"We'll start at the stoneyard."

"Not me. I'm staying away from Mina, from my foster mother. She's blaming me for what happened to Bec. Soon as Grabar convinces her that the old pud really is the gods-all-be-damned Torch, she's going to blame me for what's happened to him, too."

Galya emerged from the laundry with a huge, linen-covered basket slung over one arm. "Sounds to me like she's got a right to blame all of you for what's happened to her son. Men! When will you learn? Life is *not* a game! Bet here, throw the dice there, turn the cards and see what happens . . . That woman needs someone to stand beside her. Let's go."

"She's got Batty Dol sitting with her— That's another froggin' good reason not to climb up to Pyrtanis Street," Cauvin protested, and looked to Soldt for support.

The assassin shook his head. "If you think Lord Torchholder's there," he said and, with a shrug, disappeared into the laundry, emerging moments later in his black cloak.

Soldt and Vex followed Galya out of the inn. Cauvin seriously considered returning to the Maze but followed the dog instead.

The stoneyard gate was closed but not bolted. Cauvin shouldered it open. He saw the brown horse tied by the water trough and Flower, still harnessed, standing in front of the work shed before Batty Dol came out of the kitchen with her skinny arms wrapped around a too-heavy jug. Batty screamed, and all ten of Hecath's hells erupted as the yard dog—that no one had remembered to chain up for the day—took exception to Vex and Soldt and maybe even Galya.

Batty had dropped the jug while dodging the yard dog, breaking it beyond repair. The brown horse panicked. It broke free and charged through Mina's herb garden *and* knocked the chicken coop off its stone piers. Not to be outdone by sheep-shite lunatics, women or horses, Flower—froggin' *sensible* Flower—kicked until she was half out her harness and had tipped the cart over. And all the while, the two dogs went at each other. Cauvin's clothes were torn and his arm was bloody before he got the yard dog chained. Vex, the assassin's dog, trotted back to its master, wagging its ratty tail as though nothing had happened.

The mule didn't appear to have hurt herself, but she would if someone didn't get her untangled quickly. Batty had vanished, along with Galya. Soldt went after the horse, which left Cauvin to deal with Flower, since neither Grabar nor Mina—not to mention the Torch—had made an appearance.

He was grappling with leather straps and buckles when Soldt showed up to help. Together they righted the cart, which made unharnessing the mule simpler but which had been more than Cauvin could do by himself. Soldt noticed the Torch's blackwood staff on the ground when they finished.

"We've got a bigger problem than we thought," he said, picking up the staff.

Cauvin looked up at the sky. "How much bigger? Is it going to rain fish?"

"Seriously, that's an Irrune horse wearing an Irrune saddle and bridle."

"Froggin' shite. The Irrune and the Hand. I'd've sworn that's the *one* direction we didn't have to worry about. Twice froggin' shite."

"We can't conclude that the Hand's got allies among the Irrune, just that at least one of those who went out to the ruins at dawn went there on a horse from the palace stable."

"Say what?" Grabar interrupted on his way through the gate. He was panting and carrying a steamy pot that smelled of meat and leeks and plenty of garlic—soup fit for an Imperial Lord. "You're Soldt, aren't you? What's this about the Irrune and the palace?"

Soldt repeated himself, adding, "Where's Lord Torchholder?"

Grabar hooked his thumb backward at the work shed. "In the loft. Damned bad idea, if you ask me—but no one did. I was for putting him inside—in my own bed, mind you. And the wife was for it, too, until him and her started jabbering away in Imperial. Next thing I know, it's 'rig a sling, husband, and haul him up where he wants to be.' Damned near killed him getting him up here. He passed out once. I thought he was dead, then those wild eyes sprang open and he was telling me to pull harder. Then him and the wife send me down the Stairs for a bucket of green soup—nothing in *our* larder, nothing on the whole street to tempt an Imperial appetite. That's one troublesome old man," Grabar concluded, catching Cauvin's eye with a hint of understanding. "No wonder he's lived so long. The gods don't want him telling them how to run paradise—or Hecath's hells, either. You're sure that's Irrune gear?"

"Irrune gear on an Irrune horse. Could've been stolen, but there's a hundred men no more Irrune than you or me who walk into those stables every day. Half of them could walk out with a saddled horse, no questions asked."

"I know a guard, Gorge—you know him, too, Grabar—" When it came to the Hand, Cauvin trusted that he and Gorge would be on the same side.

"Not yet," Soldt cautioned. "Not until I've taken a look at the corpses. You didn't move them, did you?"

Grabar said, "No, just left 'em there. If we can't trust the palace, then what about the priests of Ils . . . Savankala, too. Somebody's got to be told, somebody with power to do something. They've got my boy, Soldt." He closed his eyes and shrank a little, as if a great pain had just returned to haunt him. "The Hand's got my boy. I've got to do something more than fetch soup."

The pain returned to haunt Cauvin as well. He put his arms around Grabar. "It's not too late."

"How would *you* know?" a shrill, familiar voice demanded. "Look what you've done, Cauvin. Look what you've done to us. To Bec. To *Lord* Molin Torchholder, himself—"

"Lord Torchholder would blame himself for what's happened." Soldt tried to defend Cauvin; Cauvin could have told him not to bother.

Mina turned on Soldt, snarling, "And who are you to be knowing that? Another one of Cauvin's whoreson friends?"

Grabar freed himself from Cauvin's comfort. Without exchanging a word, Cauvin knew Grabar was as guiltily relieved as he was not to be the target of Mina's desperate temper.

Soldt, though, took Mina seriously. "I'm the man Lord Torchholder charged with protecting his heir, your foster son—so a word against Cauvin is very much a word against Lord Torchholder's judgment—and I'm very confident, mistress, that you would not want to question Lord Torchholder's judgment."

Soldt had Mina there.

"Our boy?" Grabar whispered. "What can we do to save our boy? I can't stay here in the yard, not when I don't know what's happening to him."

Cauvin could have said it wasn't any easier, knowing what the Hand could do, but said, "I'm going to the palace. I'm going to find an Irrune who'll listen. I'll drag froggin' Arizak over here to see the froggin' Torch."

"Not yet," Soldt insisted. "Lord Torchholder's risked everything to keep them out of this. If you need to do something, Grabar, take Cauvin's advice—go to this guard, Gorge. Take him out to the ruins. Vex and I won't need much time out there."

Cauvin disagreed. "I'm going to talk to Gorge. He knows me well enough—"

"I want you with me. You know the way it was. You'll know if anything's changed."

Never mind that Cauvin had left the ruins before Grabar, Soldt was a man who could give orders when he had to. Grabar straightened his work clothes and headed off for the guard post beside the palace gate. Galya took the soup bucket from Grabar and herded Mina into the kitchen, where, she said, there was solace tea steeping on the hearth. She returned a few moments later with a strip of bleached linen.

"I imagine you'll be wanting this. I got it off the boy's bed," she said, offering the cloth to Soldt. It vanished within his cloak. "Be careful," the laundress advised before returning to the kitchen.

"I guess I'm ready," Cauvin said, when he and Soldt were left alone in the yard.

"Not dressed in yesterday's shirt. Clean yourself up. Any of those cuts deep enough to worry about?"

Cauvin shook his head. "I've only got two froggin' shirts and this is the froggin' best between them. Galva gave it to me just yesterday." He examined his cuffs and saw a few stains, from blood and grime, but not enough to demand washing. "It's still clean," he insisted.

Soldt wrinkled his nose. "You're not. Wash yourself off, at least."

Little as Cauvin wanted to waste time at the trough, a glance at Soldt's face convinced him that he'd waste more time arguing. His wounds stung when he dipped his arm in the trough. They bled freely, but not too freely. He intended to ignore them and had the shirt stretched over his head when Soldt ordered him to stop.

Cauvin froze more from surprise than obedience. Soldt dug into the basket Galya had left on a pile of unfinished stone and hauled out a length of snowy linen. He tore it into strips.

"Keeps the swelling down," he explained as he wound the cloth over Cauvin's forearm. "And keeps your shirt clean, if they open up again."

Cauvin flexed his fingers. Shite for sure, he couldn't remember how many times he'd been bloodied, but bandages weren't a usual—or comfortable—part of his healing. They'd protect his linen shirt, though.

"How come you're not wearing bleached linen?" he asked, carrying the blackwood staff to the ladder.

"I don't need to. Stop dawdling."

The loft was never brighter than twilight. Cauvin's eyes needed a moment to adjust. Mina and Grabar had made a wreck of his quarters. They'd dragged the pallet into the center of the loft—where, if it started raining again, the Torch would be driven mad by roof drips. Unless the geezer was already dead. The dark lump nested in Cauvin's blankets wasn't moving until Cauvin got within an arm's length. Even then, he couldn't truly see his chest rising, only hear the raspy, shallow rhythm of his breath.

"It's your fault, pud," he whispered. "Galya was right—it's all games to you, and you thought you could win one last round. Damn you to Hecath's coldest, darkest hell."

Cauvin supposed he couldn't blame his foster parents for mistaking his new breeches for bedding. He laid the staff beside the Torch's shoulder and took the cloth with both hands to yank it free. The Torch's eyes opened—maybe from the sudden movement, maybe from the staff. He said something, but not anything that

Cauvin understood, then those eerie moonlight-and-fire eyes closed again.

"If anything's happened to Bec, you'd best be dead the next time I see you."

He switched breeches and pulled on the linen shirt.

"Do you *own* a comb?" Soldt asked when they were face-to-face again.

Cauvin didn't answer, but slicked his hair down with water on his way past the trough.

# Chapter Seventeen

Cauvin and Soldt took the high road to the ruins. They had a clear view of the city, its harbor, and the tide coming in over the sea flats on either side of the harbor. The Ilsigi galley rode high beside the wharf. She'd dumped her ballast, but her crew didn't have her laded yet. She'd miss today's tide and depart tomorrow . . . without Cauvin . . . without Leorin.

He didn't mourn people. He'd seen many of them die. Dreams were rarer in his life, especially pleasant dreams. When one died, as Cauvin's love for Leorin was dying, he felt the loss with his entire heart. Had they been going to Land's End, where the road hugged a cliff to the sea, he might have run to the brink. But they were simply on the high road, far from danger, and headed for the ruins. Despair nailed Cauvin to the ground.

Soldt clapped Cauvin on the shoulder. "Time to move."

Cauvin shrugged free. "I understand it now," he whispered, as much to himself as the assassin. "Why the Torch chose me, a sheep-shite stone-smasher. This froggin' heir nonsense—I thought he was giving me things—coins, weapons, even words written on parchment. But it's not that at all. It's more like smashing bricks out of the ruins and rebuilding a house for Tobus. He's rebuilding *me* with froggin' sorcery. When he finally stops breathing, he's not really going to die, he's going to move into me. *I'm* the sheep-shite fool who's going to find himself dead— No, not dead, just gone."

"I don't think the sorcery goes that far." Soldt clapped Cauvin and, this time, gave him a tug toward the ruins.

"You don't know."

"I know that for years, when Lord Torchholder's spoken of

death, it was a threat; secretly, he didn't expect it to happen, not to him. Since I got back and found him dying, he speaks only of preserving what he's nurtured and passing on what he can. Not a word about a second chance in a young man's body. And—trust me on this, Cauvin—if Lord Torchholder planned to replace you within your flesh, he'd have said something to me."

Cauvin tried to be reassured, but the effort failed.

They approached the ruins in silence. Soldt knotted a long leather lead to Vex's collar, the first restraint he'd placed on the brindle dog; and just in time. They hadn't gone a hundred paces when Vex lowered his nose to the ground. The leash snapped taut and Soldt's shoulder got a workout keeping the dog in line.

"He's gotten a blood scent, a man's blood," Soldt explained. "Vex can find a corpse that's been buried ten feet deep or weighted with stones and dropped in a river."

"Tell him to look for Bec. I can show you the corpses."

But Cauvin couldn't show Soldt anything. The four fire-blasted bodies were gone. The ground where they'd lain had been carefully scoured. When Grabar led Gorge up from the city, they'd see that the ground had been disturbed, but they wouldn't see traces of blood or gore, and the only footprints would be Cauvin's, Soldt's, and the dog's.

They left the cellar for the ruined bedroom with its view of Sanctuary.

"You think I'm a froggin' liar," Cauvin said before Soldt leveled the accusation.

"Not at all. One ruin may look like another, but Vex scented blood. They can fool our eyes, but not his nose. In a way, they've made our job easier. The fainter the trail, the easier it is for him to follow. When there's too much blood, too much scent, he gets confused . . . Don't you, Vex?"

The dog looked up at Soldt. It shook its head, almost as if it had understood the words and disagreed with them. Only for a moment. They all heard a sound back near the cellar. Vex strained on the leash and Soldt let the dog pull him into the brush beyond the cellar. The dog seemed to have a scent, but when they got to the next hilltop there was nothing except a deer grazing in one of the Land's End fields. It was too far away to have made the noise they'd heard. Soldt commanded the dog to sit and, with a protest whine, it did.

"Next time I'm bringing a bow. Nothing like fresh venison on the spit." Soldt gave Vex another foreign-word command, and it followed him toward the ruins.

"Venison!" Cauvin exploded, catching up with them. "You're thinking about *venison*? The Hand's got Bec. They've covered their tracks. Turn that dog of yours loose. Tell him to find my brother."

"In time. First we wait for your foster father."

"What for? There's nothing here!"

"All the more reason to wait. You don't want him looking like a sheep-shite idiot in front of the watch, do you? We may still need their help. Besides, the muddle's different now. The Hand's come back; they know they've made a mistake. They know someone's moved Lord Torchholder. Do they think he's alive? Did Bec tell them Lord Torchholder's still alive? Have they guessed that your brother isn't Lord Torchholder's heir?"

"You think Bec's answered their questions?" Knowing how the Hand asked its questions added weight to Cauvin's heart.

"Doesn't really matter. Bec's a clever boy, but he's no sorcerer."

"Froggin' sure, I'm no sorcerer either—"

Soldt froze Cauvin with a glance. "Just pray the Hand realized their mistake sooner, rather than later."

"And that they'll be looking to swap Bec for someone else?"

"That's one possibility." Soldt jumped up on the windowsill. Staring down at the city, he shielded his eyes and cursed. "There he is, your foster father, coming up the General's Road . . . by himself. No need to wait now. We can meet him halfway and get back to the stoneyard. With luck, the Hand will come looking for us."

Cauvin led the way and caught Grabar's temper while it was still fresh.

"—If we had a daughter who'd gone missing. Or if we were rich. Oh, then they'd bestir themselves. But for the son of an honest man living on Pyrtanis Street? The sons of Pyrtanis Street run away all the time. The guards have better things to do than look for my son—unless I've got twenty shaboozh to bond their efforts. If they find him dead or enslaved, they give me my shaboozh back, but if he's just 'wandered'—that was Gorge's word—well, they'll keep the shaboozh for their effort! Damn their eyes!" Grabar thrust his fist in the air, then lowered it. "I ought to have dragged them up to the ruins—"

"Better you didn't," Cauvin said. "There's nothing up there. Someone— The Hand's been through. Gathered up the bodies, cleaned up the blood."

Color drained from Grabar's face. Cauvin reached out to steady him. "We're going back to the stoneyard. Soldt thinks the Hand knows they've made a mistake grabbing Bec. He thinks they'll come looking for us."

Grabar went paler still. "Mina!" he gasped. "Mina, she's alone!"

She wasn't—Galya had probably stayed with her, Batty Dol, too; and there was the Torch himself tucked up in the loft. But Grabar's point was well taken. The three men strode along a dry creek bed that got them to the Hillside breaches and into the city.

The gate was shut and the stoneyard quiet, until Vex and the yard dog laid eyes on each other again. Mina came out to scream at the dog and fairly flew into Grabar's arms when she saw him. Ten years living at the stoneyard and Cauvin couldn't remember another time when his foster parents had embraced each other. Even now, it wasn't affection or relief that held them together. Mina was wild with fear. Once they were inside the yard, the men found Galya and Batty Dol guarding the kitchen with a pitchfork and a mallet between them.

Galya explained: "We had a visitor while you were gone. You'd better come look."

A boy Cauvin didn't recognize—a boy about Bec's age—sat by the hearth, looking as frightened as Mina. The first thing he did when he saw the men was leap to his feet.

"I don't know who it was," he proclaimed. "I never seen his face before. He asked me if I knew the way to Pyrtanis Street, and when I said I did, he said he'd give me ten padpols to carry a package to the stoneyard. Five padpols straightaway when I said yes, and another five when I came back. That's all I know, all I did: I brought a package to the stoneyard. Follow me, if you've got to; I'm supposed to meet the man at Othat's. But let me go. I've got to get home. I've got to get my five padpols; I earned them. I earned them honest."

"We weren't about to follow him ourselves, so we've kept him here, waiting for you to get back." Galya finished her explanation.

"What was in the package?" Soldt asked, faster than Cauvin or Grabar could get the question off their tongues.

Galya shook out a wad of folded cloth which Cauvin immediately recognized as Bec's shirt. One sleeve hung loose and a dark, hard-edged stain stiffened the collar. Mina wailed and would have fallen had Grabar not kept his arms around her. Batty Dol's cries were softer, but there was no one to comfort her.

"Nothing else?" Soldt asked. "No message?"

"None," Galya replied. "Other than the boy's insistence that he's owed another five padpols when he returns to Othat's, wherever that is."

"He sells oil in the Crook." The boy volunteered the name of the notorious Hill-side market where, some said, slaves were still bought and sold in midnight transactions.

"How long has he been here?" Soldt asked Galya, then turned to the boy, "Did you come here straightaway?"

"Not long," Galya answered quickly, but the boy hesitated before admitting that he'd gotten himself breakfast, then stashed what was left of his five padpols in an alley bolt-hole before making his way to Pyrtanis Street.

The boy's voice faded as he realized his mistake. He was whispering when he said, "Maybe he's still there? He never said I should come running. Maybe Othat seen him. Othat sees most everything in the Crook—for silver."

No one in the kitchen answered the boy. They looked to Soldt, and Soldt just shook his head. The assassin was in favor of forgetting about Othat and either letting the boy go or locking him in the chicken coop.

"We know what they wanted us to know: They've got Bec, but they're not ready to negotiate. When they are, they'll send another message, with a *reliable* messenger."

The Hiller boy had heard enough. He broke for the door, shoving Batty Dol hard against Soldt, scattering stools, and overturning anything he could reach. The boy was quick and, froggin' sure, he'd had practice running away, but Cauvin had mastered the same lessons. Leaping and shoving himself, Cauvin reached the kitchen door a few strides behind the Hiller. His longer legs would give him the advantage across the stoneyard to the gate.

The boy was just beyond Cauvin's grasp when someone—Soldt—grabbed his shirt.

"Let him go. We don't need him."

"Frog all—" Cauvin protested.

He writhed within his shirt. His old shirts would have torn from the strain, but Galya's linen was strong, her seams, stronger. The Hiller hit the closed gate like a panicked cat, scrambled over the top, and disappeared.

"You want to follow that boy into the trouble that's waiting for him on the Hill? Do you want to save *his* life or your brother's?"

Cauvin swallowed hard and ceased struggling. "We can't just wait around here. We're not saving Bec this way."

The others had filed out of the kitchen wearing the wary looks of sheep-shite folk who didn't trust their leaders but weren't ready to challenge them.

"Is Lord Torchholder still alive?" Soldt asked.

"He was, last time we looked," Mina replied. "Before that boy came."

Soldt led them into the work shed; Cauvin led them up the ladder.

"He'd better be dead," he muttered.

No luck there. The Torch's weird eyes were open, watching Cauvin as his head cleared the floor.

"What was all that noise?" the old man demanded. "Did you find anything out at the ruins; or had the Hand scoured everything? I heard a boy—not the missing one. What did he want? Was that him going over the gate?"

The Torch had made a miraculous—or more likely sorcerous—recovery. He still resembled a skeleton wrapped in rotting skin and crowned with wild, silver-gray hair, but there could be no doubt that his mind had cleared.

Soldt gave Cauvin a prod, and he swung up into the loft before answering the Torch's questions. "Some sprout from the Hill. He brought Bec's shirt, torn and bloody. Soldt said he was going to lock him up, then let him go instead."

"He had the shirt, Lord Torchholder, nothing else. He was a

pawn. If he's lucky, he'll be dead by sundown," Soldt added, as if that settled everything; and it did, for the Torch.

"Does the Hand know I'm here?" the Torch asked.

"They know you're not in the cellar. The place had been scoured. Hard to tell, though, whether they knew that when they sent the Hiller; he took time for breakfast and to hide the padpols they'd given him."

The Torch repeated Soldt's verdict, "Pawn," then targeted Grabar, who'd just heaved himself off the ladder. "They've told you they've got your boy. Now they're giving you time to think about how much you want him—"

"I don't need time—"

"Will you surrender me?" Grabar gaped at the question; the Torch pressed on. "I would. It would be a good bargain—if the Hand would offer it. If they don't realize I'm more dead than alive and won't last long enough to satisfy them or their deity. More likely, they've realized the stoneyard son they want is Cauvin. He's not quite your son, is he? Would you give them Cauvin to get Bec?"

Grabar didn't twitch, and Cauvin's heart stopped beating while Mina called up from below, "If it's him or my boy, he goes."

The fiery white eyes turned to Cauvin. "There you have it, lad. We're down to our last chances, Cauvin. I'd hoped for more. Damn Vashanka—I'd hoped it would never come to this. Are you ready to turn the key in the lock? I have a plan to keep you alive."

Cauvin glanced across the loft. Mina wouldn't meet his eyes; Grabar was pleading silently. "Me or you?" he asked, and immediately thought of the S'danzo, Elemi. "Do I have a choice?"

"There is always a choice. You could choose to run, like that boy just did. Who's to say, you might find a hole deep enough to hide you for the rest of your life."

Cauvin thought, *I should have died in the pits. I should have begged this man to send me back there,* but he hadn't done either, and the habit of living was too hard to break between one breath and the next. "All right. What's your froggin' plan?"

"Here." The Torch sat up, steadying himself with his blackwood staff—drawing strength from it. He held out a closed hand.

Two steps separated Cauvin from the dying priest. Right foot forward, then left. Cauvin didn't feel either one. Shite for sure, he felt the Torch's cold, dry flesh when their hands touched, and it took all his strength not to run, screaming, from the loft. Something colder still, hard, and not at all key-shaped landed in his palm.

"Put it on the third finger of your right hand."

The Torch's gift was a ring. In the loft's twilight, Cauvin couldn't be certain, but he'd wager it was the black-onyx ring that he'd retrieved from the rubble in the froggin' temple of froggin' Ils.

"See if it fits."

Cauvin thrust the golden hoop down his finger. It passed the first knuckle easily, but jammed on the second. Should he pray? To whom? To Ils? What had any of Father Ils's eyes done for Cauvin? To *Vashanka*? When the Torch himself was cursing that god's name? The metal cooled. It slid easily to the base of the third finger of Cauvin's right hand.

"It fits. Nothing happened. I don't feel any different."

"That's good. Go to the palace. Show it on your hand to the majordomo. Tell him that Arizak, chief of the Irrune and lord of Sanctuary, wishes to see you. Show it to Arizak the same way, then *do what you're told*. After that, Cauvin, you're on your own."

"Froggin' shite," Cauvin muttered. He turned around, saw three faces staring at him, each different with worry and all the same with expectation, and cursed again.

Soldt spoke first. "You want company?"

Cauvin shrugged. He was good at doing what he'd been told to do. Had Elemi foreseen how easy the choice would be? He stood over the hole in the loft's floor and dropped to the straw-covered ground beneath.

"There's soup on the hearth," Galya told him, as though she'd heard nothing of what had happened above her head.

"I'm not hungry."

He got out of the way, letting both Grabar and Soldt use the ladder to leave the loft.

"You should eat before you go the palace," Galya persisted. "No ring is going to get you to Arizak without a long wait first. You'll think clearer if your mind's not distracted by your gut."

Cauvin tried arguing, but he *was* hungry, and he could slurp down a bowl of soup—even the thick, creamy soup Galya ladled out for him—in less time than it took to object to it. Or he could have, if everyone hadn't been watching him, and Galya hadn't followed the soup with a snowy white bundle of linen.

She shook the cloth out and held it against Cauvin's shoulders. "If you're going to stand before Arizak, you need to look your best."

There was nothing fancy about the shirt, no gold-thread patterns or lacy fringes, just fine-woven cloth and rows of tight stitching.

"Sweet Sabellia!" Mina complained, snatching a sleeve for closer examination. "Where'd you get the soldats for this? Look me in the eye and tell me your hands are clean."

Mina got an eyeful of Galya instead. "I keep what gets left behind at the Ravens and I do with it as I see fit. If I charged Cauvin ten soldats for making a shirt or a single shaboozh or nothing at all, that's *my* affair. Would you rather Cauvin pled for his brother's life in *rags*?"

The sleeve slipped through Mina's fingertips. "You don't forget who took you in when you had no place to go. We fed you and kept you in clothes. Treated you as our own. Don't you forget that when you're standing in the damned palace."

Cauvin had no intention of forgetting. He didn't blame her for her choices, either. He'd have made the same ones. Shite for sure, his own mother would have chosen Bec over him.

The new shirt fit Cauvin perfectly. Galya produced a tortoise-shell comb and dragged it through his hair. Batty Dol pronounced him a "right handsome young man." Cauvin turned to Grabar.

"You coming with us?"

Grabar looked at his hands. "Lord Torchholder didn't give me his ring. I'm minded to visit the Crook and see if I can find this Othat. Could be he did see something."

"The Hiller was right—he'll see more if you dangle a shaboozh or two in front of his eyes. There's a broker's purse under my pallet, under the Torch. It's full of the money I collected from Mioklas yesterday—" Cauvin wouldn't be needing it any time soon.

"Who gave you—"

"Wife!" Grabar silenced Mina. "No need to disturb the old man. We've got shaboozh in the hidey."

"You ready?" Cauvin looked at Soldt.

Soldt shrugged. He seemed on the verge of saying no, then shrugged again and followed Cauvin onto Pyrtanis Street.

"What do you know about this ring?" Cauvin asked.

"I've never seen Lord Torchholder without it. If it's sorcery you're looking for, look at his staff."

"Aye, I've noticed. What about Arizak?"

"He's not the man he was, especially on days when his leg's bad. Best hope today's not one of the days when he's chewed black-poppy seed or it could get dicey. They've made promises, one to the other; I don't know what they are."

The quickest way from Pyrtanis Street to the palace was, as Cauvin had told Gorge, across the Promise of Heaven and in through the old God Gate. But quickest wasn't easiest, not for Cauvin. The God Gate was the gate the Hand had used when they crept out of the palace, looking for anyone who'd displeased the Bloody Mother, anyone who caught the Whip's eye. He hadn't retraced those steps for nearly ten years.

"Having second thoughts?" Soldt asked when Cauvin hesitated in the God Gate's shadow.

"It's been a long time."

"We can go around to Governor's Walk and the Processional Gate."

"No, the froggin' gate's here, whether I walk through it or not, and so are the memories."

There were no guards at the Promise end of the God Gate but there were two of them where it opened onto the palace forecourt, both of them Irrune with rust-colored hair and ruddy faces. They spoke Wrigglie well enough to challenge a Sanctuary native, but the truth was that well-dressed, well-groomed men weren't seriously challenged, regardless of their language.

When Cauvin said he had to see the majordomo because Arizak was expecting him, the guards were unimpressed, until Cauvin added—

"But we're not sure where to find that worthy man. Can you tell us where he'd likely be at this hour?"

The taller Irrune pointed across the courtyard. "In the Exchange."

"So, that's what they're calling it now," Cauvin said, mostly to himself.

When the Hand ruled Sanctuary, they'd called the gray-stone

building an armory and kept some of their weapons in it. The whole forecourt had smelled of sweat and shite, with slop buckets fermenting in the sun, flayed corpses hung on iron hooks until the crows picked them apart, flies everywhere—except in winter—and rats the size of a man's forearm.

The rats kept their distance by day but come darkness, they'd ooze out between the stones, looking for food. When it came to cleanliness, the Mother of Chaos was a man's god. Food for rats collected in every corner of the Hand's palace, in every open space, too—but there were so froggin' many rats. The Hand's rats were as scrawny as its orphans. If you caught one brushing against your leg, it was all bone and gristle, scarcely worth the effort of splitting it open and sucking dry.

But Cauvin had . . . whenever he could, because food was food, and if he hadn't, someone else would. He'd been big for his age from the time he stood up, but when the Hand caught him, he'd been one of the younger orphans. His first years in the pits were the darkest. By the end, when everyone older had either died or gone behind the walls with the Hand, he knew how to survive.

Impulse spun Cauvin around. Except for their color, deep blue instead of black, the Justice Doors of the palace hadn't changed. They still swung outward, still three times the height of the tallest man, still a frame around darkness. Whoever had built Sanctuary's palace had laid it out so sunlight never crept more than a few paces beyond the Justice threshold. Inside, Arizak might be holding council or the great altar of Dyareela might be leaking blood onto the marble floor.

In the right half of the forecourt, in a line that ran between the God Gate in the eastern wall and the flagstone path to the Processional, Cauvin spotted the scars of the pits themselves. Another man might not see the slight depressions in the dirt, the slight difference in color, darker and redder than the rest. Another man, even noticing the differences, might not grasp their meaning. Cauvin was not another man. He shivered when a stabler led a horse across a rusty scar.

If Batty Dol shivered like that, she'd say, *Someone's walking on my grave*. The pits weren't Cauvin's grave, but they'd been the death of so many others . . .

"See someone you recognize?" Soldt asked, tugging gently on Cauvin's sleeve.

How to answer? He'd seen a girl, a few years older than he'd been.

*The summer sun had just risen, but already it turned the pits into ovens and she was too weak to crawl out of its light, too weak to whisk away the flies buzzing around her eyes and mouth. She'd been sick for a week. Now she was dying, not quickly enough. If she couldn't climb out of the pit when the Hand overseers lowered the ladders, they'd drag her out and take her to the Mother's altar.*

*"Please? Please?" Her lips formed the words. She was too weak, too parched to make a sound. Her hand twitched, reaching for his?*

Cauvin couldn't remember what had happened next. He didn't remember them dragging her to the altar. Maybe that was memory enough. He stared at the sky and blinked.

"No, no one."

"Come on, then. Let's find this majordomo."

"Right," he agreed, and turned back toward the exchange.

The Hand never did an honest day's work, not when they had a steady supply of orphans to order about. Cauvin and the others hauled jugs of water and jugs of night soil. They baked the bread, and they washed the linen, whenever some mighty Hand decided it needed to be washed. They scrubbed the floors around the Mother's altar, and they climbed onto the steep, slippery roofs after every storm looking for broken tiles. No froggin' way some mighty Hand was going to have water dripping on his or her froggin' face at night.

The roof hadn't changed much and the tiles were still apt to break in a gale-force wind and men still had to check them after every storm. They worked in three-man teams, linked by long ropes. Two men with steady footing hugged the crest and guided a third man, who worked his way up and down, back and forth. If the third man slipped—and it was a man slipping that had caught Cauvin's eye—the ropes snapped taut. Froggin' sure he'd have busted ribs and rope burns along his flanks, but his two keepers had kept him alive.

Cauvin would rather have cleaned the middens than check the roof tiles; and the same storms that loosened roof tiles flooded the middens. At first, he'd found ways to get put on midden duty, but Whip—damn him to Hecath's foulest hell—figured out that Cauvin feared heights. After that he was climbing ladders every time it rained, humping tiles before the last drops had fallen. He wasn't ever the only orphan scrambling across the roof, but they didn't work in teams and the only ropes were those each orphan used to lower the broken tiles and fetch up new ones.

It was late autumn—same time of year as now. Cauvin and the other roof-crawlers were barefoot. The tiles were so froggin' cold his feet were numb to his froggin' knees. The Hand had him working the lower courses of tile, the rows closest to the edge, the rows that frightened him more than the high courses near the crest. He'd spotted a cracked tile below his knee and the temptation was to pretend he hadn't seen it—but that was risky. The Hand weren't just brutes and bastards, they'd been truly consecrated by the Mother of Chaos and any one of them might be looking at the roof through his eyes at that very moment, seeing what he saw, waiting for him to shirk, waiting for him with the long, thin flaying knife when he got down to flat ground again.

The worst kind of death the Hand delivered wasn't when they peeled an entire skin. That froggin' bastard screamed and howled, but he was *dead* long before they finished. No, the worst was when the Hand flayed just an arm or a leg or peeled a circle of skin they called the "Mother's Face" off some poor pud's belly. Froggin' sure, the red flesh underneath would swell and weep. It would draw flies, turn black, and stink like the rotting meat it was until the pud died. That could take a month.

So, Cauvin had scrabbled down to the very edge and gotten to work prying out the broken tile. Bits of broken, baked clay clattered to the brink and disappeared. If they landed on someone's head . . . well, that was one of the few froggin' things that wouldn't be his fault. It was different, though, up on the roof. The crawlers staggered themselves, so the ones working the upper courses weren't dropping tiles on those working below. And they shouted warnings, "*Ware, heads!*" whenever they were chipping.

Of course, sometimes scrabbling alone was enough to make a tile crack and shed a froggin' chunk of clay. Or maybe Cauvin had just been so intent on getting his tile out—so afraid of falling—that he hadn't heard Tashos shout his warning. He'd never know. What Cauvin knew—what he remembered—was that something sharp and heavy had struck his anchoring arm. He lost his grip, was sliding toward the edge, maybe screaming, maybe praying, his fingers desperately seeking something to cling to.

Tashos slid by. Tashos *was* screaming: "*Help me! Stop me! Cauvin!*"—For a heartbeat, the boy hung from the brink, then the edge tiles broke from the strain, and he was gone. Cauvin heard a thud.

He didn't fall. His fingers had latched around the lip of a tile that held. Cauvin didn't think he'd ever make them move again, but the Hand had other ideas. He hadn't finished replacing the broken tile that he'd found and, by the Mother Herself, there were the four tiles Tashos had broken in his fall. The Whip shouted up that Cauvin would fix those fast, if he knew what was good for him.

Cauvin knew.

"You're sure you're not fevered?" Soldt asked. "You've gone pale and broken a sweat."

Cauvin's arm hurt where Tashos's tile had struck it years ago. He massaged the muscle, then looked at his fingers, half-expecting to see them slicked with blood. Froggin' sure, there was none, but his fingers were trembling, and his heart was pounding in his gut, not behind his ribs. "Let's go. I can do this."

With every step Cauvin remembered more. He might easily have been walking in two times: the present and his past. He'd dwelt in the pits for ten years, and it wasn't as though someone had died every day. But that was the way his sheep-shite memory served it up, face after face, moment upon moment when life had *stopped*. Cauvin blamed the froggin' Torch. He blamed him for singling him out and keeping him alive when he could have died with the other orphans. And he blamed him for reopening all wounds he'd thought were healed.

Cauvin fought his memories. He reminded himself that the only face he wanted to see, the only life he wished he could save was Bec's. He concentrated on the present, on the horses, the stablers, the rich merchants in lush silk robes standing on the shaded porch outside the Exchange. No one had worn silken robes while the Hand ruled Sanctuary. If there was wealth in Sanctuary, it belonged to the

Bloody Mother, for Her glory, for Her return to the mortal world.

One particular silk robe caught Cauvin's eye. It rippled with the colors of the rising sun. If Cauvin had favorite colors, they were the colors of sunrise: red becoming orange becoming gold. The merchant wearing the sunrise robe was talking to a younger man in the loose-fitting breeches and half-sleeved leather coat of the Irrune. When the Irrune gestured at the palace doors, Cauvin got a good look at his face and realized he was Naimun, the sour-looking youth he'd seen at the Torch's funeral. Naimun laughed as he turned back to catch the merchant's next words.

The merchant held Cauvin's attention, too; and the longer he looked, the less he noticed the sunrise silk. Cauvin would swear he'd seen that face before, right here in the palace courtyard. But that couldn't be— Hadn't Leorin described in great detail how she'd gutted the Whip with his own knife on the road out of Sanctuary? And, even if Leorin had lied—which Cauvin knew wasn't froggin' unlikely—the merchant's hands were paler than his face. The Whip's hands had been stained scarlet, front, back, and halfway to his elbows.

No way the Whip could show his hands in Sanctuary. But—could two men share the same nose and chin, the same jabbing gestures as they spoke?

Naimun, son of the most powerful man of Sanctuary, took a step backward to avoid the merchant's stabbing finger.

Cauvin stopped. "Do you know that man?"

"Naimun," Soldt replied. "Nadalya's eldest. Thinks he was born to rule."

"No, the pud he's talking to."

Soldt scratched his chin. "He's a merchant—more of a ship's broker. He's Ilsigi, from Ilsig, but his name doesn't come to me. Works mostly for Caronne and Aurvesh, exchanging their wines for Land's End grain—at no risk to the Serripines, mind you. He used to stay at the Ravens. Stays at the palace these days . . . for obvious reasons. Galya might know his name, or your friend Lord Mioklas. They're in the same circle, always buzzing around Naimun."

"He's always been—what did you call it?—a ship's broker here?"

"Not here. I don't remember seeing him here until about two

years ago. But he's got connections all along the western coast, from the Hammer clear up to Caronne and across the Sparkling Sea to Aurvesh. That sort of web takes a lifetime to put together, maybe your father's lifetime and your grandfather's—"

Cauvin stopped listening. Two years. Two years ago, Leorin had reappeared in Sanctuary.

*No!*—Cauvin chided himself. He was imagining things, feeding suspicions for no good reason, other than he was here, where he'd been before, and the Hand had Bec. Cauvin struck off again, walking faster than before.

Maybe that change in determination attracted the broker's attention. Or something else. Or nothing at all, and the man wasn't truly giving Cauvin the once-over, as though he saw something vaguely familiar coming toward him. Grinning, the broker touched his right forefinger to his temple. The Hand greeted one another that way: *May Dyareela keep watch over you.* But half of Sanctuary used the same gesture to invoke Eshi's blessing or to simply say, *I see you.*

Then Cauvin got the itch, the froggin' itch at the base of his froggin' neck, the itch that told him he wasn't alone. It wasn't always a bad itch, but here at the palace, with a man who looked like the Whip making Bloody Hand gestures and him not able to hide—

Cauvin pointed himself at the Processional gate and started walking. "Frog all, Soldt. I can't do this."

"Nonsense." Soldt got in front of Cauvin to stop him. "You've got the ring. If Lord Torchholder says the ring is the key to getting the help you need to rescue your brother, then, if I were you, I'd believe him. Follow his instructions—"

"I can't." The words hurt his throat. "All my froggin', sheepshite life I've done what I'm told—"

"Then do it again. Do what you've been *asked* to do one more time. Now's not the time to quit, Cauvin."

"Froggin' shite for sure, it's the right time." Cauvin struck out for the gate again. "What do I do *after* the majordomo takes me to Arizak? You heard the Torch; I'm on my own. Tell him my little brother's missing and we froggin' think the Bloody Hand of Dyareela's got him 'cause we know the Hand's back in Sanctuary 'cause they tried to kill the Torch . . . Froggin' sorry, but no, that wasn't his body you burnt the other night.

"Shalpa's midnight cloak, Soldt—he'll have me thrown in the dungeon! And if he doesn't—what? The Hand isn't just in Sanctuary, the Hand is *here,* in the froggin' palace. They *got* the Torch, Soldt. They didn't kill him straight off, but they froggin' sure got him. His plans aren't perfect. He doesn't know everything. And me—I don't know sheep-shite about anything."

They passed between the great iron-wrapped Processional doors. Cauvin veered left, toward Pyrtanis Street.

"I'm going home, Soldt. If Grabar's still there, he and I can go looking for Othat in the Crook."

Soldt stayed with him, saying nothing until they were well beyond the gate and its guards, then Soldt spun Cauvin against the wall and held him there with an implacably extended arm pressed to his breastbone.

"Can you hear yourself? Othat is nothing. The Hill is nothing. The Hand *is* in the palace, and I believe you, Cauvin, if you say you recognize them, feel them. And that's why you've got to get to Arizak. He's the only one who can root it out."

Cauvin twisted the Torch's ring from his finger, then swept his forearm to the inside of Soldt's elbow. The assassin's arm bent and Cauvin got away from the wall. "Then *you* take the gods-all-bedamned ring to Arizak. *You* do exactly what Arizak tells you to do!" He brandished the black ring in Soldt's face.

"Don't be foolish." Soldt sidestepped Cauvin's arm. "You're the chosen one."

"Frog all, he's been complaining about me since I hauled his bony ass out of the Thunderer's ruins. You know these people. You live in their world. You take the Torch's place."

"I was born on a boat, Cauvin; I don't *live* anywhere. You do. Sanctuary's your home. You're not going to leave—"

"Watch me." Cauvin forced the ring into Soldt's hand. "*You* do it, Soldt, or it's not going to be done. I was born sheep-shite stupid. I'm afraid of my own memories. I'm afraid to remember what I did and why."

"Cauvin—you made a mistake; everybody does." Soldt clasped Cauvin at the wrist, but muscle for muscle, Cauvin was the stronger man, and Soldt couldn't make him open his fist or take back the ring. "You trusted Leorin. You trusted the woman you love, and she betrayed that love. Now you've got to make it right."

"Bec got picked up by the froggin' Hand. I can't make that right. I'm stupid, I'm afraid, and I'm a gods-all-be-damned coward."

"You're wrong, Cauvin. You're neither stupid nor a coward, and if you're afraid, we're all afraid."

Their argument had begun to draw attention from the passersby on Governor's Walk. Soldt released Cauvin's wrist. He took a backward step, blocking the way to Pyrtanis Street, but giving Cauvin all the room he needed to return to the palace . . . or the Maze.

There was one mistake he could make right.

Striding along the Governor's Walk, opposite the palace gate, again, Cauvin dared a backward glance. The black-clad assassin was gone. He shouldn't have been surprised or angry—he'd declared his freedom—but he was both.

"She ain't come back yet," the Stick snarled from behind the bar when Cauvin entered the Unicorn's commons.

Cauvin left the tavern without another word, crossed to the opposite corner, and studied the Unicorn's outer walls and windows. Unlike most of the buildings in the Maze, the Unicorn shrank as it rose, retreating from the nearby streets rather than leaning over them. There were shutters on every second-story window, and a single ledge running beneath them. Once Cauvin had determined which shutters blocked Leorin's room, it was simple enough to wait until the street was clear before making his way to the ledge. He stuck the blade of his Ilbarsi knife between the shutters and popped the latch.

For one gut-churning moment Cauvin thought Leorin was asleep in her bed, but it was only her clothes. She'd emptied her baskets onto the mattress and seemed to have been sorting their contents into piles before she left with the chore unfinished. He cleared himself a space among them and settled in.

The sun came around. It poured through the shutter slats and made bright lines on the floor. Light never reached the mattress, never reached the gray emptiness where Cauvin tried to hide from his memories. In time the sunlight faded and the emptiness of Cauvin's mind filled the room.

A familiar voice rang down the corridor not long after sunset. Two familiar voices: Leorin and the Stick.

—"I had my own affairs to attend to." That was Leorin.

"What about *my* affairs?" That was the Stick. "You have chores to do during the day—this place doesn't clean itself! You're not here by day, you don't work by night." The barkeep's voice shrank to a whisper, but they were on the other side of Leorin's door, and Cauvin heard every word. "You're a risk, Leorin. If I've got to take a risk, I've got to take more money. Say a shaboozh . . . a soldat or two?"

"Keep your threats to yourself. I don't owe you another padpol until midsummer. I'm *here,* little man, whether you like it or not. Talk to your master, if you don't believe me."

The latch hook rattled. Cauvin tucked his knees under his chin. Light flooded the room when the door opened—Leorin had a froggin' lamp in her hand. She swept it back and forth as she entered the room. Her eyes showed white when she saw Cauvin on her bed, but she swallowed her surprise—and kept a firm grip on her supper trencher as well. She shoved the door shut with her foot and leaned against the jamb.

"Stay in there," the Stick snarled, and pounded the door for good measure. He never guessed there was a man waiting in his risky wench's room. "Stay there until midsummer, but don't show your face downstairs until *I* say you can."

Leorin closed her eyes and kept them shut until the Stick's heels were pounding the floorboards, then she studied Cauvin. He couldn't make sense of her expression, but possibly his was no easier to read. He had no intention of being the first to speak. It had the makings of a long, quiet night until Leorin set the trencher and the lamp on her dressing table.

"Sorry I'm late. I thought I could settle my affairs in one morning. I forgot, this is Sanctuary. Everything takes longer."

"Affairs?" Cauvin asked, taking one word and turning it into a question, the way the Torch or Soldt would.

She hesitated. "No need for secrets between us, is there? I had a few coronations and bits of jewelry with a goldsmith down on the Wideway. No way I leave anything valuable here; this place leaks like a sieve. And no reason to haul my wardrobe onto a boat and off again. I'd only have to replace it anyway when we got to Ranke—or Ilsig. Which passage did you arrange?"

"I didn't," he admitted.

"If you need more money—" She reached between her breasts

for a jingly leather pouch. "I can loan you a coronation or two."

Cauvin's love hadn't lessened, it had simply retreated. He couldn't hate her or trust her, but he was curious, in a cold way, to hear her lies. He cast his net to pull them in.

"It's not money. I didn't go down to the wharves today—"

Leorin scowled and quickly tucked the pouch in a dressing-table drawer.

"There were problems when I got back to the stoneyard. My brother's disappeared."

"You don't have a brother."

"Bec's my brother." He'd been surprised by her tone, but not left speechless. "We figured out that he'd been outside the city walls when the storm began. We can't know for certain. All we know is that he was gone when the storm broke, and he hasn't come back since."

"That's terrible," Leorin said, and managed to make the words sound sincere. "Mina and Grabar, they must be in a frenzy. Their precious little boy wandering outside the walls where he doesn't belong. Who knows—" She paused. "In Sanctuary, you have to think the worst. He could have gone to a neighbor. That crazy woman— What do you call her? Batty Something? She lost all her children, didn't she? I wouldn't trust a son of mine around that woman."

Poor Batty Dol, but maybe, if Cauvin hadn't known what had happened, he would have been willing to suspect Batty. And maybe Leorin didn't know what had happened to Bec. Whatever else she'd done, Cauvin didn't think she'd gone out to the ruins.

Cauvin said, "Batty's harmless and as frantic as Mina," then he cast another net. "At first light, Grabar and I went out to the ruins where I'd hidden the Torch—"

"Now there's another one I wouldn't trust. Like as not, he took off with Bec, and you'll never see either one of them again."

"No, the Torch was still there, surrounded by corpses."

Cauvin watched Leorin's whole body stiffen—with surprise? Disappointment? Panic?

"Sweet Mother of Night! How could that happen? You said the froggin' pud was wounded and dying! How could he kill anyone who came after him? I mean, did he say what happened? Was he still alive? Is he still there, or did you move him?"

Cauvin's nets were half-full. Leorin knew what should have happened overnight, but not what had happened. She was the one casting nets now, because the Hand always looked for a scapegoat when it failed: The Bloody Mother had to be appeased.

One moment Cauvin didn't know what to say. The next, his thoughts seethed with lies.

"He's dead . . . now. He looked me in the eye, and said, 'Cauvin, I name you my heir,' with his last froggin' breath. Me, a sheep-shite stone-smasher, heir to the froggin' Torch, and him the richest man in Sanctuary. I hid his body— We've got to find Bec, first. But afterward, when that's settled, I'm taking his froggin' corpse to the palace. Shite for sure, I won't get the Torch's whole treasure, I'll get something else, I'll tell the whole city Arizak burnt the wrong froggin' corpse. I swear to you, Leorin, when we step off the ship in Ranke, we'll start our new lives in fine style."

"We don't need the Torch's money."

Any doubts lingering in Cauvin's mind vanished when he heard those words from Leorin's mouth. He couldn't think of a time, even before the Hand, when gold and silver hadn't been foremost in Leorin's thoughts. She didn't want him talking to Arizak.

Leorin didn't want him looking for Bec either. "That boy will turn up in a day or two whether you're out looking for him or not. He'll tell his parents some sweet story, and you'll get the blame, same as always. How long have you been here? You must be hungry." She ripped into the bread on her trencher. "Sweet Mother, I've had it with the Stick. I can't wait to get out of this place."

Cauvin took the piece she offered him and wondered if she thought he hadn't heard what had gone on between her and the Stick in the corridor.

"I get so tired of him and his threats," Leorin continued. She brought the trencher over to the bed and set it on a heap of her clothes beside Cauvin. "Help yourself. Imaging him, telling *me* not to come downstairs tonight! Does he think that Twandan whore can keep the peace in the commons? Let her try! Mark me on this, Cauvin: They'll be breaking tables before the night's out. And the Stick'll be climbing the stairs on his knees, begging me to come down to make everything right again."

Leorin plucked a good-sized morsel of meat from the stew. She leaned across the trencher, dangling it a few inches from Cauvin's mouth. He reached, intending to take the morsel from her hand, but she snatched it away and hid her hand behind her back. When Cauvin lowered his hand, Leorin let him see hers again.

Frog all—she wanted to play lovers' games, which reminded Cauvin of the scolding he and Soldt had received from Galya. Galya probably wouldn't approve of Leorin. Shite for sure, Mina didn't.

When Mina served supper, she served it the Imperial way with four trenchers, four knives, four spoons, and four dainty Imperial forks for capturing food that couldn't be speared or ladled. At the stoneyard, two to a trencher was uncivilized; a man and woman sharing one was froggin' indecent. If Grabar wanted a morsel from Mina's trencher, she'd jab it up with her fork then deposit it on the edge of his trencher and, shite for sure, she wouldn't *dare* look at his face while the morsel was moving.

No froggin' wonder, then, that Cauvin had daydreamed of sharing his trencher with Leorin, whose table manners were far less Imperial than her looks. He'd wasted whole evenings imagining a trencher shared on this very mattress. And now, when the moment was in his froggin' grasp, he wasn't in the mood to enjoy it.

"Oh, stop worrying about Bec!" Leorin chided. "I'm telling you, he'll turn up. There's no reason to worry anyway. He's *not* your brother." The morsel fell back into the stew; Leorin returned to her dressing table. "What you need is wine."

Leorin had brought a flagon up with the trencher. She shook a few drops of water from a goblet already standing on the table, then filled it from the flagon. From his perch on the mattress, Cauvin couldn't see the either the goblet or the flagon, but he could see Leorin's arms. By watching their movements, he knew she'd added something to the goblet she handed him with a parted-lips smile.

"This will get you in the right mood. Drink up!"

"A toast," Cauvin suggested quickly.

He offered Leorin the first sip and was bitterly unsurprised when she rushed to the table. She came back with the flagon in her hand.

"To our future!" she proposed, and when Cauvin was slow to respond, added. "To my *husband*. Tonight's the night! Forever and always, I give my life to you."

Cauvin listened as Leorin recited a vow of marriage. He couldn't move. The room spun, as if he'd drunk poison through his fingertips. He wanted to hurl the froggin' goblet at the wall—but that would expose his suspicions before he'd gotten enough out of her to save Bec.

"Cauvin—it's just wine. It's not going to *kill* you. Aren't you happy . . . excited."

"I am," he muttered, adding: "and surprised," before he could stop himself.

Shite for sure, Leorin was most likely telling the truth: With the Torch dead—because he'd told her—and him declaring that he was the Torch's heir, the last thing Leorin wanted was his froggin' corpse on her mattress. What she'd want was him completely under her control—asleep? unconscious? paralyzed? obedient?

Obedient would be best, then she could simply lead him to the Hand. There were potions that could make a man cut out his own froggin' heart, but they were sorcerous in nature, and sorcery was froggin' expensive. Leorin never wasted money. She wouldn't have an obedience potion hiding among the perfume bottles on her dressing table unless she needed it. Leorin couldn't have known. Shalpa's froggin' midnight cloak, she *couldn't* have known he'd be waiting in her bedroom! The same reasoning weighed against unconscious or paralyzed, but not against asleep.

Leorin did suffer from nightmares; so did Batty Dol. Batty mixed up her own sleeping powders and sold them for a padpol each—Cauvin knew because he'd bought them, sometimes, for Pendy. Leorin would part with a padpol. She'd have sleeping powders on her dressing table.

Cauvin thought a moment. He could handle a sheep-shite sleeping powder.

"To our future," Cauvin agreed, tipping the goblet against the flagon. "To my *wife*. Forever and always, I give my life to you."

He put the glass against his closed lips. Peering over the rim, he could see that Leorin needed both trembling hands to steady the larger flagon against hers. She wasn't smiling when she lowered the flagon. Shite for sure, Cauvin had never seen anyone look more frightened. They were playing games, the froggin' most dangerous games imaginable; and Leorin, in deep with the Hand, had more to lose.

Wedging the goblet between the mattress and the wall, Cauvin seized his new wife by the arms and hugged her tight. Leorin fumbled the flagon, spilling wine on him, her, the clothes, the mattress, the trencher, and everything in between. She made mewling sounds, like an orphaned kitten.

"There's nothing to worry about," he reassured her.

With one arm Cauvin clutched her tight; with the other he swept the wine-soaked clutter onto the floor. Then, while kissing his bride and easing her onto her back, his fingers found the goblet and tipped it sideways—just another stain sinking into the feathers.

Froggin' sure, Cauvin had never imagined that their first time would be like this, tainted with betrayal and poison, but he was a man and Leorin was a willing woman who knew her way around a mattress. Cauvin could play the part of an eager husband. After a moment, it wasn't playing, even though each kiss, each caress, each pounding heartbeat scarred him worse than ten long years in the pits.

Cauvin collapsed onto Leorin's shoulder with a groan.

"Cauvin?" Leorin whispered in his ear. "Beloved? Are you asleep?"

The question cut through Cauvin's soul. He held her tight and clenched his teeth to keep from screaming. She kissed his lips, his eyes, along his neck. Cauvin rolled onto his back. Leorin's long golden hair swept his skin, softer than silk and shimmering in the lamplight.

"I love you so much, Cauvin, I wish I could die right now."

"Me too," he agreed and held her steady as she balanced above his hips.

"Cauvin? Cauvin, are you asleep?"

He wasn't, but the time had come for silence.

Limb by limb, Leorin freed herself from his weight. She sat up, cradled Cauvin's head in her lap, and wound herself around him. He felt her breasts and her tears; and, for a moment, he thought he had been wrong about everything. Then she slid off from the mattress.

Cauvin scarcely breathed while Leorin dressed. He heard her lift the latch. Then she was gone.

# Chapter Eighteen

Cauvin searched for his cast-off clothes. Leorin had scrambled the clutter, and finding them was more of a challenge than he'd expected. He meant to follow his betraying bride, but he would have failed from the start if the Stick and Leorin hadn't struck up a shouting match while she was still on the stairs. Though the barkeep didn't win the argument, he slowed Leorin down. Cauvin was on the window ledge—black cloak flapping, breeches unbelted, boots in hand, and the Ilbarsi knife hanging by a single thong—when Leorin stormed onto the street.

She took a torch from the bucket, lit it from the lantern hanging over the Unicorn's entrance, then strode east, the shortest way out of the Maze. Cauvin pulled on his boots and dropped to the ground. He didn't dare carry a torch, even if he'd had the time to grab one. Instead, tightening his belt along the way, Cauvin barely kept up with his bride.

The Hand hadn't felt a need for stealth when they searched for corruption and impurity, so stalking wasn't an art that they'd bothered to teach their marauding orphans. Cauvin worried about the noise he made while walking the shadows. Twice within sight of the Unicorn, he tripped over the gods alone knew what, but Leorin never hesitated, never took a glance behind. He kept her in sight.

Leorin turned left on Shadow Street, striding past dives that made the Vulgar Unicorn look respectable. Her golden hair caught the attention of a pair of derelicts just past Slippery Street. One of them lumbered up like a baited bear at Anen's springtime carnival. Before he could question his own instincts, Cauvin was running to Leorin's aid, the Ilbarsi knife bare in his hand.

He needn't have worried. Leorin knew the bear was behind her. When he got close—but not too close—she spun around, showing off a shiny knife of her own. The bear wasn't drunk enough to impale himself on a lethal length of steel. He called her a "froggin' witch" and retreated. His unsteady path brought him within a few arm's lengths of Cauvin, who could have taught him the price of corruption, if he'd wanted to.

But Cauvin's wants were limited to keeping pace with Leorin. He thought she might be headed for the bazaar and didn't look forward to tracking her through a quarter where outsiders sometimes disappeared after dark. Fortunately, Leorin turned right, toward the palace gate, not left, toward the bazaar, when Shadow Street butted into Governor's Walk.

Cauvin faced different problems on the Walk, where the guard kept the peace from two towers, one on either side of the palace gate. The guards were no more blind to Leorin's golden beauty than the derelicts had been. They offered to protect her from any froggin' Wrigglie skulking in the shadows behind her and weren't likely to be cowed by a knife in her small, woman's hand. Not that Leorin needed a knife to bend them around her fingers. While Cauvin flattened against the palace walls, she laughed and swayed and persuaded a stout fellow—an officer, to judge by his short cloak and shiny scabbard—to be her personal escort, carrying her torch past the other guards.

Cauvin couldn't keep up from the shadows. He decided to risk walking down the center of Governor's Walk as though Wrigglies had every right to be there. He'd have been in trouble if Leorin and her officer had entered the palace. The great, iron-banded doors closed at sunset, and a man had to be someone to get through the narrow watch gate. A woman had only to be beautiful, and Leorin was Imperially beautiful.

He thought there was a good chance she was headed for the palace. Froggin' sure, the palace was the quarter of Sanctuary that the Hand knew best. And, froggin' sure, if that silk-wrapped Ilsigi he'd seen earlier wasn't the Whip, then he was the Whip's twin.

The officer stopped in front of the watch gate. His arm found its way around Leorin's waist. *He* wanted to take her inside, but she eluded him. Reclaiming her torch, she continued along the Walk.

Her jilted escort made Cauvin the target of his frustration. Who was he? What was he doing near the palace? Where had he been? Where did he think he was going?

The rousting could have been worse. Cauvin's shirt had escaped the worst of the spilled wine, and his black-wool cloak was finer than the officer's. He wasn't risking a dungeon cell, but with every question, Leorin's torch got smaller. Finally, Cauvin said he was trying to find his way to the Inn of Six Ravens. The officer gave him directions—accurate directions—and insisted he carry a torch.

Cauvin accepted the torch; the officer wouldn't take no for an answer. He followed directions, too, striding down the Processional until he could get onto the side streets and hurry back to the Walk.

"Help me," Cauvin prayed to Shalpa, for Bec's sake, not his own. "This could be my only chance. Don't let me lose her."

He cast the same prayer toward Savankala, because Bec was an Imperial citizen, then added Vashanka to his litany. One of the gods must have been listening. Cauvin was back on the Walk in time to see Leorin take her torch onto the Promise of Heaven.

Frog all, she was headed for the Hill! The Hand was holed up on the Hill! That messenger boy had been onto something after all. Cauvin ground his torch into the mud-choked ditch on the verge and headed onto the Promise, where he and Leorin were not alone.

Cauvin didn't remember Sanctuary before the Hand, but from everything he'd been told, the Promise of Heaven had once been a mortal paradise. No longer. The Promise he knew belonged to the sorriest of Sanctuary's denizens: women who'd lost their beauty, men who'd lost their strength. They looked for each other and for oblivion.

"Kleetel?" a bush called out as Cauvin approached.

He couldn't hear if voice came from a man or a woman, a seller or a buyer. Kleetel, the poor man's *krrf,* rotted the guts and throats of those who chewed its bitter, gummy leaves. Addicts lost their teeth and eventually bled to death from the inside out. But kleetel was cheap—one padpol for a bundle of leaves as thick as a man's hand—or free to those who braved the brackish Swamp of Night Secrets, where the vine grew wild. By decree, kleetel was as illegal in Arizak's Sanctuary as it had been in the Bloody Mother's, but people searching for oblivion didn't care about laws. When Cauvin mistakenly took a deep breath, his lungs filled with the stench of vomit and kleetel.

He pinched his nose and followed Leorin. Convinced that she was headed for the Hill, Cauvin would have lost her when she veered toward the marble walls of what had once been the white-walled temple of Ils. But Leorin's golden hair was unmistakable by torchlight.

She got cautious as she neared the ruins. Cauvin watched her pause several times. She seemed to be calling something, a password or a name; he was too far back to hear clearly. Each time, Cauvin expected a shadow to emerge out of the night. But none did, and, after a final hesitation, Leorin ran up the weedy steps. Her torch cast wild shadows on the inner walls as she ran into the temple's depths.

Coincidence, Cauvin told himself. Froggin' coincidence had returned him to the very place where he'd found the Torch. And maybe it was, but Cauvin stuck to the shadows, slipping into the temple from the side and staying far from the light until it flickered and vanished. Suddenly, Cauvin was blind and forced to shuffle through the rubble. He searched for the hole into which Leorin had disappeared and hoped not to fall into it by mistake.

Cauvin found what he was looking for in a recess made by a fallen column and a corner of the temple's rear wall. There was a shoulder-wide gap into the paving stones and a rope ladder dangling into the pit below. The rope felt new, but the anchoring rings were rusted. The broken marble at the pit's edge was damp and flaky when Cauvin put his weight against it. The whole area—the column, the walls, the floor, the pit, and the tunnel presumably at its bottom—had been rotted by rain and seepage. A few minutes' work with an iron-headed hammer, and any sheep-shite stone-smasher could have brought it all down.

Very reluctantly—Cauvin descended the ten-rung ladder. Once at the bottom, he felt his way along a dripping, absolutely dark and unbraced tunnel until it split into two branches. Each of the branches branched again within ten paces. The left-side branches had knee-deep trip-pits, as well. If they marked the path Leorin had followed, then she knew it very well because there was no trace of her in the tunnel, not even the scent of smoke from her torch.

He returned to the temple and found a place where he could see or hear anything rising out of the pit but where—he hoped—torchlight wouldn't find him.

*She's gone to tell them that she's got me drugged asleep in her room at the Unicorn. She'll come back this way, because if there were an easier way, she'd have taken it. And she'll come back soon, 'cause she can't know how long I'll stay asleep—*

*And then, what? And then, what?*

The question pursued Cauvin as he sat with his cloak pulled tight. Would he confront Leorin? Demand that she take him to Bec? Could he hurt her? Leave her bleeding or disfigured? What if she truly didn't know where Bec was? What if she wasn't alone when she emerged from the pit? What if there was another way out of the bolt-hole?

Cauvin pounded his head against the temple wall. He was sheep-shite stupid, not meant for thinking, and his little brother was paying the price. Three times, he convinced himself he was wasting precious time. Three times Cauvin stood up, determined to leave, and three times he sat down again because he couldn't think of any place better to be. He was almost ready to stand up a fourth time when ghostly light arose from the pit.

Leorin emerged with a torch, but before Cauvin could decide to confront her, three other figures—men, by their size and movement—rose behind her. Confrontation was no longer a possibility, so Cauvin tailed them from a safe distance, straight back to the Maze. The Unicorn was busy, which was more of a problem for Leorin and her three companions than it was for Cauvin who, staying in the shadows, retraced his path to the roof outside Leorin's window. He had his ear against the shutter when the latch clicked.

"He's all yours," Leorin advised, as lamplight flickered through the slats.

Cauvin squeezed his fist so hard around the brass he wore at his throat that he almost missed what the men had to say.

"Where is he?" Cauvin didn't recognize the voice, nor could he easily distinguish it from the others who said, with increasing anger. "The bed is empty." "There's no one here." "This is a poor jest, Leorin." And, finally, in the threatening tone that was the Hand's natural voice: "You brought us here for nothing." "You've risked everything for nothing."

Leorin quickly replied, "I gave him a doubled dose. He was—"

Her explanation stopped, cut short by a sound Cauvin did recognize: a well-made fist striking an unprotected gut. Leorin tried to scream for help, but they covered her mouth before anyone other than Cauvin could have heard her plea. It hadn't been many moments ago that Cauvin had been asking himself if he could hurt Leorin. He had his answer—he couldn't, but he wouldn't risk his life to save her, either.

Cauvin waited until the three men had left before climbing into the room. By the light of the lamp the three men had left behind, Cauvin found his wife alive, but unconscious, on the floor beside her bed. They'd beaten her carefully—no blood, no blows to her face, nothing that wasn't meant to heal without scars. Which meant, in the Hand's brutal language, that they hadn't cast her out.

He could have stayed with Leorin until she regained consciousness, but then he'd have to say something to her, and there wasn't anything he could say that would change anything. He could have gone downstairs and told Mimise that Leorin needed help, but then he'd get the blame for her injuries—assuming, of course, that Mimise or any of the other Unicorn wenches would lift a finger on Leorin's behalf. He could have at least laid her on her bed, but he'd already squandered too many moments on the woman who'd betrayed him while the three men who might lead him to Bec were getting away.

Two trios had their backs to the Vulgar Unicorn when Cauvin's dropped down to the street. One trio, with two torches among them, was headed toward the harbor. The other, without torches, set a fast pace toward the palace. Cauvin followed the second trio. One man split off at Slippery Street; the second at a Shadow Street alley. The third kept Cauvin's hopes alive until the dark expanse of the Promise was in sight, then he took the Split harborward.

Cauvin almost followed the third man. The Split passed close to Copper Corner, and he could almost convince himself that the Hand had a bolt-hole in that quarter, but almost wasn't enough. He crossed the Promise instead and entered the Temple of Ils. The Hand had covered its tracks, literally. A scaffold of wood and ragged cloth had been dragged over the pit and against the broken column, concealing the metal rings. It was flimsy. Cauvin pushed it aside one-handed, but it was enough to fool quick observation.

He considered leaving the pit exposed and could almost hear the Torch and Soldt both telling him not to start something he couldn't finish. He considered climbing down the ladder again. The voices in his conscience grew louder. Maybe Soldt had taken the Torch's ring to Arizak after all. Cauvin wouldn't hesitate to follow ten or twenty men like Gorge into the tunnel. And maybe, Grabar had gotten the gods' own luck on the Hill.

Cauvin made his way from the crumbling temple to Pyrtanis Street. He scaled the stoneyard wall, whispering the yard dog's name as he climbed. It was waiting, a wag in its tail, when Cauvin swung his legs over the top and let him into the yard without raising a ruckus. The house was shuttered up and quiet. Cauvin knocked lightly, got no response, and retreated to the loft, hoping the Torch was dead.

Never mind that the froggin' pud had nothing to do with what Leorin was—what she'd been all along. Or, that Cauvin realized he was better off betrayed than otherwise. The Torch had destroyed his dreams, and he wished him dead. His wishes were worthless. Three floating embers, two small and close together, the third, large and getting brighter greeted him at the top of the ladder.

He started to ask, Aren't you dead yet, pud? but got no farther than the first word before a wind struck his chest. Cauvin staggered backward, striking his head on a roof beam, before sitting hard on the floor.

"It's me, pud—Cauvin. Frog all, I *live* here."

"Where have you been?" the Torch demanded, a hoarse voice in dark.

"I've tracked the Hand to their lair—almost. You're not going to froggin'—"

"Where's my ring?"

The third ember in the loft—the amber knob atop the Torch's staff—brightened and the third finger of Cauvin's right hand became uncomfortably warm.

"What did you do with my ring? I gave you my ring! I gave

you instructions—simple instructions: Go to the palace, talk to Arizak. Was that too complicated?"

Cauvin put his right hand behind his back. The burning lessened, but didn't end. "Listen to me, pud—I know where the Hand is!"

"I didn't send you on a wild-goose chase, I sent you to the palace! I asked you to do what you were told. Did you? No. No, you got cold feet and took off!"

"Froggin' shite, pud—Soldt and I went to the palace and saw all the wrong men once we got there. The *wrong* men, no matter what Soldt told you. I recognized a man from when I used to live there, in the froggin' pits. Soldt didn't recognize him, not for what he was. Shite for sure, *you* wouldn't have recognized him, but *I* did. The Hand's in the palace, pud. That's how they got you."

The third ember faded. Cauvin's finger cooled.

"I haven't seen Soldt since he left with you."

"Then how did you know I didn't go talk to your froggin' Irrune friend?"

"Because I'm alive, Cauvin. I'm *still* alive. If you'd done what you were told, you wouldn't have come skulking back here, and I'd be dead by now, damn it. Strike a light. What *did* you do?"

"I saw a man I recognized from before . . . we called him the Whip and Leorin told me she'd killed him herself—slit him open with his own knife. He was different—ten years different, with pale hands and a silk robe—but . . ." Cauvin found his lamp, struck sparks for the wick, and made a nest for it in a sand-filled box—a man couldn't be too froggin' careful with fire in a loft. "Leorin told me the Whip was dead. I couldn't take the chance; I needed to see her—"

"That does not follow, Cauvin," the Torch scolded. The only color in his face came from his weird eyes; otherwise, his withered face was white as ice.

"It followed for me," Cauvin countered. "I went to the Unicorn. We talked; we more than talked. She put something in my wine; I didn't drink it. Leorin left once she thought I was asleep, but I wasn't. I followed her to the Promise of Heaven—"

The Torch hummed with curiosity.

—"She went into the old Temple of Ils, all the way to the back and down into a tunnel. I waited. She came out with three men. I'm froggin' sure they were Hand."

"They must have been quite disappointed to find you among the missing. And none too grateful to your beloved Leorin."

Cauvin grimaced. "They gave her a warning."

"Only a warning? You know what this means, don't you?"

"They weren't ready to give her to the Bloody Mother. They think she might still be useful to them."

"Cauvin, you sheep-shite fool, you knew what she was before you took her clothes off. A wise man does not swive with a Dyareelan! You've given her a part of yourself and who know what it might grow into. Of course, Leorin's still useful to them, even if they trust her no more than you do. For a month, at least, maybe longer, if she's caught you in her belly."

"Shalpa's midnight cloak—Leorin . . . Leorin . . ." Cauvin groped for words that wouldn't scald his mouth as he said them. "Leorin's *barren.* She's said so herself: If she could have children, she'd have had a passel of them by now. I'm the one who held back."

"Until tonight. Need I remind you that you've shared your beloved with the Bloody Mother all along? If barrenness served Dyareela, then your Leorin was barren; if not, then quite possibly, not. There's no guessing what can happen with a god's blessing."

"No, Leorin would never give them a child," Cauvin insisted—though how could he convince the Torch when he couldn't convince himself?

He covered his face. Better a child not be born that it be born to the Hand—but *his* child . . . How could he have done that to *his* child? The shame was excruciating. Behind his hand, Cauvin closed his eyes and couldn't say a word.

"You are well aware, I assume, that *if* you had done what I told you to do, none of this would have happened. Now you're ashamed. By the gods, I should leave you to wallow in your juices until you truly know the depth—and futility—of shame. But I haven't the time. There are two treasures left, Cauvin—*listen to me!* Two treasures. One is sacred to all men of Ranke—the Savankh. You'll find Sanctuary's Savankh in a small storeroom out at Land's End. Getting it away from the Serripines won't be easy, but you'll manage. The other is the Necklace of Harmony which once graced the neck of Ils, Himself—

"Oh, not the *real* one, of course—if there were such a thing. There are as many Necklaces as there are Savankhs, maybe more—there's no denying that Ils is older than Savankala. Or that His priests have lost a Necklace or two along the way. The one that Ils in Sanctuary wore when I arrived here was stolen by a woman—a tiny creature, a competent thief, but a better curse: a veritable black bird of death. Take *Ischade* to bed and you'd be dead before the sun rose. Not her fault, you understand, the best curses never are.

"We made a new Necklace after that—couldn't have the Wrigglies losing faith in their great god, could we? That's what matters, after all: faith. The gods are real enough, but it's mortal faith, mortal prayer, and mortal sacrifice that gives Them power—Ah, Vashanka—until They break faith . . ." The dying priest retreated into himself, then continued—

"Arizak's wife, Nadalya, wants the Savankh and the Necklace together for her son, to legitimize his expected rule. We've disagreed on this, but debate is a luxury Sanctuary can no longer afford. As his god wills, Arizak's wound may not kill him for another five years, but if he's got to root the Hand out from beneath the Promise of Heaven, he's going to have to anoint a successor—or maybe two: Give the Irrune to the Young Dragon and he to them, but give the Savankh and Necklace to one of Nadalya's city-bred sons.

"The Necklace is ours—I'll tell you where it's hidden. But the Savankh is out at Land's End. Serripines won't surrender a brass soldat if he thinks it's going to the offspring of a Dark Horde chieftain—never mind that the Irrune suffered more from the Horde than he did. You're going to have to handle him carefully. Try not to lie—but a little deception—"

"Games!" Cauvin erupted. "Galya's right. The Hand's got my brother, and you want to play froggin' games with rich, old men. I'm not playing games any longer. I've got better things to do."

"I'm giving you the keys to power in Sanctuary. What could be more important than that?"

"Killing my own snakes!" Cauvin shouted.

Beneath the loft, the mule stirred, and outside, the yard dog began to bark.

"*Shhsh!* You'll wake the dead. What snakes?"

"Leorin."

"Porking bastard!" the Torch shouted, lapsing into Imperial, though Cauvin was quite familiar with the insult. "Leorin's a problem because you didn't think ahead, didn't plan your moves and everyone else's too. You'll resolve Leorin *after* you've taken care of larger issues. A resurgence of Dyareela bloodletting would be a catastrophe for Sanctuary. The city needs someone in the palace who *commands* respect. *Get the Savankh! Get the Necklace of Harmony!*"

"Get them yourself, pud. If Arizak's sons are worth respecting, they'll take care of the Hand without treasure and toys to bribe them. Frog all, Arizak did."

"Frog all, Arizak got tribute for his trouble! He led the Irrune to Sanctuary because the city promised him—*I* promised him—the palace *and* enough treasure to choke his favorite stallion if he dislodged the Hand. If the Hand had offered more, he would have taken their offer. Pay attention, Cauvin—a man like Arizak does what he wants. It's up to you to make him want what you want."

"Arizak got *tribute*?"

"Three coronations for each rider. More for fathers and grandfathers. Much more to Arizak himself. And all of it paid for by the 'rich, old men' of Sanctuary—which is why, Cauvin, you've got to keep them happy, too. It's not *games,* Cauvin, it's life—diplomacy when it works, war when it fails. And if it fails this time, forget about Bec. Forget Leorin, too."

"Shite." He was almost persuaded, but no—"Maybe I can walk away from Leorin—for now. But not Bec. The Hand's got my brother, and I don't give a froggin' ring on a froggin' rat's tail for what happens to Sanctuary until he's safe. So you'd better help me figure out how to get him away from the Hand, 'cause I'm not doing anything else first."

"There is only one way. Get the Savankh and the Necklace."

Cauvin began to pace in and out of the lamplight. "Where's Soldt?"

"Soldt comes and goes. You're the one who walked away from him. He could be anywhere by now . . . or sitting on the roof listening to every word we've said. It wouldn't be—"

Cauvin wasn't listening.

"Pay attention!" the Torch pounded his staff on the floor. "Saddle that horse and ride out to Land's End. You can be back here with the Savankh by dawn."

"You mean locked in a Serripines storeroom. Forget your games, pud—help me think of a way to rescue my brother or shut up."

"You can win my *games,* pud. You say you know where the boy is; you're lying. If you knew, that's where you'd be. Seems to me, the only one who might know where Bec is, is that woman—"

Cauvin agreed. "Leorin knows. She's still the key. If I can get to her—"

"You'll regret it for the rest of what's left of your life. When it comes to games, pud—that woman's shown you how she plays. You weren't there when she brought the Hand to take you—she's not going to think you got bored and decided to take a walk in the night air, not after dosing your wine. She'll cut her losses, pud, especially if she can't deliver you on her second try. Think about what I'm saying, Cauvin—the Hand made her."

"They made me, too, and I'm . . ."

"You're what, Cauvin? You're cleverer than your ladylove? Well, maybe you are, but she's not giving the orders, she's taking them. The Hand's come back to Sanctuary. They've killed me. Don't let them kill you, too—"

Cauvin said, "The froggin' Hand never left, pud," because it might shut the Torch up, not because it was true.

"Nonsense— Maybe we missed a few . . . your woman. Vashanka's mercy—you aren't thinking *she's* the chosen one in Sanctuary? Two days ago you swore she wasn't with them at all."

"Leorin left Sanctuary with the Whip; she came back with him. Froggin' sure, she's been chosen." Cauvin swallowed hard. His throat was tight, but he got the words out: "The Whip chose her long before you bribed the Irrune."

"Cauvin," the Torch drawled, making the name an insult. "Cauvin, shake that notion out of your head. You didn't see the Whip or any other priest of the Mother at the palace dressed as an Ilsigi merchant. His hands were stained bloodred, weren't they? He's not doing business with the majordomo, not with bloodred hands."

"Wouldn't you say the Whip's beloved of Dyareela?" The words seemed to form in Cauvin's mind; he merely repeated them. "Then there's no telling what he might be with the Mother's blessing, right? If the Bloody Mother can quicken Leorin, She can cleanse the Whip's hands. I know what I saw yesterday afternoon. Unless you've got an idea that doesn't rely on treasure, bribes, or stealing a relic from Land's End, I'm going after Leorin, and I'm not giving up until Bec's back here at the yard."

"Think of Sanctuary—" The Torch began, but didn't finish. "No, why bother? Why should you care about this gods-forsaken city? Because it's your home? No, I've lived here longer than you, and hated every moment." The fire dimmed in the old pud's eyes. His hand trembled, and for the first time in their acquaintance, it was the Torch who couldn't hold a stare. "We're tired, Cauvin. You've been on your feet for a day and a half and I'm . . . I'm dying." He said the last word softly, as though it were the first time the idea was more than a means to an end. "Get some rest before you go acting rash."

"Can't," Cauvin shot back, unimpressed by the old pud's sudden meekness and not trusting it, either. "You're in my bed."

"I only suggest that you reflect on your plans."

"I did all the *reflecting* I need to do outside Leorin's window while they pounded the snot out of her. I don't know why I bothered to come back here—except to realize that confronting Leorin and getting Bec out is something I've got to do myself."

Cauvin swung a leg onto the ladder and began his descent. The Torch tried to call him back with dire warnings about "unforeseen consequences," but Cauvin kept going, out of the work shed and onto the streets of Sanctuary. Frog all, if a man started worrying about unforeseen consequences, he'd waste himself worrying and *that* would be the consequence.

Leorin had found her way to her bed when Cauvin popped her shuttered window open. She moaned softly as he stepped down into her room, but didn't make another sound until he'd lit the lamp on her dressing table.

"You!" The word carried many meanings, not the least of which were that Leorin blamed Cauvin for every bruise, every ache.

"Surprised?" he replied, which wasn't what he'd planned to say. "I was when I woke up and found you'd gone."

"I wanted more wine. I didn't think you'd notice." Leorin covered herself with a blanket and excuses. "You were sound asleep."

"I should have been, shouldn't I? After drinking the wine you'd dosed for me."

"Frog all—what are you talking about?" She tidied her hair. If Cauvin hadn't known what she'd been through, he wouldn't have guessed from how much each movement must have hurt. "Come over here. Sit beside me. *Lie* beside me. I missed you when I got back."

"I wager you did," Cauvin countered. "You and the three men behind you."

"Three men? What three men? What are you talking about, Cauvin? Have you been drinking?"

Cauvin shook his head. "No," he said softly. His anger was gone, replaced by something harsher, yet colder. "I went to the Temple of Ils on the Promise of Heaven. I waited until you climbed out of the pit, then I followed you and the three men back here. I was outside"—he hooked a thumb toward the open window—"when you opened the door."

"Damn you!" Leorin threw her pillow. Cauvin beat it harmlessly to the floor.

"You're with them," he continued, not raising his voice. "With the Hand. You've lied to me for two years, Leorin, and last night when I told you about the Torch, you went running to the Whip. But someone made a mistake. They left the Torch on the ground and snatched my brother instead. You see, I know it all. I didn't want to believe it—froggin' gods be damned, I didn't. When I came here last night, I still hoped some part of you loved me, that you'd choose me, instead of the Hand. Everything's been lies. You haven't told me the truth, not in two years."

"I wanted it all to be true, Cauvin. I swear it. Strangle— You called him the Whip because you weren't told the name the Mother gave him. She named him Strangle—"

"What's yours, Leorin? What name did the Bloody Bitch give you?" Cauvin demanded, unable to keep a fist from forming or his nails from biting into his palm.

Leorin looked away before admitting, "Honey."

"Because you attract men." It was not a question.

"I wanted to tell you. I've *always* wanted to tell you, but I was afraid. I'm not like you, Cauvin. You were strong, even when you were a boy, and you weren't ever afraid. No matter what they did to you—even when they brought you before the Mother—you never broke. I broke, Cauvin. When they gave me the choice between sacrifice and submission, I couldn't be strong like you, so I chose submission."

"It didn't take strength to say no, Leorin. All it took was eyes to see what the Hand was, what I would have become. The choice was between a quick death and a slow one."

"All life is a slow death, Cauvin, and I'm afraid to die. It's not about Purification or the World's Rebirth. It's about giving someone else to the Mother when She's craving, before someone gives you. Strangle hasn't asked for much. I give him what he wants, and I've stayed alive."

"Until you tried to give him the Torch . . . and me. And missed both times."

"That was a mistake," Leorin admitted, twisting the blanket into a tight coil. "When I came back, and you were gone, I knew—even while they were hitting me—that I'd misjudged you. Everyone's misjudged you. You're not strong because you're too sheep-shite stupid to be afraid. You're not stupid at all; and your strength is real. I thought I could trick you, but, in the end, you tricked me. No one's ever done that to me, Cauvin. No one!

"Do you know what that means, what it *could* mean, if you'd let it?" She reached for his hand.

Cauvin didn't let Leorin catch him; didn't let her answer, either. His silence didn't discourage her.

"With your cunning and my knowledge of the Hand, not just here in Sanctuary but all along the coast, we could make Sanctuary ours, starting with Strangle. Sweet Mother, I *do* despise him, but we all need partners before the Mother's altar. Listen to me, Cauvin—" She got out of bed, put her arms around him, and went to work caressing his shoulders. "Between us, we can do it—"

"Don't," Cauvin interrupted. He peeled her arms away and held her at arm's length.

"It wouldn't be like before, Cauvin. What happened before, that was because *men* led Her worship. The Mother is different when women lead. There doesn't have to be blood every day, every week, or even every month. A few sacrifices— Murderers, rapists, thieves, their blood's as good as anyone else's. Good people, ordinary people have nothing to fear from Dyareela. Sanctuary will still be Sanctuary—only better, with the Mother's blessing to protect it. No one we love will ever be sacrificed."

She was mad, Cauvin decided. Not raving mad or harmlessly mad, like Batty Dol, but hollowed-out mad, missing all sense of what the world looked like through another person's eyes.

"Cauvin"—Leorin pasted herself against him—"Cauvin, I *love* you! Dyareela loves you. You can have a better future than you ever imagined."

"Is that what you were thinking when you straddled me or when you powdered my wine?" He shed her again, this time less gently.

"I'd never let anything happen to you, Cauvin."

"Frog all, Leorin, what were those three men here for? Supper?"

"If you'd *agree,* Cauvin. If you could see that serving the Mother of Chaos is serving yourself. The age of Ilsig is over, the age of Ranke, too. The Torch is the dying priest of a dead god. Don't devote yourself to the dead. Serve the Mother, and you serve the future. Everything can be made right."

"Froggin' sure, I don't *serve* the Torch or his god. I don't serve any one, any thing, or any god." Leorin's room was too small for pacing, Cauvin simply swayed. Thoughts swarmed like wasps in his head, but only one was important: "What about Bec? Can everything be made right for Bec?"

"He's not too young to serve Dyareela. The Mother loves children."

Cauvin froze. The wasps had formed a pattern. He could see a way to save his brother. "Bec gets out. He's got nothing to do with the froggin' Torch, nothing to do with the froggin' Mother. I'm the one you want, right? If I accept Dyareela, then Bec walks away. Froggin' right? That's if he's unharmed. If Bec's hurt, nobody gets anything."

The change in Leorin's smile was chilling. "You'd truly accept the Mother? You'd become my true husband before Her? Don't lie,

Cauvin— She'll know if you're lying. Strangle will know."

"No lies. I see where I belong. I shouldn't have walked away the first time."

Leorin flew into his arms. "Everything can be made right— Trust me," she pled, which was the last thing Cauvin intended to do.

"Take me to them," Cauvin whispered in his wife's ear before he kissed her.

They unwound slowly. Leorin sat down on the bed. Suddenly, unexpectedly, her face was dark with doubt.

"If I take you, I can't—I can't swear that Strangle will let the boy go. After we've sacrificed Strangle, then Bec can leave, if he wants, if he chooses not to serve. But for you, Cauvin—if you think you're tricking me—once we're underground, it's submit or sacrifice. You won't come up again, except with the Mother's blessing."

"You trust me, Leorin, I froggin' trust you."

Leorin nodded and reached for cloak. Her bruises had swelled, and she had stiffened. She couldn't lift the heavy garment. Cauvin wrapped it around her shoulder and carried her over the windowsill, as well—neither of them wanted a confrontation with the Stick.

Leorin stood on the eaves, arms wrapped under her breasts, hands hidden inside her cloak.

"Just step off. I'll catch you," Cauvin said from the street.

She didn't trust Cauvin any more than he trusted her but, like him, Leorin was desperate. She yelped when she leapt and again when Cauvin's arms closed around her, catching her before her feet touched the ground but not sparing her battered ribs. Walking was impossible without Cauvin's arm around her waist to support and steady her.

Cauvin could easily have carried Leorin across Sanctuary. They would have reached Ils's Temple at his pace rather than hers. She didn't ask, and he didn't offer, though he did carry their torch. The eastern horizon had brightened by the time they reached the Promise of Heaven. Cauvin let his wife sit on a chunk of Ils's arm while he dragged the scaffold away from the pit.

"It's all Strangle's fault," Leorin whispered when he helped her to her feet again. "It was him, not the Mother. None of this would have happened if he hadn't promised a blessing to whoever brought down the Torch. Strangle's will isn't Dyareela's will. Pilfer died because he listened to Strangle, not the Mother."

They were mad, Cauvin thought as he climbed down the rope ladder, and soon he'd be one of them . . . or dead. It didn't matter much, so long as Bec was free.

"I'll catch you," he promised Leorin for the second time. She fell into his arms and fainted from the pain. Cauvin chafed her hands and cheeks to rouse her. "Don't you froggin' *die* on me!"

The golden-amber eyes fluttered open. "I won't, Cauvin, I swear I won't. Help me up."

He did. "You're sure you can find the way?"

"Just stay behind me. Walk where I walk, nowhere else."

"What about torchlight?"

"What about it? They know we're here, Cauvin. The temple belongs to Dyareela. There's always someone watching."

That stopped Cauvin in his tracks as he recalled his earlier visits. The Hand must not have recognized the Torch, or maybe they weren't as vigilant as Leorin believed.

Steadying herself with her right hand against the tunnel wall, Leorin led Cauvin into a maze. Cauvin had never imagined that Sanctuary was built on a hollow hillside, but that seemed the best explanation for the wormlike passages. The torch he carried revealed shiny ribbons of stone that looked like silken draperies. He longed to run his hands over them, but Leorin, with her right hand always touching the passage wall, limped on.

Though most of the passages were bone dry, several were flooded to ankle depth. The water flowed from cracks in the passage walls or seeped up through the raw-stone floor. Living near rivers and the sea, Cauvin thought he knew all the ways in which water could kill, but he'd never imagined that a man could *drown* underground until they entered a cave that was little wider than the stream roaring through it. A waist-high rope had been slung across the turbulent water, leading from the natural arch where they stood to a dark keyhole carved out of the opposite wall.

"When it rains above, the water flows here," Leorin explained. "Yesterday, we couldn't have come this way, but it's safe now—slippery, but not very deep."

Leorin hitched up her skirt with a moan and grasped the rope with her free hand. Her feet had no sooner touched the rushing water than she lost her balance. A hard fall left her stunned and sliding toward the hole where the stream reburied itself in stone. Cauvin didn't have hands enough for the torch, the guide rope, and Leorin. He let go of the rope. The stream wasn't deep—the water didn't cover his knees—but slippery didn't begin to describe the stone over which it raced. He lost the torch during his struggle to grasp Leorin and keep his balance.

If the Hand *was* watching—Cauvin could have used some help finding the way out. He was drenched before he found first the guide rope, then the keyhole exit.

"Ice is slippery," he complained as he helped a shaky Leorin into the pitch-black passage. "That was worse. Can you get through that?"

"Yes," Leorin said grimly.

The carved passage was meant for crawling, not walking, and on their palms and knees. But it was no more than twenty feet in length—the longest twenty feet Cauvin had ever crawled—and ended in a cave that was lit by a pair of oil lamps hung from a ceiling too high to see by their light. They picked up an escort coming across that chamber—at least one man whose footsteps echoed in the darkness. Cauvin loosened the bronze slug from his neck, but the escort stayed out of sight.

There was another keyhole passage, this one high enough for walking, and at the end of it, a well-lit chamber. Leorin had told the froggin' truth about one thing, at least—Cauvin had just two choices tonight: submit or sacrifice. There would be no turning around.

The Hand's bolt-hole beneath Sanctuary was a sprawling cavern some twenty feet high and divided by a rushing stream, probably the same stream Cauvin and Leorin had crossed earlier. Lashed and floating planks bridged the stream. Judging from the length of the bridge and the high-waterline shining on the sloped floor, the stream had been a foot higher not long ago.

On the far side of the stream, at the limit of torchlight, the Hand had raised an altar to the Bloody Mother of Chaos. It was a small altar compared to the one Cauvin remembered at the palace, barely longer than a man's spine, but it was ringed with enough chains to hold any man in place while they cut out his heart. The Bloody Mother's face had been crudely carved into the cave wall behind the altar—Grabar could have done a better job. Unlit candles, mounted on spears, stood in ranks between the altar and the carved face. Skulls and long bones were piled at the base of each spear. And atop the altar, glimmering in firelight, the golden bowls that held the knives and collected the blood of those Mother desired or who got in the way.

The altar and its furnishings were revealed by five great lamps hung along the cavern walls. A dark keyhole passage opened beneath each lamp, and, one by one, the survivors of Hand emerged to greet their visitors. Cauvin counted five men and three women before a tall man strode into view. His head was bald and his hands were pale, but even if Leorin hadn't hailed him as Strangle or he hadn't carried a coiled whip below his waist, Cauvin would have recognized the Whip. Put a wig on his head, exchange his breeches and shirt for silken robes in sunrise colors, and the Whip became the Ilsigi broker Cauvin had seen in the palace talking to Prince Naimun.

"So, your sleepwalker came home," the Whip said to Leorin. "Good for you." Then he turned his contempt on Cauvin. "Ah, Cauvin—full-grown at last. And why have you come to us, Cauvin? True love? A change of heart? A need for rebirth? Something simpler?"

Leorin tried to speak for him, but Cauvin's voice was stronger. "Something simpler. I came to offer myself in exchange for my brother. I'm the one you want. I'm the Torch's heir."

"So we've heard. But, can you prove it, Cauvin? Your word isn't nearly enough."

That was a challenge Cauvin hadn't expected. Froggin' sure, other than the Torch's word—which wouldn't count for much with the Hand—all he had for proof was an old knife, dreamy conversations with dead men and dead gods, and a knack for reading languages he couldn't speak. He hadn't even kept the Torch's damned black ring!

Before Cauvin made a sheep-shite fool of himself, Leorin got between him and Strangle.

"I'll swear Cauvin's not the man he was last week. He's been transformed. He has what we need, and he's sworn to submit to

Dyareela—in exchange for his brother, who we know isn't the heir."

"I'm sure you'll swear it, Honey. You'll swear anything to have him in your bed every night." Once again he turned immediately to Cauvin, asking, "She is very good, isn't she? Worth waiting for? Worth dying for?"

Watching Leorin stiffen, Cauvin believed she did hate Strangle to the core of her icy heart. It wasn't enough to make him trust her, but there was a chance that they faced a common enemy. He felt bold enough to say: "I'm not answering any of your froggin' questions until my brother's out of here."

"You're in no position to dictate terms, Cauvin," Strangle said. When Cauvin didn't blink, he shouted, "Show him!"

Another six men entered the altar cave, two of them emerging from the passage behind Leorin and Cauvin. They came in pairs, one carrying a torch and the other a short spear with a barbed point. Although the men appeared to be roughly his age, Cauvin was a little surprised that he recognized none of the faces.

"Go ahead, kill me—and you'll never know what the Torch knew and who he told. And you'll never know where he's stashed enough treasure to raise an army ten thousand strong."

Cauvin sealed his doom with that empty boast, but it was worth it to watch the Whip's greedy eyes narrow and hear him shout another order:

"Fetch him! Fetch the whelp!"

Two women hurried into a dark passage. Cauvin clenched his fists to keep them from shaking while he waited—not long—for the women to reappear with Bec. The boy walked tall despite a rag tied over his eyes, his hands bound behind his back, and a noose tied around his neck. He was shirtless—that was to be expected—and filthy. There was a scabby cut on his forehead and two bloody welts crossing his narrow chest. Otherwise, he seemed unharmed, though surely there were bruises under all that dirt. A whip had made the welts, and Cauvin knew who'd wielded it.

Leorin had told the truth about one thing: He wasn't the man he'd been the week before. That sheep-shite fool would have charged across the stream, attacked the Whip, and gotten himself killed before Bec was home free. The man Cauvin had become stood his ground, and said—

"Untie him."

Not one of the boy's captors twitched toward the knots, but Bec recognized Cauvin's voice. "Cauvin!" he shouted. "Don't listen to them, Cauvin! Don't believe them! I didn't tell them *anything*!"

Cauvin kept his attention on the Whip. "I said, untie him. He's free now."

The Whip cocked his head to one side. "What is it about children," he asked with gentle malice, "that makes strong men weak? They're untempered . . . unfinished. They can always be replaced, and so pleasurably."

"No answers until he's free and out of here."

The Whip sighed. "Unbind him."

Bec blinked when the blindfold came off. He spotted Leorin. "Furzy feathers! Cauvin, what are you doing here with *her*?"

"Never mind." Cauvin opened his arms. The boy scampered over the floating bridge. Cauvin hunched down, embracing him face-to-face. "You get out of here—*now*!" He spoke softly, even though he knew the froggin' Hand could hear his thoughts if they wished. "Put your left hand on the passage wall behind me and keep it there—except when you come to a cave with water in it. Then, feel for a rope and hold on tight as you cross the stream. Got that?"

The boy frowned so deeply that the cut on his forehead began to weep. "Cauvin? Cauvin, you can't stay *here*. Not with *her*? Cauvin, you've got to come with me."

"Once you're in the temple, run straight to the stoneyard. You hear me?"

"Cauvin— Don't you know who these people *are*? You can't stay with them! Grandfather—"

"Grandfather's dead! They made a mistake when they took you, Bec. They want me. I've got to stay; you've got to *leave*." Cauvin gave his brother a good shake and shove toward the passage. "Put your left hand on the wall and run. Don't stop running until you're in the stoneyard."

"But—"

"Get going!"

Bec stood firm. Cauvin backhanded him across the face. The boy staggered and crumbled. When he stood, his mouth and nose were bleeding and tears streamed over his cheeks.

"Cauvin . . ."

"Frog all, Bec—run!"

Bec whimpered, then—finally—he ran.

"Grandfather, is it? How touching," the Whip purred, when Cauvin faced him again. "And you're the witch's son?"

Cauvin shook his head. "No witch. The Torch made me his heir."

"Priests don't transform heirs, Cauvin. Only witches can do that. If the Torch made you his heir, the question is: Did he make you into a witch, too?"

A part of Cauvin wanted to shout that froggin' sure he wasn't a witch, except he wasn't sure at all, so he said nothing.

The Whip laughed. "No matter, Cauvin. Witchblood is sweet on the Mother's tongue, but the Torch's soul is what She's hungered for." He turned to Leorin. "Sorry, Honey, but—you can't have him, not as a lover or a weapon against me. Take them both."

The spear-carrying man at Cauvin's back surged, and though Cauvin was willing to trade his life for Bec's, he couldn't trade it meekly. The best knife in the world was no match for a five-foot-long spear. Cauvin seized the torch from the spearman's partner, kicking him in the gut as he did. Then he brought the flames to bear on the knuckles of the spearman to thrust at him. The Hand howled as he dropped his weapon and ran for the stream.

Cauvin had a heartbeat to savor his victory as Leorin lunged for the dropped spear, but rather than stand beside him against those who wanted to sacrifice them both to the Bloody Mother, she leveled the barbed point at Cauvin's breast—or tried to. The beating she'd taken in the Unicorn left Leorin unable to hold even a light weapon steady. She'd have been useless as an ally and wasn't a threat as an enemy. Cauvin easily wrenched the spear out of her hand, but by then it was too late. The two other spearmen with their torch-carrying partners on the Whip's side of the stream had crossed the floating bridge, and the two on Cauvin's side had recovered their nerve.

Even with a spear in one hand and a torch in the other, Cauvin was no match for six men obeying their master's orders. Before he knew it, his weapons were gone, there was steel pressed into his throat, more hands than he could count pinning his arms behind his back.

His captors dragged Cauvin to the floating bridge, which was nowhere near wide enough, nor sturdy enough for the lot of them. Cauvin had nothing to lose by writhing in captivity, trying to trip his captors into the stream. He kept his balance long enough to break free and draw the Ilbarsi knife, then he grabbed Leorin and held her—spine against his chest—with the Ilbarsi knife at her throat.

From start to finish, it had been a blind, desperate move, and its success gained Cauvin nothing. There were still six men coming after him, and Leorin was not a willing hostage. She clawed at Cauvin's forearm and stomped on his foot. If the Hand hadn't beaten her earlier, she would have gotten loose.

"I'll give you everything the Torch has given me—" Cauvin shouted to the Whip, who was, at that moment, crossing the stream.

A spearman feinted; Cauvin used Leorin as a shield. She bit down hard on his arm.

"Or what?" the Whip asked patiently. "Cauvin, Cauvin—no cleverer now than you were ten years ago. You have nothing to bargain with. The Mother has decided: She hungers for you, Cauvin. She hungers *now*."

The Whip gestured toward the altar. Cauvin dared a glance. Women were lighting the ranks of candles. The Bloody Mother's carved-rock eyes had begun to glow.

"I'll kill her. I'll kill Leorin—Honey." He tightened his grip while she kicked his knees and elbowed his gut.

"You can't; you love her." The Whip walked between the spearmen. He came within easy reach of Leorin and the Ilbarsi knife. "Even if you didn't, even if you could—we all go to the Mother sooner or later. Don't we?" He caressed Leorin's chin. "You made a mistake, and you tried to correct it. Sacrifice will complete your redemption, Honey."

Leorin reacted to that by holding tight to Cauvin's arm and ramming both heels into the Whip's groin. The stunned man folded his arms over his injury and struggled to stay on up his feet. Leorin's heels caught him a second time on the chin.

Before he could take advantage of his wife's swift vengeance—

Before the Hand could react to their master's collapse—a steel-tipped arrow erupted outward between the Whip's eyes. Dead on his feet, the bald Hand dropped like stone into the stream. Rushing water swirled away the blood trickling from the wound.

Leorin screamed and went limp in Cauvin's arms as panic spread among the Hand. A spearman tried to pull the Whip's body out of the water. As he did a gout of fire sizzled out of nowhere and struck him in the chest. The flames engulfed the man with unnatural speed and continued to burn even when he flung himself into the water. Another gout from another quarter of the cave struck a second spearman, while a third hit one of the unarmed Hand on the altar side of the stream and a fourth enveloped one of the candle-lighting women.

All natural flames winked out. The only light came from the Bloody Mother's glowing eyes and the four living, wailing torches. Cauvin heard footfalls stumbling over themselves. He relaxed his grip on Leorin; returned the Ilbarsi knife to its sheath.

"We're saved," Cauvin said to Leorin. "We can get away." He offered his hand to his wife.

She grasped it left-handed and let him pull her upright. "It could have been perfect, but you destroyed it. You ruin everything! Even as a boy, you ruined everything. You killed your own mother with your blundering, but you'll never kill me!"

Leorin slashed across Cauvin's body with a right hand that had suddenly sprouted steel. He dodged, taking the steel along his forearm before knocking Leorin to the ground, but failed to shake free and she slashed again.

"Damn you!" she sobbed, the light of burning men aglow on her face. "Damn you! Take him, Sweet Mother! Take him *now!*"

Cauvin didn't wait to see if the Bloody Mother would heed Leorin's prayer. He lunged for the temple passage, set his left hand on the wall, and began to run. He hadn't gone three strides before all the light was behind him. The darkness of the passage was absolute, deeper than midnight on a moonless, overcast night. Cauvin's vision didn't end at his elbows or his knees, it simply didn't exist.

He'd slowed to a fast walk and was growing fearful that he'd missed the passage to the water-filled chamber when a hand closed over his right sleeve. Cauvin struck fast with the Ilbarsi knife.

"Easy! I'm on your side."

Cauvin recognized Soldt's voice, but his panic was such that moments passed before he could stop struggling and even then, he couldn't speak.

"This way."

Soldt tugged, and Cauvin's left hand lost contact with the stone around them.

"Left hand," Cauvin protested, barely coherent. "Left-hand passage."

"Takes too long. Come on."

Cauvin resisted. "Bec? Did you see Bec? Did he come this way?"

"Don't worry about Bec. Vex is with him. The dog won't let him get lost . . . or hurt. Now, *come*!"

Soldt's temple passage was narrower and steeper and, though every bit as dark, it was somehow easier to follow. When the duelist warned, "Careful here, there are pits in the floor. Keep to the right until you're past the first, then move quickly to the left—" Cauvin remembered his own explorations and knew they had made it back to the Temple of Ils.

Once topside, Soldt attacked the rope ladder with a boot knife, but Cauvin had a better idea. He rammed his shoulder against the undermined marble column.

"Help me. We can bring it down and seal them in."

"They've got other ways," Soldt insisted, but he attacked the column from a different angle.

Bits of stone and dirt rained into the pit. Cauvin felt the column begin to shift.

"Once more, Soldt. Once more and run for the Promise. The whole outside wall could follow."

It didn't, but several blocks of marble tumbled from the roof piers and followed the column into the pit. Rats and mice could still use the passages to the Hand's bolt-hole, but larger creatures were sealed out.

Safe on the Promise of Heaven, Cauvin was ready to congratulate himself when Soldt said—

"Your arm's bleeding."

Cauvin had forgotten Leorin's parting gift. His sleeve was slashed and blood-soaked. He'd ruined another shirt. But the gash itself wasn't serious—just a flesh wound.

"Hang on," Soldt advised, "I'll clean it out." He extracted a leather bottle from a scrip beneath his cloak. "You'd better sit down for this."

"Not now. I've got to get back to the stoneyard. I've got to know that Bec's safe—"

Soldt rapped Cauvin on the breastbone. He staggered, tripped, and wound up where Soldt wanted him: sitting on the weedy steps of the Temple of Ils.

"First things first, lad. Lord Torchholder charged me with keeping you alive, and I'm not about to fail him. The only thing the Hand loves more than blood is poison. It's second nature to them, like breathing—"

"Leorin didn't have time to load her knife," Cauvin protested and started to rise.

Soldt rapped him again. "It wasn't her knife, she pulled it off the corpse. Sit still. You're fortunate that I know as much about poisons as the Hand."

"You saw?"

"I put that arrow through his skull." Soldt opened his cloak, letting Cauvin see the odd-looking bow slung below his shoulder.

"And the fire arrows?"

Soldt shook his head. "Not mine. Not arrows, either." He unstoppered the leather bottle with his teeth. "We had help back there."

"Friends of the Torch?"

"Not hardly," Soldt snorted. "That fire stank of magic, and I can't say that Lord Torchholder's got any friends among the wizards and hazards, but the Hand hunts magi with a special vengeance, and they return the favor. I didn't think there were any master magi holed up in Sanctuary, then again, I didn't think there was a nest of Dyareelans under the Temple of Ils, either. Brace yourself, lad—this will sting a bit."

Frog all, the thick, green ooze Soldt squeezed on Cauvin's wound did a lot worse than sting. It blackened his flesh and filled his nose with acid vapors. Burning agony shot up his arm while Soldt advised the impossible—

"Try not to move," and squeezed out another knuckle-sized dollop.

The pain spread up his arm, worse than the first time, and then, thank all the god-damned gods, Cauvin felt nothing at all.

# Chapter Nineteen

"Furzy feathers! Dog! Stop pulling!"

Bec put both hands on the leather strap binding him to the huge brindle dog. The dog looked over its shoulder but, rather than give Bec another chance to loosen the strap that bound them together, the dog lowered its head and pulled harder.

Bec had had a chance to get free at the bottom of a pit that turned out to be inside the old Temple of Ils on the Promise of Heaven. The dog hadn't wanted to climb the shaky, rope ladder hanging in the pit. With nowhere to go, Bec could have sat in the dirt and worked the knot loose, climbed out, and left Soldt's dog behind. But there at the bottom of the pit, when he hadn't been certain whether the Hand was chasing him, Bec hadn't wasted time on the knot, he'd gotten behind the dog and pushed it up the ladder.

Truth to tell—Bec didn't really want to loosen the knot. He'd welcomed the dog's strength and its confidence underground. He'd been living a nightmare—caught in a sack, dumped in a cage, yelled at, threatened, dragged in front of a *horrible* statue that was half-man and half-woman. Then—when he'd thought the nightmare couldn't get worse—there was Cauvin side by side with Leorin (who was Hand, through and through), saying things that *couldn't* be true, knocking him down, and telling him to get out . . . or else.

Bec had run for his life. He hadn't wanted to leave Cauvin, but Cauvin was so different, and he was so scared. He'd even forgotten which hand Cauvin had told him to keep on the wall by the time Soldt found him.

*Follow Vex.* Soldt had said, tying the strap around Bec's wrist. *He'll take you to the stoneyard.*

Bec tried to tell Soldt what had happened, but Soldt whispered a few foreign words to the dog. It started pulling, and it hadn't stopped.

"Dog! Slow down!"

Bec pulled back on the strap again. It was morning—maybe a couple hours past dawn—and they were charging toward Pyrtanis Street—which was good. Except people were coming out of their houses with night jars and there'd be trouble if a boy and a dog tripped someone carrying a night jar. Especially a big, ugly dog and a filthy boy who'd lost his shirt. Momma always said that the safest children were the cleanest children, the quietest children, the children who didn't race about or get in the way of adults. Bec couldn't control the dog, replace his missing shirt, or wash away the soot he'd picked up in the underground, but he could keep quiet.

He did more than keep quiet, he prayed to Shipri because She was supposed to take care of children.

Shipri must have been listening because none of the scowling mothers or fathers along the Split tried to stop him or the dog. Better still, the stoneyard dog sensed them coming along Pyrtanis Street. It barked up a challenge which Soldt's dog answered with bone-chilling howls. That led to best of all, Momma and Poppa coming out the gate to meet him!

Bec didn't recognize the stout woman who opened the gate, but the dog did. When she said, "Vex!" and another word Bec didn't catch, the dog planted its tail on the ground and sat like a statue until Poppa cut through the knot at Bec's wrist. Momma was crying. Her eyes were so red, it was a wonder that her tears weren't red. Because she would touch him, then pull her hands away as though he was steaming hot, Bec feared she was more angry that he'd run off than glad to see him home.

He shouted, "I'm sorry!" and promised that he'd never run away, but that only made her cry harder.

Then Poppa scooped him up, and all the fear and pain, the cold, and even the hunger Bec had kept hidden from himself since Grandfather told him to hide in the bushes escaped. He forgot that he was too old for hugs and clung to his father with arms and legs together.

All of upper Pyrtanis Street must have known he was missing and must have heard the dogs announce his return. Batty Dol;

Honald—the potter, not the rooster; Teera; Cauvin's friend, Swift; Bilibot, Eprazian and the rest of the early-morning regulars at the Lucky Well, they all crowded into the stoneyard. Questions flew like summertime flies: What had happened? Where had he been? Had he been lost or stolen? How did he get away? Did he have help? Who . . . ? How . . . ? Where . . . ?

Bec tried to answer, but he couldn't string three words together before there was another question. Momma noticed that the cut on his forehead was bleeding again. She called for cloth and water and latched on to her son's ear—not gently at all—to get a better look. He told her that the cut didn't hurt nearly as much as the welts on his chest where the man they called Strangle had struck him with a long, nasty whip.

Those words were no sooner out of Bec's mouth than everyone wanted to see the marks, and Momma was trying to pull him out of Poppa's arms. It *was* Momma tugging on Bec's arms and he *did* know everyone in the yard—except for the stout woman holding on to Soldt's dog. Still, the tugging hurt, and all those voices, hands, and faces getting too close were frightening; and Bec had used up all his bravery. He did what he hadn't dared do underground: He closed his eyes and screamed.

Suddenly, Poppa was shaking sideways, like a baited bear, shouting at Momma and everyone else to back off. That only panicked Bec more. He couldn't think outside his terror until, after many long, black moments, he heard Poppa's voice saying:

"Easy. You're safe. No one's going to hurt you. No one."

Bec stopped screaming. He opened his eyes and found himself in Poppa's lap, in the kitchen, with Momma on her knees beside the chair and nobody—absolutely nobody else nearby. Momma had a mug of cider in one hand and a strip of linen in the other. She'd stopped crying, but her cheeks remained shiny wet. Bec took the mug when Momma offered it. He flinched when she touched his forehead with the damp linen.

"Patience, wife! Let the boy breathe. Do you want to start him off again?"

Momma started to cry again. Between sobs, she said, "My baby's hurt . . . my baby's hurt . . ." and neither Bec nor Poppa could stop her from daubing away the soot on his arms.

The water was cold because the hearth was cold. In all his life Bec had never known his mother to let the kitchen hearth go stone cold. He knew then that Momma had been as scared as he and gave her a hug, before wiggling out of Poppa's lap. Standing on his own two feet, Bec told them that he had to get to the ruins straightaway.

"Cauvin said Grandfather's dead. I've got to know—" Bec couldn't finish his thought. "I've got to go out there."

Momma said, "Cauvin. Cauvin! Lying again!" in her angriest voice, but fell quiet when Poppa snarled at her.

"Cauvin's been gone since yesterday, Bec, but Lord Torchholder's up in the loft. After the storm, when you hadn't come home, Cauvin took me out to the ruins. We were looking for you, but I brought Lord Torchholder here—"

Bec lunged for the door. Poppa caught him by the belt. Bec struggled, but there was no getting away from Poppa.

"Lord Torchholder's at death's doorstep. He didn't wake up when I looked in on him at sunrise and, son, it's not likely that he will wake up again. Cauvin told you the truth—"

"No-o-o-o," Bec wailed and stopped struggling. "He *lied*. He *lied* about everything. He had to."

"The Torch was a very old man, Bec—he was an old man when I was your age."

Bec slipped toward blind fear again. If Grandfather was dead, then Grandfather had lied when he'd promised that "*Nothing's wrong. There's nothing to fear*" right before Bec sneaked off to find a hiding place. Bec had known, of course, that something was wrong when he was hauled out of his bramble-bush hiding place, but Momma and Poppa both said that sometimes a thing had to get worse before it got better, so he'd held on to his belief in Grandfather's words. Until now.

"It's not *fair*!"

"Not many things are, Bec," Poppa said, and relaxed his grip on Bec's belt.

That was all the wriggle room Bec needed. He was out the kitchen door in a flash, running past Batty Dol, the stout woman, and Soldt's dog; past a horse he'd never seen before and up the ladder to Cauvin's loft shouting, "Grandfather!" at every step.

A thousand spiders, at least, had spun their webs over the loft hole. Bec couldn't see the spiders, but he felt the webs—sticky strands that stung wherever they touched his skin. When he opened his mouth to shout "Grandfather!" they stuck to his tongue, where they tasted gagging awful. He started crying again—twice in one day!—but he drove himself through the webs, shouting, "Grandfather!" between sobs.

Four rungs from the top of the ladder, Bec got his head into the loft where the air smelled of thunderstorms. Cauvin's pallet was in the center of the loft, and there was something shaped like a sleeping man stretched across it.

"Grandfather? Grandfather, are you awake? Are you alive?"

A faint voice came from the pallet. "Boy? Is that you, boy?"

"I'm not 'boy,' I'm *Bec*—!"

"Fetch my staff, boy. It's on the floor between there and here."

If Grandfather was giving orders, then Grandfather was himself, and Bec was reassured. He found the blackwood staff scarcely an arm's length from the pallet. He nudged what he thought was a shoulder and leapt away when Grandfather opened strange, fiery eyes. Without thinking, he held the staff crosswise before him.

Grandfather groaned and his bones crackled as he sat up. "Where have you been?"

Bec opened his mouth, but he found himself unable to speak unless he admitted that he didn't exactly know. "They tied a cloth over my eyes, but I was in a cave and in a temple on the Promise of Heaven when I got out."

"Who were you with?"

He had to be truthful, perfectly truthful, or his tongue simply wouldn't move. "A dog. A *big* dog. He pulled me through the cave tunnels, then he pulled me home."

"Before that, boy—who tied the cloth over your eyes?"

"I think—" Bec's tongue grew thick and clumsy but he slowly got the words out: "I think it was the Hand, the Bloody Hand of Dyareela. Leorin was there—Cauvin's Leorin. She was with Cauvin . . ." Bec didn't want to tell Grandfather what Cauvin had said and done, but he had to tell the truth. Had to. "Cauvin *stayed* with them, with *her* and the other bad people, but he made me leave. When I wouldn't leave without him, he hit me—he hit me harder than all the Hands put together—and told me you were dead and the Hand had made a mistake taking me instead of him. I was scared, Grandfather—I didn't know what to do except run away before he hit me again."

"And the dog? Did Soldt give you the dog?"

"Yes," Bec answered truthfully, but there was more. He didn't know how he could have forgotten, but Grandfather's questions were like keys unlocking doors in his memory. "I had help," Bec whispered. "Cauvin told me to keep a hand on the wall, but I forgot which hand and I went the wrong way. I ran into a *monster*!"

Furzy feathers, Bec couldn't describe the monster without using his arms to show Grandfather how big it had been. He put the staff down.

"Don't let go of the staff!"

Bec snatched it up again.

"Now, tell me what you saw."

"I didn't *see* it." Bec kept his hands tight around the wood. "I ran into it because it was as big as the whole tunnel. And it had *arms*! Lots of arms—well, *maybe* arms but maybe legs, too—like a crab's? They were hard and sharp, kind of cold and wet. They made *noise* when they picked me up. It had strange eyes—" Bec clamped his teeth together, but the need to tell the truth was stronger than his jaw muscles. "Like yours, Grandfather, kind of. They were sunset-colored and they *glowed* in the dark and they *moved*—" Bec desperately wanted to show Grandfather how the glowing spots had drifted apart from each other, but Grandfather had told him to keep hold of the staff, and he was afraid to disobey.

"Did this monster say anything to you?"

Bec thought *yes,* but "Maybe" was the word that came out of his mouth. "I heard a voice, but—but it didn't seem to come from the monster."

"A man's voice?"

Bec nodded confidently, "Deep, deeper than Poppa's."

"What did he tell you to do?"

"He said I was going the wrong way. He said I should turn around or I'd be back where I started."

"And did you turn around?"

"Furzy feathers, Grandfather! It was a *monster*. It would have *eaten* me if I didn't!"

Grandfather laughed—Grandfather hadn't been there in the dark; it hadn't been at all funny, even though the monster had told Bec the truth, and he'd found Soldt again shortly afterward. Then Grandfather coughed and started to choke. Bec dropped the staff. He knelt beside the pallet and pounded gently between Grandfather's shoulder blades. The spasm slowly stopped.

"Are you better now, Grandfather?"

"Better? I'm alive, that's better than death. Pick up the staff." Bec did and offered it to Grandfather, who refused it. "What did you tell the Hand, Bec?"

Bec sprang to his feet and shouted, "Nothing!" but that was an outright lie, and immediately he felt his veins filling with fire. "All right! All right! When she saw me—when she recognized me—Leorin gave me something to drink. I wasn't sure if I could trust her, so I took a baby sip and it was *vile,* so I spat it out. She made men hold my arms and pull my hair back 'til I couldn't keep my mouth closed no matter how hard I tried, then she poured it into my mouth. I tried to spit it back at her—I *tried,* but the men, they held my nose and I swallowed. I *had* to swallow. I couldn't *not* swallow. They didn't care when I told them that my stomach hurt afterward, just asked lots of questions—like you're asking now—only they wanted to know about you and Cauvin and what we did at the ruins.

"I wouldn't answer, so they brought another boy to sit beside me. He answered the questions. I yelled at him to be quiet, but my stomach was real sore, and I couldn't stop him, no matter how hard I tried. Some of the things that other boy said were stupid lies, but he told the truth, too. I couldn't make him stop."

Grandfather shook his head. "You need not blame yourself that you answered their questions truthfully. They gave you a potion to separate your conscience from your knowledge. There was no other little boy—"

"There was!" Bec insisted, and his blood didn't boil. "He didn't even look like me. I wouldn't talk to *her*. I wouldn't talk to any of them!"

"Very well, there was another boy. Did that other boy make any promises? Did he promise to do something at another time or when he saw or heard some specific thing—a word, perhaps, or an image?"

"No!" Bec replied, still indignant. "They tried. They twisted my arm until it hurt real bad and the big, mean one—Strangle, I think, was his name—he lashed his whip across my chest and told me that there were bugs in the cave and they would burrow into the cuts he'd made and they'd eat me from the inside out. Then they heated an iron poker in the fire 'til it was red-hot and held it so close to my eyes that I could feel the heat coming off; and Strangle said he'd stick it in my eye if I didn't promise to do what the other boy promised to do. But I scared that other boy away and told Strangle to sit on his froggin' poker! That's when *she* tied me up again and dumped me in a cage. Strangle said they'd come back; and they did. And I was afraid because . . . because I didn't know if I could scare that other boy off again. Then I heard Cauvin and thought everything was going to be all right—

"But it's *not,* Grandfather—it's *not*. The questions they asked—it didn't matter what the other boy said, because no matter what they did to me, I didn't know what they wanted to know. I told them your stories— The other boy told them. But they weren't what Strangle wanted. He asked questions in languages I didn't know. Cauvin won't know them either, but he told Strangle he was your heir. Grandfather—he *lied* to them . . . He's made himself one of them, but he *lied,* too. And when Strangle asks those questions, he won't be able to answer them. He doesn't even understand Imperial. Strangle will hurt—" No, that wasn't the truth. "Strangle will *kill* him. Strangle and Leorin will kill Cauvin!

"You *lied* to me! You *lied*! You said nothing was wrong, that everything would be all right. It's not. It's not—!"

"That's enough!" Grandfather declared. "Give me my staff now." He pulled the blackwood out of Bec's hands. "You were in no danger of being eaten. That man you met in the tunnels—and he is a man, no monster. That man is the greatest mage in Sanctuary and, perhaps, the entire world. His name is Enas Yorl and, as Vashanka will be my judge, I thought he'd escaped this city years ago. But my loss—his loss—is Sanctuary's gain. Do you know the empty corner between here and the Crossing?"

"Batty Dol says it's haunted. Momma says it's not, but she won't let me play there."

"I think both are right. That's the corner where Enas Yorl's house stood, and if he's still in Sanctuary, then his house is, too—sometimes. And it would seem, as well, that he still pays heed to what happens to his neighbors—"

Bec saw hope. "Does that mean he's killed Strangle and Leorin, crushed the Hand, and gotten Cauvin safe away?"

Grandfather took Bec's hand in his own. Being touched by him was as bad as being touched by that monster-magician, but Bec held his breath and didn't have to run away.

"I don't know, Bec, but if I believe you—and I know I can—then Soldt and Enas Yorl were both watching out for you and Cauvin. They saved you, with Cauvin's help—"

Bec pulled his hand away. "That's not good enough, Grandfather. Can't we do something?"

"A dying old man and a boy short of his full growth? No, Bec, there's nothing we can do except wait . . . and pray. Have you prayed?"

"I prayed to Shipri on the way home." Bec lowered his eyes, ashamed to be his mother's son and admit that he prayed to a Wriggle goddess.

"Then pray to Shipri again. Pray to them all. I prayed to my god when I knew I was dying. He sent me Cauvin. If he ever decides to claim it, your brother has everything that's mine to give, including my luck. And except for leaving Sanctuary, I've been a very lucky man—though I was an old and dying man before I understood—"

"Bec!" The voice was Momma's, and she was below the loft. "Becvar! I'm making breakfast. Fresh eggs and all the rashers of bacon you can eat!"

Bec's mouth watered. He glanced longingly at the hole in the floor. The ladder creaked—

"Furzy feathers! Momma! Don't!"

Momma didn't like spiders. If she got caught by the webs Bec had battled, she'd fall for sure. But her head and shoulders grew through the hole, no trouble at all.

"Come down from here. It's all—" Momma said, then she noticed Grandfather sitting up with his staff raised beside him. In her best Imperial, she said, "Lord Torchholder. You're—You're—What can I do for you, Lord Torchholder?"

"You can bring your son's breakfast to him when it's ready. He will be eating it here with me."

"Yes, my lord. The eggs are fresh, my lord, and the bacon's the best we can afford, but our bread's gone stale, and we have no wine that's worthy of a lord."

"Don't worry yourself, mistress; I shall not be eating. I've eaten enough for one lifetime. Now, hurry, mistress, he's a boy, and he's hungry!"

Bec had never seen his mother overwhelmed before. She begged Grandfather to taste her eggs and bacon, or maybe her porridge. It was Momma's life wish, she said—her late father's life wish—to serve a great lord a meal from her table. Grandfather relented and asked for a single egg, boiled in water.

"An honor, my lord. The honor of my life," Momma said on her way down the ladder. "I shall be forever grateful."

Once she was gone, Bec scampered over to the hole, looking for spiderwebs.

"What are you doing?" Grandfather asked.

"There were spiderwebs when I came up the ladder." He stirred his arm in the empty gap. "Sticky, stinging spiderwebs. Momma hates spiders. She's afraid of them. Where'd they go?"

"Your Momma hadn't been consorting with the Bloody Hand of Dyareela."

Bec stiffened. "I did *not.* I'm not old enough to consort!"

"But you had been within their sphere, and they had both tried and tempted you. The warding detected that."

"Warding?" Bec folded his arm close against his belly. Bilibot told tales about warding in winter, and Eprazian claimed he could cast a warding spell, though he never had. "Would I . . . ?"

Grandfather nodded.

"Why can't I feel it anymore?"

"Because you are a very brave young man. We wouldn't be here right now if I'd had the wit to set wards like that before the storm."

"Is it still there?"

"Very definitely. When Soldt and your brother return, we shall likely hear some very rude language."

Bec stared at the floor below. "Unless he *succumbed.*" Grandfather didn't reply. Bec waited a few moments before asking: "Are you dying, Grandfather?"

"I'm past dying, boy. I should have died yesterday. I would have—if your brother had listened to my directions and gone to the palace instead of visiting his ladylove. Now, I could say that was bad luck all around, or I can count myself fortunate to have one last breakfast with you, because, sitting here, I realize that I've forgotten to tell you a story. It's a very important story, especially if our prayers aren't answered.

"I need to tell you the story of a man who waited—"

Bec wasn't interested in a story. "If you die, what happens to the warding?"

"It will last a little while."

"And then? What happens to Momma and Poppa and me if our prayers aren't answered?"

"They will be— You must have faith if you expect the gods to answer your prayers. Cauvin will know how to set wards. He'll struggle at first. The knowledge won't come naturally to him— He'll need your help. Imagine I showed you a letter written in Old High Yenized. Could you copy it? Not read it or write a reply, only copy it, letter for letter, word for word?"

Bec nodded. "Can you teach me how to copy wards, Grandfather?"

"No, but I tell you what—when I'm gone, you can have my staff."

"What if Cauvin doesn't come back?"

Grandfather closed his eyes. He rubbed the wrinkles between his eyebrows and groaned a little. When he reopened his eyes they were noticeably dimmer. Patting the straw beside him, Grandfather said, "Come, Bec. Sit beside me. Let me tell you the story—we haven't much time."

With a groan of his own, Bec dragged his feet to the pallet. "If you say so, Grandfather."

"If only your brother felt the same way. The man I'm going to tell you about was named Hakiem—"

"Was? He's dead?"

"I should think so. He was some years older than I, and I've become the oldest man I know not cursed with eternal life. But perhaps he still sits comfortably in a Beysib garden. The last time I saw him—which I did not know would be the last time—he said the climate there was better suited to a man's declining years."

"Beysib? Hakiem was a *fish*?"

"Not at all. Hakiem was born in Sanctuary, just like you. We were very much alike, Hakiem and I, though I did not realize that for many years, each men of fixed desires whose lives wandered far from the courses we'd charted in our youths. Of course, my desire was to build a great temple for my god atop Graystorm Mountain overlooking the Imperial city. Hakiem's desire was to get drunk as often as mortally possible and as cheaply . . ."

Some men could command respect dressed in nothing but fishnet and rags. Other men might dress themselves in the finest silks, visit the most skilled barbers, but wind up looking no better than a man dressed in fishnet and rags. Hakiem was one of the latter such men.

He was short of spine, of legs, and of arms; paunchy and sway-backed, cursed with a fickle beard and a head of hair that was neither bald nor full, straight nor curled, black nor gray. The gods had cheated him out of a second eyebrow; he suffered beneath a single bushy ridge that spanned his entire face and kept his eyes forever in shadow. His lower lip was pendulous, his teeth were crooked and the color of ancient ivory. His feet were splayed like a duck's and he waddled when he walked.

Not surprisingly, Hakiem pursued a sedentary life, preferably in the corner chair at a corner table with a good view of the commons—and all the doors—of a lively tavern where the wine was sweet enough to drink on an empty stomach. His favorite tavern, an establishment which met each of his demands with room to spare, was the Vulgar Unicorn, deep in the Maze. Unfortunately for Hakiem, the Unicorn's keepers would not let him sit in his favorite chair unless he bought a mug of wine to sip while he sat.

This uncompromising policy meant that before Hakiem could settle in for the day's main activity—getting drunk on no more than two mugs of wine—he needed to procure a small handful of copper padpols, or padpools as the little copper coins were known in those days. He could have gone to work for any number of merchants or artisans; Hakiem was literate in Sanctuary's two main tongues; Rankan and Ilsigi, and had a keen head for numbers, especially the numbers of profit. But, as he would explain to anyone who asked, working *for* someone else's establishment inevitably led to expectations and disappointment; and working for himself would have been worse.

Hakiem could have gone begging, except begging in Sanctuary meant giving away two coins for every three collected: one to whoever owned the spot where the beggar begged and the second to Moruth, the self-styled beggar king from Downwind. Hakiem knew the cut of Moruth's sails well enough to steer clear of him. Besides, though less than handsome, Hakiem wasn't disfigured, deformed, or simpleminded; and he had too much pride, too little patience for sitting behind an empty cup *begging* strangers to drop a coin in.

He chose a more active path to his daily encounter with the Unicorn's wine. Each morning, well after dawn, Hakiem would hie himself to wherever the largest crowds of Sanctuary were apt to congregate, settle his rump on the cushion he invariably carried under the folds of his wrinkled robe, and proclaim:

"Stories for the day. Stories of lovers. Stories of heroes. Stories for children, for women, and men. Histories and fantasies. Epical or poetical. Pay what you please—satisfaction guaranteed!"

Standing in the shadows of a rope-maker's stall, Molin Torchholder watched and listened as Sanctuary's only successful storyteller gathered his small crowd. Hakiem baited his audience with snippets from his best-known tales: the wedding of Ils and Shipri or the wedding of Savankala and Sabellia; the history of the world and the history of Sanctuary; the rise and fall of Jubal and his hawkmasks, the rise and devoutly hoped for fall of Tempus and the Stepsons. The pudgy little man got his audience vying against itself—a padpol for my favorite story; no, two padpols for mine; three, then four, until, finally, when Hakiem stood to earn seven padpols—more than enough for his daily libations at the Unicorn—for whichever story he told, he began the tale of the old fisherman and the giant crab for six padpols, divvied among his audience.

The tale of the fisherman's quest was a good story, a true one, and a short one. Molin had scarcely begun to sweat within his woolen robes when the audience dispersed. Hakiem collected his cushion and his coins. He began the waddle from the wharf where he'd told the story to the Unicorn.

Molin fell in step beside the storyteller.

"My Lord Archpriest! To what do I owe the honor of your august presence?" Hakiem bowed with a flourish that was more insolence than honor.

"Lord Molin will be sufficient. I would like to buy you a mug of the finest wine the Vulgar Unicorn can offer a thirsty man. I have a business proposition to discuss with you."

"If you're buying, then the finest wine can found on the Street of Red Lanterns—"

"But the houses are no place for men like ourselves to discuss business."

"You wish to have business with me?" The storyteller's mockery became concern. "At the Unicorn?"

"Stranger things have happened at the Unicorn. Will you accept my offer?"

"Depends on what it is, Lord Molin," the storyteller said, but he led the way to the Maze tavern.

Molin ordered a table jug of the Unicorn's best—and only—vintage. He paid for it with Imperial silver and left the change—a heap of Ilsigi padpools—on the table. He offered a toast—"May Anen see you home by starlight!" that brought a smile to the storyteller's lips.

The wine was Ilsigi; no Rankan god would claim it, though it was not unpleasant: a bit harsh, a bit rebellious—a good match for salt-sea air or a raw, winter's night. Molin topped off his mug before he began the discussion.

"I have been watching you, Hakiem, since I arrived in Sanctuary—"

The single eyebrow became a bushy, worried arch, which Molin ignored.

"I have seen how the tales you tell spread through the city until they become the truths that everyone believes. I've seen, too, how you never tell a fully tragic tale, but always leave a glimmer of hope and justice for the ending. That, too, spreads through Sanctuary."

Hakiem fussed with his empty mug, "The storyteller's art—"

"Is optimism." Molin reached across the table to replenish the storyteller's wine. "And you are a master." He tipped his mug. "Of storytelling *and* performance. Though your listeners do not seem to realize it, they rarely hear the stories they request. They hear the stories you wish to tell. Do they not?"

"The art is more than telling, it's listening. I hear what they want to hear; I tell them what needs to be told."

"Exactly!" Molin crowed. This was going better than he'd dared hope. "What the denizens of this gods-forsaken city need to hear. And I propose to give you a stipend—two minted-in-Ranke soldats each week—and two more right now in earnest, if you will tell specific stories to Sanctuary's denizens." He pushed four soldats across the table.

Hakiem puffed up his plump, pigeon breast. His cheeks bulged, and his knuckles were white as he pushed himself away from the table—away from a scarcely touched mug of wine.

"Keep your Rankan money," he snarled. "It can't buy me."

Molin's personal instinct was to let the storyteller go, but it wasn't personal need that brought him to the table. He pinched the tender spot on the bridge of his nose to lessen the throbbing pain that conversations in the local Ilsigi dialect so often produced. "I did not mean to insult you, Hakiem," he said with more difficulty than the storyteller could imagine. "Please, sit down. Let me try again. I've come to you because, of all the men I've met in Sanctuary, you're the only one who—I think—would choose to remain here, had you the opportunity to live somewhere else. You *love* this city. I'm not going to ask you to tell stories glorifying me, my prince, or my Empire."

The storyteller scooted his chair close to the table and took a swig from his mug. "Very well, I'm listening. If you don't want Imperial pandering—what stories, exactly, *do* you want me to tell?"

"I'll leave that up to you, of course."

Hakiem leapt to his feet. "I will not be made a fool of!"

"Then sit down," Molin hissed.

He was a priest of Vashanka. He'd commanded armies in the north and he could command a simple storyteller without raising his voice or leaving his chair. Hakiem's rump hit wood with an audible *thump!*

"I am not interested in the particulars of your stories—well told and entertaining though they may be. I'm interested in the *effect* of your stories over time. Let it also be said that when I commission a master, I do not waste his time or mine telling him how to apply his craft. I care only for the result: the propagation of needful stories throughout Sanctuary."

Molin checked the two mugs on the table and found that his own was lower. He topped it off and continued—

"As an archpriest of Vashanka I am not only a priest of some stature, but also a commander of the Imperial army and a member of the Imperial court. Through my wife and by my own initiative I have acquired considerable property—none of which, I might add—lies in Sanctuary. As result of my far-flung interests, I stand at the confluence of communications flowing through the Empire and sometimes beyond its boundaries. In short, Hakiem: I hear things. I see things. I perceive patterns in events that others might consider unconnected. And of late the patterns I perceive have taken an ominous turn; throughout Ranke and beyond, the omens have been uncanny."

The storyteller's interest was piqued. "What does a man of your 'far-flung interests' consider *uncanny*?"

"The usual—two-headed roosters, hermaphrodite calves and lambs, a pig born without a heart, a boy-child born with its heart beating outside its ribs. I am, of course, able to conduct my own auguries here in Sanctuary. They're less dramatic, but somewhat more precise, and reluctantly I have concluded that dire days are coming throughout the Empire, especially here in Sanctuary."

"Worse than the hawkmasks?" Hakiem asked scornfully. "Worse than the damned Stepsons? Worse than a harbor filled with ships filled with people who don't *blink* and whose women bleed poison?"

"Regrettably, yes. Though it is true that Vashanka's priests are not generally known for their prognostications, I am convinced that we're confronting nothing less than a collapse of all things proper. I have intimations of tears in the fabric of existence—inversions of life and death, sorcery everywhere, and the annihilation of gods themselves."

Hakiem sipped his wine. "What can I possibly do to forestall the death of a god?"

"Nothing," Molin admitted. If he'd performed the rites properly, then the god marked for annihilation was his own god, Vashanka, and it would be regarded as a blessing by one and all, including—presumably—himself when it came. "There is an old Rankan proverb, older than the Empire: When two dragons fight, it does not matter which dragon wins, the grass will be scorched. I want you to fortify the grass."

"Fortify the grass?" the storyteller's eyebrow rose to a dangerous height.

"Yes, tell them stories about simple joys that cannot be taken away. Remind them that the genius of Sanctuary is its incorrigibility. If the city will not consent to be governed by tyranny or anarchy, then it must, in time, triumph over both. Make sure the people remember who they are—the children of slaves and pirates, yes, but survivors. Hakiem—so long as the people of Sanctuary do not forget who they are and what they can do simply by being themselves, then they will survive. That is what I expect for my two soldats a week—stories that will help Sanctuary survive the hard times I foresee."

Hakiem scowled and squinted. He looked at the soldats, then at Molin, and back again. Molin was certain the storyteller would scoop the coins into his purse. Instead, he pushed them away.

"No deal."

"What?" Molin sputtered. He knew Sanctuary's insolence—he'd just praised that very quality—but he'd thought there was a limit to its self-destructive stubbornness, individual and collective. "I cannot believe what I'm hearing. Have you ever been offered two soldats a week for *anything*?"

"Never," Hakiem admitted.

"Have you even the sense of an ant? Bad times are coming . . . horrid times. Sanctuary *needs* you, Hakiem. I'm offering you the means to serve your beloved city! Have you listened to a word I've said?"

Hakiem nodded. "Every word. Now, you listen to mine, Lord High-and-Mighty Molin Torchholder. I will not take your soldats because you're right—Sanctuary is my home, and I do not need coins to serve her. I would do anything in my power to 'fortify' my neighbors if even half of your dire omens came to pass. But that is not the only reason; I won't take your Rankan money because conscience cannot be bought."

"I am appealing to your conscience, not trying to buy it!"

"And I am not speaking of *my* conscience, Lord Molin. I'm speaking of *yours*. I see it in your eyes, hear it in your voice. You believe you have been cursed by Sanctuary and you think that by giving me two soldats each week, you can free yourself from the curse. Have you listened to yourself? You say that you despise Sanctuary, but your passions betray you. Look at yourself—you're not a golden-haired, golden-eyed Rankan. Your fellow priests resent you. The Imperial court suspects you. And your wife's glorious family regards you as no better than . . . no—*worse* than a gutter-scum Wrigglie off the streets of Sanctuary.

"You've come home, Lord Molin. You love Sanctuary as I love it, but you can't admit it, so you call your love a curse. More's the pity, Lord Molin—you've blinded yourself to happiness, and I will have no part of it."

"Not at all," Molin protested. "You're wrong. I'll be gone from here before any of what I've foreseen comes to pass. I'll be gone. I won't die here. I won't—

"I won't die here. I won't—"

Grandfather slumped sideways on the pallet. His whole body trembled.

"Momma!" Bec shouted, because he'd heard her lurking at the bottom of the ladder, waiting for Grandfather to finish his story. "Momma! He's dying, Momma! Grandfather's dying!"

The box was a masterpiece of woodcarvers' art, inlaid with stones carefully chosen to complement the wood grain. The scrollwork vines and leaves were so lifelike that Cauvin expected to hear them rustle when he touched them. Yet for all its advanced beauty, the box was kin to the boxes he'd received from Sinjon at the Broken Mast and dug out of the bazaar dirt. When he place his thumbs on the familiar spots, the vines and scrolls separated, and the lid opened.

"What's in it?"

"What has my friend the Torch been hiding all these years? Where does he keep his gold?"

The first voice was Soldt's, the second belonged to Arizak per-Mizhur, lord of the Irrune—the man who had brought Cauvin to this bright, sunlit room on the southeast corner of the palace.

"Nothing—" Cauvin began, because in such a box a scrap of dirty parchment was nothing.

Then, before Cauvin could mention the paper, his nostrils filled with the scents of flowers, spices, and the sea. With the scents came . . . memory. He knew where the Torch's treasure was—all the places, all the gold, the jewels, and the names of Arizak's mistresses—all of them. To say nothing of the thousand other secrets the Torch had hoarded.

Cauvin braced himself. The myths of the Empire and Ilsig alike were lousy with men who'd lost themselves to gods or sorcerers but the assault on his sense of self didn't happen. He was simply the Torch's heir, beneficiary of property, not personality. Cauvin figured he'd need the rest of his natural lifetime to sort through his inheritance, but he could already feel a difference.

How else had he known—not guessed, but froggin' sure *known*—that he remained himself?

"What about it, Cauvin?" Soldt asked. "I see something in there."

Cauvin unfolded the parchment. "It says, 'Fortify the grass.' "

Soldt's comment was, "Odd," while Arizak, a true herdsman, said, "Only a complete fool builds forts on grass."

But Cauvin remembered his friend—the Torch's friend—Hakiem in a hundred different conversations, all of which ended with the same sentiment: *We certainly fortified the grass today, didn't we?* He hid a smile behind his hand and returned the paper to the box.

"We're done here," he told the other two men.

"He was a strange one," Arizak said, leading them slowly from the room.

The Irrune used a padded crutch to get around and never put any weight on his heavily wrapped foot. Cauvin wondered if there even was a foot within the bandages. His inheritance quickened, and he recalled the night when he—or rather the Torch—sat by Arizak's shoulder, holding his hand while a physician summoned from Caronnne performed the amputation.

This would take some getting used to.

He missed the start of Arizak's eulogy.

—"To call him friend was to give your fate to a summer storm.

Are you certain the Hand invades Sanctuary from below? All this burrowing in rock and hardened sand, it would not be a problem if we dwelt in tents. Live in a tent, and your enemies can only come at you like the wind."

Cauvin waited until he was certain Arizak had finished speaking—the inheritance let him know that the froggin' Irrune never interrupted their froggin' chief—before saying, "We're sure. And the Hand's not just below the palace, *Sakkim*—" that was the froggin' Irrune word for sheep-shite leader-of-many-chosen-by-all. "The Hand's *in* the palace, too. I saw your son, Naimun, speaking to the very bastard Soldt killed with his arrow."

Arizak hobbled away, saying nothing. Cauvin guessed he'd froggin' offended the man. There was another Irrune word, *Bas*-something, for the *Sakkim's* sons but just because he knew the right words didn't mean Cauvin was going to froggin' use them. He wasn't Lord Molin Torchholder. They were in a ground-floor corridor, headed for Arizak's private quarters, before the Irrune chief spoke again.

"I am disappointed in my son, but not truly surprised. He is the image of my wife's brother, and it would appear that he has Teo's love of treachery, as well. Verrezza will rejoice, but the one Naimun should truly fear is his mother. Nadalya won't forgive treachery. But that's family. What am I to do with these Hand below the palace?"

"Smoke them out," Cauvin suggested. "Build a wet-wood fire in the pit at Temple of Ils, then use bellows to drive the smoke through the warren. Post your men throughout the city and outside the walls, too—to watch for men escaping. And smoke—wherever they see smoke, they'll find an entrance to the warren—"

Both Soldt and Arizak stared at him.

"It works with froggin' rats," Cauvin explained. And Teera the baker did smoke out the storerooms every fall, but the idea hadn't come from Teera. The Torch had used wet-wood fires to flush the enemy out of caves along the Empire's northern frontier some sixty years earlier.

"Throw some camphor wood on your fire, and you can use dogs to help you sort the Hand out," Soldt added.

Arizak wasn't comfortable with the plan. "This will be a very large fire. Very dangerous."

"For the Hand. The other choice is to send your men into the dark."

"Ah, yes, it would be very dark underground. Without light, men could get lost, killed. Better those men are not Irrune, not Wrigglies." As far as Arizak was concerned, all the people of Sanctuary were Wrigglies—it was an improvement over the Irrune word for anyone not born into the tribe.

"No matter what we do," Cauvin warned, "a few will escape—just as they did last time. We got lazy. We can't make the same mistake again. The Hand won't go away, not in our lifetimes."

"Not in mine," Arizak agreed. "I will speak with my commanders—only Irrune, at least until we've winnowed the Hand from the palace. My wife Nadalya will say that we need that Savankh she's always talking about. How else to know whether a Wrigglie is lying?" He looked Cauvin in the eye. "Can you bring my wife this great Savankh?"

Yesterday, the Torch had been ready to turn over both the Savankh and the Necklace of Ils. Cauvin wasn't the Torch. "I'll see what I can do."

"Listen to him!" Arizak exclaimed to Soldt. "He has an idea—He'll see what he can do—I have heard this all before. Next he will be telling me that he is but a poor man and reminding me that Sanctuary is the least of the Imperial cities. He does not have my old friend's voice, but already he has begun to talk like him!"

It was late afternoon before Cauvin left the palace, finally satisfied that the Irrune were hauling green wood over to the Promise of Heaven. They'd have a smoky fire burning by sunset, which might be too late, but was the best they could do. Soldt agreed to stay with Arizak. The duelist wasn't pleased to be seen in the company of Sanctuary's prince, but Cauvin had been a night without sleep before he'd opened the Torch's froggin' box. The weight of the old pud's memories had left him pillow-walking and scarcely able to string a thought together in any of the odd languages whose words were rattling around in his mind.

Arizak had suggested he settle into the old pud's palace apartment—three unremarkable chambers, including the one where he'd opened the ornate box. Cauvin would use them, or more accurately, he would use what they contained. The Torch was a froggin' pack rat—

Had been.

The Torch *had been* a froggin' pack rat, and Cauvin was still a sheep-shite stone-smasher. He wouldn't hazard a guess how he'd feel in a month or a year, but for the time being, Cauvin didn't want to sleep in a dead man's bed no matter how tired he was. Cauvin wanted to go home, to the stoneyard, his foster parents, and—especially—to Bec. His hand still stung from striking his brother. It had been the right thing to do; he hadn't known Soldt had followed him and Leorin into the warren or that the magician, Enas Yorl, had his own quarrels with the Mother of Chaos. Still, right or not, Cauvin had to apologize.

The stoneyard gate was closed and barred. Cauvin didn't have the strength to scale the wall. He rang the bell and waited for someone to let him in. The yard dog set up a racket, but there was a second dog in the chorus.

Vex.

If Vex was in the stoneyard, then Bec was, too. Since he'd come to on the steps of the Thunderer's temple, Cauvin hadn't allowed himself to think anything else. Soldt swore the dog was dependable, but Soldt also insisted that Cauvin had to go to the palace before he went home.

Vex was barking. Vex was here. Bec was home. Bec was safe. Cauvin slumped against the wall and began to shiver. He straightened up as the gate swung open, but couldn't stop shaking. Grabar looked Cauvin over in silence and made him feel like a ghost—an unwelcome ghost. Grabar had come to the gate with a stone mallet in his hand, and he wasn't about to let his foster son cross the threshold.

"Bec?" Cauvin asked, suddenly fearful that he'd leapt to the wrong conclusion when he'd heard a second dog barking.

"Here," Grabar answered. "The boy said you'd gone over to the Hand. That your woman had been over for years."

Mina, standing beside Grabar, added, "You struck him. You knocked him down and made him bleed." Her look said she would never forgive Cauvin for that.

That was more injustice than Cauvin intended to bear. He

pounded his fist against the gate planks. Mina jumped back in surprise, while Grabar tightened up on the mallet.

"I was trying to save his life!" Cauvin complained. "Bec wouldn't *go*. He wouldn't leave without me unless I scared him or hurt him or both, so I hit him. I hit him good, and he started running." The inheritance assured Cauvin that his plan was nothing to be ashamed of, it didn't assure his foster parents. "Froggin' sure, I'm sorry I hit him. Shite for sure, I thought I was going to die, and you froggin' know I'm not made much for thinking."

Neither Mina nor Grabar was convinced.

"The boy said you'd gone over to the Hand," Grabar repeated. "Don't see how we can trust you."

"I froggin' didn't go 'over to the Hand.' I told Leorin I'd submit to the froggin' Mother, so she'd take me to their lair. I told the froggin' Whip I'd submit, so he'd let Bec go. I froggin' told Bec, so he'd get the froggin' hell out of there. I didn't think I was getting out of there alive, but, no froggin' way did I go 'over to the Hand.'

"Shite for sure, didn't Bec tell you that Soldt was there, too? That's Soldt's damn dog I hear barking! Soldt put an arrow through the skull of the Hand's high priest. There was a magician there, too—maybe Enas Yorl himself—lobbing fire left and right. If I'd froggin' known they'd be there, I'd have done froggin' different. When Soldt and I made it out, we went to the froggin' palace first—I'm sorry about that, too; I froggin' should've come here—but Arizak believed me. Arizak's got the guards and his Irrune building a wet-wood fire in the Temple of Ils. Go up to the froggin' Promise right now if you don't believe me—"

Grabar lowered the mallet and let Cauvin into the stoneyard—over Mina's scowled objection. "We only know what the boy knew."

"Shite." Cauvin could have dropped to the ground and slept for a week, but he couldn't, not yet. "Where is he? Where's Bec? Where have you got the Torch laid out? Arizak's sending a cart for the body. There can't be another funeral, but he's claiming it just the same."

"Comes now, it comes early. Lord Torchholder's not dead yet."

"Frog all?"

Cauvin spun toward the work shed just in time to see Bec coming out with the Torch's big black staff in both hands. The staff was longer than the boy was tall. When Bec tried to point it, spearlike, at Cauvin's heart, the amber finial bobbed unsteadily. Cauvin wrenched it effortlessly from Bec's grasp.

He asked, "Do you know what this is? What it does?" because Cauvin knew that the Savankh Lord Serripines kept in his Land's End vault was the Savankh of Sihan in the northeast corner of the Empire. The Torch had stuffed Sanctuary's Savankh down the shaft of the blackwood staff.

"It makes you have to tell the truth."

"So, froggin' ask."

"Are you one of them—a Bloody Hand like *her*?"

"No. Not now, not ever."

That was all Bec needed to hear. He ran straight at Cauvin, and maybe it was simply that Cauvin was bone-weary, or maybe Bec had grown some in the past few days, but Bec knocked Cauvin off-balance and they wound up on the ground.

Cauvin had told the shite-for-sure truth while he held the blackwood staff, not that it mattered. The Torch could lie left and right when he held his staff and the Savankh within it. Cauvin had inherited that treacherous, little ability. But the other powers of the staff—how it started fires where fire shouldn't ever burn and the way it had kept the Torch alive since the attack—those were shrouded secrets. Cauvin would need time—not to mention sleep—before he understood them, if he ever did.

Just then Cauvin used the staff's most ordinary strength and steadied himself against it as he stood.

"Grandfather said I could keep the his staff"—Bec held out his hand—"because I might be needing it, if— But you're back! And everything's going to be just the way it was—except you're going to get rid of the Hand . . . and *her*?"

"Arizak is," Cauvin replied. He doubted that anything was going to be the same, but there was no reason to say that—the staff didn't compel him to tell the truth. "And Grabar tells me the Torch isn't dead yet. Maybe he'll change his mind about giving you the staff. Maybe you will—if it means you've got to tell the truth all the time."

Bec's jaw dropped, and so did his arm. Cauvin kept a straight face until Grabar started laughing. Mina scolded them both, but even that sounded good to Cauvin—a sign that some things wouldn't ever change.

Cauvin went up the loft ladder first, pausing to clear out a gods-all-be-damned infestation of spiderwebs that had sprung up overnight. His shoulders hadn't cleared the floor hole when the Torch whispered his name. The lamp was lit and sitting in the sandbox near the Torch's head. Shite for sure, the old pud didn't look that much worse than he'd looked eight days before in the Temple of Ils. His breathing sounded odd, though, and the fire was gone from his eyes when he opened them.

"Come here, Cauvin." The Torch's skeletal arm rose a handspan above the straw.

Cauvin knelt. He took the old pud's hand, but didn't say anything. His mind was crammed with memories of a life he hadn't lived and, despite its moments of heroism and sacrifice, Cauvin wasn't tempted to say "thank you" for the rest.

"Do well, Cauvin. Do better than I did."

Cauvin squeezed the hand he held. He still had nothing to say, but breathed in the Torch's slowing rhythm until the old pud's chest no longer moved. Cauvin let his held breath out with a sigh and swept his hand over the sightless eyes to close them.

"Is he . . . ?" Bec asked from the ladder.

Cauvin nodded. "It's over for him."

With a rending wail, Bec fell across the Torch's body, but for Cauvin, it was just beginning.

# Epilog

Winter had settled into Sanctuary. A raw wind blew off the sea, and snowflakes swirled through the air, never touching the ground. Two months had passed since Cauvin's first visit to the Torch's rooms. Most of the furnishings had been claimed by those who lived full-time in the palace. Only camp stools, scroll-filled racks, and a herd of locked chests remained.

Cauvin stood back from the open window, avoiding the worst of the wind and beyond the sight of anyone in the forecourt who might be looking his way. His hands were cold and the finger that bore the Torch's black-onyx ring was coldest of all. He wasn't used to the ring. It got in the way when he laid red brick for the front of Tobus's new house. Most days he left the ring buried in the lamp-box sand in the loft.

Cauvin wore the ring when he went about on the Torch's business or when he wore "good" clothes. This day he was doing both: honoring the old pud's memory and wearing the soft suede breeches and linen shirt that Mina—not Galya—had stitched up for him. They'd come to an understanding, he and Mina—or she'd come to an understanding once she'd realized that Cauvin had the power to do more for her and Bec than she could possibly hope to do to him. Mina called him "son" now, and divvied the bacon equally among her three men.

A blare of trumpets commanded Cauvin's attention. He abandoned a daydream—less a daydream than another voyage through the Torch's memories—to watch four carts rumble under an archway on the far side of the courtyard. There were twenty-three men and woman in the carts—the survivors of Arizak's campaign to purge Sanctuary of Dyareela's reborn influence. The wet-wood smoke and subsequent searches flushed out forty-one disciples of the Bloody Hand, but when it came to interrogations the Irrune needed no lessons from their prisoners.

And when it came to executions, Cauvin couldn't help but think that Leorin had been right: There was nothing wrong with a little terror, infrequently applied against those who everyone agreed deserved it.

The twenty-three prisoners had been bound hand and foot before they entered the forecourt. They were clothed in bruises and rags and fully aware of what awaited them. Of the twenty-three, Cauvin counted three who loudly maintained their faith in the Mother of Chaos and two who'd experienced a conversion and were invoking the entire Ilsigi pantheon. The rest were silent, resigned to their fates. One by one they were pulled down from the carts and sewn into lengths of bright Irrune tent carpeting. Then the rolled carpets were dragged in the center of the forecourt where they were arranged in a pattern that Arizak's shaman brother, Zarzakhan, had divined from the entrails of a snow-white goat.

Directly beneath Cauvin's window, the Dragon and his cohort kept their horses on short reins as Arizak's shaman brother, Zarzakhan, walked among them exhorting their god, Irrunega, to keep them safe as they administered the tribe's justice by riding their horses back and forth through the forecourt until every traitor was dead and their blood had soaked through the carpets into the sand. Zarzakhan and the Dragon had reason to be worried. Treason was a rare and usually solitary crime among the Irrune. They'd never had to ride their horses over so many lumpish carpets, nor in the close quarters of a palace forecourt.

Arizak and Zarzakhan had considered other punishments. They could have tied the traitors limb by limb to the tails of horses who were then driven in four directions of paradise, but that would have been just as dangerous in the forecourt. Nadalya had suggested impalement over burning straw, but that was reserved for women who committed adultery and men who raped virgins.

Shite for sure, Leorin had had a valid point.

Cauvin's hands were clammy as he waited, and he wished he'd skipped breakfast. Froggin' sure, he wished he was laying bricks or smashing stone somewhere, but when a man didn't kill his own snakes, he at least had to watch those who did.

"Odd," Soldt said. The duelist stood a half step behind Cauvin. "Once they're rolled up like meat pies, they stop struggling."

"That's because they're dead."

Soldt and Cauvin spun together, both reaching for weapons, though only Soldt had his drawn before recognizing Arizak's youngest son, Raith, who looked the way Cauvin's stomach felt.

Cauvin asked, "You were able to persuade your father?"

"No, but I've paid the men with the needles and thread to strangle the prisoners as they finish. There's no reason to prolong suffering, even for the Hand. Besides, there are more traitors than my brother has riders. The horses will balk before the punishment's complete."

"Strangle," Soldt mused. "How appropriate. Ah—they've rolled the last one: Twenty-three rugs in a row."

Raith sat on one of the stools. "There'd be twenty-four, if Mother had gotten her way."

"Your father and uncle agreed that wouldn't accomplish anything," Cauvin said gently. "Better to leave Naimun alive—a baited trap attracting all manner of vermin."

"I hope you're right. You don't know Naimun."

Raith was right that Cauvin didn't know Naimun. He'd successfully resisted that honor and would have done the same with Raith himself, but Arizak had insisted. The Torch had made Cauvin the heir of his secrets, his wisdom, his wealth, and—above all else—his headaches.

Arizak wasn't so bad, and Raith was already a friend, but his mother, Nadalya, was Mina with real power. And then there was Vashanka. The Torch's exiled god had started appearing in Cauvin's dreams. Cauvin couldn't say which was worse: the god's visits or the mere fact that he was dreaming regularly, vividly, and that sometimes, in his dreams, he did things that resembled witchcraft.

Cauvin marveled that no one had suspected the Torch of witchcraft. Froggin' sure, there was no way the Torch's luck could be explained by prayer, especially prayer to a banished god. Cauvin wasn't a witch; at least he didn't think he was. Vashanka said, in Vashanka's nightmare way, that the Torch's witchblood hadn't kindled until he was older than Cauvin and that Cauvin knew as much about his ancestors as the Torch had known, which was to say froggin' nothing. Vashanka had also reminded Cauvin that the mortal world was very small and very young. Everybody was related to everybody else; everybody had a drop or two of witchblood hiding in the pit of his heart.

How many drops did it take to steal a soul?

The trumpets blared again. The Dragon raised his war cry and led his cohort in a gallop across the forecourt. One of the horses balked on the first pass. In the press and confusion, it went down with its rider. Their screams echoed in the Torch's bedchamber. Raith bolted from the room, and Cauvin turned away. Soldt was unperturbed.

"Raith was right. There should have been twenty-four carpets out there, not counting Prince Naimun."

"She escaped," Cauvin replied, icily.

"You're a fool, Cauvin, if you think she's not coming back, and coming back for you."

"I might be wrong, but I'm not a sheep-shite fool. I'll be ready for her, whatever she decides to do."